The Sins Of Eden

THE SINS OF EDEN

Iris Gower

ROWAN

A ROWAN BOOK

Published by Arrow Books Limited
20 Vauxhall Bridge Road, London SW1V 2SA

An imprint of the Random Century Group

London Melbourne Sydney Auckland Johannesburg
and agencies throughout the world

First published in Great Britain by Century
Rowan edition 1991

Filmset by Deltatype Ltd, Ellesmere Port
Printed and bound in Great Britain by
Cox & Wyman Ltd, Reading, Berkshire

ISBN 0 09 984430 3

To my brothers Billy and John, and my
sisters Jean and Chris,
with love.

1

The Monkey Run, a wide promenade running between the golden curve of the bay and the Mumbles railway track, a meeting place for the young people of Swansea. At the Slip, the promenade petered out, giving way to cramped streets housing the triangular frontage of the Bay View Hotel.

Lying eastwards of the town crouched the unevenly spaced houses of Lambert's Cottages, darkened now in the moonless night and with a light shining from only one of the windows. Within the sparsely furnished room, Kristina Larson confronted her stepfather.

'You can't make me marry Robert Jenkins. I hardly know him.'

'You'll do as you're told!' Thomas Presdey's voice rang out ominously. 'I won't take backchat from the toughest man on the dockyard and I'm not taking it from you.' He moved his heavy frame towards a seat near the dying fire and slumped into it, staring balefully at Kristina. He was constantly reminded by her looks that she was not a Presdey but the daughter of another man, and a foreigner at that.

'Please Tom,' Ceinwen Presdey said. 'Let her think about it. You can't rush a young girl into marriage, it's not right.'

He turned on his wife angrily. 'You were young enough when you saw fit to go to the bed of that foreigner, so be quiet!' He returned his attention to Kristina. 'And you, my girl, will make friends with Mr Jenkins whether you like it or not.'

'I won't stay here!' Kristina said desperately. 'I'll leave home, I'll go to Aunt Liv in Norway.' She saw the desperate appeal in her mother's expression and fell suddenly silent, her defiance vanishing.

'Get out of my house before I take the belt to you!' Thomas shouted, his eyes gleaming, his face mottled with drink and anger.

Kristina opened the door and started to run. She knew Thomas meant every word he said.

She paused at last for breath and looked around her. The Monkey Run was silent now, the sea whispering secret messages to the shore. A hound bayed mournfully into the night sky, echoing her own misery. Kristina sat on the coldness of a dew wet bench and stared into the pewter restlessness of the sea. What a mess she had made of her life. How could she even think of marrying Robert Jenkins or any man when she was already in love with Eden Lamb?

She moved from the seat and turned towards the uneven skyline of the sprawling town; Swansea was asleep, only the shimmering pools of streetlights offering relief from the darkness. 'Oh Eden!' she whispered, covering her face with her hands. 'If only I could come to you.' Last night she had been so close to him, had lain with him beneath the sheltering beams of the pier. He had made love to her so gently and she had clung to him, thirsty for affection. They had been lovers now for over a year, the happiest year of her life.

She sighed. What would Thomas say if he knew the truth? He disliked her enough as it was, he took great pains to tell her so often enough. And Kristina acknowledged that she was different from the rest of the family, not only in name but in every particular.

She was very tall and she considered herself plain and ungainly, but she had a mane of bright hair that gave her an unexpected sheen of voluptuousness. Although she did not realize it, she was very beautiful, the product of a union between a Norwegian immigrant father and a

8

Welsh mother. But when she opened her mouth to speak, her soft, musical Welsh accent marked her out at once as a Swansea girl born and bred.

She had not been happy at home ever since her mother had married Thomas Presdey ten years ago. Her step-father took great delight in baiting her, blaming her for any small or imagined sins. She was his whipping boy, but she was young and resilient and, she reasoned, it directed the weight of Thomas Presdey's anger away from her mother. That was the one reason she would never run away from Swansea; who then would be the buffer between her mother and her stepfather?

She remained for a long time staring at the sea, waiting for Thomas to fall into the heavy sleep that always followed his drinking bouts. The sun was rising, the earth warming into the brightness of a May morning when she moved across the track of the LMS railway line and on to the sand dunes. She would look at the sea for a few more minutes and then she must make her way back home.

She stretched her arms above her head, trying to shake off the dark thoughts. She must force herself to be patient with Thomas, to try to placate him and pray that he would forget the threat, made in a mood of anger and alcohol, to marry her to a man she didn't love.

Robert Jenkins had come home with Thomas on several occasions, but only recently had he shown any interest in Kristina. Robert had once been overseer at the patent fuel works, a place of horror where the skin became scarred and pockmarked by pitch from the fuel brick. He was marked by the works not only in the faint scar across his cheek but in character. He was a man who had been brought up to be tough and to survive in a harsh world, and yet there was an unmistakable kindness in him that in spite of herself touched a chord within Kristina.

Now he was works allocator on the docks, in charge of the 'capping out', the method by which the dockers were chosen to work. The men would stand in a semicircle around Jenkins, and any man branded a shirker would be given the rottenest cargo that came into Swansea Docks. Thomas Presdey had worked on the docks for many years, and he saw in Kristina a way to secure for himself an easy living. Jenkins had expressed interest in his stepdaughter and that was enough encouragement for Thomas to begin making absurd plans.

Kristina walked briskly now back through the lightening streets of Swansea, past the Patti Pavilion in Victoria Park and along Oyster-mouth Road towards Lambert's Cottages. She sighed softly as she crept into the house, wondering how to deal with her stepfather's absurd ideas. She would forget Thomas's threats, for whatever happened she would never marry Robert Jenkins. But for now she needed to sleep before she went to work at Libba's shop.

The grocery store stood on the small roadway flanking the sprawling docklands, and every time she walked into the dimness of the interior, the smell of ground coffee and the overriding odour of paraffin was familiar and welcoming, for she had worked in Libba's shop since she'd left school at fourteen.

For the next few days, Kristina kept out of Thomas's way. She worked long hours in the shop and then came home, and after a meal of bread and potatoes went out again. She was wise enough to know that the time would come when Thomas would put his threats into action and Robert Jenkins would be invited to the small house on the docks with a view to them stepping out together.

In the mean time, she crept around the house quietly when Thomas was at home, and she looked forward to the soft spring evenings when she would be alone, walking for hours over the dunes or along the pier where she would stare out to sea and think about Eden.

It had been inevitable that she would end up in his arms, she had known him so long and loved him for what seemed to her for ever. When she was a child, her mother would take her up to the big house and Kristina would sit in the kitchen while her mother worked as a domestic for Mrs Lamb. Sometimes Eden, who had seemed then to be much older than she, would sit and talk to her and she would come alive. Roggen, his sister, was more aloof, very conscious that she was a lady and Kristina only the daughter of one of the servants.

And now, as she stood on the promenade, the dust of the day washed from her and the early evening sun shining on the sea, Kristina felt hope rise within her. She would explain to Robert Jenkins that she did not want marriage; he would surely understand. Never mind that Thomas had been waiting for her last night and had told her in no uncertain terms that Robert Jenkins would be calling and that she would be there to meet him. Of course she would, but that didn't mean she couldn't give him some plain speaking. She glanced around her, becoming aware of the crowds of young men flirting with the girls, and she felt so much older than they were.

She stood near the Cenotaph where she had arranged to meet Nia Powell, her loyal and closest friend. Kristina hoped she would come soon, she felt in need of company.

On the prom, small groups of people had gathered to argue over politics, for election fever was in the air. Mr Ramsay MacDonald was standing against Sir Stanley Baldwin, with no one giving the Welshman Lloyd George any chance. Most hotly debated was the controversial decision that young women of twenty-one and over should be allowed to vote for the first time.

From the open window of one of the large houses on the Mumbles Road blared the sound of a gramophone, piercing the quiet evening air with the strains of 'Sonny Boy'. The Monkey Run was littered with song sheets bearing the Conservative electioneering song that matched the tune.

> England for the free,
> Stanley Boy!

11

You're the man for me,
Stanley Boy!

Kristina caught sight of Nia with Roggen Lamb, Eden's sister, and her heart sank.

'Those words are simply rubbish!' Roggen was saying. She had the dark, Iberian look of many of the Welsh and was short and small boned with fine olive skin. Roggen spoke with the certainty of youth, raising neatly plucked eyebrows over fine dark eyes that were alight with derision. She looked up at Kristina quizzically.

Nia bridged the silence quickly. 'I told you I was meeting Kristina, didn't I Ro?' She tucked her arm through Kristina's, and Roggen turned away as though she had lost interest, although in fact she was wondering at the way Kristina seemed to attract the attention of the men on the prom. As a child she had been so plain, so pale and washed-out looking with her fair hair and golden eyelashes. But lately she had blossomed into quite a beauty.

Roggen broke the silence, ignoring Kristina and speaking directly to Nia who, though living in one of the humble cottages, was the daughter of the vicar, and was well educated and intelligent.

'I hear that Lady Astor pushed the Home Secretary into a corner, ticking him off about the lack of women's rights.' She paused. 'Lady Astor was the first woman MP, of course.' She glanced briefly at Kristina before continuing, 'With the result that Sir William Joynson-Hicks announced that women would be placed on electoral equality with men! So now not only old women of thirty can vote, but younger women too.'

Kristina sighed as Roggen continued her chattering. She did like to show off.

'One foolish woman,' Roggen went on, 'decided she would vote for Winston Churchill because he had the same breed of dog as she did. Isn't it a hoot! I can't wait to be old enough to vote. I'd show the world that Stanley

Boy is out and Ramsay MacDonald is in. He'll be certain to make the world a better place for everyone.'

Kristina wasn't listening. She was remembering the conversation she'd had with Thomas last night.

'Look, girl.' His tone had been conciliatory. 'Robert Jenkins has got an eye for you, mind, and him a fine catch for any woman. It would make all the difference to my job, see, me and your mam and the girls would be sure of having a living if I keep in Jenkins's good books.'

Kristina had found his reasonableness more difficult to deal with than his anger, and at last she had grudgingly agreed. Afterwards her mother had taken her aside and warned her not to make any promises she couldn't keep.

'No one can make you marry this man, or even like him, *cariad*,' she said softly, 'so think of yourself for once.' She had paused. 'It might even be for the best if you got out of this house and out of Thomas's way.'

Kristina became aware that Roggen was staring hard at her. She was smiling in her rather superior way, glancing over Kristina's shoulder. Kristina turned and saw a group of men coming towards them. One of them caught her eye and lifted his hat, and Kristina looked away with only the barest acknowledgement, but she was suddenly flustered, for she had recognized Robert Jenkins, done up in his best clothes and staring at her in a way that confirmed only too well all that Thomas had told her.

Roggen, unaware of Kristina's feelings, lifted her hand to touch the fashionably short hair beneath the neat hat a little self-consciously. 'I see you have an admirer,' she said. 'A chappie from the patent fuel works by the look of him, just your sort I would have thought, Kristina.'

The men strolled past them and Kristina averted her eyes. She did not want to encourage Robert Jenkins in any way. How could she when she already belonged to Eden Lamb?'

'There's Richard James,' Nia said quickly to Roggen. 'I know he's attracted to you, just see the way he looks at you. And you at him!'

Richard James was so different from Robert Jenkins. His clothes were well cut and expensive, his shoes handmade leather, he exuded affluence. He risked a smile in Roggen's direction as he moved past the three girls. Kristina watched as Roggen met Richard's eyes. It *was* quite obvious that the two were attracted to each other.

Kristina smiled at Nia, grateful for her presence. It was rarely that the three girls came together, and now she wished Roggen would go away. It was bad enough putting up with her superior attitude, but there was the added fear that Roggen might know something about her and Eden. Nia Powell, on the other hand, was a good friend. She had grown up in the vicinity of Lambert's Cottages and as her father had taught her at home, she had remained unspoiled and quite without any airs or graces.

Nia's father still held the courtesy title of 'vicar', and indeed he had once preached in the local church, but that was before the matter of his running an illegal book had come to the notice of the deacons. Ejected from his living, Ambrose Powell had moved into one of the small houses in Lambert's Cottages, and from there had continued with his illegal betting practices.

Nia had never known what her status in the life of the community should be. As a child she had been educated by her father to an exceptionally high degree, taught Latin and Greek and introduced early to good literature. She had been afforded the respect meted out to the daughter of a minister of God, but when her father had been divested of his office, she had become simply one of the cottagers, most of whom were dockers and labourers.

And yet, because of the nature of his business, Ambrose had the regard of many of the wealthier families in the area, some of whom enjoyed a flutter on the horses as much as did the working people who were Ambrose's faithful punters.

Roggen spoke briskly. 'What about this meeting, Nia?

You *are* coming to hear the Labour MP David Williams speak, I hope.'

'*Duw*, you go on, Nia,' Kristina said quickly. 'I'd better be getting home anyway.' She made an effort to speak lightly.

Nia shook her head. 'Please come with us, Kristina. You don't have to get home for an hour or two, surely?'

'I really should be getting home, help Mam put the girls to bed.'

Kristina put her hands on her hips, and her full breasts strained against the soft material of her dress. A young man whistled between his teeth, his fedora hat pulled low over his eyes.

Kristina ignored him as Nia shook her arm. 'You must come with us, Kris,' she urged. 'You need to get out a bit.'

'Well, I'm not really keen on meetings, but I'll come with you if you like.' In any case, Kristina wasn't in any hurry to get home. She made an effort to join in the conversation. 'Are you really going to vote Labour when you're twenty-one, Nia?'

Nia shrugged noncommittally but Roggen shook back her short hair impatiently.

'Well *I* am. I'd vote for Ramsay MacDonald any day of the week.' Roggen spoke forcefully. 'I think he's a wonderful man. He was MP for Aberavon for some time, so he knows the special needs of the Welsh valleys.'

Nia pursed her lips for a moment and then spoke almost reluctantly. 'My father said not to waste a vote on MacDonald, and even poor old Lloyd George is a loser these days. He did some good in the past but he's betrayed the people once too often, falling down on the promises he made so eloquently.' She glanced ruefully at Kristina. 'But then eloquent men often tell lies.' It was evident she was thinking of her father.

'And why should *you* want a Labour government in power, Ro?' Nia asked. 'Your family is so rich I felt sure you would have voted for Baldwin.'

Roggen shook her head. 'No fear! Him and his

broccoli!' She moved on along the ribbon of road, glancing out to sea where on the horizon the hull of a large ship gleamed hazily in the May sunshine. 'Foolish man!' It was clear she was longing to enlarge on her statement, but it seemed at the moment no one was giving her a chance.

Roggen was a conceited, opinionated young woman, Kristina thought, so different from Eden. Neither was she anything like their mother, who had always been considerate to those less well off than herself. Until after she was widowed, then it seemed as though all the verve that came from her Spanish blood had gone, leaving a sad shell of a woman.

Kristina knew that after his father had died it had fallen to Eden to take up the reins of the business, which he did with great reluctance but with every success. He was dark haired and dark skinned like his Spanish mother, but with a voice like a Welsh deacon, deep and resonant and full of power. Kristina hugged the thought of him to herself.

Roggen was striding along the prom, her skirts swinging, her head high, a right Miss Hoity-Toity. Even as a young girl, she would tease Kristina unkindly about her crush on Eden, but of course it had always been more than just a crush.

'What's this about broccoli, then?' Nia asked at last, aware as Kristina was that Roggen was waiting eagerly for an opening.

'Surely you've seen the jokes in the papers?' Roggen smiled triumphantly, happy to air her knowledge. 'They are of Mr Baldwin sporting a broccoli in his buttonhole; he gave the cartoonists a field day when he opened his mouth and put his foot in it yet again.

'We all know the country's in a depressed state,' Roggen continued. 'Unemployment is rising, the steel, coal and shipbuilding industries are in trouble and the Government puts out a fatuous election slogan like "Safety first"!' She paused, staring round her expectantly. 'And Mr Baldwin talks about the farmers of Cornwall selling broccoli to Europe, as though that alone would save us all from poverty.' Roggen sometimes got on her soapbox a little too vociferously.

Kristina looked around. The last of the young men had disappeared from view and the Monkey Run was almost deserted. The sea ran softly into the embracing arms of the curving shore, darkening the sand, leaving a ragged tide-mark of seaweed and small, glistening shells. Following Nia and Roggen along the prom, she stared seawards to where the coast of Devon lay gentle and misty on the horizon. She sometimes felt the call of the sea, the wish to travel beyond the confines of Swansea and reach out to the wider world that lay across the soft waters of the bay. Perhaps one day she would visit her father's land, the land of the Norsemen after which Swansea had been named.

As a child, Kristina had dreamed that her tall, red-headed father was the pirate Sweyne who, it was said, sailed to the shores of Wales in a strong ship and using the inlet as a place to rest named the town Sweyn's Eye. But then her father had died and Thomas Presdey had taken his place.

Women needed rights, Kristina thought, Roggen was correct in that respect, but the right to vote would alter nothing in the Presdey household, not when Thomas had the drink in him.

The town hall was surrounded by men, some of them carrying banners bearing anti-women slogans. When the three girls approached the doorway one of the men stepped forward, barring their path.

'I'm advising you not to go inside there, ladies. A political meeting is for men, it might just get a little rough.'

His eyes met Kristina's and she realized with a feeling of panic that this was Robert Jenkins, the man who, if Thomas had his way, would become her husband.

'I would have thought that the daughter of a docker

would have better sense,' Jenkins said mildly. 'Don't you know these meetings often end in uproar?'

'Excuse me!' Roggen said, on her high horse at once. 'Don't you dare talk to us that way. Please move and let us pass before I call a constable.'

'Be careful, Roggen,' Kristina said in a low voice, fearing an angry scene. There was enough of that to contend with at home.

Roggen ignored her and thrust her way past the men, with determination in the hard set of her mouth. 'How dare they!' she said angrily. 'I felt like slapping the man's face.'

'You might have started something then, mind,' Kristina said quickly. 'Perhaps he's right and the meeting might get a bit rowdy.'

'Come on,' Nia said from behind Roggen. 'Now we're in let's find a seat, shall we?'

In the body of the hallway there was an air of calm. Only the soft hum of whispered voices and the occasional scrape of a chair leg against polished floorboards disturbed the silence. Four dark-suited men were seated behind a table on the platform, all neatly dressed with white shirt collars and dark ties. There were very few women in the hall.

'It makes me so furious,' Roggen said. 'Women have been given the vote and what do they do, sit at home twiddling their thumbs, letting the men have things all their own way.'

Kristina shrugged. She knew nothing about politics and cared less, but she respected Roggen's judgement even though her methods were a little high-handed.

Nia's hands were twisted together in her lap. She knew Roggen's views well enough but wasn't sure that she agreed with them. Ramsay MacDonald might be a good enough man, but he'd had one opportunity to run the country when the first Labour government was returned in 1924. According to her father, he'd made a complete botch of the job, and after only nine months Labour was out and the Baldwin administration back in power. She decided to keep her views to herself, however; though Roggen was a dear girl, sometimes she could be quite overwhelmingly outspoken, almost devastating with her sarcasm.

Nia rubbed at her ankles. She had been up more steps and knocked on more doors than she cared to remember, all in order to bring in her father's winnings. Some money she'd collected today, enough to buy her a brand new winter outfit. It would be all right if the money was her own, but it only went into Father's secret safe place behind the chimney wall.

It was then that the germ of an idea began to grow in Nia's mind. Her own betting office, why not? She would, in a few years time, be old enough to vote, so surely she was now old enough to set up on her own? There were many customers whom her father had turned away for one reason or another. She could begin a book on them, perhaps on the side, to start with.

The MP for Swansea East began to speak, his public school tones filling the hall. But before he'd gone very far, Richard James was on his feet and, to laughter from his friends, began to heckle the politician.

There was a sudden noise from the doorway. 'Throw that man out if he's going to disrupt the meeting!' Robert Jenkins pushed his way towards where Richard James was standing. Some of the young men in the audience rose to their feet, and Kristina's heart was in her mouth as she watched. Robert was right, there could be trouble in the hall, bad trouble.

'Shut up and sit down!' Richard said. 'I have the right to speak if I wish. This is a free country, is it not?'

Jenkins pushed his way to Richard's side. 'You call that speaking?' he asked fiercely. 'I call it rabble-rousing.' He turned to his followers. 'Let's show these so-called gentlemen what we think of them, boys,' he said, staring over the heads of the crowd to where Kristina was sitting, and her mouth was suddenly dry. Then he was pressing forward at the head of his supporters.

Richard, threatened, launched himself forward, his fist aiming for Robert Jenkins's jaw, but Robert parried the blow easily, just as a scuffle broke out between the other men.

Kristina heard the sound of chairs being overturned, and then she was jostled by the crowd, losing sight of Nia in the confusion. She almost fell backwards over an upturned chair, then suddenly Robert was at her side, grasping her arm and pushing his way through the crowd. She tried to pull away but his hands caught and held her.

'Get out of this fight,' he said breathlessly. 'I told you this was not the place for women, didn't I?'

Kristina felt herself being bundled unceremoniously towards the door. 'Let me go!' she said, her voice shaking. 'I can look after myself.' The last thing she wanted was to be beholden to Robert Jenkins. She stared at him. He was very close to her and she realized they were the same height so they were looking straight into each other's eyes. He smiled at her.

'About time you learned some sense, young woman,' he said. 'Now, be a good girl and get out of here before you get hurt.'

'And just who do you think you are?' The voice, heavy with sarcasm, the words punctuated with authority, fell into the sudden silence. Eden Lamb stood in the doorway, his tall figure and stern manner demanding the attention of the people in the hall.

'Mind your own damn business.' Robert still held on to Kristina's shoulders as he stared angrily at Eden. 'I know who *you* are, the rich and influential Eden Lamb. You never stop ramming it down the throats of anyone who'll listen, but this is none of your business, get it?'

'What on earth are you doing here, Eden?' Roggen, grasping Nia by the arm, had hurried to her brother's side. Her hair was ruffled and she seemed breathless. 'Have you been following me?'

20

Eden pointed to the car standing at the kerbside. 'Get in and wait for me,' he said. Roggen gave him a quick rebellious look and then glanced uncertainly to where Richard James was watching her from the doorway of the hall.

'Go on,' Eden said. 'You too, Nia. I'll take you home.'

Eden's eyes met Kristina's and she saw that he was very angry. Did he blame her for the way Robert Jenkins had been holding her?

'You'd better come with us,' he said almost grudgingly, his tone abrupt, and without a backward glance he moved towards the car.

Robert spoke near Kristina's shoulder. 'You don't have to take orders from him, you know.'

Kristina stared at him angrily. 'And I don't have to take orders from you, either,' she said. Once in the car, she didn't look back even when she heard Robert's voice calling to her.

'I'll see you later, Kristina. I've been invited to your house for supper, remember.'

She saw from the corner of her eye that Eden was glaring at her and then, to her relief, Roggen broke the silence.

'You *did* follow me here, didn't you?' she said to her brother. 'You were spying on me.'

He shook back his hair. 'Mother was worried about you, she told me you'd gone to this meeting. I thought you were crazy to mix with such riffraff, and I was right.' He quickly covered the short distance between the Slip and the docks entrance and drew the car to a stop outside the row of cottages.

'Right.' He slid from behind the wheel and opened the door. As Kristina brushed past him she was so aware of him and was sure he was very conscious of her nearness.

Nia alighted from the car. 'Thank you so much, Mr Lamb.' She ran her hand along the shining metal in a touch that was almost sensuous. How could she even look at the car when its owner was standing so tall and handsome and commanding in the May sunshine? Kristina thought wistfully.

His eyes were upon her then and in spite of her height, Eden Lamb stood head and shoulders above her. 'It's a good thing my mother was worried about Roggen and told me where she'd gone or all three of you would have been in for some rough handling,' he said abruptly. 'And I should keep out of Jenkins's way if I were you,' he continued. 'From what I hear, the man's almost a communist.'

Kristina longed to tell him she had no interest in Robert Jenkins. Quite the contrary, she wanted only to avoid him. Why couldn't she speak out? Was it because she mustn't compromise her own position, or was it to protect Eden? How hateful was this hole-and-corner romance, why had she never seen it before? She and Eden, snatching moments in hidden places, never able to walk in the sunshine or speak openly of their love.

She forced herself to turn towards her home and raised her hand at Nia's called farewell. The sun shone on the pitted roadway and the windows of the cottages gleamed brightly, curtains moving as old women in parlours looked nosily at Mr Eden Lamb bringing folk home in his shining car.

At the door, she paused to gather her wits. Her stepfather would be home from the public bar soon and he was bound to have heard of the skirmish at the meeting hall. It would soon be the talk of the docklands, involving Jenkins as it did. And then, when Jenkins arrived for supper, Thomas would attempt a heavy-handed discretion and leave them alone together. It would be dreadful.

Kristina sighed heavily, and pushing open the front door stepped from the sunlit evening into the gloom.

2

Eden Lamb stared out of the office window into the bright sunlight, breathing in the scent of the sea and the docks drifting in on the hot May air. Spices from an Indian merchant vessel mingled with the smell of tar melting in the heat, evoking memories of his childhood.

The Lambs had been a happy family of four, Roggen being born when Eden was ten years old. His mother had been filled with laughter then, but since the sudden death of his father she had changed, becoming withdrawn and sometimes irritable, talking in her native tongue, the Spanish difficult to understand because, when agitated, his mother was inclined to rush her words.

Eden stared down at a book open before him on the desk, not seeing the name of the Lamb and Singleton shipping firm that was facing him. He had not wished to go into the business; he had always longed to go to sea, to captain a ship and ride the waves, but his father's untimely death had altered all that. Everything had changed over the past years. Roggen was a woman now, a rebel, following the absurd socialist ideas which, if she had to put them into practice, she would soon abandon. Whether she realized it or not, Roggen was not one to live in poverty, she liked her comforts too much for that.

The door of the office swung open, startling him. He turned abruptly to see Roggen framed in the sunlight, letting in a rush of spring air. She looked fresh and pretty in a white cotton dress that was perhaps a little too short, and her smile was somewhat apprehensive as she came further into the room. Eden leaned back deliberately in his chair, tapping the desk with his pen and waiting for her to speak.

'I've been trying to talk to you for days,' she said. 'I'm sure you've been avoiding me.' When he didn't reply she spoke again in a rush. 'Thanks for coming to our rescue the other night. I did appreciate it really, and you were a brick tackling that ruffian the way you did.'

She perched on the edge of the desk, her slender legs in the pure silk stockings swinging to and fro, a sure sign that she was agitated.

'I have to talk to you, Eden.' She hesitated, biting her lip, and he knew she was about to say something he wouldn't very much like.

'It's about this thing going on between you and Kristina Larson. It's not suitable at all, Eden, you must see that.'

'This "thing" as you call it is none of your business, Roggen.' He was angry at once. 'And I don't appreciate you meddling in what doesn't concern you.'

'But Eden, a girl like that, the daughter of a docker, how could you?'

He leaned forward slowly, his eyes on those of his sister. 'Are you serious about these socialist ideas of yours, or is this just another of your whims?'

'I'm serious, of course,' she said abruptly. 'What has that got to do with anything?'

'For a socialist, you are a real little snob,' he said slowly, and she had the grace to blush.

'Being socialist doesn't mean I don't have moral standards,' she said, smiling at him appealingly to soften her words. 'Please, Eden, just think about the effect this affair would have on Mama if she found out.'

'You are a little prig, aren't you?' Eden said, and Roggen's smile vanished.

'Don't patronize me, Eden,' she said quickly. 'I'm a woman, remember, not a child, and if I think you are acting like a fool I feel I've a right to tell you so.' She paused. 'Anyway, on the matter of politics, I must think for myself. You might be content to be old-fashioned and stick to the worn-out principles of the Baldwinites, but I can see there are many wrongs in the world that need to be put right.'

Eden shook his head. 'And you think this Scottish fellow Ramsay MacDonald is the one to cure all the ills of the world?' he asked, and he was aware of the sarcasm in his tone. 'He couldn't run a flower show, let alone a country. Don't you realize his first Labour government lasted precisely nine months?'

Roggen levered herself from the desk and stood beside him, and he could see by the two spots of colour on her cheeks that she was furious with him.

'Isn't it about time that he was given another chance, then?' she asked indignantly. 'MacDonald's a good man, Eden, he has principles and at least he doesn't go around during what is a deep depression bleating about broccoli!'

'Trite phrases, gutter press language, is that all you can come up with?' Eden said. He was suddenly impatient. 'Anyway, I can't debate political issues with you any longer. I'm busy.' He saw her hurt look, and relented. 'The truth is I'm expecting Colin Singleton any minute, he's coming back from the Cardiff office today.'

'I see, then I won't keep you any longer.' Roggen paused. 'Tell me, Eden, are you in love with Kristina or are you just having a fling? Either way you're not being fair to her, have you thought of that?'

'Leave it alone, Roggen, before I . . .'

A loud knocking on the door interrupted him and Eden called out irritably, 'Come on in, for God's sake, don't stand there hammering the door down.'

'Bad moment?' Colin Singleton was smiling disarmingly, his fair hair falling over his brow. 'I heard the sound of raised voices but no one takes a little spat between siblings seriously, do they?'

He patted Roggen's shoulder. 'Hello there, Ro. Giving your brother a piece of your mind, I see. He needs it, my partner is far too serious for his own good.'

Eden rose to his feet, hand extended. 'Colin, good to see you back. The trip was a success, I take it?'

'It was indeed, my boy. We've got a whole lot of new orders in, and by the look of it we'll be shipping fuel out of the docks for some time yet.'

Eden smiled. 'Not a very pleasant load, but it seems to be paying off. Good thing that the fuel is needed abroad.'

A loud tooting from a car horn sounded from outside on the harbour, and Colin smiled widely. 'That's Bella.' He glanced over his shoulder and waved through the open doorway. 'Come along in. Eden's here and he's waiting to meet you.'

Colin smiled mischievously at Eden. 'Bella is one of my cousins from Cardiff,' he explained. 'I thought I'd bring her down with me for a visit, and I thought it was about time you met a nice woman and settled down. You're not getting any younger, you know.'

He disappeared before Eden could speak, and Eden shrugged his shoulders, accepting Roggen's smile of derision with good grace.

'Perhaps he's right,' she said. 'Colin may well have a point; a good wife could work wonders for your disposition.'

Bella moved into the office in a cloud of perfume, her fashionable hat drawn down over her clear brow, her silk and lace gown stopping well above her shapely knees. She stared at Eden with calm grey eyes, hand extended, and he was on his feet before he knew it.

'This is my clever and beautiful cousin.' Colin's voice was triumphant. He was well aware of the impact she made when she gave a fellow one of her looks.

The hand in his was firm and cool, and Eden smiled politely even as he sized her up. She was no silly flapper in spite of her fashionable appearance. Her level gaze and the high brow spoke of intelligence, which in a woman was always a good thing.

After a few minutes spent exchanging pleasantries, Colin whisked Bella away, but Eden could still smell the scent of her even when the door closed behind her. He returned to his seat, well aware that his sister was scrutinizing him with amusement.

'You look bemused!' she said irritably. 'You are not going to fall for that trick of Colin's, are you?'

Eden felt annoyance at his sister's habit of meddling in his life. 'I like Bella, yes,' he said, though he wasn't sure he liked her at all. 'Not that it's any business of yours.'

Roggen lifted her hands in mock resignation. 'All right, don't vent your spleen on me. I'm just going, I know when you're in one of your moods.'

After his sister had left, Eden sat staring at his books without seeing the rows of figures in front of him. What was he going to do with his life? He enjoyed the times he spent with Kristina; seducing her had been so sweet. She was a lovely girl, and yet not the sort he would marry. Roggen was right about that, at least.

He rose abruptly from his chair. It was too nice a day to sit in the office staring at figures. He could murder a pint of cool ale; he'd take a walk across to the Burrows and forget about women.

The object of his thoughts was sitting on the bed she shared with her two young sisters. Kristina's face smarted from the slap Thomas had given her, and she could still hear his voice ranting and raving at her. They had been arguing angrily, her stepfather displeased with her rather cold response to Robert Jenkins last night.

Robert had behaved very well. He had said nothing about the trouble at the meeting, and his conversation at supper had been almost enjoyable. If only Thomas wasn't trying to push her into marriage with him she might even have enjoyed Robert's company.

She leaned forward and looked in the cracked, damp-speckled mirror of the wardrobe. At least he had not marked her face, she looked all right except for shadows of fatigue around her eyes. Looking round, her gaze took in the faded lino with the rag mats covering the worst

27

parts; the bare little room was not really home to her, not since Thomas Presdey had become master of the house.

Kristina sighed. She was not willing to take the brunt of Thomas's anger any longer. She was a woman now, she must be allowed to make up her own mind about the man she would marry.

'Come on down, love.' Her mother's voice rising from the foot of the stairs cracked with fatigue and concern. 'The kids have gone back to school, and we'll have a bit of peace to eat our dinner.'

Kristina entered the kitchen and looked at her mother bending over the gas ring, her shoulders slumped as though life had beaten her into submission. Ceinwen Presdey had once been a beautiful woman. Small and dark as the Welsh usually were, she had a shrewdness of eye and a smile so full of understanding that she aroused a feeling of happiness that encompassed all her family.

She looked up and with a small click of her tongue came to her daughter, taking Kristina into her arms. 'My love,' she said softly, 'there's sorry I am. I swear I'll kill that man if he touches you again.'

'It wasn't your fault, Mam,' Kristina said softly, love overwhelming her.

'Here, drink this tea while it's hot.' Ceinwen Presdey handed her a cup and rubbed at her eyes with the corner of her apron. She sat at the table then and faced her daughter, her eyes pleading. 'You must leave home for your own safety, love,' she said, 'though how I'm going to bear life without you here I don't know.'

'Mam,' Kristina said softly, 'I know you're right to tell me to leave, and in any case I don't think I can take it any more.' She paused, trying not to let her anger show. 'He's no right to hit me. I'm a woman grown, most girls are married with children of their own by the time they're my age.'

Her mother sniffed. 'Aye, and worn out by the time they're forty like me,' she replied. 'I want something better for you, my girl, with those looks you could have

28

anybody, even a fine gentleman like Eden Lamb. I know there's something between you, love, I'm not blind.'

When Kristina didn't reply, she continued speaking. 'Follow your real father, you do, and I think that's why Tom takes his anger out on you more than on the other girls.'

Kristina smiled and shook her head. 'Mam, don't worry about it, I can sort out my own life. When and if I marry it will be a man of my own choosing.'

'*Duw!* Any man would be lucky to have you, my girl.' She touched Kristina's long hair tenderly. 'Can't help it but I got a soft spot for you, you being my first born and Bent's only child. I would like to see you safely married even though I'd miss you badly, mind.'

At that moment, the door was pushed abruptly open and Thomas Presdey staggered into the room. His face was red, his eyes blurred and it was clear he'd been drinking.

'Married, who is talking weddings, then?' He belched loudly. 'Funny thing but Mr Jenkins is thinking on them lines, I'm sure.' He grinned. 'Most kind he was, sent me home early he did, said you was a lovely girl. Yes, you he meant, madam.' He waved his hand towards Kristina, and she was suddenly tense, wondering at the apparent good humour in Thomas's slurred voice.

Thomas slumped in a chair and leaned forward, and he smelled of the fuel he'd been loading on to the ships. 'Wants to come here and meet you again does Jenkins, he's very impressed with you,' he said, tapping the side of his nose with his finger. 'Best thing that could happen to you, madam, marriage to a fine man, and Jenkins in a position to give you a good home, him with a secure job in charge of the dockers.'

Kristina stared at her stepfather in dismay. 'Jenkins, is it, well I don't want to marry him, can't you understand that?'

Thomas's grin became a scowl. 'Shut up and listen,' he said. 'I've told you often enough that it's up to Jenkins

29

which man works every day, and I can't afford to cross him, do you understand?'

He rubbed his eyes with fingers engrained with dust. 'He's coming here for tea after work, that's why he let me off early, see, and you'll be nice to him or it will go worse for you and your mam there.'

Kristina looked desperately towards her mother, her eyes warning Ceinwen not to protest. She must handle this situation her own way, and quickly she made up her mind to agree with Thomas. She would sit nicely through tea and then when she was alone with this man Jenkins she would let him know in no uncertain terms exactly what she thought of marriage to him. He must have no false hopes.

'Right then, Dad, you go up to bed and have a rest, and Mam and me will do a bit of cooking,' she said, her tone conciliatory. 'We'll show Mr Jenkins that here in Lambert's Cottages we can put on as fine a spread as anyone.'

Her mother gave her a grateful smile and breathed out softly. She rose from her chair and turned up the gas ring under the kettle.

'Have a nice cup of tea first, Tom, and then a wash it is?' she said, and he shook his head, rising to his feet shakily.

'It's me for my bed, girl,' he said. 'I'll wash before Jenkins comes round. Be sure to get the younger girls out of the way, mind, I don't want the man frightened off with a load of kids running around his ankles.'

He moved unsteadily to the door leading to the stairs and turned for a moment to look Kristina up and down. 'Aye, not a bad looking girl, are you?' he said. 'I'm glad I didn't mark that pretty face of yours, though you deserved putting in your place, mind, and I'd do it again like a shot if it was called for. If Jenkins saw your tantrums he'd think again about wedding you, but as it is he will never need to know I've had to raise my hand to you. Don't want him thinking he's getting a sour woman do we?'

The door closed behind him and Kristina looked at her mother, shaking her head in despair.

'I won't marry Jenkins, Mam,' she said flatly. 'Not if hell had me!' She rose and put her arms around her mother's thin shoulders. 'He's just like Thomas in some ways. He's the sort who thinks a woman's place is in the home, just waiting like a good wife for him to come in every evening.'

Mrs Presdey sank into her chair and put her hands over her face. 'I don't know what to do, my girl,' she said. 'Everything is piling in on top of me. I'll just drop dead one day with the worry of it all, then Tom will be sorry.'

'Mam! Don't talk like that, please,' Kristina said softly, putting her hand on her mother's shoulder. 'Mam, what is it, there's something you're not telling me.' Kristina sat beside her and drew her hands away from her face. 'Come on, out with it, are you sick?'

'In a way, love.' Mrs Presdey made no attempt to dry the tears that ran down her face. 'The truth is, love, I'm with child again and afraid to tell Tom in case he goes into a rage.'

Kristina felt anger rise within her, almost choking her. 'Oh, Mam,' she said in despair, 'and at your age too!'

'Aye, the worst of it is I won't be able to keep my cleaning job on up at Ty Coch. I'll have to let Mrs Lamb know so that she can get someone else at least temporary like.'

Kristina sat back in her chair. 'You worry about yourself, Mam. Mrs Lamb would be the first to understand.' She chewed her lip thoughtfully. 'What about me, Mam?' she said, hope rising within her as a way of escape presented itself. 'I can leave Libba's shop and ask to live in at the Red House. That way I'd be out of Tom's sight and perhaps he'd forget all this rubbish about me marrying Jenkins.' And she would be so near to Eden, Kristina thought with a sense of excitement.

Mrs Presdey grasped her daughter's hands. 'It would be an answer to both our problems, and perhaps later on, when Tom is over this foolish idea, you could come back home, couldn't you?' Her tone was pleading.

'Of course, Mam. It would just be for the time being, until Tom forgot all about this marriage business. Anyway, you must give in your notice. You're not fit enough to clean that big house, not now.'

'I think I'll go on up to Ty Coch in the morning and ask Mrs Lamb what she thinks about the idea of taking you on instead of me. I'm sure she'll be pleased to have a nice, respectable girl like you. For now let's put our minds to what we'll give Mr Jenkins for his tea. Put on a good show we will, and perhaps it will keep Tom in the boss's good books, depends on him for work Tom do, see.'

'I know, Mam, and I'll go easy on him,' Kristina said, knowing quite well she would have to try to be tactful if only for her mother's sake.

It was late evening when Robert Jenkins presented himself at the door of the small cottage. Kristina stared up at him, a smile fixed on her lips though her every instinct was to tell the man to go to hell and leave her family alone. Behind her, Thomas Presdey loomed, smiling ingratiatingly, practically pulling his forelock to the man.

'Come inside,' she said, leading the way into the tiny parlour. 'Sit down. Tea isn't quite ready yet.'

Jenkins ran his hand round the stiff starched collar of his striped shirt and looked as uncomfortable as she was.

'I'm glad you've agreed to see me again,' he said. 'I'd like to get to know you better, Kristina.'

She stared at him in silence and he shifted uncomfortably on the upright horsehair sofa.

'If I'm not welcome, I'll go,' he said. 'Won't be beholden to anyone, me.'

'No.' Kristina held out a restraining hand. 'My mam's gone to such a lot of trouble to make a nice tea, a bit of *teison lap* and some Welsh cakes, you can't disappoint her.'

He subsided on to the hard sofa and smoothed his

trousers over his knees as if to remove the creases. 'It's a pity about that scene at the meeting hall. It got us off on the wrong foot.' He reached forward and touched her long hair, and she resisted the urge to pull away from him.

'Well that's all past now,' she said softly. 'It wasn't all your fault, and what's said and done in the heat of the moment can't be held against a man, I don't suppose.' But I do hold it against him, she thought stubbornly. He had no right to say a woman had no place in a political meeting.

She leaned back in her chair and appraised him. Robert Jenkins was not a bad looking man in spite of the pitch-damaged skin. He had a fine head of dark hair and strong features, his nose a little hawk-like. He caught and held her gaze, and smiled at her.

From the kitchen, her mother's voice called to her. 'Tea's ready, Kristina. Bring Mr Jenkins in by here, there's a good girl.'

Relieved, she led the way along the cool dark passage, aware that the green and brown paintwork was peeling from the walls, revealing the black mortar beneath. She felt Jenkins's presence behind her and suppressed a shiver; surely she couldn't be pushed into marriage with this man?

It was warm and pleasant in the tiny kitchen, with a fire glowing in the grate, and the old wooden table covered by a clean chintz cloth. Jenkins sat next to her and drew his cup towards him, nodding his thanks while his eyes still rested on Kristina's face.

'We got off to a bad start, *merchi*, you and me,' he said, 'but perhaps I can remedy that. Will you come to the Empire with me Wednesday night? Good variety show on there at the moment, by the look of it, and we'll have the best seats, mind.'

Kristina's first impulse was to tell him to go to hell. She glanced at her stepfather who was almost visibly rubbing his hands.

'There's kind of you to ask,' she hesitated, and then saw the pleading in her mother's eyes. 'It would be very nice,' she said lamely.

'Right then, that's settled, I'll pick you up at about half past six. That'll give me a chance to get rid of the smell of the docks.'

Kristina looked away from him, resisting the urge to tell him not to bother, since he wasn't going to get that close to her.

'Good, let's have that cup of tea then, missis.' Thomas Presdey's voice was full of good humour, and Kristina's lips tightened. He was so transparent, so ready to lick the boots of his boss.

She sat back in her chair with her cup of tea held in her hand, and tried to ignore the presence of Robert Jenkins, though as he talked so interestingly about the docks and shipping and the cargoes transferred from one port to another, she could not help but listen.

Still, he must not think she was softening towards him. She had agreed to go out with him for the sake of peace in the house, but he need not make the mistake of thinking she would ever marry him. She sighed softly, and then felt her mother's hand cover hers and squeeze a warning. Kristina flashed her a smile of reassurance.

'Have a piece of *teison lap*, Mr Jenkins,' Kristina said with a forced smile, and though she was rewarded by the relief in her mother's face, she was worried. How far would this farce have to go? Thomas might press her, and Robert Jenkins try to woo her with fine words and invitations to go out with him, but no one and nothing would force her into a marriage that she didn't want.

3

Ramsay MacDonald was coming to Newport to make a speech to the party faithful, and Roggen intended to be there. She glanced at her reflection in the mirror and pulled at her skirt, easing it more neatly over her hips. She turned sideways, inspecting her hair, and saw that the bob cut was growing out, curling in fans of black against her neck. She frowned; the short style called for severity, but her wavy hair annoyingly refused to conform. She pulled down her hat, picked up her handbag and hurried down the stairs into the hallway.

She failed to see the light falling through the window, splashing the Indian carpet with brilliance. The fresh smell of polish, too, was lost on her. She took her home for granted – the high-ceilinged rooms, the imposing dining room with its huge, intricately-carved furniture – just as she took for granted the fact that there would always be someone there to clean and cook for her.

Roggen was in her last year at training college. She would soon qualify as a teacher, and as she came from one of the most influential families in Swansea, a post was ready and waiting for her. She knew she would enjoy instructing the neatly-uniformed children attending the private school on Cwmdonkin Hill.

As Roggen opened the large front door, the smells of the docks drifted towards her, the King's Dock to the front of the house and the Prince of Wales Dock to the left. She stood for a moment looking seawards, where the sky was cloudless and the waters still and blue, and decided there was no need to take a coat. Hurrying along the roadway, she stopped at one of the cottages on the docks. She had asked Nia to accompany her to Newport, and after some persuading, Nia had agreed.

Nia Powell's house was small, but neat and clean. The interior was well furnished, and good, heavy curtains hung at the windows.

'Come in, Roggen.' Nia was looking a little pale. 'I hope you don't mind, but I can't come with you today.' She paused in the passageway, her voice low. 'My father isn't very well and I don't think I can leave him alone.'

'I am sorry, Nia,' Roggen said slowly. 'It's such a shame, I was looking forward to having company on the train.'

'Well, there's something else,' Nia said. 'I'd asked Kristina to come with us.' She smiled. 'She did some extra hours in the shop and I think the money is burning a hole in her pocket. I hope you don't mind, at least you'll have someone to talk to.'

Roggen forced a smile. 'But I thought she was a working girl, nose to the grindstone and all that.'

'She's got to have time off, you know,' Nia said in amusement.

Roggen bit her lip. She didn't have much in common with Kristina, but at least it was better to go with her than to go alone.

Kristina was sitting in the kitchen, talking quietly to old Ambrose Powell whose slippered feet were stretched out towards the fire.

'Goodness, it's hot in here,' Roggen said, smiling politely at Nia's father. He was an imposing man with an iron-grey beard and shrewd eyes, but he didn't look well, his face was flushed and he was lying back in his chair as if he was very tired.

'My old bones feel the cold,' he said. 'It's all right for you youngsters with your health and strength to keep you warm.'

Nia led the way to the front door and Roggen paused before stepping out into the sunlight.

'I hope your father will be all right. I'll call in when we get back, tell you all about it.'

Roggen watched Kristina as she stepped out into the sunlight, her gleaming hair falling in unfashionable waves to her shoulders.

'If we don't get a move on we'll miss the tram, it's a good walk to the Tumpkin, mind,' Kristina said, glancing back over her shoulder.

Roggen sighed. 'We've got plenty of time. We can even have an ice cream at Di Marco's if we want one.' Nevertheless, she waved goodbye to Nia and hurried to catch up with Kristina as she moved out of the docks entrance and on to the busy street.

'What's wrong with your mother, Kristina?' she asked, making an effort to be pleasant. 'She hasn't come up to the house for a few days now and we've been quite worried about her.' She paused. 'And for heaven's sake slow down, will you. We haven't all got legs like a pony.'

Kristina looked back, her face suddenly sober. 'Mam's not well,' she said softly. 'Well, you might as well know the truth. She's going to have another baby, and at her age too, I'm worried sick about her. Let's hope it's a boy this time, then Thomas Presdey might leave her alone.'

'I thought you seemed preoccupied.' Roggen felt a surge of pity for Mrs Presdey who must be past forty, the wrong age to be pregnant. 'I suppose your mother will have to give up coming up to the house for a while at least. I'll miss her cheerful smile.'

Kristina rubbed at her high cheekbone with a slim fingertip. 'If I had my way, Mam wouldn't work at all. But Thomas's job is a bit up and down, some days he works, some days he doesn't. He's got friendly with Robert Jenkins, you know, the man who made a scene in that meeting we went to? Thomas is trying to get into his good books so that he'll have work.' She sighed. 'I suppose I'm weak, but I've agreed to go out with Jenkins to the Empire tonight.'

Roggen stared at Kristina. The girl was so foolish. She

was already involved with Eden, and now she was allowing herself to be pushed into the arms of some other man.

'You don't have to do anything you don't want to,' she said dryly. 'You're of an age to make up your own mind about such things.' Roggen warmed to her subject. 'You mustn't let men subjugate you. They will try, make no mistake about it, but women are as good as men, if not better, remember that!'

'I'll try,' Kristina said ruefully, 'though it's hard to feel superior when a man is slapping you across the face.'

Roggen was shocked. She had never realized that Kristina was treated so badly, but then Kristina and she scarcely ever talked. She was Nia's friend, though what they had in common Roggen could never imagine.

'You must learn to stand up for yourself, Kristina, don't be so soft.'

'There's things you don't understand.' Kristina spoke softly. 'Jenkins has the power to say if Thomas has a job or not, he chooses the dockers to work on the ships, he's like God himself to the men.'

Roggen was about to respond angrily when she saw the expression almost of bitterness in Kristina's eyes.

'If Thomas doesn't get work, he's at home taking it out on Mam.'

'That stepfather of yours must be an unfeeling brute.' Roggen felt anger rise within her. Why did women allow themselves to be dominated by men? 'Why don't you and your mother fight back?' she said, and was puzzled by Kristina's quick look of derision.

'It's all right for you,' Kristina smiled without humour, 'but where's my mam to go if Thomas puts her out on the road? And then there's my sisters, they're only young, mind, and Mam keeps the peace as much as possible to give them a happy home to grow up in.'

'Yes, but it seems to be you who catches the brunt of that man's anger,' Roggen said fiercely, not understanding Kristina's reasoning. Why didn't she just up sticks and get out of the house?

Roggen was growing impatient, so she let the matter drop. 'Come on, let's get a cornet while we're waiting for the tram. It's so hot and my mouth's as dry as dust. Thank goodness I didn't bring a coat!'

The sun was rising higher in the sky and Roggen was suddenly determined not to let Kristina's problems spoil the day. She felt a tingling sense of anticipation; she had looked forward for so long to hearing Ramsay MacDonald speak. It was said that he was an orator of the first order, better even than the Welshman Lloyd George. He was a man of the people, even though he'd come from a very good home and was a gentleman, and that thought was comforting to Roggen.

A different kettle of fish from Keir Hardie whose aims had been laudable enough, but who had, apparently, worn a cloth cap to Parliament, and that Roggen considered an affectation in the wrong direction.

The tram rocked and rolled into sight and Roggen sighed with relief. Her feet, in their Cuban-heeled shoes, had begun to ache, and she felt sure that one of her silk stockings had come undone.

She sat near the window and stared out at the shops around the Tumpkin, feeling the sun hot against her cheeks. In spite of herself her mind turned to the subject of Kristina's problems as she tried to envisage a life lived in one of the small, two-up-two-down cottages where the only water supply was an outside tap and the privy down at the end of the garden. Worse was the stranglehold the men seemed to have on their womenfolk, especially men like Thomas Presdey who bullied their way through life, expecting and receiving obedience, even submission, from their wives and daughters.

'You're going out with this man Jenkins, then?' she said, forgetting her resolution not to discuss Kristina's affairs. Kristina looked at her, shaking back her bright hair in resignation.

'Aye, I'll go out with him, I'll smoke his Players and eat his sweets and lead him on up the garden path, but if he puts one hand out of place I'll slap him down so fast he won't know what hit him.'

'Well, I don't understand you,' Roggen said. 'I'd stay a mile away from him.'

'Well, we're all different, I suppose.'

Kristina turned away and Roggen concluded that she had finished with the subject, which was her privilege, she supposed.

As Roggen alighted from the tram she stared round her at the busy Swansea streets and breathed in the colour of it all – the big stores flourishing along the High Street, and the cockle women with huge baskets over their arms, calling raucously over the noise of the traffic. Swansea was her town and Roggen loved it dearly. She could never imagine moving away from the seaside and living inland.

'There's the station,' Kristina said, unable to keep the note of excitement out of her voice. 'I've never been on a train before, is it dangerous do you think?'

Roggen smiled. 'Don't be silly! We've had trains in Swansea for over seventy years. What makes you think the railway is suddenly going to become dangerous? Not a very intrepid explorer, are you?' She laughed as she guided her into the station at the top of the High Street and on to the platform. 'We're only going to Newport, mind, and it's not the back of beyond, I assure you.'

Kristina climbed eagerly on to the train which puffed and gushed smoke and cinders as though it were a living monster. Watching her, Roggen smiled. Kristina was a strange person, so reserved and mature in some ways and yet very much like a child, unable to conceal her excitement.

Roggen could never be like Kristina, who was friendly to the point of being uninhibited. Roggen blamed her own strict upbringing for the inhibitions she had grown to expect as normal. She would only kiss her mother or her brother chastely on the cheek. At the boarding school she had attended, the girls had been expected to be in control of their emotions at all times. Even tears of homesickness were frowned upon. Roggen had received an excellent education, but those years away from home had left their mark on her, and not in a way she thought desirable.

But they had given her a sense of independence, of knowing how to look after herself. Kristina, on the other hand, had gone no further afield than the school at Day y Graig, returning home each day to her family.

'There's quiet you are,' Kristina said softly. 'Not worried by the clackety-clack of the wheels, are you?'

Roggen smiled at her. 'Just lost in thought, that's all.' She leaned forwards in her seat and looked out through the grimy window at the sprawling eastern side of the town where the many factories and foundries huddled along the banks of the River Tawe. It was a long river and wide, tidal and busy, and it was all a part of the Swansea she loved.

If she were to go into politics, Roggen thought, she might improve the lot of women, and indeed men, too, for some workers laboured for twelve hours a day in filthy jobs, with little to show for it at the end of the week except for a long food bill in Libba's shop. She smiled a little at her own temerity. What made her think she could change the world? But she could try her level best, and as far as she could see the beginning was to follow Ramsay MacDonald's Labour Party.

As the train clattered through the small towns of Neath and Port Talbot, Roggen settled back in her seat. The carriage was filling up, and the two young men opposite them in natty suits and smart fedoras were admiring Kristina's long slender legs. Roggen glanced at her companion, who was still staring out of the window, unaware of the attention she was receiving. She was quite natural and totally unconceited, Roggen thought.

An elderly woman climbed aboard at Cardiff, her feet overflowing the sides of her black patent shoes. Around her huge bosom lay a heavy necklace of jet beads that clattered as she sank into her seat. Her entire outfit was in black, Roggen noticed. She was obviously a woman who took widowhood as a lifelong condition. Probably because she knew that she didn't have any of the charms necessary to beguile another man.

Roggen stifled a giggle. She wished she could communicate her thoughts to Kristina, but the fat woman was jammed in beside her and was looking with open disapproval at the fashionably short skirts both Roggen and Kristina were wearing.

At Newport, the sun was shining even more brightly, and Roggen alighted thankfully from the train. The heavy scent of lavender perfume worn by the fat lady at her side had become almost unbearable.

'*Duw*, is this Newport then?' Kristina said in disbelief. 'It looks ordinary enough to me, not that much different to Swansea is it?'

Roggen smiled. 'Don't be disappointed, I dare say there will be some flowers and a bit of red carpet on the platform to greet Ramsay MacDonald. Come on, let's follow everyone else.' Roggen's sense of excitement grew as she felt herself jostled along by the noisy crowd, for there was an almost festive feeling on the station that was contagious.

'There's excitement for you,' Kristina said, her eyes alight with the fun of it all. 'I always knew I'd like travelling, got my father's blood in me all right. Never seen so many people in one place. There must be five hundred here if there's one!'

Roggen suppressed a smile. She would hardly call a little over sixty miles from Swansea travelling, but then she'd been to London, had seen the streets there teeming with people, had shopped at the huge stores and attended shows at theatres that were the best in the country, perhaps even in the world. It was good to go away, but it was wonderful to return home; that was something Kristina would learn one day.

'There's a train coming, I can see it puffing around the bend ahead.' Kristina had the benefit of her unusual height, aided still further by standing on her toes. 'Someone is waving a flag through the window, it must be him!'

The crowd fell silent as the train drew to a noisy halt, steam and cinders gushing forth on to the track. One of the carriage doors was opened, and a man with a heavy moustache and with a soft hat pulled down over his forehead stepped on to the platform to the noisy cheers of the crowd.

Ramsay MacDonald was smaller than Roggen had expected him to be. He held up his hand for quiet, and Roggen felt an unexpected lump in her throat.

'We're witnessing history here,' she said softly, and then fell silent as the politician began to speak.

'My friends,' he said, and his voice was sombre, carrying well through the crowds, 'I know you had expected an address but my supporters have begged me not to wear myself out by trying to speak at any length in the open air, and I intend to take notice of that advice.' He paused and looked around, and Roggen felt a sense of disappointment. It seemed she had travelled for several hours just to catch a glimpse of the man before he was whisked away.

'But I have proof now,' he continued, 'that after the thirtieth of May, Newport is going to be Labour!' There was more loud cheering and he held up his hand again.

'I am delighted to see you, and glad that you are all so happy and enthusiastic. I will await the results at Newport with great expectation and confidence.'

'Is that all?' Kristina said as the man turned to speak quietly to one of his aides. 'I expected something more, though don't ask me what.'

A rustle of whispering ran through the crowd. 'He's leaving by road for Aberavon.' Kristina, who could see more than Roggen, sighed softly.

'Aye, he's going all right, led away by all those men and chains of office hanging around their necks.'

Roggen tried to appear more cheerful than she felt.

'Never mind. Now we're here, let's go and have a cup of coffee and something to eat at one of the cafés outside the station.'

As they moved forwards slowly behind the crowds, Roggen would not admit, even for a second, that she was bitterly disappointed there had been no rousing speech, calling the faithful, especially the women, to stand behind him. She saw the brightness of the sky and the sun-splashed roadway, and her spirits rose. This was only the beginning, great things would be achieved by the new government, she was sure of it.

Kristina had enjoyed the day out with Roggen much more than she'd first believed she would. Although she had little in common with the sophisticated young woman who lived in the big house, her doubts about the day had soon faded. She had liked the travelling, quickly becoming used to the motion of the train, and was possessed by the old urge to sail across the seas to the land where her father had been born. But now, as she walked towards the small cottage where she lived, her sense of euphoria was quickly evaporating at the thought of home. She dreaded to see her mother's pale, drawn face and to endure Thomas Presdey's ill temper.

She was very conscious that in a few hours she would meet Jenkins and go with him to the Empire or, if they couldn't get in, spend a couple of hours in the Castle Cinema. In any case she expected to be bored with his company and then afterwards to have to fend off the unwelcome advances he would surely make. Thomas Presdey had made her feel like a loose woman, offering her to Jenkins in exchange for security in his job. Well, Roggen was right about one thing; she would need to be firm and make sure she wasn't trapped into going out with the man a second time.

As she opened the door, she heard Thomas's voice complaining. 'This tea's stone cold, woman. Why don't you ever make me a fresh pot?'

Kristina saw at once that her mother was having a bad day. She was lying back in her chair as if too weary to even lift up her head as her daughter came into the room.

'I'll put the kettle on, Mam,' Kristina said at once. 'There's a lovely day I've had, you should have seen the crowds down at Newport station, hundreds of people were there.'

If she had hoped to divert Thomas, she was disappointed. He looked grimly towards her and scratched at his stomach with both hands.

'And why aren't you at work, madam?' he demanded. 'There's bloody marvellous it is to have the women folk lazing around while I work my guts out on the dock.'

'Libba gave me time off,' Kristina said reasonably, and then she smiled with false cheerfulness. 'In any case, I have to make myself look nice to go out to the theatre tonight, don't I? Can't let you and Mam down.'

Thomas nodded. 'Aye, I don't want you disappointing Jenkins, that's right enough.' He leaned back in his chair. 'Where's that tea? I'm parched, and what about some grub? Been slaving I have, loading ships all day, and those damn Chinkies bowing and scraping with their stupid plaits swinging down to their arses, look real fools, they do.'

Kristina made the tea quickly, glad to have Thomas take out his spleen on the unknown Chinese sailors. Not that she had ever found them stupid; they were always polite and deferential as they made their way to and from their ships; but then it didn't do to argue with her stepfather.

She gave him his tea and then handed a cup to her mother. 'Drink up, Mam, and then go to bed. I'll see to the food.'

'What does your mam want to go to bed for, girl?' Thomas almost spat out a mouthful of tea in his anger. 'Done nothing all day but sit around nursing her belly.'

Kristina forced herself to remain calm. There was more than one way to deal with Thomas Presdey. 'Unless Mam gets some rest,' she said softly, 'I can't see my way clear to leaving her alone and going with Jenkins to the Empire.'

Thomas looked as though he'd suddenly tasted something very sour. His features twisted in a grimace, but after a moment's hesitation he relented. 'Aw, for Christ's sake get up to bed then, woman!' He rose to his feet and pulled on his cap and scarf. 'I don't know why you need all this cosseting, anyone would think no one ever had a babba before.' He jerked open the door. 'I'm off to the Burrows for a pint, I've had enough of mewling women.'

As the door closed behind her husband, Ceinwen Presdey gave Kristina a look of gratitude. 'Just give me an hour, girl,' she said softly, 'then I'll be right as rain.' She paused at the foot of the stairs. 'The younger ones have had their tea, out playing on the patch. Keep an eye on them won't you, love?'

Kristina towered above her mother as she rested a gentle hand on her shoulder. 'Go on, Mam, I'm not exactly helpless, mind.'

She sat alone in the kitchen, staring into the fire, the prospect of an evening with Jenkins quenching her usual optimism. She could not make up her mind how to handle events; should she tell the man flatly that she had no interest in him, that she did not intend to start up any sort of relationship with him? Then she thought of her mother's pale, weary face, and knew she could do no such thing. Thomas would take out his anger on his wife as well as on Kristina, and the house would be hell to live in, especially if, as a result of her actions, Thomas could get no work.

She would have to tread carefully, not offending Jenkins but offering him no encouragement either. The problem would be solved if Kristina was to get the job at Ty Coch, for although the Red House was only a matter of a few hundred yards away from Lambert's Cottages, it was barrier enough, especially if she was allowed to live in.

She filled a bowl from the tap outside and carried it

back to the kitchen table. It was about time she started to get ready for her meeting with Jenkins, she could not put off the moment indefinitely.

In her room, she dressed carefully in her one and only pair of silk stockings, but as she fastened the suspenders, the stud holding the stocking in place broke away and rolled out of sight. She pulled her dress over her head, then hurried downstairs, clicking her tongue in annoyance. She glanced at the clock, aware that time was moving much too swiftly for her, and quickly searched in the tin box for a button. With a sigh of relief she found one just the right size and slipped it in between the silk and the metal, and it held fast.

She called from the doorway for her sisters and they trailed in from the patch, knees grass-stained, hair escaped from neat plaits falling in curly tangles around grubby faces. Kristina smiled at them. Sarah and Jayne were like peas from a pod, dark-haired and blue-eyed, with their mother's good nature. It was just as well that neither of them took after Thomas for bad temper.

'Off you go outside and have a good wash before I call Mam from bed, or there'll be the devil to pay.'

The two girls held hands and walked through the kitchen and out into the back yard without argument, and Kristina heard the swish of water and the sound of laughter with a sense of sadness. The only time her sisters were at ease in their own home was when Thomas was out.

Gently, she woke her mother. 'Come on, Mam,' she said softly. 'I'll be going out soon.'

Ceinwen looked up at her and pushed back her greying hair. 'There you are, I feel better already,' she said, forcing a smile. Her eyes were deeply shadowed and she winced as she sat up and pushed back the heavy covers. Kristina looked at her in concern.

'Shall I stay in, Mam?' she said. 'I can tell Jenkins that you are not feeling well.'

'No, go you,' her mother said quickly. 'I'd rather avoid any rows with your father tonight.'

Kristina was just returning to the kitchen when the sound of the front door knocker reverberated through the house. She straightened her shoulders, took a deep breath and moved slowly along the passage. The moment had come when she had to face Jenkins, and now there was no going back.

4

The Empire Theatre was stuffy and heavy with the smell of cigarette smoke. The curtains hung in folds over the stage, the dust and discoloration of the heavy velvet concealed by the diffused lighting. The musicians were tuning their instruments, the discordant notes drifting to where Kristina sat in the centre of the auditorium, uncomfortably aware of Jenkins at her side.

The seats seemed huddled together, and she felt his knee against hers and glanced at him, not sure if this was a deliberate ploy on his part, an unsubtle way of making a suggestion. She decided to ignore it, and stoically faced the front.

'Good crowd in,' Jenkins said, leaning towards her. 'I've heard it's a damn fine show, a sell-out. There are some famous foreign singers here and they're only in Swansea for a few days.'

Kristina nodded, not really interested. She did not particularly like the enclosed atmosphere of the theatre. She preferred to be walking the sands or climbing the rough slopes of Kilvey Hill to survey the panorama of the docklands and, far across the way, the twin curves of Mumbles Head. The stretch of sea reaching as far as the coast of Devon gave her a feeling of space and freedom. In the warmth and dimness of the theatre, she felt unbearably restricted and somehow smothered by the heavy figure of Jenkins as he loomed over her.

She glanced into his face, realizing that to some women he would appear almost handsome. His hawk-like nose gave him an exotic, almost Arabian look, and his jaw was

49

firm and square. His thick hair was dark and slightly unruly, and the pitch damage to his skin scarcely mattered at all. She wondered how he had come to leave the fuel works and find a job of such responsibility on the docks. Probably he was the ruthless sort, the kind of man who would get his own way in everything. But not with her.

She was slightly puzzled by him. His attitude this evening was so different from what she'd expected, and there was a gentleness about him that surprised her.

'Here,' he said, as though sensing her thoughts, and a cardboard box was placed in her lap. She glanced down at the Fry's chocolates and felt a momentary sense of pity. Jenkins was trying hard to impress her.

'There's no need to have gone to such trouble,' she whispered, and the gift was like a heavy weight, a link in a chain that was trying to imprison her.

The orchestra struck up a rousing tune, and even Kristina felt a sense of anticipation as the curtains swished apart to reveal the stage. She settled back into her seat and decided the best tactic was to pretend she was alone and lose herself in the colour and music and in her apparent enjoyment of the line of chorus girls high kicking their way across the boards to a backdrop of incredible mountains and lakes.

She became caught up in the music and movement and was transported from the theatre into a comforting make-believe world where everything was fun and laughter. Beautiful young girls in splendid costumes danced and sang, and a portly tenor, his voice rising thrillingly to the gods, held the audience spellbound.

In the interval, the lights went up, and Kristina stared around her half blinded. Jenkins leaned forward without speaking, staring intently at her as though trying to gauge her mood, and for a moment the unreality of the action on the stage seemed to be continued in Kristina's thoughts and she smiled unguardedly.

Jenkins blinked rapidly as though hardly believing the

evidence of his eyes, and then Kristina sat back in her seat and deliberately held out the box of chocolates as though it could form an effective barrier between Jenkins and herself.

For the rest of the show, Kristina kept a tight hold on herself. She told herself that the man and woman singing so passionately to each other on stage, holding hands and gazing longingly into each other's eyes as cruel fate wrenched them apart, were only acting a role. Nothing in the theatre was real, it was all an illusion, as was the softening of her hostility to Robert Jenkins.

She was relieved when it was all over, for in spite of herself she had become ensnared in the web of make-believe and heightened emotions portrayed by the actors. She moved into the crowded aisle, wanting only to get out into the fresh air and into the world of reality where men were not romantic heroes but demanding bullies.

'I'll take you home,' Robert said, and Kristina stared up into the star-filled sky, breathing in the scent of flowers from a window box as she tried to ignore the sounds of revelry from a group of men pushing their way from the Bay View past the crowds of theatre-goers.

'No, it's all right, I can get home on my own, thank you.' She was aware that she sounded childishly belligerent, but somehow she couldn't help herself. It seemed that Robert managed to bring out the worst in her.

He held out a protective arm as a drunkard almost barged into her, and Kristina found herself in the embarrassing position of having to agree to his suggestion that he accompany her along the darkened roadways. She was rarely outside the confines of Lambert's Cottages at this time of night, and on reflection she did feel apprehensive at the thought of making her way to the docklands alone.

They walked in silence for a while, leaving the busy streets behind them. Kristina searched her mind for something polite to say as Jenkins led the way along

51

Oystermouth Road to where the twin piers of the docks came into view, but all the words stuck in her throat.

Kristina sighed as the sea moved restlessly into the shore and on the horizon there gleamed the distant lights of a ship waiting for the outgoing tide. She felt again the old urge to leave the familiar shores of Swansea, to go away and find adventure, a new life perhaps, far from Lambert's Cottages.

'Thank you for taking me to the Empire,' she said, glancing towards Jenkins's dark shape. 'You needn't come any further, I know my way blindfold, from here.'

'I'm taking you to the door,' Jenkins said, and his voice brooked no argument. Kristina held back a sigh, knowing that this was what she deplored in men like Robert Jenkins; their unshakeable belief that they were always right.

'I told you,' she said with an edge to her voice, 'I'll be all right. I'm not a child and neither am I a fool.'

She began to walk ahead, her long legs covering the distance quickly. Roggen certainly had something in wanting equal rights for women; how dare Jenkins, a virtual stranger, treat her as though he were superior? She had no time for the likes of him, and if Robert thought an evening at the theatre and a box of Fry's would make her fall in love with him, he was sadly mistaken.

As she reached the West Pier, a figure lurched out of the shadows and confronted her. She stopped, dismayed, but spoke out clearly. 'Get out of my way!'

'Uppity, is it?' A slurred voice spoke, and the fumes of stale ale drifted to where Kristina stood. 'Come on, what are you walking the docks for if you don't want to make a shilling or two, then?'

As Kristina opened her mouth to speak she became aware of a hand on her shoulder.

'The lady is with me,' Robert said evenly. He didn't make any move but his very calmness was a threat.

'*Duw*, Mr Jenkins, is it? Sorry, sir.' The man seemed to vanish into the shadows, and anger rose within Kristina that she had once again put herself in a position where she was beholden to Robert.

'Well, you were right,' she said ungraciously. 'I do need someone to see me home. Thank you, Mr Jenkins.'

'Call me Robert, will you?' he said. 'You make me sound like a church deacon.'

Kristina didn't reply, but walked in silence towards the cottages, where the lamps from the windows shone like fireflies in the darkness. At the door to her own house, Kristina stopped and turned to speak to Jenkins. She was the same height as him and they stood eye to eye. It was she who looked away first.

'I won't ask you in, if you don't mind,' she said. 'My mam is not very well and it's getting a bit late.' Before he could reply, the door was flung open, and Kristina's stepfather was revealed in the wash of light. For once he seemed in a good humour as he stood back invitingly.

'Come on inside,' he said. 'I've got a bottle of Ceinwen's parsnip wine waiting.'

Jenkins bent his broad shoulders and moved into the house, and Kristina bit her lip in frustration. She had hoped to end the evening without incident and so far that hadn't been too difficult, but if Jenkins got the drink in him he would doubtless be as uncontrolled as any other man in his cups.

'I've sent your mother up to bed,' Thomas said with false heartiness. 'She's very tired, going to have another babba, see.' He laughed uproariously. 'There's life in the old dog yet, eh Mr Jenkins?'

Kristina winced at his crudeness, and glanced at Robert, who was seating himself at the table as though he was one of the family. He wasn't joining in the laughter as she'd half expected him to, and as his eyes met hers it seemed there might be a glimmer of understanding in them.

'I'll just have one to be sociable, like,' Robert said, taking the glass Thomas held towards him. 'I've got work in the morning, Tom, and so have you.'

Kristina, reading behind his words, knew that she could not make her escape yet. It was clear the Robert expected her to be with him till the bitter end of the evening. And what then, a snatched kiss in the doorway?

Thomas sat at the table, big legs spread apart, his thick fingers clutching a glass. 'Well, if you say I've got work tomorrow, Mr Jenkins, then that's lovely by me.' He spoke fawningly and seemed reluctant to leave the company of the man who was the virtual power on the docks.

It was Robert who brought the evening to a close as, with a quick look at Kristina, he rose to leave. 'Will you see me out?' he asked, and Thomas immediately leaped to his feet.

'There you are then, I'll go to bed, leave you youngsters alone for a bit. Nothing like having young blood roused by a drop of parsnip wine.' He winked at Robert before leaving the room, and Kristina felt the hot colour suffuse her face.

'Well, I'll say good night then.' Kristina opened the front door pointedly. The houses opposite were in darkness as if all the occupants had long since gone to their beds, and it somehow made Kristina feel very alone. Robert took her hand, and she tensed, expecting to have to fight him off, but he just looked into her face as though memorizing her features. She realized suddenly that he hardly ever seemed to smile.

'I'm not one to make speeches,' he said, 'but I have enjoyed taking you out. I hope you've forgotten our quarrels and that we can be friends, at least that will do for a start.' Kristina remained silent, and he spoke again. 'Can we try to forget our differences, then, and make a fresh start?'

Kristina's strong sense of fair play came to the fore, and she found herself nodding. 'Aye, we could be friends, perhaps, but nothing more, mind.' She gave him a direct look. 'This is not what I want for myself.' She waved to the two rows of low-built uneven houses crouching against the docks. 'I want to be free of Lambert's and free of my stepfather. I want to see something of the world outside Swansea, and I won't be tied down, not by anyone.'

'*Chwarae teg*,' Robert replied with a glimmer of a smile. 'Fair play. I'm not asking you for anything except to forget the bad start we made.'

Krisina felt a little foolish. 'I know,' she said quickly. 'I'm sorry.'

'We seem to make a habit of apologizing to one another,' Robert said softly. He stared at her for a long moment.

'Good night, Kristina,' he said, and then he had turned and was striding away into the darkness. Kristina felt a sudden sense of anticlimax as she closed the door against the night.

Thomas was peering into the room even as she moved towards the stairs. 'Well, when are you going out with him again?' he said eagerly.

'I'm not,' Kristina replied, and bit her lip as Thomas's face darkened. He entered the room and stood before her, a ridiculous figure in his long underpants and a vest that revealed his corpulent belly.

'I got a good mind to take the belt to you.' He came up to her and caught her shoulder, and Kristina pulled away from him in sudden outrage.

'You touch me again, Thomas Presdey, and I'll swing for you!' She glared at him fiercely. 'Your little plan to marry me off has worked in my favour because in Robert Jenkins I've found someone who can protect me even from you.' She was heady with her own sense of power as Thomas fell back, uncertainty written across his face.

'Robert wants me to like him,' she continued. 'He'll do anything for me, and if I say there's no work for Thomas Presdey there will be no work.' She wasn't at all sure that Robert would pay the least bit of attention to anything she said, but Thomas didn't know that.

She lowered her voice, fearing her mother would hear.

'There are going to be some changes round here, mind, or I'll want to know why.'

He turned away from her then, shoulders slumped. 'What's the world coming to when a daughter turns and bites the hand that's fed her for all these years. Gratitude! By God, there's not a scrap of it, no thanks for all the times I've slaved in a stinking hold to keep food in your belly.'

'I've more than paid you back, mind.' Kristina refused to feel guilty. 'I've helped in the house since I was a child, scrubbing and cleaning alongside Mam so that she didn't have to wear herself out looking after you. And since I've been working,' she paused, 'ever since I was fourteen, I've handed over my wages from Libba's, not keeping any-thing back for myself. Well, Thomas, that's all in the past. Now I'll be having a fair share of what I earn.'

He moved away from her without another word, and climbed the stairs heavily. She heard the creaking of springs as he climbed into his bed.

Some of the tension eased from Kristina's shoulders. It had been a strange night, a night of compromises. She had given way a little, in spite of herself, feeling almost sorry for Robert Jenkins, but she had also won a battle against her stepfather. She smiled wryly as she extinguished the lamp. It seemed that some good had come of her meeting with Robert Jenkins after all.

The thirtieth of May was a day of brilliant sunshine. Blossoms clouded the branches of the trees with puffs of colour, and the late daffodils scattered the grass verges with brave splashes of yellow. And it was the day the fate of the Labour Party would be decided.

Roggen stood in the sitting room, staring into the garden, her thoughts on the coming election. It was surely a foregone conclusion that Ramsay MacDonald would win. People were tired of false promises and meaningless rhetoric; what the voters needed now was a strong leader, a man of vision who would take the country forth with hope into the new decade of the thirties.

She had left her mother and Eden talking in the dining room over a desultory breakfast. Eden was in no rush to get to the shipping office, and that was a decision Roggen regretted because she could foresee an argument ahead. She was not wrong.

'So there you are, Roggen.' Eden came into the room, tall, yet moving smoothly, quietly. His voice had the usual ring of authority about it, and his dark serious eyes probed hers. 'Not really going through with it, are you?'

She turned her back to him, her skirt swirling above her knees as she moved. She was unaware of her natural charm, the glow of vitality that gleamed from her thick, bobbed hair, and the air of suppressed energy in her movements, the latter an idiosyncrasy she shared with her brother.

'If you mean am I canvassing votes for Ramsay MacDonald, the answer is yes.' She tried to keep the edge of impatience from her voice, but Eden was more perceptive than most.

'Don't get annoyed,' he said reasonably. 'It's just that I'd like to try to tell you a bit about the aims of the socialists. They're all for redistribution of wealth, for one thing. Take from the rich to give to the poor, in fact a misguided Robin Hood syndrome.'

Roggen glanced up at him. 'Is that such a bad thing?' she asked, and watched his face as he replied.

'In theory, no,' he said, 'but it's just like communism. If you shared out the wealth of the country today, in a few years there would still be rich and poor, because some would work hard at making a go of things, while others would just fritter the wealth away.'

'You are not giving people much credit for intelligence, are you?' Roggen said, turning to face her brother. 'All right, I agree some people would be useless whatever anyone did for them, but others, given the chance, would make something of their lives.'

Eden shrugged. 'People with initiative will do it on

their own just as our grandfather did. No one gave the Lambs a leg up. What we've got we've earned.'

Roggen sighed. 'All right, you are much cleverer at words than I am, but I still feel that MacDonald can't make a much worse mess of things than Baldwin and Lloyd George have done. Give new ideas a chance, Eden, let's see how things turn out.'

He came to her and rested his hand on her shoulder, and on an impulse Roggen reached up on tiptoe and kissed him.

'Please, Eden, don't say any more. Let me be my own woman rightly or wrongly?'

After a moment, he drew her to him and hugged her close for a moment, before releasing her and moving to the door. 'It goes against the grain, but good luck to you anyway, enjoy your first experience of the political arena.' At the door he paused. 'Would you like a lift somewhere?'

Roggen shook her head. 'Thanks, but I'm meeting Nia in a minute.' Roggen frowned. 'Kristina Larson, too. I bet you'll be even more keen to give us a lift now. By the way, Eden, what do you think of Mama's plan to take Kristina on here instead of her mother?'

Eden frowned. 'I shouldn't think Kristina will want to clean house for us. She's a lovely young woman, she shouldn't spend her time chasing around after anyone.'

Roggen shook her head. 'For an intelligent man you can sometimes be lacking in common sense.' She smiled indulgently at her brother. 'Apart from the obvious inducement of working near you, Kristina is not happy at home. Her stepfather picks on her, I think sometimes he's even violent towards her.'

Eden was silent for a long moment, a brooding look on his handsome face.

'I'll speak to mother about it later,' he said at last, 'but there will be no problem. Kristina's got a job here whenever she wants it.'

And he wasn't too displeased by the idea, Roggen

could see, but she did not give voice to her thoughts. Eden was a private man and would not take kindly to any further probing into his feelings.

'I've got to go,' Eden said. 'I've got a business meeting at the Mackworth, and then I suppose I'll have to treat the client to a good luncheon.' He smiled, and Roggen thought how handsome her brother was. He would be a catch for any woman.

'Poor you,' she said, her voice heavy with sarcasm. 'What a difficult life you do lead.'

He caught her by the collar, a look of feigned anger on his face. 'Why I put up with lip from a little squirt like you, I don't know. Get into the car.'

They picked both Nia and Kristina up outside Libba's shop. Kristina's face lit up when she saw Eden, and in that moment Roggen felt almost sorry for her. Roggen watched, noticing how Eden held the door for Kristina, his eyes on her lovely face. He seemed unaware of the heavy smell of paraffin that clung to her clothing.

'Been working this morning?' Roggen asked, somewhat superfluously, and Kristina nodded.

'It was very busy at Libba's this morning, so I went in for a couple of hours.' Kristina grimaced. 'Wish she'd put me on grinding coffee rather than doling out paraffin, mind, but there it is, somebody's got to do it.'

'Well, not any more,' Roggen said, aware that Eden was looking at her with raised eyebrows. 'Eden agrees that you'd be the ideal person to do the job at our house in place of your mother, don't you, Eden?'

He glanced at Kristina. 'What I actually said was the job is yours if you want it.'

Nia edged her way beside Roggen while Kristina sank back beside Eden against the leather upholstery in the front of the car, her eyes shining, her face flushed. Watching the fall of Kristina's golden hair, Roggen felt a momentary stab of apprehension, wondering if she had just made a big mistake. By trying to take a rise out of

Kristina, all she had done was to ensure that she and Eden would be thrown together.

But then, nothing serious could ever come of their attraction to each other. Eden needed a wife who could grace a dinner table, speak well and confidently to his business associates, in short be an asset to him in his career.

Shock waves rocked through her as the realization dawned that she was nothing but a snob. Here she was spouting about votes for women making them equal, but at the same time perpetuating the old prejudices of the middle classes. She felt like a heel, and actually reached out a hand towards Kristina who misunderstood the gesture.

'Thanks for speaking up for me,' she said, turning round in her seat. 'I'm a good worker, I'll keep your house as spotless as my mam did, you'll see.'

Roggen was glad when Eden stopped the car outside the polling station.

'David Williams is the candidate for Swansea East,' she reminded her companions. 'He's a good chap and I'm sure he'll get in.'

Eden glanced at her as he slid easily from behind the wheel. 'Sure, and a real working class man too, coming as he does from the respectable, middle class area of Brynmill.'

The sarcasm in his voice was not lost on Roggen, but she chose to ignore it. She was still too unsure of her own views on class distinction to enter into an argument with her clever brother.

'Don't listen to him, girls,' Roggen said, smiling at Nia who seemed preoccupied with her own thoughts. 'Eden is a clever talker, but he's quite biased in his opinions.'

The hall was empty, the meeting was quite obviously over, and Roggen realized with a feeling of chagrin that she must have got the time wrong.

'No one's here,' Kristina said, and there was a trace of relief in her voice. 'There's a shame.'

'Damn!' Roggen said. 'I was so keen to give my support, a fine canvasser I am.'

Eden was still standing beside his car and he smiled as they left the hall. Roggen glared at him.

'I bet you knew I'd got the time wrong. You mean pig, you could have told me.'

Eden shrugged. 'Can't tell you anything when you get the bit between your teeth.' He took her by the arm. 'Come along, I'll treat you to some tea at the Mackworth, make up for the disappointment.'

Roggen sighed. 'Come on, then, I'll accept your offer. It isn't often you put your hand in your pocket, brother mine.'

It was almost a week later when Roggen, picking up the newspaper, saw an item about David Williams. She felt a sense of triumph as she read the article, in which Williams was offering his thanks to the voters who had elected him. He gave his special thanks to the many people who had contributed to his success. On the same page of *The Post* was a quote from Ramsay MacDonald, who gave every credit to the women of the country for their sound common sense in voting Labour in the election. As Roggen read his words, she felt tears blur her eyes.

'Thanks are due,' she read, 'to the women who voted for a policy of social reconstruction at home, and peace abroad.'

As she put down the paper, she felt vindicated. All her fruitless arguments with Eden seemed not to have been in vain. She looked up to see her brother enter the dining room.

'Well sis,' he said, 'you've got them in, but remember this, you may have caught a tiger by the tail and it's all of us who will have to live with the results.'

Suddenly Roggen's elation faded away. What if Eden was right? Had a big mistake been made on that sunny day in May that she and many others might live to regret?

5

The hot June sunshine washed the streets of Swansea with contrasting splashes of light and shade; between the buildings lay deep cool shadow, but the surface of the roads seemed to shimmer with heat.

Nia Powell would have liked to take off the linen coat she wore over her short summer dress, but that was not practical, for it was a specially designed coat. Inside the lining were huge reinforced pockets for carrying the illegal cash handed to her with the slips of paper used for betting.

She waited for a tram, brushing back her hair in weariness. Her one consolation came from the knowledge that the money she collected during the next hour or two would be her own. Ambrose would be mortified if he had any inkling of what she was doing, but he did not suspect for one moment that his daughter was taking a cut of the business for herself.

Nia suppressed a smile as she saw the tram come into sight, snaking its way along the road between shimmering rails. She had collected her father's bets, enough to make him happy, and now she would approach his cast-off customers on her own account.

Ambrose had a rigid code of practice; if clients let him down with a payment, he ceased any contact with them. He told Nia that a man who did not pay his gambling debt was worse than a thief, for it was a debt of honour. Nia had found these customers only too ready to take a second chance, and they were confident that old Ambrose Powell's daughter must be trustworthy with the might of

62

her father's business behind her. Little did any of them know that she was venturing out alone, taking grave risks whenever she took a bet that was a little high, for it would wipe out her entire month's takings if it should be called in.

But her customers were, for the most part, losers, amateurs who gambled recklessly on a whim, and so far she had been fortunate, taking in much more than she ever had to pay out, which was why there were scarcely any failed bookmakers, she decided.

She had to be cautious because the law was against both her and her father. While it was legal for the rich to gamble with credit, it was still illegal for bets to be taken for cash. Nia climbed aboard the tram and sat carefully on the wooden seat, trying not to rattle the heavy coins in her large pockets.

It was even hotter in the tram than out on the roadway, and Nia felt perspiration break out on her brow. Her discomfort was caused not only by the sun shining through the window but also by the sight of the constable wheeling his cycle on the roadway outside. It seemed she had caught the tram just in time to avoid him.

She was aware that it was suspicious, to say the least, for a young woman to be paying calls on the same houses day after day on a regular basis, and so she kept out of sight of the law as much as she could. Some days she carried a basket on her arm and wore a light shawl around her shoulders and the small black straw hat of the cockle seller. No one but her customers knew that beneath the snowy cloth lay not seafood but the fruits of her illegal trade.

Nia alighted from the tram and made her way, sighing wearily, towards Brynhyfred. She had many customers living in the small houses bordering the square and she felt too hot to work. Still, this was for herself.

She resisted glancing uneasily over her shoulder as she walked along the pathway to the door of one of the neat houses and lifted the knocker. It wasn't likely that the constable would come this way. A dog barked in the back regions of the building and then Nia heard the sound of slippered feet coming along the passageway.

'*Duw*, it's you, Nia. Come in, there's a good girl. My Bertie was just saying he hoped you was coming, got a good tip, so he has.' The plump housewife led the way into the kitchen where, in spite of the summer sunshine, the fire glowed redly in the grate. 'Here's the girl you've been waiting for, Bertie, now I'll just get a cup of tea going while you two sort out your business.'

The man shuffled the pages of a newspaper between his fingers, and glanced up at Nia, smiling. 'Wish I'd put a bet on the outcome of the election then, would have won hands down, I would. I said old Ramsay would get in this time and he has.' He laughed smugly. 'Stanley Baldwin has just resigned officially, so it says in here anyway.'

Nia smiled noncommittally; she had voted for Stanley Baldwin herself, but it was not politic to say so to one of her best customers.

'What horse you got in mind today then, Bertie?' Nia found she dropped into singsong Welsh when speaking to her customers. They would not readily understand that she was fluent in Latin and Greek, and could read and write in French as well as she could in English or Welsh. Fortunately she had a gift for languages, and it was this which had kept her home when her father had been bent on sending her to a boarding school. She had coaxed and cajoled him, emphasizing that no one could teach her as much as he could.

Nia had learned her lessons well, though she had been more fascinated with the intricacies of the betting world than with learning art or history. She could work out an Accumulator or a Yankee as well as any man, probably better, and knew how to prejudge the odds a horse would be given just before the start with amazing accuracy.

She had bought a book on law and betting, and intended one day to work with the law on her side, opening an office legally in a respectable part of the town.

She would be taking bets from the more affluent, those to whom she could afford to allow credit. Perhaps she would end up with a string of offices all over Swansea. She certainly intended to try.

'Sixpence on the nose for Gold Bar, is it, Bertie?' She looked at the slip of paper he had given her. 'You must be confident of this one, then.'

He winked. 'Oh, aye, from the horse's mouth as they say. Put a sixpence on him yourself, Nia, do yourself a bit of good.'

'I might at that.' Nia smiled but she had no intention of doing any such thing. She had seen too many 'sure things' fail to reach the post, and her information was that Gold Bar, though good on the soft, was not a winner on the hard-baked earth which was the going at Chepstow today.

'Oh, I've just remembered,' Bertie handed her his money, 'the chap next door, young Joe Barnes the coal, has asked me to give you the nod.' He smiled. 'Got a convert there, I have, he'll be a good customer if you take him on.'

Nia nodded, concealing her eagerness. 'His name's Joe, did you say?' She jotted down his name in her neat handwriting, along with the number of his house.

Joe Barnes, coal merchant, that sounded promising. If he took to the betting he might become a regular customer, and that was just what Nia needed; clients with some security behind them.

'Thanks, Bertie.' She made her way from the hot kitchen, shaking her head at the proffered cup of tea. 'No thanks, Mrs Harries,' she said warmly. 'I can't drink tea everywhere I go or I'd be running to the privy all day!'

She left the heat of the little house and stood for a moment looking towards Kilvey Hill looming up across the River Tawe and dreaming a little, enjoying her fondest hope of one day being rich and respected. She longed to shake off the shame of being the daughter of a disgraced vicar. She would show the people of Swansea that she was somebody to be reckoned with.

Her knock on the door of the next house yielded a quick response. A surprisingly good-looking young man was staring down at her, his dark eyes regarding her steadily.

'I'm looking for Joe Barnes, coal merchant,' she said, feeling her colour rising at the admiration in the young man's smile.

'Then you've found him,' he said. 'And you are Nia Powell?' He held the door open wider. 'I think you'd better come inside for a bit. I can see old Peter Plod coming up the hill wheeling his bike.'

Nia glanced quickly in the direction of the constable and stepped at once into the shadowy passageway feeling at a distinct disadvantage. It was humiliating the way she had to creep around, hiding from the law, but it wouldn't always be like that, she promised herself.

'Bertie next door put me on to a sure thing,' he said, leading the way into the coolness of a neat parlour. 'Gold Bar, was it?'

Nia shook back her brown hair. 'If you'll take my advice you'll leave Gold Bar alone and put your money on Red Fin. He's an outsider, but good, and with a fine jockey riding him. The odds are at ten to one right now, but they may drop to seven to one which would still bring you in a good profit.'

It was rare for Nia to give away such a gem of advice, but she wanted Joe Barnes to be a regular, and there was nothing like a good win at the start to make a convert out of a beginner.

Joe looked at her shrewdly. 'Have you told Bertie about this Red Fin?' he asked, and Nia had the feeling he saw right through her. She shook her head.

'I can't afford to give all my customers tips.' She decided that honesty was her best policy. 'I want to have you on my books as a regular, that's why I'm giving you special consideration.' Her smile said that, apart from that, she found him an attractive young man, and Joe responded in the way she hoped he would.

'Right then, we'll have a guinea on this Red Fin, and if he wins perhaps you'll help me to celebrate?'

'Why not?' Nia said, mentally preparing to lay this bet off on her father. It was too big a risk for her to take with her slender resources, but Ambrose would accept the man as a casual, not questioning Nia if she gave him some story about meeting the man through one of Ambrose's regulars.

As Joe Barnes opened the door for Nia, he smiled down at her. 'You're a very unusual young lady, and I like a girl with some guts who's not afraid to push out on her own. I wish you the best of luck and hope I'll see you again soon.'

She glanced around her and saw with relief that there was no sign of the police constable. She continued her round, walking along the flatness of Neath Road, calling from house to house and looking longingly towards the cool waters of the River Tawe. Perhaps she should call it a day and go home. The pockets of her coat were satisfyingly heavy, and she would have plenty of book-work to do for Ambrose and herself, which would occupy a great part of her evening.

She had promised to go down the Monkey Run later on with Kristina, but she felt weary of walking, and perhaps an early night would be of more use to her than the parade along the Prom looking for men to ogle. It had been fun in the past when they were younger, and it had become something of a habit, but she really felt far too mature to be parading like some dizzy young thing harbouring a futile hope that Mr Right would come along.

She continued along the Neath Road until she reached the Hafod Bridge where she heaved a sigh of relief. From here, she could take a bus right down to the bottom of Wind Street and then she would be almost home. Just a short walk along the docks to the cottages and she could divest herself of the coat that had become a dead weight.

Her friends, she thought, did not know they were born.

Not for them this tramping the streets in a humiliating search for customers. For a moment, she almost resented Ro, with her rich home and fine background, and even Kristina, with her more simple way of life. Then she dipped her hand into the hidden pockets and felt the money nestling there, and she smiled.

Nia had been calling on Joe Barnes for several weeks when he made a suggestion that they go into business together.

'I respect your judgement,' he said, leaning with both his hands on the table. He was smart in a white shirt and neat tie, his strong legs covered with a pair of hound's-tooth check trousers. 'You gave me a good tip about Red Fin, didn't you? Won a tidy bit of money, I did.'

'So?' Nia smiled at him, waiting for his next words. She had become interested in Joe. He was quite different from her usual customers; well heeled, almost affluent, owning not only the house in which he lived but several other houses in the area. She had learned that he was not simply a coal merchant but was also a man of great intelligence with the added advantage of fine good looks.

'So, I have contacts with people through my coal rounds,' he said. 'I can provide some financial backing as well as premises suitable for a legal office. You, Nia, can provide the know-how.'

Nia sank into one of the plush chairs. It was cool in the well-furnished parlour, and on an impulse she slipped off her coat. It was a measure of how much she trusted Joe, she thought with surprise, for she had never before allowed anyone to see the hidden pockets containing the shillings and sixpences collected from hours of hard slogging around dusty streets.

'What do you know about betting offices?' she asked, a little disconcerted that Joe had taken the initiative and had looked into the matter.

'Well,' he smiled, and Nia thought again how handsome he was, not a tall man, but well set, with a narrow waist and broad shoulders, his face almost swarthy from being out in all weathers, 'I know that, in theory, making a book is a simple affair.' He smiled. 'I said "in theory", remember. The idea is that whichever horse wins, the pay-out should not exceed the total money customers have staked.'

Nia looked at him carefully. 'That's correct,' she said a little sharply, 'but remember, a bookie like me can't set his own prices or odds. I can only copy those laid down by the big on-the-course bookies. I have to stay with the small punter to make the thing work; one big winning bet would ruin me.'

'You don't think an established office a good thing, then?' Joe asked, and Nia bit her lip, considering his suggestion.

'Would you be prepared to offer the punters credit terms?' she asked at last, and watched as Joe turned to stare out of the window, a thoughtful look on his face.

'Aye, I could collect their money on weekends, along with the payment for coal. Is credit part of it, then?'

Nia smiled in relief. Joe did not know that much about betting after all. 'While it's illegal to collect cash bets,' she explained, 'it's within the law to take bets on credit, but I daren't allow my customers credit. If they were to lose their money a few times and grow disheartened, they'd simply not pay, and would take their wagers to some other back street bookie. There's always someone around just waiting to poach the punters.'

She paused. 'I tell you what, you get me new customers who are willing to pay on the button, and I'll cut you in for a share of the profits. When we're a big enough business with a list of well-heeled punters, then's the time to think in terms of an office.'

Joe moved round the table as Nia rose and picked up her coat. 'Here, let me help you.' He stood beside her looking down at her, a smile lighting up his blue eyes. 'You know something, Nia Powell,' he said quietly. 'You are a very remarkable woman.'

She knew he was going to kiss her, and she stood still, unable to move for fear of spoiling the moment. Joe drew her close until his arms were tightly around her, and then slowly he bent his head.

Nia felt a sudden glow as his lips touched hers. This was not her first kiss but it might well have been for the excitement that filled her. Joe was so strong, so sure of himself, and he admired her, more, he cared about her. That was so important, a balm to the times when she felt hurt and alone, an outcast almost from society; Nia Powell whose father was a disgraced vicar and who walked the streets collecting bets for a living.

When Joe released her, they stared at each other in silence for a long moment. Joe spoke without touching her again. 'Here's to our future together, whatever it might hold.'

Nia left his house in a state of euphoria, hardly noticing the walk home, her thoughts on the moment when Joe had held her in his arms. She savoured his words of praise, each one a pearl to cherish.

When she entered the parlour, her father was waiting in his high-backed chair near the window. He held her ledger in his hands, and there was a page full of figures before him. He looked up over his spectacles at Nia, and there was a strange look in his eyes.

'Done well for yourself today, Nia?' he asked. 'You look extra specially pleased, you must have found yourself some new punters.'

'What do you mean, Dad?' Her mouth was suddenly dry. She looked at Ambrose and saw that he was smiling gently.

'Don't dissemble, my dear, you can't con an old con man. Come and sit here and tell me just how you've been doing over these past months.'

Nia obeyed him and stared at him defiantly. 'I haven't been cheating you, Dad,' she said quickly. 'I've still been doing your work, but I took up some of the customers you didn't want, that's all.'

'I'm not blaming you.' Ambrose put the ledger down on the desk, and placed his fingertips together. He didn't seem angry, just faintly amused, and that made Nia uncomfortable. 'Indeed, I commend you for using your initiative.'

Nia was suddenly angry. Her father had sent her out on the streets collecting bets ever since she was a child; surely she deserved something for herself after all this time.

'Don't be on the defensive, my dear.' Ambrose seemed to sense something of her feelings. 'You've been a dutiful daughter, even if you haven't been a loving one, and there is no reason on earth why you shouldn't line your own pockets as well as mine.'

Nia felt the old aching feeling of pain rise up within her. She not a loving daughter? That was rich. She rose and walked to the door, feeling the tears burn her eyes. She paused and turned to look back at Ambrose who sat so self-satisfied and unshakeable.

'Let he that is without sin cast the first stone, isn't that what you once preached, Dad?' she said raggedly. 'You talk to me about love, but when did you ever take me in your arms and tell me you loved me?' She swallowed hard, determined not to break down now, not after years of hiding her feelings from the old man seated before her.

'You taught me a lot, I'll give you that,' she continued. 'You taught me Latin and Greek side by side with law breaking. I was the only girl in the whole of Lambert's Cottages who could speak French fluently and who learned as a child how to evade the constable.'

She placed the bag with his takings on the desk before him. 'Here, Father, this is the last time I collect for you, get someone else to be your runner, you've used me long enough.'

'Man's inhumanity to man,' her father murmured, and Nia faced him squarely, her hands clenched to her sides.

'Oh, yes, you know how to quote someone else's words all right, but when did you ever have kind words to spare for your child? Even when my mother died from the

71

shame of seeing you cast from the church, I had no comfort from you. The very day of Mam's funeral I was sent out to collect your bets!'

She moved closer and stared down at him, and he seemed to have shrunk into his chair. 'Well, you gave me my knowledge of figures, you taught me the trade of the bookie very well, and I'm going to use that knowledge to build up my own business.'

She opened the door. 'You talk of me being a dutiful but not a loving daughter, when all I longed for from you was a little love.' She sighed softly. 'Why bother to talk? It's too late for that, much too late. As soon as I can, I'll get out of here. You can hire a paid housekeeper and a paid runner, and in the meantime, you can add up all that you owe me for the years of work I've done for you.'

She closed the door before he could speak, and hurried up the stairs to her room. Then, sinking down on to the brightly coloured quilt that covered her bed she put her head in her hands, holding back hot, painful tears.

After all this time, the bitterness in her had overflowed, released by her father's criticism of her. If only once he had taken her in his arms, kissed her, shown her a little human feeling, she could have forgiven him everything.

And yet, today a man had held her in his arms, a man with clear eyes and a strong jaw. Joe Barnes had kissed her and told her she was a remarkable woman. The tears came then, rolling salt into her mouth. Nia lay on the bed and the sobs were wrenched from her in painful gasps. She cried until she felt there were no more tears in her, and then she moved to the basin on the table and washed her face in cold water.

It didn't take her long to pack her small case. She lifted the floorboard in her room and took out her savings book, staring at the figures in satisfaction before tucking the book safely away in her handbag.

She stood for a moment, staring out of her window at the back of the house, not seeing the huge rubbish bins at the bottom of each garden and the small privys ranged along the back like a line of dilapidated sheds. She knew she must get away from here, she could not remain in the same house as her father, not now he knew her real feelings towards him. Her bitterness had surprised even herself, and she could not bear to be constantly reminded of her past hurts by the sight of her father sitting like a miser counting his money.

She knew where she was going, and she had not a doubt in her mind that she would be welcome. She moved to the door, looking round the spartan room with its worn Indian carpet and dusty curtains, and realized she had not really seen it for some time.

It was clear that Ambrose Powell had never been a man to waste his money on fripperies. Well, now she would be well out of it, she would miss nothing of her home life. She paused for a moment. She would miss her friends; Kristina had always seemed to understand her loneliness, but then she had her own life to lead, and they were no longer children playing together around the docklands.

She moved downstairs and felt the sun on her face as it fell through the fanlight above the door. For a moment she was blinded, so that at first she did not see her father standing in the parlour.

'You're leaving.' Ambrose spoke softly, and it was a statement, not a question. 'It hasn't all been bad, has it, Nia?'

There had been good times when Mam was still alive and when Father was the vicar of the old established church near the docks. She remembered her mother's pleasure when she saw Ambrose teaching their daughter to be a scholar, but Mam hadn't known then about the bookmaking, the surreptitious bets taken by Nia, and the secret ledger kept by her husband in the same desk at which he sat to compose his sermons.

'There were some good days,' she conceded in a tone more sorrowful than truthful. 'But those days are over now, Dad. I've got to be my own woman and you must manage as best you can.' She paused, her hand on the doorknob. 'You've never needed anyone else, have you, Dad, not emotionally anyway, and I'm sure you'll soon find someone to run around for you.'

He took her hand and placed a purse of money square on her palm. 'You've earned this, it's yours. I've saved it for you.' He gestured around him. 'One day everything will be yours, you must realize that everything I've done was for you.'

'But the price was too high, Dad.' Without another word, she opened the door and stepped out into the street where the long evening shadows stretched between the uneven rows of houses. She had never really been part of the street, she had always been a little bit of an outsider. She had recognized that fact very early on.

She was aware that her feet were aching. She had walked several miles on her rounds. Wearily, she made her way out of the docks entrance and along the roadway to the Tumpkin. There she leaned against one of the shop windows and waited for the bus that would take her away from her past.

When it came, she climbed aboard without a backward glance. She felt no regrets, no sense of sorrow, just a great feeling of release.

She sat on the bus and closed her eyes, and refused to think any further ahead than the next step. She was washed clean by her tears, she felt like a blank page of paper waiting for words to be written that would give her life meaning.

She felt the bus jolt to a stop and lifting her case she moved quickly to the doorway. Over the small houses at Brynhyfred, the sun shed its evening light, rosy and comforting.

Nia sighed and moved forwards towards the small row of houses that stared out at Kilvey Hill. The path had never seemed so long, not in all the time she'd been collecting money. She knocked on the door and put down her case, waiting patiently, expectantly.

Joe Barnes looked at her and then glanced down to the

74

case at her feet. Taking in the situation at once, he held out his arms, and as Nia moved into his embrace she heard him whisper softly, 'Welcome home, *cariad*.'

6

Victoria Park was fragrant with the scent of the roses blossoming in the well-kept gardens. The squat shape of the Patti Pavilion cast but little shadow, for the sun was high in a cloudless sky. Across the road at the Slip, a gentle tide washed into the golden crescent of sand, and on the horizon, cargo ships were faint shadows in the haze of heat.

'So you've actually left home to go and live with this coalman?' Roggen spoke in wonder, staring at Nia curiously, unaware of the implicit snobbishness of her question.

'Joe's not just a coalman!' Nia said, and her hands were white as they clutched her black patent handbag. 'He's a fine man. He works hard and . . .' She broke off as Kristina reached out towards her in sympathy.

'Well I think it's very brave of you to defy your dad, and him a preacher, too,' Kristina sighed. 'And there's a romantic story if ever I heard one, love at first sight, *duw*, I do envy you, Nia.'

Roggen rose from the wooden bench and stared out across the busy Mumbles Road. If she was honest, she too envied Nia her astounding good fortune in finding, in such unlikely circumstances, a man she could love enough to live tally with. Roggen found it difficult to believe that she herself would ever be so swept away as to live with a man without the respectability of a gold wedding ring.

'I suppose it *is* very brave of you, Nia,' she said, 'to defy not only your father but convention too. I doubt if I would have the courage.'

She saw Nia glance at her with raised eyebrows. 'What have I to lose?' she said softly. 'I'm already a sinner in the eyes of the people of Swansea.' She·spoke bravely, but there was a blush in her cheeks that belied her air of bravado.

Kristina shook back her long hair, her green eyes full of sympathy. 'You can't help it if your dad was thrown out of the church, can you?'

Nia's smile was forced. 'You know what the good book says, the sins of the father shall be visited upon the children. Anyway, I've been a runner for my father for as long as I can remember, and it isn't exactly a respectable occupation, is it? I'm forever hiding from constables and taking money illegally. If you ask me, Joe's too good for me.'

'But do you love him?' Kristina asked anxiously. 'This Joe you've found, he sounds a fine and handsome man, a good man, but you have to be sure you love him, mind.'

Roggen watched the two as they sat, heads close together, talking in wonder of love and romance. A fat lot of romance there would be in a small cottage in Brynhyfred with a man who worked in filthy coal all day. She couldn't believe that her friends wanted so little from life. She sat down and abruptly changed the subject.

'Mother tells me you are moving your things up to our house tonight, Kristina,' she said. 'What does your stepfather have to say about you leaving?'

'I think he's relieved.' Kristina turned a troubled face towards Roggen. 'I've always got on Thomas's nerves, and perhaps with me out of the way he'll be a bit better tempered with Mam.'

Roggen doubted that. Thomas Presdey was a drunk and a bully, and his sort would never change, but it wasn't for her to interfere in Kris's business. 'How's your mother coping with her pregnancy?' she asked, and Kristina smiled.

'Mam's over that sickliness now, feeling much more human, so she says. Growing a bit, she is, too, putting on weight. It's strange to think of Mam with another baby, mind.'

Roggen sat in silence for a moment, staring at the full-blown petals of the roses without seeing their silky bloom. She was bored and her mind drifted to the meeting, wondering if either of the girls would come with her tonight. There was to be a lecture on the Labour movement in Swansea, given by an aide of the Labour MP David Williams.

'I'm going to the Royal Institute tonight,' she said, breaking into the conversation. 'Anyone feel like coming?'

There was a long silence that seemed to stretch on for ever, and then Kristina smiled. 'Aye, I'll come, got nothing better to do anyway.'

Nia shook her head. 'I'm staying in with Joe. We've got a lot to talk about.' There was a softening of Nia's expression, a glow in her eyes that gave Roggen a pang of envy in spite of herself.

'Proper little love birds, aren't you?' she said. 'But for heaven's sake, don't allow yourself to get pregnant. There are several methods of contraception available to us now, so be sensible and find out about one of them.'

She saw the colour run into Nia's face and realized the girl was embarrassed at her frankness. 'For heaven's sake!' she said impatiently. 'I'm sure you two are not going to live together in the same house without anything intimate happening, so all I'm saying is be careful.'

Kristina rose to her feet. 'Well, I know it's Saturday afternoon,' she said, 'but I've still got a lot to do, especially if I'm to bring my things over to your house tonight, Roggen.'

'I'll have to make a move, too,' Nia said quickly. 'Come on, if we hurry we can all go to the bus stop together.'

Roggen glanced at her watch. 'You two go on,' she said. 'I want to do some shopping, and then Eden's picking me up. See you about seven then, Kristina. Come over to Ty Coch with your stuff and I'll show you your room.'

She waved her hand in farewell and stepped briskly out of the park gates in the direction of Oxford Street. Perhaps she would stop in the café near the hospital and have a cup of iced coffee. It really was a very hot day and she had an hour to kill before she met her brother.

She sat in the coolness of Cascarini's ice-cream parlour and stared out at the church opposite. It towered above the road, casting a shadow over the surrounding buildings. Further along the road, towards the centre of town, the Swansea Hospital stood in splendour, fresh new trees growing at the gates. She loved Swansea and felt sure she would never move away from the town.

Roggen felt the tensions ease away. Perhaps she had been hasty in condemning Nia's sudden love affair with this man, Joe. She might have been a little kinder; could it be that she was more envious of Nia than she'd realized?

Early marriages were so romantic, but regrettably they were not usual in her own family. Take Eden, for example, a fine man, in the prime of life, but not yet engaged. He'd had lady friends, of course, and perhaps indulged sometimes in feminine company that was not so ladylike, but he was willing to wait until the right woman came along before committing himself. He was now walking out with Bella. Could she be the right one for him?

Her brother was choosy, and that was her way, too, Roggen decided. She would be patient and wait for the right man to come along. The thought was a small crumb of comfort to her.

She was about to collect her gloves and handbag and leave, when a shadow fell over her. She looked up into the face of Richard James smiling down at her. He had a good face, Roggen thought, and a wide intelligent forehead, and further, he shared her political views.

Roggen didn't afterwards know if it was the backwash of Nia's love story or Richard's own charm that made her return his smile. Encouraged, he took a seat beside her and leaned forward.

'May I buy you another one of those?' He indicated the empty glass, and Roggen nodded.

'That would be very nice. It's iced coffee, please.' She admired his air of confidence as he raised his hand to the waitress behind the counter who hurried, blushing, to do his bidding.

Roggen leaned back in her chair and watched Richard with interest, wondering about him. She knew him by sight, of course, and she recalled clearly the way he had stood up to the man Jenkins at the meeting some time ago, but now she felt she would like to know more about him.

He was obviously from a good family; he was dressed in a light worsted suit, well cut and fitting him admirably from his broad shoulders down to the heels of his shining shoes. He was not traditionally handsome – his jaw was perhaps a shade too square for classic good looks – but he had clear eyes and a disarming smile, and she judged him to be in his late twenties or early thirties.

'Tell me something about yourself.' Roggen took the glass he held towards her and smiled.

'I'm a teacher at the grammar school.' He leaned back and stared at her directly. 'I live on the hill at Cwmdonkin, I'm free and unattached, and my intentions are strictly dishonourable. Will that do?'

Roggen realized he was poking gentle fun at her. 'It will do for a start,' she said, lowering her eyelashes in what she knew was a coquettish gesture. 'I'm a teacher too, strangely enough,' she said. 'I take the little ones, need a firm hand, they do.'

They indulged in small talk, and all the time Roggen was sizing Richard up.

'I'm going to the lecture at the Royal Institute tonight,' he said. 'Will I have the pleasure of seeing you there?'

'You may well do. It's certainly my intention to go,' she said, meeting his gaze.

'Perhaps I may call for you?' he said, an easy smile on his lips as though he was not really bothered if she accepted or not.

'I would like that very much, but I have a friend coming with me.'

He immediately leaned away from her, his eyes half closed, concealing his thoughts. 'I see. It was presumptuous of me to expect you to be unattached.'

'My friend is Kristina Larson,' Roggen said.

'Ah, I remember,' Richard said softly. 'The lovely girl with the long hair.'

Roggen felt a flash of something like jealousy. 'Kristina is going to work as a domestic at our house,' she said quickly.

'Well, perhaps I could see you both there at the meeting,' Richard said. 'I certainly wouldn't object to being in the company of such lovely ladies.'

Roggen thought about it for a moment and came to the conclusion that Eden would probably object to Richard James knocking on their door out of the blue. He was a stickler for convention, and she and Richard had not been formally introduced.

'Yes, I'll see you there. I live so near to the Institute that it's only a few minutes' walk away.' She added quickly, 'Though it would be nice if perhaps you could keep seats for us.'

'It will be my pleasure,' Richard said, and rose to his feet. 'As for now, might I drop you somewhere? My car is right outside.'

Roggen rose to her feet with a smile. 'That would be very nice,' she said, pulling on her lace gloves. 'I have some shopping to do in Oxford Street; perhaps you could take me as far as the market?'

His car was high bonneted and shining, and in spite of herself, Roggen was impressed. The car reaffirmed her impression that Richard must have good family connections. He certainly would not be able to afford a car like that on a teacher's salary.

It was good to be driving along the shimmering roadway towards the market. The heat was intense, and Roggen hoped that her expensive perfume was keeping her fresh. She glanced at Richard who drove confidently, his hands firm on the wheel. He really was nice-looking and very sure of himself as well. In too short a time, they pulled up outside the market entrance, and he turned to look at her.

'Thank you,' Roggen said, embarrassed to have her scrutiny returned. She alighted from the car as he held the door open for her, aware that her short skirt had ridden up and was showing a little more leg than was proper. But if Richard noticed, he made no comment. They were standing very close together and she could smell the masculine scent of him as he smiled down at her without speaking. She felt her colour rise as she reluctantly turned away from him, knowing she'd wanted very much for him to kiss her.

She walked away as gracefully as she could, wondering if he was watching. In the market, she strolled aimlessly between the stalls, not seeing the colourful rows of fruit and the crisp greenery of the vegetables brought every day from the farms of Gower. She was thinking of Richard, and wondering excitedly if he would turn out to be more than just an attractive friend. That he liked her was obvious, she thought with a feeling of happiness.

She dawdled over her shopping so long, unable to concentrate on what she was buying, that she was five minutes late meeting Eden. He was standing near the car, arms crossed over his spotless shirt; a tall, handsome man was her brother and she was proud of him, but she had no intention of telling him about her tryst with Richard James. She knew he would disapprove.

Tryst. What a lovely expression, she thought as she gave Eden a small peck, standing on tiptoe to reach his cheek.

'Thanks for coming to meet me, brother,' she said, and

allowed him to take her parcels and put them on the back seat of the car.

'To tell the truth I thought you'd be laden down with bolts of material and ribbons and things, but you've not bought very much, have you? Miracles still happen, I see.'

'Don't be sarcastic, Eden,' she said, but she was smiling, lost in thought, considering what she would wear to meet Richard.

'I understand from mother that Kristina's coming up to the house.' Eden's voice broke into her reverie. 'I hope you'll be kind to her and won't try to interfere in things that don't concern you.'

'I've spoken to Kristina, and she's moving a few things up to the house later, as a matter of fact,' Roggen said, seeing an opportunity to make an excuse for going out. 'I thought perhaps I could take her out for an ice cream somewhere.' She didn't like lying to Eden, but she wasn't going to tell him that she was meeting Richard.

She sank back in her seat and closed her eyes, unwilling to say any more in case Eden thought of questioning her. She allowed her thoughts to drift, and in her mind's eye she could see Richard James's smile, and feel the excitement of being near him. She felt the urge to giggle; perhaps she and Nia were experiencing a delayed reaction to spring fever. She could almost feel sorry for Kristina with her tangled love life – it was a strange new sensation, and one that Roggen rather liked.

Kristina picked up the small parcel of clothing that lay on the bed, and stared around the familiar room with a strange constriction in her throat. She had happily shared the small bedroom with her two sisters, cuddling close in the cold dark nights of winter, laughing, crying with them, and now she was preparing to leave home. She was glad the girls were out playing on the patch. She didn't want any tears.

She moved towards the door, telling herself that Roggen would be growing impatient, perhaps standing at the window of the big house at the edge of the docks, shaking back her bob of dark hair in the imperious manner of which she was quite unaware. Kristina felt beholden to her – she owed her something for putting in a good word about the job at Ty Coch – but Roggen could be a little intolerant and difficult, Kristina had no illusions about that.

In the kitchen, Kristina walked slowly to where her mother was bending over the fire, poking up a flame to boil water for the tin bath standing before the hearth. Kristina felt a flash of resentment. It wouldn't hurt Thomas to do that for himself now that Mam was expecting again.

'I'm off now, Mam.' She saw her mother glance at the parcel, an anxious question in her pale blue eyes.

'I'm taking my things over to Ty Coch,' she explained, unnecessarily, for Mam knew exactly what she was doing, which accounted for the mistiness that was quickly wiped away on the corner of a spotless apron.

'I won't be far, Mam,' she said quickly, 'and I'll still be able to nip over here and give you a hand with the girls and all that.' She hugged her mother warmly. 'Look, I'll be out of Thomas's way and that's the best thing I could do for you. I wish I'd thought of getting out of here years ago.'

Her mother returned her embrace wordlessly, and Kristina sensed the conflict within her; she did not wish to be disloyal to her husband, and yet she had to agree that Kristina's presence was a constant source of irritation to him.

'Go on, you.' Ceinwen freed herself reluctantly. 'I'm a foolish old woman, acting as if you were going for ever. Don't take any notice of me.' She patted her small rounded stomach. 'Carrying makes you go all weepy, *cariad*. It's hard to explain, but you'll understand when you're married and having a babba of your own.'

'That won't be for some time yet, don't you worry, Mam,' Kristina said wryly. 'I haven't even met my Mr Right, remember.'

'I think you have, *cariad*, you just won't admit it, even to yourself,' her mother replied softly.

Kristina left the house quickly and hurried along the dirt road. She avoided the square of bare ground aptly named the patch, where her sisters were playing, but hearing the sound of happy childish voices, she felt suddenly uncertain of the rightness of what she was doing.

She hesitated a moment and then moved towards the big house near the entrance to the docks. Ty Coch. The Red House. It was well named, for the walls were red and glowing in the evening sun. It was the most imposing house in the area, built to withstand the vagaries of the weather.

Kristina felt tears burn her eyes and rubbed at them impatiently. She would not be far away from the little house in Lambert's Cottages, and yet nothing would ever be the same again. She would never be part of the household, she would soon become little more than a visitor.

'There you are, Kristina. I've been waiting for you.' Roggen held the door open, a formal smile on her face. She looked particularly smart, her light blue frock with a white sailor collar edged with matching blue suiting her to perfection.

'Thank you,' Kristina said as she stepped into the hallway of Ty Coch, feeling strange at the thought that this was to be her home.

'Come along and see your room. I think you'll like it.' Roggen was clearly making the point that she was the mistress and Kristina the servant.

Kristina followed Roggen as she hurried up the wide staircase and along a passageway that was deeply carpeted and had fine paintings hanging on the walls. Ty Coch was a lovely house, old and mellow and much larger than it appeared from the outside.

'Here,' Roggen swung open a door, and as Kristina followed her inside she was struck by the spaciousness of the bedroom and the way the light spilling in from the large window gave an impression of brightness and warmth. The curtains and bed coverings matched the upholstery on the large chair that stood near the elegant fireplace. It was splendour to Kristina, who had helped her mother clean the room often enough but had never imagined sleeping in it herself.

'*Duw,* there's a lovely room. Is it all mine, just for myself?' she asked.

'Well, of course.' Roggen answered the question with an attitude of surprise. 'Who do you think you're going to share with? Not me, and I don't think it would be proper if you were to share a bedroom with Eden, would it?'

Roggen was well aware of the situation between Kristina and Eden, she was making that quite clear. Kristina straightened her shoulders and stared directly at Roggen, and the girl had the grace to look away.

'Are you still going out with that Jenkins man?' Roggen asked, and Kristina nodded.

'Aye, I've been with him to the Empire a few times, and he's been to visit me at Mam's house.' How could she explain that she'd gone with him for the sake of keeping the peace? Roggen simply did not understand the situation. And really, Robert wasn't so bad. Kristina had come to realize that he was quite a sensitive man. He knew the way Thomas's mind was working and so he had deliberately kept the situation between them light and friendly.

'Well, you must settle yourself in, I suppose.' Roggen moved to the door. 'I hope you'll be happy here,' she added as an afterthought.

'I will be!' Kristina said, trying to sound enthusiastic. 'I can't get over it, having such a big room all to myself. It'll be so peaceful.' She looked round her, thoughtfully. 'This house is going to be a lot to clean, mind, but I'll soon get used to it.'

Roggen moved to the door. 'Well, Eden's thought of that. He's employed one of the young Williams girls to come up and do the rough work. See how my brother is looking after you? Special treatment for you, it seems.'

Kristina saw Roggen's eyebrows rise and her clear eyes regard her steadily. Roggen could freeze over the water in Swansea Bay with such a look, Kristina thought ruefully. She returned the gaze speculatively. She had seen Roggen sitting in Cascarini's ice-cream parlour with Richard James, laughing and having fun. She was a strange girl; the hoity-toity Roggen Lamb one minute, and next just a young girl wanting some fun.

'I'll leave you for now,' Roggen said, 'but do hurry and get changed or we'll be late for the meeting tonight. You are coming along, I take it?'

'Yes, I'm coming,' Kristina said, 'I'll be ready in two ticks.' She changed hurriedly, not wanting to keep Roggen waiting. She knew quite well that she was acting as second best to Nia, and indeed if it wasn't for Nia's intervention, Roggen probably wouldn't consider going out with Kristina at all.

In the meeting, Kristina hardly listened to the speaker bumbling on about politics and how the Labour government would soon have the country on its feet even though it seemed to Kristina that nothing much had happened yet. There was still a depression, a great deal of unemployment, and some believed it would get worse. And what this man was saying about great prosperity being round the corner for all seemed far removed from the streets of Swansea, where folk went about their own business and if they were hard up solved their own problems by making a visit to the pawnshop.

She glanced covertly around her to see if anyone else was as bored as she was. Roggen appeared to glow with fervour, but if the feeling was aroused by the speaker or by the closeness of Richard James who was sitting next to them, Kristina could not be sure.

She caught the eye of a man across the other side of the room and sat up straighter in her seat, quickly looking away and pretending she hadn't seen Robert Jenkins's small nod of recognition. *Daro!* Did he have to be here? The man seemed to dog her footsteps, following her everywhere she went or else knocking on the door for her. Well, she doubted if even he would have the gall to come up to Ty Coch, not after the way Eden had treated him.

The speaker resumed his seat to a scattering of applause, and with a sigh of relief Kristina realized the lecture was over. She shifted in her seat, hoping to be first out of the hall, but out of the corner of her eye, she saw Jenkins making his way towards her, pushing chairs aside in his haste.

'Evening, Kristina,' he said as he stopped beside her. 'How's your mother, all right is she? Perhaps I can see you home and call in on her?'

Kristina saw Roggen turn, frowning at Robert, and she spoke up quickly. 'Mam's doing very well, thank you, but I'm not at home now. I've got a living-in job.'

Roggen was hurrying from the hall, talking swiftly to Richard James, probably telling him all about how Kristina had been walking out with Robert Jenkins. Kristina bit her lip. She didn't want a scene, all she wanted was to creep into the privacy of her own bedroom up at Ty Coch and be allowed to live her own life.

Robert Jenkins accompanied her from the hall. Outside, a crescent moon sliced through the darkness, an illuminated nail paring against the inkiness of the night.

'Can I see you to where you work, then?' Jenkins asked, and Roggen was suddenly beside her.

'Richard has just offered us a lift. He's starting up the engine of his car. Hurry, if you're coming with us, I don't want to keep him waiting.'

Kristina nodded gratefully. 'That's very kind of him.' She turned apologetically to Robert Jenkins. 'Thanks so much,' she said politely, for whatever she felt about him, she didn't wish to be rude, 'but as you see, I have a lift.'

But Jenkins wasn't that easily put off. 'I can't offer you a car ride,' he said, 'but we could have a drink in the

Burrows before you go home, and remember,' he smiled, 'two's company, three's a crowd.'

Kristina looked uncertainly at Roggen. She had not thought that she might be in the way, and on reflection, she didn't want to play gooseberry to Roggen and Richard James.

'All right. I'd be pleased to have you walk me home, but as for going into the Burrows, no thank you, I don't want to be out late. I've got to get up for work in the morning.'

'Kristina!' Roggen said in a low voice. 'You must come home with us. Don't let this man browbeat you.'

'It's all right,' Kristina replied. 'Really, go on, you, I'll be all right.'

'On your own head be it, then!' Roggen said and turned huffily, striding away. She climbed into the car and for a moment her head was bent close to Richard's. Kristina sighed with relief as he slid the car into gear and pulled away from the kerb.

'What did you think of the speaker?' Robert said conversationally as they began to walk towards the docks.

'I was bored stiff,' Kristina replied, a little angry with herself for encouraging him, even though it had been for the best of reasons. She certainly hadn't wanted a clash between Jenkins and Richard. They'd had a confrontation once before and there was no knowing what sort of scene would result. She felt a sudden warmth; it was clear that Richard could not cope with the like of Robert Jenkins and the thought was somehow cheering.

'I think your friend disapproves of me,' Robert said, his voice intruding into her thoughts.

'Well, she's not really my friend, more my employer. I suppose she doesn't see things the way we do.'

'I suppose not,' Robert said dryly. 'Though she does imagine herself a socialist or she wouldn't come to the meetings.'

'I suppose so.' Kristina had never thought of it that way

before. Probably the only reason Roggen put up with Kristina's company was because it gave her the belief that she was being democratic in her outlook.

When she came to a stop a little way off from the big house, Kristina realized that Robert would now know exactly where to find her. She turned to him and spoke as honestly as she could without offending him.

'There's no point in you wanting to see me again, mind,' she said softly. 'I'm not ready to go courting, not with anyone. There's soft you are bothering with me.'

'I don't want anyone else.' He paused. 'I wish our first meeting had been different.' There was so much real regret in his voice that Kristina felt a pang of sympathy for him.

'You see, Kristina,' he continued, 'I think I've fallen in love with you.'

Before she could stop him, he had taken her in his arms. 'I wouldn't hurt you for the world, I'd be a good husband, mind.'

As Kristina tried gently to free herself she heard the sound of a car engine and felt the beam of headlights wash over her. 'I've got to be ready for work in the morning,' she said in confusion, knowing that the driver of the car must be Eden.

She pushed Robert away. 'I must go.' She hurried towards the house, her mind racing. She had tried her best to be kind to Robert and now she had provoked a declaration of love from him.

As she entered the hallway of the house, Eden was hanging up his hat. He looked piercingly at Kristina and she sensed the way she always could that Eden was not in a good mood.

'Got a follower in that fellow Jenkins, then?' Eden's tone was brisk. 'After the way the man has behaved, I would have thought you'd keep well clear of him.'

'It's not like that,' Kristina began to protest, and then closed her lips firmly. Eden would not understand the power Jenkins had over the people of the docklands. He would be like Roggen and tell her not to allow a man, any man, to subjugate her.

'He's not my follower,' she said lamely. 'I don't want to get tied up to anyone.'

Eden smiled suddenly. 'That's my girl! Don't get burdened with a load of children as do most of the women round here. Look for a better life, Kristina, make something of yourself. You're too good to waste on the likes of Jenkins.' He stared down at her for a long moment, and Kristina wished she knew what his thoughts were. Then he moved away into the sitting room and closed the door.

As Kristina let herself into her room, she saw that a fire was burning low in the grate. She kicked off her shoes and sat before the embers, knowing the glow in her cheeks was not from the heat of the coals. Her lips curved into a smile. She did believe that tonight Eden had been a little jealous of Robert.

She sighed softly. Eden was right, perhaps she should try to make something of herself. She was not content to wait around for marriage. She wanted more from life than a house full of children and perhaps a man like Thomas coming home each night the worse for drink.

She slipped out of her clothes, and washed in the water that stood in the elegant porcelain jug alongside a matching basin on the marble-topped table. Tonight was her first night under the same roof as Eden and already she felt she was a different person.

As she climbed into bed and switched off the light, her door opened quietly and she saw Eden silhouetted against the light from the landing. She moved over in the bed and made room for him, and she could not wait to hold him close to her.

7

Nia coughed a little in the damp chill of the morning, drawing her woollen coat closer around her slim figure. Already, the reinforced pockets inside her coat were full of money, for many of the men from the docks were keen on backing the horses, betting half a week's wages on a sure thing. Would the punters never learn that there was no such animal as a sure thing? Horses had their vagaries just the same as people; were off colour, in poor spirits or just plain awkward; but so long as it pleased the punters to believe they might make a fortune, they would continue to put out money with a readiness that for Nia meant instant profit.

She moved along the edge of the King's Dock where the trimmers were dark mysterious figures half hidden in coal dust and the mist. One or two dockers stood on the quayside, smoking their early morning Woodbines. One of them glanced at Nia and spoke in a gruff, throaty voice. '*Duw*, Nia Powell, come like yourself, girl, frightened me half to death you did, looming up like a ghost there.'

'Hello, Mr Presdey, waiting for work, are you?' Nia adopted her usual singsong voice that she thought it politic to use when talking to her customers. It didn't do for them to think she put herself above them.

Thomas Presdey pushed back his cap. 'Aye, waiting all right. Mr Jenkins is a bit late this morning.' He pulled nervously on his cigarette. 'I've been watching the trimmers,' he continued. 'Loading a self-trimmer they are today, and thankful for it, easier work it is, see, *merchi*.'

Nia watched as coal rushed into the hold, the flow directed by men with strangely shaped shovels like inverted shields.

'They are a race apart from us ordinary dockers, mind.' Thomas Presdey's voice was hoarse in the early morning. 'I bet some of those men are your best customers, paid in gold guineas are the trimmers, with their own accountant who sees to their money.' He paused and dragged heavily on his cigarette. 'Work like mules for it, they do. I don't envy them. Loading ships with coal is a murderous job, especially if the ship's not a self-trimmer. They have to get down in the square hold and level the coal off from the corners, with all the dust going into their lungs, poor sods.'

He thrust his hands into his pockets. 'Half the work it is if the hold is the bowl shape of the self-trimmer. The coal settles at the right level on its own then, see.'

Nia had little time for Thomas Presdey. He had given her friend Kristina a dog's life before she left home to work at Ty Coch, and yet as she saw the sweat beading his forehead and the anxious glances he threw from time to time to the gate where the works allocator would arrive, Nia could not help but feel a little sorry for him.

'Having a flutter today then, Mr Presdey?' she asked. 'A win might cheer you up a bit.' She dipped into her pocket and brought out a slip of paper which she put surreptitiously into his hand. 'Good tip there, just between us,' she said. 'Put sixpence on the nose of that horse and I think you'll be a winner today.'

'Aye, all right girl, I'll do that.' He brought a coin from his pocket. 'Perhaps you'll bring me luck. I haven't worked for three days now, Mr Jenkins not selecting me. Getting short of money is me and the missis, and her with another babba on the way too.'

Nia nodded and smiled, putting the money in her pocket. It was almost a certainty that Sonny Boy would win. She calculated that the odds would be very low, Sonny Boy being the favourite, and she knew she could

93

afford to pay out from her takings without losing very much. Not that she owed Thomas Presdey anything, but it was his wife and children Nia was sorry for.

The coal trimmers were sweating as they called cheerfully from the ship being loaded in the King's Dock. Chutes spewed forth black streams of coal that were directed by the trimmers into the bowels of the vessel, sending clouds of dust rising up to mingle with the morning mists. Banjos, the trimmers' name for the huge wide-bladed shovels, lay on the quayside, unwanted on the self-trimming vessel. Blackened faces smiled a welcome as Nia moved along the edge of the murky water, for she was a familiar and welcome diversion from the loading.

She collected a fair amount of money from the trimmers, and her coat began to sag around her legs. It was a reassuring feeling to know there would be a good profit for her from today's takings.

On her way back across the docks, she saw Thomas Presdey lift his cap to her and jerk a thumb into the air. It was clear from his attitude that he had been chosen to work, and Nia smiled to herself. It seemed she had brought him luck after all.

She wondered if Kristina was keeping Jenkins the selector at bay, now that Roggen had given her the job of cleaning at Ty Coch. The problems of her friends seemed so insignificant now, almost childish compared with her own experiences.

As Nia thought of Joe a warm glow settled over her. She was so lucky, Joe was a good man and she loved him so much. The first night beneath his roof she had been frightened, a virgin in all senses of the word, but he had been sensitive and caring, and as Joe had slowly divested her of her clothes, so her inhibitions had fallen away. Afterwards, she had felt not the expected guilt, but a sense of fulfilment; she was a whole woman perhaps for the first time in her life.

If there was one cloud on her happiness it was that Joe

had not proposed marriage. He loved her, she was sure of it, but if he had only put a gold ring on her finger she would have been the happiest woman in the whole of Swansea.

She paused as she reached the edge of Lambert's Cottages, and stared towards the dark windows of the house where her father lived. They had not communicated in any way since she had walked out, and now, overflowing with love, Nia felt it was time to make her peace with her father.

She let herself into the house and smiled wryly; he had not changed the door lock. It must be the only house in the whole of the uneven rows of cottages that had a lock at all, for in Lambert's no one locked their doors. But then, Ambrose Powell was a man apart, a man of culture and breeding, and a man who had a safe full of ill-gotten gains.

He was sitting near the fire, his slippered feet stretched out to the blaze. Nia stared at her father from the doorway, and he looked up from his paper, registering no surprise at her sudden appearance. It was almost as though he'd been expecting her. His trained eyes took in at once the full pockets, and after a long and hard scrutiny, he smiled.

'Come in, Nia, you're very welcome,' he said, leaning forward and pushing the kettle on to the fire.

There was a constriction in her throat, but Nia swallowed hard and moved forward to sit at the table, the money chinking solidly in her pockets.

'I see you're doing well then, girl?' Ambrose pushed his spectacles down on his nose, peering over them to see her properly. 'In more ways than one,' he added, and Nia felt the colour run into her cheeks.

'You've doubtless heard I'm living tally?' she said a little defensively, and Ambrose smiled, eyebrows lifted.

'I see you're adopting the idiom of the uneducated, Nia,' he remarked. 'Living in sin is what I would call it.' He paused and eased himself upright in his chair, and Nia realized his rheumatics were bothering him.

'Call it what you like, Father,' she said, but without hostility, knowing that he was not judging her, merely stating what he saw as a fact. 'I suppose I've lived in some sort of sin all my life, being your daughter.' The words were without rancour, and Ambrose acknowledged them with a tilt of his head.

'But at least, Father,' Nia continued, 'you taught me how to make a living for myself. I'm that rare woman, a financially independent one, which means I can order my own life, be mistress of my own destiny.' She smiled, aware of her choice of words, and after a moment, Ambrose returned her smile.

'Then I've given you a great deal,' he said. 'But remember this, independence is not only a matter of finance, it's a matter of troublesome emotions. Keep your head, girl, and keep your own money separate from that of your lover.'

He held up his hand. 'I know, don't tell me, in the first flush of love, you are ready to trust your instincts to the limit, but listen to your father. Don't I always talk sense?'

Ambrose was rubbing at his legs with knotted hands, the knuckles swollen, and Nia saw him in that moment as she'd never seen him before; a man growing old alone. On an impulse, she reached out to him, and for a long moment their fingers remained entwined, then Ambrose drew away.

'Don't become too soft, girl. A business head needs that edge of hardness and a clear mind uncluttered by sentiment.'

Nia felt the old familiar pang of rejection as she sat back in her chair. Her father had never offered nor expected displays of affection. Ambrose was, from choice, a man apart.

'I'd better be going,' she said. 'Is there anything you want from the shop?'

Ambrose shook his head. 'Thank you, no, I pay one of the little Williams girls working at Libba's to bring me all

I require, so you see there is no need to feel any guilt at leaving me alone. I can manage quite well.'

Nia moved to the doorway and looked back at him. 'And your book, is the Williams girl doing your running for you too?'

'No need,' Ambrose said smiling. 'The bar at the Burrows serves me very well indeed.' He lifted his hand. 'By the way, you've got competition for the dockers' business.'

Nia tensed. 'What do you mean, Father, competition?' she asked, and her mouth was a little dry as she waited for him to reply.

'Oh, not from me,' he said. 'I don't poach on another man's preserves.' He shook his head. 'All I'm saying is there's some other bookie after the dockers' bets, so keep your eyes peeled, girl.'

As Nia let herself out into the street, she saw that the mist was dispersing and the pale sun of autumn was warming the walls of the houses, shining on glass window panes so that they sparkled like diamonds from conscientious washing. This was the place of her childhood, she had played on the patch with the other children of the area, and yet she had always been different; Nia Powell, daughter of the defrocked vicar, a curiosity who spoke posh like the English and who always had decent shoes to her feet and a good coat on her back. But it was pointless to dwell on the past. She had her future to think of now.

She was puzzled by her father's warning. Was it genuine, or was it his way of paying her back for taking up with his old customers? Well, if that was the case, she couldn't blame him, and if there was some strange bookie in the area, so what? There was enough trade for all of them.

As Nia walked away, she smelled the scent of coffee from the grocery store and breathed in the tang of salt drifting in from the sea. The house where she now lived with Joe, just off the square at Brynhyfred, was not far in distance, but it might have been a million miles away, so different was it.

She began to walk with swift steps over the uneven ground towards the docks entrance, nodding her head to the constable who strolled towards her. He was a familiar figure but always one to respect, for Dai could turn difficult and insist on searching her before she left the docks, if he so chose. However, Nia knew this was unlikely, for Dai had been one of Ambrose's customers for as long as she could remember. The docks policeman had always turned a blind eye to Ambrose's activities and hopefully would to hers. He nodded affably as she walked past, pockets bulging with illegal bets.

The sun was rising higher in the sky as she made her way back to Brynhyfred. Joe was at work but Nia liked this part of the day when she saw to the house and planned the meal she would make for Joe when he returned home. It was almost like playing house, Nia realized that, and realized too that she would quickly become bored if that was all she had to occupy her time. Her business filled her world, and her ambition to one day own a string of legal betting offices had not diminished with the coming of Joe.

To her surprise, Joe was at home, sitting near the table with a map spread out before him.

'Hello love, back so soon?' he said, looking up at her. She moved to him and putting her arms around his neck kissed the top of his curly head.

'This is a nice surprise,' she said softly. 'I thought you'd be at work.'

'Got something to think about, Nia,' he said. 'Been offered another mine, a bit of a risk it is, but there's a good crop of Red Vein to get out if it's worked properly.'

'Well, what's the problem then if there's good coal there?' Nia carefully removed her coat and set it down on the armchair, deciding to deal with the bets later. She sat beside Joe and looked down at the map, which seemed quite meaningless to her.

'The seam runs here under the hill,' Joe said, 'but the mine has gone to the dogs and filled up with water. It's been neglected for months so it would mean a lot of hard graft and a good bit of investment to get the place working again.'

'Well?' Nia said. 'If you've got the capital to do it, and if you think it's a good investment, why not take it on?'

Joe frowned. 'It's a good investment for sure, but my money is all tied up for the moment, and as the place is going for a song it needs to be snapped up straight away before anyone else gets to hear of it.'

Warning bells began to ring in Nia's brain. Her father had told her not to let emotions interfere with business, and he was right. She knew it in her head and yet her heart told her not to mistrust the man she loved. She hesitated, and Joe spoke again in his slow thoughtful way.

'I will give myself a day or two to think about it. It's not wise to rush into anything. I'm sure the owner is not in *that* much of a hurry.'

It was like a reprieve, and Nia sighed with relief. She didn't have to commit herself, not at the moment. She wound her arms around Joe's neck and put her cheek against his. The dark curliness of his hair brushed her face and she closed her eyes in a sudden rush of emotion. How she loved him, surely he was worth putting her trust in. He had given her so much without asking anything in return. Perhaps her father had been speaking urged on by his own cynicism.

'Look, Joe,' she said quickly, 'you can have the money for the mine. I've got enough to buy it outright so you won't have to wait.'

He drew her on to his lap and held her close. 'I don't want your money, *cariad*. The day I can't fend for myself they can put me in the ground.'

There was such a rush of gratitude welling within her that tears pressed behind her tightly closed lids. Joe was a real man, not one to be beholden to any woman. How could she ever have doubted him?

'Come on then, Nia,' he said, 'how about a bite to eat for a hungry man. I'm starving!'

'You!' She pushed him away playfully. 'Always thinking of your appetite.' She pressed her mouth against his and suddenly the laughter died away as the embrace became passionate.

Joe kissed her mouth, her eyelids, her throat, and pushing aside the soft cotton of her blouse touched her breasts with his lips. She wanted him so much, Joe had taught her so well the delights of the flesh. She sighed softly as he lifted her in his arms and carried her to the stairway.

'On second thoughts,' he said raggedly, 'food can wait.'

The moon hung in the sky, shining through scudding clouds, peering through the swaying trees from which the wind was sweeping the last leaves.

Joe Barnes walked swiftly towards the Gloucester public bar, his hat pulled down and a white scarf knotted around his throat. It was good to get out of the house. Nia was very sweet and he had to admit she had taught him a great deal about horse-racing, but she could also be a little cloying.

He had enjoyed educating her in the ways of love; she was a ready and able pupil and ripe for the plucking. If it had not been him, some other man would have come along before long and taken her virginity.

He saw the welcome lights of the bar spill on to the pavement and quickened his step, eager for the first taste of cool ale. As he pushed open the door, piano music and Woodbine smoke drifted towards him, embracing him like welcome arms, and drawing him inside. This was a man's world where he could be completely at ease.

Joe took off his hat and nodded to the men seated round a table playing cards. He ordered his ale and took a long draught of it before moving to the far corner where the dockers were receiving their pay-out. For a moment he watched the long-winded way that the money was being counted. It was like a child's game; one for me and one for you, until the pile of cash was shared evenly. He waited patiently until the dockers had some beer inside them and then he moved forward and sat across one of the stools, elbows on the table.

'Well then, boys,' he said, 'who's going to have a little flutter with me, then? I've got a hot tip straight from the horse's mouth, as they say.'

He lit up a cigarette as the dockers vied for his attention. Yes, Joe thought smugly, little Nia had taught him quite a lot.

Roggen sat in the chair opposite the fire and stared defiantly at her brother.

'I don't know what you've got against Richard,' she said. 'He's a law-abiding man and has very good qualities. I like him very much.'

'More than like him from what I can see.' Eden leaned forward earnestly, a fall of dark hair almost covering one of his eyes. 'You're too young to allow yourself to be involved with any man,' he said. 'I don't want you being led astray, Roggen.'

'Please, Eden,' she said desperately, 'give me credit for some sense, will you? I don't "allow" anyone to influence me one way or another. I make up my own mind.'

She watched him ease himself back into his chair and shake his head. 'You won't be told, will you? I just don't want some man taking advantage of you.'

Roggen frowned. 'But you're not above taking advantage of women yourself, are you?' She watched as Eden took a cigarette from a slim gold case and tapped the end of it angrily.

'Look, brother mine,' she said, 'I'm a teacher now, a working lady. I'm no silly helpless young girl any longer.'

Eden regarded her steadily. 'What I do and what you do are two different things. All I'm saying is don't allow your feelings to get the better of you. You're young and impressionable, and this James man is following the wrong sort of politics for my liking.'

'Oh, don't start that again!' Roggen looked up with a sigh of relief as the door of the sitting room opened and her mother entered the room. Marie Lamb always made an entrance, pausing in the doorway, her dark, watchful eyes missing nothing. Her hair was white but still abundant, swept upwards in plump rolls away from her face in a style reminiscent of the Edwardian. She was upright in carriage, imposing in her unusual height, a woman not to be ignored.

'*Madre*,' Roggen rose to her feet, 'come and sit near the fire. Where's your shawl? You'll catch cold.'

'Stop fussing, *muchacha*, I'm not in my dotage yet.' Her accent was heavily Spanish in spite of the years she had spent in Wales. She glanced affectionately towards her son and spoke to him in her native tongue.

'Are you reading your sister a lecture yet again, Eden?' She allowed herself to be settled in a chair and accepted the brightly crocheted shawl that Roggen placed around her knees.

'Yes, Mother, he is,' Roggen answered for her brother. He can't accept that I'm an independent woman with views of my own.'

'Tut, you are not going on about boring politics again, are you? How silly to wear yourself out with such nonsense.'

Roggen lifted her eyebrows as she met her brother's gaze, and he shrugged indulgently.

'We will not talk of politics if it's going to bore you, Mother. What topic of conversation would please you?'

Marie smiled disarmingly, as though she were a young girl flirting with her lover. 'You know what will please me, Eden, the news that you are going to be married and give me grandsons. What has happened to the lovely Bella? Is she coming to visit us tonight?'

'Stop matchmaking, mother,' Eden said, but he smiled to soften the words. 'And to answer your question, yes,

Bella is coming to visit.' He turned to look levelly at Roggen. 'I expect you to be here to meet her.'

'Of course Roggen will be here,' Marie said. 'But surely Bella is not driving that dreadful monster car here on her own, is she?' Marie shuddered. 'I don't know what young girls are coming to these days.' She glanced at Roggen. 'If you only knew how I worry about you both now that everyone worships speed.'

Roggen bit her lip in irritation. So Bella was coming over yet again. That meant she would have to stay in and be polite and not meet Richard at Cascarini's as planned. She caught her brother's eye and saw the amusement there, and realized he knew exactly what she was thinking. She made a face at him and turned away, feeling her colour rising.

'I'll go and talk to Kristina for a while if no one minds,' she said, wondering if the girl could be persuaded to take a message to Richard. She dutifully kissed her mother's smooth brow and quickly left the room.

Kristina was not in the kitchen, which was silent and empty, smelling of soda and freshly-baked bread. Roggen noticed that the square tiles of the floor had recently been washed. Kris was nothing if not conscientious. Of Anita Williams, there was no sign. The girl certainly did not believe in working too hard.

She hurried upstairs and along the passageway, and knocked perfunctorily on the door before opening it. Kristina was sitting curled up on the bed, poring over a book.

'What are you reading?' Roggen found it difficult to keep the surprise from her voice. She had not thought Kristina would be interested in books.

Kristina looked up and smiled. 'It's about anatomy,' she said. 'Come and see – this is what the inside of a heart looks like.'

'Ugh, no thanks!' Roggen sat in the basket chair near the fire. 'That's not what I call light reading. Don't you like novels, or something a little more entertaining?'

Kristina looked at her from under long silky lashes, her green eyes inscrutable. 'I've got ambitions, Roggen, just like anyone else.'

Roggen felt as though she'd been put in her place. She stared blankly at Kristina for a moment, wondering what she could say without sounding patronizing. Kristina had very little education and what could she hope to achieve without it?

'Well, that's all very laudable,' she said. She sat on the edge of the bed and leaned forward earnestly. 'If I can help you in any way, then I would happily do so.'

Kristina smiled, and Roggen felt again the flash of envy that assailed her whenever she saw afresh the beauty in Kristina's face.

'*Duw*, if you mean it, then help me with my English,' she said softly. 'I know I speak it roughly compared with you. You sound so posh and cultured.'

'Don't be silly,' Roggen said, 'you've got a lovely accent.'

Kristina sighed, pushing her long abundant fall of hair away from her shoulders. '*Duw*, I wish I had, but I've got a lot to learn, haven't I?' She leaned back against the pillows and stared for a moment up at the ceiling.

Roggen rose from the side of the bed. 'I'll bring you home some books on grammar,' she said with sudden inspiration. 'There are quite a few spares in my classroom cupboard.' Roggen felt elated. She had always liked to teach, and Kristina would be a challenge, her speech patterns formed from years of speaking English in the Welsh idiom. It was something Roggen personally thought was a charming part of her make up, but if Kristina wanted it changed, so be it.

'Now you can do something for me,' she said. 'I was to meet Richard in Cascarini's, and now I can't go out. Will you give him a message for me?'

Kristina rose from the bed in a swift graceful movement and stood looking down at Roggen. 'Course I will.' She smiled mischievously. 'I'd be delighted.'

Roggen smiled. 'That's good! You sound very posh indeed. Now, have you got a piece of paper so I can scribble a note?'

She bent over the marble-topped dressing table and wrote swiftly. 'You can read it if you like.' She glanced over her shoulder. 'There's nothing really personal in it.'

Kristina took the folded note and slipped it into the pocket of the jacket she'd taken from the wardrobe, and Roggen saw that she had no intention of reading her letter. On an impulse she put her hand on Kristina's shoulder. She wanted to say how glad she was that they had achieved a more friendly understanding but the words were too difficult, so she contented herself with a smile.

'Thanks.' It sounded bald but Kristina was sensitive and understood her perfectly well.

'Why are you always so, so . . .' Kristina paused, not knowing how to express herself, and Roggen smiled.

'So restrained? I think it's something to do with the way Mama and Eden have expected me to be, self-sufficient always.'

'Well there's nothing wrong with a bit of affection, mind,' Kristina said. 'Everyone needs loving.'

'Ah, but there you are lucky,' Roggen replied, moving to the door. 'You have always been able to show your feelings, and I envy you that.'

'Well perhaps you envy me just a little bit, then,' Kristina said smiling. 'I'm going now or your Richard will think you've let him down. See you when I get back, Roggen, hopefully with a message from your follower.'

She ran down the stairs and hurried through the door, a bundle of beauty and energy. As Roggen heard the front door close, she stared down at the book her friend had been reading and wondered just who was the richer; she with her education, or Kristina with her gentle and loving spirit.

8

The sky was overcast with low grey clouds drifting round the peaks of Kilvey and Townhill, and the houses in Lambert's Cottages were veiled in darkness. Except for one where lamplight spilled from an upper window, casting a stain upon the virgin snow.

The chill of the winter night penetrated the thick walls of the house in the middle of the row. Intricated webs of silver frosted the window panes even though a bright fire burned in the grate of the small bedroom. In the bed the woman closed her eyes, sweat beading her forehead as she laboured to give birth to her child.

Kristina stood beside her mother, holding her hand and talking softly, encouragingly, knowing by the look on the face of the old midwife that the birth was not going well.

'It won't be long now, Mam, soon you'll have your new baby in your arms. There's a Christmas present for you.'

Ceinwen Presdey moaned a little, turning anguished eyes to her daughter. 'Thank God you came, Kris, something's wrong, I know it is. Look after the girls if anything happens to me, promise now.'

Kristina forced back the tears. 'Nothing is going to happen to you, Mam.' Her voice was strong, firm. 'You are going to be all right. It's just that you're a bit older now and everything takes a little bit longer, mind.'

A contraction caught Ceinwen and racked her weakened body, and the midwife bent forward sympathetically, old hands moving gently and expertly, eyes half closed in thought. After a moment, she jerked her head towards the door.

'I won't be long, Mam,' Kristina said. 'I'll just get some more hot water, and don't worry, it will soon be all over.'

'It's no good.' Outside on the landing Mrs Carey dried her hands on her apron. 'We'll have to get the doctor in. She's going to lose her life's blood if we don't do something quickly.'

Kristina quickly calculated how much money she had put aside in the savings box in her room at the big house. Would there be enough to pay a doctor?

'I'll run over to Ty Coch,' Kristina said at once. 'Eden will go in his car to fetch the doctor, I'm sure.'

She ran downstairs, pausing only to pull on a coat before hurrying out into the darkness of the night. The cold air caught her face, searing her lungs as she breathed deeply trying to calm the panic that raced through her. Mam couldn't die, it was unthinkable.

She didn't stop running until she reached the door of the big house, almost falling into the warmth of the hallway. The huge tree dominated the room, hung with pretty baubles and heavy with packages prettily wrapped in coloured paper.

'Eden!' Her urgency brought him quickly from the study. He was fully dressed and it was clear that he had not yet gone to bed in spite of the lateness of the hour. He took one look at her face and caught her icy hands in his.

'What's wrong?' As Kristina gulped air into her lungs, he drew her closer, brushing back her hair.

'It's Mam,' Kristina said. 'We have to get the doctor for her. Please help me, Eden.'

'Go home,' he said at once. 'I'll bring Dr Mayhew, he's a good man to have around in a crisis.'

'We can't afford much, mind,' Kristina said at once, knowing that the doctor Eden spoke of attended only the rich and privileged of the community.

'Don't worry about that. Go on, I'll be with you as soon as possible.' He reached for his coat and Kristina heard the jangle of car keys as he removed them from his pocket. She moved to the door, and as Eden opened it to let her through, Kristina was halted by Roggen's anxious voice calling her name.

'Kristina, what's happening, is someone sick?' Roggen hurried down the stairs, her warm red dressing gown wrapped around her slim figure. Her dark hair was tousled, her eyes heavy with sleep.

'What is it?' she repeated. 'What's wrong, Kris? You're as white as anything.'

'It's Mam,' Kristina replied. 'Her time's come and the birth isn't going right. Eden's going to bring the doctor.'

'Shall I come to the house with you?' Roggen asked. 'I could see to the children or something, couldn't I?'

Kristina nodded. 'That would be a great help. If they're awakened by all the comings and goings the girls will be so frightened.'

'Go on ahead then, while I get dressed.' Roggen turned back to the stairs. 'And don't worry, Eden and I will be with you in a couple of minutes. You won't be alone for long, I promise you.'

As she hurried back over the snow-frosted ground, Kristina listened to the sound of the car engine revving into life, and felt somehow that Eden had the power to make everything all right.

As Kristina returned to the warmth of the bedroom, she saw that Ceinwen was breathing heavily, her closed lids seeming almost transparent in the light from the lamp. The midwife was standing before the fire, arms folded across her ample breasts, waiting. Kristina moved quickly to her mother's side and took her hand, and the blue shadowed lids fluttered open.

'The doctor is coming, Mam, you'll be all right now.' Some of her faith appeared to transfer itself to Ceinwen and she smiled, nodding her head slightly, unable to summon the energy to speak.

It seemed an eternity before the sound of footsteps on the stairs heralded the appearance of Dr Mayhew. If he was unused to such humble dwellings he showed no sign of it as he calmly and efficiently examined Ceinwen Presdey.

'The child is presenting in a breech position,' he said quietly to the midwife. 'But I expect you know that. We must make a few incisions to facilitate an easier delivery.'

He turned to look at Kristina. 'Are you sensible enough to help? If not, I'd prefer it if you left the room.'

'I'll help,' Kristina said decisively. She washed her hands and moved to the bedside, watching the doctor work swiftly and efficiently. He wielded the scalpel with precise and sure strokes, and then the midwife was busy with swabs of cotton wool in her hands. After a moment, she gave Kristina a bowl with the used swabs and returned to her task of assisting the doctor.

Kristina found herself absorbed, her attention riveted on the doctor's hands wielding the silver instrument. There was a sheen of perspiration on his forehead as he fought to bring the child into the world.

'Is everything all right?' Ceinwen's voice was thread-like, and Kristina moved to her side quickly, reassuring her mother in gentle tones. She didn't see the child being born, but she saw the doctor relax and the midwife bend forward. Dr Mayhew sighed and shook his head. Slowly, footsteps dragging, Kristina walked to the end of the bed. The baby lay still on the stained white towel, the umbilical cord around the tiny throat.

The child was perfect in every respect. Tiny hands with pearl-like nails were spread open as though the infant was reaching out for something to cling to. The eyes were closed, with a fan of lashes resting against rounded cheeks. Kristina stared at the baby with tears in her eyes, unable to believe that her mother's desperate struggle had been in vain.

'Tell me, Kristina.' Her mother's voice was stronger, anxiety evident in the way she leaned up on one elbow and stared with wide eyes first at her daughter, then at the doctor.

'I'm sorry, Mrs Presdey.' Dr Mayhew moved to her side. 'We did all we could.'

Ceinwen began to weep and Kristina held her close, the roles of mother and daughter strangely reversed. 'There, there, Mam, perhaps it's for the best,' Kristina said softly.

Dr Mayhew was washing his hands in the fresh bowl of hot water the midwife had placed on the marble-topped table. 'Your daughter has a great deal of common sense,' he said. 'The child might well have suffered damage as a result of the difficult birth.'

'Was it a son or a daughter?' Ceinwen asked in a whisper as the midwife moved forward and began to wash the dead infant.

'There, a fine little girl, she is,' she said gently, 'as pretty as a picture. Give her a name, Mrs Presdey, and then the little one can be buried with decency.'

Ceinwen was weeping softly, shaking her head as though in shock. 'I don't know what to call her,' she said raggedly. 'I can't think of anything at all, I was sure it was a boy this time.'

'What about Eira, which is Welsh for the snowy weather she was born in?' the midwife suggested, and Ceinwen nodded distractedly.

Kristina felt tears burn her eyes as she looked down at the perfect child swathed now in a lacy shawl, looking as though she were simply asleep. She had petal-soft skin and a mass of dark hair, and it was difficult to believe that there was no breath of life in the child.

'I shall give you a sedative to help you to sleep, Mrs Presdey.' Dr Mayhew took a syringe from his bag and held it up to the light. Ceinwen made as though to protest, but the doctor waved his hand to quieten her.

'You need rest in order to recuperate, my dear lady,' he said. 'And think of your other children awaiting your recovery. It is to them you must look now.'

Kristina sat with her mother, holding her hand until Ceinwen's eyes began to close. She tucked the bedclothes

110

warmly around her and rose to her feet, and only then did she feel exhaustion flood over her.

Downstairs, Eden and Roggen waited anxiously. Kristina bit her lip, trying to frame an acceptable way of breaking the news. 'The baby was stillborn.' The words came out hard and bald, and then Eden was at her side, his arm around her shoulders.

'Come back to the house and try to get some rest,' he urged. 'Roggen can stay here to look after things.'

'Yes, you go, Kris,' Roggen said at once. 'You look as though you'll drop soon if you don't listen to good advice when it's given.' She pushed her towards the door. 'Don't worry about a thing. The midwife will be staying for a while, so I shan't be alone.'

Kristina allowed herself to be led out of the house. She felt empty of emotion, as though she, not her mother, had laboured to bring forth a dead child into the world. She climbed into the car and felt the cold air sting her face through the open window as Eden drove her the short distance to Ty Coch.

'Come on, to your room with you.' Eden helped her into the house, past the Christmas tree that seemed to mock her with its cheerfulness, and up the deeply carpeted stairs. 'Now get into bed, I'll bring you a hot drink.'

Kristina sank on to the bed, unable to think clearly. She stared into the dead embers of the fire in the small grate and wished there was a glow of coals at least to warm some life into her. She was shivering, though whether from cold or shock she didn't know.

She didn't afterwards remember how long she simply sat in the soft glow of the lamplight, staring at the empty fireplace and seeing only the small perfect form of the stillborn child.

The door opened and Eden stepped into the room, shaking his head as he saw her sitting there fully clothed. 'Come along.' He knelt down before her. 'Let me take off your shoes.'

She saw his dark head bent before her and longed to reach out and touch him. She wanted simply to be held close, to feel the warmth of another human being. Slowly and gently, Eden took off her blouse and undid the buttons of her skirt.

'Where's your nightgown?' he asked, and Kristina shook her head, unable to think.

'Well, it doesn't matter if you sleep in your petticoat for once,' he said softly, his voice suddenly ragged.

Kristina leaned against his shoulder and he held her gently, patting her arm, talking in a low, soothing voice, and she was grateful to him for his tenderness, offered just when she needed it most. He lifted her into the bed and covered her with the warm blankets, and then he sat beside her, holding her hand.

'Don't worry, your mother will be all right. Dr Mayhew is a first-class doctor, there's nothing to worry about there.' He stroked her wrist. 'I'm sorry about the baby. I know it's a blow to you as well as to your mother, but perhaps it's for the best.' He stood up and smiled down at her, and Kristina loved him so much it hurt. He had stood by her when she needed him and so, surprisingly, had his sister. Roggen had been ready and willing to do all she could to help, and Kristina would never forget to be grateful.

'Try to get some sleep now,' Eden said gently. 'You look washed out.' He left, closing the door quietly behind him, and Kristina wondered if this was to be the pattern of their lives now that Eden was seeing Bella regularly. Would he stay away from her bed for ever more?

And then she was ashamed, worrying about herself when Mam had suffered so much this night. She closed her eyes but sleep would not come, and so she stared up the ceiling, trying to close her mind to the thoughts that leaped and tumbled through her mind like shadows.

Eden moved towards the glittering crystal decanter and poured himself a drink. The brandy trembled in the glass

112

as he raised it to his lips. He had meant to talk to Kristina, to tell her about Bella, to explain things to her, she deserved that much. But how could he in the circumstances?

Bella was so tranquil and yet so stimulating to talk to. She was a lovely woman, not with the wild, passionate looks Kristina possessed, but with a beauty that was more than skin deep. Suddenly he wanted to see Bella, to talk to her, hold her in his arms. He moved swiftly, picking up his coat from the hall stand and letting himself out into the cold winter air.

Bella had taken a house on the slopes of Mount Pleasant to be nearer to Eden, and as he drove through the streets towards her home there were men abroad walking to work. Dockers, trimmers, and capped and booted miners, early morning faces washed clean of sleep. Those lucky enough to have jobs took care to be at their posts early, for these days unemployment was a constant threat.

If Bella was surprised to see him so early in the morning she did not show it. It was clear that she had been awoken from sleep, her hair was tousled around her small oval face and she wore a warm woollen dressing gown that fell down to her slippered feet. A feeling of tenderness swept over him as he took her in his arms. 'I'm sorry,' he said softly, 'I didn't mean to wake you but what I have to say couldn't wait.'

'Come on into the sitting room,' Bella said, smiling, her clear eyes shining as though already she knew what he was going to say. 'Mary has just lit the fire in there and it will be warmer than standing here in the hallway.'

She took his hand and he went with her into the large high-ceilinged room furnished sumptuously in heavy-carved furniture. The rich brocades and velvets were jewel bright and the scent of lavender polish permeated the room.

Self-consciously, Bella pushed back her hair, trying to tame the unruly locks that curled around her face. 'But I'm not dressed, I must look a sight!'

He took her in his arms once more and held her close, smiling down at her. 'You look very lovely, Bella, and at least I know what my future wife will look like first thing in the morning.'

'Oh, Eden!' She stared at him wide-eyed, fully awake now. 'You are sure about this, aren't you?'

Instead of replying, he took her face between his hands and kissed her mouth. She eased herself away from him and looked into his face. 'Are you sure, really sure? We haven't known each other all that long.'

'It's almost a year now, isn't it?' Eden said, neatly avoiding a direct answer. Was he sure? At this moment, he felt sure of nothing except that Bella was the right sort of wife for him.

'Just so long as you know what you're doing, Eden,' she said softly. 'Marriage is for keeps, mind.'

'As practical as ever, that's my little Bella.' He kissed her nose and then moved away from her as the young maid came into the room balancing a tray on her arm.

'Something smells good!' He looked down at the tray; a teapot issued steam from a delicate spout, and beside it was a plate piled with hot buttered toast. Suddenly he realized he was hungry.

'Have some breakfast,' Bella said, her level gaze meeting his. 'You look as if you could do with it. Had an eventful night?'

He smiled. 'You could say that, but it's nothing for you to trouble yourself with.' He saw the doubt still in her eyes and he leaned forward and took her hand in his. 'I'm sure I want you for my wife. I have no doubts about it at all and you mustn't have any doubts either. We'll make a terrific couple.'

She moved towards him then and wound her arms around his neck, and as he held her, Eden felt that he had everything in the world he could possibly want.

9

The Carlton Cinema was dark and warm, a secret world where two people could sit and hold hands safe in the knowledge that they would not be seen by inquisitive eyes. Roggen smiled to herself. She and Richard had been going out together for some months, growing closer to each other, learning, sometimes coming near to quarrelling with each other.

They had argued endlessly about world politics; from the Wall Street Crash that had sent a cyclone heading towards Britain, to the poor efforts of Margaret Bondfield the first woman Cabinet Minister, who, as Minister of Labour, was in charge of unemployment.

'Fine mess she's made of it, too,' Richard had said in exasperation. 'Unemployment has more or less doubled since she's been handling it.'

'Well give her a chance!' Roggen had been indignant. 'At least she hasn't walked out on the party in disgust the way that Oswald Mosley did in May.'

They had often disagreed, but at least they had never been bored. And now in the dark world of the cinema, they sat very close together. Roggen hardly watched the flickering images on the screen. She was more interested in the way her pulse had quickened when Richard had taken her hand in his, stroking her wrist gently with forefinger and thumb. It was an essentially erotic gesture, and to Roggen, who had never before experienced the symptoms of arousal, it was a gesture so intimate that she knew she and Richard must be meant for each other.

She found herself wondering what it would be like to

be made love to. The surrendering of a girl's virginity was no light matter, but if the way her senses responded to Richard's touch was anything to judge by, it would be an enthralling experience. It would be strange if she should follow in Nia's footsteps and find herself a lover. Nia had obviously cast aside her chastity without a second thought, for she was openly living in sin with Joe Barnes and seemed to care little for the opinions of her former neighbours in Lambert's Cottages.

And there was Kristina, of course. She had been Eden's mistress for some time and she also had Robert Jenkins setting his cap at her. He had continued to pursue Kristina with a doggedness that brooked no argument, and as far as Roggen could see he would not be such a bad catch. He was a figure to respect, a man of considerable power in his own small world of the docklands, which was perhaps the best Kristina could expect. Unsophisticated as she was, Kristina was far more experienced in love affairs than Roggen, yet Roggen felt that Kristina should discourage Eden's attentions; a girl in Kristina's position should make the most of an advantageous marriage, for the only jobs open to her were those of shop assistant or maid in one of the big houses, which was more or less what Kristina was doing now at Ty Coch.

Roggen was not entirely unaware of the distinction she was making between Kristina's prospects and her own. But she did not mean to be snobbish, she told herself, only realistic.

Roggen felt Richard move closer to her; in the warm womb of the cinema they seemed to be alone, lost in a secret world where nothing existed except the two of them and the wonderful web he was weaving about them. His shoulder touched hers and she felt his breath on her face and slowly she turned to look at him.

It seemed an eternity before his mouth, so close, actually touched hers. Shock waves rippled through her and she realized that this was the first time she had been kissed. At least, the first time that it had been more than a fleeting touch of mouth to mouth. Richard's tongue probed hers and the intimacy thrilled Roggen even as it shocked her. His hand was on her breast – somehow he had opened the buttons on her blouse without her knowing – and his fingers caressed and teased as she leaned closer to him.

Her breathing became ragged. Roggen forgot that she was in a cinema as she focused all her attention on the sensations of the moment. She seemed to be fused to Richard, emotions she did not know existed flared through her, and she understood for the first time in her life the meaning of desire.

It was Richard who drew away first. 'I wish to God we were alone,' he said, and his voice was husky.

Roggen sat up feeling almost dizzy. She brushed back her hair and straightened her clothing with shaking hands. How foolish she was to have allowed Richard such familiarities. Was she a weak woman that she should succumb so easily to the stirring in her blood. 'It's just as well we're not alone!' she said, not without a touch of humour.

'Don't worry,' Richard was whispering in her ear, 'what you feel is perfectly normal, people make love to each other all the time.'

Was he right and was she being an old-fashioned prude? She must have time to think. 'Let's get out of here and have a coffee,' she whispered, and before he could reply she was making her way past rows of knees, wondering if anyone had witnessed her disgraceful moment of abandon. She must keep a tight rein on herself. It was quite obvious she had hot blood in her veins that must come from her Spanish mother, she decided, unable to help feeling faintly smug.

'You were like a frightened little rabbit there.' Richard caught her arm, but Roggen felt safe now outside the darkened cinema, with the light from the street lamps bringing a sense of reality and the summer air warm and balmy on her cheeks.

117

'Not at all,' she said as though it was every day she was kissed and caressed in such an intimate manner. She did not want Richard thinking she was gauche, nothing more than a silly flapper.

'It's all right, I like your reticence,' Richard said, drawing her close to his side and tucking her arm through his. 'I'd enjoy teaching you all about love, Roggen. Perhaps I may one day have that honour.'

'Don't count on it!' Roggen was more than a little nettled by his assumption, however correct, that she was a virgin.

'Oh, dear, have I offended you?' Richard's voice revealed amusement. 'Perhaps I'm wrong and you've had countless lovers, all of whom would willingly die for you.'

'Perhaps,' Roggen said flatly, not sure that she liked that assumption any better than the first.

'There's the coffee shop, let's go inside,' Richard said lightly, obviously changing the subject.

They sat like strangers then, one at each side of the table, Roggen avoiding Richard's eyes, not wanting to see the laughter there. 'It wasn't a very good film was it?' She struggled to speak lightly, to make conversation, and she heard him laugh.

'I don't know, I don't think I actually saw any of it, did you?' He leaned across the table pushing aside the cup of cooling coffee. 'Roggen, don't be in a bad mood, now, there's nothing to be ashamed of or to feel foolish about in two people wanting each other.'

She looked into his eyes, unable to conceal her feeling of vulnerability. 'But I am frightened, frightened by my own feelings, can't you understand that?' She sighed. 'But then it's so different for a man.' She glanced away from him. 'A woman can become little more than a scalp on your belt instead of a flesh and blood person with deep feelings.' She felt him take her fingers and explore them one by one with his tongue. She wanted to snatch her hand away, for the unfamiliar sensations were stirring in her once more.

'No,' he said after a moment, 'it's not different for a man, don't make that mistake, Roggen. Don't you think I feel a little afraid, afraid I'll disappoint you, fail to live up to your expectation? Perhaps it's even more difficult for a man, for he is supposed to lead, to know all about love, to be the initiator.'

Roggen met his eyes once more. 'Is that really how you feel, Richard?' she asked, a warm glow filling her at the prospect of having a man want her so badly that it frightened him.

'It's how I feel when I'm with you,' he said. 'I know already that you don't suffer fools gladly, that you have a mind of your own and will not allow anyone to influence your opinions on matters like politics, for instance.' He smiled. 'You see we have a meeting place to start with; we both follow the Labour lead in spite of our fairly well-to-do backgrounds.'

He drew her to her feet. 'But to hell with politics, we have more important ties between us. Let's get out of here, Roggen,' he said. 'I want to hold you and kiss that pouting mouth. You don't know how desirable you are.'

Roggen followed him into the street and stood for a moment looking back at the brightly lit coffee shop. In there was a world of safety, the place of childhood pranks when Sunday School was out or when a girl daringly played truant from school. Here in the darkness was the unknown, the glittering path to womanhood from which there would be no turning back.

Kristina sank on to the bed and kicked off her shoes. She was very tired tonight and the air was hot and heavy with the promise of thunder. She lay back on the pillows, too tired even to pick up her book and study a little anatomy, or read some of the classics that Roggen had loaned her.

Kristina sighed heavily, wishing she was back at home in the little cottage with the soft breathing of her young sisters in the bed beside her. Mam had grown stronger since the stillbirth of the baby at Christmas, and what a dreadful Christmas that had been with one disaster after another.

Shortly after the death of the baby, Thomas Presdey had been suspended from the docks, caught carrying out brandy and packets of cigarettes from one of the ships. Robert Jenkins had spoken up for Thomas, claiming that there were mitigating circumstances, and although the most he could promise was that reinstatement might be possible, Kristina had warmed to him, grateful for his help.

The shame of it had been almost too much for Ceinwen Presdey to bear. She had sat for hours on end staring into the fire, ashamed to venture out of doors in case she should meet one of her neighbours. It was Kristina who faced the curious stares of the people in the street, and it was Kristina who brought her mother the necessary groceries from Libba, whose attitude, as always, was unswervingly friendly.

But now with the coming of summer, matters had improved. Thomas had been given a second chance; the charges against him had never been proven and so he was again employed at the docks. The conditions were that he should be watched at all times and if so much as a lump of coal was missing he would face instant dismissal. At least he was gainfully employed once more and bringing wages into the house.

She sighed. Eden had paid most of the doctor's bills out of his own pocket, and though she had protested at the time, she realized now that she could never have managed to pay them all herself.

She was thoroughly disheartened. There seemed little point in studying now that she had no money left. It was as though the store of savings had been a bolster to her pride, making her feel she could accomplish great things. Now she could not pay for an apprenticeship even if one came along. In any case, she was probably too old to be trained. She turned her face into the pillow, suppressing tears that she recognized were ones of self-pity. That sort of indulgence did no good at all.

She had become interested in the idea of becoming a herbalist. She had learned quickly and well the matters of the body from her book on anatomy. Her mother had given her a book on old herbal remedies which contained receipts claiming to cure all sorts of conditions. Perhaps if she couldn't become a real nurse in the hospital, she might be able to work on her own, offering home remedies to those too poor to pay for professional advice. It was still the practice of some of the older women to turn to a herbalist rather than risk calling out a doctor, and there were few pregnant women who didn't consult the local self-made midwife who often had no other training than sheer practical experience passed on from mother to daughter.

There was a knocking on her door and Kristina sat up abruptly. 'Who is it?' she asked, and Anita Williams peered into the room, a smile on her freckled face. Anita had become part of the Lamb household, taken on now as a live-in maid-of-all-work. She was a cheerful girl and Kristina smiled at her, waving her into the room.

'It's a follower, Kris,' she said. Her eyes narrowed in laughter. 'A man at the back door to see you, and me not knowing you had a fella, there's a sly one you are.'

Kristina slipped on her shoes quickly. She guessed at once who it would be – there was only one man with the nerve to come up to Ty Coch to call for her, and that was Robert Jenkins.

'All right, Anita, tell him I'll be there in just a minute, will you?' She washed her face quickly and rubbed at her skin with one of the soft towels that abounded in the Red House. The standard of living was so different from anything Kristina had ever known, and while she wasn't unduly acquisitive, she realized that it was easy to become used to comfort and a convenient way of life.

Robert was standing outside in the kitchen garden, smoking a Woodbine and not one whit abashed by the elegance of Ty Coch.

'Hello,' she said softly, and as he turned and smiled at

her she realized afresh that he was an attractive man in a rugged way that might appeal to some women. But not to her; she was in love with Eden.

'There's nice to see you,' he said, not moving towards her but staring with unnerving curiosity at her slender figure in the thin summer frock. 'I've got good news. Your father has been reinstated on the docks,' he continued, throwing away the glowing cigarette end.

A sense of panic filled Kristina. The old trap was closing in on her, the need to offer gratitude to the man who held sway over the dockers. She moved towards the garden gate, very much aware that she and Robert might be clearly seen from the kitchen window.

'Thank you, Robert.' She didn't meet his eyes. 'Mam's told me the news and I really am grateful to you. I can't tell you how much it means to us all to have Dad working again. Good thing I was privileged enough to have a job up here at the house.'

'Aye, privileged,' he said softly. 'You were very privileged to have to keep your entire family on one small wage each week, weren't you? I did my best for your father, Kristina, knowing that you were going to have to carry the burden for ever otherwise.'

Kristina put her hand out to him at once in an impulsive gesture. 'I really am pleased that Thomas was reinstated, and I know it's all due to you, Robert. You're a good man, we don't deserve your help.'

He held on to her fingers for a long moment and then dropped her hand. 'Would you like to come with me to have a drink?' he asked and held his hand up as Kristina moved to speak. 'No, not in some small smoky public bar. I was thinking about the Grand Hotel or the Mackworth, somewhere nice.'

Kristina felt so tired that all she wanted to do was to fall into bed and sleep, but it would be churlish of her to keep on refusing Jenkins when all he wanted to do was spend a little time with her.

'All right,' she said. 'Come on then, the Grand sounds very nice. I don't think I've ever been in there.'

'Oh, it's very plush,' Jenkins said proudly, almost as though he owned the place himself. 'I don't think you'll have to worry about compromising yourself, not in such a respectable place.'

She fell into step with him, keeping up easily with his long, almost loping stride. He moved solidly, one foot planted firmly in front of the other, as though he were on a mission and determined not to be outwitted or outdone. He was so different from Eden, both of them manly but in such contrasting ways. Eden was a thoroughbred and Robert a carthorse. Kristina smiled at the thought, and Jenkins looked at her questioningly.

'A private joke,' she said at once, the laughter draining away from her. 'I'm sorry, don't take any notice of me.' She felt suddenly homesick for Eden. She wanted to be with him, and much as she had grown to like and respect Robert, he was no substitute for Eden Lamb.

The Grand was indeed plush, with soft carpets and softer lighting, and in the background a pianist was playing a haunting tune. As she sat beside him, Kristina suddenly felt sorry for Jenkins. He wasn't a bad sort, not really. It was that first meeting when he'd been so high-handed that had turned her against him.

'Why on earth do you bother with me?' she asked quietly, and he looked down at her, eyebrows raised. He stared hard at her for a moment, his eyes roving over her face and figure and resting on her long slim legs.

'There are many reasons,' he said, 'the main one being that I don't like anything to beat me.'

'What do you mean?' Kristina asked, puzzled. He smiled and lifted his hand, and the waiter moved quickly forward, taking his order with a deferential air. When the waiter had gone, Robert leaned forward and stared into her eyes.

'You are a challenge to me,' he said, 'and I don't like being beaten, so I will persist until I make you like me.'

'But why should it matter if I like you or not?' Kristina said, frowning. 'Surely you've plenty of women who simply long for your company?'

'Aye, that's true.' Jenkins's smile might have been mocking, Kristina couldn't be sure. 'But to answer your question, I want you to like me because one day I mean to marry you.'

She stared at him in disbelief. 'You can't be serious?' She leaned away from him wondering if he was still mocking her, and decided that he must be teasing her in his clumsy way.

'I am deadly serious,' he said, and now he was not smiling. His eyes appeared very dark as they looked into hers, and Kristina didn't know if she should be amused or angry.

'There's soft you talk,' she said. 'I don't intend to get married for a long time, if ever, so you might just as well look for someone more suitable.'

'You are suitable,' Jenkins said. 'I don't mean to be on the docks all my life, mind.' He waved his hand around him. 'But through my carefully run enterprises on the docks, I've gained a lot. For instance, I've been able to get part ownership in this hotel, and I mean one day to own much of the property in and around Swansea. I'll be as rich as Lamb himself, perhaps richer.' He caught her hand and drew her closer to him.

'Lamb will do you no good, you're not his sort, mind.' He paused as Kristina tried to draw away from him, holding her fast. 'All he wants is a quick tumble with you and then away to someone more his style, like that woman he drives about in his car. Engaged they are, mind, she wears a great big sapphire on her finger and I'll bet she's let him into her bed in payment.'

'When did this happen?' Kristina quickly drew her hand away from him, biting her tongue against the angry words that rose to her lips.

'Recently, as I understand it,' Robert said softly. 'I'm sorry, Kris, but you must face the truth.'

Kristina couldn't begin to deny the hurt that flooded through her. Eden might have told her about such a momentous decision himself.

'You must have a very low opinion of me,' she said slowly. 'If you have guessed about Eden and me, you must think I'm a harlot.'

He shook his head. 'You are no harlot, Kristina, that's one reason why I mean to marry you.' He smiled. 'You are the sort of woman who honours the vows of marriage, just like your Mam, who should have thrown Thomas Presdey out into the street years ago.'

Kristina looked away from him, he had summed her up very well. She bit her lip. The thought of Eden's duplicity had struck a deep chord of pain within her.

'If Eden is engaged, why haven't we seen an announcement in the papers about it?'

'Well, for the time being, I suppose it's unofficial. Perhaps Mr Lamb is afraid of committing himself to any woman.'

'Then how do you know all about this?' Kristina asked, hope rising within her. 'If it's such a secret, how are you in the know?'

He leaned back in his seat, frowning, and she knew he would not have spoken of the matter unless he was sure of his facts. Kristina felt her hope evaporate, to be replaced by a feeling of dejection.

'The jeweller from whom Lamb bought the ring is a good friend of mine. He tells me any bit of news he might think interesting.'

'I see.' Kristina could not help the slight tremble in her voice, even though she told herself that it was to be expected that Eden would one day find himself a wife. And yet she had felt part of him, her destiny inexplicably bound to his.

'Well, that's his business,' she said abruptly. 'What he does has nothing to do with me or with you, come to that.'

'You're right, and as you must be just as anxious as I am to get on in life, we'd suit each other very well.'

Kristina looked at him, all her pain and anger welling up in her. 'I'll never marry any man.' The words came out clipped and harsh. 'I mean it, Robert, I won't make the mistake my mother made of marrying a dock worker and struggling to bring up children on a pittance. I'll make my own way alone in the world before I'd rely on a man. I'm the independent sort, I can work for myself.'

His slow, understanding smile infuriated her still further and she rose to her feet, unaware that her voice had risen and of the inquisitive eyes focused upon her. 'I don't need anyone!'

'That only makes me more determined to have you,' he said. 'Run away if you must, but one day you'll be my wife, make no mistake about it. I'll get you in any way I can.'

Kristina turned and walked out of the hotel, her head high. She felt the colour burn in her cheeks and told herself that Robert Jenkins didn't know what he was talking about. Of course Eden wasn't engaged. So Bella had been to the house a great deal recently, but that meant nothing, did it?

She moved along the moonlit roadway towards Ty Coch, wanting nothing more than to be alone in the sanctuary of her room. She walked quickly, looking neither to left nor right, seeing nothing, hearing nothing, for pounding in her head was the pain of Eden's betrayal.

As she stepped out on to the roadway leading to the house, she came to a sudden halt at the sound of tyres screeching against the roadway.

'God, Kristina, what are you doing?' Eden was at her side, catching her arm, hustling her back on to the pavement. 'You almost got yourself killed then.'

She drew away from him, anger mounting within her. 'Don't touch me!' she said harshly. 'I never want you to touch me again, is that clear?'

'Come here.' He propelled her towards the car and

126

pushed her into the front seat. 'Come on, Kris, nothing can be that bad, can it?' He smiled down at her, and she wondered how he could smile with such charm, knowing he had betrayed her.

She shook back her hair. 'I understand that congratulations are in order.' Her tone was sarcastic. 'You *are* engaged, aren't you?'

He sat down beside her and attempted to put his arm around her shoulders, but she drew away from him. She knew the gesture was one of almost childish defiance but she could not bear him to be near her.

'Don't shut me out, Kristina. It's true that Bella and I are engaged. I should have told you myself, but I didn't want to hurt you.' His voice was soft and she glanced at him, wanting to believe him.

'I need a wife like Bella. She's a fine woman with a lot of good qualities, but selfishly, I suppose, I wanted you as well. You know I'll always love you in my own way.' He was very close, his profile was strong, his jaw clean cut, and Kristina's arms ached to hold him. She wanted to reach up and kiss his mouth but she couldn't, he was no longer hers.

Kristina took a deep breath and rose from the seat of the car, quite calm now. She avoided Eden's eyes and stared away into the distance.

'It's over.' Her voice was cold. 'You can't have both of us.' She paused a moment, wanting him to say something to put matters right, but of course he didn't. She climbed out of the car and walked away from him, her head high but the tears were brimming in her eyes.

She heard him call her name but he did not come after her. She walked towards the house and let herself into the polish-scented hallway, the warmth wrapping her as though in protective arms. She put her hands to her face feeling the salt damp of her tears and knowing that if only Eden could still in some small way be hers, she would give up everything to have him in her arms.

127

10

For Roggen, losing her virginity and coming to what the world termed womanhood had been the most disappointing experience of her life. If she had expected whirling ecstasy and the moving of the earth, then her expectations were to be dashed.

She had gone to bed with Richard, at last succumbing to his and her own urgent feelings of desire, in a small room in a seedy hotel on the Strand. She had flatly refused to accept that what she expected to be the most momentous experience of her life was to happen in the back seat of Richard's car.

It had been difficult, almost impossible, to summon up in the small dingy hotel room the glow of desire that she usually felt when she was in Richard's embrace. Outside the window they could hear men relieving themselves, to the accompaniment of expletives, in the privy positioned in the yard of the hotel. Added to which was the coldness of the arrangements. The certain knowledge that this time their sweet moments of love would culminate in the final act left her almost paralyzed with nerves.

He had been patient and gentle, and Roggen was grateful, but in spite of her love for him she could not truthfully say that there was any glorious flash of joy when he finally entered her and they became what the Bible had promised would be 'one flesh'.

It had been a painful and embarrassing experience, and the fact that Richard cried out in ecstasy at the crucial moment did little to compensate for her own lack of enjoyment. When he had rolled away from her she had felt nothing but relief and an overwhelming sense of guilt that somehow she must be lacking.

Richard had taken her gently in his arms, reassuring her that it was always difficult the first time, and that the next, he promised, would be better. She didn't believe him and when he turned to her once more, his desire evident in the way his body hardened against hers, she was proved right.

It was surely strange, she thought, that the preliminaries of the act always thrilled her; the kissing and embracing, the gentle stroking and touching, left her breathless with longing. But when, at the moment of their joining, her happiness should be complete, desire seemed to vanish like mists before the sun.

As the long hot months of summer sun had changed to the gloom of winter the situation had not improved. She still felt the same sense of frustration when Richard left her bed as she had the very first time.

She sat now in the hotel room, which had become less dingy with familiarity, looking towards the bed where Richard lay, one arm flung above his head, his eyes closed. He was a handsome, well-built man and there was no doubt that she found him attractive, so why this awful failure in her to enjoy his lovemaking? The necessity for taking precautions had the effect of cooling her ardour before she was really aroused. Was there an essential element missing that doomed her always to this sense of frustration?

'You're very quiet.' Richard had opened his eyes and was staring at her, his expression shrewd. 'Still waiting for the bells to ring, aren't you, Roggen?'

She shook her head. 'I'm sorry, Richard, I didn't think that I would turn out to be frigid.' She looked down at her fingernails scarlet with varnish, and wished she could lie to him.

He was out of bed in one movement, and she turned her eyes away from his lean flanks and muscular back as he dressed. She felt an ache of love within her, so why did the climax of it all escape her?

'These things take time,' he said softly. 'You are not frigid, my love, I think you are simply tense and worried, that's all.'

Perhaps he was right and she should simply enjoy and make the most of what they did have; a sound friendship, as well as a love for each other. Wasn't that enough for her? And more, mightn't it have to be enough for her, if her suspicions were correct?

He stood before her, and taking her hands pulled her to her feet. 'Put on your shoes and we'll go to the Mackworth for some supper,' he said smiling. 'We can put the world to rights in comfort then.'

He drove her along the Strand and up a steep lane heavy with rain into the width of the High Street. Light spilled from the doorway of the Mackworth where a liveried commissionaire waited to admit them with a courteous bow, his breath hanging on the cold air like puffs of cigarette smoke.

On each table stood a candle dispensing glimmering pools of light on the damask table cloth. A pianist was playing a soulful tune and suddenly Roggen was near to tears.

'What shall we have to eat?' Richard asked, leaning over and touching her hand gently. 'Come along, cheer up, you seem very quiet. I'm letting you down somehow, aren't I? Roggen, come on, you can tell me the truth. You've realized you don't love me after all, is that it?' He seemed so vulnerable with his hair falling across his brow, and a rush of love sent rich colour into Roggen's face.

'Oh, don't think that!' she said, her fingers entwining themselves in his. 'I do love you, Richard, I promise you that. It's me that's at fault, I feel I'm letting you down so badly. I'm so sorry I'm a failure, Richard.'

A waiter approached them and Richard was in control once more, consulting the menu and ordering in a low steady voice as though he were not vulnerable at all but a man in full command of himself.

Roggen watched him with a sense of pride. He was easily the most attractive man in the entire room. She had not failed to see the discreet looks cast his way by some of the other well-dressed, confident-looking women who sat in the dining room. She wondered if they too had experienced frustration, and smiling a little she imagined herself walking up to one of them and asking if they had achieved fulfilment, or was it all some myth spread about by men and the lie kept a deadly secret by women.

And yet she was proud to be seen in Richard's company. She loved him so much and if only she could get the other, secret part of their lives right she would be content.

They ate in silence and Roggen, though she had little appetite, pretended an enjoyment for Richard's sake. The pressed beef he ordered was well cooked with bay leaves and mace and just a hint of allspice. It had been pressed and brushed with a glaze and garnished with small shapes of pâté d'Italie. The wine was good, clear and sharp, cleansing to the palate, and Roggen drank more freely than she usually did.

When the meal was cleared away, Richard led the way into the large sitting room of the hotel and indicated that Roggen should sit close to him on the huge leather sofa. He leaned forward, his expression one of earnest concentration.

'Let's not talk about ourselves, perhaps too much introspection only makes matters worse.' He smiled and touched her hand lightly.

'I was reading the paper the other day and it was full of this man Stafford Cripps. I can't understand where he has suddenly sprung from,' he said, obviously steering the conversation on to the subject of politics, their common meeting point. 'Did you hear anything about him prior to his sudden rise to Solicitor-General?'

Roggen felt in her state of lightheadedness that she

didn't really care a damn about politics, but she made an effort to respond intelligently.

'Well, he was a leading practitioner at the parliamentary bar, and apparently he was a correspondent in the last war.'

'Oh, then you know more about him than I do.' Richard sounded just a little piqued. 'Anything else?'

'Well I've heard a rumour from my brother that Stafford Cripps will be contesting the by-election in Bristol in January.'

Roggen took a gulp of wine, wishing to drown the flurry of futile anger that rose within her. Why was she different to other women? Her friend Nia, always a prim little miss, had found love in the backstreets of Swansea, and absolutely glowed with contentment. She drank more wine and held her glass out towards Richard.

'I want to go back to the hotel.' She spoke softly, and if her words were slurred, Richard seemed not to notice. He rose to his feet immediately. Roggen didn't remember how they got back to the seedy room, but then she was in Richard's arms, panting and eager.

'I haven't anything with me, no protection, you know,' Richard said, but she didn't listen. She held him close and with a groan he pressed her back on to the bed.

Even intoxicated as she was by the wine, there was still no burst of stars or ringing of bells, and suddenly Roggen wanted nothing else but to go home. She felt sick and headachy, and Richard's presence seemed to overwhelm her. She simply wanted to be left alone to sober up and sort out her muddled thoughts.

She sat up and Richard looked at her in surprise. 'I want to go home,' Roggen said. 'I feel ill.'

In silence, Richard dressed and led her down the stairs. Outside, the cold air made her feel even less in control of her senses. She stared at the car waiting at the kerb and moved towards it as though her feet were dragging in honey.

'You're drunk,' Richard said, and the note of censure in his voice stung Roggen into a sharp reply.

'So what? Haven't I the right to get drunk if I want to? I'm an emancipated woman, so what's the odds?'

Richard helped her into the car and his face, she realized, was grim, his mouth set in a straight line so that suddenly he appeared mean and bad-tempered. She wondered if it was her over-indulgence in alcohol that had set him off, or if he was annoyed that she hadn't moaned beneath him in ecstasy? In any event, Roggen found that she did not like him very much, not in this mood.

'For heaven's sake!' she said as he put the car jerkily into motion, grating the gears in his impatience. 'Stop acting like a little boy whose favourite toy has been taken away.'

He turned to look at her as though she had grown two heads, and his eyebrows lifted in astonishment. 'That's rich!' he said. 'You are telling me not to act like a child when you can't even control your drinking. Well, it has to stop right here, I will not be embarrassed by your behaviour again, do you understand?'

Roggen sat upright in her seat. 'I don't need this,' she said. 'I don't want to be under any man's thumb and if I can't be allowed free expression then this relationship has to end right now.'

She half expected him to show remorse, to tell her she was right; a little drop too much was no big problem, most people indulged in drink far more often than she did.

'Fine!' The word came out clipped and sharp. 'It's your loss, not mine. I don't want a woman who can't behave properly in public hanging like a millstone around my neck.'

Roggen was so hurt that she felt the need to strike back twisting like a burning knife inside her. 'And who would lose more?' she demanded. 'You would no longer have me as an easy means of gratification!' She stared at him, her eyes burning with unshed tears. 'And what would I lose? Nothing but a lousy lover!'

As soon as the words were spoken, she wished them unsaid. She put her hand to her lips and looked at Richard. His face was white and set in the light of the moon.

She hunched miserably in her seat, not knowing how to make things right between them. She had said what she realized was the unforgivable; to malign a man's competence in bed was the worst thing any woman could do. Roggen thought of the times he'd held her close, whispering how much he loved her, and she knew that the physical side of any relationship was not, could not be, the only part of it. She had so much with Richard; a companion, a man with whom she could talk freely, a friend and lover; and who knows, given time their relationship in bed might have improved. Now she had ruined everything.

When the car drew up outside Ty Coch Richard flung open the door without speaking, and miserably Roggen climbed out on to the frost-rimmed pavement. From the house, light spilled on to the pathway where the patterns of frosting were like icing on a wedding cake. Only now there wouldn't be a wedding.

'Won't you come in?' she asked in a desperate effort to make amends. Richard stared out of the car at her, his expression unreadable.

'You must be mad,' he said harshly. He slammed shut the door and without another word drove off, sending up a shower of diamond slivers of ice from the thrust of his tyres.

Roggen moved inside into the warmth of the hallway and stood for a long moment looking at her reflection in the mirror. She was very pale, her eyes shadowed with blue, her hat was askew on her dark curls and her coat hung from her shoulders like a tent. Had she lost weight? It appeared that she was thinner in the face with hollows beneath more prominent cheekbones. That's what loving a man did to you, she thought bitterly.

'Roggen!' The voice of her brother startled her and she

turned to face him, her eyes filling with tears. He came to her side at once and put his arm around her shoulders. She wished she could bury her face against his broadness, lean on him and confide all her fears and troubles, but the years of instilled control took over and she moved away from him.

'What's wrong?' he asked as he took her coat gently from her shoulders and hung it in the hall closet.

'Nothing much,' she said, and realized that now she was completely sober. 'I've just had a row with Richard, that's all.'

'Lovers do have tiffs, cheer up sis, it's not the end of the world.' Eden led her into the sitting room and drew her towards the cheerful glow of the fire. 'I'll see that you get a hot drink and then you must get yourself into bed, you're freezing.'

It was true, she was trembling with cold and she had begun to feel ill. 'Has the fire in my bedroom been lit?' she asked and Eden nodded.

'Yes, Anita banked it up with small coal a little earlier.' He paused. 'I'll ask Kris about a hot drink, you'll feel more cheerful when you're warm again.'

She heard him leave the room, then buried her face in her hands. She had made a shambles of her life, sleeping with Richard and giving him her all, and then alienating him so that she felt sure he would never speak to her again.

Kristina came into the room a short time later. She looked pale and drawn and there were dark circles beneath her eyes. 'I've brought you one of my medicines,' she said. 'It's only made of herbs so there's nothing to be afraid of. *Duw*, you don't look well.'

'Don't say "*Duw*",' Roggen corrected automatically. She smiled. 'I can't help sounding like a teacher, Kristina, I'm sorry.'

'I think you'd better go up to your room and get into your nightgown,' Kristina said in concern. 'You look really bad. I'll fill a hot water bottle for you, how does that sound?'

'As if you were trying to humour me,' Roggen said, smiling. 'But for once I feel like being humoured, I'm tired and I feel sick and I'd like nothing better than to climb into a warm bed.'

Later, as she snuggled against the pillows, Roggen felt a great deal better. The herbal medicine had taken away the last remnants of the alcohol-induced confusion and she could think quite rationally about the events of the evening. She had made a real mess of things and in all probability Richard would never forgive her harsh words. And she needed him so much, what a fool she was to herself.

Eden looked in on his way to bed and she smiled at him reassuringly. 'I had a little too much of the booze with my supper,' she said. 'I'll be just fine in the morning, don't worry.'

He kissed her brow and she looked up at him, wondering what he would say if he knew she had slept with Richard. A feeling of unease crept over her as she remembered that in her drunken state she had allowed Richard to make love to her without taking precautions.

Shortly after Eden had left the room, Kristina came in with a hot water bottle and Roggen looked at her closely. 'You don't look too well yourself, you seem very down in the mouth. It's something to do with my brother, I'll bet.'

Kristina shook back the mane of hair that gleamed red-gold in the firelight. 'There's nothing between us, not now,' she said almost reluctantly. 'I can't help being bitter at the way Eden's treated me but I suppose it's my own fault for being weak. The sad thing is, I still love him.'

'Love isn't all it's supposed to be.' Roggen patted the side of the bed. 'Please, I've got to talk to someone. I've been foolish, I've slept with Richard,' she said abruptly, sitting up and hugging her knees. 'But Kristina, it's not at all what I expected. It's something of a disappointment, in fact, and I'm wondering if there is something wrong with me.'

136

'I shouldn't think so,' Kristina said, and if she was surprised at Roggen's revelation she didn't show it. 'I'm sure it must be very difficult to adjust to the ways of a man, any man, but at least you're lucky that he's not playing you false.'

Roggen sighed, scarcely hearing what Kristina was saying. 'We quarrelled tonight,' She chewed her lip, 'and I said the unforgivable; I told him he was a rotten lover.'

'Oh, dear.' Kristina looked down at her hands. 'I should think that hurt him very badly.'

'I suppose so,' Roggen said miserably. 'Oh God, how can I make it right?'

Kristina's green eyes were brimming with tears. 'Go and see him,' she said, her voice thick. 'Forget your pride, apologize to him, there's no quarrel worth ruining your life over. If only I could settle things between Eden and me so easily, I wouldn't hesitate.'

'You're right,' Roggen said, and she felt better at once. Richard was a civilized man, a sensible human being, surely he would not repulse her if she went to him and begged his forgiveness?

It would be a difficult enough thing to do in all conscience. She was not used to humbling herself, but perhaps that had been a bad thing. Look how she'd always thought of Kristina as beneath her, an ordinary working girl, and yet here Roggen was now seeking her advice and getting sensible answers to her questions.

Kristina moved away from the bedside. 'Try to sleep now, you'll see things clearer in the morning.' At the door she paused. 'He seems a very nice gentleman, your Richard,' Kristina said softly. 'He might be mad with you but he can't eat you, can he?'

'I suppose not,' Roggen said, snuggling down into the bed. 'You're right, I must try to get some sleep. And Kristina, thanks for everything.' When the door closed quietly behind Kristina, Roggen closed her eyes against the memory of the scene with Richard. The entire evening had been a disaster from start to finish, how could she have acted so badly? She had flung herself at Richard with complete disregard for his feelings and then when he failed to satisfy her she had blamed him. And worse, she had risked getting pregnant. What a fool she had been.

Outside the door, Kristina was standing against the wall, her entire body shaken by sobs. Little did Roggen realize that she had stirred up a fresh rush of anger and despair with her confusion about her own love affair.

Kristina looked longingly along the corridor to the room where Eden slept. What she would give to go to him and to be in his arms. They had not spoken a word to each other since she had told him it was over, and Kristina knew that she would have left her job but for the fact that she would have to go back to Lambert's Cottages and put up with Thomas's carping criticisms.

At last, she moved quietly into her own bedroom and sank into a chair. She was tired but she knew she would not sleep. She took up her book on herbs and began to read, and the ache within her was eased as she lost herself in the pages before her.

By January the weather had turned grim and grey with sleet falling in cold showers and threatening to turn to snow. The roadways were rimmed with heavy black ice and traffic crawled along the roads, tyres skidding and spinning on the treacherous surface.

Sir Stafford Cripps had fought and won the Bristol by-election and had gained, as expected, the safe seat of Bristol East. But the Government was in turmoil, Mr Churchill was becoming wildly popular in opposition, and Ramsay MacDonald was simply soldiering on in blind hope that a cure for all ills could be found. His prospects at the next General Election were very poor. Promises had been made and broken, and unemployment, starting off at just over a million, had, in eighteen months, become two and a half million.

But Roggen had put politics out of her mind, for she had more pressing matters to think about. Richard had refused to see her, she had not even had the chance to speak to him since before Christmas, and her worst fears had been realized; she was pregnant.

It was clear that she would have to confide in someone and ask for help, but to whom should she turn? Kristina had done her best to advise by advocating a swift reconciliation. But Roggen had lowered her pride once and tried to make amends. She would not do it again, especially for a man who so clearly did not care for her at all.

It was in her brother that she finally confided. Eden had just come in from work for lunch and paused in the doorway of the sitting room, staring at her in concern as she made an effort to hide her tears.

'Eden,' she said, 'will you give me a minute of your time.' He came into the room and closed the double doors behind him, sensing at once that something was badly wrong. Crying into her hands Roggen begged some unknown source of power to make him understand and help her.

'Come on now, sis.' Eden took her in his arms and smoothed the curls away from her damp face. 'Don't let Mother see you like this or she'll have one of her attacks of the vapours, you know anything sets her off these days. Tell me what's wrong and perhaps I can put it right.'

Roggen drew a shuddering breath. 'Eden, I'm pregnant,' she said, and bit her lip as she saw his face tighten in anger.

'That bastard Richard James is responsible for this, isn't he?' Eden turned away from her, thrusting his clenched hands into his pockets. 'I ought to beat the living daylights out of him.'

'No!' Roggen said quickly. 'Please don't blame Richard. It was all my fault, it happened the night I got drunk.'

Eden sighed and took her hands in his. 'I'm sorry, love, I shouldn't be blaming anyone. I should be trying to help. I suppose you are going to marry Richard as soon as possible? Arrangements will have to be made, but it'll all be taken care of, don't you worry. You'll have the smartest wedding this side of the Bristol Channel.'

Roggen shook her head. 'No, I'm not marrying him. We've quarrelled. I did try to talk to him but he didn't want me, and I can't blame him.'

'It's your life, you don't have to get married, you know that, Ro.' He paused. 'In fact, I'd much prefer not to have that jumped-up social climber as part of the family.' He took her face in his hands. 'And I don't want you to have your life ruined by being saddled with a child. You must be realistic.' He smiled reassuringly. 'The only other alternative is an abortion, and then this one mistake will all be over and done with.'

Roggen bit her lip. 'I don't know what's the right thing to do. Please, Eden, tell me what I should do.'

'I'll tell you what you don't have to do, and that's have this child. You are a young woman, and a fine teacher in a very good school. You'll lose all that if you continue with this pregnancy.'

Roggen knew he was talking sense. She looked up at him pleadingly. 'Help me, Eden, please help me, I feel so lost.'

He pulled her close and held her against him, smoothing the hair from her brow.

'Don't you worry about a thing. I have contacts, people who know the right doctors for this sort of thing. You won't be in any danger, I promise you.'

She clung to him, not knowing what to think or feel any more. She had completely lost sight of what was right or wrong, all she felt was blind panic. She was not competent to cope with a baby; she didn't even want one, not now, not like this.

Eden turned her face towards him and looked into her eyes. 'Now this is entirely up to you, sis,' he said. 'If you feel strongly that you want this child then so be it, we'll think of some story to cover up for you.'

Roggen thought of the lies, the deceit, the curious

140

stares and dawning disbelief, and she knew she could not go through with it.

'I'll see a doctor,' she said. 'I don't want a baby, Eden, I just couldn't cope with one. I don't know the first thing about motherhood.'

'Then don't worry,' he said softly. 'We'll soon have you out of this scrape.' He kissed her brow almost absently and Roggen felt so grateful to him for taking matters out of her hands that she hugged him in an entirely uncharacteristic manner.

'Eden, what would I do without you?' she said softly. 'Thank you for caring about me, I won't forget what you've done, ever.'

'Don't talk nonsense!' he said at once. 'It's only what any brother would do, and the entire thing would be unnecessary if James had shown even a scrap of concern for your welfare.'

'Well you won't be seeing him around here any more. I've finished with him,' Roggen said bitterly. And yet she missed him, missed his laughter and his fine clarity of mind, and she even missed the lovemaking which, although not entirely satisfactory, had at least made her feel part of Richard and part of his life.

'I'm going out now,' Eden said, 'but you are not to worry, I'll see to everything.'

Roggen heard her mother's voice in the kitchen, rising excitedly as she tried in her broken English to show Anita Williams for the umpteenth time how to make the spiced meat dishes of which she was so fond.

Roggen moved upstairs and on the landing met Kristina, who was carrying a broom and a handful of dusters, and who smelled faintly of lavender polish.

'Are you all right, Roggen?' Kristina asked softly, and Roggen nodded her head.

'Yes, things couldn't be better,' she said brightly. She had grown to like Kristina, even had a real understanding with her now, but there were certain things she could not confide to anyone who was not family.

She went into her room and closed the door. If only she could shut out her problems so easily. She lay on the bed and closed her eyes, and once she was alone her fears rushed in on her. The tears came hot and bitter then, running into her mouth.

'Oh Richard, why aren't you here to help, to tell me what to do?' she whispered, but the only sound was of the coals shifting in the grate, and Roggen felt that she had never been so desolate in all her life.

11

Roggen sat on her bed staring into the fire, but she wasn't seeing the blue and green flames beneath the cast-iron hood, nor did she hear the coals shifting in the grate. She was trying to imagine the ordeal that was before her. How was an abortion procured? Would there be pain, and afterwards the sharper bite of remorse?

She shivered, her hands cold in spite of the warmth of the fire. Her pulse quickened in fear as she contemplated the next few hours.

There was a light tapping on the door and Roggen grew tenser. Her teeth bit into her lip as fear washed over her in waves. She wasn't prepared, not yet, she had to think a bit longer, build up her litany of excuses for what she was about to do. But it wasn't Eden who entered the room, it was Kristina. 'Tell me to mind my own business if you like,' Kristina said, 'but there's something very wrong, isn't there?'

Roggen looked up at her and knew that Kristina was too wise to believe any lies. 'I'm all right,' she said. 'Except for the fact that Richard no longer wants to know me, I'm fine.'

'Roggen, it's no use pretending. I've heard you in the bathroom in the early morning and I've seen my own mother in the same state you're in now. Please talk to me, it might help.'

Roggen's lips trembled. 'You're right,' she said, 'but I can't have this baby, I just can't.' Roggen whispered, 'It would kill my mother, the shame of it. I must take the only way open to me and get rid of it.'

Kristina stood beside her, an expression of urgency on her face. 'You could have the baby adopted, give it to someone who is longing for a child. You don't have to keep it, not these days.'

Roggen shook her head doggedly. 'How could I let my baby go to strangers?' She felt the tears constrict her throat. 'Look,' she said desperately, 'it isn't even a baby yet.'

Kristina brushed back her hair. 'Listen,' she said softly, 'it's got a right to life, just as you or I have.'

Eden entered the room and paused, his eyes searching Kristina's face. She looked away from him but not quickly enough to avoid the charming half smile that curved his strong mouth. 'Come along, Roggen,' he said softly, his arm around his sister's shoulders, 'let me take you out to the car.'

Roggen could scarcely think or feel. She was aware of rising to her feet and picking up her bag and gloves, and somehow reaching the door. Eden took her arm and was leading her down the stairs. Her legs moved automatically though her being cried out in protest. She no longer knew what to do. Was she making the right decision, or would she regret this day for evermore?

Numbly, she left the house and stared around her. The old house looked mellow and splendid, a place to bring up a family, yet she was about to end a life before it was begun.

Eden drove swiftly and Roggen was aware of his anxious glances but he said nothing, allowing her privacy to sort out her confused emotions. She was grateful to him for his silence. She wanted no more outside pressures, she simply wished to be at peace with herself.

The tangy smell of the docks drifted through the window, the spices, the salt sea air, scents and memories of childhood. These were some of the experiences she was denying her unborn child.

The house of the anonymous doctor looked as ordinary as any other, and yet the large doorway with a heavy bronze knocker in the shape of a lion's head, and the shuttered windows like blank eyes sent a shiver of alarm through Roggen.

She allowed Eden to help her from the car and watched as he lifted the lion's head and let it drop heavily against the dark wood. From within came the sound of footsteps and then Roggen found herself swept inside the large hallway by a nurse in a blue and white uniform who neither smiled nor looked unduly curious.

'I'll be back for you in about an hour,' Eden said, his arm comfortingly warm and tangible around her shoulders. 'Don't worry, you're going to be just fine.' As he left her she stared around, feeling trapped, a mouse on a treadmill unable to resist the ceaseless motion of the wheel.

'In here, please.' The nurse was elderly with grey hair protruding from beneath her cap. But she was briskly efficient, leading Roggen into a room of antiseptic whiteness where silver instruments glared under large lights.

In the corner was a screen of Chinese silk worked with muted colours to a dull jewelled effect. It was the only bit of colour in the room and Roggen fixed her eyes upon it as though she were drowning and clutching at straws.

'Undress over there, please.' The nurse indicated the screen. 'Take off your suspenders and lower underwear and just pop on the towelling robe, and then I'll prep you.'

Roggen did as she was bid, feeling that the ordeal was happening not to herself but to some stranger who had no ability to think rationally or to resist. She placed her silk underwear on the rattan chair behind the screen and drew on the robe, shuddering a little in the coldness of the clinical room.

'Come along, I'm sure you must be ready by now.' The voice, if not irate, was impatient, and Roggen moved from behind the screen to take her place on the high couch that dominated the room.

The nurse held an enamel bowl of steaming water and a frightening looking rubber tube that dangled onimously from her hand. 'I'll just shave you, this won't hurt a bit,' she said quickly, realizing that Roggen was trembling.

The indignity of having her pubic hair shaved would remain with her for ever. Roggen stared up at the ceiling trying to distance herself from what was taking place. She felt angry that she was allowing this to happen. Panic flared through her as the razor scraped against her flesh, and she closed her eyes tightly, trying not to imagine what the rubber tube was for.

'I'll have to give you a good cleansing,' the nurse said. 'It might feel a little unpleasant but it won't really be painful.'

Roggen opened her eyes and stared up at the ceiling in terror as if it offered answers to unnamed questions. She concentrated on details of the rose, the centrepiece around the light which was worked with intricate patterns of leaves and flowers twisted together like lovers' knots. Lovers. That was ironic. She and Richard had been lovers but now that she needed him he wasn't here.

'Move to the edge of the table, if you please.' The impersonal tones rang through Roggen's head. 'Come along, right to the edge so that I can work properly.'

Roggen realized quite suddenly that she could not go through with it. She sat up straight and tried to draw the robe around her nakedness, and covered, she felt less vulnerable.

'What's wrong?' The nurse dropped the bulbous part of the rubber into the bowl and stared at Roggen as though she had taken leave of her senses. 'You can't have the operation unless I prepare you first.' She sounded almost sympathetic. 'I know it's not very dignified, but neither is giving birth to an unwanted child.'

'There must be another way,' Roggen said, sliding to the edge and climbing down from the high couch with difficulty. 'I just can't think any more. I'm not even sure that what I'm doing is the right thing.'

The nurse smiled for the first time. 'I see many girls in here, trollops for the most part, eager and willing to get rid of an innocent unborn child so that they can go on with their way of life as before. Late, some of them come, when the child is formed, and then it can be a nasty job, believe me. But you are not like those unthinking hussies. I can see you are simply a nice girl who's got caught out.'

She began to pack away the razor. 'Don't do it if you've got any doubts, that's my advice. Go on home, think it all out, a few days won't make any difference. I'll make up some excuse to the doctor, tell him you've got a cough or a chill or anything that will put off the decision, give you time to consider, for once it's done there's no turning back.'

She began to wash her hands in the sink, and the water swirling round in the china basin like a whirlpool had a mesmerizing effect on Roggen. She didn't know what to do, wasn't there someone who could help her?

The nurse continued to talk. 'If you still feel the need to rid yourself of the baby, then come back the day after tomorrow, but I hope you'll not do that.'

'What else can I do?' Roggen was no longer in charge of her life, her youthful confidence had vanished. 'I don't want the baby and yet I can't, I don't want to destroy it.'

'Look, I'm Nurse Freeman and here's my address.' The nurse spoke with some warmth. 'I think I might know a way to have the baby adopted. We'll see.'

Roggen dressed quickly. Her hands were still trembling but she felt the block of ice within her thawing. She pulled on her stocking carelessly, snagging the silk, but it didn't matter. All she wanted to do was to get out of the house, away from the smell of Lysol and the sight of the paraphernalia of abortion.

The nurse was holding the door open for her. She put her finger to her lips in warning. 'We can't talk here. Come along and see me at my house some time this evening.'

It was good to be out in the fresh air with the feeling she had done nothing irrevocable. She had at least given herself time to think and if, after she had spoken with the nurse, there was no acceptable solution, she could always return to the doctor and go through with the operation.

She walked into town and made her way towards the beach. The sunshine was bright and warm. It was a day of sudden sunlight, when the town of Swansea was for a time a place of warmth and light. A day that made the winter seem far away.

By the time she returned home, Eden was pacing the hallway, frowning, his eyes half closed with the worried little-boy look he sometimes unconsciously adopted.

'Where did you get to?' he said. 'I've been worried out of my mind about you. What happened, why didn't you wait for me to bring you home? You must have known it was dangerous to walk about after . . . after what happened.'

Roggen paused, giving herself time to think. It was clear that Eden thought she'd gone through with the abortion. 'The nurse wants to see me this evening,' she said vaguely. 'Oh, Eden, you don't know how awful it was in that room with the bright lights shining down on all those gleaming instruments.'

Eden's eyes were suddenly steely. 'I blame the bastard who got you into this mess. He needs a good horse-whipping.'

The sitting room door opened suddenly and Marie Lamb stood regal, if a little bowed, in the doorway. 'Eden, what's all this shouting about, and in the hallway too. Do you want the servants to know all our business?'

'Mother, for heaven's sake!' Eden said. 'What servants? There's only Kristina and Anita Williams here, and I should think both of them are too busy to listen to me.'

'Well, what are you *ninos* quarrelling over now? Children! I don't know what to do with you any more.' Marie Lamb lifted a thin hand to brush away her wispy hair. She appeared much older than her sixty years as she stood frail and small in the light from the sitting room.

'It's nothing, Mother,' Roggen said quickly, moving towards the stairs. 'I'm just going to have a bath and a rest, but I'll have to go out for a while this evening.'

As Marie retreated to her seat near the fire, Eden caught Roggen's arm, his eyes anxious. 'How do you feel, are you in any pain?'

She didn't want to lie to him and yet she hadn't the courage to tell him the truth; that she'd run away without solving anything. She just shook her head and moved slowly up the wide staircase.

Later, as she sat in her room, brushing dry her short dark hair, she felt as though she had in some measure washed away the indignities of the day, and yet, as she looked down at her still slender body, she felt panic engulf her. How could she bring a bastard child into the house? The shock would kill her mother.

Kristina came into the room with a tray on her arm, and looked at Roggen anxiously. 'How are you feeling?' she asked, and Roggen raised her eyebrows in derision.

'How do you think I'm feeling? Lousy, of course.' Roggen looked away. She didn't want Kristina reading anything from her expression –the girl was very shrewd. She felt she didn't want to talk to anyone about what had happened, and especially not to Kristina; she might not be speaking to Eden at the moment but that was a state of affairs that might not last.

'Have a nice hot cup of tea, you'll feel much better then, I'm sure,' Kristina said softly.

'Everything is so simple with you, isn't it?' Roggen was a little irritated. 'Nothing is grey, it's all black or white. Well, you'll soon find that childlike philosophy doesn't always work.'

'Perhaps you're right,' Kristina answered gently. 'I'm sorry, I should mind my own business.'

'No, I'm sorry,' Roggen relented, 'I'm picking on you and I know it, but I've been through the mill today, believe me.' Roggen shivered. The whole thing had taken on the proportions of a nightmare. She didn't want to think about it any more. She rose to her feet and stared out of the window. Kristina moved to the door at once and Roggen gave her credit for having a fine degree of sensitivity.

'Is there anything else I can get you?' Kristina asked, and Roggen shook her head, regretting that she'd let Kristina trap her in the first place into admitting she was pregnant.

'No, nothing, thanks,' she said quickly.

When she was alone, Roggen sank down on the bed, her head in her hands. What a God-awful mess she'd got herself into, and she was the very one who had everything in her grasp with a good career and a fine family behind her. And now she was throwing it all away because of one foolish night of drunkenness with Richard James. How could she have been so stupid?

But recriminations were serving no useful purpose. She could tell herself a hundred times that she had been silly and irresponsible but it wasn't going to make the problem go away. Could she go through with the abortion? Could she go through with the pregnancy?

She would have to give it some thought when she was calmer, but sometime soon she would have to see the nurse and give her a decision, and at this moment she was not entirely clear in her own mind what that would be.

'You can get dressed now, Mrs Barnes.' The nurse spoke politely and Nia was not sure if the title was given her out of courtesy or if Nurse Freeman really believed she was married to Joe. The nurse had been recommended to her by one of her more well-heeled customers, and as she lived a little way outside the town in all probability Nurse Freeman would not know anything about Nia's background.

'I'm sorry, Mrs Barnes, it's not good news.' She was washing her hands as she talked, and Nia watching her felt a chill at her words. 'You are not pregnant, indeed, I don't think that it will be easy for you to conceive a child. There seems to be a tilting of the womb.' She smiled. 'It can sometimes correct itself, mind.'

Nia felt her old sense of inferiority coming to the fore, she felt that she was flawed in some way. She dressed quickly, unable to speak. The nurse was at her side at once.

'It's nothing for you to be ashamed of, my dear,' she said. 'Many women are in the same boat as you and they solve the problem sometimes by adopting a child.'

Nia shook her head. She knew Joe would never agree to that. She wasn't even sure that he would want a child of his own, let alone someone else's. She herself had harboured mixed feelings when her periods had stopped; she had felt panic and fear, and yet one little part of her had thought how fine it would be to become a mother. She had not expected to be told that she would have difficulty conceiving, and somehow she felt cheated.

She felt a flash of resentment against Joe as if somehow this was his fault. He was having things all his own way at the moment. She was cook and cleaner as well as doing her own work, and then in the nights she was expected to be an eager mistress, until now a role she had been willing to play.

She had not been aware that tears were running down her cheeks until Nurse Freeman handed her a handkerchief. 'There, there, cheer up, there's always hope, you know.'

'Yes, I suppose you're right,' Nia said anxiously, and Nurse Freeman smiled.

'I can't raise your hopes, but my advice is to put it all out of your mind. Put your energy into other things, my dear, and the miracle might just happen.' The old woman sighed. 'It's so sad that the girls who don't want children come to me, and then someone like you who would be a fine little mother is disappointed. But then the Lord works in mysterious ways.'

'We could have given a baby such a good, secure background,' Nia said distractedly. It would have been so different to her own, she would have made sure of that.

'Well,' The nurse's tone had become brisk and Nia realized she was keeping her from her other duties, 'don't set your heart on anything in this life, dear, but just keep on hoping, that's my advice.'

Nia rose to her feet as Nurse Freeman moved towards the door. It was clear that the interview was over.

'Thank you so much, Nurse Freeman,' Nia said automatically, then paused. 'Do you think it would be worth while me seeing a specialist, have a second opinion?'

The nurse looked at her carefully. 'That's always a way open to you, Mrs Barnes, and if it would make you feel better that's the right thing for you to do. Good day to you.'

Nia moved into the street, unaware of the noises around her. She felt locked into a world of sadness, knowing in her bones that the old nurse probably knew her job better than any doctor.

As Nia left the busy street where the nurse lived, she thought with impatience of the long walk home. It was not the walk itself – she was well used to that, doing her rounds, collecting bets as she did all day – but she was impatient to talk to Joe. All right, so there was to be no baby, but at least they could come to some understanding about their future together.

When she reached the lights of the town, she breathed a sigh of relief, and at the bottom of Wind Street, she caught a bus that would take her to Brynhyfred.

Joe was in his shirtsleeves, sitting at the wooden kitchen table with the map of the new mine spread out before him.

'Hello, love,' he said, glancing up at her. 'I've decided I'm going to buy into the mine,' he went on, tapping the map, 'but I need a partner. How do you feel about that?'

Nia's thoughts were confused; she'd been going to

speak to Joe about personal matters. 'I don't know, business hasn't been so good lately.' Nia slipped out of her coat. 'My punters seem to be falling off. I suppose I can blame my father for that.' She sat beside Joe and rested her head against his shoulder.

'We have to talk, Joe.' She looked at him levelly and impatiently and he shook out the map before him.

'Well, yes, I want to talk too, about the mine.' He stared at her, frowning. 'Is anything wrong?'

'I went to see the nurse today. I thought I was going to have a baby.' She felt again the grip of disappointment, and swallowed hard. 'It was a false alarm, but still, it made me think. We should be married by now, Joe, we've been living together long enough, haven't we?' She despised herself for the pleading note in her voice but somehow in the face of Joe's stony silence she was unnerved.

'A false alarm, was it,' he said at last. 'Thank God for that, then.'

She felt hurt and anger rise within her and rising to her feet she faced him angrily. 'I get the feeling you're just using me, Joe,' she said, her voice shaking.

'Well, I don't know what to say.' Joe looked up at her from his chair, frowning. 'I thought we were getting on just fine together. I didn't think you'd be the sort of woman to want a baby, not with your career ahead of you.'

'Well, perhaps I'm not really the maternal sort,' she said, 'but I felt that a baby would have made us a real family, Joe.'

'Perhaps,' Joe said, 'but have you thought that it might drive us apart? You should be getting on with your business interests, you are too intelligent to sit at home and nurse a child.'

She moved around the room restlessly. 'Perhaps you're right, Joe,' she said, and perhaps he was. Why didn't she just accept that he wasn't the marrying kind? He didn't want a wife or a family, in short, he didn't want any responsibilities. She sat down opposite him, her hands clasped together.

'I'm going to take your advice. I'll open a betting office, have the rich phoning in their bets to me, make everything legal instead of tramping around the streets in fear of the law.'

He hugged her then, his smile warm. Joe certainly knew how to turn on the charm.

'That's my girl!' He kissed her mouth and, as always, Nia felt herself respond to him. She clung to him for a moment and then drew herself away from the warmth of his arms. They still had a great deal to talk about.

But he was putting on his coat, swinging his silk scarf around his neck. He obviously intended to go out, and somehow she felt cheated. He took a roll of money out of the drawer in the dresser, and Nia felt a sense of shock; she hadn't known that he had that much money, let alone that he kept it lying about in the kitchen. It really was careless of him.

'Where did you get all that from?' she asked in surprise.

'I earned it, of course, on my coal round,' he added hastily. 'I'm off now to do a bit of business and put a deposit on the mine. I'm really keen on digging out my own coal. I'll be a business man then, Nia, and we'll have that much more in common.'

He paused at the door. 'Oh, one thing, Nia. Will you lend me the balance of the money, just for a few weeks?'

'Of course I'll lend you the money, Joe!' she said hotly. 'I'll get it for you just as soon as you put a ring on my finger!'

She watched him walk down the path and stride angrily away towards the public house, and then, slowly, she closed the door. She sank into a chair and rested her head in her hands. She had offered Joe an ultimatum. What would he do now, put her out into the street?

Suddenly she was weeping, hot bitter tears that ran salt into her mouth. Everything in her life was going wrong and she didn't know what to do to make it right again.

12

The roadway along the dockside was enveloped in a cold mist that rose menacingly from the water. The gentle wash of the hidden sea was an eerie accompaniment to Kristina's footsteps, but she didn't feel nervous, even though the swirling mist concealed buildings and distorted scenery. She knew every inch of the dockland, had played there since she was a child, and her progress was sure as she moved towards the cottage where she had been born.

'*Duw*, there's lovely to see you, Kris.' Her mother moved from the fire and hugged her. With a sigh of relief Kristina put the heavy bag of groceries on the table. The potatoes had weighed heavily, pressing against her side, and the smell of the onions had almost brought tears to her eyes.

Her young sisters were having supper, and Kristina bit her lip as she saw the plate of bread and scrape. Beside the mugs of weak tea stood the open tin of condensed milk and as she watched, Jayne put out a small finger and scooped up the drips running down the side of the tin.

'Still no work on the docks?' Kristina asked, knowing with a sinking feeling inside her what the answer would be.

'Aye, but there'll be ships in soon,' Ceinwen said quickly, knowing that her daughter would be blaming herself. 'Even if you were to give in and go courting with Mr Jenkins, I don't think it would make things better now. Times are hard on the docks, Kristina, and there was me thinking that once we moved into the thirties and with a Labour government at the helm, everything would improve.'

'Improve indeed,' Kristina echoed. 'The Labour government resigned like cowards once things were too tough to handle!' Kristina had never held such hopes. She had accepted the views put forward by Roggen without question at first, but then perhaps she had a more cynical eye than her friend, because she could not see the lot of the worker changing much whoever ran the country.

'I've brought you some fresh bread and some potatoes,' she said, changing the subject. 'There's a quarter of tea there too, and a bag of sugar. Don't worry, I haven't stolen the food. Eden gave it to me before I left the house.'

Kristina sank back in her chair, and looking into the fire saw that it was kept alight with pieces of wood and cinders. She must try to get some coal delivered to Mam, even if she had to pay for it herself. She would ask Nia's man friend Joe to deliver a load to the back of the house; that would keep Mam going for a while.

'Where's Thomas now?' she asked, and Ceinwen rubbed her hand on her apron in an apologetic gesture.

'He's down the public with that brother of his. Tom only sees him once in a blue moon and then he usually wants something,' she said. 'But there, he might as well be in the pub as laying about the house.' She smiled. 'Won a little bit of money on the horses, Tom did. He put on the bet with some man, and Tom says old Ambrose Powell and his girl Nia will have to look to their laurels if they want to stay in business. This Joe Barnes, he lets folk owe him, see, then he takes the stake money out of the winnings.'

'What about the losers?' Kristina asked, resisting the urge to say that Thomas shouldn't be spending anything on such trivialities as backing horses.

'Well, they pay up when they get their dole or the assistance. Not many fail to pay a gambling debt round here, you should know that, Kristina.'

Kristina sighed. 'Aye, because they know no one else will take their bets if they do.' She pushed back her long hair thoughtfully. 'I suppose Joe Barnes is collecting money for himself. He must have taken over that side of the business. Nia's opened a betting office, very private it is, mind, wouldn't know the place was for betting at all.'

Ceinwen set the teapot on the table, covering it with a brightly coloured cosy. She put her chin in her hands, ready to listen to some gossip, anything so long as Kristina forgot to be angry with Thomas.

'What does she do in the office, then?' she said with interest.

'I'm not sure, Mam,' Kristina hooked her finger in the cup handle, 'but she's well set up by the look of it; a posh desk and a telephone and lovely carpet. I think she just has to sit there all day and take calls and write out bets. A bit different from when she had to walk all over Swansea to get her money in.'

'And what's happening up at the big house, then? How's Mrs Lamb, keeping well is she?' Ceinwen didn't wait for an answer. '*Duw*, I miss them all up there mind, even Roggen Lamb, who I must admit can be a bit uppity at times.'

Kristina poured the tea and watched the amber liquid steam from the cups. 'To tell the truth, Roggen isn't so snobbish these days, Mam. In fact I'm quite missing her now she's gone on a teaching course in London.'

Had she? Kristina wondered, or was she hiding away somewhere? Kristina could not be sure what had happened, for Roggen had gone back to Nurse Freeman, returning home chastened after some hours, and telling Kristina that she never wanted to speak of the subject again.

'But there's marvellous to go off to London, what an adventure, mind.' Ceinwen looked fondly at her daughter. 'And you would love it there I'm sure, you always did want to travel. You were so excited when you went to Newport that time to hear Ramsay MacDonald.'

Kristina smiled. 'I suppose I was, though I felt Roggen was only putting up with me on sufferance because Nia couldn't go with her.'

She looked around the room and thought with sadness of the old piano that had gone from the parlour, leaving a mark along the bare wallpaper, and of the other pieces of furniture which had had to be sold, along with anything else of value, before the family had been allowed to claim public assistance.

'The money my stepfather spends on beer and gambling could be better spent on the girls,' Kristina said, her tone suddenly sharp, and her mother looked away.

'I'll freshen up the tea,' Ceinwen said as she pushed the kettle on to the fire in preference to using the gas ring.

'Why do you put up with it, Mam?' Kristina asked quietly.

Ceinwen poured the boiling water on to the tea, keeping her face averted and her hands busy. 'He's my husband, Kris. I took him on for better or worse, and now that things are bad, what can I do? Leave him? And where would I go with my little girls to look after? At least Mr Lamb has reduced the rent for us and we have a roof over our heads.'

It was news to Kristina and she felt warmth wash over her. 'Eden has reduced the rent? I didn't know.'

'Well,' Ceinwen smiled, 'we are not supposed to say, favours this household he does.' She sank down into a kitchen chair, her work-roughened hand clasped on the bare wood of the table.

'I remember when you were a little girl and I couldn't afford to buy you school clothes, he went out he did, and him only a young man, and bought you an outfit, even down to little woollen socks. Moved to tears I was, I'll never forget him for that kindness.'

Kristina too remembered the incident well, the pleasure she had taken in the pristine blouse and the finely pleated skirt. And it was true, Eden did single out her family for special treatment, but that was because she had always been up at the Red House, getting under everyone's feet while Mam did her cleaning. Perhaps the fact that he felt guilty about making her his mistress had something to do with it too, though he had not come to her bed since his engagement to Bella.

'I'm sorry for old Mrs Lamb, mind,' Ceinwen was saying. 'Always been sickly she has, ever since her husband died.' There was a tinge of compassion in her mother's voice and Kristina felt anger harden within her. It was all right for Mrs Lamb to go all sickly and unable to cope because she was cushioned with plenty of money, a luxurious home and a fine son to look after her. But Mam had no such comforts. Ceinwen had worked hard since the day she was first widowed and continued to do so long after an age when she should be putting up her feet and enjoying some of the pleasures of life. But then, public assistance didn't cater for pleasures.

The door swung open and Thomas moved into the room. He was sweating and his eyes were moist. He appeared to be dissolving, an ugly man and fat, Kristina thought grimly, soon he would be nothing more than a pool of lard on the slate floor of the kitchen.

Suddenly she tensed. Entering the room behind Thomas was the tall figure of Robert Jenkins, his size dominating the kitchen, and Kristina wondered if he had somehow known that she was visiting her mother.

'Get these kids off to bed, Ceinwen,' Thomas said, planting his portly figure before the fire, hands thrust into pockets, belly bulging over the old leather belt that encircled his large waist. He showed little sign of being underfed, Kristina thought angrily.

Robert moved to her side and leaned over her, and she looked up at him warily. 'I was telling Tom here that there's a few boats in the Kings that need dockers.' He smiled. 'I know things are tough on the assistance.'

He looked prosperous. His top coat was of good heavy cloth and his shoes were neat and well heeled.

'That's very kind of you,' Kristina said, warming to

159

him. He did not have to put himself out for Thomas, it was very good of him to bother.

He took a chair and drew it towards her but Kristina rose at once to kiss the girls good night. Jayne clung to her. 'Will you be here again tomorrow, Kris?' she whispered. 'Daddy is always nicer when you come.'

'I'll be here, don't you worry.' Kristina hugged her close and followed them upstairs to the bedroom.

'Go on down, you,' Ceinwen said anxiously. 'Just humour Tom and that Mr Jenkins too, it's so good of him to get Tom work.' She rested her hand on Kristina's shoulder. 'I know you don't want to get too serious with Robert Jenkins but be nice to him while he's here, there's a good girl.'

Kristina sighed and moved towards the stairs. 'All right, Mam, for your sake I'll try to make conversation and then we'll keep Thomas in a good humour.'

She descended the stairs slowly, feeling once again like a whore offering herself to Jenkins in exchange for Tom's job. But poverty was all around her and there was no food in the larder, and a few weeks work would put all that right.

She smiled as she returned to the kitchen, and made a point of sitting beside Robert Jenkins. 'We haven't been out to the pictures for a while now, have we?' She smiled at him and he leaned forward, his hand on her arm.

'I was just about to say the same thing.' He smiled, and for an instant he seemed almost handsome. But it was a trick of the light, the glow from the fire, an illusion.

'There's a good film on at the Castle,' Robert said, his face close to hers, his eyes shrewd as they rested on her. 'And after we could go for a coffee or perhaps even a drink. What about tomorrow night?'

Kristina nodded at once. 'Yes, tomorrow will be lovely, thank you.' Might as well get it over with as quickly as possible.

'*Duw*, don't the girl speak nice, then?' Thomas was

practically crawling to Robert, and Kristina felt a mixture of pity and revulsion.

'Aye,' Robert said slowly, 'she's a real lady and I'd be proud to have her as my wife.'

Kristina looked up at him, her pulse beating swiftly. '*Duw!* I certainly don't want to get married for a long time yet,' she said breathlessly. She tried to quell the feeling of panic that was rising within her, there was no way she could be forced into a marriage she didn't want, she told herself firmly.

'Well, don't leave it too long, girl,' Thomas said, irritation plain to see in the creases on his fat brow. 'Or otherwise you'll end up on the shelf a vinegary old maid, and you're too fine looking for that, isn't she, Mr Jenkins.'

Robert Jenkins smiled slowly. 'I don't think there's any fear of that,' he said. 'Kristina's not your ordinary run-of-the-mill woman, mind, she's got some quality that I can't quite explain, dignity, I think it is.'

Kristina felt her colour rising and she was relieved when Robert Jenkins turned away from her and spoke to Thomas.

'Report first thing in the morning then, Tom, we'll see what can be done.' He rose to his feet, a slim yet broad-shouldered man, well set up and handsome, and a man who intended to get on. Why, then, couldn't everything be simple, why couldn't she fall in love with him and solve everything?

'I'll walk you up to Ty Coch,' Robert said, and it appeared to be more of a command than a request.

'Now there's a good idea.' Tom was fawning again, and Kristina turned away from him in disgust. She moved towards the stairs.

'I'm going now, Mam,' she called. 'See you sometime tomorrow, all right?'

Ceinwen hurried to kiss her daughter, her eyes anxious. 'Mr Jenkins walking you home, is he?' she asked, and guilt lay like a heavy mantle around her shoulders.

'Yes, that's right, Mam, and we're going off to the pictures tomorrow night. It's about time I went out a bit, saw something of the world, instead of sitting in my room looking at the four walls.' She was attempting to reassure her mother and Ceinwen was well aware of it. She squeezed Kristina's hand and followed her to the door.

'Come on back here, Ceinwen!' Thomas said in irritation. 'She's a woman now, mind, and she's not tied to her mammy's apron strings.'

'See you tomorrow, Mam.' Kristina's smile did not include Tom. 'I've got some material over at the house that you can make up into nighties for the girls.'

The clouds and mist were even thicker as Kristina stepped out beside Robert Jenkins. He took her arm in a possessive way and drew her close to his side. She did not pull away; better to humour him, just until Thomas was settled back into the job, but one of these days she would really give him a piece of her mind and put him in his place.

'You could do worse, you know,' he said, drawing her so close that his arm was around her waist, almost touching her breast. 'I'm quite well off these days and I'd be very good to you.' Taking her silence for compliance, he continued speaking softly, coaxingly.

'I'm no womanizer, mind. I'm the faithful sort, I want a good wife and a nice home, and I'm getting very tired of living alone.'

'Give me time,' Kristina said as he stopped walking and drew her close, his breathing ragged.

'But it's so hard to wait, Kristina,' he said. 'I want you so much that it's like a hair shirt on my back. I want to make love to you very much indeed, but first I want to make you my wife.'

'I can't say anything now.' Kristina felt his hardness against her and tried to draw away. 'I'm so confused. Please, Robert, just give me a bit of time.'

'I know you're too honourable to continue an affair with Eden Lamb now that he's engaged, so there's no one else in your life, is there?' He nuzzled his chin against her hair. 'Be my wife and let me give you children. We'll put your past behind us.'

'Look, I'll see you tomorrow.' She finally managed to extricate herself from his embrace. 'Perhaps we can talk then, when my mind is clearer, please, Robert.'

'All right,' he said heavily. 'I'll call for you tomorrow and then we can look into each other's eyes and you can tell me to my face that you find my embrace repulsive.'

'But I don't!' Kristina said at once, and surprisingly it was true. Robert did have the power to arouse her. But then if she rationalized the situation, she was a young healthy woman needing a man, way past the age when most girls of her class were married. It was an instinctive response, an animal response, that was all.

When she let herself into the silent hallway of Ty Coch, the light was on in Eden's study. Kristina stood outside for a long time, wondering if she had the courage to do what she longed to and talk, really talk to Eden and ask him to reconsider the way his life was going; did he really love Bella, or was she just what Eden considered a suitable wife.

She was startled when he suddenly appeared in the doorway, a glass of port in his hand. 'Kristina,' he said, 'what are you doing lurking about in the hallway?'

'Nothing,' she said quickly. 'I was just going to bed.' She looked up into his face as he approached and put his arm around her shoulders.

'You're like a lost little soul there.' He smiled down into her eyes. 'I've missed being with you, Kristina.' He took a sip of the port and the ruby liquid glowed darkly in the light from the stairway.

Kristina made an attempt to smile. She was very aware of his arm warm around her, she longed to reach up and hold him, to rest her head against his shoulder. Didn't he know, couldn't he feel the strength of her love for him?

He bent and kissed the top of her head. 'I don't think you realize what a temptation you are to a man, any man,

163

but especially me.' He put his glass down on the hall table and put both his arms around her, smiling so tenderly that she wanted to burst into tears. Kristina felt suddenly happy, he still cared, still wanted her, and she made an impulsive move to put her arms around him.

He deliberately paused before slowly lowering his mouth to hers. 'Kristina,' he said thickly, and then he was drawing her up the stairs towards her room.

As he closed the bedroom door, Kristina clung to him, her scruples forgotten as she revelled in the happiness his touch brought her. His hold tightened, his mouth was passionate against hers, and she felt as though she had come alive again. His hand on her breast was gentle and she strained closer to him, loving him so much that she felt tears burn her eyes. He kissed her neck and then her mouth, and her pulse seemed to be beating inside her head. She felt tinglingly alive and it seemed her nerve endings were bare so that every touch brought her joy.

'You are so lovely, Kristina,' he said raggedly, 'such a beautiful woman, and I want you so much.'

His head bent over her proud breasts and his mouth was like fire on her nipple. Kristina hadn't known she could feel like this, so happy and yet so near to tears.

She arched herself against him, wanting as well as loving him. She could no longer think of Bella, or of right or wrong. She had to grasp this moment, hold on to it, treasure it. What would happen tomorrow she neither knew nor cared, but for now, for one magic night, Eden Lamb was hers.

The force of Eden's desire was unexpectedly fierce, and Kristina was suddenly breathless. He took his time, he was perceptive, and a good lover. She realized instinctively that this was his way of saying goodbye; he would love another woman from now on, but Kristina would be the one who loved him best.

13

Roggen sat near the rain-washed window, staring out at the misty outline of Worm's Head. It seemed so long since she'd left Swansea, the months passing with unbearable slowness. She was feeling frustrated and claustrophobic, her swollen body was anathema to her and she wished the whole damn thing was over and done with.

Nurse Freeman had been sure in her arrangements, planning the future for Roggen as though it were a wartime strategy. Once she was five months pregnant and with her waistline thickening, Roggen had claimed to be going to London on a course when actually she was staying with a family, obviously relations of Nurse Freeman, at Rhosilli, a small seaside village approximately seventeen miles from the town.

For the actual delivery, she was booked into a small private clinic nearer Swansea, and from there her baby would be legally adopted. Roggen did not think beyond that moment, she simply wanted to be free to resume her life in as normal a way as was possible.

It was a good thing she was not short of money. The venture had taken most of Roggen's allowance and some of her savings, but it was worth it. She would have sacrificed anything to be free of the child growing within her which had taken her over, threatening to ruin her life. If she had realized when she had lain with Richard that this ignominy would be the outcome, she would have taken flight at the first sign of passion. And it had not even been a worthwhile experience, for in the end Richard did not love her.

A knock on the door intruded into her thoughts and Roggen pushed herself upright, adjusting her loose smock so as to conceal as much as possible the gross swelling of her body.

'Do come in,' she said, attempting a pleasantness she was far from feeling.

'I wondered if you'd like some tea and biscuits.' Mrs Rogers was the image of Nurse Freeman, it had been clear from the start that they were related. Uncharitably, Roggen wondered how much of the money she'd paid to the nurse went into the pockets of her landlady. It wasn't that she expected to be housed and fed for nothing, but she could have rented a room in one of the best hotels at far less expense.

'There's a letter for you, Mrs Lamb.' The title was a courtesy one. Mrs Rogers spoke with an almost professional smoothness, her tone that of a kindly aunt to a rather backward child.

'Thank you.' Roggen took the envelope with little interest. If only it was from Richard she would not feel so depressed. One word of comfort or support and she would forgive him everything. But how could he write? He had no idea where she was.

'Yes, I'd like some tea, please,' she said, turning the letter over in her hand. It was from Eden, his strong, bold writing almost leaping with energy from the page. The postmark showed it had been written almost a week ago. Naturally it had taken a while to reach her as it had been diverted via a London address, another matter arranged by the good nurse.

She handled the envelope curiously, wondering what her brother had to say. He had swallowed the story that she was going to London on a course, not questioning her plan to acquire experience in teaching the disadvantaged. He had allowed her to make up her own mind; after some of their early wrangling over politics, he had realized that interference was not welcome.

The letter contained bad news. Mother was not very

well, her health was failing almost daily, and she longed for Roggen to come home. He did not labour the point, he did not need to. Roggen recognized a distress signal when she saw one. She bit her lip, she could not go like this, much as she longed to. Oh, God, if only the thing was over!

Eden ended his letter on a lighter note. Nia had been asking after her and would probably be in touch some time, but she was very busy with the new betting office she'd opened. Bella was well and sent her love. The news from home brought a lump to Roggen's throat.

The pages fluttered into her lap and Roggen looked up absently as the tea tray was brought into the room and set on the table. The china was delicate and fine, the tray cloth spotless. 'Thank you,' she murmured and waited patiently as Mrs Rogers poured the tea.

Nia was doing well in business if not in her love life. Poor, foolish Nia had obviously fallen under the charm of this man Joe Barnes who cared nothing about her reputation or he would have married her by now. Well, Roggen told herself, she at least would not be so foolish about men in the future. She had made one mistake that had taught her a lesson for life.

She rose awkwardly from her chair and moved closer to the rainswept window. She suddenly saw herself reflected in the glass, a lumbering creature with no more speed and grace than a cow. How she hated the way her clothes strained around her body. She hated everything about her pregnancy.

Roggen gasped as the movements of the child within her almost made her vomit, and prayed for the labour to start. It could not be over soon enough for her. She sank on to the bed and quite without warning, she began to weep.

It was almost a week later that an urgent message arrived in the shape of Nurse Freeman herself.

'I have to tell you something very upsetting, *merchi*.' She spoke softly. 'Now sit down and try not to get hysterical, it won't do you or the child any good.'

167

'What is it?' Roggen's mouth was dry as she sat on the edge of one of the upright chairs near the small polished table.

'It's your mam. I'm sorry, but there's no other way to say it. She passed away last night, quite painless it was, mind, there was no suffering.'

Roggen clasped her hands together. Mama dead, it couldn't be possible. She was frail, it was true, but Mother had seemed indestructible.

'The pneumonia it was; this misty, rainy weather doesn't help the elderly you see, goes straight to the bronchials and sits there causing trouble, especially in the frail.'

Roggen wished the nurse would stop talking. Her head was pounding with confused emotions. Mother was dead, and Roggen had been tied here, isolated by the fact of her pregnancy.

'I must get back to Swansea,' she said in agitation. 'I must be with Eden, he will need me.'

'Now think,' the nurse said softly, 'will you ruin all these months of secrecy?'

'It doesn't matter, not now,' Roggen said dully. 'It was mostly for my mother's sake that I took this way out.'

'And what about your future?' Nurse Freeman said carefully. 'Do you wish to bring up this little baby yourself then, because if you're seen in Swansea, everyone will know about your pregnancy and there will be cruel talk when you have it adopted.'

'I don't know.' Roggen closed her eyes and the nurse sympathetically patted her shoulder.

'You don't want a child, nothing can alter that. You want to live your life as you did before this . . . this accident. Don't act hastily now and ruin it all for yourself.' She played her trump card. 'You'd be the subject of a lot of malicious gossip, mind, and I don't think you want to upset your brother and bring down your family's good name now, do you?'

All that Nurse Freeman was saying was right, and yet

how could Roggen stand aside and miss her own mother's funeral?

'I feel I must at least go to see my mother buried,' she said wearily.

The nurse sighed heavily. 'Think very carefully then, my dear.' She went to the door and called for a fresh pot of tea.

'I have thought,' Roggen said, 'and I'm going to Swansea.'

'I'll take you myself, then,' the nurse said in a tone of resignation. 'We'll catch the morning bus on the day of the funeral.'

'No,' Roggen said, 'I'll hire a car and a driver for the day. It will be all right.'

'Very well, but I insist on coming with you.' Nurse Freeman handed her a small tablet. 'Take this with your tea, it will help you sleep, and don't worry, *merchi*, soon all this will be behind you like a bad dream. You're young and attractive and very clever, you'll get on in the world, you'll see. I can always tell the winners.'

The day of the funeral was unexpectedly sunny when somehow Roggen had expected greyness and rain. As the car drove along the winding roads from Rhosilli to Swansea, Roggen stared with a feeling of sadness at the lush hedgerows and the occasional glimpses of lovely coastline down below the hills. She knew that nothing would ever be the same again.

Because of Richard she had suffered so much, and he would come out of it all unscathed. Resentment mingled with longing for him. How she needed him at this moment. She swallowed hard, trying to force back the tears. Now she had even been deprived of being with her mother at the end.

As the car drew to a halt, Roggen saw that the cemetery was alive with people. It seemed everyone had come to the funeral of Mrs Marie Lamb who for so long had been the lady bountiful of the docklands, giving of her largesse in times of poverty, handing out large sums of money to charity when a soup kitchen was needed.

Roggen peered through the windows of the car, reluctant to get out. She saw her brother then, his tall figure standing out from the crowd of mourners. His dark head was bent and at his side, Bella slipped her arm through his as though in support. Not that Eden needed support; he was strong, a man of iron will, and Roggen knew that however much pain he felt at the loss of their mother, he would never reveal his feelings in public. In that they were very much alike.

Roggen took a deep breath and moved to the edge of her seat. She must force herself out of the car, brave the curious stares of the townspeople.

The pain struck as she leaned forward, and Roggen gasped in sudden fear. She bent over, clasping her swollen stomach, and bit her lip hard. When the pain subsided, Roggen looked at the nurse questioningly. The older woman had summed up the situation at once. She called out a command to the driver and the car was set into motion.

'It's not time,' Roggen said shakily. 'The baby isn't due yet. Are you sure I'm in labour?'

'I'm sure,' Nurse Freeman said. 'The baby is arriving a little earlier than expected but we're quite near the clinic. There's no danger, we'll have you in bed and made comfy before you know it.'

The car was driven swiftly through the streets and into a faceless square of large buildings, one of which was distinguished only by being larger than its neighbours. Roggen found herself being led along silent corridors and she gagged at the smell of antiseptic that permeated the hallway.

She was taken into a small, clinically bare room, where the pale pearl light creeping in through the small window seemed misty, unreal as the pain that wrapped itself around her body. The brief sunlight had disappeared and the day was dull with grey clouds racing across the sky, a

170

day of death and a day of new life. There was no way out, no turning back, she had to face the greatest ordeal of her life alone.

She undressed as the young nurse who had followed her into the room indicated, and drew on a striped towelling robe which strained around her tightened stomach. She bent over, the pain washing through her. When it subsided, she climbed into the bed and sank back staring into the gleaming lamp above her head.

The nurse bustled around the bedroom, her attitude encouragingly efficient. 'Now, don't you worry, you're in the hands of experts here. You are young and strong and everything is going to be all right, you'll see.'

The young girl smiled, her face rosy beneath the white cap. 'We've had many mothers through here. It's all quite straightforward and should be over perhaps before morning if you work with us. Just try to relax.'

Roggen allowed herself to be helped to an almost comfortable position against the pillows. How could she try to relax when, if she had her way, she would be out of here and back home in Ty Coch, grieving as was right and proper over the death of her beloved mother?

She was left alone then to watch the slow darkening of the sky outside through the window of dimpled glass that hid her effectively from the rest of the world, and suddenly the tears began to flow. It was like being isolated from reality, Roggen thought, imprisoned in her own pain and discomfort.

A little later, she was given some medication which didn't seem to help much. The pains were becoming stronger, tearing at her, dominating her thoughts as she tried to prevent fear from overwhelming her.

'When will the baby be born?' she asked the same pretty nurse who had tended her earlier. 'I can't wait to have it over and be out of here.' In the darkening of the girl's face, she read disapproval and something else. 'What's your name?' Roggen asked on an impulse.

'Just call me Dot,' the girl said. 'Everybody calls me

Dot.' She fussed with the sheets, smoothing them as though they were full of creases. 'I know I shouldn't ask, but don't you want your baby, then?'

'No, I most certainly don't,' Roggen said. 'In that I'm no different from any of the other mothers here, am I?'

'No,' the girl said doubtfully, 'I suppose not.'

From another room Roggen could hear the low moans of a woman in labour, and the fear rose up in her afresh, a nameless monster that made her hands icy cold and bathed her forehead in sweat. She realized with a sense of panic that there was worse to come.

But she must be calm. Nurse Freeman had told her what to expect and Roggen tried to rationalize the situation, telling herself that if the ill-educated women of Lambert's Cottages could accomplish childbirth without difficulty, then she could too. Any fool could produce offspring, so Roggen Lamb would not break under the strain.

By late afternoon, she felt she was no longer in control. It was then that Nurse Freeman came into the room and rested a hand on her forehead.

'There's good you are, doing well, just as I knew you would.' She smiled down at Roggen encouragingly and then began her examination.

'That's it, all going as it should be, no complications with you, young lady.' She paused and there was sympathy in her dark eyes. 'It won't be long now, soon everything will be over and you can have a well-deserved sleep.'

Roggen felt a strong contraction coming, and took a deep breath. The pain grew stronger, squeezing, compressing. Roggen cried out in fear. There was a strange, warm sensation at the base of her stomach, and then it was as though her life's blood was flowing away.

'There, nothing to worry about, your waters have gone,' Nurse Freeman said with satisfaction. 'That'll make the labour pass all the quicker for you. I'll just give you something that will make you a bit woolly but more relaxed, like.'

172

From then on, it seemed to Roggen as though she was sucked into a morass of confusion. She was aware of being wheeled along a corridor, of long white cotton socks being pulled on her legs, and then of the voice of the nurse urging her to bear down.

It seemed that her body took charge and she heard herself uttering guttural groans like some wounded animal. It went on and on, the pain, the effort of pushing, and with her strength slowly ebbing away she fought to be free of the child within her. All she wanted was that separation so that she could be herself again.

Daylight had come and gone, the early hours of morning stretched ahead and Roggen thought she could not go on any longer. She felt sweat bead her forehead and her eyelids drooped; she hadn't the strength to look up at the world of whiteness and lights and silver instruments that she had no desire to see.

Then, suddenly, there was release and into the heavy silence came a cry, raw and animal-like, the first cry of a newborn child. Without stopping to think, Roggen held out her arms and the baby was in them, lying surprisingly heavy and vulnerable against her breast. For a moment they were close, she and her child, and the strangest emotions were running through Roggen's consciousness.

'Right then, be a good girl and let me take the baby away for a nice wash, then.' Nurse Freeman's wide smile was reassuring and reluctantly Roggen gave up the baby to be wrapped in a thick warm towel. She was tired, so tired, and her heavy eyelids refused to stay open.

After a time, Roggen was moved into a bedroom, sparse and featureless with pale curtains and furnished only with a bed and a locker. The young nurse who had seen her earlier came in with a cup of tea and placed it beside Roggen, smiling comfortingly.

'You will be all right now, Mrs Lamb,' Dot said. 'You came through it very well especially considering this was your first time.'

Roggen drank the tea thirstily. Her mouth was dry and

there was a strange dragging sensation inside her. She felt again the small child heavy against her breast and heard the frantic, helpless cry.

'What did I have, a boy or a girl?' Roggen's voice sounded thready, hesitant, and the nurse avoided her eyes.

'I don't know, to tell the truth. I wasn't on duty in the delivery room.' She moved quickly to the door.

'Wait!' Roggen said, lifting herself up on one elbow, her heart beating swiftly with sudden fear. 'Ask Nurse Freeman to come in, would you?'

A long time passed before the door opened and the old nurse came into the room, a small bowl in her hand, a bland smile on her face.

'Rest now, is it?' she said softly. 'You've been through a great deal in the past hours, I doubt that you're thinking right.' She held up a syringe and indicated with a wave of her hand that Roggen should turn over.

'What is it for?' Roggen asked apprehensively.

'Just something that all new mothers need. Don't you worry now, everything is going to be all right.'

The needle was sharp and the effects almost instant. Roggen felt herself fall into an abyss of darkness. Her mouth felt as though it was filled with cotton wool as she tried to speak, and her tongue would not frame the words. Then the nurse was tucking the blankets around her, patting her shoulder reassuringly and moving away to the door. She stood for a moment whispering to another nurse who was biting her lip as though in sympathy.

'It'll take a bit of time,' Nurse Freeman was saying, 'but she'll get over it and then she'll be able to live her life as she wants to.'

Roggen tried to concentrate but the room was misty, wavering before her face, and sleep would no longer be denied. Her eyes closed and she did not hear the rest of the nurse's words.

'The baby is not strong, the poor mite has got

174

breathing difficulties, sucked some fluid into her chest, if I'm any judge.' She sighed. 'Right, let's get on, we've other mothers to see to, mind.'

Dot sang as she washed the babies, one of them newly born and very delicate. A sweet little girl, with a mop of unruly dark hair. The infant was very pale, she seemed in distress, and quickly Dot ran to find Nurse Freeman.

'It looks bad,' the old nurse said softly. 'Better get the minister here and warn the undertaker.' The nurse leaned over and took one of the infant's tiny hands.

'Poor little mite,' she said and her voice was trembling. 'It looks as if you won't be with us for very much longer.'

When Roggen woke it was to find Nurse Freeman standing at the foot of the bed, hands folded, eyes sad. 'There have been some problems,' she said softly. 'A very sad time for us here at the clinic.'

'What's wrong?' Roggen said quickly. 'What's happened to the baby?' Suddenly Roggen was flooded with fear.

The nurse shook her head. 'Put on your dressing gown, Mrs Lamb, and come with me.'

Roggen felt weary as she dragged herself out of bed and pulled on her robe. There was something dreadfully wrong and she bit her lip, fighting the weakness that threatened to overcome her.

Slowly, her slippers dragging against the hard stone floors of the corridor, she followed the nurse into a dark, silent room where a tiny figure was lying inert and pale, wrapped in a white sheet from head to toe.

'I'm sorry,' the nurse said gently, 'I'm afraid your little girl died in the night.'

Roggen drew back the sheet and stared at the tiny child. She was beautiful, doll-like, a perfectly formed baby with thick, strong hair curling around her face. But there was no breath of life to colour the cheeks and the small rosebud mouth. Roggen gripped the edge of the table, feeling faintness engulf her. Her child was gone, the baby she'd held so briefly against her breast was dead.

Roggen began to weep. 'It's my fault,' she said brokenly. 'I didn't want her, I resented carrying her and now I'm being punished.'

'A normal reaction,' the nurse said softly. 'It's difficult to believe that your baby has died. Don't worry,' she seemed genuinely moved, 'you are young and strong and when the time is right, you'll have another child.'

'Never.' Roggen's voice lacked power. Within her was an awful sense of loss for the still baby lying before her.

She turned away at last from the closed, lifeless little face, and moved heavily back into the corridor. Within her a voice screamed silently for someone, anyone to help her, but she was answered only by the rain on the window, and the cold, spartan furnishings of her room.

14

Swansea was in the grip of the depression that had swept the world. Women stood in queues at the pawnbrokers with furtive bundles wrapped in aprons, and men crouched ashamed in the gutters, playing at pitch-and-toss, the clatter of the old bent pennies against the stones sounding like the death rattle of a dying man.

With the coming of September 1935 the Nuremberg Laws were passed in Germany outlawing the Jewish people and making the swastika the official flag of the country.

In November, in Britain, the Silver Jubilee of George V was celebrated and the people of Swansea joined in as best they could, for they didn't seem to have much else to celebrate.

Nia Powell sat near the curtained window of the house in Brynhyfred and counted herself lucky that she was still solvent amongst so much poverty, for the rich were still placing bets, using her now legal betting office, well situated in the High Street, to the full.

She pushed away the book of figures before her and ran her hands through her glossy hair. It was time, so it seemed, to open another office, for the workload was getting too much for the one establishment to cope with.

Thank goodness she was unencumbered by children. Suddenly Nia's thoughts flashed back to the time when she had sat in Nurse Freeman's room and heard the news that she was not pregnant and probably would never be. The tears had flowed in a frenzy of self-pity until Nia had pulled herself together and got on with her life.

At first, her apparent inability to have children had been frustrating. She felt that somehow she was failing as a woman and more that Joe would somehow blame her. Now she faced the fact that marriage was not part of Joe's plan in life. He wanted to be unfettered and, strangely enough, Nia felt that she did not want marriage either. Once respectability had seemed all important, but not now.

She looked down at her books. She was doing quite nicely, she could support herself more than adequately and even the money Joe had coaxed her into lending him had been repaid in full. She closed her book with a sigh of satisfaction. Financially, she was doing so well that perhaps it was time she considered buying a larger house in a more salubrious quarter of Swansea, perhaps at the sea front, overlooking the large expanse of bay. She could laze in the neat garden and grow brown and sunkissed under the summer sun.

She shivered. The summer seemed very far away in the depths of a winter's night, with the wind blowing outside the house and the ice forming patterns on the panes. Nia moved to the fire, adding more coals and creating a blaze of light and warmth that washed over her face as she closed her eyes, locked into her thoughts.

So far, Joe had refused to move from the house in Brynhyfred. He was unwilling to give up his own home, feeling it was a matter of retaining his independence. It was possible that he resented Nia's rise to a financial position surpassing his own, and yet at night, when they lay together beneath the sheets, they were so happy, so in tune, both of them enjoying the physical contact that ended always in satisfaction and on Nia's part in a flowing of the love she had felt for him from the first time they met.

Nia glanced at the clock. Joe was late, his dinner would be drying in the oven. She pushed back her hair and uncrossing her legs from beneath her rose from before the fire, making her way to the kitchen and, somewhat impatiently, switching off the gas. Slowly, she returned to the small front room and looked around at the four walls which seemed to be closing in on her. She was alone a great deal lately and the realization came almost as a surprise to her.

The door opened quietly and Joe entered the room, bringing with him the scent of the December air, the coldness, the hint of frost, along with the excitement Nia always felt when looking at him.

She moved to his side and hugged him. 'You're late, Joe. I was beginning to get worried.'

Joe's kiss was perfunctory as he set her aside. 'Let's get to the fire, girl, it's freezing out there.'

'What kept you out so late?' Nia asked. 'It's getting to be a bit of a habit lately, Joe.'

He turned on her, his face darkening with anger. 'I'm a man grown, mind,' he said. 'You may be earning more money than me but it don't mean you can wear the trousers, right?'

Nia looked at him in surprise, and a trickle of fear halted the angry reply that rose to her lips. Was Joe resenting her success so much that it was affecting his love for her? She put her arms around his waist and leaned against his chest, hearing the strong beat of his heart.

'I worry about you, that's all. Sometimes I'm afraid of losing you, Joe,' she said, and her voice was almost a whisper. After a moment's hesitation, his arms closed around her.

'There's soft you talk, girl, what's all this about losing me?' He tilted her face up and kissed her lips but when she would have clung, he put her away from him.

'I'd better get my dinner, my stomach thinks my throat is cut.'

As he moved towards the kitchen, his words rang of disapproval and Nia bit her lip, holding her temper in check. It was his fault if he wasn't home to have his meal on time.

She sighed. How could she explain to Joe that the evenings were long when he was out, and that she was finding it increasingly difficult to keep at bay the questions that she longed to ask.

'I'm going to bed,' she said crisply and she was aware that she was stamping on each stair as she mounted it, venting her temper on the unfeeling fabric of the house. It was cold upstairs in the bedroom, the fire in the tiny inadequate grate having little effect on the punishing December winds that sought out every crack and entrance to the tiny room.

She *must* find a house, she decided. Apart from the freezing cold of the place, she wanted a better environment for herself, a gracious home in which to live and be comfortable. She had come to hate it in the small house in Brynhyfred, knowing that her business status demanded better. Nia was aware of the snobbishness in her reasoning, but she had grown up with the advantage of a good education which offset a little the disgrace of being illegitimate. If Nia couldn't persuade Joe to move to a better house, she might as well cut her losses and leave him. On an impulse, she hurried back down the stairs.

Joe was eating his dinner, seemingly unaware that the meat and gravy had dried around the edges and that the vegetables had become soggy. Nia made a cup of tea and sat beside Joe at the scrubbed white table, resting her chin on her elbows.

'We have to talk, Joe, it's no good just avoiding issues that need to be settled,' she said, and Joe avoided her eyes, knowing at once where the conversation was leading. 'Joe,' She put her hand on his arm, 'it's important that we talk about this. Isn't it time that we were settled in a house more suitable for our needs?'

He pushed his plate away, irritated by her argument, and lit up a cigarette.

'For God's sake, girl, you'll give me ulcers.' He attempted to make light of it. 'A man shouldn't talk about business matters when he's eating his dinner.'

180

'Joe, you always stop me talking about moving house. Is the idea such a bad one?' She paused, but he was taking off his boots and stretching his legs towards the fire, delaying his reply as long as he could.

'No, girl, it's not a bad idea at all, but then I don't want to look like a man who is living off a woman's money, see?'

'That's just silly!' Nia felt herself growing angry. Joe was adept with excuses and he had the ability to turn everything against her.

'We have a great deal in favour of us living in a better part of town, Joe,' she said urgently. 'We are both doing well and look what a fine life we could make for ourselves. Is it so wrong to want nice things around me?'

Joe looked at her through the smoke of his cigarette. 'But listen to yourself for a minute, girl, you even talk different to me.' He sat up and leaned forward in his chair. 'You want what I don't, a posh house. Well, you've had a posh education, mind and I haven't. I want only a simple life with an ordinary woman, can't you see that?'

Nia bit her lip, what was he saying? 'Do you mean you'll never want to move ahead with me, ever?' The words were thready, her voice shaking with the importance of the awaited answer.

Joe ran his hand through the thick springy hair. 'I don't know, girl! Don't push me into a corner all the time. That's all you ever talk about these days – buying houses and moving out of Brynhyfred – and I'm getting sick of it.'

Nia put her hand over her eyes, rubbing away the tears. She didn't want Joe to see her losing her dignity completely.

'There, that's it!' Joe said cruelly. 'Turn on the tap, that's always a woman's answer whenever she can't get her own way, isn't it? You want what's best for you, but have you thought about what's best for me?' He paused and rubbed at his eyes. 'Haven't you ever considered the fact that I might not want to spend the rest of my life with you?'

'Joe!' Nia stared at him in dismay. 'How can you talk like that after the time we've been together. I thought you'd committed yourself to me.'

He didn't answer, and Nia shivered. Joe was telling her he was not in love with her. She'd been a blind fool all this time. She stared at him, trying to see him objectively. Good looking, yes, but not by any means well dressed or refined in any way; and yet none of that really mattered, if she was truthful with herself. Or did it?

'Tell me the truth, Joe.' Her voice was level. 'Did you ever intend me to be anything other than your temporary mistress?'

'For Christ's sake, woman, let it drop!' He got to his feet and moved restlessly around the kitchen. 'You've got to pick, pick, pick like a little kid picking at a sore spot. Can't you be content with what we've got here?'

Nia rose to her feet. 'I could kill you, Joe!' Her voice was heavy. 'You know I wanted better than all this.' She gestured around the small room. 'Respectability I was willing to forgo. I haven't pressured you to marry me, have I? But I wouldn't have come to live with you at all if I'd known it wasn't a real partner in business you wanted, but a docile mistress to warm your bed.'

'Oh, mind now!' He thrust his jaw forward. 'You were quick enough to hop between the sheets with me, I didn't have to do no coaxing, now did I?' He thrust his hands into his pockets. 'A right little hot blood you were, just couldn't wait to get your hands on me! Well, you are not the only one, believe me!'

Nia stepped back a pace in horror. 'I love you!' she said in anguish. She sat down at the table and put her head into her hands. What was happening? Was her life breaking up into tiny pieces before her eyes? She wished she could move back in time to the moment when she'd closed her books, waiting patiently for Joe to come home to her.

'Christ! I can't stand this,' Joe said. 'I'm getting out of it before I smother to death.' She heard him open the back door and slam it shut, and then his heavy footsteps moving off towards the roadway. She couldn't cry, even though his words rang around her head, his insults, his insinuation that she was not the only woman in his life. The thoughts were all tangled up with pain and rejection, the old rejection that dogged her always. What was wrong with her that no one wanted her for very long? It must be that there was some flaw in her, some implicit fault that made her unlikeable and worse, unlovable.

She put out the gas light and moved heavily upstairs to the bedroom, and though she remained dry-eyed and awake until dawn crept through the ice-patterned window panes, there was no sign of Joe.

Joe stayed away for three days in all, three long, empty days when Nia felt she would lose her sanity. And yet through it all came the strength of knowing that should it come to the worse and she was left alone, she could cope.

When he returned, he was sheepish and repentant and he caught Nia in his arms, holding her close.

'My lovely,' he whispered, kicking the door of the bedroom shut, 'there's never been a girl like you, there's sorry I am to have been such a fool.'

Nia kissed him without speaking, feeling joy flood through her as his hand touched her breast. It wasn't so much her own desire, she realized, it was that he still wanted her after all the angry words that had been spoken between them.

'I've missed you so much,' he said raggedly, his lips against her throat. Nia moved against him, wanting to devour him with her love, to regain the feeling that she was important to him, more important than anything in the world.

'And I've missed you, Joe, but we've got all night to make up.' Nia raised her mouth to his and as his tongue probed hers she felt her anger dissolve. Joe had never meant any of the harsh words he'd spoken. He wanted her, and by God she wanted him.

He lifted her and carried her to the bed and gently set

her down, his hands deftly unfastening the buttons on her blouse. His mouth was a flame on her nipple, bringing it to a peak of hardness, and Nia moaned as he expertly divested her of her clothes.

He was a fine big man, so handsome and vigorous, how could she ever think of living without him? She wanted him and needed him so much. He teased her into an ecstasy of desire and she clung to him as he came to her at last, possessing her, making her whole as no other man would ever do. He was her Joe, for better or for worse, and even with all his failings she would want only him.

Her thoughts drifted into a limbo where there was nothing but sensation. She thought she cried out as she clung more tightly to his shoulders, but there was only the silent cry of fulfilment and then tears, hot and unexpected, pouring down her cheeks as she lay still now with Joe safely back in her arms.

That Christmas Day was one that would remain forever in Nia's memory. She and Joe in each other's arms, opening brightly wrapped parcels, laughing in sheer childish delight. They ate dinner at three o'clock; freshly killed chicken, succulent and tangy with herbs, and surrounded by crisp sprouts and sweet carrots. Afterwards, Nia played the piano and Joe stood behind her singing in his rich, deep voice. They sang carols and hymns until the music and the heat of the fire and the taste of the wine lulled them into a mood of sleepiness and then together they went upstairs to the bedroom.

'Right, my lovely,' Joe took her in his arms, 'now it's going to be the finishing touches to Christmas Day for you.' From his pocket he drew a small box. 'Here you are, Nia, and that's only the start, right?'

In the box nestled a ring, the small diamond shimmering at her in the light of the fire.

'Oh, Joe, it's beautiful!' He caught her hand, holding it tightly as he slipped the ring on to her finger, then he lifted her hand and kissed her fingertips.

'That's the first step towards making you my wife. Does that make you happy, my girl?'

'Joe!' She didn't know what to say. She'd wanted a partnership, not a marriage. Yes, she wanted security, the security of her own house, her own property; but marriage was something different. If Joe was not prepared to move house, how could he expect a marriage to work?

Joe lifted her into bed and softly but persuasively kissed her mouth. 'Hush now, there's more important things to think of, *merchi.*'

Later, Joe rose from the bed and declared his intention to have a drink with the boys down at the King's Arms.

'Oh, Joe, do you have to go, tonight of all nights?' she asked, but the protest was half-hearted for she was filled with the warmth of the release she had found in Joe's arms, and so she curled herself into a snug ball in the double bed and fell asleep.

The New Year came in with cold winds and sleet blowing across the River Tawe and sending the waves of Swansea Bay sweeping restlessly up the ice-rimmed beach.

Roggen crouched in a chair before the fire, her feet tucked beneath her, her dressing gown pulled close around her. She was suffering from a sore throat and a violent headache and it seemed she had never been really well since she'd given birth to her child. But it was all a very long time ago that the baby had died, and so why did she constantly feel this searing guilt, the feeling that she had abandoned her baby before it was even born?

Roggen was quite sure that had the baby lived, she would have brought her home and damn the consequences, convinced that once Eden had seen the child he would accept her too. But there was no point in such speculation; there was no child. Roggen had come home, supposedly from London, and resumed her life, at least outwardly as though nothing had happened.

And yet the entire episode had changed her. She was no longer the self-centred young girl she once was. The more she thought about her past, about her high-handed ways and opinionated views, the more she disliked the Roggen Lamb of the past.

Even Eden had noticed the softening in her and often he would look at her in a puzzled way, as though wondering what had changed her. Perhaps he put it down to the death of their mother and of what he thought of as Roggen's inability to get home in time for the funeral. She took a deep breath; it hurt her whenever she thought about the funeral, how she had been sitting in the car, watching the minister stand over the grave like a bird of prey, grieving for her mother and yet unable to pay respects to her mother's memory.

And tied up with her thoughts of the funeral was the nightmare of giving birth to her child, holding her for a brief time only to learn that the baby had died. She tried to brush the thoughts away but the memories persisted. Memories remained, too, of Eden's bewilderment at her absence at such a time. She had excused herself by telling him that she had been taken sick and couldn't travel, and though she felt that he didn't really believe her story, he never pressed her on the matter.

Of Richard she had heard little, and that too had the power to hurt. He had gone from her life so completely, never even knowing the damage he had done. And yet she could not blame him for that, for her own pride had stood in the way. She should have gone to him, insisted on telling him about the child he had fathered. But it was far too late for that now. Richard had risen to a high position in the local council and was about to become the next mayor of Swansea. He would scarcely want his past raising its ugly head.

Politics, once so important, seemed so trivial to her now. What did politics really matter when it was everyday life and death events that most affected people's lives?

186

She did wonder sometimes how Richard would have reacted had she given him the opportunity to know about her pregnancy. Would the embarrassment have proven more fierce than the joy of parenthood? She feared so, but then perhaps she was being unfair to Richard. She would never know.

Kristina came into the room, a hot drink on a tray. She smiled at Roggen and held the tray towards her. 'Here's some lemon and honey, it'll do your throat good.' She put down the tray and rubbed at her cold hands. '*Duw*, this winter seems to be lasting forever, but thank goodness Thomas has got work on the docks. At least Mam and the girls have a decent fire and plenty of food in the cupboard.'

Roggen coughed, making an effort to clear her throat, and spoke huskily. 'Still seeing Robert Jenkins, are you?' She sipped at the hot lemon and gasped a little at the sharpness of the drink.

'Aye, still seeing him,' Kristina agreed. 'Not allowing him any liberties, mind.'

Roggen studied Kristina's face. 'You do know that Eden plans to be married in the spring, don't you?' Roggen wasn't sure of the state of affairs that existed between her brother and Kristina. That Kristina still had a crush on Eden was without doubt. Roggen had seen her eyes light up whenever he came into the room.

Kristina nodded. Although they were on better terms than they had ever been, there was still a barrier between her and Roggen, and she didn't give anything of her feelings away. From Kristina's offhand response, Roggen guessed that it really was all over between the two of them now; either that or they were being far more discreet about the affair.

She wondered if Kristina had ever guessed the truth behind the elaborate plans she had made to conceal her pregnancy. If she had, there had never been any reference to it, but then Kristina was nothing if not discreet.

'Sit down, Kristina,' Roggen offered. 'It would be good

to have company for a while.' She did not like to admit how lonely she sometimes felt, the need to confess all about her child to someone was often overpowering. She might even have been indiscreet enough to talk to Kristina had the girl not shaken her head.

'I've got loads of work,' she said. 'We can't all sit around enjoying ourselves.'

'Lots to do?' Roggen asked, aware that there was a tinge of colour in her cheeks. She felt put in her place by Kristina's remark.

'Enough,' Kristina replied. 'Especially as the little Williams girl is homesick again. She seems to get very bad colds in the winter and it's no good her spreading it all around the house.'

Kristina moved to the door, then paused and looked back. 'Any special dishes you'd like for supper? I think Eden has asked Mr Singleton to come over again tonight.'

'I see. Well, that was silly of Eden. I, for one, don't feel up to entertaining anyone, not even Colin, nice as he is.' And he was nice. He was based in Swansea now and had been calling at the house for some time, obviously with a view to getting to know her better, and while Roggen liked him well enough and felt that any man's attention was a balm to her battered ego she knew she was not up to making small talk tonight.

'Shall I make Mr Singleton's favourite dinner of saddle of beef?' Kristina asked.

'For heaven's sake, call him Colin!' Roggen smiled in mild exasperation. 'You make him sound as old as Methuselah.'

'Are you going to marry him?' Kristina asked and then blushed hotly. 'I'm sorry, it's none of my business.'

Roggen smiled. 'And here was I thinking that you were the soul of discretion, not one to meddle in other people's affairs.' She leaned forward, suddenly serious. 'I don't know if I'll marry him or not, he might well be my last chance. And talking of last chances, I hope the thing between you and my brother is over now,' Roggen said.

'All you've had from him is a few small gifts and the fear of an unwanted pregnancy. It's not good enough for you, Kristina, you deserve much better.'

Kristina sighed. 'Don't worry, I can take care of myself.' She smiled and adeptly changed the subject. 'Now my mam is joining in with Tom urging me to marry Robert Jenkins because she's afraid I'll end up an old maid!' Kristina smiled, 'I'm still only in my twenties, which is young in the circles you move in, but an old maid for anyone living at Lambert's.'

'That's silly, you don't have to get married, you'd be a good catch for anyone. In any case, you've made yourself quite well known for your herbal recipes. You could make a little business of that, I should think. My advice if you want to get married, though, is to get out a bit more. There's nothing more certain than that you won't meet anyone else while you hedge your world between your mother's house and Ty Coch!'

'Don't worry about me,' Kristina said. 'I get over to see Nia from time to time, though of course she's very busy now with her business. In fact, come to think of it, I haven't seen her since before Christmas. She's very tied up with Joe, and him doing the dirty on her from what I hear.' She smiled ruefully. 'They all do the same thing, it seems, promise the earth and give nothing.'

Roggen sank back in her chair. 'How is Joe "doing the dirty" on Nia?' she asked, frowning. 'What have you heard?'

'He's not only carrying on with Anita Williams, blatant about it he is, too, but he's been cheating on Nia another way by taking her customers from her.'

Roggen bit her lip thoughtfully. 'But Nia has a legal office now, surely it doesn't matter if Joe is doing a bit of bookmaking on the side, does it?'

Kristina shook back her thick tawny hair. 'Maybe not, but Joe took them away before Nia ever had the office, and him not telling her a thing about it. The worst of it is, she thinks it's her dad who's been pinching her

189

customers, and that's a pity. Ambrose Powell may have done all sorts of bad things, but taking his daughter's customers is not one of them.'

Roggen sighed. 'Ah, well, we can't all choose to love wisely or even well.' She smiled ruefully.

Kristina picked up the tray and the empty glass and moved towards the door. 'It seems to me that we all have to make a compromise,' she said. 'We must take what we can have and forget what we can't.'

As the door closed behind Kristina, Roggen stared thoughtfully into the fire. By accepting Colin Singleton's tentative courtship, she was most certainly making a compromise, but then she had known what was laughingly called true love, and look what it had turned out to be; infatuation, a sham, an ethereal feeling that vanished the moment difficulties arose. Well at least with Colin she had trust; she knew he would stand by her come what may, and surely that was worth a lot more than a temporary spine-tingling facsimile of love? Perhaps she should grasp hold of him while there was time.

Later, when Colin arrived to see her, carrying a box of chocolates, she greeted him warmly but turned away when he would have brushed her cheek with his lips.

'Don't kiss me,' she urged, her voice still hoarse. 'I don't want to pass my sore throat on to you.'

As he shrugged off his coat, Roggen caught his faint smell of tobacco and soap. Colin was a real man, she thought, a solid reliable man, husband material, not a leaf blown anywhere in the wind like Richard had been.

Colin sank into a chair and stretched his long legs towards the fire. 'One thing I like about winter is that I don't have to go off across the world with the cargo!' He grinned. 'Not even that slave-driver of a brother of yours expects that of me.'

He leaned forward, suddenly earnest. 'I can't wait any longer, Roggen. We're not children, and I want you to know I would like us to get married as soon as possible.'

'Why not?' Roggen said half in amusement. 'We've known each other long enough.' She realized then that he was serious. 'But on the other hand, we haven't had much of a courtship, let alone an engagement.' Colin looked disappointed. 'What if we talk to Eden about it,' Roggen said. 'I'm sure he can't raise any objections, but I feel we should discuss something so important with him.'

Colin rose and planted a kiss on her lips, and even though she tried laughingly to push him away, he persisted. At last he released her and she moved away from his arms.

'If you get a cold it'll be your own fault,' she said sternly. She sank into the chair opposite him, curling her bare feet under her. That was one thing in Colin's favour, she was so used to him, she could be quite at home in his company. Their's might not be the most passionate of marriages but at least it would be based on good solid friendship. So why couldn't she say yes?

Colin took out his pipe and looked questioningly at Roggen. 'Will it bother you if I smoke, don't want to go making the old throat any worse.'

She shook her head. 'You carry on. I think Kris's lemon and honey elixir has brought me over the worst.'

'You know why I want us to be married quickly?' he said. 'Well, things are looking bad in the world at the moment.' He puffed smoke through the briarwood pipe. 'This chap Adolf Hitler we're hearing so much about lately is getting to be quite popular with the German people. He'll need watching, his views are quite extreme.'

'Oh, Hitler, he's a little nobody, a jumped-up pip-squeak. He won't get very far,' Roggen said earnestly. 'Surely you don't see him as a world threat, do you, Colin?'

Colin pushed back the fall of blonde hair from his high forehead. He was an intellectual as well as a good businessman, and Roggen respected his opinions.

'Give the man a little time and he'll be ruling Germany with an iron rod,' Colin said seriously. 'He's the stuff

191

dictators are made of. He wants an elitist society, Ro, a hand-picked human race. He's a very dangerous threat, believe me.'

Roggen shivered and drew her dressing gown more closely around her. 'Well, I'm glad we live in this part of the world then, at least he can't touch us here.'

She looked at Colin's closed expression and a thead of fear ran through her. 'He can't touch us, can he, Colin?' she asked. He leaned forward after a moment and touched her hand.

'Course not. You don't think I'd let Adolf Hitler frighten my girl, do you?' He smiled warmly, but in spite of the cheerfulness of his words, Roggen was left with a strange sensation of dread.

15

The waters of the Prince of Wales Dock were driven into small scalloping waves by rough winds; the houses in Lambert's Cottages had a shuttered look, curtains drawn, lamplight shining in warm pools through close-curtained windows. And it seemed strange to Nia to be visiting her father's house again.

Since the day she had walked out, she had returned only a few times, and Ambrose always made a point of telling her she had a rival bookmaker in the area. She bit her lip, knowing very well who her rival was; who else but Ambrose himself would know anything at all about bookmaking?

But now Ambrose was sick, very sick, and it was her bounden duty to visit him. Hadn't Joe insisted on it, even suggesting that she should stay the night with her father?

Nia walked towards the familiar doorway with a strange sensation gripping her. It was as though she were a small girl again and the butt of the spiteful gossip that had surrounded her when her father was shamed and disgraced, forced to move from the comfortable manse to the lowly cottage near the docks.

Ambrose was not in bed but was seated near the fire. He seemed shrunken in his woollen dressing gown, his bare feet, grey and bony against the brightness of his slippers, emphasized his vulnerability.

'So you've come to see your father die?' He forced a smile and Nia moved towards him quickly.

'Dad, don't talk like that. There's been a great deal of

wrong passed between us, I'll admit it, but I don't want to see you sick and alone.'

He stared at her steadily. 'There's not a great deal of choice, Nia. You have your home and your man to think about and I don't expect you to give anything up for me.' He paused and smiled at Nia who searched for something to say but found words of comfort elusive.

'The nurse comes in to see to me every day,' Ambrose said softly, 'so don't feel too badly.' He paused, smiling a little. 'And I wouldn't want you witnessing my lost dignity, but I would appreciate a visit from you whenever you can spare the time.'

Nia felt a tightness in her throat. Ambrose might not have been the perfect parent but by his own lights he had done his best, and after all, there was the bond of blood between them. She rested her hand on his shoulder. 'Dad, I'd like to come and stay with you, tonight. I'm sure Joe won't mind.'

'I don't suppose he will.' Ambrose spoke with an irony that Nia didn't understand, but then he had always been a strange man, locked into his own thoughts much of the time.

On an impulse, she bent down and kissed his cheek. The skin felt dry and thin, and Nia realized in that moment just how sick her father was.

Ambrose touched her hair. 'You know what I believe, Nia?' he said quietly. 'You can count yourself mature when you can forgive your parents for the wrongs they wittingly or unwittingly did you.'

'Dad, don't talk like that, you make me feel so guilty.' Nia drew a chair near to where her father sat and took his hand, though the simple act left her feeling foolish. 'I shouldn't have neglected you all this time. I've been no sort of daughter to you, have I?'

'You've been no worse a daughter than I've been a father,' Ambrose replied, 'so I'd say we were quits. Now, enough of all this sentiment. Tell me, how is the betting office doing?'

'It's going well,' Nia said, swallowing hard. 'Legal betting pays much more than illegal betting, and it's not half as much work.' She smiled. 'No pounding the pavements until every stone is a boulder through your shoes and your pockets weigh you down until it feels there's a yoke across your shoulders.'

'Is the business in your name?' Ambrose asked, and the very casualness of his tone alerted Nia to some hidden reason for his asking.

'Why, dad?' She paused, resenting his question, and then reluctantly replied, 'No, not entirely. It's between Joe and me, is that wrong?'

Ambrose sighed. 'I thought I'd taught you better than that, Nia. In business you don't trust anyone, not even your nearest and dearest.'

'Joe's all right.' Nia defended Joe quickly, but icy fingers along her spine told her that her father had a reason for asking the question, and he was the shrewdest man she knew.

'Just be on your guard, Nia,' Ambrose said. 'I sit here alone most of the time and yet the gossip comes my way just the same. Nurse Freeman comes in to look after me now and she's got a fund of stories, believe me.'

Nia felt suddenly cold and afraid. 'What's the nurse been telling you? Has she been talking about me or Joe?' she asked.

'Oh, nothing about you, Nia, but I'm afraid she's vociferous about Joe Barnes. You ought to watch what he gets up to. I have tried to warn you before about rivals.'

Nia digested his words in silence for a moment; did her father mean that it was Joe who was usurping her customers and not himself as she'd believed?

'Joe, taking bets?' Nia asked in a small voice, and Ambrose sighed heavily. 'I don't want to hurt you, but I don't want you risking your future either, not with a man who does not merit your confidence in him. All I'll say is that I've heard gossip, and it's up to you to find out anything you can. You've never been guilty of acting stupidly, Nia, don't be a fool now.'

The front door opened and the nurse came into the kitchen, her apron, crackling with starch, tinged with colour from the blue bag. She smiled and nodded at Nia. 'How are you today, Mrs Barnes?'

She dumped a bag of groceries on the table, not waiting for Nia's reply. 'And how's the patient feeling today?' She placed the back of her hand against Ambrose's brow and smiled and nodded. 'Fever's down, not too bad, Ambrose. You'll see me out yet.'

She went to the pantry and brought out a heavy black pot. 'I'll just warm up a bit of this soup for you, and there's fresh bread from Libba's in the bag. A hot meal before you settle down for the night will do you the world of good, won't it then?'

Nia sat back in her chair, the heat from the fire warming her cheeks. It was some time since she'd seen Nurse Freeman. The woman looked not a day older, but then Nurse Freeman had never seemed young, her hair had been grey, her face round and highly coloured ever since Nia could remember.

'*Duw*, it only seems the other day that you were so proud of your new daughter, Ambrose, and here she is grown up.'

Nia saw in the slightly raised eyebrow and a certain look in the nurse's eye that she didn't think Nia much of a daughter. But then she didn't know too much about Nia's upbringing, she was only called in when babies were being born or folks were sick.

'Aye,' Ambrose said, 'I was proud indeed, so happy to have a child, though after Nia's mother died it wasn't easy.'

'I know,' Nurse Freeman was still bustling about the kitchen, 'children do take up a lot of time, though they don't always appreciate it themselves.'

She placed the bowl of soup before Ambrose, and Nia bit her lip. The nurse was right, Nia hadn't thought of the difficulties her father had faced bringing up a daughter alone.

Watching her father carefully, it seemed to Nia that he had lost all his strength. His hand holding the spoon trembled, and the nurse had to reach out and guide his hand to his mouth.

'I'd made up my mind to stay the night,' Nia rose to her feet, 'but I see that you are being well looked after. Is there anything I can fetch you in the morning, Dad?'

'No, love.' He shook his head. 'As you say, Beattie here looks after me very well.' He smiled, and it was clear that there had been at some time much more than a nurse-patient relationship between the two. 'But come again soon, I'd like to see a bit more of you.' He didn't add 'before I die', but the words seemed to hang in the silence.

Nia left the house and paused for a moment before crossing the patch towards Ty Coch. She might as well call in on Roggen, it would be churlish to pass without seeing how she was.

It was Kristina who opened the door, as tall and slim and lovely as ever. In that moment, it seemed that nothing had changed and they were back in the easy days when there were no problems other than deciding which man to make eyes at, and when everything in life seemed to be simple.

'Nia,' Kristina smiled in her usual open-hearted way, 'it's ages since I've seen you. Come in, don't stand there on the step. Roggen will be so pleased that you've called.'

The old house carried the same scent of polish and had maintained its air of sumptuousness, in spite of the depression that had racked the town. There, men sat on street corners playing shove-halfpenny, or stood in long queues at the labour exchange, while the womenfolk did their best to stretch the meagre supplies of food to nourish ever-increasing families, for children, it seemed, were the one growing product that came out of the depression. But none of it had touched Nia or the Lambs, cushioned as they were by their money.

Roggen's dark hair was longer now, sweeping across thinner cheeks, but otherwise she looked just the same.

'Nia, you've become quite a recluse since you've had a man to look after. Does Joe keep you chained to the cooker or something?'

Nia shrugged. 'Not quite, but what with the business and everything, I don't seem to get much free time.' She sank into a chair and relaxed against the plump cushions. 'I've been to see Dad. He isn't well and I'm rather worried about him.' Nia realized she was understating her concern but she didn't want to sound too dramatic.

Kristina came in with a tray of tea and stood near the door. 'Mam told me that Ambrose hadn't been out of the house much lately, and that Nurse Freeman is back and forth there. Mam wanted to go in to see what was wrong but your father is a man for keeping himself to himself and she didn't like to push herself on him.'

'I know,' Nia said softly. 'It's my place as his daughter to keep an eye on him and I've been wrong neglecting him the way I've done.'

Kristina put the tray on the table and stood back almost diffidently. 'Shall I bring you some Welsh cakes. Anita's just baked them, hot out of the oven they are.'

'That would be lovely, Kris,' Nia said quickly. She sensed that Kristina was not happy, her eyes were shadowed and her usual warm spirit seemed to be subdued.

When Kristina had left the room, Roggen turned to Nia. 'I keep telling Kristina she should marry Robert Jenkins. If she's not careful she'll end up being an old maid.'

Outside in the hallway, Kristina paused. Marry Robert and everything in her life would be all right. How wrong Roggen could be. Kristina had seen a great deal of Robert in the last months. He had become a regular visitor to the house in Lambert's Cottages, and though she had grown to like him, Kristina could never consider herself in love with him.

She still loved Eden and even though she knew he was engaged to Bella and would soon marry her, Kristina could not break free of her relationship with him. She knew she was weak and foolish and that she was going against all she believed in by continuing to sleep with him, and yet she lived for the times when she was in his arms.

As she moved into the kitchen, she saw that Anita Williams was not alone. Robert was leaning against the sink, talking to her. He smiled when he saw Kristina and came to her side at once.

'I've just been down to your mam's,' he said. 'Took her some fish I had from the docks. She was like a dog with two tails, you'd think I'd given her a chest of gold.'

'That was good of you, Robert.' Kristina smiled at him. 'Sit down, have a cup of tea with us, I was just going to make a fresh pot anyway. Will you put the kettle on, Anita?'

Anita pouted. 'I wanted to finish early today, mind, got to meet my boyfriend, I have.'

'All right,' Kristina said, smiling. 'But just take that plate of cakes through to Roggen.'

It seemed, Kristina thought, that whatever she did, fate was conspiring to throw her together with Robert. He smiled at her, catching her eye, and unexpectedly she felt a sense of warmth.

In the sitting room, Nia was drinking her tea, feeling it was time to get back home and talk to Joe. But she knew it would be rude to rush off so quickly so she attempted some small talk with Roggen.

'I'm surprised the Williams girl is still working here. She never seemed to me to be the type for domestic work.'

Roggen nodded. 'Yes, we're lucky she stayed. We took her on to help Kristina with the heavy work. She's not bad if a little flighty with the men, lucky girl!' She laughed. 'Who would think that a plump little thing like Anita Williams would be so attractive to the opposite sex?'

Nia leaned back in her chair. It was strange how mature Roggen appeared to be now, she was not so arrogant as she used to be, and there was an air almost of humility about her that Nia found very endearing. But then, Roggen had faced a tough time of it when her mother had died and like them all, she was getting older.

Nia glanced round as she heard the door opening, anxious to see Anita Williams for herself. The girl who entered the room, cheeks flushed, a tray on her arm, didn't look very much like a *femme fatale*. She had high round breasts and she was just as Roggen had described her, plump and short. But she had large eyes, heavily fringed with light lashes, and a mop of bouncy childish curls.

Her eyes flickered over Nia with something like hostility, and Nia looked away, wondering if she'd been rude staring so hard. She accepted a cake from the tray.

'I understand you want to get off early, Anita,' Roggen said amiably. 'If it's all right by Kristina, then it's all right by me.'

The girl lifted her head, her shoulders stiffening defensively, and she seemed to be addressing her remarks directly to Nia.

'I've been going out with him for a long time now,' she said. 'He's going to buy me a ring for my birthday, there's every chance we'll be married before the year's out.'

'Oh, dear,' Roggen sipped some of the tea from her cup, 'I suppose that means we're going to have to find someone else to look after us.'

'Well, there's nothing to worry about there, miss.' Anita's attitude changed at once. 'I've got sisters, mind, and times is hard, see; any one of them would love a job up by here with you.'

Roggen put down her cup. 'Well, we'll face that hurdle when we come to it. Go off to see your friend, Anita, and don't bother about the washing up, I'll see to it.'

'One thing more, miss,' Anita said, twisting a ringlet of fair hair between her plump fingers. 'I think I'll go home to my mother's for tonight, if that's all right by you.' She flashed Nia a venomous look and Nia frowned in bewilderment.

'Yes, that's all right,' Roggen said, 'just so long as you get here early in the morning.'

As the door closed, Roggen sighed. 'And if I believe that excuse I'd believe that apples grew on Christmas trees. Why do I feel so old when I listen to Anita. God, I feel like Methuselah.'

Nia forced a laugh. 'I think it's her high spirits,' she said. 'Anita seems so full of life she makes me feel ancient too.'

Nia was puzzled and strangely apprehensive; first her father's warning and now this chit of a girl apparently having a dig at her. What was going on? Doubts began to trickle into her mind. Joe and Anita, it couldn't be possible, could it?

She flinched when Roggen teased her about being modern and 'living in sin'. She felt a sense of overwhelming insecurity, all her doubts about Joe and their life together suddenly intensified. Damn it! Just when she thought she had found her niche in life and the uncertainies of her childhood had slipped away from her, all these doubts turned up to confront and bewilder her.

'You've become very quiet there, Nia,' Roggen said, leaning towards her. 'My trivial talk must be very boring to someone who has her own home and business and copes with life so wonderfully well.'

'I'm not at all bored,' Nia protested. 'I was just thinking how much I appreciate being with you. I'm happy to be sitting here with you gossiping again as if it was old times.' Roggen appeared not to notice the agitation that Nia was sure was evident.

'We'll have a little drink of sherry, shall we?' Roggen rose and padded across the deep carpet in her bare feet, lifting the shining decanter and pouring two drinks, and it struck Nia very forcibly that Kristina was not invited to join them. Strange how she'd always been a bridge between the two girls, being half in one camp, half in the other and never really sure where she belonged.

Nia sipped at the sherry, not really liking the taste. In any case, it was high time she was getting back if she was to catch Joe before he went to the pub. He wasn't expecting her home. Perhaps that was just as well and she might learn something about what was really going on. Or was she simply being silly and over-imaginative, making up problems where there were none?

She replaced her empty glass. 'I suppose I'd better be getting home,' she said, sighing. 'I've enjoyed being with you so much. I don't think you can realize how much I feel I've got into a rut, so much so that I'm practically taking root!'

She rose from her chair, knowing that if she were to be truthful she would have to admit that everything was going wrong. She had loved Joe for all his faults, and even if he was taking in some bets, was that so bad? She had her office now and soon she would be opening another one, she could do without the illegal betting. But was there something more serious that Joe was hiding from her?

'Don't bother to see me out, you just sit here in the warmth and put your feet up. And Roggen, thanks for the welcome.'

It was dark in the street and very cold with the wind coming in from the sea, and Nia took off her hat and tucked it under her arm. It was probably too late for a tram but if she walked briskly, she would soon be home with Joe and the warmth of their house, and everything would be all right again.

By the time she reached Brynhyfred, her cheeks were glowing and Nia felt warm through with apprehension. She was anxious to be with Joe to have his reassurances that he was not being unfaithful, that nothing was further from his mind.

She moved quietly into the house and saw that he'd riddled the ashes and set the fire for the morning, and a smile curved her lips. Didn't that prove to her that everything was normal? From upstairs, she heard a sound. So Joe had not gone out, that was a relief. She moved to the stairs and hurried to the bedroom, wanting only to be in his arms and forget her fears.

As she pushed open the door, she saw them naked and in her bed. She stopped, her senses refusing to believe the evidence of her eyes.

'Joe!' She didn't know if she whispered or screamed the name but then he was sitting up, staring at her, and clinging to him was the plump Anita, her pale eyes wide with triumph. It was clear that this confrontation was exactly what she had hoped would happen.

Roughly, Joe pushed the girl away from him. 'Wait, Nia, I can explain. It means nothing, I promise you!'

She stared at him, her eyes hard with the hurt she was feeling. She wanted to lash out to humiliate him as he'd done her.

'I suppose this is all you can attract!' she said scathingly. 'A foolish, fat little girl without a brain in her head. Well, you are welcome to her, Joe, she's all you deserve. I'm leaving, and I hope you both burn in hell.'

As she slammed the door on the sight of Joe naked in bed with another woman, she felt as though her world had come to an end. He had deceived her in more ways than one and she had been gullible, a blind fool. Well, she would go to Lambert's Cottages to her father. Ambrose had tried so hard to warn her, he knew what had been going on so would not be surprised to see her.

As she stood in the darkness trying not to scream and cry and break up into tiny little pieces, she vowed that she would never in all her life put her trust in any man again.

16

The air, soft with the scent of night stock, drifted in through the open window of Kristina's bedroom. She lay, arms stretched above her head, exquisitely tired, her eyes heavy with sleep. Beside her was Eden and she could hear by his regular breathing that he was asleep. She moved towards him and his arm immediately encircled her, though there was no sign that he had stirred from his sleep.

She lay against his warmth, the silk of his shoulder against her cheek. She loved Eden, so why did she feel so unhappy? It was because of Bella, of course, and the proposed marrage that would take place very soon. She must begin to face facts and take the decision to end the relationship. It was the only realistic and honest course she could take.

She must have drifted back off to sleep because the sun was shining in her eyes when she opened them, and Eden had gone. He always disappeared to his own room before the household was awake and Kristina was torn with disappointment at his absence, seeing it almost as a form of betrayal. But she rationalized the situation, telling herself he only wished to be discreet.

She sat up in bed and suddenly the room spun in vivid circles around her, nausea swept over her, and she stumbled out of bed and towards the bathroom on the landing, clinging to the walls for support.

Later, she washed her face in cool water and stared at herself in the mirror, her mind analysing and assessing what was happening to her. She did not deceive herself;

she had studied her herbal remedies too long, spending hours over her remedy books, not to know the symptoms. She was pregnant.

After a while Kristina left her room and went downstairs. It was time she saw to the breakfast, for Anita Williams had slept at home last night and might not have come into work yet. But the kitchen was warmed by a stove long since lit, the floor shone with cleanliness and the smell of frying bacon permeated the room.

'*Bore da*, Kristina.' Anita was swathed in a white apron, her long hair tied back with a brilliant red ribbon, she appeared cheerful and her brown eyes were shining. 'I've taken the breakfast in.'

'Glad to see you were early. I take it you had an enjoyable night off.' Kristina turned away from the full frying pan, feeling the pangs of nausea once more at the sight of the fat bubbling round the strips of bacon. She lifted the brightly knitted cosy, touching the china pot beneath. It was hot, and quickly she poured herself a cup of tea.

'Well, enjoyable isn't exactly the word.' Anita seemed in the mood for confiding as she skilfully slid the bacon on to a plate and broke an egg into the pan.

'What do you mean?' Kristina turned her eyes away from the sight of Anita basting the egg with fat, turning the yellow to white.

'We was caught last night, me and Joe. *She* came home and found us in bed together.'

'Anita!' Kristina looked at her in surprise. 'You mean this thing with Joe Barnes has gone that far?'

'What did you expect, that we'd just hold hands? He was upset at first, mind, but when *she'd* gone, Joe soon got over it and said she could go to hell for all he cared. A real man he is, mind, not like these daft young boys you see about the place.

'*Duw*, I didn't expect to see her sitting in this very house, mind, nearly dropped the tray when I saw her. Thought she'd found out about me and Joe and had come to make a fuss, but just in case she was in any doubt I put my two penn'orth in. A prim madam, she is, mind. Joe would never marry her, see, waiting for me to come along he was all the time, he says.'

'Where did Nia go in the middle of the night, have you thought of that?' Kristina rose to her feet and walked to the window. Perhaps she should have warned Nia, but then she hadn't realized just how far the affair had gone. In any case, she couldn't bear to hurt her friend.

Anita shrugged. 'I don't know, back to her dad's house in Lambert's, I suppose, but then that's none of my business, is it? I can't help it if Joe prefers me now, can I?'

Poor Nia. 'You'd better look out,' Kristina said soberly. 'A man like that would betray anybody.'

'No, he won't betray me,' Anita said smugly. 'Loves me, he does, says I'm like a breath of fresh air, and what's more I don't make him feel small, see?'

Kristina felt a sudden, fierce anger against Joe. How could he be so heartless as to take another woman into the bed he shared with Nia?

'I think he's a rat!' she said heatedly. 'He's taken plenty of her money and now he can't even be faithful to her. You'd better get out of that situation before he does the dirty on you.'

Anita was very red in the face. She moved to the window and stood alongside Kristina, her small mouth pouting. 'I told you, Joe wouldn't do anything to hurt me, he loves me, he's told me so often enough.'

'And you believe him?' Kristina said shortly. 'Well, after the way he's behaved you're more of a fool than I took you for.'

'Before you talk, you want to look nearer to home, mind.' Anita paused to gauge Kristina's reaction. When she was sure she had her full attention she continued. 'We all know that Eden Lamb comes to your bed every night that it pleases him. He spends the evening taking his fiancée to somewhere posh and spending lots of his money on her while you get nothing. He's using you, mind and you too soft to see it.'

Kristina clenched her hands so hard that the nails bit into her flesh. Colour flowed into her cheeks. If Anita knew the situation then so would everyone else in Lambert's Cottages. The thought of people gossiping about her – and gossip they would because Anita was not one to keep things to herself – shook Kristina to the core. She should stop handing out advice to Anita and deal with her own situation. Kristina bit her lip. She was just as foolish as Anita, more so because the girl was young and naïve and Kristina was old enough to know better.

'My situation is different,' she said, knowing even as she spoke that it was pointless trying to justify herself. She didn't believe her own words which rang hollowly in her ears. 'It's not the same thing at all.'

'Not the same? Well I don't see any difference in you stealing Eden off that nice Miss Bella and me taking Joe from Nia Powell. As far as I can see, you are worse than me because my man isn't married and Mr Eden Lamb is going to be married soon to Miss Bella, isn't he? Oh, aye,' she continued, 'you talk about me being soft, but you're the talk of the place, you and your carryings on!'

Anita would have continued but Kristina held up her hand for silence. 'That's enough.' Her voice was calm, almost cold, but the warning behind it was enough to stop Anita's flow. She turned away and began to clear the dishes, grumbling to herself as she clattered them into the sink.

Kristina moved through the hallway, her heart beating so swiftly she thought it would suffocate her. She didn't see the sun slanting in through the window, or smell the scent of lavender polish. Only last night Eden had come to her bed and made love to her without either of them speaking about his forthcoming marriage, though it had lain like a stone between them. Well, it was over. Everyone knew about her affair and she must be the laughing stock of Swansea, but she would put an end to it right now.

She walked into the dining room, and with one look at her face, Roggen rose and moved towards the door. She glanced briefly at her brother and spoke with a hint of anger in her voice.

'The time of reckoning has come, Eden, as I said it would, and it serves you damn well right!'

'It's over, Eden,' Kristina said, 'completely over. You must have known that everyone was talking about us, discussing our affair in all the public bars, no doubt. But why should you worry, I'm only your little bit of fun on the side, aren't I? Go on, try to deny it, you never took me seriously, so why should you care who talks about me behind my back. I've only got myself to blame for being so weak as to give in to you.'

He rose and held out his hand to her but Kristina drew away from him. 'Don't touch me.' Her gaze never left him as he thrust his hands into his pockets, his face averted.

'Well,' she continued, 'I'm going to save you the embarrassment of sacking me.' Her voice was hard. 'I'll pack up my belongings and go.'

'No!' he said quickly, and he looked then into her face. 'I want you to stay, you need the job here.'

'I *have* to go and you're a fool if you can't see that. Even if I was willing to be under the same roof as you and your new wife, how do you think she'd feel with you keeping your mistress just along the corridor from the bridal suite?'

He was perfectly aware of the scorn in her voice and his face hardened. 'I didn't intend that,' he said. 'Shortly I will be moving out to a house of my own and you would be quite all right here.' He moved a pace towards her. 'Do you really want to go back to living under Thomas Presdey's iron fist?' He spoke softly, his tone suddenly conciliatory. 'I'm sorry that I hurt you, but it takes two to make or break a bargain.'

She shrugged off his hand and opened the door. 'Well, I've been informed this morning that I'm the laughing stock of Lambert's Cottages, so there won't be any more "bargain". From now on, it's finished, for ever.'

Her green eyes were unforgiving as she looked at him. 'And if you try to interfere in my life again, I swear I'll kill you.'

She hurried up the stairs and into her room, and as she drew her clothes from the drawers she heard the door open behind her. She spun around, angry words on her lips, but it was Roggen who entered the room.

'I'm sorry, Kristina,' she said quickly. 'I can understand why you're going but I'll be sorry to lose you.' She came to stand next to Kristina. 'If you want to return to work here again when Eden gets a home of his own, you can always come back to Ty Coch, you know that, don't you?'

Kristina finished packing her few clothes into a soft bag and shut the clasp with a click of finality.

'I'm going to miss living here,' she said softly. 'I don't relish the idea of going back home to be under Thomas's feet again.'

'What will you do, get another job?' Roggen asked. Kristina sighed, thinking with a feeling of panic of the child she was carrying.

'I suppose I'll end up giving in and marrying Robert Jenkins,' she said, her voice hoarse.

'There's many a true word spoken in jest,' Roggen said, 'but you don't have to get married, you can work away at your herbal remedies or perhaps find a job in a store or something.'

Kristina sighed, Roggen was so naïve in many ways. Didn't she realize that in such a depression jobs were like gold?

'I'll come to you when I want references.' Kristina picked up the bag and then on an impulse turned to Roggen. 'Everything is falling apart,' she said softly. 'My life has changed so drastically this morning, but at least I've done the right thing by everybody.' And a fat lot of comfort that thought would be to her over the coming months, she thought ruefully.

She moved down the stairs and stood for a moment in

the spacious hallway, looking around her, feeling hope-
lessly lost and alone. Of Eden, there was no sign. Then
she opened the large front door and walked out of Ty
Coch, her head high, her shoulders straight. She felt as
though she would take on the world and spit in its eye if
challenged.

She crossed the patch and smelled the tar and the spices
from the ships, and tasted the coal dust that hung in the
air, and as she drew nearer to the small house in
Lambert's Cottages, she felt her courage evaporate.

'Hello Mam.' She stepped into the kitchen and put her
bag on the table, and her mother's smile of welcome
changed to one of concern.

'You've had the sack?' she asked, her voice shaking.
'Oh *Duw*, and Tom without work an' all, times is going
to be very hard without any money coming in.' She
paused and rubbed at her eyes and then held out her
arms.

'Come here, my lovely, there's a welcome from your
mam, me telling you my worries straight off without
listening to yours first. Sit down, I'll put the kettle on and
we'll have a nice cup of tea.'

'I haven't been sacked, Mam,' Kristina said. 'I've left of
my own accord, I can't stick it up there any more.'

'I thought you wouldn't have the sack. Eden Lamb's
too fond of you for that.'

Kristina sank into a chair wondering how much her
mother actually knew about her daughter's affair with
Eden Lamb. Everything, probably, just as everyone else
did.

'Well, I'd better make up a bed for you on the floor of
the girls' room,' Ceinwen said thoughtfully. 'They're
both grown so big now they take up all the room in the
bed.'

'That'll be lovely, Mam,' Kristina said reassuringly. 'It
won't be for very long so don't go making any fuss.' She
sank down into a chair and put her head down on her
hands, smelling the scrubbed pine of the table and

knowing with a feeling of dread that she was in deep trouble. She had no job, no home of her own, and she was going to have a child. The tears came then, hot and bitter, and in that moment she felt that she hated Eden Lamb with all her heart.

That night, she managed to avoid Thomas by going to bed early. Kristina felt worn out with the momentous discoveries of the day. Anita's attack on her, coming on top of the realization that she was pregnant was too much to bear, and she longed for sleep to come and blot out reality. But it was dawn before she slept, and even then she dreamed that she was walking up the aisle of the church on Eden's arm, as his bride.

The weeks passed in a haze of desperation as Kristina tried to find herself a job that would pay enough wages to make her independent. Libba would have taken her back just as a favour but she couldn't afford to pay very much, and so Kristina was forced to look further afield in the more busy parts of Swansea. She wasn't helped by Thomas's constant harping accusations that she was lazy, had adopted grand airs and felt herself too good for her own folk. And always with her was the knowledge that soon her pregnancy would begin to show.

She thought of Eden constantly, she missed his love-making and she missed like the breath of life his presence. It was as though he had never been, or she had lived with him in some other, more wonderful life.

Eden's wedding morning dawned bright and with a pale sunshine warming the day. Kristina knew it would be a painful experience to see him marrying another woman, and yet she could not keep away from the church in Sketty.

She stood on the fringe of sightseers and watched him step out with Bella clinging to his arm. She looked every inch a bride, in a close-fitting coffee-coloured lace cap and matching lace gown, and a small veil hanging over her shoulders. She looked adoringly into Eden's face, her hand bearing the gold wedding ring clinging to his arm.

Kristina thought for a moment that he had seen her, that their eyes met over the heads of the crowd, but then he was striding away and she told herself she must have imagined it. She heard in a haze the sound of voices speaking close behind her.

'*Duw*, thought Mr Lamb would never get married, been keeping that nice lady on a string for ages he has, and him carryin' on behind her back as well. It's a sin and a shame, I say.'

She moved towards the bus stop without looking round, and stood as though frozen as the car, gleaming in the early sunlight, carried Eden back towards Lambert's Cottages. Nothing could have underlined more firmly the difference between their stations in life as the opulent car passing where she stood among the crowd on the cold pavement waiting for a bus to come along.

Kristina told herself that now was the time to say goodbye forever to Eden in her heart and mind and soul; he belonged to someone else, their love affair was dead, finished.

When Kristina reached Lambert's Cottages, she found to her dismay that Thomas was sitting in the kitchen with Robert Jenkins. Both of them looked up when they saw her.

'So there you are, gel,' Thomas said with false heartiness, and it was just as though he had never for a moment bullied her, forcing her spirits to new depths with his criticisms. 'Come and sit by here, I'm just going to get the coal in, I won't be long.'

'Where's Mam?' she asked ignoring the chair he offered her, and he smiled. 'Well Robert there gave your mam a bit of help with the shopping, like. She's down at Libba's now getting some groceries.'

Kristina sighed. That meant Robert had handed over some ready cash, for the bill at Libba's was so high her mother could not ask for more credit.

Bumbling, Thomas made an awkward exit, but then carrying the coal scuttle out the back was not in his usual line of work.

'Hello, Kris.' Robert looked at her steadily. 'You're a bit of a stranger these days. I haven't seen much of you, though not for want of trying on my part.' He studied her, his head on one side. 'You're looking a bit pale, has Thomas been keeping on at you?'

'No more than usual.' Kristina sat reluctantly, knowing that the money he had given her mother somehow made her beholden to him. She wanted nothing so much as to go to the bedroom she shared with her sisters and cry out the anguish of seeing Eden leave the church with another woman as his bride.

Robert took her hand. 'I mean to have you for my wife, Kristina,' he said, 'and I won't give up whatever you say or do.'

She stared at him for a long moment. 'I'm pregnant.' The words, bald and flat, fell into the silence and Robert's face was suddenly drained of colour.

After a long silence he spoke. 'I take it the man is not going to marry you.' His voice was harsh, he leaned closer and she could understand the pain in his eyes because it reflected her own.

'No, he isn't going to marry me,' she said. 'I've been a fool, gullible and blind, thinking that he loved me when he was only using me. There now, Robert, what do you say to that, do you still want me?'

He put his hand on her shoulder. 'It's a lot to take in, I'd be a liar if I said different.' He rubbed at his eyes. 'But, yes, I still want you, Kris, any way I can have you.'

She felt a flutter of pity for him. 'It would mean bringing up another man's child, mind,' she said and he faced her steadily.

'One thing I have to know, the father is Eden Lamb, am I right?' He watched her face anxiously and after a moment Kristina nodded.

'Yes, you've a right to know that much.' She smiled thinly. 'Indeed you know more than he does and if I have my way Eden will never know that I've borne his child.'

Robert Jenkins nodded slowly. 'In a way then, I shall

213

have one up on him; he might have had you first, but I will have you last and for always. Agreed, Kristina? No changes of mind and no divorce. We will be man and wife for keeps.'

She held out her hand to him as though confirming a business deal and he took it in both his own. 'It's agreed,' she said softly.

As though waiting for a sign, Thomas came into the room dragging the scuttle behind him. '*Duw*, this blasted thing is heavy,' he said putting it near the fireplace. 'Damn near gave myself a hernia, I did.'

'It's only what Mam and us girls do every day,' Kristina said but Thomas chose to ignore the sharpness of her tone.

'If you've finished talking by here Mr Jenkins, then perhaps we could go down to the Burrows and have a pint. Could murder one, I could.'

'I don't think so, Thomas.' Robert smiled at Kristina. 'I've proposed to Kristina and she's accepted. I think it's her I should be taking out for a drink, don't you?'

'Well then!' Thomas literally beamed at Kristina. 'You've come to your senses at last then, and about time too. Who could ask for a finer man than Mr Jenkins and him able to give you a nice home and a comfortable living.'

Kristina rose to her feet and moved to the door. She was eager now to leave the house and the jubilant Thomas behind. As she stepped out into the spice and tar scented air of the docklands, Kristina wondered what her life would be like as Mrs Robert Jenkins. At least she would be able to hold her head up again, and whatever Robert was, he was not a womanizer, so she could be sure of him. And he was willing to give her child his name.

In sudden gratitude, she turned to him and took his arm, and the pleasure in his eyes made her realize that however little she deserved it, he loved her. The thought was like a healing balm easing a little the ache that had plagued her since she'd realized what a fool she'd been remaining Eden's mistress for so long. And yet the charm of Eden's smile, the look in his eyes when he made love to her, all of this had been so precious to her.

Well, all that was in the past. Robert Jenkins was her future and she would do all in her power to be a faithful, obedient wife.

17

The marriage of Kristina Larson to Robert Jenkins took place on a fine sunny day in May when the blossoms were falling like a snow maiden's tears and the breeze blowing in from the sea was hot and balmy.

They stood together in the church bordering the busy Mumbles Road and made their solemn vows to each other with unfaltering calmness. Kristina wore a soft blue frock of lace and silk and Robert was tall, almost austere, in a good suit and a white shirt with a starched collar fastened with silver studs.

The church was crowded, for Robert Jenkins was a well-known figure in Swansea. While still holding the powerful position on the docks of works allocator, he now was involved in many business enterprises in Swansea. He was a man who could give favours, each one of them set by and stored like a precious stone, the debt to be called in whenever Robert chose.

Nia stood at the back of the church and as she watched Kristina take the marriage vows there was the tightness of tears in Nia's throat and just a trace of envy in her eyes as they rested on the bride, so tall and beautiful, her oval face pale but composed.

Nia had returned to Lambert's Cottages and was living once more with her father. She had quickly become part of the fabric of the docklands again and a few weeks after leaving Joe Barnes it was almost as though she'd never been away. Almost but not quite.

She had lost weight, she was now very slim and her cheek bones were high and prominent. Her mousy hair had darkened and she was more attractive than she had ever been, although she was quite unaware of it.

She glanced towards the doorway and saw Roggen's small figure against the splash of light. There was a man with her and for a moment Nia thought it was Eden. But no, of course Eden wouldn't come to Kristina's wedding. Nia's lips twisted bitterly; men were not to be trusted, that much was apparent to her now. Joe had taken her money to buy himself a mine, had poached many of her customers and played with her affections for years, but none of that had been enough to keep him from straying. God only knew how many times he'd been unfaithful to her.

And yet it was strangely peaceful living with Ambrose, and much to Nia's relief, her father had welcomed her warmly.

'I wondered how long it would take you to find that man out,' he'd said in satisfaction. 'I knew my daughter wasn't one to be fooled indefinitely, and that bounder has been cheating on you for years.'

Nurse Freeman, or Beattie as her father insisted on calling her, had become quite a regular visitor to the Powell household, and as Nia had suspected, there was more than a casual friendship between the nurse and Ambrose. It was doubtful if there was anything of a passionate nature between the two – the nurse was quite old and Ambrose too frail – but perhaps in the past there had been passion aplenty, though it was difficult to imagine it now.

Nia found herself grateful for the nurse's help. She tended to Ambrose diligently and his condition had improved a little over the last few weeks though Nia was warned by Nurse Freeman that such a remission from his sickness could only be a temporary state of affairs for Ambrose.

Kristina was coming down the aisle and she looked gorgeous. The blue silk and lace clung over her superb breasts, curved in at her tiny waist and fell in pretty folds around her knees. The outfit wasn't what Nia would have chosen had she been the bride but then, as Kristina had said, she was no flighty young girl but a mature woman. Perhaps she was right, and yet Nia in Kristina's place would have loved to wear a diaphanous gown of white with lots of bows and tucks and frills, and an elegant veil.

The rousing organ music brought tears to Nia's eyes as she watched Kristina leave the dimness of the church and step out into the sunlight. Her hair blazed, a golden aureole, cut short now and curling thick and silky around her face.

Roggen touched Nia's arm. 'Hello, I thought I'd just call in to the church and see Kristina wed,' she said, smiling. 'And this handsome man at my side is Colin Singleton, I don't think you two have met.'

Nia smiled politely, taking the hand that the tall man held out to her, but she was distracted by the sight of Roggen throwing a handful of rice over Kristina.

'Are you a friend of the bride?' The voice was low and musical, and Nia turned to look up with quickening interest into the smiling face of Colin Singleton.

'Yes, I am.' She looked Colin over carefully. He had an air of breeding about him and it was obvious from his clothes that he had spared no expense there.

'I only came by to pick Ro up in the car, give her a lift back to the old homestead, so to speak.' He smiled warmly down at her. 'But I'm very glad that I did.'

'Are you, and why?' she asked archly, noting with amusement that she had adopted what her father called her 'posh' voice, the voice she had grown up with.

'You interest me,' Colin said, leaning towards her, his eyes sparkling, and she raised her eyebrows at him.

'Oh, yes? That's not a very original way of making a pass,' she replied quickly.

'No, I'm not making a pass, I mean it.' Colin was a very tall man and he had to lean towards her to keep his voice low against the backdrop of the crowd buzzing around Kristina, congratulating her noisily.

'I've been interested in you for some time, I've watched

and admired the way you've built up your business. Betting has always appealed to me. You wouldn't like a business partner, by any chance?'

A partner, that was rich. She had a partner, Joe the unfaithful. She was about to utter a flat refusal when she stopped for a moment, giving herself time to think. Perhaps, just perhaps, Colin Singleton would be prepared to buy Joe out. That was what she most wanted, to cut the ties between them entirely.

She glanced around and saw Roggen watching her with a strange look in her dark eyes. Was there something between her and Colin Singleton?

'This isn't the time or the place, but I'd certainly like to discuss your idea in greater detail.' She smiled at him politely but as she met his eyes, she realized with a small shock of surprise that he really was interested not only in the business but in her. She warmed to him and on an impulse held out her hand, then she turned to Roggen.

'I hope I'm not intruding on anything,' she said. 'If I am, please accept my apologies.'

'No apologies required,' Roggen said somewhat dryly. 'Colin and I are simply friends.' Her tone was cool and Nia didn't quite know what to make of the situation.

'What if we meet this afternoon in the foyer of the Grand Hotel and we'll talk some more. You too, Roggen, of course.'

Colin enveloped her fingers in his and a warmth flowed between them. Nia felt a surge of attraction which surprised her. She had not expected such feelings so quickly after Joe's betrayal. Watch it. Her mind ticked over. Business was one thing, becoming emotionally involved was another, hadn't her father taught her that?

She withdrew her hand a shade too quickly and Colin leaned back as though allowing her space. She realized he was that rare being, a perceptive man.

Roggen, watching them, saw the attraction as if it were something tangible. In Colin's stance, the set of his shoulders, the angle of his head, in every move he made, she could see the attraction. She bit her lip. What was it about her that made her so unlucky in love? First her affair with Richard had ended disastrously and now it seemed that Colin was very ready to turn to another woman. Well, she'd been on the point of telling him that she could not marry him, anyway. There was no passion in their relationship, nothing but mutual liking between them.

She turned away from the crowd outside the church and began to walk along the Mumbles Road towards home. Colin had forgotten all about her and perhaps it was just as well. If the lost expression in Kristina's eyes was anything to go by, a marriage of convenience was not the pathway to happiness she had supposed it to be.

'Impressed?' Robert stood near the entrance to his fine house situated halfway up the slopes of Mount Pleasant Hill and looked proudly at Kristina, willing her to appreciate what he was offering her. His pride was justified. As they entered the house together, Kristina saw that it was spacious, with high ceilings, and a window facing the splendour of Swansea Bay with Mumbles Head clearly visible in the distance.

'Of course,' Kristina said, grateful that he had not wanted to carry her across the threshold like some starry-eyed teenager. She felt the peace of the old building settle over her even as she wondered what Robert would expect of her now. Would she be asked to consummate the marriage without delay? Would he reach for her and demand his conjugal rights?

But she misjudged him. He led the way around the house, not crowding her, not touching her, simply talking quietly as he showed her round the ground floor rooms.

She sighed softly, relieved that the public part of the wedding at least was over. The reception had been an ordeal, the tear-filled eyes of her mother and the attentions of Thomas who acted the part of proud parent to the end were images fading thankfully from her mind.

The speeches had been full of lewd innuendo, an obligatory part of any wedding breakfast, and more than once Robert had looked at her expecting embarrassed blushes. But Kristina had held her feelings in check as she'd done since the moment she'd left the house in Lambert's to make her way to the church.

'I suppose I'd better change,' she said glancing down at the silk and lace frock. 'And then perhaps I can get us something to eat.' She looked at him uncertainly. 'My things are in the bedroom, aren't they?'

Robert stared at her steadily. 'I'm not going to rush you, Kristina.' He took off his good jacket and slipped it over the back of a chair and Kristina made a mental note to place it tidily on a hanger once she knew her way around the house.

'Don't worry,' she said softly, 'I'm not a child to be humoured. I made my vows in church and I have no intention of going back on them.'

He didn't bat an eyelid. 'You haven't seen the kitchen yet,' he said. She followed him along a passageway into the kitchen and stared around her in approval. She would certainly have no difficulty cooking for Robert in such attractive surroundings. The room was fitted out with every convenience, from the brand new stove with the fire alight, warming hotplate and oven, to the cupboards placed strategically around the walls.

'It's lovely,' she said, and Robert leaned on the well-scrubbed table and favoured her with one of his rare smiles.

'I'm glad you like it.' He moved to the sink and filled the heavy black kettle. 'I expect you'd like some tea.' His back was towards her. 'And I know you want to get out of your wedding finery. Go on upstairs, look around and see if you approve of the bedroom I've chosen for us.'

As she walked along the passageway and began to climb the wide stairs she found she was trembling, though with relief or bewilderment she didn't know. She had expected Robert to take her in his arms as soon as they entered the house. She'd been prepared to go through with her obligations with good grace, but now his attitude had thrown her completely off guard. She smiled ruefully. At least being Robert's wife wouldn't be boring. She never knew what to expect of him.

The upstairs rooms were furnished with good taste and a fair degree of luxury, and Kristina knew at once which was the master bedroom. Facing the sea, it was larger than the others with fine heavy curtains in old rose, and bedcovering to match. A fire burned in the ornate grate and a vase of blue irises stood on the highly polished dressing table. It was clear that Robert had the benefit of domestic help, for there were touches that only a woman would think of, such as the finely worked sets of crocheted circles protecting the silken surface of the furniture, and the brass companion set standing near the fire.

She had never set foot in Robert's house before today. It had been he who had moved her few possessions, and now as she looked in the large, ornately carved wardrobe, she saw her frocks hanging neatly in a row and her two pairs of shoes placed like soldiers in the rack beneath.

She slipped out of the wedding dress and put it carefully away. It would serve for another occasion, though she was not sure what other occasion she had in mind. Certainly not the christening of her child. The baby was not due until much later in the year, when it would be impracticable to wear silk and lace.

She dressed in her plainest frock and brushed her hair until it shone. She glanced at the clock on the wall. It was five o'clock in the afternoon and in a way she wished it was already night-time. There would be no hiatus then, it would be to bed with both of them and the consummation of the marriage would take place. She wished it was over, the moment when she gave herself to Robert Jenkins, for that would be the last betrayal, the final severing of the bond between herself and her real lover.

Eden. He had not come to linger on the fringes of her

wedding as she'd done at his. But then he wouldn't. It was not a society wedding but merely the marriage of a docker to a girl who had been in service most of her life. Nothing to be excited or curious about. And yet she had hoped that he would pay his respects, see her off, as it were, on the new life she had forged for herself.

In the kitchen, Robert was seated at the table, two cups of tea rested on the bare scrubbed boards and a plate of bread and strawberry jam stood between the two cups.

'Tea time,' he said, glancing at her, his eyes missing nothing of her appearance. 'We'll go out later and have a proper meal at the Grand.' He pushed her cup towards her and she glanced apologetically down at her frock.

'I'm sorry, I didn't know, I assumed we'd stay in, it being our wedding night . . .' Her words trailed away as Robert leaned towards her.

'I told you there's no rush, we've got the rest of our lives to find out about each other.' And yet the heat in his eyes belied his words. He wanted her, and Kristina knew it.

She drank her tea and picked at a little of the bread and jam. It was surprisingly good. It was simple food such as was never eaten at Ty Coch, where there had been sumptuous meals, whole hams or plump poultry. Not one sign of the depression was allowed to enter the house of Eden Lamb.

Why couldn't she stop thinking about Eden? She was Robert's wife now, Mrs Robert Jenkins. She was respectable and the thought gave her an unexpected sense of pleasure.

'You have lovely eyes,' Robert said. 'Green they are, like the sea when a storm is coming.' He leaned back in his chair then, as though embarrassed at revealing his thoughts.

She didn't know what to say so she looked down at her cup, watching the leaves swirl in the whirlpool of tea. She must teach Robert to use a strainer. Such insignificant thoughts. Here she was, her life changed, and she was worried about trivialities. This waiting was absurd, why play out the rest of the evening like some sort of waiting game?

Pushing away her cup, she rose to her feet and moved purposefully towards Robert. She rested her hands on his shoulders and looked down at him. His eyes were hooded, she could not read his thoughts. Slowly, she lowered her lips to his. She felt his mouth firm and gentle beneath hers. It was a pleasant sensation, Robert Jenkins was an attractive man. After a moment, he held her away from him.

'I don't want you coming to me like a lamb to the slaughter, Kristina,' he said. 'I'm prepared to wait for what I want.' He moved away from her. 'We will consummate the marriage only when you come to me with desire in your eyes. Until then, I'll sleep in one of the other bedrooms.'

She returned to her chair, nonplussed, and as Robert left the room and made his way up the stairs, she covered her face with her hands. There was more to him than met the eye, this man, her husband.

Nia felt warmed and flattered. Colin Singleton had pursued her ever since the day of Kristina's wedding. He had persisted in his intention to become her partner and at last, after several meetings, she had put her idea to him.

'I'd like you to buy out Joe Barnes's share of the business.' She leaned across the tea table in the Mackworth Hotel and touched his hand with hers. She did not know from where her confidence came, or the belief that Colin would be interested in her proposition. Perhaps it was Colin's open admiration of her, for with him she felt desirable, and more, he credited her with having some intelligence. To Joe, whatever she'd achieved, she was always the little woman, to be patronized rather than praised. With Colin it was so different, they were the same type of people, both of them ambitious, both on the same wavelength when it came to ideas.

'After that,' she continued, 'the world is our oyster.' She smiled. 'There is no reason why we can't own a chain of offices between us.'

His fingers curled around hers. 'You're right.' His eyes smiled into hers. 'We need not stop at Swansea either, what about the surrounding districts like Neath and Port Talbot?'

She allowed her fingers to remain within Colin's clasp. He was her kind of man and they spoke the same language. Life certainly had some surprising twists and turns. Who would have thought that breaking up with Joe was the best thing that could have happened to her? She'd outgrown him, she realized it now. He was a good lover, but he simply was not the marrying kind. One woman would never be enough for him.

She knew that Joe would never sell out his share to her, he would keep it out of sheer spite. He had tried several times to see her, calling at her father's house at odd hours in the hope of catching her at home. Always, Nurse Freeman turned him away with asperity, informing him that there was a sick man within trying to get some rest, and she would be pleased if he ceased knocking on the door. But if Colin was to offer an enticing sum of money, Joe would surely succumb, for he would have no idea that Colin was involved with Nia in any way.

'So are we partners?' she asked at last, knowing already what the answer would be, because Colin was looking at her as though she were good enough to eat.

'We are indeed,' he said, and his tone suggested that he would very much like to take the relationship a few steps ahead of mere partnership in business.

Later, as she returned home to Lambert's Cottages, she faced the fact that she would need to move away from the dockland and find herself a respectable address on the west side of the town. It was only fitting for the future partnership that she present as good an impression as possible. If the business grew large enough, she might need to entertain business people, and the small front room of the house on the docks was not suitable at all.

'So there you are, Miss High and Mighty!' The savagery in the voice startled Nia and she spun around to see Anita Williams hurrying behind her on her short plump legs, her breasts bouncing obscenely beneath her coat.

Anita stood stock still in front of Nia, hands on hips and glared at her with half-closed eyes, her usual sweet babyish expression vanished.

'I have nothing to say to you.' Nia spoke with dignity and attempted to pass the girl, but her way was effectively barred by Anita's bulk.

'Oh, no you don't, madam!' The girl's voice was shaking with anger. 'You've poisoned Joe's mind against me, haven't you. You've lied about me and blackened my name and now he don't want nothing to do with me.'

'I've said nothing,' Nia said. 'I haven't spoken to Joe Barnes since the night I came home and found you both together in my bed. *My* bed, remember. You took him away from me, or have you forgotten?'

Anita stepped back a pace, startled by the look in Nia's eyes. It seemed she had not expected anger to be directed back at her.

Nia moved forward. 'In any case I don't want anything to do with Joe. You can have him, gratis and welcome. I've finished with him and when you see him you can tell him that.'

'You're lying,' Anita said, but the confidence had left her voice and she seemed to be dissolving, her large eyes filling with tears, sweat beading her upper lip. Nia felt no pity for her.

'You've brought it on yourself,' she said. 'If you lure a man away from another woman's bed then you're asking for trouble. It's common sense that what he's done once he'll do again. Why should he be faithful to you?'

'But he said he loved me.' Anita bit her lip. 'I wouldn't have done it if I didn't think he loved me.'

'No? Well you've found out that you were wrong about him. Joe only loves himself. Perhaps you'll be more discriminating next time you sleep with a man.'

Nia walked past the unresisting girl and hurried towards her father's house trying to calm the racing of her pulse. Arguing with Anita in the street and over a man like Joe was embarrassing, to say the least. She hoped it wouldn't happen again.

She tried to put the incident out of her mind as she let herself into the house. The silence wrapped itself around her and she stood for a moment, taking deep breaths.

Nurse Freeman opened the kitchen door and put a finger to her lips. 'Ssh, Ambrose is asleep,' she whispered. 'I'm just going up to check on him now.'

She plodded up the stairs and Nia quietly filled the kettle and placed it on the gas ring. A cup of tea would settle her, she could still feel the force of Anita Williams's anger and dislike. But it was not important. She was carving out a new life for herself now, without Joe Barnes.

She smiled. It was good to know she could attract the attentions of a man like Colin Singleton. He was a warm, sincere man, and the way he'd looked at her just now had made her pulse beat faster.

She was better off without Joe. She should have seen what he was like a long time ago and saved herself some pain as well as some money.

A sudden, urgent banging on the floorboards startled Nia and, alarmed, she hurried along the passageway and up the stairs towards her father's bedroom.

'*Duw,*' the nurse was white-faced, 'taken a turn for the worst, he has. Your father's breathing his last, child, and he has something on his mind that he wants to say to you.'

Nia's heart was racing as she approached the bed. Beneath the quilt, her father's wasted body hardly showed. His face was thin, parchment-like, and his eyes were the only thing alive in a death's head.

'Nia,' His voice was threadlike and she leaned closer to him, fear washing over her in waves. He could not be dying, her father was indestructible.

'Don't try to talk, Dad,' she said hoarsely, but the nurse touched her arm and shook her head.

'It can't harm him now, love, let him have his say so that he can go in peace.'

'I've never shown you love, Nia,' he gasped the words, 'but I did love you, have always loved you.' He paused, fighting for breath. 'I'm sorry I left it so late in the day to say it aloud.'

She knelt beside the bed, forcing back the hot tears. 'It's all right, Dad,' she said softly, 'it's all forgotten now. We found each other before it was too late, didn't we?'

With surprise she realized that she spoke the truth. She had been closer to Ambrose since returning home from Joe Barnes's house than she'd ever been in her life. Ambrose had taken her back into his home without demur and there had never been any recriminations. They had sat and talked late into the night and she'd come to understand a little of the man beneath the hard shell.

His hand trembled uncontrollably as he held it out to her, and she took it, gently smoothing the dry skin with her fingers.

'I know so many words,' he whispered, 'but none of them suit, not now. I don't even know how to say goodbye to my only child.'

'Oh, Dad.' She bent her head, her eyes full of tears as she felt him touch her hair as though in benediction.

He sighed once, heavily, and with his eyes closed he looked so peaceful. Nia rose to her feet and stood looking down at the frail old man in the bed, a stranger now in death. The tears came then, hard and hot and washing away the bitterness held in check for so long.

'Go on away downstairs,' the nurse said softly. 'It's the living who count now, we have done all we can for the dead.'

Nia turned away feeling lost, one part of her life over for ever. At the door, she straightened her shoulders, she had to look forward now to the future. She paused for a moment and looked behind her at the still figure in the bed.

'God rest you, Daddy,' she whispered, and the tears were hot against her lids.

18

The house was still, the sounds of the docklands muted, and the sun slanted in through the windows reflecting the heat of the day, throwing shadows into corners and highlighting the motes of dust floating through the hallway.

Anita Williams had cried so many times over the past weeks that she felt drained of emotion. How could Joe do this to her when she was so much in love with him? He had changed towards her from the moment Nia Powell had walked in and caught them in bed together. Roughly he had pushed her away, cursing as he pulled on his trousers, anxious to go after the fancy piece who lived with him. But he had returned to the house alone, and Anita had been willing to comfort him. At first he had responded, but the next time they met he'd been vicious to her.

'*Duw*, there's no need to be downhearted, boy.' She'd been loving, her arms winding around his strong neck. 'You've got me now, and with *her* gone there's nothing and no one to stand between us.'

His reply had been short. 'Stupid bitch!'

But he hadn't meant the cruel words, he'd felt foolish at being caught out, that was all.

She polished the elegantly carved banister half-heartedly. No one seemed to notice how her work was done anyway, not Roggen who was out at meetings half her life, and certainly not Eden Lamb. She sniffed. He was too toffee-nosed to even speak to her. She was the domestic, a piece of the background, someone to fetch and carry until she dropped.

Since Kristina had left Ty Coch to get married, Anita had found just how difficult life in service was. She was up at first light, setting fires and, most important, cooking breakfast. Mr Eden Lamb and his new wife were very particular about breakfast. He liked haddock served with poached eggs, or sometimes devilled kidneys, while Mrs Bella Lamb favoured Welsh fare such as cockles and lava bread. The two of them ate enough food at breakfast to keep the Williams family supplied for a week.

Anita hated cooking lava bread. Even rolled in oats, the messy black food stuck to the frying pan and defied all efforts to remove it. But what Mrs Lamb wanted, she could have. There was no thought given to the difficulties that Anita faced working alone with no help around the house. She would be pleased when the Lambs moved into their own house, a move too long delayed, in Anita's opinion.

The same excuse was always given whenever Anita approached Eden for some help; that soon there would be only Roggen to look after. That was all very well, but it didn't make the house any smaller or the number of rooms to dust and clean any the less.

But what Anita most objected to about being in service was polishing the shoes. She felt really demeaned by creeping around the long passageway upstairs and quietly picking up footwear from outside the rooms. At home it was Dad who did that sort of work. Sugar Williams might be a big tough docker, but he wasn't above looking after his daughters.

And even after she had finished the early chores, there was still plenty of work ahead of her. She would have to face the extra tasks of polishing the silver and cleaning out cupboards, as well as once a week getting the huge pile of sheets and linen ready for the laundry. Of course Mam thought having the laundry do the heavy wash was a wonder of modern science. She still rubbed at sheets in a tin bath with an old rubbing board and a bar of carbolic soap.

The people of Lambert's Cottages did enjoy, however, the benefit of having their own power station on the docks. Electricity had replaced oil and candlelight several years ago, which had at least made life a little easier.

Anita sank down on to the carpeted stairs and chewed at her fingernail. She was tired of housework, at least of cleaning other people's houses. She smiled to herself; she would not mind having a permanent job cleaning Joe's house for him.

Should she make just one more effort to see Joe, try to win him back? The thought cheered her and she returned to her cleaning with vigour, anxious to get her chores finished so that she could be on her way to the little house at Byrnhyfred which one day she hoped to make her home.

The docks were alive with sounds and smells, for the port of Swansea was a hive of activity in the bewildering, ever-changing world events of the summer of 1939.

Eden stood in the doorway of his shipping office, hands thrust into his pockets, too hot and restless to work. He stared seawards to where the breast-like mounds of Mumbles Head jutted out forming a peninsula of land, an effective barrier on which the white-capped waves could expend their strength before dying into the gentle ripples that washed the beach.

The sound of dockers' voices calling to each other as they unloaded ships was cheerful, and the mingled scent of spice and tar and old rope that was so familiar to Eden seemed accentuated as he breathed in the sunshine.

He was in a good mood; he was married to a highly intelligent woman and Bella was just about everything he needed in a wife.

He thought involuntarily of Kristina with the lovely, perfect body and the honey gold hair falling over pale skin. She had made him feel ten feet tall and had aroused in him a sensual response that he might never experience again. She was married now and he was glad about that. The match was a suitable one, for the man was a docker.

It was the sight of her this morning, walking down the road to the cottages, wearing a loose smock and with her hair cut short that had made him realize how foolish he had been in making her his mistress. What if he, and not this man Jenkins, had fathered her baby? What a proper mess that would have been.

Kristina no longer lived in Lambert's Cottages but had a solid house up on the hill. It was clear she was well enough set up and he was pleased for her but also a little piqued that she had found another love so swiftly.

She had not seen Eden this morning, indeed he had taken great care to stay out of her line of vision, but he had watched her from a distance, remembering old times. They had been good times for both of them. She had been angry with him when they'd parted but he hoped that now Kristina must see for herself that their affair could never have lasted.

He returned to his desk and looked at the newspaper, trying to distract his thoughts from the image of Kristina as a mother-to-be. A piece in the small print reported that Russia and Germany had concluded a non-aggressive pact. A fat lot of good that would do. Hitler had already proved himself a Fascist dictator and he would have no scruples about tearing up agreements and riding rough-shod over any principle if it suited him.

War in Europe was coming, and in the very near future, judging by the events of the last few years. It was only a matter of months since the ending of the Spanish Civil War with the surrender of Madrid. Yet there was a fever in the very air which Eden could feel as though it were something tangible.

Governments were, as always, playing down the situation. Neville Chamberlain had gone to Munich only last year to attend a conference including Hitler, Deladier of France, and Mussolini, to talk about safeguarding the Czech frontier, but it meant nothing. There were no guarantees where a man with the power of Adolf Hitler was concerned.

Eden pushed the newspaper away and moved restlessly to the gas ring where the water simmering in the kettle was sending puffs of steam into the air. He made himself a pot of tea, and then felt he didn't want any tea after all.

'Hello there, old boy.' The door was pushed wide open and Colin Singleton breezed into the office. 'How about a beer down at the Burrows. I've got a thirst that all the water in the Bristol Channel wouldn't quench.'

Eden was never so glad to see his partner as he was at that moment. 'You've just saved me from a cup of my own tea.' He lifted his light jacket from the back of a chair. 'And that is a fate not to be recommended.'

The two men left the office and picked their way across the railway tracks that crisscrossed the whole of the docklands with ribbons of silver glinting in the sunlight.

'Reading the old *Mirror* then, were you?' Colin said. 'Full of scaremongering articles warning us all about the impending war, was it?'

'It's not scaremongering,' Eden said. 'It's a fact.'

'Oh God, not you too. Why is everyone determined to look on the black side of things?' Colin said with cheerfulness beaming from his handsome, open face.

'What the hell's wrong with you?' Eden asked, regarding his friend through half-closed eyes. 'You haven't fallen in love, have you? You certainly never look so bright-eyed when you're with Roggen.'

'Well,' Colin paused, 'Ro and I, we've always been friends and for a time it looked as though it was going to be more than that, but . . .' He shrugged and led the way into the smoky dimness of the public bar of the Burrows, elbowing his way through the crowd of dockers towards the ale-soaked bar.

Eden wondered how his sister would feel about Colin's apparent cooling off, would she really care? He doubted it. He took a seat near the doorway where a cool breeze drifted in and dispelled some of the Woodbine smoke that permeated the room. He sat back and relaxed a little, it sometimes helped to be in the company of men and forget all about women and the problems they raised.

'Here, old chap.' Colin handed him a glass. 'There's a cool pint with as good a head on it as you'll get anywhere.' He sat opposite Eden and took a long drink. 'Now,' he wiped the foam from his moustache carefully, 'to answer your question.'

Eden stared at him blankly. He'd forgotten what the question was but Colin would enlighten him, he had no doubt.

'I've met this wonderful girl.' Colin sat back as though expecting an amazed response from Eden who merely grunted and lifted his glass, allowing the liquid to glide down his throat.

'She really is something,' Colin persisted. 'Bright as well as beautiful. I think this is it, Eden, I think that Nia is the girl for me.'

'Nia Powell, old Ambrose's daughter?' Eden asked, eyebrows raised. 'Roggen and she have been friends for years. Strange, I always thought Nia was the mousy one of the two.'

'Not likely!' Colin protested. 'She's certainly not mousy.' He stared up at the ceiling as though contemplating her image. 'She's slim, with dark shiny hair and such an elfin face.'

'You really have fallen, hook, line and sinker.' Eden smiled and Colin grinned back, a foolish happy grin, and in that moment, Eden envied him.

'Well, I think you might talk this over with Roggen, tell her your feelings and then go and get your lovely Nia,' he said. 'Don't let the grass grow under your feet or someone else might beat you to it.'

'I won't let that happen,' Colin said. 'In any case, I think she's in love with me, too, strange as it may seem.'

Eden suppressed a sigh. He hoped Colin wasn't being naïve. No doubt a girl like Nia Powell, though undoubtedly well educated and even comfortable in her own way, would look upon Colin as a catch, a step up the social ladder. He did not express his views out loud, he knew that he would immediately be accused of being a snob, and perhaps rightly so.

'Do you think Roggen took my calling on her as a seriously romantic gesture?' Colin asked doubtfully. 'We did a bit of kissing and cuddling, it's true. Perhaps I have been misleading her.' He smiled. 'But I'm sure she'll understand.'

Eden lifted his arm and the landlord nodded and brought two fresh pints of ale to the table.

'*Bore da*, Mr Lamb,' he said amiably. 'Think that this war is ever going to be more than a horror story, then?' He set the glasses down and took the note Eden handed him without question, tucking it away with the dexterity of a pickpocket, knowing that the change was his. '*Duw*, talk has been going on about it for so long, I don't think it will ever happen.'

'It will happen,' Eden said, 'and soon. That man Hitler wants to dominate the world.' He leaned forwards. 'Hitler's troops have already occupied Bohemia and Moravia. Slovakia has been placed under what the man likes to term his "protection" and Germany has seized Memel from Lithuania.'

Colin joined in the argument. 'Aye, but Britain and France have agreed to support Poland if Hitler invades, surely that's deterrent enough for any man.'

Eden shook his head. 'Not for Hitler, he's a megalomaniac.'

The landlord moved away to serve other customers and Eden sank back in his seat. Colin looked worried.

'What will be our role if there is a war?' he asked, and Eden shook his head.

'I'm not sure. I should think most shipping lines will be taken over by the Government. We'll certainly have enough to do.'

'Well, if war is ever declared, I shall enlist,' Colin said at once, rubbing his moustache thoughtfully. 'Men like us will be needed to lead the troops.'

Eden allowed himself a smile. 'Some felt needed in the Spanish Civil War,' he said, 'but not us.'

'Ah, well,' Colin was at a loss but only for a moment, 'it's different when a man's own country is concerned. Surely you can see that, Eden?'

'Maybe so, but Poland isn't our own country, is it? If Hitler chooses to invade, what makes it our business?' He enjoyed tying Colin in knots. It wasn't that his partner lacked intelligence but he was sometimes so naïve about world affairs.

'But we've given our word,' Colin said triumphantly.

'Aye, so we have,' Eden agreed. Colin was a man whose word could be trusted every time, he was undoubtedly an honourable gentleman. Eden sighed. He himself wasn't so honourable, but at least he had the sense to look after his own hide.

Anita dressed carefully in a fluffy concoction of pink organza, one of Roggen's castoffs. It was too tight across Anita's plump breasts but that was not a disadvantage. The skirt swirled around her plump knees, and admiring herself in the mirror, Anita felt so desirable and smart that she knew Joe couldn't fail to be impressed. That the frock was more suited to a soirée and to a woman several pounds lighter, didn't bother Anita. She felt wonderful as she sauntered from her bedroom and down the elegant stairs towards the front door.

Anita sometimes played a game of being mistress of Ty Coch. It wasn't difficult, she was alone in the house so often. Once the heavy breakfast was over Eden went to his office, Roggen to her teaching job and Bella, the one thorn in Anita's flesh, usually left the house after a cooked luncheon followed by fruit or cheese and several slices of thinly cut bread. Anita often wondered how Bella Lamb stayed so slim when she herself put on weight just by looking at food.

She brushed her hair until it stood out fine and curled around her face, making her apple cheeks appear more rounded than usual. She felt wonderful, quite unable to see that she looked like an overdressed, overweight street girl instead of the *femme fatale* she believed herself to be.

She caught the bus at the bottom of Wind Street and preened when the ticket collector gave her a saucy wink. Now she knew she was looking her best.

Joe Barnes entered the house and the silence engulfed him. He cursed as he struggled to light the fire, grit and coat dust chafing his skin beneath his caked clothes. It had been a hard morning. Humping bags of coal into people's houses wasn't one of the most enjoyable aspects of his business, but this morning it had been a necessity, for two of his men were off work through sickness, so their wives claimed. More likely too much booze was the cause. Yesterday had been pay day and his men liked to waste most of it up against the lavatory walls of the Cooper's Arms.

He finally had the fire burning and the big kettle bubbling steam on the hot coals. He divested himself of his clothes and stood in the tin bath, spending a good half-hour trying to rid himself of the dust that clung stubbornly in the creases of his body.

He cleaned up the kitchen, and realizing how hungry he was, opened the larder door. The loaf of bread had sprouted mildewed spots and the cheese stank to high heaven.

'Blast!' He was tired of this, he should never have allowed Nia to walk out of his life. He missed her, damn it. Nia had always been his girl, dark-haired and so full of warmth and love. He'd been a fool to let his natural urges make him indiscreet.

Why couldn't women realize that it was normal for a man to have a fancy piece. And he wasn't *married* to Nia, was he?

With a shock he realized that's where he'd gone wrong; he should have married her and she would have thought twice about running home to her dad. Joe had heard of the old man's death and had cherished the hope that Nia would now come back to him. The hope had lasted two days and then he realized that she was made of sterner stuff than he'd imagined.

Perhaps if he called into Lambert's Cottages again, this time she might relent and see him. Once he had her in his arms, she would be unable to resist, she had always been as eager as he to get in between the sheets.

He looked at his reflection in the mirror. He had the scrubbed look that Nia liked. His hair was sprinkled with drops of moisture and swept crisply back from his face. He looked well, he decided with a feeling of smug satisfaction. He forgot about food and let himself out of the house into the street. It was a sunny afternoon with a cloudless sky above him. The warmth was pleasant now, but earlier when he'd been carrying coal all morning, the sun had been a killer.

He sat on the bus and stared unseeingly through the dusty window. He wondered how to approach Nia. Should he throw himself on her mercy, vowing not to stray again? He doubted if she would swallow that. Perhaps an honest confession that he had wronged her would be enough. By now she must be missing him like hell.

He thought he saw someone waving to him and glanced quickly towards the roadway. He did not at first recognize the plump girl frantically waving both her arms in an effort to attract his attention, and then with a shock he realized who it was.

Anita! Thank God he was on the bus and could pretend not to see her. He deliberately turned away, sweating a little as the sun struck hotly through the glass. God! How could he have risked everything for that little floosie? He must have been mad. He thought uncomfortably about the moment when Nia had walked into the bedroom and confronted them; he naked as the day he was born, and Anita with her big breasts pointing proudly, practically on top of him. No wonder Nia was taking her time about forgiving him.

He was glad to alight from the platform of the bus and feel the breeze gusting in from the sea. A short walk took him to the docks and to Lambert's Cottages, and he paused for a moment at Nia's door before rapping loudly.

If she was surprised to see him, she didn't show it. She looked at him in polite enquiry and didn't ask him to step inside. Play on her conscience, instinct told him, and he smiled in what he hoped was a self-deprecating manner.

'I'm sorry, gel,' he said, 'I know this is an unexpected call but I think you should at least listen to what I have to say. In the past, I've been wrong and very selfish, I've wanted my freedom, you see, but now I know I want you more.'

'Really?' Nia said with complete lack of interest. He would have to think fast or she would be closing the door in his face as she'd done before.

'Come on, Nia, I took you in without question when you needed me, didn't I? Be fair now, *merchi*.'

She was wavering, and after a moment she stepped back a pace. 'All right, come on in, but don't get any silly ideas, will you?'

The house smelled musty as if old Ambrose Powell still inhabited it, and Joe shuddered. How could Nia live here now her father was gone. It was as if she read his thoughts.

'I shall be moving soon and I want to make it clear that you will not be welcome to call on me. What's past is past and I just want to forget it.'

He had not intended to move so fast but he could see the moment slipping away from him. Any second now she would be turning him out. He moved towards her and took her in his arms, and after a moment's pause, just to get her aroused, he lowered his mouth to hers.

If he'd expected unleashed passion at his touch, he was sadly mistaken, for Nia appeared made of stone. She neither accepted nor repulsed him, but simply stood, waiting for him to release her.

'I know what it is,' he said harshly. 'You've found yourself some other man to warm your bed, that's it, I'll bet.'

'Think what you like, Joe,' she said, unruffled, 'but please accept that it's all over between us. It was the moment I saw you in my bed with another woman.'

'That was a mistake,' Joe said desperately. God, what did he have to do to get through to her? 'I'll admit I was wrong, foolishly wrong, and *Duw*, I've suffered for it since, believe me.'

'That makes two of us then.' She was implacable. She moved away, putting the table between them. 'If that's all you've come to say, then it's time you went.'

'But I love you,' Joe said. 'Don't you understand I want to marry you?' He wasn't really keen on marriage but it was worth trying it out if it made Nia come back to him. He was sick of coming home to an empty house. Her silence encouraged him. 'Just think of it, Nia, me and you walking down the aisle together, setting up home, perhaps somewhere away from here, having children . . . we could be a real family.'

'It's a bit late in the day to think of that, Joe,' Nia said softly, and she placed her hands squarely on the table as though to emphasize the point.

'It's never too late,' Joe said. 'Please, Nia, won't you just think about it? You don't have to answer now, give it time.'

She shook her head. 'No, Joe, I don't love you, I don't suppose I ever did love you. It was just that you were the first man I ever had and you were so good in bed that I mistook passion for love.'

'But I could make you love me, Nia, I know you did once, don't deny it. There was that magic between us at first, wasn't there?'

'Perhaps, but you soon spoiled all that, Joe. First you cheated on me by taking my punters, and then you wrangled money out of me for your mine that you've never worked from that day to this, and lastly you were unfaithful to me.' She gave a short laugh. 'What makes you think I'd even consider marrying you, Joe?'

He moved around the table swiftly and caught her to him, his mouth burning down on hers, and after a moment she pushed him away. But she had responded, he might just have found a chink in her armour.

'Please leave me alone, Joe, I don't love you. It's all over, why can't you just accept that?'

'Because when I hold you and kiss you, I can tell you still want me,' he said triumphantly.

'That's just the response of a normal woman,' Nia said, her cheeks colouring. 'Sheer physical attraction, nothing else. Now go away, Joe, I don't want you, not now, not ever. I can't make it any clearer than that, can I?'

'Why are you so keen to push me out of your life?' Joe asked, his eyes narrowing. 'There's another man, I know there is.'

'And what if there is, what right have you got to talk? You and your precious Anita Williams. If I want another man I'll certainly have another man.'

'I bloody well knew it!' Anger poured through Joe as if wine was coursing through his veins. 'I just knew you were too much of a hotblood in bed to be on your own for long. Out with it, who is he?'

'It's nothing at all to do with you, Joe,' Nia said forcefully. 'I'm free, remember, unencumbered by a wedding ring. You had your chance, Joe, and now it's too late for any reconciliation, far too late.'

He wanted to catch hold of her by her slender neck and force the man's name out of her. 'God, it didn't take you long, did it?' he said scathingly. 'Two minutes and you've got another man in your bed. Who says you're any better than Anita?'

'Talk on, Joe,' Nia said. 'Insult me all you like, it will only make me more determined not to bother with you again.'

'Smug, that's what you are, self-centred and smug.' Joe was furious now, he could feel the blood pounding in his head. 'You've always thought you were a cut above everyone else, haven't you, but I could do anything with you once I got you into bed.'

'Maybe once, Joe, but all that's in the past, you might as well accept it first as last. Now get out before I call the constable.'

'All right, I'm going, but I won't give up, I'll be back.' He strode out of the house, his anger blinding him to the sights and sounds of the docklands. He was angry, yes, but there was a feeling of emptiness inside him that he knew would take a long time to go away.

Anita was becoming impatient. Joe must have seen her waving to him when he was on the bus. Of course she could tell by the direction in which he was travelling that he'd been on his way to Lambert's Cottages. It was obvious that he wanted to see her, beg her forgiveness, ask her to come to live with him. She would agree, of course, but only after a lot of coaxing.

She had come to Brynhyfred with a set of ready excuses; she had left some of her things behind in his house and she needed them at once. She wanted him to see her again, to remind him of the happy times they'd spent together, to show him what he was missing. But she was getting fed up of waiting for him, he should have been back long ago. It was a good thing no one locked their doors in Brynhyfred or she would have been waiting on the step like a little child.

She glanced in the mirror and smiled as she primped her hair. She felt she was looking especially pretty today in her lovely dress. Joe liked to see her in bright colours.

She tensed as she heard his footsteps coming rapidly along the path, and her heart started to pound. She couldn't wait to be in his arms again, how she loved him. She turned to face the door but her smile faded as he walked him. His brow was furrowed, his eyes, usually so blue, seemed dark and heavy.

'What the hell are you doing here? You've caused me enough trouble already.'

'Joe, my lovely, what's wrong?' she asked innocently. 'I thought you'd be glad to see me, but I only came up here to get my things, mind. Still annoyed with you, I am, you weren't very nice to your little Anita last time we met, were you?'

He moved swiftly towards her and then she felt a stinging blow on her face. 'Don't give me so much lip, you little bitch!' he said, and then he was shaking her like a madman, throwing her away from him. She reeled and fell to the ground, her lovely skirt torn, riding up above her plump thighs.

'Joe, don't hit me, I love you so much!' She saw the clouds clear from his eyes, he shook back his hair and stared down at her, and then he reached for her, and lifting her in his arms pressed his mouth roughly on hers.

She could feel by the hardness of his body that he was aroused. There was nothing of the tender lover about him as he crushed her breasts with his big hands. He was forcing her legs apart, thrusting himself at her as though he could not wait another minute.

In the midst of her pain, she felt exultant. He wanted her, and that was all that mattered. She groaned and clung to him. Joe, her Joe, had come home to her.

19

Kristina was sitting in the window seat, looking out over the sheer beauty of Mumbles Head and the splendid curve of Swansea Beach. She had felt strange all day; a sort of brooding loneliness had crept over her from early light when Robert had let himself out of the front door. As she'd heard the click of the latch, she had panicked. She was alone, and she felt so strange.

It was September, the early autumn weather fine and sunny, luscious fruits ripening on apple trees and in blackberry bushes. The summer had passed so quickly and Kristina had not yet become Robert's wife in anything but name. Now that she was big and heavy with her pregnancy, she did not expect him to come to her bed, and yet, strangely, she felt she was failing to keep her part of the bargain.

The heavy dragging sensation in her back that had plagued her since morning had intensified but she dismissed it as one of the discomforts of carrying a child. It meant nothing, the baby was not due for several weeks yet.

She made herself a jug of raspberry leaf tea. She had worked enough with herbs to know that it was helpful for expectant mothers to drink as much as possible of the scented brew. It tasted quite pleasant and, putting down her empty cup, she rose and moved to the doorway, longing to feel the fresh morning air on her face.

She wished Robert was home. It was true that theirs was no love match, at least not on her part, but she had grown accustomed to him. She looked forward to the evenings when they would sit and talk together about his work, about his plans to leave the docks eventually and be his own man. Of her plans they spoke little, she had no plans except to be safely delivered of her child. Her child and Eden's.

Not once had Robert referred to her past, he had neither reproached her nor discussed the fact that she had been Eden's mistress. Kristina had not thought of herself in that context, except in retrospect, for while her affair with Eden had been going on, it had been romantic, a dream which would end in a white lace dress and a golden ring. But now she could see it for what it was, a union in which she did all the giving and Eden the taking.

And yet she still thought about him. She had caught sight of Eden one day in the street and her heart had leaped with the pain of remembering. He had been striding along the docklands like a king, his head high, dark hair falling across his forehead. His easy way of walking, with panther-like grace, was distinctive as his long legs covered the ground swiftly. He had not seen her and she had stood still for a moment, wondering why she had ever loved him.

And she *had* loved him; lying in his arms, close to his strong body, his breath mingling with hers, she had been transported into another world. It was a world of make-believe that took her away from the greyness of her everyday life. But he was a married man now and she a married woman. There was no way back.

She gazed down the pathway to the road outside. It was a constant throb of hurt, the knowledge that she had made a fool of herself over Eden, and she knew she should go down on her knees and thank the gods for giving her a strong man like Robert for a husband. On the docks he might be a tyrant, a powerful man, a force to be reckoned with, but in the home he had chosen for her, he was gentle and patient, and she did not yet know the depths of him, she was quite sure of that.

A pain caught her low in her stomach and she gasped

with sudden fear. She looked around. The street outside was empty, the windows curtained with net for privacy were bland and uncaring. The big house seemed to close in around her as pain caught her in its grip once again. She was going into labour and she was alone.

She looked around her with a sense of panic, why hadn't she allowed Robert to install a telephone? When he'd suggested it, she'd shaken her head, feeling strangely frightened by the thought that anybody could interrupt her life by the mere lifting of a receiver. She did not want the disembodied voices of strangers entering her home. He'd laughed and called her old-fashioned. 'Everyone has a phone these days,' he'd said mildly. 'It's only being businesslike.' But he'd conceded graciously, accepting that a telephone was not vital to their way of life.

She leaned against the door jamb and stared along the street. It wound away from her, running downhill, disappearing behind a row of tall houses. If only she was back at Lambert's Cottages there would be no fear of being alone. Mam would be fussing around her like a mother hen and the girls would be sent to fetch the midwife. And Thomas Presdey would be there, upsetting everyone with his sharp tongue, she reminded herself.

A figure had appeared in the distance, and even from far off she could tell it was Robert by the way he strode forward, an irresistible force, expecting and receiving no opposition. By the time he reached her, she was doubled up with pain, hands clasped around her stomach as though to staunch the flow of broken waters. He did not speak, but lifted her in his arms and carried her gently into the room she had prepared for the birthing.

Beneath the pristine sheet, brown paper crackled, a tip from Nurse Freeman to preserve the mattress, and Kristina made an effort to smile. 'How did you know?' He did not answer as he gently drew off her shoes, but there was no need for words. Robert had appeared when she most needed him. He was big and comforting and he was here with her and now she knew everything was going to be all right.

Roggen left the classroom with a feeling of thankfulness. The little horrors had been worse than usual today. The children appeared to be wound up, talking about war at every turn, too old for their years, some of them. She brushed chalk from her hands as she entered the staff room and sighed tiredly, feeling strangely depressed and out of sorts. She saw that a tray had been left for her, with the pot covered by a brightly knitted cosy, and a cup upturned in the saucer, and she felt a warm rush of gratitude to old Mrs Price who 'did' for the staff of Cwmdonkin Private School.

She caught sight of herself in the old, damp-speckled mirror and saw a woman with short, thick hair curling darkly to her neck, and eyes that somehow lacked lustre. An old maid by many standards.

It was strange how she had had so little success with the men in her life. Richard had loved her once, had made her pregnant, and somehow she had thrown it all away. And Richard had never known about the baby. He had never seen their beautiful child, had never even known that it had existed. But then he was only the father, far removed from the reality of the situation.

Roggen still felt the pain of it, not so much for the child, still and beautiful in death, but for the lively baby who for so brief a time had lain against her breast. That time she remembered on days such as today when the world seemed colourless, lacking in light and love.

Her mouth twisted into a wry smile as she thought of Colin who, though not exciting, had seemed to be in love with her. He had soon become all cow-eyed when Nia came into his line of vision. His regard for Roggen, so he said, had always been that of a brother. She took leave to doubt that but it was no good brooding. He had not been in love with her, at least not in the way a lover should be, and if she was truthful, she had seen him as a compromise, a last chance to lead a normal married life.

She had her work. Teaching other people's children could be quite rewarding, but not today. Today she felt old and alone.

Roggen still occasionally attended political meetings, and inevitably she came face to face with Richard some of the time, but he usually managed to ignore her. He would probably be the next mayor of Swansea, a man who at thirty years of age had become a little portly, with grey hair growing in distinguished wings of pure white at the temples. He was engaged to be married to the eminently suitable young daughter of Comfort's Welsh Brewers, a very old established family with good connections all over the country. It seemed that Richard had found all he ever wanted from life.

Family ties, it seemed everyone had them except her. Roggen smiled ruefully, she was being indulgent today, wallowing in self-pity. It did no good, but it was a luxury that she allowed herself from time to time.

She left the school and began the walk down the steep hill towards the Uplands. From there she would catch a bus that would take her most of the way home. It would be good to be home in the familiar house that would wrap her protectively in the remembered security of her childhood.

As she walked, she wondered if perhaps she should buy herself a little car, a second-hand Austin maybe, she could well afford it. And yet the thought of learning the intricacies of steering and changing gear was daunting, even though Roggen was usually eager to face a new challenge.

The bus ride was uncomfortable, hot and airless. She glanced at the man seated in front of her. He was reading a newspaper and she could not help studying the print over his shoulder. Uneasily she read that the women and children of London were being evacuated, just as a precautionary measure, and she judged that the long talked about war must be a very strong possibility indeed.

When she had alighted from the bus and reached the familiar dirt road leading to Lambert's Cottages, Roggen paused for a moment, staring out towards the sea. Was she destined to live out her life in the comfortable but dull surrounding of her docklands home, growing older with the prospect of someone of her own to love growing ever distant?

Once inside the well polished hallway, she saw from the coat hanging near the door that Eden was at home. Her spirits lightened, at least for now she had the company of her brother and his wife, but soon they would move to a house of their own and she would be left, a solitary figure rattling round the empty rooms of the Red House. Perhaps Ty Coch should be sold and she should move somewhere smaller, but then she would be alone *and* among strangers, not a pleasing prospect.

Eden looked up from his newspaper and smiled warmly. 'You're looking tired, Ro, shall I get you a cup of tea?'

'Please.' She sank into one of the plump upholstered chairs and kicked off her shoes. 'The children in my class have been horrors today, all talk of war and fighting. It seems they've caught some sort of fever and are unable to settle down to proper study.'

Eden's face darkened. 'There's going to be a war, no good hiding our heads in the sand about it.'

Roggen felt a chill of apprehension. She had heard the talk, read the signs, and yet she couldn't believe that war would touch the soft shores of her own country.

Bella came into the room, a light coat over her arm. 'I'm just going into town,' she said. 'Anybody want anything?'

'No thanks.' Roggen smiled. The more she saw of her sister-in-law the more she liked her.

'Right then,' Bella kissed Eden's cheek, 'I'll be off. See you later.' Eden saw her to the door and then looked round at Roggen.

'I'll get your tea myself. Anita seems more than a little preoccupied these days.'

'Thanks, Eden,' Roggen said gratefully. She stared into the fire sinking low in the grate, and picking up the tongs she placed coals strategically over the embers. She felt suddenly as though a chill wind was finding every nook and cranny in the old house.

When Eden returned with the tray, he handed her a cup of fragrant tea. 'Drink this, it'll do you good. You seem so tired, Ro, everything all right?' There was such sympathy in his voice that ready tears welled in her eyes.

'Is it Colin?' Eden asked, smoothing back his wave of unruly hair that would fall across his forehead whatever he did.

She could have laughed in his face. 'Good God, no. If I'm to be honest, Colin was the last hope, the biggest compromise you've ever seen in your life.' She shook back her hair. 'I suppose I was a little put out when he took up with Nia so suddenly, but not worried enough to break my heart over it.'

She stared at him evenly and his eyes were clouded. 'What about you?' she said softly. 'Any regrets?'

He moved away from her quickly and thrust his hands into his pockets. 'I'm not grumbling. I've a good wife in Bella, and a man can't ask for more.' He changed the subject.

'When the war does come, I think it'll be the navy for me,' he said, moving aside the paper that lay crumpled on the small table beside him. 'I've always loved the sea.'

Roggen felt a chill once more as she thought of the implications should war come to Swansea. 'Will we be very much affected here, do you think?' she asked in a small voice.

'There's no denying that Swansea will be a target because of the docks, but I should think if it comes to that, there will be masses of evacuations here, just as in London.'

'I don't want to think too much about it,' Roggen said in a small voice. 'I feel so frightened and so alone, Eden. Why haven't I got a fine husband who would give me a

251

brood of children to love? Why can't I be part of a family?'

'You *are* part of a family,' Eden said softly, 'and don't talk as if life has passed you by.'

'As far as I'm concerned, it has,' she said, examining her fingernails carefully, noticing that the polish had chipped again.

Eden took her chin in his hand and forced her to look at him. 'I hope you're not still pining for Richard James?' Eden was frowning heavily. 'I still blame him for being so irresponsible, making an abortion necessary.'

'Don't waste your energy,' Roggen said flatly, her cheeks suddenly full of colour. 'There was no abortion.'

Eden stared at her with eyebrows raised. 'What are you talking about, Roggen?'

She sighed. 'Remember the time I went away to London on a course? Well, there was no course and no abortion.' She paused, chewing her lip worriedly. 'The plan was that the baby would be adopted.' She swallowed hard. 'But it didn't come to that, the child died shortly after it was born. I didn't want to upset you by telling you the truth, and as for Richard, he never even knew I was having the child.'

After a moment, Eden took her by the shoulders and drew her into his arms. 'You should have told me before.'

'What was the point?' she said softly. 'It was my problem and I wanted to solve it my own way. I tried to be so independent and all the time I was scared stiff. But now you know why I couldn't come home when Mama was sick.'

And the experience had changed her in some indefinable way, though if the change was for the good or bad she didn't know.

'Sorry, brother,' she said, 'but I think I needed to talk about it now. It must be the thought of war coming and all of us being in danger.' She gave a watery smile. 'I'm going to my room now, I feel quite exhausted. Thanks for the sympathy.'

252

As she hurried up the stairs she felt lighter. The burden was removed from her shoulders, Eden now knew the truth, and to Roggen, the telling of her secret had brought a great sense of relief.

It was later that evening that Eden Lamb left the house and moved purposefully along the docks towards the main road. There were people he had to see, a job too long put off. Richard James would be punished. Whatever Roggen said, the man had been irresponsible and had gone his way unscathed. Well now he must pay for his carelessness. Eden had contacts, favours owed him and now was the time to use them to his advantage.

The labour was a long one and though the nurse worked hard, her face beaded with perspiration, progress was slow.

In a haze Kristina heard Robert asking anxiously if anything was wrong. The old nurse washed her hands in the water steaming in the white enamel bowl, and shook her head.

'Nothing wrong, Mr Jenkins, but first babies do take a long time, mind, especially if it's a big lump like the one your wife is carrying. Don't worry, when the time is right, the child will come out, there's no rush, mind.' She rolled down her sleeves. 'Now, how about making us a nice pot of tea, then? Keep yourself occupied, that's the ticket.'

Kristina heard Robert leave the room and she wanted to call him back, but her mouth was dry, seemingly full of cotton wool, and she swallowed hard.

Nurse Freeman was at her side at once, dabbing her lips with cooling water. 'Keep your spirits up, girl,' she said softly, 'you're doing well but it's a slow babba, must be a boy, too lazy to come out, see.'

Kristina's heart lifted. A boy, how she would love a son. She felt another contraction coming on and she grew tense. The midwife's hand was on her swollen stomach, pressing downwards as if to ease the baby on its difficult journey.

The pain swamped her, drowning her, taking charge of her. She bit back a scream and instead growled low in her throat, and all the time the nurse was urging her on.

'That's a good mother, you're doing nicely, we're doing well. There,' she said as the contraction subsided, 'wasn't that a good effort, then? Soon you'll be able to push and that's the last part where you work very hard and the baby comes into the world. You'll feel better soon, I promise you.'

Kristina sighed as the pain left her, and wondered at the way she felt almost normal in between contractions. She was tired, very tired, but elated too, knowing the time was near when she would hold her child in her arms. Her child, and Eden's, she thought guiltily.

Robert returned to the room and placed the tray on the table. She gave him a reassuring smile. 'Not long now, Robert,' she said, as though she needed to set his mind at rest. 'It'll soon be over. What time is it?'

'Gone midnight,' he replied coming to her side and taking her hand. 'Have courage, Kristina, you're coming along like a true mother. I'm proud of you.'

Suddenly there were tears in Kristina's eyes. Robert was not even the father of her baby and yet here he was treating her with every consideration, so unexpectedly kind. Would Eden Lamb, she wondered, have been capable of offering such a strong, reassuring presence?

'Robert,' she said holding his hand tightly, 'I don't know how to say this, but . . .' He placed his finger to her lips.

'Hush, *merchi*, save your strength for better things.' He gave her one of his rare smiles and she felt an unexpected surge of affection. And then the pain began again, washing over her, crushing her body unbearably. It felt as though the bones of her spine were being pulled apart. Was childbirth always like this?

'Good girl!' encouraged Nurse Freeman. 'That's the way, come on now, every pain brings the baby nearer to

254

this world, remember that. Be sensible, try hard, and it will be over all the sooner.'

Slowly the pains changed from the aching, racking sensations and there now came the irresistible urge to bear down. She growled low in her throat and the midwife tapped her arm.

'Don't put all your strength into your throat, girl, keep some of it for your child. Gather yourself together now and push!'

Sweat beaded Kristina's forehead and she gripped Robert's hand more tightly as though his strength could communicate itself to her. She closed her eyes and concentrated on the sensation low within her, the age-old struggle to bring forth new life.

When the sensation receded, she fell back gasping and exhausted, wondering how she could go on. But there was no choice. Her baby must be born, and only her own efforts would bring that about.

She was aware of Robert bathing her forehead in cold water and she looked up at him gratefully. She didn't speak, she had no strength, but she knew that he would read her well, as he always did.

He was born at last, a fine, healthy nine-pound boy, and she held him in her arms very tenderly, happy that Robert was there with her, crouching admiringly at her side.

Kristina's son was born at precisely three-thirty on the morning of September the third, 1939. The same day Britain and France declared war on Germany.

20

Roggen stared at Richard James with her head on one side. He had scarcely changed; his hair was touched with grey and he carried more weight, perhaps, but he still retained his clean good looks, and the high intelligent forehead was still smooth over clear eyes. Once she had lain in his arms, experienced his passion and now, years later, she felt the same tugging at something deep within her.

He was angry. 'Your brother has seen to it that I will never be mayor of Swansea.' His tone was clipped. 'If he'd done this when we first quarrelled I could have understood it, but why after all this time does he want to harm me?'

Richard had come to Ty Coch obviously seeking a confrontation with Eden, who had moved only a week ago into his own house. Roggen could not help feeling thankful that her brother was not present. She wanted peace, not more bad feeling.

'Sit down, please,' she said softly. 'There's something I think you should know.' She rubbed her hands together. Telling him was going to be so difficult.

'What is it?' Richard did not take a seat but moved towards her until he was uncomfortably close, and stared down at her, waiting.

'I should have told you all this before,' she said helplessly, 'but I had my pride, you know, and it did seem all over between us.'

'Just get on with it, Roggen.' Richard was still, an air of waiting about him that made her uneasy.

'I became pregnant with your child,' she said, and held up her hand as he would have spoken. 'I'd decided on an abortion.' She looked up fleetingly, begging him with her eyes to understand. 'There was no future for you and me and I would not pressure you into something you didn't want.'

'But Roggen, destroying our child...' Richard's hostile stance had changed at her words, and now he looked uncertain, concern evident in his eyes. He paused as she held up her hand.

'Wait, before you speak, the abortion never took place.' She swallowed hard. The fact of the baby's death did not come any easier with the passing years, if anything, it became ever more painful.

'I went through with the pregnancy, with a view to having the child adopted.' She looked down at her hands, there was only one way to say it. 'The baby died shortly after it was born.' She felt again the child moving so restlessly, so full of energy against her breast. Would she never forget that feeling? 'I came home alone, it was as though nothing had happened.' She shook back her hair. 'At least, it appeared that way to my brother.'

Richard took a step towards her, pain etched into his face, but Roggen turned away from him deliberately. She didn't want his pity.

'Eden knew about the pregnancy, of course, but I lied to him, let him think the abortion had been carried out.'

'Oh, Roggen.' Richard ran his hand distractedly through his hair. 'I suppose I was a thoughtless oaf in those days. I can't honestly say what my reaction would have been if you'd come to me. If you asked me now, I'd say I'm ashamed and so sorry for what you went through alone. No wonder Eden has it in for me.'

'Eden has only just learned the truth of it all,' Roggen said quickly, somewhat shy of this softer side of Richard James. 'I'm afraid I blurted it out to him thinking that after all this time the bitterness would be gone. Obviously I was wrong.'

Richard rubbed a hand over his eyes. 'Roggen, how could you keep it from me all this time? I had a right to know.' He turned to her at once, his hand held out towards her.

'God, that was selfish of me! I had no rights, I'd forfeited them.' He touched her arm. 'You must have hated me for the way I went out of your life so completely.'

'It's all in the past now,' Roggen said, 'it's over and done with.' But it wasn't, she would never forget.

Richard stepped back a pace. 'I can't ever make it up to you, Ro, and I suppose I could expect nothing else but revenge from your brother.' His tone was bitter as he turned away from her.

'Don't go,' Roggen said at once, holding out her hand. 'Let's talk. I've been so lonely just for someone to talk to about the baby.' To her horror, her face crumpled and tears fell hot against her cheeks.

Without a word, Richard took her in his arms and held her close, smoothing back the tangled hair from her face. He cared, and a flash of hope flared through her. He cared about the loss of the baby, and why shouldn't he? He was the father, after all. If anyone could understand her anguish, surely it was Richard James.

Eden paced the floor of the shipping office, frowning. Should he take the step he longed to and enlist in the Merchant Navy? The inevitable fall of hair swept across his brow and he pushed it back impatiently. Anger burned within him, coupled with a sense of frustrated outrage at the events of the last few weeks.

On the third of September Neville Chamberlain had announced in sombre tones that the British people were at war with Germany. Ten hours later, the Donaldson ship *Athenia*, evacuating women and children to the United States, had been sunk without warning off the coast of Ireland. Kapitan-Leutnant Fritz Julius Lemp, commander of the U-boat, claimed to have mistaken the ship for an armed merchant cruiser, but five days later the first Welsh ship, the *Winkleigh*, was lost in the North Atlantic. It seemed the battle of the seas had begun and it was going to be a dirty one.

At the end of September there had been the beginnings of retaliation by the land forces when the British Expeditionary Force of 158,000 men had been sent to France, but so far there had been no news of any great victories.

Eden did not fool himself, there were difficult times coming and he intended to be a part of them. He stared through the window at the plethora of ships in the dock, feeling the sway of the deck and tasting the salt of the breeze. He could not wait to go to sea. Colin could hold the fort at home, make sure their ships continued to carry supplies in and out of Britain. Unless the rumours he'd heard were correct and the Government intended to requisition all private shipping.

The door to his office was opened suddenly and Roggen stood staring at him breathlessly, her slim figure outlined in the fall of afternoon sunlight. She was angry, her cheeks were flushed and her eyes bright, and Eden sighed inwardly, knowing full well what was on her mind.

'How could you be so cruel to Richard?' she said, facing him squarely, her small hands clenched tightly. 'What passed between Richard James and me was none of your business.'

He sank into a chair and picked up a pen, tapping it against the desk. 'You made it my business when you confided in me your pain at bearing a stillborn child,' he said evenly.

Roggen shook back her hair which was long now, curling thickly against her shoulders. 'But did you have to destroy his dreams?' Her voice quivered a little and he looked at her intently.

'Did he have to destroy yours?' he countered. He watched her move restlessly about the small room, the sounds of the docks a background to the clipping of her heels against the polished floor.

'It was all so long ago, Eden,' she said helplessly. 'Why punish him after all this time?'

'He deserved what was coming to him,' Eden said shortly. 'It was worth biding my time to repay him in full.' He sat up straighter. 'In any case, there's more to think about now than anyone's petty ambitions in politics.' He regarded her steadily. 'It may have escaped your notice, but we are at war with Germany.'

'I know that as well as you do,' she snapped, 'but so far it hasn't affected *us*, has it?'

'You are not very well informed,' he said. 'We have begun to lose our ships already. This war is serious, Roggen, it's not a game, and Richard James will soon have more to think about than a minor disappointment such as being denied the position of mayor in the town.'

'You're so hard, Eden.' Roggen spoke softly. 'I sometimes wonder if you have any feelings for anyone.'

'Look, Ro,' He spoke more softly, 'what did you expect me to do? I was so angry when you told me that Richard James wasn't even interested enough to find out that you were pregnant. He left you alone, took the easy way out. I had to do something, surely you can see that?' He leaned forward. 'I wasn't going to let the man think he could treat my sister with complete disregard and go unpunished. I love you, Ro.'

He held out his arms, smiling so charmingly that after a moment Roggen relented and went into them. Eden hugged her close. She was his only family, apart from Bella, of course. Bella, waiting so coolly in the sitting room of their new house high on Mount Pleasant Hill. She was a good wife and surely soon she would begin to bear him sons.

The name of Lamb had always been a proud one, and as far as Eden was concerned it was up to him to see that the good name was perpetuated. He needed sons, especially now with a war on and life expectation an unknown quantity. He sometimes worried a little that there might be something wrong with Bella, though he never for a moment allowed her to see his impatience.

Roggen leaned back and looked up at him. 'You must be fair to Richard. He never knew about the baby, I've told you that so many times before.' She sighed. 'But don't worry, he won't be a thorn in your flesh any more. I hear he is going to England, it seems he's going to join the Air Force.'

'Well, at least he has some guts,' Eden said, releasing Roggen and moving to the window to stare out into the late sunshine. 'He's going to need them, the Germans are much better equipped for war than we are.'

He turned to face his sister, smiling once more and she thought how handsome he was. She was proud of him for all his faults.

After Roggen had left, Eden stood morosely near the doorway, his restlessness increased by the news that Richard James had taken a decisive step and was going to become an airman. Eden moved towards his desk and stared at the order book, one of his ships was scheduled to take a load of coal to Monaco. He tapped his pen against the page thoughtfully, it would be a good idea if he were to accompany the ship on her crossing and find out for himself what sort of conditions prevailed at sea in wartime. He would simply sit back and watch, leaving all the decisions to the master and crew of the *Chware Teg*. It was time he got up off his arse and met this war face to face.

Richard made a point of seeing Roggen before he left for England. He talked about the past and was a most sympathetic listener. He was contrite about the way he had let her face her ordeal alone, and wanted nothing more than to make up for it. His engagement, he said, was ended, it had been a mistake from the beginning.

'I've regretted our separation every day of my life.' It was raining and Richard stood before her in the doorway of one of the shops in Wind Street, his bulk sheltering her from the worst of the weather. 'I've seen other women, I can't deny that, Roggen, but I've never once forgotten that precious magic we had in the beginning.'

Roggen reached up and touched his cheek. 'We both made foolish mistakes. We were so young then.'

'It's not *that* long ago.' He smiled and nuzzled against her, and a splash of cold rain ran from his cheek on to hers.

'It seems a lifetime,' Roggen said softly. She smiled suddenly. 'I know, let's go and have tea in the Mackworth. It'll be just like old times.'

'You'll get soaked,' he protested. 'It's raining cats and dogs.'

Roggen looked over his shoulder to see the rain beating a tattoo against the cobbles, dancing in spikes from the roadway.

'Come to the house, then, to Ty Coch,' she said on impulse. 'No one will be there, we'll have the place to ourselves.' Roggen wondered then if she'd been too forward. Was her invitation likely to be misconstrued? But in any case Richard was shaking his head.

'I might not be able to keep my hands to myself, Ro,' he said seriously. 'If only you knew how much I want you, you wouldn't put temptation in my way like that.'

'Please Richard, I need you.' Perversely, she wanted him to make love to her. It had been so long since she'd been in a man's arms, been shown any passion at all, and the thrill of it was more than anything physical could offer. She wanted to be desired, it proved that she was still alive, part of the human race. She'd been so afraid of becoming a vinegary old maid.

'I'll run and fetch the car,' Richard said. 'You stay here out of the rain, I won't be long.'

While she waited, she felt breathless, almost a young girl again in the throes of love. But was it love she felt for Richard, or the remembered emotions of the past? Whatever it was, Roggen was determined to make the most of it.

He took her home but he would not step inside the doors of Ty Coch. On that he was adamant. He took her fingers in his and kissed the tips, and she warmed to the admiration in his eyes. She remembered reading somewhere that first love is always precious, stored away like a dried flower, ready to flourish again at the first sign of nourishment. She watched him with mixed feelings as he climbed into his car, a little battered now, the shine gone from the paintwork, a mark of the time that had passed like a desert between them. He turned and waved, and then as she stood on the step she felt the reaction of loneliness almost instantly and she hurried indoors, not wanting anyone in the street to see Roggen Lamb in tears.

She did not see Richard for one long week during which her feelings fluctuated between uncertainty and happiness. He had gone to his base somewhere in England but he would be back, he'd promised her that.

When he did return, he had a special licence in one hand and a beautiful antique diamond ring in the other.

'I want to marry you, Roggen,' he said soberly, 'if you'll have me.'

The *Chware Teg* left harbour in the dusk of a cold November evening, her cargo coal bound for Monaco. The craft huddled as though for warmth in the wake of a small coastal convoy that would take her into deeper waters. There would be the added strength of a larger convoy for the run down to the Straits of Gibraltar.

The master was uneasy, for even with the best efforts of his engineers the *Chware Teg* would not be able to reach, let alone maintain, the speed of nine knots specified by the convoy commodore. The master was further disturbed by the presence of the ship's owner, for Eden Lamb had a reputation for being a hard and exacting man.

The journey did not progress well. The Welsh ship was a persistent straggler, limping along at barely eight and a half knots. Visibility was poor, landmarks few, and after

263

a nightmare journey towards deep waters the master decided to strike out alone for Gibraltar.

Eden rested in his cabin. He had been without sleep for several nights, realizing that John Davies had an impossible task before him in his attempt to keep pace with the rest of the convoy. Eden trusted the master of his ship implicitly. John was a good man, a seasoned sailor, but too much was being asked of the *Chware Teg*, and that was something John did not like. Eden had been aware of the dangers of striking out for deep water without the protection of a convoy, but he had too much respect for John's judgment on the matter to interfere.

He must have slept for many hours, because when he opened his eyes the ship was moving in the gentle corkscrewing motion that would develop into a lazy roll when she turned beam-on to the swell. He guessed that the *Chware Teg* had entered the waters of the Bay of Biscay, and from all the signs the weather was fine, so visibility must be good. That, at least, would keep John Davies happy.

Eden shaved his several days' growth with difficulty, unused to the pitch of the boards beneath him. Fortunately he was a good sailor untroubled by sickness and he even enjoyed the challenge of an occasional storm.

Eden frowned at his reflection as he thought of his wife's fear when he'd told her he was going to sea. Bella seemed lately to be looking to him for reassurance of his love. He tried to be understanding, knowing that her failure so far to conceive a child was probably at the root of her insecurity.

John Davies gave him a nod as Eden came up to the bridge. 'Had a good rest?' His tone was gruff but with the good-natured kindliness that characterized the man.

'Aye, you could say that.' Eden leaned against the door jamb, unwilling to distract the master from his job, but John seemed in a mood to talk.

'I've set a course well clear of the land,' he said,

'making for a point about a hundred miles off Cape Finisterre.'

Eden scratched his newly shaved chin, trying to chart the layout of the land and sea without the benefit of the master's experience. John nodded, as though confirming the information to himself.

'Then it's due south to the Straits of Gib. I'm hoping that by staying in the blue waters as long as possible the ship will go unnoticed by the Jerries.'

Eden knew that by 'blue waters' John was referring to the Atlantic, and the plan seemed good to him.

'Of course,' John continued, 'I would usually hug the Spanish and Portuguese coastline, but that's in peacetime conditions. Mind, there's no telling where the swine will surface, we take a blutty chance whatever.'

Eden nodded, he respected the man's knowledge of the sea. John had been a master for long enough to weigh up the risks and decide on the best course of action.

John Davies lit his pipe and fell silent, apparently lost in his own thoughts. He was a short, thickset man with a shock of red hair and a beard that flamed around ruddy cheeks. He was an extremely capable, even gifted, sailor, and Eden would have trusted him with his life.

'I think I'll get below and find someone to have a hand of cards with.' Eden felt he'd be intruding if he remained too long on the bridge. He would not like John to get the idea his actions were being monitored.

'Yup.' John did not look at Eden. The men had formed an understanding and words were sometimes unnecessary.

Eden looked out to the swell of the sea. It was tranquil, with no sign that beneath the waves lay hidden dangers. The distance from the home coast to Monaco by sea was about two thousand miles. He sighed; many of the natural dangers of such a journey had been negotiated, but there was a long way to go yet before the cargo was safely delivered, especially as there was the added danger now of the German U-boats that searched the seas for unwary prey.

Eden went below, and the smell of tobacco reached him at once along with the tang of rope and tar and coal dust. It was a good world, a man's world, and Eden wondered as he'd done many times before why he had not pursued a more active career on the sea. It was not too late to start, not now in wartime when men would be needed in all the armed services. If Eden had to choose between the air, land and sea, he knew that he would choose the sea every time.

The even tenor of the journey had lulled the crew of the *Chware Teg* into a false sense of security. The ship was abeam but not yet in sight of Cape Finisterre. A moderate swell was running, indicating a blow far out in the Atlantic, and yet the weather, so far, continued fine.

The young officer was grateful that soon he could leave his post and get some rest. Eden joined him on the port wing of the bridge, drinking coffee, hot and black, out of a tin mug.

'Nearly bedtime, Gary.' Eden was not tired; he felt tinglingly alive, his senses alert, and as he leaned forward to peer out of the wheelhouse window he felt at peace with the world. His life was a good one, he could not deny it, he had a fine wife at home and for that he should count himself a lucky man.

He leaned closer to the window and suddenly swore under his breath in disbelief.

'Christ! Look at this, Gary.' Eden pointed to where a beautiful trail of silver bubbles, seemingly phosphorescent in the moonlight, cut across from the port beam to the bow of the ship.

'*Daro!*' Gary exploded, 'we're going to be hit.' But as the two men watched, the line of bubbles crossed the bow from port to starboard and disappeared into the night.

Eden followed as Gary threw himself into the wheelhouse and caught hold of the voicepipe, and within minutes John Davies was on the bridge, taking command.

'It could have been a torpedo,' he said slowly, 'or even

266

the wash of the U-boat's periscope, but we won't take any blutty chances, whatever.'

Eden watched silently, keeping out of the way, knowing the master was well equipped to handle matters.

John gave an order. 'Helm hard to starboard.' His voice was brisk and cool and it was clear he was not a man to lose his head in a crisis. It was good to watch as he swung the ship through an arc of ninety degrees, putting her stern-on to the estimated position of the U-boat.

'There's no chance of outrunning the swine,' he said conversationally, glancing at Eden, 'not with our best speed eight and a half knots, but we can make things damn difficult, mind.'

Another wake of silver bubbles brought a frown to John's weathered brow. He acted at once, and a series of urgent blasts rocked the silence.

'Got to think of the safety of my crew, see,' he said evenly. He smoothly gave orders that the signal be sent out to warn other shipping in the area of the danger of attack, and to give the position of the *Chware Teg*.

Eden watched in fascination. It was a joy to see the man work so courageously as he repeated his earlier move and presented his ship's stern towards the estimated position of his attacker.

'Jerry's wasting his torpedoes,' John said with satisfaction. 'Keep it up, *boy bach*. We'll waste a few more Reichsmarks with pleasure.'

Eden felt exhilarated, alert and aware of the danger. And yet he felt fear too, burning low in his gut, and he looked at John wondering how the older man remained so calm.

'*Daro*, Jerry's coming up,' John said. 'See her there, surfacing on the port quarter at about 250 yards.' He swung his binoculars to his eyes. 'Aye, there they are, little bastards running along the casing towards the deck gun.'

Even as John spoke, a shell arced with a screech towards the ship but fell away harmlessly into the sea.

The next shell hit home, bursting into the superstructure, and now they'd found the target once, the shells began to be aimed without mercy. It was only a short time since the alarm had been sounded, but with startling suddenness John Davies was ordering the lowering of the lifeboats.

Eden helped as best he could and to his admiration the seamen worked swiftly but without panic. The boat-swain knocked away the gripes, but even as the order was given to lower away, a shell exploded close by, sending bodies hurtling into the sea like so many rag dolls.

'Bastards!' Eden heard his own voice hoarse with anger, and realized he was shaking. He felt the wetness of blood on his forehead but he felt no pain, only a longing to take the enemy and strangle each and every man with his own hands.

Eden began to usher some of the remaining men into the starboard boat, and they moved quietly and with proud dignity. The second lifeboat was safely launched with all remaining crew on board, and crouched in the stern Eden heard the slap of the waves against the small boat as it drifted dangerously near to the U-boat which was still shelling the crippled *Chware Teg*.

'The Jerry swine are contravening the Geneva Convention,' John Davies said harshly. By the sound of his voice, Eden knew that the master was near to tears. It was hard for a man to lose his ship.

'The enemy has won,' Eden said flatly, 'but not without cost. I reckon the German commander's superiors will think he's used a sledge-hammer to knock in a nail.'

The U-boat turned and was heading silently away, careless of survivors as she drifted into the darkness.

The men in the lifeboat watched in silence as their crippled ship sank slowly beneath the waters, and Eden's throat constricted with tears as the last wash ran towards them from the doomed *Chware Teg*. He knew he didn't grieve for the loss of the actual ship or her cargo, much as the loss would affect him financially, but for the bravery of the seamen seated with him, who had to a man fought to keep the ship out of danger for as long as possible, hoping for help that never came.

The darkness seemed to close in around the pitifully tiny craft. The waves were moving restlessly with the deep swell of the blue waters and it was easy to feel fear.

A voice began to sing, quietly at first, and then with growing conviction, rising powerfully on the night air.

> Eternal father, strong to save,
> Whose arm hath bound the restless wave,
> Who bidd'st the mighty ocean deep
> Its own appointed limits keep:

Other voices joined in and the singing grew louder, more defiant. And Eden, swallowing hard, began to sing too.

> O hear us when we cry to thee
> For those in peril on the sea.

He didn't know where he was or where he was heading, or even if he'd get out of this alive, but one thing he did know; he was proud to be in the company of such men. And if his face was wet with tears, there was only the sea and the sky and the darkness to bear witness that Eden Lamb, ship owner, was weeping.

21

The news of the sinking of the *Chware Teg* with Eden Lamb on board spread like wildfire through the houses huddled on the docklands, and to the inhabitants of Lambert's Cottages the news struck particularly hard. Eden Lamb was sometimes a difficult man, but always a fair one. A man who, as landlord of some of the properties on the docklands, could be relied upon to be forebearing in the face of late rents. Above all, he was a local, one of their own, and the docklands grieved for him.

Kristina heard the news from the baker's boy who stood on her doorstep, a basket of hot loaves in his arms.

'You used to live in Lambert's didn't you, Mrs Jenkins?' He was just a boy, a cowlick of hair hung over his eyes, and his thin face, bearing little evidence of manhood, was as smooth as a child's. He had been calling on Kristina ever since she and Robert had moved into their house, showing proper respect to the wife of the works allocator from the docks.

'Folks are saying there's been a terrible accident at sea.' He spoke in heavy tones, but Kristina was more concerned with listening for the baby – he had been crying fretfully through the night – so what the boy was saying didn't register immediately.

'Mr Eden Lamb's ship sunk, and with him on board, mind, torpedoed by them Jerries, so they say.'

Kristina didn't remember taking the hot bread and placing it in the wooden bin in the kitchen, neither was she conscious of wrapping Verdun in the shawl, Welsh fashion, and leaving the house. Her mind refused to accept what she had heard. She only knew that she must see Roggen, find out what had really happened, be reassured that Eden was safe, for the alternative was unacceptable.

She hurried down the hill and along the sea-blown road leading to the docks, telling herself that everything was all right. The boy was mistaken, he *had* to be, he was only giving voice to rumours, after all.

She knocked on the door of Ty Coch with fingers that trembled, and the moment she came face to face with Roggen she knew that the rumours were true.

'Come inside.' Roggen's voice was heavy as though she had been crying for a long time. In the hallway, she turned and looked at Kristina, her eyes red-rimmed and anxious. 'Come into the sitting room and put the baby down on the sofa, he's heavy for you to have carried all this way. I'll make us a cuppa in a minute.' She was struggling to remain calm but after she had watched Kristina tuck the baby into the softness of the cushions, her composure deserted her.

'I can't believe it, Kris.' Roggen's face was white and strained. 'Eden can't be dead, he just can't be.'

Kristina turned to her. 'Be calm, now, tell me exactly what you know.'

After a moment, Roggen took a deep ragged breath. 'It seems that a tramp steamer that answered a radio call from the *Chware Teg* found pieces of timber from one of the lifeboats.' She swallowed hard. 'Worse, there were some bodies caught up in the wreckage. Oh Kris, I know how you've always cared about my brother.'

Kristina, pushing her own dread to the back of her mind, attempted to reassure Roggen. 'Nothing is certain, not if they haven't found Eden.' Her voice shook. 'They haven't, have they?' Relief poured through her as Roggen shook her head dumbly. 'We mustn't panic,' Kristina continued. 'Eden is a strong, resourceful man, he'll be all right, you'll see.'

Roggen nodded, agreeing silently but her eyes were uncertain, underlined by dark shadows.

Slowly, she straightened her shoulders and moved to the door.

'I'll make that tea,' she said shakily.

Kristina sat on the sofa and stared at her baby. Verdun slept soundly now, making up for the lost hours of the night, but Kristina suddenly felt weary and drained of energy. She would not allow herself to think of Eden, the coldness of the sea and the danger he might still be facing. Instead, she studied her son's face minutely, searching for the many likenesses to his father she saw in him.

Roggen returned to the room with a silver tray in her hands. She put it down and poured the tea, and without looking at Kristina, began to speak.

'I don't know if you've heard, but Richard joined the Forces. He's been sent to Singapore.' She set down the silver teapot. 'I'm supposed to be joining him as soon as possible but how can I leave the country not knowing what's happened to Eden?'

'You must go to be with Richard, it's your duty as a wife, mind.' Kristina attempted to smile. 'Anyway, you must be missing him like nobody's business.'

'I suppose I am, Kris.' Roggen smiled ruefully. 'In any case, I feel I should be at his side at this moment.' She shook back her hair. 'He's not in any danger though, he won't be on active service, apparently his age is against him. Isn't it ridiculous, they are giving the plum jobs to youngsters of nineteen and twenty.' She sighed. 'And I know Richard, he must feel bitter about being given a desk job.'

She sat down and sipped her tea. 'To think that before I heard about the loss of the *Chware Teg* my only worries were about the sort of clothes I should take abroad with me. How trivial it all seems now.'

'Don't blame yourself for thinking normal thoughts, Ro, you weren't to know what would happen. Anyway,' she forced a lightness into her voice, 'it's very exciting for you, going on a journey to Singapore, and it all sounding so foreign.'

Roggen smiled. 'Of course it's foreign. You are funny, Kris.' She refilled her cup and smiled, obviously trying to behave as though nothing had happened. 'What about you, how's marriage and motherhood treating you?'

'I'm managing all right.' Kristina frowned. 'Though talking about travelling, Robert has suggested that I take the baby to my relatives in Lillehammer. It might be a good idea, Norway is a neutral country after all. And Robert wanted her to go, he wanted her safely away from Swansea. She warmed at the thought of him; Robert was a fine man in every way and she didn't deserve him.

Roggen nodded. 'Why not? You've always wanted to see the land your father came from.'

'Yes, but I didn't think it would take a war to send me across the North Sea,' Kristina said ruefully. Verdun stirred in the folds of his shawl and opened his eyes, and after a moment began to wave a small fist angrily in the air, a cry of protest rending the peacefulness of the room.

Kristina picked him up and adjusted the shawl so that it encompassed both of them, binding them together. Slowly she moved towards the door. 'I'd better be going now, Ro. I know it's a useless thing to say, but try not to worry too much.'

'All right, I'll try, and thanks for coming.' Her mouth trembled a little as she tried to smile.

As Kristina left Ty Coch, she came face to face with Bella. She paused, her mouth dry, not knowing what to say to the woman who had married Eden.

'I'm so sorry,' she said at last, in an almost inaudible whisper.

Bella's tone was cold. 'There's always hope, isn't there?' Bella's eyes swept over the baby, and Kristina, sensing the raw hunger in the other woman, understood it only too well. It was no secret that Bella longed for a child and now it might be too late. Kristina felt a momentary unease, wondering if Bella, a shrewd woman, would see how like Eden the baby was.

She hugged Verdun closer to her. 'I'd better get off home then, only came to give Ro my sympathies.' She saw no softening of Bella's white face and she turned, hurrying away.

She walked briskly up the hill to her home, the baby held firmly in her arms and a mixture of sadness and hope warring within her.

Once indoors, away from prying eyes, she put Verdun in his crib and left him to the silence of the bedroom. She sat alone in the kitchen, staring into the fire and at last allowing herself to think about Eden. The idea of him being lost at sea, perhaps injured and suffering was painful to her, and she realized that there was a large part of her that still cared for him. Now Eden might never see the son he had sired, would not even have the comfort of knowing he was a father. Perhaps she should have told him the truth.

Then she told herself not to be foolish. Eden had married another woman, it was best he did not know that the boy was his. Even if he came back from sea unscathed, he must never be allowed to learn the true facts. *If* he came back, a small voice said within her head. Kristina tried to rationalize the situation to herself. She must not allow herself to grieve — Eden had a wife to wait and grieve for him — it was none of her business.

The day she heard the news that Eden was missing was the day she made up her mind to become Robert's wife in fact as well as in name. She owed him such a debt of gratitude that it could never be fully repaid, but she would make one last try to save her marriage. From now on, her husband's happiness must be her chief concern, for with the war encroaching on all their lives, who could tell how long they had together? Robert might well decide to enlist — he had spoken of it several times — though he could stay safely at home if he chose because of his work on the docks.

But the war was demanding more and more of Britain's

resources, there was no indication of when it would end, and a rush of patriotism was sweeping the town of Swansea like a wave. If Robert did enlist, she would definitely take Verdun to Norway, she decided, but for now she would do her best to be an ideal wife.

She walked silently up the stairs to check that the baby was still asleep. He was peaceful beneath fluffy blankets and Kristina looked down at him, marvelling afresh at his likeness to his father. His hair had grown thick and dark from the moment of his birth and his eyes when he looked at her were like Eden's, clear and piercing.

She knelt at the side of the crib and let memories wash over her. She was in Eden's embrace where she had longed to be ever since she was a child, for even then she had loved him. But they were meant to go separate ways; it was like walking along a preordained trail where there were many twists and turns, but only one way forward for each of them. They were not destined for each other. From different classes, almost different breeds of people, they would have made an incongruous couple.

She heard the door open, and then Robert was in the hallway, taking off his coat and cap, uncompromisingly a working man in spite of the rise in his fortunes and the comparative grandness of his surroundings.

She hurried downstairs. She would have his meal ready by the time he had washed away the grime of the docks. Then later, in the marriage bed, she would become Mrs Robert Jenkins, and memories of the past would be laid to rest like so many insubstantial ghosts.

Bella returned to the new house Eden had bought for her, a feeling of anger rising within her. She closed the door on the outside world and stared at herself in the hall mirror. She saw a woman with a mouth that trembled and with a darkness in her eyes. She saw again in her mind's eye the meeting with Kristina Jenkins on the doorstep of Ty Coch. She could not have failed to observe the protective way Kristina had held her child close. Eden's child.

Bella had always suspected that something had gone on between the girl and Eden. There had been no mistaking the tingling spark generated between them whenever they were in the same room. And much as she had fought to make Eden hers, she knew she had never really possessed him. Perhaps no one would ever possess him.

She had asked him once and once only about his feelings for Kristina. He had held her in his arms and smiled down into her eyes, and assured her that she was his wife, his only love, and that there was no one else in his life. After that the subject had never been raised again. But the meeting earlier with the girl had confirmed her worst fears; the baby boy was the image of Eden and the wonder was that no one else had noticed it. Perhaps they had, it was possible that everyone in Lambert's Cottages knew about the child and she, the wife, was the last one to learn of it.

What gave her the most pain was the thought of her own failure to bear Eden a son. If they'd had a brood of infants running around their cold and lonely home, it would have bound them closer and she would have made him truly happy.

She moved into the sitting room and dropped her coat carelessly over a chair. Bella had been brought up to expect others to clear up after her. She was not selfish so much as thoughtless, taking it for granted that her role in life was to be waited on. She sank down into a chair and kicked off her shoes. She had managed to conceal her chagrin from Roggen, had talked with her about Eden and his chances of survival, both of them agreeing that he must be safe. His body had not been found and so neither of them would accept his death until there was proof of it.

Roggen had been in tears and Bella had speculated on the scene between her sister-in-law and that awful Kristina. Doubtless they would have talked about Eden, they would have comforted each other and shared, really shared in their grief. Bella accepted that Kristina was an inevitable part of the closed community that was Lambert's Cottages, but it was a heavy yoke to bear.

The horror of her husband's disappearance washed over her afresh. Eden's ship torpedoed. No sign of survivors. Widowhood. The very word was cold and harsh, but the reality would be even harsher. She would be a woman alone with no chick or child to live for while that low-born woman had everything – Eden's child and a doting husband who had provided her with luxury and even a position of sorts in the town.

Bella tried to push her anger aside but she could not. She thought of Eden with that girl and the pain tore at her. Kristina was so stunningly beautiful, so tall and with such an air of innocence about her that must be quite enchanting to a man. And she, this common girl from one of the small cottages on the docklands, had given Eden what Bella had singularly failed to do, she had borne him a son.

The anger and jealousy rushed and pounded in her head. Bella wanted Eden here so that she could confront him with the proof of his infidelity. Would he deny any knowledge of the child? Perhaps he really *didn't* know that this girl had borne him a son. She chewed her lip. It was possible he took it for granted that the child was born of Kristina's marriage.

The anger drained away. Eden might even now be dead, drowned by the uncaring seas. She, his wife, should be praying for his return, not blaming him within her heart for his past affairs which in all conscience had nothing to do with her. Eden had come to her marriage bed having forsaken all others, Bella was sure of that at least. There had been no betrayal of marriage vows or of Bella's trust. What had happened before their marriage was none of her business.

Bella leaned forward, her head resting wearily in her hands, and the tears so long denied came tumbling unchecked down her cheeks. It was true she would never possess his soul, but all she wanted in that moment was to have him safe in her arms.

Kristina was aware that Robert was regarding her carefully when she entered the kitchen after putting Verdun down for the night. The muted light gave a soft glow to Robert's handsome face, highlighting his strong features and adding a gleam to his eyes. She knew he was wondering whether she had heard about Eden's ship and she felt him search her face for any sign of tears. But there wouldn't be any, her crying for Eden was within her, locked away out of sight.

'How was work?' she asked him as she always did, and he brushed back his shock of dark hair and sighed.

'It's been a damned difficult day.' He sat down at the table. 'When I went back this afternoon there was a ship in, so that meant capping out, choosing who would work, and leaving the other sods to idle away the day. It's getting me down, I'm so sick of it all. It'll be a good thing when some more of the men join up and there's not so many queuing up for work with hunger written all over their faces.'

Kristina poured his tea, hot and strong and sweetened with condensed milk just as he liked it. She hated condensed milk, it clung to the spoon and ran down the sides of the tin. However careful she was, she always dripped some on to the fresh tablecloth.

She didn't have to ask Robert what he meant. Kristina knew the capping-out routine by heart. Her stepfather had thrown it at her enough times for her to fear it almost as much as the dockers did. It was a primitive ritual, almost barbaric in its simplicity. The men waiting for work would stand in a circle around the figure of power, the works allocator, Robert Jenkins, and would be chosen or rejected for work that day or any day. If a man fell foul of the dockers' code, he could be rejected indefinitely and reduced to the soul-destroying act of touting for any sort of work.

'What's to eat?' Robert said predictably, and Kristina smiled. They had both fallen rapidly into the ways of an old married couple and without once sharing the same bed. And yet lately a change had come over Robert, he was distant, more inclined to pick on small things, so ready to quarrel with her – and who could blame him? He had all the problems of married life without any of the privileges.

But tonight it would be different. She would go to his room, share his bed and consummate their marriage. There was no telling how long they would have together as man and wife but she needed to feel that she had made him happy, if only for a short space of time.

'It's cawl, Robert, can't you smell it?' she said, setting out the deep soup dishes. 'Cawl filled with good beef and carrots. And then to follow I've made some Welsh cakes.'

If he was surprised at the warmth of her voice, he gave no sign. He drew towards him the bowl of rich smelling cawl freshly ladled from the huge cooking pot, and took up a thick slice of bread.

Robert was a fastidious man and he ate with surprising delicacy, a habit of which Kristina approved. Her stepfather had been a pig, inelegantly slopping food into his mouth and then rubbing the plate with a piece of bread to finish his meal. But she need not worry about Thomas any more, she had Robert to care for her now, and she'd been a fool to risk jeopardizing her marriage by her neglect of her duty all this time.

There was no excuse, she was well over the birth of the baby, and her strength had returned much more quickly than she had anticipated. She glanced shyly at Robert, wondering what he would say if she blurted out the fact that she intended to sleep with him from now on. Would he repulse her? The thought was frightening.

She barely touched her food. She was as nervous as a young, virgin bride, which was just foolishness, she told herself. She was an experienced woman, had known a lover and the pangs of motherhood. And yet her hands shook as she took away the soup and brought out the Welsh cakes, still hot from the griddle and smelling deliciously of sultanas.

Robert had warned her to conserve her dried foods. He forecast that there would be shortages of imported goods, and so far Kristina had scarcely taken any notice. But now, with the sinking of the *Chware Teg*, war seemed to have become a reality.

She pushed the thought aside; tonight she must concentrate all her energy and emotion on becoming Robert's wife. She washed up the dishes quickly and efficiently, her mind not on the task but going over and over the moves she would make towards Robert.

What she would wear to bed had become suddenly very important. She had but few nightgowns, most of them plain, well-washed cotton, but there was one made of silk. She had bought it on a whim when she had childishly imagined that one day Eden would marry her. It was a honeymoon gown, slim fitting and sensuous to touch. It dipped down in the front, revealing her full breasts and was edged with real lace. She had not looked at it since her marriage to Robert and had only brought it with her to her new home because she did not want to leave it behind at Lambert's Cottages.

'I'm going to wash and go up to bed,' she said softly. 'Turn out the lights before you come up, mind.'

He scarcely glanced up at her from the paper he was reading and, somehow disappointed, she tiptoed up-stairs, not wanting to waken the baby. She washed and undressed in the coldness of the bathroom and stood shivering with apprehension as she allowed the fine silk to slip over her head and fall shimmering to her feet.

She heard Robert come upstairs and go into his bedroom along the landing, and she peered at herself in the mirror. Her reflection showed a woman with shining hair and a sensual body, but all Kristina saw were the shadows beneath her eyes and the trembling of her lips.

Taking a deep breath, she stepped out on to the landing, and padded silently along the corridor. Robert's door was ajar and through the small aperture she caught sight of him sitting on the bed, his head in his hands.

Quickly, anxiously, she moved into the room and touched his shoulder. 'Robert, there's something wrong. What is it, please tell me, *cariad*.'

He groaned as he saw her and turned his face away. 'For God's sake, Kristina, don't torment me like this, will you?' His voice was savage. 'I'm only human, mind, how can I keep myself under control if you come to me looking like that?'

She cupped his face in her hands and moved closer to him so that her silk-clad body was close enough for him to touch.

'I don't want you to be under control, Robert,' she whispered softly. 'I want you to be my husband.'

'Why now?' he demanded. 'Is it because Eden Lamb has been lost and you think I'm all you've got left?'

She shook back her hair, trying to excuse his hurtful words, understanding that they arose out of his own pain.

'I don't know why now, Robert, it just seems right. I want us to be man and wife. I always intended it to be that way, you've got to believe me.'

Without rising from the bed, he put his arms around her slowly, almost reluctantly, and drew her closer to him. His head was against her breast and he sighed heavily.

'I hope you mean it, Kristina,' he said, 'because once you are mine, I'll never let you go.'

'I mean it,' she said simply and bent her head to touch the springy hair with her lips.

He kissed her breasts, pushing aside the silk gown with his mouth, and she felt with an almost sensuous thrill the scrape of his unshaved cheek against her soft flesh. She groaned. It had been so long, so very long since she'd lain in a man's arms; she was young and hot blooded and she recognized in that moment that she needed Robert as much as he needed her.

He pushed her gently back against the pillows and leaned above her, his lips exploring her breasts, her neck

281

and finally her mouth. She felt her breathing become ragged as desire flowed through her. She was used to Robert, the scent of him, the look of him, and yet never until now had she known the tactile pleasure of his hands caressing her intimately, his body hard against hers.

She was lost in a mist of desire. Love, uncomprehendingly, was mingled with the physical urge to be one with this man who was taking command of her in such a compelling way. He was fierce in his pleasure, almost rough, so urgent was his need. And yet Robert waited, held back, bringing Kristina's desire to such a pitch that she thought she could not bear any more of the exquisite sensations he was bringing her.

She cried out and clung to him as Robert held her close. Was this love? It surely could not all be lust? The climax when it came drew them both into a vortex of pleasure. Kristina felt she was possessed utterly, abandoning herself to the glorious feelings of her body. Robert held her to him as though he could never penetrate deeply enough to dispel the barriers that had been between them. In the afterglow they clung together, breath mingling like children spent from too much playing.

It was several moments before Robert leaned on one elbow and smiled down at her, pushing her tangled hair away from her face.

'Well, Mrs Jenkins,' he said softly, 'I think I can safely say that you are now my wife.'

And that was just how she felt, she was truly a wife at last.

22

Nia sat in the window of her new home and stared around her as though assessing the images of fine furniture, rich hangings and soft carpeting objectively, through the eyes of a stranger. This was her fourth home and she wondered if she might find happiness in the large, elegant house perched on the shelving slopes of Mount Pleasant. It was a large house with long windows overlooking the five-mile sweep of Swansea Bay and the huddled hills of Mumbles Head jutting out into the sea. And it was her own.

Her first home had been the vicarage, a spacious house filled with books, smelling of old leather and pipe tobacco. The Vicarage held mostly painful images for she had left it with her father under a cloud of disgrace. The vicar's crime was not so much in dealing with illegal bets as in being found out.

She had moved to a smaller, less elegant home on the docks, spending her blighted childhood among the uncritical people of the docklands. She had grown to live and breathe the scents of tar and rope and sea winds, and had taken for granted the comparative comforts offered by her father's ill-gotten gains.

And then she had moved up to Joe Barnes's house in Byrnhyfred, had lived out her girlish dreams as she had stared across the wide Black Road and watched the River Tawe flow to the sea. There in the simple cottage she had known contentment and had become a woman in Joe's arms. There too she had known disillusionment and heartache, the pain of betrayal. But now all that was past.

She was living in comfort, a businesswoman respected in the community and being courted by the eminently suitable Colin Singleton.

She moved restlessly. Colin had been so busy since the disappearance of his partner, and the strain was beginning to show in his face. The talk of Eden Lamb's shipwreck still haunted the shops and public bars of Swansea, and Nia had come to realize that such speculation was something to be turned into hard cash, but certainly not by her. She had been horrified that other bookmakers were taking bets on Eden's fate. Was he drowned or was he safe somewhere? There was a great deal of money being staked on the matter but Nia refused to have anything to do with it all.

Colin knew nothing about her job except that she ran a couple of perfectly legal betting offices where the wealthy could place bets without cash changing hands. He had brushed aside her explanation that credit betting was legal with a dismissive wave of his hand.

'You know what you're doing, Nia.' His smile had been warm. 'I trust you to handle your business in a proper manner.'

A proper manner. Proper, wasn't that what she had always wanted to be? Respectable, accepted among the eminent business people of Swansea. At last she was well on her way to realizing her ambition.

Then why wasn't she happy? She could not explain her present mood of restlessness even to herself. Was it that almost a week had passed with no word from Colin? But then she knew and accepted that he was heavily committed to the shipping business. Now that there was a war on, the business of the docks was even more vital and pressing.

Nia sighed and studied her immaculately manicured nails. Was it marriage she wanted, or simply love? Could it be that she had not quite shaken off the feelings she'd had for Joe Barnes. He had given her physical joy but emotionally he had left her barren.

As she rose and studied herself in the oval mirror hanging over the marble fireplace, the telephone bell rang out stridently from the hallway and Nia was momentarily startled. It took a bit of getting used to, having a phone in the house. She wondered if she would ever become accustomed to an instrument that allowed intrusive voices into her home.

'Hello?' She spoke quietly but with an air of authority that she was not conscious of. 'Who is it?'

'I must see you.' The voice was harsh, disembodied, Joe's voice. 'Please, Nia, don't hang up. I'm desperate.'

She caught back a sigh. 'What's wrong, Joe?' She spoke carefully, not wanting to show signs of softening and yet reluctant to appear entirely hostile. He had, after all, been part of her life for some time.

'I didn't realize how much I would miss you, Nia,' he said quickly. 'My life is so empty now that you've gone. I know it's too late for us to get back together, but if you'd only let me see you, speak to you, it would mean so much to me.'

'It would be unsettling, Joe,' she said softly. 'What happened between us is over, it's history.'

'You're right, I know you're right, but at least see me, let's talk. It's not much to ask for old times sake, is it?'

Nia sighed, glancing at the clock. Time was passing so slowly and the day stretched before her long and empty. She could, of course, take a trip to one of her offices but to what purpose when they were run on oiled wheels by her hand-picked managers?

'All right, come over, Joe, but you are not to stay long, mind.' She sounded like a reproving schoolmarm but Joe did not seem to notice.

'You won't regret it, I promise you.' He put the phone down before she could reply and slowly she retraced her steps into the sitting room, biting her lip thoughtfully. An unexpected flutter of excitement brought colour to her face as she stood before the fire, staring at the coals. The flames were burning low, needing replenishment, and she rang the bell absentmindedly, hardly hearing the strident sounds echoing through the house and below stairs.

The 'maid' was an old woman by Nia's standard, drawn and lined, her eyes faded as though they had looked too long on the trials of life and wanted to see no more.

'Mrs Preece, would you build up the fire?' Nia sank into a chair and studied the woman's stooped shoulders as she knelt in the hearth. It had been Colin's idea to take her on, but then he was soft-hearted, given to helping the less fortunate, which didn't always pay, Nia had found.

'We must find you a young girl to help with the heavy work.' She did not want to sound too sympathetic – sympathy was mostly unwanted and misguided – and yet she did not relish the sight of such a frail woman struggling with the coal scuttle. Irritation with herself and the woman rose to the surface and Nia bit her lip against the rush of angry words. 'Go on, leave it now, that will do,' she said, and immediately Mrs Preece rose and self-effacingly made her way from the room as though apologizing for her existence.

'Damn!' Nia took up the slim silver case from the table and extracted a cigarette, lighting it impatiently and sucking in the smoke greedily. Damn Colin for playing on her emotions. Why hadn't he taken the woman into his own household if he'd been so anxious about her welfare?

Her face softened to a smile as she pictured Colin's tall frame, his long legs which appeared always in the way, and the tilt to his head. She supposed she loved him, enjoyed his gentle lovemaking, but she did not respond to him the way she had responded to Joe. The earth-shattering rush of feeling that came when Joe took her in his arms was gone. Perhaps it came only once in a lifetime and in the end it had proved false.

But what would it be like to experience it just once more? She probed the thought as though probing a sore tooth with her tongue, and shivered. She dared not allow herself to fall into Joe's clutches again, she had proved him false and she would be a fool to trust him again. Wouldn't she?

She wandered upstairs and into the bedroom and stood looking into the full-length mirror. In the reflection the colours of the room were muted to soft shaded greys, grey carpet and soft grey curtains touched here and there with a warm rose. It was a good room, a tasteful room, and yet it lacked vibrancy, just like her life.

The doorbell rang and Nia glanced at herself quickly. She wore a frock that hung just above her knees and clung to her curves as though moulded there. She still had the figure of a young girl, but then why shouldn't she? She had borne no children, she was barren.

Mrs Preece was calling up the stairs to her, and taking her time Nia walked down to the hallway, aware of Joe on the step watching her hungrily.

'That's all right, Mrs Preece,' Nia said, and led the way into the sitting room. Joe followed without any sign of hesitancy, unaffected by the grandeur surrounding him, and firmly closed the large double doors. He had isolated himself and Nia in the room together as though asserting his old claims to her. She was having none of that.

'Do sit down,' she said distantly, and stood above him, her eyes expressionless. 'And what do you have to say to me so urgently?' She might have been talking to a stranger, but Joe was not easily subdued.

'Nia, I've no right to ask anything of you.' He spoke softly and his eyes travelled over her slim figure longingly. Nia could not resist the surge of triumph that washed through her. He had thrown away her love so lightly but now he wanted her, and the taste of revenge was sweet in her mouth. She could not resist it.

'The thought of the plump and silly Williams girl is no longer so enchanting, is that it?'

Joe brushed back his thick springy hair. 'She offered herself to me with open arms,' he said shrugging. 'Any man with good red blood in his veins would have to be a saint to resist.'

287

Nia felt the old anger, the old sense of inferiority rise to choke her. 'You found it difficult to resist such a cheap, common little floosie?' Her tone was venomous and Joe half smiled.

'She meant nothing, a moment's distraction. If only you hadn't found us that day it would have died a natural death.'

'But I did find you, and in *my* bed. Can't you even now see the depths of your betrayal, Joe?'

'I was a fool.' He looked up at her appealingly. 'I didn't stop to think what I was doing to us, but Nia, I've realized since just how much I love you and need you.'

He rose and slipped his arm around her waist, and Nia pushed his arm away quickly. He persisted, drawing her closer, and she stared up at his firm jaw, the broad neck and the well-muscled shoulders with something like curiosity. Could he still rouse her to the heights of passion?

His hands were softly caressing her spine and she allowed him to continue, waiting expectantly for the rush of feeling that would not seem to come. His mouth was upon her forehead, his lips brushing against her eyelashes, touching her neck. His hands slid to her breasts, cupping them, rubbing gently at the nipples that were erect beneath the silky material of her frock.

In spite of herself, Nia felt her breath quicken, her arm crept round his shoulders and then she was pressed close to his maleness. How well she remembered the scent of Joe, the Woodbine taste of his mouth and the clean-washed smell of his skin. She felt sensation rise within her, his touch filling her with desire. He was urging her towards the door but she resisted, not wanting to take him to the private tranquility of her bedroom. He must not be allowed to invade so far into her life.

'No.' She tried to draw away but Joe held on to her insistently, pushing her downwards on to the soft pile of the carpet. 'No,' she said again, but he was already lifting the skirts of her frock, his hand brushing beneath the elastic of her suspenders, fingers probing intimately as though it was his right.

Nia tried to twist away but her mind told her it was already too late. She had allowed him to go too far, he would not, could not stop now. He mounted her with a smile of triumph, his hands gripping her hips.

'There's soft we were to stay apart so long. You want me as much as I want you.' He gasped as he thrust deeply, his eyes dark and unseeing in passion. He tore at her bodice, freeing her small breasts, and grasped her nipple in his hot mouth.

Nia began to feel passion ebb away from her. Joe was like a rooting pig, he lacked finesse. She was used to Colin now, his gentleness, his delicate touch rousing in her love as well as desire. She was a fool allowing herself to be used, manipulated by Joe Barnes. As he heaved above her she saw him for what he really was; a man out to grasp greedily at life, taking like a child unable and perhaps unwilling to give even a little part of himself. What would come later, the soft touch perhaps? The not-so-subtle hint that some money would not come amiss?

He pushed away at her and Nia felt disgust for Joe and for herself. She wished for nothing now but for the self-revealing episode to be over. She had no one to blame but herself, but now her curiosity was quietened. She knew that she had never loved Joe Barnes. The layers of lust and the childish rose-coloured spectacles had been torn away and now she could see him for what he really was; an adequate but insensitive lover who at the earliest opportunity would be making love to some other woman, any other woman.

He rolled away from her at last and lay gasping at her side. Carefully, Nia picked up her torn lace knickers and removed the laddered stockings, and left the room.

When she returned a few moments later, Joe was standing near the window, his coat carelessly thrown on so that his braces were revealed. He looked like a working man, awkward at finding himself in such dainty surroundings.

'That's that,' Nia said matter-of-factly. 'Perhaps you'd like to go now.' She had spoken with deliberate casualness and Joe turned quickly, looking at her as though she had grown two heads.

'Go?' he said foolishly, and the air of a male having brought a female to panting submission vanished. 'But why, Nia, I thought . . .' His voice trailed away as Nia walked to the door and opened it.

'I think we both learned something today,' she said softly. 'I learned that I don't need you, can't even see why I thought I loved you, and you, well, you have learned that you can't rule the world with your genitals.'

'You cow!' He spoke disbelievingly. 'You've just played with me, treated me like . . .' He searched desperately for words.

'A whore?' supplied Nia. 'Well, now you know what it feels like, perhaps in future you'll be more caring of the women you take into your bed.' She stared hard at him. 'We have feelings, Joe, we are not just pieces of flesh put on earth for your gratification. Love begins with a two-way trust – but then you don't even know the meaning of the word. Go back to your little Anita, if she hasn't yet found you out, that is.'

He took a step towards her, his face dark with anger, his arm raised threateningly. Nia faced him without flinching.

'I wouldn't, if I were you, Joe. I have some influential men among my customers who wouldn't like it if I was attacked in my own home by some hooligan.' She adjusted the cameo brooch at her throat. 'Indeed, I think some of them might feel the need to take action against you, legal action, of course.' She half smiled. 'I can just see you in court, Joe, with clever lawyers walking all over you.'

Suddenly the tension went out of him and Joe smiled, his easy, charming smile. 'Why was I fool enough to let you go? We could have done big things together, me and you.'

'You could be right, Joe,' Nia shrugged, 'but it's all past now, water under the bridge. If ever I doubted it was finished, today has proved it to me.'

She led him towards the front door. 'See you round, Joe,' she said. He paused for a moment, his hands thrust into his pockets, his eyes lit with some inner triumph.

'One thing.' He smiled. 'That baby you always wanted by me, well, you missed the boat there, didn't you?'

She was suddenly tense, she *had* wanted a child by Joe and she didn't like to be reminded of that fact.

'So?' She held up her head challengingly and his smile widened so that she could see the neat even teeth beneath his dark moustache.

'Well, Anita has gone one better than you. She's having my baby, she's giving me something you could never give. Not that silly, is she?'

He turned and strode easily away from the house, and as Nia watched him swing down the drive she bit her lip, surprised that his words had the power to hurt her. And she wasn't fooled for one minute by his apparent coolness. Joe was furious, burning mad with her, and she would have to watch out for him. She stared out for a moment at the darkening sky, her gaze falling to the stocky figure moving away downhill towards the lights of the town.

'Goodbye, Joe,' she said softly, and closed the door with a click of finality.

The sky was heavy with threatened rain as Anita let herself into her mother's house. 'Mam, it's only me!' She pulled her arms out of the sleeves of her inadequate coat and flung it on a chair. 'Mam, where are you?'

There was a faint calling from the kitchen and Anita pushed open the door, recoiling at the rush of steam and the heavy smell of boiling linen.

'*Duw*, come like yourself, girl.' Mrs Williams rubbed her hands on her apron and smiled a welcome. 'I thought it was the rent man there for a minute.'

Anita sat on one of the wooden kitchen chairs and eased her shoes from her swollen feet. 'There's nice to sit down,' she said. 'I've walked all the way from Brynhyfred and my shoes not as good as they might be, there's a hole in one of them, see? Got a bit of cardboard have you?'

'Why don't you ask that man of yours to buy you some decent shoes, girl. He's got the money, him being a coal man and all that.'

'Joe will buy me shoes, don't worry.' Anita was on the defensive. 'I've only got to ask, mind, and he'll give me anything.'

'Aye, a good hiding maybe.' Mrs Williams brewed a pot of tea and sat down opposite her daughter. 'What do you want, love? I haven't got much money if that's what you're after, and I've got your sisters to think of. You're on your own now, Anita.'

Anita pouted and stared down at her nails. 'I came to give you good news, Mam, and you not making me very welcome.'

'Here, have a cup of tea and stop being childish. What good news? I could do with cheering up.'

Anita looked up coyly. 'Guess what? You're going to be a granny!' She gazed at her mother, disappointed at her lack of response. Wasn't she supposed to leap up and embrace her daughter and weep a few tears? But then, Mam had never been a proper mother, always wrapped up in herself and her own problems.

'That's what you call good news?' Mrs Williams sighed. 'Getting yourself in the family way is all very well if there's a ring on your finger, but without one you'll find folks looking down on you.'

'Joe and me, we're going to get married, thrilled to little pieces about the baby, he is.' She studied her figure thoughtfully. 'It'll be nice when it shows, then Joe will realize it's true.' She smiled.

'Lived with that Nia Powell long enough, didn't he, she didn't get him to marry her.' Mrs Williams glanced quickly at her daughter.

'But this is different. I'm going to have his baby.' Anita patted her stomach complacently. 'Joe will marry me all right. He knows I'm a real woman because I'm going to give him a son.' She laughed. 'He did it right with me, sec.' Her mother frowned disapprovingly.

'No need to be common, our Nita, and remember, it's easy getting a baby, not so easy keeping it when it needs clothes on its back and shoes on its feet.'

'Oh, Mam!' Anita was exasperated. 'Do you always have to be such a wet blanket? I came down by here to tell you my good news and all you've done is moan and groan about it.'

'Well, times are bad, mind,' Mrs Williams said. 'I don't know if you've noticed it or not but there's a war on. Food will be short, mind, and prices will go up, they always do, and you should have had the sense to get Joe Barnes to marry you proper like before you gave in to him. Once men have what they want they very often don't want it any more.'

'We haven't seen much of the war here, Mam, so don't be so gloomy,' Anita snapped. This meeting wasn't going at all as she'd envisaged. Where was the warm embrace, the plans to knit small garments, the good wishes for future happiness?

'Well, you're forgetting that one of your sisters is working in the Bridgend ammunition factory on them shell things, coming home all yellow from the powder, she is. Dangerous work it is, mind, one of the girls had her hand blown off in spite of the glass and steel that was supposed to protect her.'

'Well, I don't know about that,' Anita pouted. 'I got me a proper job so that I wouldn't have to go into the factory, didn't I?'

'A proper job warming Joe Barnes's bed!' Mrs Williams was flushed. 'There's a war on, mind, and you should be doing your bit like your sisters, not sitting there telling me you're having a babba.'

'Oh, Mam, don't keep on!' Anita had heard enough

about the war. She had come here to talk about herself and her baby, not something that was happening far away and had no bearing on her life whatsoever.

'Wake up, Nita,' her mother persisted. 'The war is really happening and you can't make it go away by ignoring it.'

'But do we have to talk about it all the time?' Anita said irritably. She rose and pulled on her coat indignantly. 'God in heaven, I come here to tell you about my baby and I've not even been given a welcoming cup of tea, there's selfish you are sometimes, Mam.'

'I'm sorry, love.' Mrs Williams was contrite. 'It's just that down by here on the docks we know there's a war on, what with Mr Eden Lamb lost at sea and all. Sit down, girl, I'll get you a cup of nice hot tea and a Welsh cake. You always liked Welsh cakes, didn't you?'

'Don't bother.' Anita was on her high horse, dragging the too-small coat around her plump figure. 'I'll go home to Joe, at least he don't go on moaning all the time about the horrible war, enough to make me put my head in the gas oven you are, Mam.'

'Don't talk like that, for shame, girl, and you young and healthy and with a babba on the way. That's sinful talk, that is.'

Anita made for the door. 'Sorry I came I am, mind, our mam.' She paused. 'Tell the girls about the baby, perhaps my sisters will be more interested than my mother seems to be.'

'Oh, now don't be like that.' Mrs Williams rubbed her hands together in agitation. 'Sit a while, see, it's nice and sunny outside, we'll put a chair in the doorway and you can get some fresh air while I make a pot of tea.'

Anita was mollified. She waited while her mother dragged a kitchen chair towards the door and set it in the slant of sunlight. 'All right then, but I can't stay long. Joe will be home for his tea soon, likes me to be there when he comes in from work, he does.'

The rain clouds had vanished, the sun was hot, and the

scents from the docklands drifted in from the sea on the gentle breeze. Tar and salt and spices and old rope, these were familiar and welcome scents. Occasionally when the wind was right the unpleasant odour from the fish market pervaded the cottages so badly that people closed the doors and windows.

The kettle was boiling on the fire and the tinkle of teacups soothed Anita's ruffled feelings. It was good sometimes to be pampered for if she waited for Joe, she'd wait for ever. Not that he wasn't good to her, mind. He was a little thoughtless at times, eager for his own gratification, but that only proved how much he wanted her. And he was generous, he did not keep her short of money.

She glanced ruefully at her worn shoes. It was her own fault that they had not been tapped at the cobblers, for she had taken the money and bought a silly, feathery hat with it. Still, she would coax Joe and he would give her more, especially if she asked him in bed. At such times, she found, a man would give a girl practically anything she asked for.

She heard without interest the mournful drone of a plane somewhere in the distance and took the cup of tea from her mother with a nod of her head.

'Plenty of milk in it now is there, Mam? And you know I like my tea sweet.'

Mrs Williams moved away from the door. 'I'll just get the tin of Welsh cakes from the pantry,' she said, her tone conciliatory.

The sound of the plane was louder, it seemed to be flying nearer the docklands. It was a heavy, monotonous noise as though the pilot could get no thrust from the engines. Anita put up her hand to shade her eyes and saw dimly a sharp shape hovering over her, outlined against the sun. There was a crackling sound that Anita couldn't quite identify. There were cries from the docks and figures running wildly between the sheds. And the aeroplane came onward.

Anita could see it clearly now. It seemed to be spitting fire but she was not afraid, she had no reason to fear the object high above her. Suddenly she was jerked back against the wooden chair as if a heavy blow had caught her chest. There was no pain. Another blow caught her stomach and another her shoulder.

There was a look of surprise on her face as she saw blood spurting through the print patterns of her frock. She heard her mother screaming, screaming, screaming. And then there was darkness. The war had come to claim Anita Williams.

23

The mountains were high and rugged, capped with pristine snow, the fiords glistened like upturned mirrors in the spring sunshine. Norway was a very beautiful place to call home.

Kristina sat in the house of the kindly strangers who were her father's family, holding Verdun tightly in her arms, her fingers gripping his plump hand. He had been fractious ever since she had embarked with him on the journey to Norway but now he lay sleeping peacefully, his dark lashes resting on plump cheeks.

Kristina's welcome had been warm; from the moment she had introduced herself she had been swept into the household, relieved of her baggage and plied with hot milk chocolate drinks. She had glanced around the bright living room, seated herself on the plump sofa and immediately felt at home. And more, she knew that her father's sister was a woman after her own heart.

Auntie Liv was tall and smooth-skinned in spite of her age, and her auburn hair held just a trace of white at the temples. Uncle Ulric was not at home and though it was not spoken of overtly, Kristina was aware that he was on Norwegian business, trying to stave off the complete takeover of his country by the German troops.

'It is not so happy that you come to Norway now.' Her aunt poured another creamy cup of chocolate, laced it with brandy and handed it to her. 'If we had known sooner of your visit, we could have warned you that all was not well here.' She smiled. 'Although I must say it, Lillehammer is very beautiful at this time of the year.' She waved her hand elegantly. 'Do not notice the cold, there is an unexpected turn in the weather but it will improve.'

'I love it here already,' Kristina said softly. 'And I think I would have known you anywhere, Aunt Liv.'

'And I you, so much like my dear brother.' She took Kristina's cup and refilled it. 'It is not so healthy in Norway right now, not with Quisling siding with the Germans and offering them ... what you say, our country on the platter.'

Germans in Norway. The dreaded enemy who had violated the peace of the docklands of Swansea with bullets and death were here in the country where Kristina had thought to find sanctuary. It was difficult to believe there was danger because the landscape of snows and sweeping fiords and beautiful mountains was so tranquil.

Kristina drew in a deep breath, realizing suddenly and with a sinking heart how far away she was from home. She had travelled across the North Sea from what had seemed the edge of Britain, the trip taking several days, cold, dangerous days when the heavy swell of the sea and the increasingly frosty air had made her wonder if she had been unwise to leave Wales.

It had been the strafing of the docks by a lone enemy bomber that had decided Robert that it would be best for her to go to Norway. Several dockers had been killed, one of them falling from the mast of the ship on which he was working into the grey waters of the dock. And then there had been the untimely, almost freakish death of poor Anita Williams who had been doing nothing more dangerous than sitting in the doorway of her mother's house.

'I'll be sick with worry about you all the time I'm at work.' Robert had held her tenderly in his arms. 'I'd like to think that you and the baby are well out of it, for with the docks such a prime target, we can be sure that this is only the first of many raids.'

'I don't want to leave you,' Kristina had protested and it had been true, Robert had proved himself a loving husband and he had taken to Verdun as if the little boy was his own son. But at last, when he insisted that his mind would be at rest with her away, she had agreed to go to Norway. Neither of them had known that the German army, far from honouring the neutrality of the Norwegians, was slowly, inexorably taking over the country.

'That Vidkun Quisling, he betrayed us all,' Auntie Liv said bitterly. 'He's set himself up as leader but he's nothing more than a German-lover. He's telling awful lies about King Haakon and having him hunted like an animal.' Her stern expression softened. 'So striking in good looks is our king,' she said proudly. 'Six foot seven inches tall, a fine handsome man with a distinguished moustache. Such a man it will be difficult to keep hidden for long.

'General von Falkenhorst is still in temporary quarters near Drobak,' Aunt Liv continued. 'The Germans don't trust that puppet prime minister Quisling any more than we do. They had counted on occupying more of Norway than just Oslo by now.'

She absentmindedly patted Verdun on his cheek. 'Fine baby but not like his grandpapa Olaf Larson at all. The boy's so dark, but very handsome.' She looked at Kristina. 'You child, you are the spit out of my brother's mouth, a true Larson.' She seemed to have a butterfly mind, changing from one topic of conversation to another without pause.

She rose to her feet and spoke decisively. 'We are happy to put you up a few days here, but then you must leave our country, return to England before we are overrun completely by the Germans.' She drew herself to her full, considerable height. 'We Norwegians fight the Germans, we offer our resistance with guns, even broomhandles if needed, but here there will be no place for mothers and babies.'

Kristina sighed softly. The journey across the sea had not been an easy one and with the added danger of

German U-boats in Norwegian waters the return would be even more hazardous. But she could see she would be in the way if she stayed, perhaps making life more difficult for her father's people, especially if it was discovered that she was not Norwegian but British.

'You are right, Aunt Liv,' Kristina said, 'I must take Verdun home as soon as possible.'

'I'm glad you agree.' Aunt Liv's smile softened. 'At this moment there is not much danger to any of us and it was not surprising that you got to us without being stopped.' Her aunt touched a finger to her neat plaits. 'Not many people in Lillehammer even realize yet that a very real war is almost upon us. The Germans, they do not think we have brains or courage to fight them, so they take their time over every little move.'

Kristina nodded. 'I saw the German flags flying in Oslo. The royal palace had been taken over by the army and outside there was a huge swastika, it was quite frightening. I was not sure then if I should turn round and go home or come on to Lillehammer.'

Aunt Liv leaned forward and put her hand over Kristina's. 'I'm glad you came, if only for a few days. I would not have missed meeting Olaf's child for the world.' She straightened. 'But as for the Germans, well, they will soon learn that we have outwitted them, for we mean to get our King and Government out of the country and into the hands of the Allies before the enemy have time to notice. Our gold reserves too must be saved.'

Aunt Liv glanced around as though in fear of being overheard and put her hand to her lips. 'But say nothing about this to anyone, it is only your cousin Kaare's job as manager in the bank that gives him this information.

'Come, I will take you to your room. You must be tired.' Aunt Liv smiled warmly as she led Kristina up the stairs to the room that was to be her home, at least for a few days.

Robert was standing on the docks, the sudden winds

from the sea sending ripples through his hair. The smell of petrol hung heavy in the air as the cranes lifted the volatile cargo, swinging the pallets crammed full of cans over the edge of the dock to be lowered slowly into the darkness of the hold.

Robert was a lonely figure as he stood supervising the work. He seemed to be the only man dressed in civilian clothes as he leaned against the barricade of sandbags stacked on the edge of the dock. Two men in army uniform stood ticking off the loads and a naval officer watched the proceedings, one foot resting on the edge of the ship. The dockers in the hold who manoeuvred the cargo into place were older men, not required to join the forces. Robert frowned; soon he would be a soldier too. Now that Kristina was safely despatched to Norway, he would be free to enlist.

The thought of his wife lifted his spirits. Soon, when all this nonsense of war was over, for it could not last long, he would have her back home, and the emptiness in which he now lived would be filled with her presence. She brought light and happiness into his life. With Kristina, he could drop the façade of toughness that his work on the docks demanded.

'Watch that load!' he called sharply as the crane moved too quickly, swinging the cargo dangerously close to the servicemen standing above the hold. They looked up at him in surprise and Robert moved swiftly, pushing the edge of the pallet as it almost knocked the servicemen into the abyss of the hold.

'Keep your eyes open,' Robert said harshly. 'The docks may not be the front line but it has its dangers for all that.'

The officer sniffed but the private respectfully moved back a pace. Robert shouted up at the crane driver who, though not hearing all his words, nodded in apology and moved the load more carefully down into the hold.

The officer took out a packet of cigarettes and Robert shook his head. 'No!' he said in disbelief at the man's stupidity. 'No smoking, not with petrol as a cargo.'

The young officer had the grace to look abashed as he put the packet away in his pocket. 'Sorry,' he said and looked down earnestly at his notepad.

By the time the load was stored away, Robert was tired and hungry, but he didn't want to go home to the empty house with its echoes of Kristina's voice and the sounds of the baby chuckling in his cot. Strangely enough, Robert missed Verdun very much. Although the child was not his, he had been present at the birth and had been with the baby through his small, childish ailments. When Verdun was feverish with a chill, Robert had held him, dabbing the hot brow with a cold cloth, talking soothingly to the baby while Kristina made up one of her herbal potions. It was easy, he had learned, to love the child of the man he hated.

In the warm, smoky atmosphere of the Burrows, Robert sat in a corner and drank his beer slowly, savouring the drink and the noise of the other men as they talked and argued about the war, its likely duration and Hitler's evil plans. The Führer had been underestimated by the world and treated as a harmless fanatic, but now he was proving far more ambitious and dangerous than anyone had believed possible.

From the corner of his eye, Robert saw Sugar Williams leaning against the bar, downing a pint of ale as though it were no more than an eggcupful. The man had his problems; his daughter killed on her mother's doorstep and a wife who seemed to have gone slightly over the edge with the grief of it all. Sugar was getting old but he was a good worker, a docker all his life, and his mates would close ranks around him. The dockers cared for their own in times of trouble.

Suddenly Robert felt he'd had enough. He wanted to get home and change out of his clothes that stank of petrol. He would wash away the sights and sound of the docks under the pump in the yard and then he would go to his lonely bed and think about his wife.

Aunt Liv pushed away her empty breakfast dish and

leaned forward. 'Tell me, Kaare, is it right that the gold bullion has been moved from the Bank of Norway,' she said softly, 'and that it is on its way here in bread vans and trucks and sledges, and that we shall have the honour of keeping it in the Lillehammer vaults.'

Kristina had just finished her breakfast. She put down her cutlery as she heard Uncle Ulric say something rapidly in Norwegian. Aunt Liv shook her head and glanced apologetically at Kristina.

'My husband thinks the less you know the better for you. It is not that he does not trust you but he does not want you put in danger, do you understand?'

'It's all right,' Kristina said quickly. 'I've got to see to Verdun anyway.'

She was relieved to go to the silence of her room. Every bone in her body ached and she felt lonely and homesick. She stared down at the baby tucked into the bed, sleeping soundly, and love for her child brought silly tears to her eyes. She missed Swansea, the sound of the sea on the shore, the clatter of the railway trains across the tracks, the hooting of tugs on the river. Robert too, she missed him most of all.

Suddenly she knew that even had the Germans not been on the point of occupying Norway, she could not have stayed. She wanted to go home to Swansea. Whatever the dangers the war might bring, she would face them in familiar surroundings and among her own people. And she would be at her husband's side where she belonged.

As the days passed and Kristina grew more accustomed to being with the Larsons she began to feel a great sense of pride. The Norwegian family, like her own Welsh kin, were fiercely patriotic and valued their freedom greatly.

It was quite apparent that something secret was going on, matters to which Kristina was not made privy. Then, early one morning, her sleep was interrupted by the sound of excited voices from downstairs. She pulled on her top coat and buttoned it up over her nightgown. She checked that Verdun was still asleep and tucked the blankets more firmly around his small frame. He stirred and sucked at his thumb, and she smiled and kissed him lightly before leaving the room.

In the hallway, Kaare was talking rapidly to his mother. He was fully dressed and was pulling a woollen hat over his shock of bright hair. He glanced at Kristina and smiled.

'You will have some story to take back to your Wales,' he said, then he opened the door and disappeared into the night.

Kaare Larson had become manager of the bank at Lillehammer at a very early age. He was, at thirty-five, a man who spoke several languages fluently and who could add a column of figures in his head in seconds flat. He had a fine memory and total recall of conversations that had taken place maybe months before, which was an asset in any business, for bits and pieces of information when added together sometimes made a very interesting and useful picture.

He was a man set to move to the top of his profession, perhaps becoming manager of the Bank of Oslo in good time, or maybe taking up politics and seeking a place in the government. But the coming of the Germans had put paid to that ambition, at least for the time being.

He stood now in the cold streets of Lillehammer, aroused from sleep by the chief constable to be told that outright war had begun and, excitingly, that the gold was on its way. He was not surprised. It was not in the Norwegian nature to suffer oppression without protest. How great it would be, how fine, to fool the Germans, who would wake up and find there were no reserves of gold in the whole of Norway.

The hours seemed long as they waited, standing on the steps of the bank, not wishing to miss the first sight of the convoy. Kaare had just returned from getting himself a hot drink when there was a sudden air of excitement in the small group of people waiting near the bank. The news was that the train of assorted vehicles carrying the gold bullion was in sight, drawing nearer the town.

'Damned fine job by our men.' The chief constable spoke puffing cold air like smoke with every word. 'God knows how the convoy has got here from Oslo. The bullion can't be easy to load or to move, must have worked their balls off, those boys.'

Kaare was not listening. His ear was tuned to the approach of the convoy, the low hum of many vehicles crawling through ice and snow towards the bank.

'They're here,' he said tersely. The sun had set the snow on fire, touching trees with gold and slanting brilliant light across the windows of the bank. Kaare felt emotion clutch at his throat as the first vehicle limped into sight, a milk van driven by a young boy with an elderly policeman seated at his side. The van seemed to sag sideways, the wheels slipping over the icy road, but the boy drove gamely, a grim look of determination on his young face.

The policeman alighted stiffly and stretched his arms above his head. His face was red with the cold and there were deep shadows beneath his eyes.

'Good boy, Finn,' he said as the boy, his youth and small stature evident now that he was out of the driving seat, smiled uncertainly. He was very pale and there was a smear of blood across his forehead.

Kaare stepped forward and greeted them. 'Lillehammer welcomes you,' he said, extending his hand to the policeman and then to the boy. 'Trouble?' He indicated the dried blood, and the boy nodded.

'Enemy plane,' he said, his voice was trembling with tiredness. 'Attacked the convoy, sprayed a hail of bullets at us, killed a few of the men and my father among them, the bastards.'

'Come inside,' Kaare said at once, 'I'll see that you have a hot drink with a lacing of something special.'

It was warm inside the bank where some of the women of the town were occupied keeping the supply of hot drinks going.

'Here,' Kaare took some coffee and handed it to the boy, 'drink this, it'll make you feel at least a little warmer.'

The boy put the mug to his lips but could not swallow. He looked up at Kaare with a haunted expression, and Kaare smiled in sympathy.

'I know, the old throat's seized up, just the cold.' And the shock. 'Rub your throat gently in a downward motion, that's it, can you feel the tension relaxing?'

Part of Kaare's success was his ability to handle people with tact and sympathy, and never was that ability to be put to the test more than now. He nodded to the boy and moved back to the door of the bank where the cold air struck him like a blow.

The line of vehicles snaked back through the streets, punctuated by the flash of lights from the police cars that had accompanied the convoy from Oslo. The intention now was to transfer the gold bullion from the array of vans and cars into the vaults of the bank, no easy task. It would be backbreaking and tedious, with the danger of being spotted from the air.

Kaare moved over to where the old policeman was talking respectfully to the chief constable.

'Did the enemy plane report the moving of the gold?' he asked, and the old man shook his head.

'Think they believed we were all trying to escape from the city,' he said, taking a pipe from his pocket and lighting it with maddening slowness, crushing the tobacco down into the bowl with loving fingers. 'Many were. It was only the presence of the police cutting a path through the private cars that got us here at all.'

Kaare was well pleased. The presence of the gold in Lillehammer would mean danger for all the inhabitants of the small town. Oslo radio didn't start broadcasting until eight o'clock and now it was just after seven. Until the news was broadcast, no one in Lillehammer would realize that the war against the Germans had begun in earnest.

He thought of his parents and of Kristina, his cousin, with her young baby. Damn! It was a mess.

He stared at the line of men like ants with their burdens of gold, streaming in and out of the bank, and he sighed. By dusk the gold would probably be moved yet again, every step taking it nearer to the coast and the allies who hopefully waited there to take it to safety. Kristina must take her baby and go with the convoy, it was the safest way to get her back to her homeland. He himself would drive the milk van in place of the young Bergstrom boy who was not really ready for such a responsibility.

It was much later when Kaare was able to return home. His mother, the small child in her arms, was sitting with Kristina near the warmth of the fire. She smiled but there were lines of strain around her eyes. She looked up at him questioningly as he shrugged off his coat.

'What is happening, Kaare?' she asked in Norwegian. 'Are we in any danger?'

He shook his head and replied in English so that his cousin would understand. 'We are in no immediate danger but you might as well know that we are at war with the Germans, out and out war. There will be no collaborating with them except by a few traitors like Quisling, and we intend to make life as difficult for our invaders as possible.'

He smiled at Kristina, admiring her fine looks and voluptuous body. It was a great pity she was married with a child, it was a long time since he had felt so drawn to a woman.

'Have something to eat, Kaare.' He looked at his mother, not understanding her words until she repeated them.

'You must have some hot food inside you. There is much work for you to do and it cannot be done on an empty stomach.'

'Good old mother,' he smiled, 'always practical.' He sat down next to Kristina and the scent of her was sweet in his nostrils. He watched her take the baby from his mother and then, when they were alone, he looked at her directly.

'You must be prepared to leave at any time,' he said in a low voice. 'I don't know what time or even exactly what day, but go to the coast you must, and from there to England where you will be safe, safer than here at any rate.'

He saw her hands tremble and he covered them with his own. 'I will be coming with you to the coast. I will take care of you and of your son, so there is no need to worry.'

As he looked into her green eyes, Kaare knew that he would face any danger to protect his cousin. He smiled to himself a little ruefully. He might damned well have to, for one thing was certain, it would not be easy getting her out of Norway.

24

The sea was like eternity, stretching ahead as far as the eye could see. Above, the sky blazed with sunlight, a cloudless sky with no hint of rain, no sign of a promising wind.

Eden looked around him despairingly. He was so dehydrated he had no sweat, his mouth was rimmed with dry salt, his eyes were gritty and burning, and he felt as though his head was splitting open as the small boat drifted aimlessly through the calm sea. The oppressive heat threatened to destroy him more thoroughly than the enemy guns had done, and Eden felt hope and life draining away from him.

Two of the men had died almost at once and had been tipped unceremoniously over the side. Both had been wounded and the loss of blood had weakened them so that the punishing sun proved too strong.

Eden's mind drifted and though he had counted thirteen long days since the shipwreck, he no longer knew what day or hour it was. He was vaguely aware that he was alone now in the boat; he was burning up, he must give in and allow himself to sink beneath the waves, the tempting waves.

He was leaning over the side of the boat, dipping his face into the water, he was drowning, he could not breathe. Dead men called to him from the ocean bed. Seaweed clung with strong tentacles. He was dying.

He sat up abruptly, sweat beading his forehead. The room around him swam into focus and he saw that the twisted bedclothes were entwined with his limbs. His memory returned and he knew he was home in Swansea, surrounded by the familiar trappings of his own home, the house he shared with his wife Bella. He had wakened from the nightmare, the nightmare that had haunted him over the months since he had been rescued from the lifeboat where all the others had been dead men.

It was a Spanish ship, the *Fuente*, that had picked him up more dead than alive.

'*Agua, por favor*!' he'd croaked, and at once he had been given water in small measures until at last he had recovered enough to speak to the seamen in their own language, the language of Eden's mother. He had gone with them to Santander on the north coast of Spain, a golden stretch of beach bordered by turquoise seas, and had been quickly nursed back to health.

His nurse was young and pretty with glossy dark hair, and eyes that were almost black in an ivory skin. Gloria was the daughter of the captain of the *Fuente* and had found it an obvious pleasure as well as a duty to look after Eden.

He pushed back the tangled bedclothes and moved to the window, staring out over the docklands without seeing the familiar sights of ships riding high on a full tide, and the crouched rooftops of Lambert's Cottages grey in the summer drizzle.

The temptation to seduce Gloria had been very strong, but Eden had resisted her sweet face and innocent charm. At home he had a wife, a good sensible wife and soon, once the damned stupid war was over, he would have sons.

It had been another Spanish ship that had carried him to Ramsgate, the journey so uneventful that war seemed a distant nightmare. The moment he had set foot on English soil he had longed to fall to his knees and kiss the very ground he stood on. The greenness, the mild sunshine, the soft rain, even the grey clouds, had taken on a freshness and a uniqueness that he had come to treasure.

The rain had ceased, and curls of mist were rising from the roadway as the cobbles dried. The sun slanted in through the window, falling on his bare shoulders. It reminded him of the heat and light of Santander, of the curling turquoise waves and the warm sand beneath his feet, and of the beauty of Gloria.

Bella, he had his lovely Bella, of course, with her calmness and her inner strength. Her knowledge of his faults and her ability to live with them was perhaps the secret of her success. It was disappointing to them both that she had not yet conceived a child, but that would come in time, he felt sure.

Later, when he had shaved and was dressed in his working suit, he strolled over to the shipping office and stood in the doorway for a moment, his eyes becoming accustomed to the gloom after the sunlight outside.

Colin was sitting in his chair, head bent industriously over the books, and Eden felt a surge of affection. Good old Colin, upright and honest, a man who was uncomplicated and down to earth. What a pity he could not be more like Colin, Eden thought ruefully. As soon as news of Eden's safe return had reached him, Colin had rushed to his side and once assured of his partner's good health had chatted to him about anything and everything except the effects the war was having on the shipping industry.

'Eden!' Colin looked up, his face filled with pleasure. 'Thank God you're up to coming back to work. I'm inundated here and I could do with some help.'

'My aim is to please.' Eden spoke lightly to hide the sudden rush of emotion. His brush with death had left him more vulnerable than he'd realized.

'What's been happening in my absence? I think it's about time you filled me in on all the news.'

Colin rose and took the coffeepot from the gas ring, pouring two cups before answering.

'You heard about the shooting?' he queried. 'It seems a lone bomber, Italian or German, no one seems to know, found its way towards Swansea and strafed the docks indiscriminately, killing several of the men. Oh, and some poor young woman caught it too, it was the talk of the place for a week or two.'

Eden nodded. 'Aye, I heard about it. The girl used to work at Ty Coch, little Anita Williams, and she was pregnant by all accounts.' He sighed heavily. 'No one expected civilians to be involved.'

He sank down into his chair. 'I've got to enlist, Col, I can't just sit here day after day not doing anything.'

'Me too,' Colin said firmly. 'We could get in one of the old managers to run the office.' He drew a deep breath. 'We're in real trouble here, anyway,' Colin said. 'I mean the entire shipping industry not just us.' He sat down and stirred at the coffee, frowning into its swirling depths. Then his face brightened.

'Mind, the sailors did a great job at Dunkirk. Nearly 340,000 men were successfully evacuated from the beaches by every sort of ship they could lay their hands on.'

'Aye, I heard about it as soon as I came home,' Eden said. 'I couldn't believe that a retreat on a great scale had happened so soon in the war.'

'And not without cost.' Colin looked up at Eden, his eyes clouded. 'The Royal Navy lost twenty-five destroyers, apart from the small ships that were damaged or sunk.'

Eden chewed at his lip thoughtfully. 'I suppose that means the merchant ships have no protection then?'

Colin shook his head. 'It's nothing to see twenty or thirty merchant ships take to sea with only a single armed tug as an escort. The Merchant Navy has lost sixty-one of its ships already. It seems the German U-boats are having a fine old time with us.'

'What about our own line?' Eden thrust his hands into his pockets and stared at his coffee, feeling in his bones that the news would not be good.

Colin shook his head. 'Our best ship, the *Glamorgan*, took off with coal for the Med and then went on in ballast to South America to pick up a cargo of grain.' He took a gulp of coffee. 'A nice job for the boys, hard work of course, clearing the coal and scrubbing up for grain, but away from the war so to speak.' He cleared his throat.

'The ship was on course for Falmouth, riding low in the water, a slow, easy target for the enemy.' He paused and shrugged. 'We know the ship was sunk, but the crew, well, your guess is as good as mine.'

'Did Jonesy follow the timed zigzag course of evasion in daylight? Damn! Need I ask? Jonesy was an experienced man, he'd follow instructions to the letter.' Eden rose abruptly and moved to the window, staring outside without seeing anything of the docks around him.

'The men may be safe,' Colin reminded him. 'They would have taken to the lifeboats and may well have been picked up by now, we can only wait and see.' Colin scraped back his chair and Eden turned to look at him.

'I'm going to be on the next ship out,' Colin said decisively. 'I'm going to sign on without any more dithering.'

Eden inclined his head. He understood his partner's need to be on active service, because he shared it. As owners neither of them were obliged to do anything but administer the business of their shipping line, for the bringing in of vital supplies was an essential lifeline for the country, and yet the urge to be out there fighting the Germans was undeniable.

The tension went from Eden's shoulders and he smiled. 'You're on,' he said and resumed his seat. 'I'm coming with you. Now let's forget about the war. Tell me, partner, how's your love life?'

Colin raised his eyebrows. 'Now isn't that strange?' he said quietly. 'That's just what I was about to ask you.'

Colin left the office early and strode towards the docks entrance where he had left his car. He was smiling thoughtfully, his mind on the surprise he had planned for Nia.

He had known he must go to sea the minute he'd heard Eden was safe, and he planned it then, that he and Nia would be married by special licence. That way, if anything happened to him her future would be secure. Not that Nia needed him or his money but then that was part of her attraction. She was a capable, intelligent woman and he could no longer deny it, did not want to deny it, he was in love with her.

The door to Nia's house was opened by old Mrs Preece who smiled warmly when she saw him, aware that she owed Colin her job.

'*Duw*, there's well you're looking, Mr Singleton.' She took his coat almost reverently. 'Shall I tell the missis that you're here to see her?' She would have continued to speak but Colin held up his hand.

'No, I'll surprise her.' And surprise her he did. She was at the window, staring towards the sea and across the room from her, his face darkened with anger, was Joe Barnes.

Colin pulled up short. 'Sorry, Nia, I didn't realize you had a visitor. Is it a bad time?'

She smiled at him so warmly that it took his breath away, and yet there was an air about her, something almost furtive, that was not tangible and yet was unmistakable.

'No, of course not, Colin. Joe was here to tell me some rather bad news.' She looked directly at Joe. 'I'm so sorry about Anita. If there's anything I can do to help, of course I will.'

'I've told you what you can do, Nia,' he said mutinously. 'Take me back, you know you need me as much as I need you.'

'We've said all we have to say, it's time to leave.' She moved sensuously across the large room and opened the door, but Joe Barnes stood his ground, smiling un-pleasantly as he turned his attention to Colin.

'So you are the new man in our Nia's life then, are you?' he said, his question not needing any answer. 'Well

I can tell you that you'll never satisfy our little hotblood here. She needs a real man.'

Colin felt a shock of anger at the man's insult. His first reaction was primitive, he wanted to put his fist in the man's face and knock him to the ground.

'Joe,' Nia said icily, 'will you please leave?' Her colour was high but she did not flinch as she looked at the man.

'Aye, I'll go, nothing but an embarrassment to you now, am I? But mind, you were glad enough for me to take you in when your own father showed you the door, weren't you?'

'I'm grateful to you for many things, Joe,' Nia said reasonably, and Colin admired her calmness. 'But all that is past, you know it is.'

Colin moved forward menacingly. 'The lady said it was time to go, please do as she asks.'

'Oh, aye, I'll go right enough.' Joe spoke through clenched teeth. 'But not before I tell you that only a few days ago I pleasured myself with this same "lady" on this very carpet. Ready for it she was, mind, dropped her knickers quick enough then, she did.'

Nia was silent and Colin knew the man spoke the truth. 'Out!' he said, his hand on the man's collar, rushing him through the hallway in blind anger. 'Out before I kill you with my bare hands.'

He opened the door ignoring the startled Mrs Preece and flung Joe Barnes out on to the gravel drive. 'If I ever see you round here again, I'll kill you.' His tone was level and Barnes scrambled to his feet, staring back at him with hatred in his eyes.

As he reached the end of the driveway he looked back. 'Ask her who else she's been whoring around with, she's no good, you're welcome to her.' He hurried away along the drive as Colin made a move towards him.

'Don't let me see you on a dark night, man, or you'll have the hiding of your life.'

Colin closed the door and slowly returned to the sitting

315

room. Nia was standing before her fire, her back towards him.

'Sit down Colin,' she said. 'We have to talk.' She turned towards him and now her face was very pale. 'He spoke the truth, Colin . . .' She paused. 'There are no excuses. All I can say is that afterwards I realized finally that it was all over between him and me.' She shrugged. 'I can't ask you to forgive and forget. That would be asking too much.'

He stood looking at her for a long time. 'I can't pretend I'm not hurt,' he said at last. 'But neither am I a child. I know there are always complications where emotions are involved.'

She looked at him, her eyes swimming with tears. 'Colin, why are you such a *good* man?'

He laughed shortly. 'Don't make me out to be a saint. I'm not.' He walked towards her and took her in his arms, resting his chin against her silky hair. 'But I won't let that man's spitefulness spoil what we have together. Nia, I want you to marry me.'

She reached up and clung to his shoulders. 'I'll marry you and I'll make you the best wife in the world. I've learned my lesson, I'll never look at another man as long as I live.'

He kissed her throat and her slender neck and finally her mouth and it tasted sweet and vulnerable. 'Let me take you to bed,' he said huskily.

Nia woke up to the sunlight streaming in through the window and turned to see Colin at her side. Last night had turned from disaster into triumph, she had responded as never before to Colin's lovemaking. He had been passionate yet tender, his touch so delicate that she wondered how she ever could have imagined she wanted Joe's rooting insensitivity.

She sat up, careful not to wake Colin, her eyes alight as she realized this was her wedding day. She glanced at the polished doors of the wardrobe, trying to picture what was inside. If Colin had given her more time, she could have gone to Ben Evans and chosen an entire new outfit, but as it was she would just have to choose something suitable from her not inconsiderable collection of clothes.

Colin's hand was on her arm, drawing her towards him and she smiled down at him happily.

'My love,' she said, bending her head to him. His kiss aroused an immediate response and she snuggled down beneath the sheets pressing herself against his hard body. 'Do you always stand to attention first thing in the morning?' she teased.

'Only when I'm in bed with the woman who is going to be my wife.' His mouth covered hers and she abandoned herself to the surge of love and passion that enveloped her.

He was fierce now, almost aggressive in his possession of her, and she moaned with pleasure. Her eyes were closed against the morning sun, and behind her lids fluttered particles of orange light that mingled with the explosion of pleasure that seared her at Colin's final thrust. They clung together, bound closer than they had ever been, and Nia felt gratitude deep within her that such a man should be in love with her. At last she felt she was someone of worth. The awful creeping sense of inferiority that had clung to her since childhood evaporated, and excitedly Nia leapt out of bed and danced her way into the bathroom.

She felt a little sad as later, alone in her bedroom, she began to dress for her wedding. Her close friends should be with her at this moment, supporting and helping, but Kristina had gone to Norway and Roggen was abroad in Singapore with her husband.

She chose a soft blue dress with a small blue and white jacket and a hat that was little more than a froth of lace. She had gloves of white lace to match and shoes with neat heels. She had no flowers, so on an impulse, she searched in her drawer for the little white testament that her father had given her when he was a respectable vicar.

It would be a most conventional wedding and that was all right by Nia, for afterwards she would be Mrs Colin Singleton and no one could change that.

The registry office ceremony was a simple affair with

only a few flowers in a vase to lend an air of festivity to the occasion. Eden Lamb and his wife Bella were the only guests. Nia stood in a shaft of sunlight with Colin tall beside her and listened to the beautiful words that would bind them together. He put the slim gold band on her finger and bent to kiss her, and she hugged him close.

'I love you, Colin Singleton,' she whispered in his ear, and he looked down at her smiling.

'I love you too, Mrs Singleton,' he said proudly as Eden Lamb stepped forward to congratulate him.

Nia turned at a touch on her arm. 'You look lovely, Nia,' Bella said softly, her smile warm and genuine. 'And so happy, I envy you.'

Nia glanced towards the men, they were deep in conversation. 'Surely you and Eden are a perfect couple, I've always thought so.'

Bella shrugged. 'We're happy enough, but as you and all Swansea must know, I haven't yet been able to give Eden the son he wants so much.' She turned away then and Nia sighed softly. It seemed no one could achieve everything they wanted, not even Eden Lamb.

At the Mackworth Hotel the small orchestra was playing rousing marches, no doubt in tribute to the boys who had gone to war. Looking round, Nia could see that there were very few men present, at least not young men. There were some officers in uniform, looking stiff and out of place among the aspidistras and fine china, but mostly there were women alone. War was beginning to take its toll.

'Are you having a honeymoon?' Bella asked, playing absently with the silver cutlery, her movements nervous and out of character.

It was Colin who answered. 'No time,' he said, looking apologetically towards Nia. 'We only have a few nights together at home before I go to sea. I've signed on, love, I'll be sailing with the *Castell Coch* carrying coal to the Med.'

Nia felt her hands tremble but she was rigidly controlled, always able to conceal her feelings. She met Colin's eyes and saw that there was no talking him out of it, it was his duty, and that he would never neglect. So this was the reason for the rushed marriage, the swift signing over to her of his property. Since the ordeal suffered by Eden Lamb everyone in Swansea must be aware of the danger faced by the men at sea, none more so than Colin.

Suddenly, she couldn't wait to have her husband to herself. She reached over and caught his hand in hers, urging him to his feet.

'Excuse us,' she said, forcing a smile, 'I think our honeymoon is just about to begin.'

Bella watched the couple leave the hotel arm in arm, unable to stem the flush of envy she was feeling. They were so right for each other, Colin and Nia, in spite of the differences in their backgrounds. The closeness between the two of them was apparent even to the casual observer, and Bella was far from being that.

She wished she could be closer to Eden. She wanted to know him, to learn everything about him. They had never talked about her failure to conceive a child and she wondered sometimes if he blamed her for it. Ever since Bella had seen Kristina with the boy in her arms, she'd been unable to get the meeting out of her mind. One day, Eden surely must learn the truth, and then what would he do?

She glanced at him, he had a sparkle, an energy so sexual that Bella longed to throw herself passionately into his arms. Of course she did no such thing. Instead she smiled at him and he briefly covered her hand with his.

'Oh, God!' Eden's words came almost as a shock. 'Don't look now but I think Dr Summers and his wife are coming over to talk to us. I don't mind him, but she's such a gossip.'

Bella forced herself to smile at the elderly couple and graciously she waved them towards a chair.

'How nice to see you both out together, my dear.' Mrs Summers was drawing on her gloves which was a reassuring gesture heralding her imminent departure.

Bella inclined her head, unable to think of a suitable reply, but Mrs Summers was not one whit put out. 'Of course,' she rushed on, 'we were all *so* delighted when your dear husband was brought safely home.' She glanced coquettishly towards Eden. 'So pleased to see you safely home, you did give us all a terrible fright, you know.'

'Eden is very resilient,' Bella said quickly. 'It would take more than the Germans to get rid of him.'

'Yes, well that's as maybe, my dear.' Mrs Summers looked once more towards Eden. 'You have heard about little Kristina Larson, of course?' In the silence that followed her words, the woman could almost be seen licking her lips.

'She's gone to her father's homeland. The poor dear thought it would be safe there for herself and her child.' She paused, knowing the effect she was having on her listeners. 'The news has just come through via one of my husband's contacts that the Germans have occupied Norway. Isn't that dreadful? I don't suppose the poor girl will ever get back home now, because those Germans are supposed to be quite ruthless where a pretty woman is concerned.'

'We have to go.' Bella stood up to give emphasis to her words, and Mrs Summers, satisfied, urged her husband to get a move on.

'Come along, dear, you have patients to see, we can't hang about gossiping for ever, you know.' Having dropped her bombshell she departed, and Bella sighed, resting her hand on Eden's shoulder.

'I wouldn't take anything that woman says as gospel, you know. She just loves to talk for effect.'

Eden didn't answer and Bella suddenly wished she had the courage to really talk to him about his past. And yet his affair with Kristina was over long ago, it really was none of her business.

'Let's go home,' she said softly, and as they left the hotel, she slipped her hand through his arm and he looked down at her and smiled.

'Have I ever told you how much I love you?' he said, and suddenly, for Bella, the day was filled with sunshine and happiness.

25

Life was quiet for Roggen living as she did in the married quarters that fringed Seletar aerodrome. She sat now in the shade of the trees in her garden, a book open and unread in her lap, and pondered on how different Singapore was from home. The heat was enervating, so the pace of life was slow, and the war seemed far away.

Singapore was impregnable. Facing the sea, a battery of 15-inch guns dominated the eastern mouth of Johore Strait and guarded the vast military barracks at Changi. It seemed almost indecent to be so safe and protected when the news from home was that the docklands of Swansea had been strafed with machine-gun fire, killing a number of Swansea dockers. It was even harder to believe that bombs had been dropped on the town.

To pass the time, Roggen and Richard entertained often. It was no trouble, the Malay servants were well trained, if a trifle slow in carrying out their duties. And if dinner was served late, another drink and some light-hearted conversation would fill the gap until the meal was brought to the table.

It was a life of ease and luxury even by Roggen's standards, and yet she was not happy. How could she be when she had realized some time ago that she was not in love with her husband? It had all been an illusion, a throwback to their youth, and Roggen had changed too much to blind herself to the truth.

Tonight there would be yet another dinner party, this time given by her friend Maggie Dunbar and her husband John at their palatial house within sight of Johore Strait.

Richard was delighted when Roggen had struck up a friendship with Maggie. He thought it was just the sort of diversion Roggen needed, for he must have sensed her growing restlessness.

John Dunbar had never been particularly taken with Richard but he was always polite. John was a rather thin, unassuming man who was, none the less, a brave and daring pilot, performing stunts across the Singapore skies that took the breath away. It irked Richard that he was deskbound while John and many others were fêted and fawned upon even though, as yet, they had seen very little action and were unlikely to do so if the war remained the distant non-event it had been so far.

Later that evening, Roggen dressed with care in preparation for the party, and when she entered the sitting room Richard smiled down at her in approval. 'That's my girl, you look good enough to eat.' He kissed her cheek and she smiled up at him, determined to make the evening a pleasant one. But it was a sad state of affairs when a wife would rather be in the company of friends and neighbours than sitting at home with her husband.

Maggie greeted Roggen warmly, and linking arms led her into the smoky, crowded room. Richard immediately attached himself to John Dunbar and the two men walked over to where the drinks stood on the sideboard.

'I want you to meet a lovely man,' Maggie said in a whisper. 'He's just come over from Australia and he's going to set some hearts fluttering, if I'm not mistaken.'

Mark Thornton was tanned by the Australian sun, his eyes piercing blue against the gold of his skin, and the moment he touched Roggen's hand in greeting, she knew she was attracted to him.

'Hello.' Her tone was deliberately cool; she didn't intend to be one of the women who would be what Maggie described as 'fluttering' around him.

'*Hello*.' His voice was deep and resonant and his eyes crinkled up as he smiled. Roggen felt a lift of excitement and she withdrew her hand from his perhaps a shade too quickly. Mark continued to smile down at her in a way that was disconcerting. Maggie had disappeared into the crowd and Roggen searched her mind for some light conversation.

'It's so hot tonight, isn't it?' she said, and then felt foolish. What an inane thing to say. It was always hot in Singapore.

'Well you look pretty cool,' Mark replied, and suddenly Roggen was glad she was wearing the new, simple, white cotton frock, so well cut that it shaped her body enticingly, making the most of her small breasts and emphasizing the slimness of her waist.

She became aware of Richard at her side and quickly introduced the men to each other. She was not surprised when after a few moments Richard drew her away from Mark.

'Bloody awful Aussie,' he said. 'They think they own the world, that lot.'

Roggen sighed. 'You can be so bad-tempered at times. You have no tolerance, Richard.' He mumbled something in reply but she didn't listen. She had met Mark's gaze across the room and found it very difficult to look away.

For once, Roggen was glad when Maggie's party came to an end. She longed to get home, away from the scrutiny of Mark Thornton's searching blue eyes. She wanted to put him out of her mind, he was just another uninteresting businessman. In the car, she snuggled down into her seat. 'I'm beat tonight,' she said. 'I think I'll go into the spare room.'

Richard gave her a quick look but made no comment, for which she was profoundly thankful. She'd been sure he'd raise objections as he usually did when she suggested they sleep apart. It was something that was happening more and more lately, and one day soon there was bound to be a showdown.

It was a long time before Roggen could settle down.

She tossed and turned restlessly in the bed, and found herself going over her meeting with Mark in minute detail, picturing the way his blue eyes crinkled when he smiled, feeling the grip of his hand upon hers. At last, in the early hours of the morning, she fell into an exhausted sleep.

She was sitting in the garden the next day, reading a book, when she glanced up casually to see the Malayan maid crossing the garden towards her. Then Roggen tensed as she spotted the man, tall and bronzed, his hair gleaming in the sun as he removed his hat. She almost dropped her book as she stood up, smoothing the creases from her dress, telling herself that her reaction was that of a schoolgirl. But her racing heart and beating pulse were acting independently, ignoring her attempts to be calm.

'Mr Thornton.' Her voice was cool and more than a little shaky, her hand unsteady as she held it towards him. Her fingers were engulfed and he stood smiling down at her, his eyes half closed against the sun.

'Mary,' Roggen addressed the maid whose Malayan name she could not pronounce, 'bring some iced tea, would you please?'

She became aware that her hand was still clinging to Mark's, and she moved quickly to her chair and sat down, self-consciously crossing her legs, aware that they were bare and that her small feet were encased in the unbecoming pumps that she wore around the house.

'Sorry to call unannounced,' he said, and his smile showed that he wasn't at all sorry.

The colour rose to her cheeks and Roggen turned away, relieved to see Mary approaching with a tray of drinks. She rose quite unnecessarily to take the tray from the slim brown hands of the Malayan servant. The diversion of pouring the lemon tea gave her time to gather her wits, so that when she handed Mark his glass she was able to meet his eyes.

'I saw Maggie Dunbar earlier,' Mark said conversationally. 'Her husband is sick, so it seems.'

'I'm so sorry,' Roggen said, 'but poor old John seems prone to fall ill with anything that's going round.' She felt she was talking rubbish, inane, disjointed words that spilled from her lips with no sparkle or wit or charm. Discussing a friend's sickness was not the most stimulating of subjects. Why couldn't she just be her usual relaxed self?

'I could take you over there to see how things are, no trouble,' he offered, leaning closer. 'Got a jeep outside.'

She was flustered; was it proper for a married woman to accept a lift from the most eligible bachelor in the district, even if it was to visit a sick friend?

'I don't bite, honest,' he said. 'We Australians are quite civilized when we want to be.'

She made up her mind quickly, it was too tempting an offer to miss. 'I'll just go in and change my shoes,' she said to Mark, who was already standing, tipping forward on the balls of his feet and then dropping back on to his heels as though anxious to go.

'Right.' His eyes held warm approval as he walked with her towards the house and she felt bathed in a glow of warmth, gripped by a strange sense of excitement that was hurtling her forwards into she knew not what.

The drive to Maggie's house was a short one, but the day had taken on an almost magical quality and even the breeze from the straits, lifting her hat from her brow, seemed to carry a heady perfume that filled her senses. Occasionally, Mark's arm touched hers and Roggen was tinglingly aware of him.

Maggie's face lit up with pleasure when she saw Roggen. 'Come along inside out of this dreadful heat.' She hugged Roggen's arm and drew her into the coolness of the house. The fan on the ceiling whirred pleasantly distributing the air, and Roggen sighed in contentment as Maggie waved her towards the large comfortable sofa. Mark took his place beside her as though it was his right, and to do Maggie justice she did not show any signs of surprise. Whatever her thoughts might be privately,

Maggie was not one to interfere in the lives of other people.

'Poor old Johnnie is in bed,' Maggie apologized. 'He really is laid low by this sickness, he looks like death, poor lamb.' She moved towards the door. 'I shan't be long, I'll just arrange some drinkies for us and get John a glass of boiled water. That's all he can take at the moment.'

She disappeared, and Roggen glanced at Mark who had slipped his arm very casually around the back of the sofa. She could almost touch the heat vibrating from him, and she sat bolt upright in an agony of self-consciousness. She wanted to speak, to break the heavy silence, but she could think of nothing to say and was relieved when Maggie re-entered the room and set a tray on the table as though everything was quite normal.

'John's sleeping,' Maggie spoke matter-of-factly, 'sleeping like a baby. Let's hope he's over the worst of the sickness now.'

Roggen was finding it so difficult to make conversation that she fell silent, allowing Mark to do most of the talking. When he excused himself and made for the bathroom, Maggie came quickly to her side and took her hands.

'You look thunderstruck, my girl,' she said in mock severity. 'Any fool can see you are attracted to the man. What are you going to do about it?'

'Do?' Roggen had not thought beyond the moment. 'I don't know, what can I do? I'm a married woman.'

'And when has that ever stopped anyone from having fun?' Maggie said firmly. 'Now we'll forget it and have a bite of lunch, but accept a word of warning from a friend; don't give your life up as a sacrifice to the god of respectability. It simply isn't worth it.'

The hours spent with Maggie seemed to pass far too quickly and yet Roggen's every instinct cried out to be alone with Mark. But once she stepped out of her friend's house, the magical day would be almost over and Roggen would return to her home and her husband.

At last there was no more reason for remaining with Maggie in the cosy safety of her home. Mark rose to his feet and stood looking down at Roggen. 'I'd better take you back,' he said softly. She followed him towards the hallway where the afternoon sun was slanting in through the windows.

'God, it's hot,' Maggie said taking the scarf from around her slim throat and dabbing her face with it. 'I think I shall join Johnnie in bed for an hour and have a nap. I appreciated the visit, come over whenever you feel like talking.'

The sun beat mercilessly down on the open-topped jeep and Roggen was thankful for the shade from the brim of her hat. Sweat trickled down between her breasts and she felt uncomfortably hot.

And then the ride was over, she was back home and Mark was driving away from her. She felt lost and alone. As she entered the house and moved into the dimness, she knew there were foolish tears brimming against her lashes.

It was inevitable that she would see Mark Thornton often at dinner parties and at functions held in Raffles Place, and always their eyes would meet, however crowded the room. Roggen knew she was treading on thin ice when at one of Maggie's dinner parties she sat next to Mark and allowed him to flirt outrageously with her. Richard was furious and when they got home he threw down his jacket and faced her with set features.

'Did you have to encourage that man?' he said, his eyes narrowed. 'The way he was looking at you, he'd have had you in bed in a tick if you'd led him on any more.'

'Don't be such an old grump,' Roggen said, pouring them both a drink, 'what harm can anyone do in a roomful of people?'

'Well, I don't like it.' Richard took the drink and sank into a chair. 'He's full of himself and it's women like you who are encouraging him to think he's Casanova.'

'Don't worry,' Roggen said easily, 'it doesn't mean

anything.' And yet was that strictly true? Didn't she hope with one secret part of her that Mark's attentions were more than just a little bit of fun?

Mark took to dropping in on her almost every day, and she looked forward to his visits as if they were an oasis appearing in an arid desert. They sat and talked for hours and as she began to learn more about him, she knew she was falling in love with him. It was clear in her mind that she must put a stop to his visits, and yet she couldn't bring herself to make the break. Soon people would start to notice and then the gossips would have a field day.

And then Maggie told her that people were already talking. 'Look, love,' she said softly, 'you and Mark may be as white as the driven snow, but who is going to believe that you just talk to each other when you're alone together so much?'

'I'll have to stop him calling, there's nothing else for it,' Roggen said, feeling as though the bottom had dropped out of her world. She looked at Maggie who smiled enigmatically.

'Or you'll have to be more discreet, my dear. Now, let's have some iced tea shall we, and forget about the snooping old ladies of Singapore.'

It was the most difficult thing she'd ever had to do, but as she faced Mark across a table at Raffles, she took her courage in both hands and came straight out with what she had to say.

'It's got to end, Mark.' She bit her lip as his eyes crinkled into a smile. 'I mean it, we mustn't go on meeting, we're being talked about.'

'But we haven't done anything,' Mark said in amusement, 'except talk, and I don't think that's a sin, not even out here.'

'That's not what people think we're doing, though,' Roggen said. 'It's being rumoured that we're having an affair.'

'I'd like nothing better.' He smiled into her eyes and Roggen felt breathless. She stared around the room, not seeing the other people or hearing the hum of conversation. She couldn't do it, she didn't have the same sort of courage that Mark obviously did. She shook back her hair.

'It's not that easy though, is it?' She was frightened by the intensity of her own feelings, there was a sense of exhilaration flowing through her, a feeling of gratitude that Mark so obviously wanted her. But how far did his wanting go? Roggen couldn't see herself having a casual love affair with him, she wanted all of him or nothing at all.

'Don't worry about other people,' he said softly. 'No one matters but us, it's no one's concern what we do. And don't look so harassed, I'm not going to force you into anything.'

Perversely, that was just what she wanted him to do; to make the decisions, to take charge of her life and take her away from the boredom of her marriage to a man she no longer loved, perhaps had never loved. Poor Richard. She tried to imagine breaking to her husband the news that she was being unfaithful to him, and it made her shudder. You couldn't leave a man because you were no longer excited by him. She could picture the hurt expression that would come into his eyes and she felt she could not inflict such pain on him.

'We really *must* stop meeting,' she said quickly, 'otherwise everything is going to blow up in our faces, you must see that. Maggie is right, we are giving the gossipy old women in Seletar a field day.'

He rose to his feet and held out his hand to her. 'Then let's not disappoint the gossips. If we are to be accused, we might as well commit the crime.'

She rose and went with him and didn't speak as he helped her into the jeep. She looked at him uncertainly as he set the jeep into motion and drove quickly past rubber plantations, the vehicle leaping and bounding like a live creature over the uneven roads. He turned off the main road that led to Seletar, and the question died on

Roggen's lips. She knew he was taking her to his home a few miles from the airport. If she was going to protest, now was the time, but she knew she would not. Fate was leading her headlong into an experience that she knew she could not stop.

In his house it was cool with the blinds drawn against the afternoon sun. He spoke to his elderly serving woman in Malay, and with a small bow she withdrew.

'Come here.' Mark threw down his hat and held out his arms, and without a word, Roggen went into them. His mouth possessed hers, his hands were strong, pressing her close to him. Her breath left her and her head seemed to whirl with a kaleidoscope of emotions. He picked her up easily and carried her through to the bedroom. Gently he put her down against the softness of the sheets, pushing aside the mosquito nets impatiently. Then he was beside her.

Roggen could not remember getting undressed, but in a moment they were lying together, naked, on his bed. His strong hands caressed her tenderly and she smoothed her palms against the silkiness of his shoulders, down to his slender waist and over the swell of his buttocks. He was beautiful.

He teased at her nipples with his tongue. She breathed heavily, loving him, wanting to know him. She did not think she could bear it if he did not take her soon. She was ready to give him all of her inner self, the self that she had always withheld from her husband. When he came to her, she gasped with the delight. She clung to him, head flung back as he kissed her throat, arching her body to meet him.

'Mark, I love you so much.' She whispered the words but he heard them, and the slow, easy, tantalizing movements became more vigorous. He was almost aggressive in his lovemaking, as though he wanted to fuse with her, become one being, and she responded with small cries of pleasure, lost to anything but the joy of the moment. Within her there was a sudden explosion.

330

Sensations she had never known tore into her. She was spinning in a whirlpool of feeling, her nerve endings raw, jangling with pure pleasure. Roggen clung to Mark, shuddering and moaning.

Afterwards, they lay silent while Mark smoked a cigarette and Roggen caught the netting round the bed in her fingers, imagining it was a bridal veil. She would leave Richard of course, there could be no living with him, not after this. She did not question Mark about the future, she had no need to. He would look after her, protect her, and one day when the war was over, he would take her home with him to Australia.

'What's your home like,' she asked, leaning on one elbow and looking down at him. 'I mean your real home, not all this.' She waved her hand around the faded room.

'It's sunny and warm, the sea is blue around the coral reef, and it's the most beautiful country you ever saw. You'll love it.'

Her heart warmed. She had known he would wish to take her home with him but it was good to hear him say it. She kissed his mouth tenderly and he lifted a hand and smoothed back her dark, tangled hair.

'I'm never going to give you pretty speeches,' he said, 'and I'm not a guy for flowers and perfume, but I'll look after you, Roggen, you'll be my girl.'

'I know.' She kissed him again and there were tears in her eyes. Gratitude overwhelmed her, she could not believe her good fortune in finding a man like Mark.

He rose from the bed in one easy movement of his lithe brown body and left the room, careless of his nakedness. She could hear the splash of water and then the soft sound of Mark singing to himself, and she smiled at the intimacy they shared so naturally.

Then she thought of Richard, and drew a sharp breath. How was she going to tell him? He would be hurt and humiliated that she had chosen the 'awful Aussie' in place of him. She smiled wryly, knowing that Richard would resent the loss of the social contacts they had made far more than the loss of his wife. But then that was unfair. He had been a model husband, he'd not dallied with other women the way that many of the servicemen had done when faced with the freedom of a foreign country.

When Mark returned, he was dressed in fresh clothes and looked cool and contained in a crisp white shirt and linen slacks. He stood looking down at her, a slow smile curving his mouth.

'You'd better get dressed, girl, before you give me any more ideas.' He held the net aside for her to climb from the bed, and, almost regretfully, Roggen made her way to the bathroom, knowing that the magical moment was over, fearful that something would happen to prevent her being with Mark again.

When she returned he was in the sitting room, holding the keys to the jeep in his hand. He made for the door, expecting her to follow him.

'Where are we going?' she asked a little uneasily. He led her to the jeep, and the force of the heat wrapped itself round her like a warm blanket.

'To collect your things,' he said reasonably. He helped her into the jeep and Roggen felt herself trembling.

'You mean we're going to tell Richard right now?' She tried to imagine the scene. Could she face it? Was she ready to just pack up and leave her home and go to live with Mark? Apparently he thought so, he had no doubts at all about the rightness of what they were doing.

She glanced at her watch. Richard would be at home now, probably wondering where on earth she'd got to. Doubtless Mary would have filled him in about the male visitor who had carried her off in his jeep. Mary adored Richard and would do anything for him, including informing him of all his wife did. It would be impossible for her to have an affair with Mark in secret. He was right, the only way to do it was to bring everything out into the open right now.

There would be a scandal, of course. Seletar would be agog with the story of how Roggen had run off to be with Mark Thornton, but then surely honesty was preferable to the way some of the bored wives had affairs with married men in secret?

'Please, Mark,' Roggen said as he drew the jeep to a halt outside the house, 'let me talk to Richard alone. I'll try and break the news gently.'

'No chance,' Mark said firmly. 'There's no way to break it gently. You're leaving him for me, that's that.'

Roggen entered the house, and for a moment she could not see after the glare of the sun. The sitting room was empty and the door to the bedroom stood open. Richard was buttoning up his shirt, his hair, still damp, curling around his face. He smiled in welcome and then the smile froze as he saw Mark standing beside Roggen.

'Hello,' he said with forced politeness. 'I wasn't expecting visitors.'

'I'm sorry, Richard,' Roggen said gently. 'I love Mark and I want to be with him. You must have realized our marriage wasn't working.'

He was suddenly white, his lips moving as though he would protest, and then he turned away from her. 'There'll be no chance of a reconciliation, not if you go like this.'

Roggen was sorry for him, but pity was no basis for a marriage and she couldn't allow it to change her decision to be with Mark. 'I'm sorry,' she repeated, then she glanced towards Mark. 'I won't be a minute.' She was amazed at her calmness as she went into the bathroom and collected her toiletries and her make-up bag. She would pack her case with only the few clothes she would need until she could buy more. Her new life with Mark would begin from scratch with none of the trappings of her old life to act as reminders of her years with Richard.

In the hallway, Richard was questioning Mark. 'Why are you taking my wife away from me?'

Mark said nothing until Roggen came to his side. He put his arm around her shoulders. 'We have to be together,' he said, and Richard stepped back a pace as though the words were a physical blow.

'Ro,' he said, and his pleading tone was harder to bear

333

than his anger, 'you can't leave me. I've been a good husband to you, you can't deny that. I love you, Roggen, I need you. Anyway, what will people say if you walk out on me?'

Mark moved Roggen towards the door. 'I'm sorry it's happened this way. Neither Roggen nor I wanted anybody hurt, but it happens.'

'I don't know what's going on here any more,' Richard said. 'Can't we just sit down and talk about this?'

'It's no use talking,' Roggen said sadly. 'Mark's taking me away, I'm going to live with him. That's all there is to it.'

Richard's resistance suddenly crumbled and once more Roggen felt pity well within her. 'Don't worry,' she said softly, 'I'll take all the blame. No one will turn against you.'

'For God's sake, why can't we discuss this thing?' he said. His face had taken on a pinched expression. 'Let's at least be civilized about it. You can't just go, Roggen, you must see what a scandal it would cause.'

She shook her head. 'I don't care about the scandal any more. It's over, Richard, and there's nothing you can say that will make me change my mind.'

'Go, then!' he shouted, furious now that his pleading had failed. 'Go and rut in bed with the rough, tough Australian. You'll soon get sick of his uncouth ways, and don't think you can come crawling back to me, because I won't have you.'

'Come on, Ro,' Mark said easily, ignoring Richard's outburst as he would the buzzing of a fly. He climbed into the jeep and started the engine, and quickly Roggen climbed in beside him.

As the jeep drew away from the house, Roggen glanced back to the garden, shaded now in the evening air. She was not sorry to be leaving, even though her life with Richard had been comfortable and safe and the future was an unknown quantity. She settled back in her seat and looked towards the road ahead. There could be no going back now, and the thought was a little frightening. But she would face her future with courage, because Mark would be right there beside her.

26

Kaare had been asleep on his makeshift bed in the bank for only a few hours when he heard a commotion outside in the street. There was a hoarse voice shouting protests, and the loud slamming of car doors. Kaare moved cautiously towards the window and peered out into the dullness of the morning.

The chief constable was being manhandled into a car, a boot placed firmly in his back propelling him in an undignified heap on to the back seat. Kaare felt a rush of blood pound in his head. His instinct was to run into the street and put up a fight, but that would do neither him nor the hidden gold any favours. As he watched, the mayor of Lillehammer was sent sprawling into the road, and before the man could rise to his feet the car had driven away, almost running over him.

A crowd had gathered. It was clear that news of the invasion had reached the town. Kaare hurried outside and grasped the mayor's arms, lifting him into an upright position and brushing the snow from his coat.

'What's going on?' Kaare asked quietly, and the mayor shrugged.

'Quisling's men want the chief for questioning, it'll be my turn next, I suppose.' The mayor walked dejectedly away, shoulders bowed, head drooping, and Kaare knew the man was feeling as though somehow he had failed the townsfolk.

Kaare became aware that the young Finn boy was standing next to him, looking up meaningfully at him. 'I can help,' he said, and Kaare knew exactly what the boy was getting at.

'Come inside the bank,' he replied, and obediently the boy followed him. Kaare closed and locked the door. 'There are only a few of us who know that the gold is in our vaults,' he said. 'You and I will take it in turns to stay awake and on guard until further instructions get through.'

The boy nodded. 'Aye, all right. I can call on my twin brother if we should need him. He, like me, will be proud to stand up for my country against the Germans.'

'Good man,' Kaare smiled. Peter Finn may be young, but he was every inch a man if his courage and tenacity were anything to judge by.

Kaare moved to the window and stared out into the snow. The crowd of people was dispersing, returning to their homes, none of them aware that in their own local bank lay a fortune in gold bullion, the wealth of the nation. It was much safer, Kaare mused, that it remain that way.

It was four long days before any news got through to Kaare at all, and in the meantime his regard for his cousin had grown with every visit he made to his home. She was intelligent, amusing and intuitive – all this and beauty too – and he was proud to recognize her as his kinswoman.

The news when it came was bad. The Germans were advancing relentlessly from Oslo up the Gudbrands Valley towards Lillehammer. The enemy had no knowledge of where the gold was, but they would comb every inch of Norway until they found it. The search was on too for the King, and the Government was in hiding, God knew where. Kaare could only be grateful that he was spared that burden as well as the responsibility for the gold.

General Headquarters had transferred from Oslo to Eidsvoll to the north, but if they did not move soon they were in danger of being overrun. A dispatch rider had come to Lillehammer from General Hvinden Haug who was holding the enemy at bay in the hope of delaying the onward thrust for long enough to get his King and the country's gold into the hands of the Allies.

It was vital to keep the ports of Molde and Andalsnes secure in Norwegian hands or the Allies would have no chance at all of even landing in Norway. The General promised that soon, very soon, instructions would come concerning the gold. Kaare felt frustrated that he could do nothing to stem the rush of Germans across his land, but at least he could make an attempt now to get the gold out of Lillehammer.

He nodded to Peter Finn, who had discreetly let himself in by the back door, and sighed with relief. He wanted to get home to wash away the musty smell of the bank and snatch a few hours' sleep.

When he stepped out into the street, he became uncomfortably aware that most of the young men of the town were now wearing uniform. During his days and nights in the bank, the town had become a mobilization centre, and curious looks were cast in his direction, eyebrows raised at the sight of the young man wearing civilian clothes. No one knew about the gold and he had no intention of making excuses for himself.

He was weary when he entered the house and the first person he set eyes on was Kristina. She smiled at him and his spirits lifted. What it would be to have such a woman for a wife. His mother bustled from the kitchen. 'Come bath and then eat, and then go off to your bed, you are grey with fatigue,' she said in her swift, breathless way. 'Then you must shave off that awful beard. It is not becoming to your position of bank manager.'

She was agitated and he believed he knew the reason for her nervousness. 'Mother,' he said softly, 'do not let the gossip of other people upset you.'

'I don't know what you are talking about, Kaare.' She avoided his eyes. 'No one is talking about you, what nonsense.'

'I have seen the looks I've been given in the streets,' he

said. 'Our friends are wondering why Kaare Larson has not joined up to fight against the Germans. Well, they do not know that there is more important business for me to do, but you know, Mother. Let it be a comfort to you.'

After dinner, he made an effort to speak to Kristina alone. 'It will be soon,' he said. 'The gold will be moved without warning, so I trust you are ready, whatever time of the day or night I come for you.'

Her green eyes met his levelly. 'I'm ready, Kaare,' she said in her soft Welsh voice, 'and I want you to know I'm very proud to be your cousin.'

He kissed her cheek. It was soft and blooming with pinkness for she was embarrassed by his gesture. But he believed she was pleased, too.

'I must get some rest.' He moved away from her reluctantly. 'I will have news for you soon, never fear.' He fell into bed wearily and the moment he closed his eyes, he was asleep.

His father roused him several hours later and Kaare dressed hurriedly, knowing that the young Finn boy would be almost asleep on his feet. He had been mature and responsible and Kaare had been grateful for his unquestioning help, but he could not take advantage of the young boy's eagerness to be of service.

Kaare took his leave of the family and smiled reassuringly at Kristina. 'Soon,' he said. 'It will be soon.' He could not get her out of his mind. She was a woman he would be proud to call his own, and perhaps he would never meet another like her. She had courage, he was sure of that, and she would need all her strength to endure the hardships and dangers of getting away from the Germans and finding freedom.

When he neared the doors of the bank, his pulse quickened. Men were coming out of the building, men he had never seen before. As he moved closer, one of them drew a pistol.

'Name?' The man snapped the command and Kaare responded, recognizing with relief that the silent figure

338

standing a little behind the others was that of the Prime Minister of Norway.

'I'm Kaare Larson,' he said, and he saw the tension drain from the man holding the gun.

'Good. Come inside, we have instructions for you.' The men turned and entered the bank, and Kaare saw the frightened face of Peter Bergstrom who had no idea who these people were.

'It's all right,' Kaare said to him quietly. 'Don't worry, they're on our side.' He closed the door on the snow-white street, and breathed a sigh of relief. It seemed that the waiting was over.

Sarah Williams pushed herself up from the pillows and looked down at the handsome face of Joe Barnes. He was asleep, his dark hair curling over his forehead, his long eyelashes resting against his cheeks. Her heart warmed with love with him, and yet there was the heavy burden of guilt, too, for she had betrayed Dan who trusted her, and, what was more, she had taken her sister's lover.

But Dan was a boy, young and inexperienced. She liked going out with him but in her heart she'd wanted more from life than he could offer her. And as for Anita, she was dead, killed by stray enemy bullets as she'd sat in the doorway of Mam's house in Lambert's. Sarah's eyes misted with tears. Anita had been flighty, selfish perhaps, but she was Sarah's older sister and she did not deserve to die.

Joe had come to Sarah in his grief, his face drawn and white, his eyes so sad that she immediately wanted to comfort him. He had told her how much he grieved for Anita, how angry he was that he could do nothing to avenge her death, and Sarah had put her arms around him, smoothing back his hair so tenderly that he had kissed her in gratitude. At least that's what it had been at first. Then slowly, inexorably, he had moved further and further with each clandestine meeting, until at last he'd got her into his bed.

Sarah knew she was taking a great risk. She knew nothing about how to prevent becoming pregnant, it was not something Mam would ever talk about. But Joe had said to trust him, and how could she refuse when all her instincts clamoured for this man?

He stirred, opening his eyes, and smiling, he drew her sleepily into his arms so that her face rested against his bare chest. His hand caressed her small breast and she sighed softly. She was not like Anita, she did not fall readily under his spell, indeed she was a little afraid of his aggressive lovemaking. But the knowledge that she was helping him over his grief and loneliness seemed to be enough to make her his willing partner.

'Sweet little Sarah,' he said softly, 'so delicate and small, so gentle and loving, you'll make such a good wife.'

She warmed to him. The delight of being Joe's wife, of having his ring on her finger, would wipe out all her guilt and anguish. When he rose above her and pressed his hand against her slender hips, she did not protest. Sometimes he hurt her, for she was still not used to lovemaking, but the relationship would improve. Hadn't Anita told her many times how fine a lover Joe was? It must be some lack in herself, Sarah acknowledged the fact readily. One day, perhaps when she was more used to him, the magic would come and she would be blissfully happy.

If only she didn't feel so sick and ill; some days she could scarcely get out of bed without the room swimming around her. The days spent working at the munitions factory were dreadful. She hated the noise and the smell and the sound of shouting voices as the women tried to communicate. She hated too the way her skin and hair were streaked with yellow, but then she was young and strong and she was expected to work for the war effort.

As Joe moved into her flesh she gasped, and he smiled triumphantly, thinking he was giving her pleasure. Anita had warned her always to praise a man's prowess in bed.

If a man thought he was a great lover, it did him the world of good and made him so grateful to his woman.

He closed his eyes, his hands gripped her breasts with cruel force. Tomorrow she would have bruises on the paleness of her skin, bruises she would have to conceal, for if anybody found out that she was being bedded by a man, and Joe Barnes at that, all hell would break loose. She remembered her father's anger when he'd learned that Anita was sharing Joe's bed. Sugar Williams had ranted and raged, and had threatened to beat Anita within an inch of her life. But Anita had gone to live with Joe, where she was safe from her father.

So far Joe had made no mention of Sarah coming to share his house, and she continually hoped that one day he would speak out, ask her to be his wife, take her away from the house on the docklands and give her everything she'd ever wanted – a home and children.

He was straining above her now and she screwed up her face, not in pleasure as he imagined, but in pain. And then it was over and Joe was panting beside her. He looked at her then and smiled. 'Time to go home, little one,' he said.

The house was silent. The family must have retired to bed early. Kaare moved quietly to Kristina's room and stared down at her sleeping face in the light from his torch. Poor Kris, she was in for a hard time. It would be a miracle if he managed to get her out of the country and back home in one piece. But he would try, damn it, he would try.

He touched her shoulder lightly, and immediately she was awake. 'It's time to go,' he said softly. 'Here are some suitable clothes. Put them on please, and don't worry, I'll turn my back.' He placed a pair of thick trousers on the bed. 'I've got some woollens for you, you'll need them.'

He looked away while she dressed, and she did so swiftly with no fuss. When she was ready he could not help but smile. Her slim, elegant figure had vanished under the shapeless clothes.

'Wrap the child up warmly,' he said, and she nodded obediently. When she stood before him with the baby held against her breast, he wrapped one of his own thick jackets around them both, so that in the darkness it appeared as though Kristina was a fat, shapeless being with no features or form. That was just as well since she would be in the company of a dozen or so soldiers on the journey.

He helped her into the truck and set off at once for the station. There was no time to rouse his parents, and anyway, Kaare hated fond farewells. Soon, the train would leave Lillehammer with the first stop to be five hours' journey away in Hjerkinn. By then, even if Kristina's presence was discovered, there would be no turning back.

The people of Lillehammer retired to bed early, and the streets were deserted, but near the station the steaming of the train could be clearly heard, and a little way off, Kaare stopped the truck and helped Kristina down into the snowy roadway. In the darkness, Kaare drew her along the platform towards the supply truck. He put his finger to his lips and she nodded silently. His heart warmed, she was a good sensible girl, a girl of courage. On an impulse, he drew her into his arms and held her for a moment, whispering reassuringly in her ear.

'I will be close by at all times, remember that. As for the child, there's plenty of milk aboard, powdered as well as a few churns of fresh. The boy will be all right.'

He settled her in among the supplies and covered her with a blanket. Her large green eyes looked into his and he felt her fear. He kissed her cheek, and she tasted of cold and freshness and the bloom of young womanhood.

He carefully pulled the tarpaulin sheeting over the top of the truck and returned silently to the platform. He was just in time. An officer was walking crisply towards him with a group of soldiers a respectful distance behind.

'I understand you're Kaare Larson, the bank manager,' he said. 'I'm Johan Olsen.' He saluted smartly. 'I think we should be getting away any time now. I've engaged a group of skiers, a Carl Ringe and his friends, who will act as extra protection. They are all trained in unarmed combat and I think we will need all the help we can get.'

Kaare could tell by Johan Olsen's tone that he considered the entire venture to be madness with little hope of success, but Kaare believed it could be done. If the bullion had succeeded in coming from Oslo to Lillehammer in a raggle-taggle of trucks and milk wagons, there was no reason why it could not get to the coast under the guise of a goods train.

'We can do it, sir,' Kaare said forcefully. 'We have the element of surprise on our side, and wouldn't it be an achievement if we got the gold out of Norway under the very nose of the Germans?'

'You're right, of course,' Johan said, and his voice seemed to rise with sudden excitement. 'Come into my truck with me, at least I can offer you a drink and some warmth.'

Johan's truck was furnished with a small shaded lamp, some bedding rolled in a corner and some cooking equipment nestling incongruously alongside two sub-machine-guns. Some white tarpaulin sheeting was ready to cover the truck.

As Kaare sat down against the wall of the truck, there was the loud hissing of steam, and with a jolt the train began to move. His heart lifted; he, the gold, and most of all Kristina, were on their way to freedom.

Kristina slept fitfully, lulled by the clattering of the wheels and overcome by her own sense of fatigue. Fear had swiftly given way to weariness and a deep sense of sadness that she had been unable to say goodbye to her newly-found relatives. But Kaare had been right to make her departure swift, he had picked up her bag, fragrant with the herbs she always carried, and ushered her out into the cold silence of the night.

She felt warm and comfortable beneath the thick

blankets Kaare had provided. He was a fine man, this cousin of hers. Drowsily, she snuggled down to sleep and dreams about Robert; he was holding out his arms to her, waiting for her to come to him; he was kissing her, touching her face, and she felt tears of happiness wet on her cheeks.

She woke abruptly. Kaare was shaking her shoulder. In her arms, the baby lay asleep, dark fans of eyelashes soft against rounded cheeks. Kaare smiled.

'I've got you some breakfast.' He crouched beside her with a can of mutton soup in his hand. 'We've arrived in Hjerkinn, that's the first stage of our journey over.' He knelt, helping her to sit up, taking the weight of the baby in his own arms. 'I got Johan Olsen to warm some hot soup, telling him I hadn't eaten properly for days.' Kaare smiled again. 'He gave me enough to feed three men, so come on, enjoy it, you never know when we'll have a chance of food again.'

Kristina was aware of Kaare watching intently while she fed herself and the baby, who sleepily sucked at the spoon. He seemed fascinated by Verdun, and Kristina supposed rightly that her cousin was not used to children.

'What's the next move?' she asked, warmed by the soup but nevertheless feeling the chill from the open corner of the tarpaulin above her head.

'Well, the station master tells us that the Germans are coming inland from Trondheim, but we should reach the coast long before they catch up with us. At the moment, the train is hidden in a siding beneath some fir trees, so we are quite safe, there's no need to worry.'

Kristina reached out and touched his gloved hand. 'You are a wonderful man, Kaare.' For a long moment, Kristina thought he would lean forward and kiss her, and instinctively she drew back a little. If he saw the gesture, he gave no sign, but suddenly his eyes were half closed and she knew he was quite aware of her anxiety not to become involved in something that could have no future.

'The new recruits have been given a roasting,' he said

lightly. 'They seem to think this trip is a sporting adventure but Olsen told them in no uncertain terms that military rules must apply. There must be no unnecessary movement and no noise, otherwise we shall draw unwelcome attention to the train.'

'Don't worry about us,' Kristina said softly. 'The baby is a very good sleeper. So long as he's fed and dry, he'll be all right.'

'That reminds me,' Kaare took a bag out of his coat, 'any discarded clothing from the baby can go in here and I shall see to it.'

Kristina smiled gratefully. 'It seems you've thought of everything, there's glad I am to leave everything in your hands.'

He rose to a crouching position and peered through the tarpaulin for a moment. 'It's a beautiful day, Kristina,' he said. 'It's very cold, but the sun is shining in a blue sky and the icicles on the trees are sparkling like diamonds.' He glanced back at her and there were lines of strain around his eyes. He smiled, but she had seen that he was worried.

'What's wrong, Kaare, what is it that you are keeping from me? I'm not a child, remember, but a woman. I want to know the bad as well as the good.'

'The Germans are pushing towards Lillehammer,' he said, not insulting her intelligence by prevaricating. 'Soon it will be occupied, and I wonder how my parents will deal with the situation.' He smiled a little ruefully. 'I know my mother, she's nothing if not outspoken. She's got too much spirit for her own good and she'll likely tell the Germans where to get off.'

'They'll be all right,' Kristina said softly. 'They are sensible people, and anyway, the Germans will probably be too busy to bother much with the civilian population of the town.'

'I must go,' Kaare said. 'It's going to be a long day, Kristina, you are bound to feel cramped and bored, but it's not for long. Soon you will be on board a ship heading for home.'

345

When he had gone, Kristina settled down to try and sleep, but her eyes refused to close. She lay on her back staring up at the white tarpaulin above her head, and thought about home. What would Robert be doing now? Capping out? Offering a few select men jobs on the ships. Maybe now, with the war taking hold, there would be plenty of work for all the dockers and the hated routine of allocating jobs would be unnecessary.

She must have dozed, and again it was Robert who featured in her dreams. He was calling out for her in the darkness, and she could not reach him although she strained every muscle to catch his hands in hers.

'Kristina, it's Kaare, you are safe, you have been having a bad dream.' He spoke softly, taking her in his arms, and Kristina realized she was trembling.

'I'm all right,' she said, struggling to sit up against the hard wall of the truck. She looked down at Verdun. He was awake, staring at his waving, mittened fist as though in bewilderment. She rubbed at her eyes and moved her position, realizing she was stiff and cold.

'I've brought some more hot food for you,' Kaare said. 'We are very lucky, come on and eat, you will feel better soon.'

As she gratefully ate the long thin sausages and hot beans, she listened to Kaare talking. He had an air of suppressed excitement about him and she smiled at him suddenly.

'There's something about you, Kaare. Tell me what really has happened here while I've been asleep.

Kaare looked at her levelly. 'You are a perceptive women, cousin Kristina,' he said softly. 'It is the King. He has been here at this very station, and now he is on his way to Otta.'

Kristina frowned.' Is that bad?'

Kaare nodded. 'Yes, Otta is rather close to the Germans.' He shrugged. 'But then, there was no other line available,' Kaare said quietly. 'Otta is so small that in all probability the Germans will by-pass it altogether. In any case, that is a risk we have to take.'

346

'What other risks do we have to take?' Kristina asked, her pulse quickening. She was beginning to read her cousin very well.

He shrugged. 'Some damn fool station master telephoned his wife near German lines and told her about the King, and about the train being here. All we can hope is that none of it is taken seriously.'

Suddenly, he crouched down close to her and put his hand over her mouth. Kristina tensed as she heard the ring of heavy boots against the platform and the sound of German voices in loud conversation as they strode past.

Kaare remained silent for a long time and then moved cautiously, lifting the tarpaulin and looking out. Kristina felt the rush of cold air, and shivered.

'It's all right,' Kaare said. 'They think the train is carrying arms for the Germans. Fortunately, the driver is Swedish, a neutral. They've bought his story about the train taking a load to the west coast. The Germans are even helping to move the train on to the right track.'

'You understood them?' Kristina asked, pulling the woollen scarf more firmly round her head.

Kaare nodded. 'Norwegians learn German in school, it proves an advantage at times like this. Now you stay put, don't move, try to keep the baby quiet.'

He climbed out of the truck and Kristina heard the rough sound of the tarpaulin being drawn to above her. She sighed heavily, hoping that Kaare's optimism was justified. She picked up the baby and wrapped him close against her breast. He was tired now and burrowed into her neck. She hugged him closer, loving him with every fibre of her being.

Suddenly into the silence came the sound of a single rifle shot echoing like thunder, piercing Kristina's sense of calm. She sat upright, holding her child closer to her breast. There were running footsteps thudding against the snow, shouted commands in the darkness. Voices, German voices, spoke sharply on the track beneath the truck where Kristina crouched.

She held her breath. Every muscle grew tense with her

347

effort to remain motionless. The baby gurgled softly and Kristina drew in a sharp breath. There was the sound of feet scraping wood, and then the canvas above her head was drawn back and eyes screwed up against the dimness looked down at her in amazement. She saw the glint of a steel helmet and stared up fearfully into the face of a German soldier.

He climbed into the truck and stared at her with a smile creeping over his face. He spoke in German, making a rocking movement with his arms, nodding towards the baby. Kristina realized he thought she was Norwegian and obviously he could not speak the language. She drew the shawl away from Verdun's face, and the soldier bent forward, touching the plump cheek with a gentle hand.

The rattle of machine-gun fire somewhere towards the front of the train distracted the soldier, and he stood up and heaved himself up over the side of the truck. Carefully, he replaced the tarpaulin. He had come to the conclusion, rightly, that she was some sort of stowaway, and it seemed he had no intention of giving her away.

Kristina heard the ring of his boots against metal as he jumped on to the track. She closed her eyes in relief and drew the baby close once more, pulling Kaare's coat closer round them. The machine gun rattled again, there were cries of pain, and Kristina closed her eyes, trying not to picture the scene of carnage that was going on outside on the snow cold platform.

Kristina buried her face in the baby's soft neck and tried to hold back the tears. Were they for Kaare, the unknown German soldier, or herself and her child? She did not know. All she longed for was to be home, back in familiar surroundings where her child would be with people who would care for him if anything happened to her.

She pushed away the picture of herself lying dead in a pool of blood, and her baby crying unheard into the snowy darkness that was Norway. She must be strong, for any sign of weakness or hysteria now would betray her presence on the train, and then everything Kaare had strived to do would be in vain.

27

It was a fine day, a warm, sunny day, when the water of the docks danced with light and the ceaseless motion of the tides. Coasters and tramps jostled for elbow room, rising and falling on the sparkling wash of water.

Robert Jenkins sat hunched over a newspaper in the shack that served as a canteen, and there was a worried frown on his face as he read the page in front of him. The war was dragging Norway into its relentless net, and Kristina, his wife, was in danger.

He had heard from her only once and that was a brief note to tell him she was coming home. Since then there had been nothing, and his heart as well as his loins ached for her presence. If he had not recognized good honest love before, he recognized it well enough now that he was separated from Kristina by the dangerous might of the North Sea.

He had made his decision to join the Army before Kristina's ship had sailed from the shores of Scotland. Soon he would be going away to do his training and it troubled him that he was unable to let Kristina know anything about it. He had waited in vain for concrete news of Kristina's whereabouts, hoping that even now she might be aboard a ship returning to Britain.

His attention was caught by the sound of raised voices, and he shook out his newspaper before folding it and placing it on the wooden table. He moved out of the shade of the shed and into the sunlight, blinded for a moment by the sun. Then he realized that two of the dockers were at each other's throats. They stood, fists raised, faces red with anger, sizing each other up with narrowed eyes.

'What's going on here?' he said quietly, but his voice carried authority and both men moved back a step, uncertainly.

'Come on, Sugar,' Robert urged, 'what's so important that you have to fight here when there's already war enough going on?'

Sugar Williams's arms were big and strong, he was an old docker, toughened by work and weather, and his honest face shone with sweat.

'It's 'im,' he said, 'Dan here, he's been walking out with my Sarah, see, and got her in trouble.' His eyes narrowed. 'And don't go on about it all being the fault of Joe Barnes.'

'Well, don't blame me for what another man's been doing,' Dan said defensively. 'Joe Barnes got your Anita into trouble, rest her soul, and now he's trying the same trick on with Sarah.'

'Dan here is trying to get himself out a scrape, if you ask me,' Sugar said heatedly. 'The cheeky bugger is trying to tell me that Barnes is trifling with my Sarah and seeing a married woman on the side.'

'It's true, Sugar!' Dan said earnestly. 'You ask your girl. Respectful I've been to her, so it wasn't me that did the damage. It's that Joe Barnes that's done the girl wrong, I tell you.' He shuffled the toes of his boots against the edge of the dock. 'Still, marry her I will, mind, if she'll have me.' His thin shoulders were hunched and Robert stared at him pityingly.

Joe Barnes, a troublemaker if there ever was one. Robert moved forward and stood between the two men.

'Now, Sugar,' he said placatingly, 'you know what this Barnes chap was like when he used to come creeping round here taking bets from Nia Powell. Thought he was a big man, he did, strutting about the docks as if he owned the place.' He held up his hand as Sugar began to speak.

350

'Wait now, I'm not saying he touched your girl, but find out the facts before you jump in with two feet. Go home now, have time off, I won't dock your pay. Ask young Sarah to tell you the truth, that's your best bet.'

Sugar nodded thoughtfully. 'Aye, boss, I will.' He stared hard at Dan. 'But if you're lying through your teeth, I'll take a shotgun to you and march you up the aisle myself.'

The tension eased from Sugar's big shoulders as Robert led him back towards the shed. 'Have a cup of tea, man, and then get back home. Talk to your girl, find out who's to blame before you start throwing punches, right?'

'Right enough, boss.' Sugar hung his big head. 'I did take it a bit for granted that Dan was the cause of the trouble, but if that coalman is the one to blame he won't get off scot-free, you bet. I'll wait for him with a bit of iron bar in my hand, and he'll get what for.'

'That's enough of that talk,' Robert said sternly. 'If the bobbies hear you threatening the man, you'll be in the cell before you know it.'

Sugar took the mug of tea in his big hand and drank it down in one gulp. 'I suppose I do let my mouth run away with me at times, but it's this damned temper of mine. I'm a bugger when I start.'

Robert picked up his newspaper once more and unfolded it pointedly. Sugar took the hint and moved to the door.

'Thanks, boss, I'll get off home now then, and see you in a bit.' He let himself out into the sunshine, his bulk filling the doorway and casting a shadow into the small shed. Robert frowned. He could not see the print that danced before his eyes, the small piece mentioning the plight of the Norwegians. But then, he did not need to read it, he knew it off by heart, and in disgust he threw the newspaper to the floor.

'Work,' his voice filled the shed, 'it's high time I got back to work.'

*

The honeymoon was short-lived. Nia had not known that love could be so sweet, so tender, could mean giving of herself completely, something she had been afraid to do ever since childhood. She had never before thought to give such love to any man.

Colin was different, he was a man who knew her faults and still loved her. He was so patently worthy of her love that she was moved to tears when in his arms. And now he was going away from her. Her worst fears had been realized when Colin had come home to her one evening and sat her down in the warmth and luxury of their home, his face sombre.

'I'm leaving tomorrow.' The words rang like a death knell in her ears. Nia had stared at Colin for a long time in silence and then the words burst forth like a torrent.

'Why! Why are you going to leave me alone? What about the business, how am I going to live without you?' And finally, 'When are you going to sea?'

'Soon. I had to enlist, my darling. It's wartime, there's no choice.' He took her in his arms. 'I don't want to leave you, God knows, but I have a duty like any other man. I must serve my country in some way and the sea is in my blood. It was the obvious choice.'

'I don't want you to go.' She knew the words sounded childish, foolish even, but she clung to him with tears brimming in her eyes. She wished she could be brave, but life seemed so cruel. She had at last found truth and love and happiness, only to have them snatched away from her.

'I'll only be doing what seamen have always done, taking cargoes to different lands.'

'I know,' Nia said shakily, 'but this time the cargo is not coal or grain or flour, but shells and bombs and things.'

'Not necessarily, Nia.' He stroked her hair. 'There are cargoes of vital supplies to transport. I shall doubtless do the Med run and be home quite often.'

She knew he was trying to reassure her. She felt him

place his finger beneath her chin as he forced her to look at him.

'Don't you think I'm going to look very dashing in my officer's uniform?' He was smiling but his eyes begged her to make it easier for him. Nia realized she was being selfish, and with a sigh she held him close, shutting her eyes tightly against the lies she was about to speak.

'You will look wonderful, Col, I will be very proud and happy, and of course I know you must do your duty. How could I respect a man who was a coward?' But she would rather have a live coward for a husband than be the widow of a dead hero.

The telephone rang suddenly, a strident voice in the silence of the room. Nia answered automatically and was surprised to hear the voice of Joe Barnes coming over the line.

'Yes, what do you want?' she asked coolly, and as her eyes met Colin's she shook her head and frowned.

'Joe Barnes.' She mouthed the name and Colin didn't hesitate. He moved quickly across the room and took the phone from her.

'Get off the line,' he said angrily, 'and don't call my wife again or it'll be the worse for you.'

He replaced the telephone in the receiver. 'What do you think he wanted?' he asked, and Nia sank into a chair biting her lip.

'I don't know, but at a guess I'd say he wanted money. Forget him, Colin, he's not worth bothering about.' She held out her arms. 'Come on, we've got much more interesting things to do than talk about Joe Barnes.'

Robert sat in the comfortable sitting room that looked over the sea, and stared at the shape of Mumbles Head highlighted in a burst of moonlight against the gloom of the night. It was at such times that he missed Kristina most. He had been a fool to let her go to Norway, but the news of the trouble the country was in had not reached him before Kristina's ship had sailed. Once at sea, there was no way the ship could be stopped.

He found he was missing Verdun too. The little boy had become like his own child and the circumstances of his birth had brought Robert and Kristina closer together. They had become friends at first, and then lovers. And their marriage was a good one, that could not be denied.

He did wonder if she sometimes thought about Eden Lamb. She had been in love with the man once and for that he could not blame her. In his book, the man had taken advantage of her. She was probably easy prey; a girl from a poor family, dazzled by her rich boss. But Robert had always meant to have Kristina as his wife, and once she was home again, he would make sure he put into words how much she meant to him.

He moved restlessly from his chair. It was so frustrating that he could do nothing to bring her back from Norway, but he must trust her family. If they were anything like Kristina they would be resourceful and courageous, they would make sure she was safe. He picked up his silk scarf and drew on his jacket. He would go out, he couldn't remain alone in the house any longer with his fears.

Nia was preparing for bed when the telephone rang again. Instinctively, she knew it was Joe Barnes. Her first thought was not to answer it, but then slowly, she picked it up.

'You can't fob me off with threats!' Joe Barnes's voice rang out harshly, and it was clear he'd been drinking. 'I want you back, Nia.'

'Leave me alone, Joe, please,' she was saying softly just as Colin entered the room. She hung up quickly and Colin stood for a long moment, looking at her in silence.

'I've a lot to do before I go away to sea,' he said at last. 'Pack me an overnight bag, love, I'll go up to Cardiff first thing in the morning and see to things in the office there.'

'Where are you off to now?' Nia asked nervously as Colin moved to the door. He smiled. 'Don't worry, I'm only going to put Barnes right, once and for all.'

She hurried towards him and put her arms around his waist, leaning her head against the regular beat of his heart. She felt part of this man, they had forged a life that no one must be allowed to break, and certainly not a man like Joe Barnes.

'What ever time you come in,' she said, 'I'll be waiting.' She watched him leave the house and there was a strange sense of foreboding resting over her like a cloud. She shrugged and went towards the kitchen. She stopped for a moment in the sunlit hallway and drank in the silence. She felt her mind fly above her body and knew that she was praying that she would never have to lose Colin's love.

It was late when he came in, and she was sitting up in bed, the lamp switched on, a book idle on her knees. He entered the bedroom and she went cold with fear, for there was a trail of blood across his face.

'Colin, what have you done?' She knew already. He had seen Joe Barnes.

'Only what I had to do.' He moved through into the bathroom and she heard the tap running. She bit her lip, wondering how she could ever have been so foolish as to put her trust in a man so unworthy as Joe Barnes.

When Colin returned to the room, Nia saw that his eye was turning black and his lip was slightly swollen. She slipped out of bed and put her arms around him.

'I love you so much, Colin,' she whispered. 'Please believe me, Joe Barnes might be dead for all I think of him now.' She led Colin towards the bed and drew him under the sheets, cradling him as though she were a mother and he her baby. She smoothed back his hair and dropped light kisses on to his forehead until his regular breathing told her he was asleep.

In the morning, Nia woke to the pounding of fists against her front door. She slid out of bed and glanced at

Colin, noticing that the skin around his eye was turning from black to purple. The pounding resumed and feeling a dart of apprehension, Nia pulled on her gown and hurried downstairs to where Mrs Preece was already opening the door.

Two burly policemen entered the hallway and stood self-consciously in the slant of morning sunlight, staring at Nia almost apologetically.

'Is Mr Colin Singleton at home?' the sergeant said politely. 'We would like to speak to him.'

'Come into the sitting room,' Nia said graciously, though her heart was beating rapidly. 'My husband is just getting dressed.' She turned to face the older of the two men who seemed to have the set of authority about the strong features of his face. 'What is this in connection with?' Nia asked shakily, playing nervously with the belt of her dressing gown.

'I would rather speak to Mr Singleton himself, Mrs Singleton,' the sergeant said gently, and the expression of sympathy in his eyes worried Nia more than any brisk manner would have done.

Colin came downstairs buttoning up his waistcoat and carrying his overnight bag in his hand.

'Going somewhere, sir?' asked the young constable, and something in his tone, an air of smugness, stung Nia.

'As a matter of fact, I'm off to my Cardiff office this morning,' Colin said easily. 'Is there anything I can do for you?' He addressed his remarks to the sergeant.

'I'm afraid, sir, I'm going to have to ask you to come with me to the police station on a matter of some urgency.'

Colin looked puzzled, but a feeling of dread had washed over Nia and she clasped her hands together to stop them from trembling.

'What matter?' Colin was becoming slightly irritated. 'Out with it, man, what's wrong?'

'We want you to help us with our enquiries, sir.' The sergeant's tone had taken on an edge of hardness, even though it was still polite. 'There's been a case of a fatal wounding in the town last night, and we think you can help us to sort it out.'

The constable was looking carefully at Colin's bruises. 'Been in an accident, sir?'

Colin lifted a hand to his face. 'Sort of,' he said shortly. 'But what about it?'

'The fact is, sir, a man, Joe Barnes, was fatally injured last night, and you were the last one to be seen in his company, sir. What's more, you were seen to have attacked the man quite viciously.'

Colin shook his head. 'I gave him a hiding that he deserved, yes,' he said in bewilderment, 'but I certainly didn't hit him hard enough to kill him.'

The sergeant sighed heavily. 'That will all be sorted out in good time I'm sure, Mr Singleton. Now may I ask you to accompany me to the station?' His tone implied that if Colin did not go reasonably, he would be forced to do so, and in horror, Nia watched her husband being led out of the door flanked by the two policemen as though he were a criminal.

When the door closed behind them, Nia hurried to the bedroom and flung on some clothes. She must go after Colin. Whatever he had done, he needed her support. Her hands were shaking so much she could hardly hold her clothes. Frustrated, she threw her blouse on to the bed, and then the tears came, hot and bitter, rolling salt into her mouth. This was some dreadful nightmare from which she would soon awake. 'Oh, Colin, my love,' she whispered, 'what have you done?'

The whole of Swansea buzzed with the story of how Colin Singleton, ship owner, had been taken into custody accused of murdering Joe Barnes.

Celia Williams sat in her kitchen, her head hammering, and stared before her with unseeing eyes. What did she care if a man like Joe Barnes was dead. He could not touch her, not now. Tragedy had come into her life and shaken her world the day that the bomber had flown low over Lambert's Cottages and killed her innocent daughter. That Anita had been with child had only made things worse, for Celia now would never see her first grandchild.

Anita had been buried in Dan-y Craig cemetery, laid to rest beneath the sweet earth that flanked the docks, and Celia Williams paid a visit to the grave every Sunday, giving her daughter more attention in death than she had ever done when the girl was alive. It was, she recognized dimly, a way of atonement. She placed her flowers in a vase at the head of the grave where a small wooden cross, planted into the ground, was all that was left to remind people that Anita Williams had ever lived.

Joe Barnes had got his just desserts. From what Celia had heard he'd been playing around with another man's wife before Anita was cold in her grave. Celia felt she had enough on her plate to worry about, what with Anita's death and now her man Sugar. Celia's husband had stayed out all night, and that was not like him, not like him at all. Celia had sat up till long after the lamp beside her bed had been switched off, waiting in vain for the creak of the latch on the back door.

Celia began preparing food. At least her girls would eat, even if she could not. Sarah especially had a good appetite, too good, the girl was putting on weight. Celia had only just put the kettle on the fire when Sugar came through the door, a look on his face like thunder. She did not allow the flood of relief she felt at the sight of her husband to show in her face.

'What's the matter with you now, old man?' Celia stirred the soup warming on the gas ring and wiped her face with her apron. Sugar did not see the tears that glinted on her eyelashes. He would have thought her daft grieving for her daughter who should, according to him, be forgotten.

'Where's our Sarah,' he asked roughly, and straddled the kitchen chair so that its joints squeaked in protest.

'In work, where she always is at this time of day.' She stared hard at him. 'Never mind that, I've got some questions to ask you, like where did you stay all night, old man? Getting a woman on the side at your age, are you?'

'Don't talk daft,' he said. 'I had business to attend to. Where's my tea, I'm starving.'

'You don't get tea if you don't go to work. You should know that well enough, Sugar Williams, it's a rule you made up yourself.'

'Bring my food, woman.' Sugar's voice was surprisingly soft. 'I'm in need of something in my belly, mind, feel real bad I do.'

Celia glanced at him anxiously, he was a little bit pale and there was a slight cut on his mouth.

'What you been up to then?' she asked, standing before him, hands on hips. 'I won't have you sitting in my kitchen if you've been womanizing or getting into fist fights. Tell me the truth now, Sugar.' Her voice softened. 'Haven't we always been honest with each other?'

Suddenly his face crumpled. He held out his arms to her and, alarmed, she went to him. In an uncharacteristic gesture she put her arms protectively around him, hugging his head to her aproned chest.

'What's wrong, my lovely, come on now, nothing can be so bad that you can't tell your old woman about it.' She brushed back his thinning hair, fear rushing through her. 'It's nothing to do with that Joe Barnes, is it, Sugar? Come on, you can tell me now, can't you?'

'I didn't mean to do it, Celia,' he gulped. 'Honest to God, I didn't. Some other man had already given him a good beating, see, and I didn't know. Waiting in the dark I was for him to come home, hit him with a bit of old iron bar.'

'But why, love?' Celia's eyes were wide with fear. Was there no end to the pain and suffering that had come upon her family?

'Mucking about with our Sarah, he was, mind, trying to put her in the family way just like her sister. He was a

359

bastard of a man, but for all that I didn't mean to kill him.'

'No, of course you didn't, love.' Celia felt her gorge rise. Sarah was only sixteen and not flighty like Anita had been. A nice quiet girl was Sarah, yet come to her flowering as a woman. Celia felt the sudden urge to kill Joe Barnes herself.

'I can see why you did it,' she said softly. 'Keep quiet about it, Sugar. I had old Ma Tully in by here this morning, said that Mr Colin Singleton has been arrested and taken to the station for the beating he gave Joe Barnes. He's just as guilty as you, he *could* have killed the man.'

'I can't do that, gel.' Sugar took out a big red handkerchief and rubbed at his eyes. 'What if they hang 'im?'

'Well, we'll face that when we come to it,' Celia said decisively. 'You listen to me now and don't say a word. Lay doggo for a bit, tell folks you got a bad belly or something. No one will think of you, they'll all blame this ship owner, don't you worry.'

She went back to the fire and removed the pot of stew. She was cold inside, her whole stomach seemed to have a life of its own, jumping and fluttering as if there were a bird trapped in there. Suddenly the bile rose to her mouth and she ran outside along the cinder path towards the privy.

Robert, like everyone else in Swansea, had heard about the killing. His immediate response was to think of Sugar Williams's anger when Dan had confronted him with the story of how Joe Barnes was sniffing around young Sarah. It was incredible to believe that Sugar would actually kill anyone – he was a gentle man in spite of his size – and yet knowing the circumstances, it was equally impossible to believe that Colin Singleton was guilty.

On an impulse, he went out of the shed and walked along the docks, looking for a sight of the big man who should be helping to load the *Welsh Pride* with boxes of ammunition. This morning it had been a matter of all hands to work on the ships. There had been little need for capping out since most of the young men had signed up for the army.

There was no sign of Sugar, but Robert spotted young Dan, his thin seventeen-year-old frame bent by the weight he was lifting.

'Dan!' he shouted above the noise of the docks, 'come here a minute. I want to talk to you.' He drew the boy away from the dock's edge. 'Have you seen anything of Sugar Williams?'

Dan shook his head. 'What I heard is that he's sick, pains in his gut. Why, do you want him for something?'

Robert lit his pipe thoughtfully. 'No, it's all right. Carry on, you.' It was strange that there was the murder last night of a man Sugar had been heard to threaten, and now the unheard of had happened; Sugar had not turned up for work. Perhaps he should pay Sugar a visit.

A little while later Robert was walking, deep in thought, along the perimeter of the docks towards Lambert's Cottages. There was a mystery here and he didn't like mysteries. If Sugar had killed Joe Barnes then it was an unintentional killing he was sure, and it wasn't like the man to let someone else pay for what he'd done.

He looked up and came face to face with Eden Lamb. The man stopped before him, obviously determined to speak.

'I wanted to ask you,' Eden said, 'is there any news of Kristina?'

Robert felt his jaw harden. 'What happens to my wife is my concern,' he replied abruptly.

'I'm only asking out of a sense of decency, man.' Eden spoke so reasonably that Robert was made to feel churlish.

'Well, your tone is a touch too condescending for my liking,' Robert could not resist the barb, 'but seeing as you asked, I don't know anything except that Kristina is on her way home.'

'I'm very glad to hear it,' Eden said, thrusting his hands into his pockets. He stood his ground and Robert wondered what else was on the man's mind. He was not kept waiting long.

'You would know if anything untoward was happening on the docks, wouldn't you?' Eden said slowly.

Robert braced himself. 'It all depends on what you mean by untoward,' he said. 'There's always a little bit of pilfering when the cargo is something portable like sweets or flour, but that's been an accepted code of practice among the dockers for many years. None of them would abuse it.'

'I'm talking about something much more serious than that.' Eden Lamb pushed back a lock of dark hair that had fallen across his brow. Watching him, Robert could not deny that the man was a handsome devil; no wonder he ensnared women so easily.

'Such as?' Robert was on the defensive. He had a good idea what the man was getting at, but if Eden thought Robert would betray a fellow docker then he was more stupid than he looked.

'My partner is in trouble,' he said abruptly. 'Colin Singleton has been accused of the murder of a man called Joe Barnes. Have you heard of any threats, any rumours that a docker was after the man? Apparently,' he went on as Robert remained silent, 'Barnes was struck with something made of heavy metal – perhaps a trimmer's flat spade or something.'

'You're way off the track there, man,' Robert said easily. 'You couldn't catch any docker taking off with one of the trimmer's shovels, treat their possessions like babies do the trimmers.'

'Well, have you heard anything suspicious at all?' Eden asked, losing his patience.

Robert sized him up. He liked the man for trying to do the right thing by his friend, but Eden Lamb was on a different side of the fence to the dockers, and the men who worked the ships were loyal to their own. 'If I hear

362

anything of value, I'll let you know,' Robert said coolly, aware that Eden was looking at him in disbelief.

'Oh, I bet you will,' he said, and abruptly strode away in the direction of Ty Coch.

Sugar Williams was sitting in a chair near the fire, a bottle of ale clutched in his big hand. His face was pasty, his eyes puffy, and he didn't look well. But he had the look of a man poor in spirit rather than in flesh.

'Hello boss, sorry I couldn't come in this mornin', pain in the belly, see, running to the lav I am all the time.'

Robert took a seat and looked up apologetically at Mrs Williams who was rubbing her hands in agitation. 'Excuse me calling unexpectedly,' he apologized. 'I won't stay long, it's all right.'

'*Duw*, no need to rush, mind. I'll make you a nice cup of tea in a minute, when the kettle boils.'

'Mrs Williams,' Robert spoke quietly, 'I wonder, could I talk to Sugar on his own. It's docker's business and quite confidential.'

'Oh, is that all right with you, Sugar?' The woman fluttered around her husband anxiously, sensing danger and unwilling to leave him to face it alone. Sugar was not so perceptive.

'Aye, go on woman, bugger off,' he said, his eyes downcast as he rubbed at the sides of the bottle with his thumb and finger.

'Right then, I got to make the beds and straighten the rooms anyway, so I'll leave you to it then.' She went through to the parlour and closed the door, and Robert leaned forward in his seat.

'Sugar,' he said slowly, 'you know I'm your friend and I'll help you all I can. You do trust me, don't you?'

'Aye, boss, always been fair by me you have. Why, what's up then, something gone missing off the docks?'

'No, Sugar, it's much more serious. Last night, Joe Barnes was killed, and I think you might know something about it.'

Sugar's eyes were haunted. 'I'm sorry, Mr Jenkins,' he

said, crumbling at once, 'I didn't mean to kill the man, only to teach him a lesson, like, but I hit him once and he went down like a stone.' He buried his face in his big hands and his shoulders were shaking. 'Not a killer, me, I didn't mean to do it. I couldn't even drown a kitten, never mind kill an 'uman being.'

'I know that, Sugar,' Robert said kindly. 'Think, did you look at him after you hit him?'

'Aye. When he didn't move I turned him over like, and his face was battered as if somebody had given him a damned good hiding. Black his eyes was, an' his nose spread across his face. If I'd seen that before I took the lead pipe to him, I wouldn't have touched him, honest to God, Mr Jenkins.'

'I believe you, Sugar, and the police will believe you too, I'll make sure of that.'

Sugar's face began to tremble, the trembling spread through his body, then he jerked as though in spasm and suddenly fell forward into Robert's arms.

'Christ!' Sugar's face had gone awry, his eyes were closed and his mouth was drawn down at one corner. 'Mrs Williams!' Robert called, and she rushed into the room and fell on her knees, staring with horror into her husband's distorted face.

'He's been struck with the palsy,' she said in a whisper. 'Dear God, how much more do I have to take?' She turned on Robert. 'It's your fault, you and your pestering, why couldn't you all leave my husband alone. He's a good man, I tell you, a good man.' She began to weep, cradling Sugar in her arms, and Robert rose to his feet, a sense of unreality gripping him.

'I'll call the doctor,' he said quickly. 'Don't worry, Mrs Williams, we'll soon have him fixed up.'

'He's going to die, I know he is,' Celia Williams said pitifully. 'I saw my dad go like this, a clot running through his brain, it was, and now the same thing has happened to my Sugar. I can't stand it.'

Robert walked to the door, his step heavy. Mrs

Williams was right. If he had not interfered, perhaps Sugar would not have had the stroke. He strode out towards Eden Lamb's family home; the man was probably the only one in the vicinity who had a telephone.

A thought suddenly struck him; the house had been empty now for some time what with Roggen away and Eden settled in his own home. What if the phone had been disconnected?

He hurried towards the large doorway and knocked hard, seeing the irony in the fact that he, who had refused Eden Lamb help, now wanted help himself. He would never have gone to Kristina's lover for anything, but Sugar Williams's life was at stake, and Robert had nowhere else to turn but to Eden Lamb.

28

Kaare brushed the sweat from his face. It had been an unexpected and bloody clash with a handful of stray Germans, but they had been quickly overpowered, for the Norwegians, dressed now as German officers, had the element of surprise on their side.

He walked along the platform towards the stores truck where Kristina was hidden. In his jacket was a flask of coffee, hot and black and sweet. He knew that Kristina must be frightened out of her wits by the shooting, but he could not make his progress to the back of the train too rapid or too obvious, or someone would be bound to ask him what he was about.

As he passed the station master's office, the telephone rang, and after a moment's hesitation, Kaare picked it up. '*Ja?*' he said, and a German voice rang out over the line.

'Major Holst here, speaking from Dovre. Who is this? State your name at once.'

Kaare quickly took off the German cap and looked inside. 'Hans Richter, sir, Lieutenant Richter,' he replied in German.

'Fetch your commanding officer at once,' the voice ordered, and Kaare waved urgently to Johan.

'A German officer,' he explained quickly, 'speaking from Dovre, a Major Holst.'

Johan caught on quickly and explained rapidly in German that he and his men were isolated on a small railway line and were awaiting orders. The voice over the phone barked out questions, and Kaare could guess at the nature of them by the replies Johan was giving.

'Ammunition, sir, no, not gold. Yes, sir, I examined the cargo myself, it is most definitely ammunition. I'm sorry, sir we had to delay the train. The driver, a foolish fat Swede, was very drunk, but we are ready to move at once, sir.' It was true, Bjerkelund was lying drunk on the floor of the station office, snoring like a pig.

A smile spread over Johan's face. 'Is that so, sir, the British have landed and are attacking Trondheim? That is bad news indeed. Yes, sir, I will take the train to Andalsnes, yes, we should arrive there in two hours and fifty-one minutes precisely, just as you say. Thank you, sir.'

He put down the telephone and rubbed at his eyes. 'That took some quick thinking, Larson, but at least now I have some information to go on. We must get a message to Colonel Hagen – he's the officer commanding the marines at Andalsnes – the Germans are going to attack at two o'clock. I'll code the message and you, Larson, can be responsible for sending it. When you get through to Dombas, make sure you are talking to a Norwegian operator and not a German one.'

Kaare waited impatiently for Johan to work out the coded message. It was very cold and he was worried about Kristina and the baby. She must be worried, wondering what had happened. He hoped to God that she wouldn't stir from the truck and show herself, or she would most likely be left at the small station to fend for herself.

When the message was in code, Kaare picked up the telephone. He spoke carefully to the operator, and when he was sure he was speaking to a Norwegian, he gave the coded message and put the receiver down with a sigh of relief. Now, at last, he could see to Kristina.

She was crouched against the side of the truck, her eyes wide and frightened as they rested on his German uniform. Then she sighed with relief as she recognized him.

'Kaare, I thought I'd never see you again.' She could

367

hardly speak, she was shivering so much. He took out the flask of hot coffee and held it to her lips.

'Come on, you can't get rid of a good Norwegian that easily,' he said gently. 'Kristina, listen to me, we will be arriving at Andalsnes in just under three hours. If anything should happen to me in the mean time, you must look for Colonel Hagen, he will take care of you.'

She clung to him for a moment and he touched her cheek softly. 'But don't worry, I shan't let anything happen. How could I when I've such a lovely girl to look after?' He moved away from her. 'I must go, we shall be leaving here any minute now. Take heart, Kristina, the sun is shining, the air grows warmer and soon we shall be safe, I promise you.'

As Kaare strode briskly back along the platform, he thrust his hands deep into the pockets of the German coat and frowned worriedly; had he made a mistake in bringing Kristina on this foolhardy mission to the coast? And yet, what other choice was there? As civilians they would have been stopped by the Germans, and if Kristina's identity was discovered she might even be taken for a British spy.

'Larson, get over here.' Johan was in the cab of the train, calling to him impatiently. 'Can you drive a train?' he said without preamble.

'I know the mechanics of it,' Kaare said quickly. 'If there's no one else, then I'll do my best.'

'Get out of those German clothes, then,' Johan said. 'You're a Swedish driver now and a friend of the Germans. Remember that if we should be stopped.'

It took a while to get up the head of steam required to pull a train so heavily laden, and it was past noon when Kaare began the journey to Andalsnes. He concentrated fiercely on working out the proper ratio between required average speed and lost momentum on braking due to the weight of the gold. It was a task almost beyond him, inexperienced as he was, but there was no choice. It was take a risk or remain static on the line, an easy target for any suspicious German. He pulled down his cap and was grateful for the heat from the boiler which was being stoked by one of Johan's recruits. What a way to run a train, Kaare thought ruefully, but they would get to Andalsnes if it was the last thing he did.

He was beginning to get the hang of gauging the speed and handling the train, and was concentrating so hard on his task that it was some moments before he noticed that a large barricade of logs had been laid across the track up ahead. Fortunately, the track was long and straight, and Kaare was able to pull up with a loud screeching of brakes some fifty yards away from the barrier.

Johan joined him at once. 'Trouble?' he asked as he swung himself up into the cab. Kaare pointed at the logs, and Johan frowned. 'Looks like a trap,' he said, 'but set by the Germans or by patriotic Norwegians, I wonder?' He paused. 'We'll wait here, let them make the first move.'

The silence was punctuated only by the spluttering of the boiler and occasional gushes of steam from the engine, and still no one appeared from behind the barrier. If it was a war of nerves, it certainly was a good one. Then Kaare tensed, as first one figure, then another and another, dark against the snow, became detached from the bulk of the logs, until there were about twelve Germans, all armed with sub-machine-guns, walking towards the cab. It was clear from the uniforms they wore that they were Gestapo, and the officer in charge stepped forward, gun thrust out belligerently.

'Lieutenant Richter?' the man said in a harsh voice, his eyes narrowed against the glare of the sun on the snow.

'That's me,' Johan said quickly, and Kaare gave the man full credit for swiftness of thought. Kaare had posed on the telephone as Richter, but now he was dressed in the clothes of a Swedish civilian train driver.

'What do you want?' Johan said, his tone equally sharp. 'I shall be late if I am delayed. I should be in Andalsnes in a few hours.'

The Gestapo officer eyed him up and down, and hoisted the gun into a more comfortable position against his hip. 'We both have our jobs to do,' he said, 'and mine is to search this train. It won't take more than half an hour and then you must just make up time by travelling faster.'

'I've searched this train personally,' Johan said firmly, 'and I tell you, it's ammunition we are carrying.'

'The searches may well have been made,' the officer eyed Johan with hostility, 'but you may have been mistaken. Did you, for instance, look at the boxes lower down, or did you, as I suspect, simply open those on the top of the pile?'

Johan was clearly searching about in his mind for a convincing reply, and in the silence the officer spoke again. 'Obviously the search has not been made to Himmler's satisfaction, for he personally has sent me to double-check.'

'I object to being disbelieved in such a manner,' Johan said quickly. 'I am telling you a further search is a waste of time, the gold is not on this train.'

'Then where is it?' the officer persisted. 'It is no longer in the bank vault at Oslo, it has to be somewhere, wouldn't you agree? In any case, we had a phone call from your Swedish driver, made at the last stop, and he claims that the gold is aboard.'

He gave a command, and two German soldiers dragged Kaare down from the cab. They caught his arms in a pincer-like grip and thrust him before the officer.

'Speak, man, where is the gold?' the officer said in a reasonable tone. Kaare remained silent, forcing a sullen look on to his face. A crashing blow from a rifle butt caught him on the back of the neck, and he fell sprawling on to the track, hitting his head with a sickening crash against one of the rails. For a moment he saw lights exploding before his eyes, and then he must have lost consciousness, for the world was a place of whirling blackness.

*

Robert stared around him at the bare barrack room with its rows of small beds and faceless cupboards standing like sentries against the wooden walls. Some posters had been pinned up on doors and windows in an effort to make the place look more homely, but nothing could conceal the spartan bareness of the surroundings.

He sank down on to his bed and stared at blankets folded with the minute precision which the army demanded. Never mind that men were being maimed and killed on the front lines, here in the training camp in England, rules were meant to be observed.

His body ached. His kit had weighed more and more as the day of marching and training had continued, and now it all had to be cleaned and put away. His boots must shine until he could see his face in them, his webbing would need to be blancoed, the buttons on his uniform must be buffed up until they gleamed, as must his badges. It all seemed so trivial.

It was a far cry from the docklands of Swansea, where he had been in charge of the men, looked up to and respected. Here he was just a number, a faceless being to be bullied and badgered into instant instinctive response on being given a command. It might one day save his life, or so he was constantly being told.

The sergeant in charge of his unit seemed to take an instant dislike to Robert, recognizing perhaps that here was no raw youngster but a man who needed to be taught a lesson. Robert smiled to himself. He would obey without demur, but no one was going to break his spirit.

He sighed. Well, tomorrow he was going home on leave, and he hoped desperately that back in Swansea there would be news of Kristina.

'Gawd, I've had enough of humping this monster around on my back!' Jim Bingham was a Cockney, sparky and full of personality, and he too came in for a great deal of abuse from the sergeant. 'I'm going to kick the hell out of the Germans when I get to see 'em, and every one will have the face of our beloved sergeant!' he said with feeling.

Robert removed his mud-caked boots and eased the thick woollen socks from his blistered feet. What he would give for a good pint of beer and a smoke in the bar of the Burrows. The room was beginning to fill up with men weary from their day spent marching and drilling, presenting arms, coming to attention and, if slow, condemned to an hour or two doubling round the ground, heavy packs bouncing against bruised shoulder blades.

The sergeant entered the room, his eyes going to where Robert was getting painfully to his feet, standing to attention at the end of his bed.

'You, taff,' he said, 'special duties for you tomorrow.' He stood nose to nose with Robert who felt a sharp pain of anger that his leave was obviously being cancelled. But he would not give the man the satisfaction of seeing his anger, so he remained silent. 'Thought you'd be going home to the little wifey for a bit of canoodling didn't you, taff, but the sooner you learn this is the army, the better.'

He marched out triumphantly and Robert sank back on to his bed, his fists clenched until the knuckles shone white.

'Never mind, mate,' Jim said in sympathy, 'only another few weeks to go and we'll be out of this hellhole. Let's get to the real war, that's what I say.'

Robert sighed heavily. 'Aye,' he said, 'nothing could be worse than being in this godforsaken place.'

He stretched out on the bed and stared up at the ceiling, trying to fix his thoughts on something positive, but all he could think of was that Kristina might be on the way home. She might even now be making her way to the house, looking for him, worrying about him. He tried to relax his stiff fingers. It was no good thinking of murdering the sergeant, the man was paid to be a pain in the backside. He smiled suddenly. As Jim said, a few more weeks and the training camp would be left behind for ever.

Kristina was wide awake, kneeling on a box, trying to see

out of the truck. 'Oh, Kaare, what's been happening? I've been so worried about you.' She clasped him in her arms and held him close.

'It's all right now. We had some difficulties with the Gestapo but we've dealt with them.' He touched her face lightly. 'I told you not to worry, didn't I? Everything is going to be all right. I have to go now, but later on I'll come and see you and I'll bring you some hot food. How is the baby?'

She smiled, the lines of anxiety easing from her forehead. 'Fast asleep, not disturbed by anything.' She pressed his hand. 'I'm all right too, but you, I fear for you with the Germans hiding round every bend.'

'Let's hope from here on in we won't meet any more Germans and we'll have a chance to make up for lost time.' Kaare looked at his watch. 'It's quarter to one and we've only travelled five miles. We must do better than that.' He took her face between his hands. 'Now keep down in amongst the blankets, keep yourself and the baby warm. Try to sleep if you can, it will pass the time, and whatever happens, don't show yourself.'

'I'll be careful,' Kristina said, looking levelly into his eyes.

He turned to climb out of the truck and Kristina caught his arm. 'Kaare, you've been hurt!' she said in a whisper. 'There's blood all down your collar.'

'It's nothing,' Kaare said quickly, 'just a scratch. It looks much worse than it is. I'll have a headache for a while but nothing more.'

'No, let me see to it!' Kristina searched in her bag and produced a small jar of crowsfoot ointment. She worked quickly on the wound, and once she was finished Kaare smiled at her gratefully.

'You should have been a nurse, Kristina, you have very good hands.' As he left the truck and walked slowly back along the track towards the cab, he wondered if it was worth taking the risk of telling Johan of Kristina's presence so that she could see to some of the wounded men in the party.

Suddenly Kaare saw a slight ripple of snow fall from one of the trees. He drew his gun and waited until he saw another shower of snow, and then he fired several times into the tree. A grey shape plummeted to the ground and rolled down the icy slopes. At the same time, there was the sound of a car starting up and driving away, and Kaare looked at Johan who had come to stand beside him.

'What do you think that was all about?' Kaare asked. 'A Norwegian collaborator, perhaps.'

Johan shrugged. 'We'll probably never know. Now, let's get going, the line is cleared and we have a lot of time to make up.'

Kaare hurried towards the cab and climbed inside, aware that his head ached as though a thousand hammers were striking repeated blows against his temples. He forced himself to concentrate, though the glare of the snow on both sides of the track assaulted his eyes. Time ceased to have meaning and Kaare performed the operations of handling the train automatically. He was brought out of his daze by Johan's hand on his shoulder.

'We're nearing Trollheimen now. There is a siding up ahead completely surrounded by mountains,' he said. 'It's just beyond a small station, and we'll be able to rest and have a meal.'

Kaare brought the train slowly to a halt, and looking around realized that Johan's strategy was sound. Here, between the mountains, there was no wind, it was a snug and safe hideaway and the train with its white tarpaulin was not likely to be spotted from the air. Nevertheless, they had only been halted a few minutes when there was the sound of an aircraft overhead. It circled around before flying out of sight.

'That was a near thing,' Johan said, but even as he spoke the plane reappeared. 'How the devil!' Johan was exasperated but Kaare had spotted something among the trees.

'Look, sir, a red cap,' he said. 'There's a man up there,

374

and listen, I can hear the sound of a car engine. It's probably the same car we heard way back along the track. We've been followed by a traitor, it seems.'

Kaare made to move away but Johan stopped him. 'Not this time. You take a rest, it's my turn now.'

Kaare watched as Johan, taking a few men with him, skirted the roadway where the car was standing, engine running in readiness for a quick getaway. There was silence for a time, an eerie silence that was punctuated suddenly by a single shot. Kaare waited impatiently for Johan's return, wondering what had happened, wishing that he was at the centre of events. He had no taste for sitting on the sidelines. Johan Olsen returned as silently as he had left, a red cap clutched in his gloved hand.

'The bastard was signalling with this.' He held out a mirror. 'No wonder our position was so easy to spot.'

'Is he dead, Johan, did you shoot him?' Kaare asked, but Johan shook his head.

'He was felled by a rifle but the shot you heard was me shooting the man's tyres.' He rubbed at his face. 'He was a Norwegian, a man from Dovre which is now occupied by the Germans. There's no staying here tonight, we'll have to get down to Andalsnes straight away. Our whereabouts must be well known to the enemy.'

'Shall I get going at once, then?' Kaare asked, hope rising in him that within a few hours he would have Kristina safely in the hands of English soldiers.

'Firstly I want to contact Hagen in Andalsnes,' Johan said soberly. 'God only knows what's happening there, we don't want to walk into a trap now that we've come this far. Take a rest, have a coffee break, while I get on the phone. You look as if you could do with it.'

Kaare took a piece of thick lint and some clean bandages, and with a quick look round him climbed into the truck where Kristina was settling the baby down to sleep.

'I've come to ask you to take a risk,' he said. 'Some of the less seriously wounded have been put in a truck next door to this one. One of them has started bleeding heavily. Is there anything you can do?'

'I can try,' Kristina said, 'but what about the baby?'

'I'll stay with him, he'll be all right,' Kaare said. 'Don't you worry about that.' He drew his coat from around his shoulders. 'Put this on and my cap, and be careful.' He helped her from the truck, and then all he could do was to sit and wait for her return. She seemed to be an age, but at last he heard a scratching at the tarpaulin and then he was helping her into the truck.

'I think the man is going to be all right,' she gasped, 'but you'd better go, someone is calling you.'

He was leaving the truck when Johan came into sight. Quickly, Kaare pulled the tarpaulin into place.

'I have some bad news.' Johan beckoned to Kaare, rubbing at his forehead anxiously. 'We have to abandon the train,' he said. 'I've been on to Hagen and they need another two days to reduce the numbers of German parachute troops to a minimum.' He paused, seeing the question in Kaare's eyes before he had time to voice it. 'Lorries, carts, anything and everything we can get our hands on. Kaare, I want you to shunt the train up to the goods shed until we've unloaded, and then take it back to the siding, which is where the Germans will expect to find it.'

Kaare nodded, his mind racing. He wondered if Kristina had heard. If so, she would be worrying, as he was. How in God's name was he going to conceal a woman and a baby on a lorry? Would it be better perhaps to leave Kristina behind in the town? But then he knew instinctively that she would refuse to remain with strangers, and who could blame her? Many Norwegians were sympathetic to the Germans. It would only take one collaborator to blow Kristina's cover and she would be in real trouble. No, there was no way he could leave her behind, he must take over one lorry himself and somehow smuggle her into the cab. But for now he had the dangerous job of reversing the train back into the station, no easy task with so much snow about.

The goods sheds were swarming with men, it was clear that Johan had done his work well. The reloading of the gold proceeded smoothly and efficiently, if a trifle slowly, but at least there was transport aplenty, lorries from the nearby quarry.

Kaare spoke to the station master. 'Is there anywhere we can hide the lorries if we should need to hang back for a few days?' he asked, and the man nodded.

'There's a logging camp not more than three miles from here, deep in the forest, and there's garaging there for the lorries too.'

Kaare nodded. 'Good, that sounds just the place.' He turned as Johan called to him.

'Take the train back to the siding, Kaare,' he said. 'Most of the gold is loaded, we'll start on the supplies next.'

Kaare felt cold. He was the only one who could drive the train, and yet if he went Kristina was bound to be discovered. There was nothing else for it, he would have to come clean with Johan and hope the man would understand the position he was in.

'I must speak to you,' Kaare said in a low voice, and Johan paused for a moment, on the point of saying that surely anything else could wait. The look in Kaare's eyes stopped him.

'What is it, are you sick?' Johan said as Kaare drew him to one side. Kaare shook his head.

'I have something to tell you, it's most important,' he said urgently. Even as he explained Kristina's presence on the train, he saw the look of disbelief cross Johan's face.

'You mean we've had a woman and child aboard the train all this time, through the shooting and the waiting and the bloody awful weather? How have they survived?'

'I pinched one of the stoves from the live-in tent,' Kaare said, 'and I've kept Kristina supplied with food and hot liquids.' He shrugged. 'She's from England, Johan. I guessed that Lillehammer would soon be taken over by the Germans so I could not leave my cousin there.' If he'd expected Johan to blow up into a rage he was mistaken.

'You fool,' Johan said, but his voice was tinged with admiration. 'Your Englander cousin must have a charmed life not to have been discovered by one of our own men, let along one of the Germans.'

'I've taken care to go for supplies myself,' Kaare said. 'I insisted that I was the one who knew where everything was, and no one bothered to argue with me. They were all too intent on being brave soldiers.'

'Well, look,' Johan said, 'you must go and take the train to the siding. I will come with you now and meet your cousin, and I personally will install her safely into one of the lorries. But you must be the driver of that lorry. None of the men must be allowed to know there is a woman along with us you understand?'

'That might be a little difficult,' Kaare said. 'She has tended one of the injured men. But I doubt he'll say anything.'

Kristina looked up with alarm as Kaare and Johan climbed into the truck. Kaare, looking at Johan, knew that the older man was smitten at once by Kristina's lovely face and expressive eyes. Johan bowed, and for the first time Kaare actually saw the man smiling.

'Now I can see why the good Kaare risked everything to take you to safety. You are a very beautiful woman.'

'We have to abandon the train,' Kaare said, taking Kristina's hand. 'I will be taking the train to the siding but Johan will be looking after you until I get back.'

'Wait here,' Johan said, 'I will drive one of the lorries as near as I can and then we can smuggle the lady and her child into the cab without her being seen.'

When Johan had gone, Kaare took Kristina into his arms. 'Don't worry, he's a good man to have around and if anything should happen to me, at least now I know there is someone else who would be responsible for seeing you to safety.'

'Hush,' Kristina said softly, 'don't talk about anything happening to you. We have come this far, we must reach safety together.'

Kaare simply held her. How could he explain that once she was delivered into the hands of her countrymen, Kaare's war would only just be beginning. But if he and Johan could safely see their country's fortune in gold bullion leaving the shores of Norway, they would have done more to help Norway than any man might expect in a lifetime of fighting.

In a short while, Kaare heard the sound of a lorry outside on the platform. He lifted the tarpaulin and assured himself that Johan was the driver before helping Kristina out into the cold of the day. She shivered and held her baby close, and gratefully allowed Johan to help her into the cab of the lorry.

'I'll get the train off to the siding and then make my way back,' Kaare said quickly.' He lifted his hand to Kristina in a brief salute and made his way to the front of the engine.

It was a tricky task to get the train into the siding, and when it was done Kaare stopped for a moment and looked around him. The train had been good to them and progess had been slow but fairly safe. What hazards might the convoy now meet on the open road?

When he got back to the station, the first of the lorries, driven by a local man, was already winding its way out on to the road. Twelve lorries in all made up the convoy, the back one driven by Johan himself. He stopped for Kaare to clamber aboard, watched by Kristina's green eyes. Half her face was concealed by a cap and scarf, and the baby was held out of sight in her lap. From a distance she might have been taken for a young boy.

'Good work, Johan,' Kaare said, and looking at the old man he realized that Johan was enjoying himself hugely. He winked.

'It isn't every day that a soldier gets to drive a lovely lady on a secret mission, is it?'

Kristina was wedged between her cousin and the older man who seemed to be in charge. It was his idea that she cover her face and don a cap so that she looked like a man. She felt doubly safe now, cared for not only by her brave and wonderful cousin but by this experienced officer who exuded an air of confidence that made her trust him instinctively.

From her new vantage point, she could at least see something of the road they were travelling and it was a relief, for she was heartily sick of the warm womb of the goods truck in the train where she knew by heart every item of baggage, every tin and every box. It was fresher in the cab of the lorry, not so warm but the journey hopefully would not be a long one. Soon they would be in Andalsnes and she would join a boat filled with British soldiers and be returned to her own country.

At last, the leading lorry turned off the road on to the logging track, and Johan grunted in satisfaction.

'If the snow continues to fall, our tracks will be covered almost as soon as they were made,' he said. 'Kaare, you take Kristina into the main office of the camp and keep her there while the men are garaging the vehicles. If anyone asks, that is my quarters and I wish to share them with no one.'

He glanced at Kristina with a smile. 'Don't worry, my dear. Your cousin and I will be sleeping in the next room. You will be safe with us.'

When Johan stopped the lorry, Kaare took Kristina by the shoulders and hurried her through the snow. 'I'll have the stove lit in just a few minutes,' he said cheerfully as they entered the office. 'At least there's plenty of timber round here for the fire.'

Kristina sank down on to a chair and lifted the baby high in her aching arms. For tonight, at least, they were safe.

29

The scandal of Roggen's sudden decision to leave her husband and live with her Australian lover shook the small community at Seletar to its foundations. Many of her former friends ignored Roggen entirely, siding with Richard, the deserted husband. It was only her old friends Maggie and John Dunbar who remained firm in their support and friendship.

Not that Roggen had time to worry about the reactions of other people. For the first time in her life she was almost out of her mind with love and happiness. She had been swept away by Mark's strength, and the more she grew to know him, the more she respected the iron will tempered with a fine sense of humour that her lover possessed.

She sat in their living room trying to write a letter to Eden, but she couldn't help glancing at Mark from time to time, watching the way he moved as he talked, only slowly becoming aware of what he was saying.

'There's talk that Australia may send troops over here some time in the near future.' He smiled at her. 'It'll be good to see some fellow Australians even if they are army men.'

Roggen felt suddenly chilled. 'But Mark, we're all right out here, the war isn't touching us, is it?'

'Not at the moment, love, that's for sure. All the experts say that Singapore is impregnable, with the heavy fortifications on the straits it would be dificult for anyone to attack the island.' He shrugged. 'On the other hand the Japanese are making threatening noises, and God knows what the cunning little bastards will get up to next. They invaded China in 1937 — that proves they've got the capability to be top dogs.' He looked levelly at Roggen. 'We couldn't expect any help from the Malays, that's for sure. They'd have to look after their own skins, and who could blame them?'

Roggen had been sitting near the light from the window, the pen idle in her hand. Eden had to be told about the great changes in her life and the news had to come from Roggen herself. It needed to be done quickly before Richard sent home his version of the facts. But now Roggen put down her pen and pushed the letter away from her. She wanted to hold Mark in her arms, to be reassured that her life with him was not threatened by war.

She wished Mark had not voiced his thoughts out loud, and yet she knew that part of the value of their relationship was their ability to talk honestly to each other. That was something she and Richard had never done. Perhaps once, when they were young and believed that politicians could put the world to rights, they might have had something in common. But much as she hated to admit it, she now found Richard's opinionated expression of his views boring, and the talking between them had gradually dwindled to banalities.

'Come here.' Mark held out his arms. 'Don't look so crestfallen. I guess I'm talking through the back of my neck, I don't suppose we'll ever see the war.'

As he held her, Roggen closed her eyes. He was so precious to her, and she loved him even more for trying to protect her. She reached up and kissed his mouth.

'Don't ever try to shield me from the truth, Mark. I value the honesty that's between us too much for that.' She moved away from him. 'Come on, let's get moving, we're going over to Maggie's for a drink, or have you forgotten?'

Mark groaned. 'Damn! And here was I looking forward to an early night with the most beautiful girl in Singapore.'

'Only in Singapore?' Roggen teased. 'What about the rest of the world, or are you one of those men who have a woman in every port?'

He caught her in his arms again and kissed her. 'That would be telling, my lovely, but you have the advantage over any of my other women; you are here with me now.'

She pretended to slap him, then clung to him, eyes closed, for a moment, love overwhelming her. She marvelled at the speed with which love had grown from attraction and fascination to a real, solid fact of life. She had not really known Mark when she had left Richard for him, and yet instinctively she must have seen the man beneath the hard exterior. Mark was a man of great strength of character, and when he gave her his love, though he spoke sparingly of it, he gave whole-heartedly.

Maggie Dunbar was waiting to greet them. She was every inch an English lady, from the top of her rolled-back hair to the hem of her long, sleek satin gown.

'Come in, Ro, you look marvellous.' She linked arms and leaned closer to whisper in Roggen's ear, 'That man of yours really *is* handsome!'

She drew them into the coolness of her beautifully furnished sitting room where the fan whirred on the ceiling and the open windows were covered in fine nets to keep out the mosquitoes. John Dunbar was there, elegant in a silk jacket with a cravat tied loosely at his throat.

'I hope you're feeling better, John,' Roggen said, taking the hand he offered shyly. 'Last time we saw you that wretched bug was still bothering you.'

'I'm jolly good now, Roggen my dear, jolly good.' He patted his stomach. 'Still careful about my eating habits however, don't want a repeat performance, do we?'

Maggie waved them to a seat. 'No, Johnnie is having *rijstaffel* which is much less spicy than the *nasi padang* we're going to indulge ourselves in. But more about food later, what about a little drink?' She leaned forward, her slender hands clasped over the satin gown. 'Something long and cool, perhaps?'

Roggen flashed a glance at Mark, who was leaning back, arm stretched along the sofa, smiling in his usual enigmatic way. 'I'd like an "it" with some gin in, quite a lot of gin actually.' She smiled at Maggie. 'As for Mark,' she said teasingly, 'I expect he'd like a beer.'

He ruffled her hair. 'Stop being so bossy, woman, but you're right, I'll have a cool beer.'

Maggie laughed. 'I can see you two are acting like a married couple already!' She glanced down at the large diamond gleaming on her finger. 'There's been a bit of gossip about Richard, though.' She paused. 'Seems he's been seen escorting the daughter of one of the old buffers running the aerodrome, some boring little girl with only a rich daddy to commend her.'

Roggen felt nothing, not surprise nor jealousy. 'Richard would have to find another woman if only to prove his manhood. Well, I hope it makes him happy to have a rich lady friend,' she said. 'Perhaps now he'll agree to a divorce.'

There was a discreet tapping at the door and an elderly Malayan bowed almost reverently to Maggie. She thanked him in Malay and rose graciously to her feet.

'Dinner is ready,' she said, linking arms with Roggen. 'That's good, because I'm starving.' She seemed relieved that the snippet of gossip about Richard had been delivered and well received, she was a good friend. Roggen smiled at her warmly.

'Me too,' she said. 'I could eat a horse.' She crossed the scented hallway with Maggie and was achingly aware of Mark and John walking behind them, talking about the war.

'Nothing can touch us here,' John said decisively. 'We're really impregnable, what with the guns at Jahore and the military base at Changi. I sometimes wish I could see some action. I feel my flying experience is being wasted.'

'I have a feeling we are not so untouchable in Singapore as people seem to think,' Mark said quietly. 'This end of

384

the island is well defended but what if we were attacked from somewhere else along the coastline, the north of the island, for instance? Another thing, Singapore lies between the Pacific and the Indian Oceans, we are in easy reach of India, China and Europe, we have a major port here and it will be a great asset to whoever holds it.'

Roggen didn't hear John's reply because Maggie was talking again. 'The meat has heaps of chillies added as well as some coconut cream. I do hope you like hot food, Roggen, it's supposed to be good for your love life.'

'In that case I can't wait.' Roggen smiled. 'Anyway, I've got an iron constitution, I can eat anything. If you only saw our lava bread at home, you'd realize what I mean.'

Maggie seated herself next to Roggen. 'What is it, this lava bread?' she asked, her eyes bright and inquisitive like those of a small bird. It was part of Maggie's charm that she was always so interested in even the tiniest detail.

'It's a dish made from seaweed, believe it or not.' Roggen said. 'It looks black and awful, but fried with bacon and cockles, it really is delicious.'

'I'll take your word for it,' Maggie pursed her lips, 'but it sounds dreadful.'

John was talking amiably about flying and Roggen listened for a moment, wondering at the sensitivity in Mark's make-up that enabled him to draw the best out of any company. Richard had always been difficult, moody, sometimes childishly so, and very often Roggen had stepped in and passed over a touchy moment with a tactful change of subject.

'Here, try some Javanese *krupuk* first,' Maggie said offering a dish of prawn crackers. 'They really are delicious, much better than your lava bread, Ro, I'll wager.'

'Maybe,' Roggen said good-naturedly, and took some of the food, placing it on a small saucer provided for just that purpose. The meal was tasty and well-cooked, the rice and vegetables spiced with *blacan*, a paste of dried shrimps which complimented the prawn crackers.

John served the wine and ate sparingly of his bland meal of rice containing very little spice or meat. He was still pale and there was a yellowish tinge to his skin that concerned Roggen. He was obviously still far from well.

After the meal, Maggie led Roggen back to the sitting room. 'Let's leave the men to their smoking and their boring talk about aeroplanes and war,' she said lightly. 'I have a million things I want to ask you.' When they were seated, she leaned forward, eyes shrewd, and put a question bluntly to Roggen. 'I want to know the truth, do you think you've done the right thing leaving Richard? It's such a big step, and in a way I feel responsible for encouraging you.'

'I'm not exaggerating when I say I have never been so sure of anything in my life,' Roggen said promptly. 'I love Mark to distraction and it will last even if we are never able to marry.'

Maggie sighed with relief. 'Then I'm happy too. I've spent some sleepless nights telling myself what an interfering busybody I am, I can tell you.'

'There's silly you are!' Roggen was unaware that she had lapsed into the Welsh idiom until Maggie smiled teasingly.

'How charming,' she said. 'You have such a lovely voice, Ro, so cultured, I do envy you.'

Roggen's dark eyebrows lifted. 'You with your posh English voice, how could you envy a poor little Welsh girl?'

'I do, though,' Maggie said soberly. 'I envy you Mark and his health and strength, I envy you your dark, beautiful looks, and most of all I envy the happiness that glows from you like a rainbow.'

'A lot of it is due to you, Maggie,' Roggen said. 'I'll always be grateful for all you've done and for the way you've remained a good friend in spite of other people ostracizing me.'

'Enough of this emotion,' Maggie said. 'I think the wine must be clouding our brains, don't you?' Nevertheless, she squeezed Roggen's hand before rising elegantly and lighting a cigarette from the gold box on the sideboard.

'I'm afraid I've some sad news. We may have to leave Singapore and return home.' Maggie puffed smoke into a spiral above her head. 'John is not recovering his health at all, you may have noticed that he ate very little dinner. I'm concerned and I want him looked at by the best specialists in London.'

She moved around the room with an uncharacteristic air of agitation. 'This dinner is by way of private farewell to you, Ro. I think we shall sail for home within the month.'

'Oh, Maggie!' Roggen said softly. 'I am sorry to lose you, but of course you must go home if John's health is at stake.' She found it difficult to conceal her dismay; without Maggie, Roggen would have no friends at all on the island, she would be totally isolated from all contact with other people. For Mark it would not be so bad, for he had his job at the rubber plantation, and the men who worked there for him were not the sort to care if he had a woman or not.

'I'm going to try an experiment to bring you back into the fold, as it were.' Maggie's frown vanished. 'I'm going to give a big party, invite everyone from the air base, including Richard and his young lady. That way, people will see for themselves that there are two sides to every story.'

'Maggie, do you think that's wise?' Roggen said doubtfully.

'Wise or not, we've nothing to lose, so why not try it?' Maggie's eyes twinkled. 'In any case, I always was one to take a gamble.'

Roggen smiled ruefully. 'You'd have got on very well with a friend of mine from home who runs a chain of betting offices. You and she are two of a kind.'

'I take it that's a compliment?' Maggie said, stubbing out her half-smoked cigarette.

'It is,' Roggen agreed. 'Nia is a very clever lady. She's made herself very rich by her own talents and I don't think there is anything about horse-racing she doesn't know.'

Mark and John entered the room together and John looked interested at once. 'What's that about horse-racing? One of my favourite sports, old thing.'

'Never you mind,' Maggie said. 'There's something important to discuss. We're going to give a big farewell party. Perhaps at Raffles. What do you think, Johnnie?'

'You do as you like,' John said in mock resignation. 'You always do, anyway!'

'Don't say that!' Maggie feined indignation. 'I have never failed to discuss any of my plans with you.'

'I agree, old girl, but you always tell me when things are *fait accompli*.' He sat down and stretched his long thin legs before him, and there were tired lines around his eyes. 'But we'll have a party, have six parties if it will make you happy. You know I can deny you nothing.'

Maggie dropped a kiss near his cheek and sat beside him, lighting another cigarette. 'You are a lovely old goose, I don't know what I'd do without you.' She spoke softly and Roggen, catching the underlying concern in her friend's voice, rose to her feet.

'I do think it's time we were making for home,' she said lightly. 'We're still on honeymoon, remember?' She glanced at Mark and he seemed to understand instinctively.

'Quite right,' he said, rising easily and tucking his shirt back into his wide belt. 'It's an early night for us. So long Maggie, John. Thanks for a lovely evening.'

As Mark set the jeep into motion, Roggen glanced at him. 'He's very sick, isn't he?' she said without preamble, and he did not pretend to misunderstand.

'Poor old bugger is real bad, if you ask me.' He said no more, but as Roggen glanced back at the glow from the windows of Maggie's house she felt a strange sense of sadness that refused to be shaken off even though she snuggled near to Mark's reassuring strength, glad of the warmth of his skin against hers in the darkness.

The party was set for the week before Maggie and John's departure, and as Roggen dressed carefully she was aware of her own nervousness at being with a crowd of possibly hostile people. The meeting with Richard would be tricky to handle, he was not the most tactful of men at the best of times.

She glanced at Mark who was handsome in an open-necked shirt and casual slacks. He would not dress formally even though the other men would all be wearing ties. He was not one to conform and Roggen admired him for being man enough to do what he pleased.

'You look stunning, love.' Mark leaned over and kissed the back of her neck. 'I love your hair long and curling and soft the way it is. Too many of the women around here slavishly follow the fashion, rolling back their hair to within an inch of its life, scalping themselves into the bargain. You do what you please. We're two of a kind, girl, do you realize that?'

Roggen smiled. He was right, she realized suddenly. She never had been one to be swayed by fashion except when it suited her.

'I was a typical flapper once, mind,' she said softly. 'I wore short skirts and cropped my hair like all the rest of the girls. But now that I'm an old lady I feel it's time to do what I want.' She wound her arms around his neck. 'And what I want right now is you.'

He kissed her gently and then with growing passion, and Roggen, laughing, pushed him away. 'We're going to a party, or have you forgotten?' She danced away from him and he looked at her sternly.

'You know what you are, my lady? You're a damned tease, and that's putting it politely.'

'Come on,' Roggen picked up a silk wrap, 'let's get going, get this thing over and done with.' Suddenly her lightheartedness had vanished. She felt threatened by the

389

coming meeting with their so-called friends. And she wasn't looking forward to seeing Richard again either.

Mark held the door of the jeep open for her, and she frowned ruefully as he helped her up into the seat. 'We should really get a car, Mark,' she said, smoothing down her dress. 'It's not very dignified climbing up into one of these with a skirt on.'

'Maybe not,' Mark said easily, 'but it gives me a terrific view of your legs.'

From the sounds issuing from the open windows of Maggie's house, the party was in full swing. The gramophone was playing a lively tune that Roggen failed to recognize, and above the music swelled the sound of many voices.

'I'm glad Maggie didn't have the party at Raffles after all,' Roggen said, aware of a sensation like a fluttering of many butterflies inside her. 'It's bad enough walking into Maggie's house, never mind one of the big rooms at Raffles.'

Mark took her arm and guided her firmly up the steps. The door swung open and Maggie, who must have been waiting for their arrival, stood ready to greet them.

'Come on in darlings!' She spoke unnecessarily loudly, attracting the attention of the other guests. 'It's wonderful to see you again, so glad you could make it.'

She spoke as though Roggen and Mark had a full engagement book, and Roggen smiled warmly, kissing her friend's cheek.

'Delighted to be here.' She and Mark were engulfed in a roomful of people, where smoke drifted in the air whirred by the fan and the clinking of glasses accompanied the hubbub of voices. There was a sudden lull in the conversation and then it took off again, as though the other guests were deliberately filling an awkward silence. Roggen took a glass from John and held it towards him in salute. 'Good luck, John,' she said softly.

Across the room, she spotted Richard. He had a young, plain girl clinging to his arm, with a burly man, apparently the rich father, hovering near by. Richard glanced in her direction and then deliberately looked away again.

'This is going to be a bundle of laughs,' Mark said softly in her ear. She looked up at him gratefully. She was proud to be with him and to hell with what anyone else thought.

At first, Roggen felt that she was being ostracized by the old crowd, but then, slowly, one or two of them made tentative remarks to her before moving on. It said a great deal about Maggie's clout as a friend and hostess. Roggen found herself relaxing as Richard kept his distance and occupied himself with his girlfriend and her proud father. It looked as though the evening would progress without event, and as soon as it was polite to do so she would ask Mark to take her home.

'John's looking very sick, isn't he?' One of the wives from the air base spoke to Roggen in hushed tones. 'No wonder Maggie's taking the love back home, can't get the right sort of doctors out here, you see.'

Roggen made a polite reply and found herself being separated from Mark by the crowd. She looked round for him anxiously and saw that he was in conversation with a man in officer's uniform. Her heart missed a beat. She knew instinctively that they would be discussing the war and whether Singapore would find itself threatened. But at least he appeared to be enjoying himself which was more than Roggen could say for herself. She was still a little tense, expecting any moment to be confronted by one of the elderly and very proper ladies of Seletar base and told in no uncertain terms that she was a scarlet woman.

But it didn't happen. The guests, it seemed, were on their best behaviour, primed no doubt by Maggie. Roggen felt herself sighing in relief as she accepted another drink from John who winked at her conspiratorially.

'How are you feeling, John?' Roggen asked, but she

never heard his reply, because, in the sudden lull that comes sometimes to a roomful of people, Richard's voice rang out.

'How she can show her face in decent company, I just don't know.'

The silence became profound. Roggen was aware of Mark crossing the room and standing casually before Richard.

'I was waiting for some crack from you, you holier than thou bastard,' Mark said in a deceptively soft voice. 'We came to put it to you straight on the line that we wanted to be together, and may I say you haven't wasted any time yourself if it comes to that.'

'It's none of your business what I do.' Richard was floundering and everyone in the room knew it. 'You ran away with my wife, you'd say anything to put me in the wrong.'

'And you are an old woman, indulging in petty gossip,' Mark replied easily.

'Well, what sort of wife was she anyway?' Richard demanded, 'running off with the first man to take her fancy?'

Roggen drew a sharp breath. How could Richard be so cruel? Mark took him by the collar and then after a moment released him, pushing him away. Richard adjusted his jacket and turned to see his lady friend being led away by her father. Hastily he followed, casting a look of loathing towards Mark as he passed him.

'Come on, people,' Maggie said, 'let's get on with this party, shall we?' She smiled. 'More drinkies everyone, this is not a wake, we're supposed to be having fun.'

'Well,' she said quietly to Roggen, 'I think that Richard has cooked his goose after that little display. In a way I feel sorry for him.' She linked arms with Roggen and led her over to a group of elderly ladies. 'This is my best friend, ladies. As you're new to the island I don't think you will have met her.'

Roggen was engulfed in conversation. She smiled and

made all the correct responses, but she couldn't wait to go home and be alone with Mark. He must have felt the same, because after a few minutes he came to her side and took her arm.

'I think it's time we were getting back home, Ro,' he said lightly. 'It's been an eventful party, wouldn't you say?'

He was smiling and she could have hugged him for putting the small upset into perspective. Richard was unimportant in their lives, nothing mattered so long as she and Mark had each other.

Roggen made her goodbyes to Maggie. 'Come and see us, please, before you leave,' she said, kissing Maggie's cheek. 'And you must promise to keep in touch when you get home.'

'Will do.' Maggie accompanied them to the door, hugged Roggen briefly and then returned indoors.

Roggen sighed with relief as Mark set the jeep into motion. She nestled against him and closed her eyes. 'Thank God that's over. I hope I never have to see Richard again.'

'Forget him,' Rod said easily, 'he's not worth a light.' He put his arm around her, guiding the jeep with one hand. 'Have I ever told you, Roggen, that I love you very much and I'm a lucky son of a gun to have you?'

She turned her face into his shoulder, and there were sudden tears in her eyes. 'No,' she said softly, 'that's the first time you've ever said it.' The tears trembled on her lashes and ran salt into her mouth, but they washed away all the guilt and anger she had been feeling, for they were tears of pure happiness.

30

Sarah sat alone, staring into the waters of Singleton Lake. On the surface, lilies spread green leaves like fallen fans, and here and there the alabaster of the flowers glowed against the darkness of the water. How could she have made such a devastation of her life? All she had done was to fall in love with Joe Barnes and it had ended in tragedy. She might as well slip into the waters of the pond and let them close over her, then she and her unborn baby would be out of it for ever.

'Sarah, I thought I'd find you here.' Dan looked down at her and there was sympathy in every line of his face. She turned away from him, she did not want his pity.

He sat beside her and took her hand in his. 'You like sitting here in the park, don't you?' When she didn't reply, he tried again. 'Sarah, don't look so lost and alone, everything will be all right. I know Sugar is very sick, but your father is a strong man, he'll get well again, you'll see.'

She didn't answer. Could anything be right again with Joe, her love, gone for ever? And Dad had been paid back in full for his violence. He had looked so ill, lying beneath the pristine sheets in the hospital bed.

'It's all my fault,' she said, her voice shaking. 'Dad wouldn't have gone for Joe if it hadn't been for me.'

'Now there's a daft way to think,' Dan said, putting his arm around her shoulders. 'There was Anita too, mind. She was having Barnes's baby, and what he did to you was the last straw. Every docker in Swansea is on your Dad's side, blaming that Mr Singleton, they are. He isn't innocent, is he, otherwise the police wouldn't have come for him.'

'Hush!' she said, looking around, 'we don't want everyone to know that it was Dad who . . .' Her voice trailed away and Dan leaned closer to her.

'Why were you looking into the water like that, love?' he said anxiously. 'Not thinking of doing anything silly, were you?'

'I've done enough silly things to last me a lifetime,' Sarah said sharply, and then she looked up into his worried face and was sorry. 'Look, Dan, why don't you just go away and forget me?' she said. 'I'm no good, I'm just what Dad calls a fallen woman. You don't want nothing to do with my sort.'

Dan swallowed hard. He was thin and wiry with lank dark hair, and he was not the sort of man who would behave like a knight on a white charger. And yet that's just what he was trying to do, she thought sadly.

'I want you to marry me,' Dan said. 'We can do it quiet, like, no church, no fuss, just me and you and a couple of witnesses. That way no one will be any the wiser, about the baby, I mean,' he added.

'It's good of you, Dan,' Sarah said, staring into his face, 'very good of you.'

'Then you'll say yes?' he said, and his voice shook.

She sagged against him. 'How will you keep us, Dan? You're a young man, you're earning good money on the docks, I know, but it's a boy's wage. How could we afford to rent a house for a start?'

'I could join up,' Dan said, 'put my age up. Lots of men have done it and got away with it.'

Her heart melted with pity for him and she stroked his cheek lightly. 'I'm very touched, Dan,' she said, 'but I must have time to think, you understand. What with Dad so sick and Mam out of her mind, I don't know if I'm coming or going.'

'There we are then,' Dan said, 'take all the time in the world, *cariad*, I'll be here when you want me.'

Suddenly the siren rang out over the town, wailing mournfully, heralding the approach of enemy planes. Sarah's insides turned over with fear as she looked up towards the darkening skies.

'Come on,' Dan took her arm, 'we'll have to get to one of the shelters before the planes get too near.'

He hurried her from the park and along the street, and suddenly Sarah didn't care if the bombs dropped on her or not. It would be a way out of her misery, for what was the point of living?

Crouched in the shelter on a bunk, with Dan beside her and enemy planes overhead, Sarah faced the horrors she'd kept from her mind for so long. The image of Joe with the life beaten out of him was almost too painful to bear. She imagined him lying senseless on the ground, his life blood flowing from him as he lay alone, unable to call for help, and she wanted to die.

The planes droned inexorably on overhead, bombs spiralling down on to the town, setting up flames and clouds of dust that obscured the moon and stars. And Sarah had her wish, for death came as she clutched Dan's hand in the too fragile shelter that could not withstand the impact of a direct hit.

Kristina pulled on her cap and the scarf to cover the lower part of her face, and tucked Verdun inside the large jacket Kaare had loaned her. She glanced around the office where she had spent the night. At least it had been a building with walls and windows, there had been some sense of security, but now they were to take to the road again, and Kristina felt a surge of panic. She wanted to beg Kaare to stay here with her in the safety of the logging camp, to conceal her here with her child until the war was over. But of course that was ridiculous, they would run out of food, they might be swamped by the Germans. Pressing onwards was the only solution, and she had no choice but to go along with it.

The convoy of lorries creaked out of the camp with two

drivers to each vehicle and the rest of the men from the rifle club travelling among the crates of bullion beneath the white tarpaulin taken from the train. The road wound its way upwards, and as the lorries mounted the first ridge of the Dovre Heights Kristina could see the line of trees below them. The air was colder here, sharp and clean, and Kristina, breathing it, felt cheered. She was on her way towards the coast at last.

She must have dozed because she suddenly became aware that the lead lorry had jerked to a halt. Johan was speaking rapidly to Kaare.

'We are nearing the main road.' He glanced at Kristina. 'Some scouts have gone ahead to see the lie of the land.' There seemed to be tension in the air, electric, almost tangible, and Kristina wondered fearfully what was wrong.

At last the leading vehicle began to move and the others followed out on to the wider road that seemed to Kristina to be only a little better than the mountain pass had been. But she was relieved to be on the move again, for every yard of roadway brought her nearer to Andalsnes and the ship that would take her home. The baby began to move impatiently and Kristina reached for the flask of milk in her pocket. It was cold by now and yet she knew that Verdun would drink it down greedily enough. She smiled as he sucked at the bottle top, spilling some of the milk in his haste.

There was a shout from behind and Kaare muttered an oath. 'I'll see what's wrong,' he said, looking at Johan. 'Let's hope it's nothing serious.' He returned after only a few minutes. 'Last vehicle has broken down,' he said. 'I've directed some of the men from the rifle club to stay behind with the driver while the fault is traced and repaired.'

'Good man,' Johan said. 'The rest of us must press on. At least that way there'll be a chance of most of the gold getting through.'

The swaying of the lorry had a soporific effect on

Kristina and once more she dozed lightly. Then she heard Kaare talking quietly to Johan and opened her eyes to see the road ahead filled with men dressed in white coats, for purposes of camouflage, she supposed.

A second lieutenant approached Johan and asked him who he was. Johan stepped down into the road and gave some sort of code word, and the man disappeared, to return a few minutes later with Colonel Hagen.

'You've just caught me, Johan,' Hagen said. His round face was red with cold but his smile was cheerful. He gave Kristina and Kaare a cursory glance and returned his attention to Johan. 'It's a bit of a mess at Andalsnes. The Fourth Division have been through the town clearing it of paratroopers. There's no water and no telephones but I have got two destroyers coming in to collect the gold. They'll each take a third to spread the risk, and the rest we'll have to see to later.'

'How long will it take us to get to Andalsnes,' Johan asked, and the Colonel considered for a moment.

'With good luck, about four hours, I'd say. I'll go on ahead and look for a place to conceal the lorries, preferably right on the docks. I'll be able to travel faster by car.'

Kristina understood nothing of the conversation, but when the colonel had returned to his car, Kaare explained it to her, leaving out, she was sure, any disquieting information. She waited patiently for the convoy to move off again but for some reason there seemed to be another delay. Johan shook his head in exasperation and made his way back along the line of lorries.

'I wonder what's gone wrong this time?' Kristina said softly. 'Kaare, will we ever finish this journey, and will I see Swansea again, do you think?'

He put his arm around her shoulders and hugged her close. His face was cold against hers and she felt a love for him well up in her. He was the brother she had never known. Kaare was a man who cared for her but expected nothing in return.

'I can't tell you in words how I feel about all you are doing for me,' she said with a catch in her voice. 'I am grateful and proud and . . .' Her voice trailed away as Kaare put gentle fingers over her lips.

'There is no need for words,' he said quietly. 'There is a good love between us, Kristina. I will never forget you, even if I never see you again.'

Tears rose to Kristina's eyes as she leaned against Kaare's broadness, admiring his strength. He was a fine man, the salt of the earth. Rather like Robert, she thought in surprise. But then men who were the salt of the earth did not turn the blood to water and set the pulse racing. It was the scoundrels like Eden who had the power to stir the senses, more was the pity.

Johan returned, his expression grave. 'Another of the Finn boys is dead,' he said. 'His wounds were just too bad.' He climbed into the cab, looking at Kaare long and hard. 'I want you to accept these stripes. You are now a corporal.'

Kristina sensed Kaare's amazement. 'But I have no military training,' he said. 'I am a bank manager, not a soldier.'

Johan smiled. 'Well, no one would think so the way you've handled yourself and others on this strange journey. I take it you will want to be part of the army once this mission is over and your cousin is safe?' He turned up his hands. 'Well, I am determined to keep you at my side, you're too good a man to lose.'

Kristina saw the pleasure in Kaare's eyes and surreptitiously she squeezed his hand. So he was to be a soldier for the duration of the war. That meant he would have to offer resistance to the German occupation, and suddenly she feared for him.

It was almost midnight before they reached Andalsnes, and Kristina leaned forward in the cab, staring with sinking spirits at the skeletons of burnt-out lorries silhouetted against the still glowing skyline.

Johan said something to Kaare in Norwegian, and

though Kristina did not understand the words, the tone was clear enough as Johan increased speed. Here in the streets of the stricken town, there was every chance that they would be stopped, the lorries searched and the bullion discovered.

Johan made straight for the docks, and as the waters came into view Kristina thought of her home in Lambert's Cottages where the ships rode in the harbour and the twin arms of the piers reached out into the sea.

'Damn!' said Kaare in English, 'the gates are locked.' He jumped down from the cab and a blast of cold air rushed in so that Kristina shivered. She saw Kaare being confronted by a dark figure wielding a rifle, and then he stretched his hands up into the air. Through the gloom she could see the man searching Kaare's pockets and all the time he held the weapon menacingly. She wondered if they had fallen into enemy hands on the last leg of their journey.

But Kaare was smiling, beckoning to Johan who drove the lorry through the slowly opening gates of the docks. Kaare jumped back into the cab.

'We're to pull right over to the far side of the docks where we will be concealed in some sort of tunnel,' he said.

As Johan drew nearer the dark mouth of the tunnel, he stopped the lorry and leaned out.

'He's asking the soldier what's at the other end,' Kaare explained. 'Trust Johan, he is not an easy man to convince.' Kaare smiled. 'But he's been given some keys. It appears there are gates at the end of the tunnel so we shan't be boxed in.'

Johan looked at Kristina and smiled one of his rare smiles. 'Well, young lady, it seems that this is the end of the journey for you. Tomorrow, with luck, you should be aboard an English destroyer and going with the gold, back to your homeland.'

Kristina could scarcely believe it. Was it possible that after one more night spent on Norwegian soil she would be returning home?

Johan lept down from the cab. 'I will see what the arrangements are,' he said. 'You, Kaare, stay with your cousin and her child until I can speak to someone in authority.'

Kristina looked at Kaare. 'What will happen to you when I leave?' she asked, her voice husky. 'I know there will be danger for you and I don't like to think of you facing it alone.'

'I won't be alone,' Kaare said reassuringly. 'I will have Johan and all the other men to keep me company.' He smiled. 'Perhaps we will form our own resistance party, I would like that. Ringe would make an excellent teacher. He is experienced in many things, unarmed combat among them.'

As Kristina shivered Kaare put his arm around her. 'You will be in danger, too,' he said, 'and I shall pray for your safe return home. Had the war reached Swansea when you left?'

Kristina shrugged. 'There was the attack from the air,' she said. 'The foreign plane fired at random and there was some civilians killed, but we won't have such a bad time as you Norwegians so long as we can keep the Germans on the other side of the water.'

Johan returned. 'Two lorries have been rigged out as sleeping quarters,' he said, 'but Kristina and the baby will have to remain here out of sight. You, Kaare, can bring over a few provisions and stay with your cousin if you think it necessary. With a bit of luck there's going to be water brought in and some supplies of food.' He bowed. 'For now, young lady, I'll wish you good night and God bless and keep you.' It was as though Johan was saying goodbye, and on an impulse Kristina leaned towards him and kissed his cheek. His smile was one of pleasure, he lifted his hand in salute and then disappeared into the darkness.

Kaare followed Johan silently and Kristina felt suddenly lost and alone. She realized Kaare had to go to fetch the supplies they would need for the night, but glancing around the damp darkness of the tunnel she hoped he would not be long. Kristina eased Verdun out of her stiff aching arms and put him to lie on the seat, before stretching her legs and moving her arms to relieve the ache in them.

One more night in Norway and then she would be on her way home. She couldn't believe it. They were actually at Andalsnes, and though the port was more or less destroyed, it was the last step towards leaving the country where she had come to love and respect her kinsmen. Kristina could not help the feeling of sadness that swept over her. What had become of her Auntie Liv? she wondered. Would Norway ever recover from the war and the occupation by the Germans? She smiled a little, knowing that once she was back home it would be difficult to believe all this had really happened. It was like some improbable fairy tale, transporting gold bullion by rail and road and giving it into the hands of the Allies under the very noses of the Germans. It sounded an impossible task.

She looked around fearfully at the darkened tunnel, worried that even now something might happen to prevent her leaving for home. She was relieved when Kaare reappeared and began to set up a stove in the back of the truck among the crates of gold bullion.

When Kristina took the baby into the back of the lorry she found that Kaare had made it all as comfortable as possible. He had cleared a small space between the crates for her to lie on the bedroll, and the stove threw a warm and comforting glow that made her feel better immediately.

'I shall stay with you,' Kaare said. 'There will be nothing for you to worry about, I will look after you.'

In the night, Kristina cried out in fear. She had dreamed of Robert being shot on a strange battlefield and she sat up shivering. Kaare came to her and held her close, and for the rest of the night, she lay in her cousin's arms.

The following morning Kristina was able to see through the mouth of the tunnel what devastation had been caused by the enemy. The port was practically destroyed, every installation had been bombed and there were gaping holes in the harbour walls.

'Cover your face,' Kaare said easily. 'There is the harbour master. I expect he's here to tell us about the plans for loading the gold on board ship.'

It seemed that the destroyers were weaving between the islands to avoid capture and that they would not enter the stricken port until dusk.

'The port seems deserted,' Kristina said softly. 'Surely there are no more ships coming to berth here?' Kaare shook his head.

'No, there is no air cover here. All the troop ships are using the Molde Fiord. Hopefully the enemy take it for granted that the port here is obsolete, as indeed it is. The destroyers picking up the gold will be the last ships to pass through this way.'

The day passed slowly, but at least Kristina had the comfort of the small space in the lorry in which to attend to Verdun's needs. She even managed to sleep a little herself. Lying in the warmth beside her son, she relaxed in a way she had not done since the nightmare journey across Norway had begun. And when she woke, Kaare was there with a hot meal. He waited until she had eaten, sitting crouched beside her, his big hands resting on his knees. Then he spoke.

'Not long now,' he said, and if there was a trace of regret in his voice, his bright smile concealed it well. 'It will soon be high water slack, and the British destroyer is in sight. She is well camouflaged. I was the first one to spot her.'

Kristina hugged him. 'Oh, Kaare, I wish I didn't have to leave you behind, how am I going to thank you for all you've done for me?'

His voice was husky as he returned her embrace. 'There is no need for thanks. I am only grateful that my wild plan to get you to the coast succeeded. I sometimes doubted my sanity in bringing you along on such a perilous journey.'

'You did a wonderful job,' Kristina assured him. 'I would now be in the hands of the Germans if you hadn't taken me away from Lillehammer.'

Kaare laughed. 'You have such a funny, charming

accent, Kristina, sometimes it is difficult to understand you at all.'

'That's because I am half Welsh,' Kristina said. 'I try to speak posh but it doesn't work very well, as you can hear. I often forget myself and speak as I did when I was a child.'

Kaare sighed. 'I must go, but you can watch the shipping of the gold bullion from the lorry, though ours will be the last to be unloaded. Once the gold is aboard and hidden away, I'll introduce you to the British commander.'

Kristina was suddenly apprehensive. 'What if he refuses to take me?' Her mouth was dry and her pulse quickened at the thought.

Kaare shook his head. 'He won't. Indeed, Johan has already spoken to him about you. He says you're preferable to the King of Norway who he expected to be carrying.' Kaare smiled. 'But the news is that the King is safe. He may be here on the dockside even now, but I'm sure if he was, he'd be well hidden.'

After Kaare had gone, Kristina settled herself down, wrapped once more in Kaare's jacket with Verdun tucked into its folds. She could not see much, her vision was restricted by the confines of the cab, but she could plainly hear the rumble of the trolleys and the quiet voices of the men taking the gold to the ship.

It took well over an hour for the heavy cargo to be loaded, and even though the British destroyer was carrying only a third of the gold, it took much longer than anyone had anticipated.

Finally, Kaare came for Kristina and smiled at her with a mixture of expressions fleeting across his face. 'It's time,' he said. 'Come, let me help you down from the lorry.'

The tunnel was dark and dank-smelling, and all the men had departed now to find shelter for the night and to have a good meal and enough drink to celebrate in style the successful delivery of the gold. It seemed strangely lonely with just the two of them standing together in the silence, listening to the cold slap of the sea against the wall of the dock.

'You should be with the others, enjoying yourself,' she said huskily.

Kaare took her face in his hands. 'Time enough for celebrating when I see you safely aboard the British ship. Only then can I think of relaxing my vigilance over you.' He paused and then kissed her lips lightly. 'I will always remember you for as long as I live.' He kissed her lightly once more and Kristina felt tears burn her eyes.

'I'll remember you too. You're the brother I never had,' she whispered.

He put his arm around her shoulders. 'God go with you.' He led her to the mouth of the tunnel where the cold sea air washed over them. 'Think of me sometimes, Kristina, and tell your husband he had better look after you well or he'll have Kaare Larson to deal with.'

She could just make out the outline of the ship now, a dark shape against the water. Excitement filled her, vying with the feeling of loss at her parting from Kaare.

'Come on, we're to have a drink with the commander before the ship sails. I will introduce you to him and tell him what a fine and brave woman you are.'

Kaare took her arm and led her out towards the edge of the docks. The empty space between the tunnel and the ship seemed to stretch out endlessly as Kristina walked for the last time on Norwegian soil. She doubted if she would ever return, even when the world was at peace again, for she had suffered such feelings of fear and despair over the past days, though she had managed to conceal them successfully from Kaare.

The outline of the ship grew larger and Kristina's sense of relief was heightened. Such a fine vessel would take her across the North Sea to her home with very little trouble, she was sure. If the Norwegians were entrusting their gold to the commander, he must be a great man indeed.

'You will be taken to Scotland,' Kaare said. 'From there, the commander has promised to see you safely on your journey to Wales.'

It was as though they were discussing an improbable

dream. Wales, Swansea, the scented sea breezes, the colour and noise of the docklands. Kristina remembered the innocence of three girls who had once believed that the vote for women would solve all problems; how naïve they had been then. Well, Kristina would never be the same foolish girl she once was. She had seen another side of life now, a fight for survival by a people determined not to be subdued. She had grown up.

They had almost reached the edge of the quay when there was a sharp and sudden retort. 'God, a sniper!' Kaare pushed her before him. 'Quickly, get on board, someone is shooting at us.'

Another shot rang out and Kaare stood swaying for a moment, his eyes glowing redly in the darkness. He seemed to attempt to right himself, and then slowly he slumped to the ground.

Kristina knelt beside him, clutching her baby close as she looked wildly round. She heard a round of firing and a voice calling out to her.

'Kaare,' she said softly. His eyes fluttered open and he looked up at her, mouthing his words silently.

'My dear Kristina. Remember me sometimes in your prayers.' His hand tried to reach towards her but he had no strength.

'Kaare!' Kristina bent towards him and kissed his mouth. 'I will never forget, never.'

Gentle hands drew her away, and she knew that Kaare was dead. She stared down at the still face in bewilderment; he looked as though he were simply asleep. Kristina did not remember being taken on board the ship. She could not rid herself of the picture of Kaare lying there on the cold snow-covered dock, the life draining out of him.

It was the motion of the ship, the drum of the engines, the lifting and dipping into the waves that brought her out of her stupor. And it was as if Kaare's voice was in her head, all round her, filling her.

'Kristina,' it said, 'be of good heart, for you are going home.'

31

Swansea lay slumbering under a cloud of mist, the sea shimmering with ghostly light, and a cat called mournfully from a backyard. Kristina sighed heavily, unable to believe she was home at last.

She entered the house and stood for a moment in the silence, staring around her, a wave of happiness engulfing her. The door of the kitchen swung open and Robert stood staring at her as though he couldn't believe his eyes.

'Kristina, why didn't you tell me you were coming. I would have met the train.' Robert looked strangely distant in his army uniform. He took the baby from her arms and Kristina smiled at him gratefully.

'If only you knew how glad I am to be back in Wales,' she said softly. 'I'm so happy to be home.' Her voice broke and he put his arm around her and drew her into the living room.

'I missed you.' Robert's voice was hoarse and Kristina knew by the terse way he spoke how much it had cost her husband to put his feelings into words. She touched his cheek and he turned his face to kiss her palm. He moved away from her. 'I missed this little tyke, too.' He smiled down at Verdun who was still fast asleep.

'And I've missed you, Robert.' Kristina stared at her husband, her eyes full of tears.

'I'll put the baby into his bed and then I'll make you some tea,' Robert said, his emotions hidden by the ordinariness of his words. 'Sit down you, you look washed out.'

When they were seated at the table, the tea before

them, they stared at each other for a long moment and then reached out and held each other's hands.

'Tell me what happened to you out there, Kristina, you must have been in great danger. I was so frightened for you.'

'I can't talk about it, Robert, not yet.' The pain of Kaare's death was still too much to bear. 'Tell me about you and about Swansea and what's been happening here.'

He frowned. 'Well, the war news is that most of the people of Swansea have lost loved ones. And we've had our dramas in other ways, too.'

She could see that he was troubled, there were shadows beneath his eyes and a grim terse set to his mouth that was uncharacteristic of him. 'What's wrong?' she asked with a sudden feeling of unease. He shrugged and sank into the wooden rocking chair, staring into the fire.

'Joe Barnes got himself killed, and unfortunately I know who did it.' He rubbed at his eyes. 'I've been telling myself I should go to the police, but I'd be giving away an old friend. On the other hand, how can I allow Colin Singleton to remain in custody without speaking up for him?'

Kristina shook her head. 'How could you know who the killer is?' She was bewildered.

'Colin Singleton didn't kill Joe Barnes,' Robert repeated. 'The man's innocent.' He pushed back his hair with both hands, and the thinness of his face struck a chord of pity within Kristina.

'But Robert, there's soft you are to hesitate. You've got to tell the police the truth.'

'It's not so simple,' Robert said softly. 'Sugar didn't mean to kill Barnes, and anyway, Sugar's suffered a stroke. He's in hospital, unable to move or speak, he can't defend himself, so how can I betray him?'

'There's awful for you, Robert, what are you going to do?'

Robert shook his head. 'I don't know, but Singleton

will be coming up for trial soon, and in all probability he will be hanged as a murderer if I don't speak up.'

'You must tell the truth,' Kristina said decisively. 'You should have done it straight away.' She touched Robert's hand. 'Loyalty to your own I can understand but you can't let an innocent man die.' Her fingers curled encouragingly in his. It was the first time she had seen him vulnerable and uncertain and it was a side of him she liked.

'Well, that's enough about my worries.' Robert smiled, and he was once more the strong, almost arrogant, man she'd married. 'We have some celebrating to do, we must make the most of the time we've got together, for soon I'll be going back to camp. I'm no longer a free man, I'm in the Army now.' He held out his arms and Kristina rose from her chair, and as she went into Robert's embrace, there were tears of happiness in her eyes.

It was early next morning when Robert left the house to go to the police station. He bumped into Nia Singleton and she looked up at him anxiously. 'Don't look so worried,' he said impulsively. 'Everything is going to be all right.'

She held on to his arm. 'You know something, don't you, about the murder?'

'Yes,' Robert said, 'I'm on my way to the police station right now.'

'Let me come with you,' Nia said pleadingly, and after a moment Robert nodded.

It took some time before the officer in charge of the enquiries could be found, but when he at last appeared, he listened carefully to what Robert had to say.

'Right, sir.' The officer rose to his feet. 'There's been a call from the hospital anyway. Old Sugar is able to talk and it seems he wants to clear his conscience. We'd better get over to the hospital right away. You can come too, Mrs Singleton,' he said with a note of sympathy in his voice.

Robert was shocked by the change in Sugar. He was an old man as he lay broken against his pillows. He held out a hand to Robert and his fingers trembled as Robert held them. In a slurred voice, he told his story as he had told it to Robert, and glancing at Nia, Robert saw that even she was moved to tears as she listened to the man's confession.

'It's over, at last,' she said, as later she stood with Robert in the hospital grounds. 'Thank God for that.'

A few days later, Kristina went to see Nia, and the two women embraced warmly. Mrs Preece brought in a tray and there was silence for a moment broken only by the tinkle of the bone china cups as Nia took the tray and poured fresh coffee.

'I can't thank Robert enough,' Nia said. 'It was kind of him to take me to the police station with him. He's a good man, Kristina.'

'I know, and he's going away soon, back to the Army,' Kristina said softly. 'It seems that none of the men can keep out of this war.'

Nia took a sip of coffee. 'Now that Colin's released, he'll be off to sea.' She looked at Kristina sympathetically. 'Was it hell in Norway?'

'It's a beautiful country,' Kristina said softly, 'and the Norwegians are a people to be proud of. They were caught unprepared but they have tried their best to beat off the Germans. And yes, it was hell. I lost someone very dear to me.'

'Are the Germans behaving badly, then? I thought Norway was neutral.'

'Most people think that,' Kristina said. 'Some of the Norwegian people are taken in by the German propaganda, but most of them are against the occupation. My own cousin Kaare died in the fight.' Kristina did not dare divulge anything of her involvement in the moving of the gold from Norway under the noses of the Germans. One of the last things Kaare had told her was to speak of it to no one.

Nia put down her cup. 'You are lucky to have a man like Robert Jenkins you know, Kris.' She smiled. 'I know we didn't like him at first – remember all that time ago in that political meeting – but he's turned out to be a good 'un. You chose wisely there.'

'I know.' Kristina rose to her feet and Nia looked up at her. 'Are you going so soon? Well, I hope you'll come again, we can keep each other company when the men are away.'

'I'd like that,' Kristina said, 'but now I must spend as much time as I can with Robert.'

Nia brushed up her roll of hair with slim, well-manicured fingers. Watching her, Kristina was aware that Nia was still a lovely woman.

'What happened to the young, light-hearted girls we used to be?' she said wistfully, and Nia smiled.

'I'd never put the clock back, even if I could. You know how I hated running for bets for my father.' She bit her lip. 'How I envied Roggen Lamb her easy life, and even you, Kris, though your family was hard up you were free to do what you wanted, while I was always running errands.'

'Free?' Kristina said, 'you call working at Libba's all hours of the day being free, do you?'

Nia shook back her hair. 'I realize your childhood wasn't all roses, but compared with me you were so respectable. My father was a defrocked priest and a gambling man as well. I felt so inferior as a child.' She smiled suddenly. 'But I do remember your panic when Thomas wanted to foist you off on Robert Jenkins. That meeting we went to when Robert was waving a banner and trying to prevent us from getting into the hall: God, that was a long time ago.' She moved towards the door. 'And yet here you are, Mrs Robert Jenkins for all that. It must have been fate, when you come to think of it.'

'Aye, I suppose so.' Kristina didn't care to go into that too deeply, and she was relieved when Nia saw her to the door.

411

'I mustn't keep you any longer,' she said, 'but thanks for everything, Kris.'

As Kristina hurried away towards home, she was already anticipating being with Robert again, sleeping in his arms for just one more night. And there were tears on her cheeks as she thought of the morning and of Robert leaving her and going off to war, and she told herself that she would make the most of this last night together, for she would have to remember it for a long time to come.

Kristina was alone, looking through the window into the street, and her thoughts were of Robert. It was almost a week now since he'd gone back to camp and she could hardly bear the loneliness. On an impulse, Kristina put Verdun into his pram and covered him with a warm Welsh wool shawl. She was restless, she needed to walk. Perhaps she should call to see her mother. It was some days since Kristina had been over to Lambert's Cottages.

Her mother smiled joyfully when she opened the door to Kristina. 'Hello love!' she said. 'Come on, bring the baby in by here, that's right, put him in the parlour where he'll have some peace to sleep. We'll go into the kitchen and have a nice cup of tea.'

'There's quiet the house is, Mam.' Kristina sank down into the wooden rocking chair, comforted by the familiarity of the kitchen.

'Aye, well Thomas is working, of course, they need the older men on the docks now that the youngsters are gone to war. And the girls, well they are up in Bridgend working the munitions. I don't like it, mind, but anybody without work got to go, no choice but to go there.'

It distressed Kristina to think of her sisters working in dangerous conditions. 'What if one of them comes up to the house as a domestic?' she suggested, but her mother shook her head.

'No, love, they wouldn't come. The two of them want to stick together, see, always been close they have, and won't be separated. Anyway, I think they like it in a funny kind of way, they feel they're doing their bit for the war effort, like.'

Kristina could understand her sisters' feelings only too well. In Norway she had experienced at first hand the fight against the Germans.

'Are you managing with the rationing?' It was a banal question, but Kristina found her thoughts wandering to her last night with Robert and the way he had touched her hair and the urgency in his voice when he'd told her how much he loved her.

'Oh, aye,' Ceinwen Presdey chuckled. 'You know your Dad, always able to get away with a bit of stuff off the docks. We do all right.'

'He'll be caught if he doesn't watch out,' Kristina said. 'You know he was lucky to get back on the docks after the last piece of thieving he did. It was only because of Robert that he was given his job back then.'

'You don't understand the dockers, love,' Ceinwen said reprovingly. 'They feel it's their right to take just a bit here and there when the ships come in full of stuff.'

Kristina sighed. It was pointless to argue. 'You're looking well anyway, Mam,' she said changing the subject, and her mother smiled as she pushed the kettle on to the fire.

'Aye, your father has mellowed in his old age. He's a better man these days, not so much arguing the toss, like.' She carefully warmed the brown china teapot. 'Worried he was, mind, by the killing of that man Barnes. All the dockers are on Sugar's side, of course. They say this Barnes man got what he deserved, messing around with Sugar's daughters, getting one in the family way and then taking up with the younger girl.'

Kristina watched as her mother made the tea. She was so lonely without Robert, but life went on outside on the docks and in the streets. Women did men's jobs and made the best of things.

'Here, stop daydreaming, girl, and take this cup off me,

will you?' Ceinwen's voice interrupted Kristina's thoughts. 'Far away you was then, penny for them.'

'Oh, I was just wondering what to get the baby for his birthday,' Kristina said quickly.

'*Duw*, this past year has flown by,' Ceinwen said softly. 'Your son's a fine boy, not much of the baby left in him, a sturdy chap he is.' She smiled. 'I'm glad to see you married to a fine man like Robert Jenkins. I know it was difficult at first but you are happy now, aren't you, Kris?' It was as though she sensed that Kristina's thoughts were with her husband.

'Of course I'm happy, Mam, except that I'm missing Robert.'

Ceinwen drew up her chair. 'Right, now, come on, tell me again all about your trip to Norway. Was your Auntie Liv nice to you and did you really escape from under the noses of the Germans?' Her eyes were wide. '*Duw*, this is better than going to the Empire. Come on, Kris, start right from the beginning.'

Kristina smiled. 'All right, Mam.' She was glad to talk about anything that would take her mind off the way she was missing Robert.

It was later when Kristina was home cooking dinner that she felt a sense of loss so keen it was as though she had lost a loved one all over again. Her tears were for Kaare as well as for Robert.

Soon Robert was home again, but Kristina's happiness was marred by the thought that he was on embarkation leave. Shortly he would be leaving for the shores of France. They lay together in the big double bed and Kristina was sleepy and comfortable in his arms. Suddenly, she was wide awake. She sat up in bed hearing sounds like great bursts of thunder, and her heart was suddenly beating so swiftly she thought she could not bear it.

Robert slipped out of bed and moved the curtains, staring out into the night. 'Christ!' he said, 'we're being bombed again!'

Kristina hurried into Verdun's room and lifted the sleeping child in her arms, holding him close. What were they to do, where could they run for cover?

'It's all right.' Robert put his arm around her and led her downstairs. He opened the door of the broom cupboard and helped her inside. Kristina clung to him.

'Thank God you're here,' she said softly. She would have been so frightened if she'd been alone. Once she would have had old Mrs Morgan who helped in the house for company, but she'd gone to her daughter's house at the start of the war.

'Now don't worry, we've had a few raids before,' Robert said, 'and you know they've never done a great deal of harm.' He crouched on the floor beside her. 'And they never last very long. The Germans have to come over at night because the Do 17z can only carry small bomb loads and they can't fight off our Spitfires and Hurricanes.'

'This one sounds pretty bad to me.' Kristina attempted to smile but her lips were trembling as the bombardment continued. Through the open door of the cupboard, she could see the glare of flames lighting up the windows over which Robert had placed tape that appeared like so many kisses scrawled at the bottom of a letter.

'I'm going outside to see what's been hit,' he said, and before Kristina could protest, Robert had pulled on his heavy coat and was out through the door. She sat there for what seemed an eternity, crouched over her son as though to protect him from harm. The noise was deafening but Verdun stirred once and then slept peacefully on.

It was much later when Robert returned. He gestured for her to come out of the cupboard. 'It's over.' He sounded weary as he made his way to the kitchen, 'but keep the lights out just in case there are any strays around.' He put the kettle on the ring and slumped into a chair.

'The refinery at Llandarcy has been hit,' he said. 'It'll take some time to put the fire out, maybe days.'

Kristina put Verdun in a chair and tucked the shawl around him, and he continued to sleep just as though he was still in his bed. 'Nothing bothers him,' Kristina said softly.

She made the tea and sat opposite Robert. His face was grimy and there was a smear of blood across his forehead. She touched his hand. 'If the raids get any worse than this I'll be afraid to let you go back to the Army.' She tried to smile. 'You look awful, Robert, why not go up to bed?'

'I'm all right,' he said, but his hands shook as he took the cup of tea. 'There's been some casualties,' he said, his voice strained. 'A few people have been killed.' He looked up at her. 'Your stepfather was one of them.'

'Oh, God, what about Mam?' Kristina asked.

Robert shook his head. 'Presdey wasn't in the house, the others are safe. Tom was on his way home from a late night at one of the public houses, having "afters", they were, the landlord should have closed up hours before.'

Kristina bit her lip and looked down at her hands. She had never been fond of Thomas Presdey, he had always singled her out, giving her the back of his hand on more than one occasion, but for all that she'd never wanted him dead.

'Does Mam know?' Kristina asked, and Robert shook his head. 'I expect the constable will have gone down there as soon as he could, there were others, you see.'

'I must go home,' Kristina said. 'I'll leave Verdun by here with you. I'll have to be with my mother, you do understand, don't you?'

'Aye.' Robert nodded. 'Go you and get dressed, I'll just look out to make sure the All Clear was the real thing.' He reappeared in a few minutes and nodded his head. 'Right, go on, but be careful, I don't want anything happening to you.'

Kristina moved through the darkened streets towards the docks, her heart missing a beat whenever she saw a smoking ruin of a house or heard the sounds of weeping from distraught women. It was as if she was in the grip of some horrible nightmare, and anger against the faceless enemy rose up within her. And then she remembered the German soldier in Norway; he could have given her away but had chosen to remain silent. He was a good man, a kind man. Not all Germans were cast from the same mould.

The lights were out on the docklands but Kristina knew every nook and cranny of the area where she had been raised and she found little difficulty in picking her way over rough ground and railway tracks towards Lambert's Cottages.

Her mother had obviously heard the bad news and sat stunned in the wooden rocking chair, her daughters around her.

'You know?' Sarah asked, her eyes filled with tears, and Kristina hugged her.

'Yes, Robert told me. I came over straight away, I knew how you must be feeling.' She saw her young sister's face cloud with unhappiness.

'But you can't know. Dad wasn't your real dad, was he? You lost your father when you were little,' There was a hint of reproach in Sarah's voice, and, hurt, Kristina went towards her mother and put an arm around her shoulders.

'If there's anything I can do, Mam,' she said, and Ceinwen looked at her almost blankly.

'No, love, I'm all right by here with the girls. Don't you worry, you got a husband and a boy to look after, go home you.'

Kristina felt rebuffed, almost as though she were an intruder. Her place was home with her own family, she knew that, but she'd only wanted to comfort Mam and the girls, tell them that she was there if they needed her. But it seemed they didn't. The small family group, with Mam in the chair and the two girls around her, seemed to be shutting her out.

'Right then, I'd better go,' she said softly.

Ceinwen nodded, raising her pinny to her face to wipe

away a stray tear. 'Thanks for coming, love, it was good of you,' she said woodenly.

As Kristina let herself out into the roadway she felt a sudden sense of panic. Everything that was familiar was crumbling. She stumbled over some debris and almost fell, and strong hands held her.

'Watch out there!' A familiar voice spoke close to her ear, and she looked up quickly.

'Eden!' He held her very close, as though he would kiss her, and for a moment she stood frozen, looking into his face. 'No!' she said quickly. She pushed Eden from her and started to run. Her breathing was ragged and once she glanced over her shoulder in fear. But the streets were empty, Eden had not followed her. She was alone.

32

Nia picked her way through the devastated streets of Swansea, a shopping bag over her arm. Some of the buildings in Wind Street were still smouldering, and King's Dock had clearly taken a direct hit, and several houses had been flattened. A child's shoe lay in the street and Nia picked it up, feeling tears start in her eyes. When would this madness end?

And yet Nia found that she was becoming accustomed to it. All the bombing and the now familiar scenes of fires flaring across the town were just an unpleasant fact of life. What was important now was that Colin, after being at sea for several months, was coming home on leave.

She joined a queue at the greengrocers and stood patiently waiting with the other women. It gave her a feeling of being one of them, part of the war effort. She could usually get what she wanted from contacts in the black market, but today she had felt the need to be out in the streets to be free of the silence of the house. Although she had plenty to occupy her – running her offices, albeit from a distance, took up a good deal of time – what she really needed was someone of her own to hold her and love her. She wanted Colin.

She suddenly felt dizzy and the earth seemed to spin around her. She felt herself fall sideways, and then she was on the ground with a chatter of concerned voices around her.

'You all right, love?' One of the women put a coat beneath her head. 'You're as white as a ghost, bless you.'

Nia struggled to sit up, staring around her in

confusion. 'I'm all right,' she said. 'I just felt a bit faint, that's all.'

'Having a babba, I expect,' the woman said kindly. 'You can always tell by the eyes, mind.'

Nia left the queue and in a daze made her way back home. Could it be true? Nurse Freeman had told her it was unlikely she'd have a child, unlikely but not impossible. The sickness in the mornings, the sudden swings in mood . . . how could she have been so blind? She let herself into the house and sank into a chair as Mrs Preece entered the room with a tray of tea. She must have been watching out for Nia – the old lady was frightened of being alone these days.

'You all right, Mrs Singleton?' she asked in concern. 'You look awful white, mind, shall I call the doctor?'

Nia shook her head. 'No, I'll be all right, thank you, Mrs Preece.'

She sat for a long time staring into the fire, trying to work things out in her mind. Colin had been gone about two and a half months, and since then she had not seen her courses. And yet could she really be pregnant? She was almost thirty-three years old.

Joe, of course, had never wanted her to have a child. He'd always claimed it would spoil their lives, and she'd accepted that. But now, to have Colin's baby would be the ultimate joy. And yet she was frightened too, worried about the bombing, because now it would not only affect her, but her child too.

But before she jumped to any conclusions, she must see the doctor, make sure she really was going to have a baby.

Nia was dressed in her best red wool frock as, the next morning, she waited for Colin to come home. She had brushed her hair until it shone and had outlined her mouth with lipstick and rouged her cheeks to conceal her paleness. She sat in the window, staring out at the roadway and rubbing her hands together in a fever of impatience. And then she saw his tall figure striding towards the house. She rose to her feet, her heart pounding with excitement, and unable to contain herself went into the hallway and flung open the door. And then she was in his arms, held close to him, breathing in the familiar scents of him.

She drew him into the house and kissed him again and again until he laughed and held her at arm's length.

'I've only been gone a few months. I don't really deserve a hero's welcome, you know.'

'You do in my eyes,' Nia said softly. 'Sit down, Col, I've got wonderful news for you.'

She sat beside him and gripped his hands tightly. 'We're going to have a baby.' She looked at him anxiously. 'You are happy about it, aren't you?'

'You bet I am!' He held her close and kissed the top of her head. 'I'm bloody worried too; I'll be leaving you alone at the time you most need my support.'

'I'm a survivor, Col,' Nia said earnestly. 'I'll be all right. It's yourself you want to worry about, out there on the seas with the enemy aircraft overhead and the submarines beneath the waves. How do any ships ever get through?'

'We go in convoys for the most part.' Colin spoke reassuringly. 'You can see for yourself how many vessels come safely into the Swansea docks.' He rose and poured himself a drink, and then suddenly he put down his glass and came towards her, taking her gently in his arms.

'I'm thrilled to bits.' He nibbled her ear. 'Now, put your feet up and take it easy while I go and get changed, and then we can spend all our time talking about the future. We'll put this damn war right out of our minds, at least for the time being.'

They sat and talked until the small hours of the morning, and when Nia was lying beside him in bed, she forced herself to remain awake. She cuddled against Colin's warmth, drinking in the comfort he brought just by being there.

The two days of his leave passed all too quickly, and

Nia stood once again on the doorstep, watching him walk away from her. She felt tears burn against her eyelids but she forced them back. He would not take away with him the memory of her in tears.

Kristina's feelings of guilt were almost overwhelming. In the cold light of day, she wondered about her instinctive responses to being in Eden's arms. Her first thought had been to cling to him, and then, frightened, she had run away. But she was married to Robert, she loved *him*, so why did she still feel this attraction for Eden Lamb?

She covered her face with her hands. 'Oh, Robert, why don't you write to me?' she said softly. She was worried. She'd had a few letters from Robert that she treasured and read almost every day, but there had been no letter now for some weeks and she had no idea where he had been posted. She wrote to him daily at the address he had given her but there was no response and she wondered if he'd ever received her letters.

She had written several times to Aunt Liv, too, and though the reply was a long time in coming, it seemed she and Ulric were safe. The fight against the Germans was continuing, but even the presence of the Allies had not prevented the towns of Dombas and Storen being taken by the enemy. Kristina still grieved for Kaare, and Aunt Liv's pride in her hero son was very evident in the glowing way she wrote about him. She asked after Verdun and sent her love and hoped they would all meet up again at some happier time.

Kristina wished Aunt Liv could see Verdun now. He was growing into a fine, healthy boy. But as he grew older, the likeness to Eden became more pronounced, and it was a wonder to Kristina that no one suspected anything. Not even her mother noticed the similarities between Eden and Verdun, but then Ceinwen Presdey was still suffering from the shock of losing Thomas.

On an impulse, Kristina decided to telephone Nia. Although they had not met for some time now, they remained close friends, able to take up the threads of their relationship with ease. But they had not been in touch for some while and it was high time the situation was remedied. Kristina realized it was her own selfish wish for company that prompted her telephone call to Nia, but after all that's what friends were for.

Nia was delighted to hear from her. 'Oh, Kris, you are just the person to cheer me up!' were her first words. 'I'm missing Colin so much, you wouldn't believe it.'

Kristina smiled to herself as she made arrangements to go to Nia's house. It seemed that her need for a friend was reciprocated.

'I'll be over this afternoon,' she said. 'I can leave Verdun with Mam for a while and we can have a nice quiet hour together. We can unburden ourselves to our heart's content.'

It was good to sit in the peaceful surroundings of Nia's sitting room with the softly coloured furnishings a backdrop to the huge windows that overlooked the curving golden crescent of Swansea Bay. The peninsula of Mumbles Head was misty in the dampness of the autumn weather, and the timid sea washed inwards in small waves.

'It's lovely here,' Kristina said, leaning back in the plumply cushioned chair. 'I don't know why I haven't been here more often, do you?'

Nia smiled. 'I suppose we have our own lives to lead, but we should remember that worries seem magnified when they're not shared.' She kicked off her shoes and swung her legs up on to the scroll-backed sofa. 'Well, you first. What's all your news, Kris.'

Kristina smiled. 'I don't know what to say, Nia. Now that I'm here I feel so foolish and childish. Perhaps you don't want to hear my petty worries after all you've been through.'

'Nonsense!' Nia said. 'You'll take my mind off things. Come on, let's pretend we're silly young girls again, sharing secrets. Me first, then. I'm going to have a baby!'

Kristina smiled in amazement. 'You sly old thing! And

me daring to come here to moan to you. Forget my silly old worries and tell me all about it.' She hardly paused for breath. 'I bet Colin's like a dog with two tails, isn't he?'

'Of course he's thrilled,' Nia said, 'and so am I.' She glanced at Kristina. 'I could hardly believe it, and me no spring chicken either. When are you going to have another one? It's about time you gave young Verdun a brother or sister.'

Kristina smoothed the wool of her skirt over her knees. It was an old skirt and a little too short, but in every magazine and even on hoardings there were warnings that material was in short supply and clothes must be made to last.

'I won't be having another baby, not for a few years anyway.' She swallowed hard and Nia leaned towards her earnestly.

'Come on, out with it, what did you come here to say? I'm selfishly going on about myself and I think you're very troubled. What is it, Kris?'

'I feel exactly like a silly young girl now,' Kristina said. She looked directly at Nia. 'There's you so happy and secure in your marriage, and I've been very happy with Robert too.' She shook back her hair. 'The trouble is I met Eden Lamb the other night, bumped into him really, and the attraction is still there, Nia, however hard I try to deny it.'

Nia looked at her hands for a long time in silence, and Kristina began to think that she had shocked her friend. At last, Nia looked up at her, eyes shadowed.

'Physical attraction does strange things to you,' she said. 'It doesn't mean you have to love the person you're attracted to. I was actually unfaithful to Colin. I wanted to know if what Joe and I had together was really over, and so I slept with him one more time. It was a disaster.' She shrugged. 'So you see, I'm the last one to offer advice.'

Kristina sighed. 'Well at least I know I'm not the only foolish one around.' She leaned back in her chair.

Nia smiled. 'You always did have a crush on Eden,' she said, 'and I honestly think that's all it is now, Kris, a

424

hangover from when you were young and impression-able. But you're still a woman, and a woman without her husband. It's going to be a hard time for all of us.'

'You're probably right,' Kristina said softly, 'and I do feel much better for having talked to you.'

Some time later, as Kristina was just about to leave, the telephone rang out stridently from the hall.

'I won't be a minute,' Nia said, and there was a touch of anxiety about her voice that she couldn't conceal. Kristina understood it at once. Nia was worried about Colin, for every moment that he was at sea he was in danger.

When Nia returned to the room, her face was glowing with pleasure. 'That was Colin,' she said softly. 'He's on leave, he'll be home this evening.'

'Oh, love, there's thrilled I am for you.' Kristina moved towards Nia and hugged her. 'I'm going now, leave you to prettify yourself for Colin.' She envied Nia her obvious happiness.

As Kristina walked back home with Verdun sleeping in his pram, she paused to stare out to where the coast of Devon lay on the horizon. The softly folding hills were bathed in autumnal light, so different from the craggy snow peaks of Norway where she had been swept away from her everyday existence into some sort of dream world where adventure and death had become realities. It still hurt to remember Kaare and the courageous way he'd faced death. The knowledge that he'd given his life trying to save her made her very aware of how precious life was.

She would go home, write to Robert, then she would feel nearer to him. She walked more briskly now, as though with renewed purpose, and her head was high as she entered the house where she'd come as Robert's wife.

Nia bathed in scented water and washed her hair until it squeaked clean, using the last of her precious supply of sweet smelling soap. She felt like a bride again as she dressed carefully in a red woollen dress that fell softly over her hips. Her figure was still slim with no sign of the small life growing within her. She slid her hands over her stomach, and there was so much happiness that it was hard to bear. She shivered, deliciously anticipating the moment when she would be in her husband's arms.

She brushed her glossy hair with rhythmic strokes, planning what she would say to Colin, how she would hold him in her arms, and how she would tell him she loved him so much it hurt.

He was late. Nia sat in the darkness, listening, waiting and then, at last, there was the sound of a key in the front door lock.

He stood in the hallway, tall and rugged in his navy sweater and heavy coat. He stepped across the space between them and took her in his arms. She sighed heavily, clinging to him, drinking in the scent of him, unable to believe that he was really here in her arms.

They ate their meal, both of them picking at the food. Colin poured some wine, glancing with raised eyebrows at the bottle.

'I didn't know my wife was into black market goods these days,' he said playfully.

'Oh, I have my contacts. I can usually get hold of something when I want it badly enough,' she said, smiling.

'Oh, dear, now I've got a black marketeer for a wife.' Colin pulled at her hair playfully and Nia turned her face, kissing the palm of his hand. He came to her, pushing aside the wine, and took her in his arms.

'I think I would like an early night,' he said, his hands cupping her face. She looked up at him, her eyes bright.

'Me too,' she said. The telephone rang in the silence and Nia frowned in displeasure, resenting the intrusion into their privacy. 'Don't answer it,' she said quickly, and then realized how foolish she sounded. 'If anyone wants to call on us, put them off,' she added.

Colin came back a few minutes later. 'It was Bella,' he said. 'My cousin has had a disaster; her lights won't work and she doesn't know what to do.'

'Can't she get a tradesman out?' Nia said eagerly. 'Oh,

Col, we have such a short time to be together. Let Bella call on someone else.'

'At this time of night?' Colin kissed her brow. 'I'll have to go over. It's probably something very simple. In any case, I won't be long, I promise you.'

She stood on the doorstep and watched him walk along the street away from her, and there were tears of disappointment trembling on her lashes.

It was perhaps an hour later that Nia heard the drone of a squadron of aircraft overhead. She told herself they must be British planes for there had been no warning sounded. She sat in the window, looking out at the street, willing Colin to come into view.

The first bomb burst deafeningly up on the heights of Townhill. More bombs fell, closer now, the rumble of the blast echoing along the hillside and into the valleys below. Nia closed her eyes, covering them with her hands. She waited, long hours she waited, making all sorts of excuses to herself.

When morning came, she was still seated near the window staring out into the pale dawn, seeing the last dying flames from the incendiary bombs that had been dropped near by.

The knock on the door was like a death knell, and Nia moved woodenly to answer it. A policeman stood on the step, his face blackened with smoke, his tin hat shading his eyes. Behind him was a young constable.

'Bad news, Mrs Singleton.' It was the constable who spoke, the older policeman happy to leave the task to him. 'A bomb fell on Eden Lamb's house . . . there was a fire . . . Mrs Lamb and Mr Singleton . . . dead.' The words were fragmented as they fell into Nia's consciousness. She heard them singly, not as part of a sentence, and yet they rang out clearly, cutting in their finality.

She heard herself saying ridiculous things, thanking the men politely for coming to break the news. The constable was speaking again, saying something about asking a friend to call, and then she closed her eyes as the welcoming darkness overwhelmed her.

427

33

The spirit among the townspeople of Swansea was magnificent. Bombs might fall, houses might be destroyed, but no German air force was going to defeat the inhabitants of the area that had once seen greatness as the metallurgical centre of the world. Christmas had come and gone and the air raids had intensified in ferocity. The New Year crept slyly upon the town accompanied by two hundred incendiary bombs and twelve high explosives.

Kristina knew fear such as she had not experienced even in the snows of Norway, for now there seemed no escape from the terrifying sounds of enemy planes overhead and the whine of bombs heading for the buildings around Swansea.

She sat in her bedroom and stared out at the moonlit port of Swansea held in the grip of ice and snow. Cold air blew in from the sea and frosted the windows, and the stark branches of trees pointed heaven-wards as though begging for release from the freezing conditions. And Kristina had still not heard a word from Robert. She wrote to him every day, letters of hope and comfort, homely letters that she prayed would bring a little normality to Robert, wherever he was.

The drone of planes sounded overhead. The raid was not unexpected, for the night was cold and clear with just a few wisps of snow-filled clouds hanging over the town.

Most folk slept defiantly in their beds, but Kristina took Verdun in her arms, wrapped him in a Welsh shawl, and looked down towards the docklands which were now in darkness. The electricity in the area of the docks was generated separately from the rest of the town, and Kristina always knew when the enemy planes were drawing near because the docks became a patch of darkness against the restless sea.

The attack was the worst so far. Bombs were dropping indiscriminately over Hafod, Cwm Road and the King's Dock, and as Kristina watched, terrified, fires flared against the night sky.

She hurried down the stairs, spurred on by the whistling noise that seemed to be right over her head. There was a shattering blast and Kristina huddled against the wall, her son heavy in her arms. She heard the crack of fire above her, and the acrid smell of smoke poured towards her down the stairs. She felt the wall beside her shudder and move, and even as she covered Verdun with her own body, there was a blinding flash, and then the house seemed to fall in on top of her.

The morning saw a town devastated. Huge craters loomed where houses had once stood, and the Home Guard, mounting a rescue operation, were hampered by the terrible weather conditions. The dazed survivors, white-faced, sought among the ruins for loved ones, but the spirit of the townsfolk was undefeated by enemy bombs. It had been a bad night for Swansea and the worst was still to come.

Eden's ship had come into Swansea with the morning tide, but it was several hours before he was free to go ashore. He strode through the docklands, staring with disbelief at the still smoking ruins of the town beyond. He stumbled over a pile of rubble and cursed the tears that blurred his eyes. Bella was dead; the news had come some weeks ago via the radio operator, and Eden had sat alone in his cabin trying to imagine life without his wife. He had loved her so much, loved her fund of humour and common sense, and he grieved that he had not been there to take care of her.

And there was the devastating sense of shock that while he was away his wife and his best friend were both dead and buried, almost as though they had never existed. He had been given no time to come to terms with the tragedy, for the sea journey had been hazardous, with little time for thoughts or even for sleep, and it was a miracle that the ship had come home unscathed.

He let himself into Ty Coch. The house, shut up for so long, smelled musty and dank, but a few open windows and some well-built fires would soon take care of that. He shrugged off his coat and set about freshening up the house. He worked automatically, his mind on other things. He wondered with a sudden sense of pain how Kristina was, and whether she too might have become a victim of the vicious bombardment. He would go to see her as soon as he had visited the graves of his friend and his wife. He would have to visit Nia, too, to offer his condolences. He imagined she would be grief-stricken, for she and Colin had been so much in love.

Soon the house blazed with cheerful fires. Eden sank into a chair, a brandy in his hand, and stared at the flames. He was overcome by a sense of inertia. There was so much he needed to do, so many difficult situations to face, and he needed some time to gather his strength.

A knocking on the door roused him and he felt a momentary sense of irritation at being disturbed. And yet there was relief, too, for being alone meant facing cold hard facts.

An old woman stood on the doorstep, her arm in a sling, her face bruised. She stared up at him for a long moment in silence.

'Can I come in?' she said at last. 'I'm Nurse Freeman. There are some things I think I should tell you.'

He stood his ground, his bulk barring her way into the house. 'What is it?' He knew he sounded hard, but he had foolishly hoped that it would be Kristina who was standing on his doorstep.

'There's a way to greet a woman who is bringing you

good news.' She spoke with asperity. 'And, *duw*, don't you know how the cold puts the ache into old bones?'

Eden found himself stepping aside, admiring the old woman's spirit. When she stood in the warmth of the hall she turned to look up at him.

'It's about your son,' she said, and watched his face, knowing that her words would be a shock. 'I'm the midwife who delivered him, and I think you have a right to know about it before the Germans kill us all off. Now, do you want me to talk about it out here in the hall, or can I take the weight off my poor legs?'

'Come in.' A strange sensation was sweeping over him. He looked at her as she hobbled into the sitting room and knew that this woman was somehow going to change his life. 'Please sit down.' He indicated a chair. 'What have you got to tell me?' He stood over her, and she smiled at him almost pityingly, easing her arm into a more comfortable position.

'The Germans should have finished me off, done me a favour.' She patted her thin chest. 'I've had my days, lived too long already, I have. Be glad to go, but must get things off my mind first, see.'

He sat down then and knew he would have to humour the old woman. She would tell him what she wanted him to know in her own good time. But it came sooner than he had expected.

'Kristina Jenkins, she's the mother of your boy.' She paused. 'Oh, everyone thinks the child was fathered by Robert Jenkins, but you can't fool an old midwife.'

She was overcome by a bout of coughing, and Eden rose and brought her some brandy. 'Here, it will warm you up,' he said, and his hand shook as he gave her the glass. 'Go on.'

'The child was conceived before the marriage. I was there at the birth; he's your son all right.' She sipped the brandy. 'You've only got to look at him – spit out of your mouth, he is.'

431

'How can I believe you?' Eden asked. 'Why didn't Kristina tell me this herself if it's the truth?'

'Married, weren't you? The girl had her pride and she needed a father, legal like, so that her child wouldn't be labelled a bastard.' She looked at him over the rim of the glass with something like amusement in her eyes. 'Almost three years of age he is now, and like I said, he's the image of you. How folks don't see the likeness for themselves, I don't know, but then people only see what they expect to see.'

Eden knew instinctively that the woman was telling the truth. But why come to him now? 'So,' he said, 'supposing the story is true, what do you expect me to do?'

'Look after the boy and his mother,' she said reasonably. 'Robert Jenkins joined up in the Army. Missing he's been this past month, probably dead as a doornail if you ask me.' She paused and rubbed at her eyes. 'The girl has always been a favourite of mine, and now she's fallen on hard times, see.'

Eden rose and stood before the fire trying to sort out his confused feelings. He actually had a son, a boy of three, and Kristina had never given him a hint of it.

'Thank you for what you've done,' he said. 'I would like to give you some sort of reward.'

She shook her head. 'I've no chick or child to leave anything to. Just promise you'll bury me decent when I go, for there's no one else to ask.'

'That's a promise.' He wanted her out now. He needed to be alone to think. Joy flared in him, for in his grasp was the one thing he had always desired – a son and heir.

'I didn't know if I should come or not at first,' she said as he led her towards the front door. 'Not everyone wants to know about past mistakes, but I felt it was your right to know the truth, and in any case, I think you should look after Kristina and her boy. Suffered enough, she has.'

'You did right,' Eden said decisively, 'and I can only thank you again for coming. I shall see my solicitor about all this in the morning. You should get home out of this cold weather as soon as you can. You have to look after your health, you know, and then the burial you are concerned about won't need to take place for a very long time,' he added with a smile.

Nurse Freeman grimacd. 'You don't give a damn about me and why should you?' She shook her head. 'I've got very little time and I know it. I'll be gone before spring, and that's if the German bombs don't finish me off first. We had another raid last night. Don't know who copped it this time, though.' She stepped out into the chill air. 'Do what's right by Kristina now.' She lifted her hand. 'Good day to you, Mr Lamb.'

She hobbled away, her figure small and somehow defenceless huddled against the sharpness of the winter air.

Seated near the fire once more, Eden wondered how he could have remained ignorant of so many important facts for so long. His son was almost three years of age; how could he have not known? He would have to see Kristina, tell her that he knew everything. He doubted that she would lie to him, it was not her way. But of course she would have to give up the child to him. He would hire the best nurse he could find, have her take the boy into the country where he would be safe from the air raids. Kristina might object at first, but surely she would eventually see that he could give the boy every chance in life?

He stretched out his long legs to the blaze. He was so tired he could hardly think straight. He had been at sea for months, dodging the enemy at every turn, threatened by enemy aircraft and enemy submarines. He had lost his wife and his friend, and now he'd been given the shattering news that he had a son. It was too much.

'Blast the war and blast the Germans!' His voice rang out in the empty room and he took another sip from his glass. The war could not last for ever. Soon he would return to the peacetime business of the shipping office and a normal life. He would watch his son grow up into

433

manhood, teach him all he knew about the business, make a man of him.

What was his son's name? It was strange, he didn't even know that much about him. Later on, sometime during the week, he would go over to the fine house nestling among the hills and he would see his son for himself. But for now, the warmth of the fire and the brandy, and the effect of nights of sleeplessness were catching up with him. He was so tired, he had never been more weary in all his life. And yet deep within him there was a glow of warmth. He had a boy of his own, and by God he would not be deprived of his son, not by anyone.

Kristina had regained consciousness slowly, aware that there were sounds of voices around her. She moved carefully and in the darkness touched her child's face.

'Mammy.' His voice was plaintive but strong, and Kristina felt his limbs and body with a sense of gratitude. It seemed he was unhurt. 'Dark, Mammy,' he said, his silky head close to her face.

'It's all right, boy *bach*,' Kristina said. 'Some kind men will get us out. I'll just call them.'

She had gathered all her strength and shouted at the top of her voice, 'Help me, I'm in here!' The tapping on the slabs of concrete that had fallen in a tent-like position above her ceased.

'Where are you, *merchi*?' a strong voice called. 'Keep on talking, love, and we'll soon have you out.'

The next few hours were the longest Kristina had ever known. She could hear the men working above her but they seemed to be getting no nearer. Then, suddenly, a shaft of light poured in, and Kristina was blinking in the sudden brightness.

'There you are, gel, we'll have you out of there in two ticks.' Strong hands lifted Verdun from her, and then she was caught and drawn free of the wreckage that had once been her home.

'Any relatives to go to, love?' One of the men from the Home Guard asked kindly, and Kristina nodded.

'Yes, Ceinwen Presdey down at Lambert's. She's my mother.' She found it difficult to stand. She had been trapped so long in a crouching position that her legs seemed to have lost their flexibility. She sank down on to the rubble and wondered if her own face was as dirty and dusty as those of the men who had rescued her.

'Come on then, *merchi*.' The man helped her to her feet. 'I'll take you down to Lambert's. Your mam will be glad to know you're safe.'

Some weeks later, Kristina was still living in her mother's house, though she hoped the arrangement was a temporary one. She was setting the table for dinner. It was rabbit stew again, a good nourishing meal filled with potatoes and swede, and it was Verdun's favourite.

'Have you washed your hands now, Verdun?' she asked, and her son nodded solemnly as he climbed up on to his chair.

'There's a good boy,' she said softly. 'Now how about a bit of rabbit, then, and if you eat that all up like a big boy I'll give you some pudding with a bit of jam on.'

The door opened and Ceinwen entered the warmth of the kitchen, rubbing her hands gratefully. '*Duw*, love, there's cold it is, glad to get in I am.' Ceinwen put her bible away carefully for she had become very religious of late, attending chapel meetings and singing hymns about the house whenever the mood took her. Other things had changed too. Bill Presdey, Ceinwen's brother-in-law, had seemed to take up permanent lodgings in the house. Sometimes, Kristina was made to feel very strongly that she was a visitor in her mother's house.

Ceinwen kissed the top of Verdun's head. 'There's lovely it is to have you both by here with me,' she said. 'Keep me company, you do, now that the girls are married and off about their own business.' She looked tentatively towards Kristina. 'No word from your husband, then?' She sat down and eased off her good stout shoes. 'Never mind, love, you know what they say, no news is good news.'

Kristina felt a stab of pain. Robert, good honest Robert, had left her life so completely that she could scarcely believe they'd been married. She still wrote to him every day. Posting the letters had become almost a ritual, giving her hope that he was still alive.

The dreadful night her house had been destroyed was etched into her mind for ever. The drone of enemy planes, the screech of bombs, the thunderous explosions. She had been grateful to escape with Verdun safe in her arms and only later had she realized how desperate was her position. Robert's assets had been mostly in property, his papers had been lost in the rubble of their home, and anyway, what price bricks and mortar with a war raging?

Ceinwen sank back with a sigh of relief. She was pale, the shadows beneath her eyes etched with the blue lines of her veins. 'Put some stew out for me, there's a good girl. You don't know what a comfort it is to have you home.'

A comfort. Kristina smiled ruefully. A burden, no doubt, with a grown woman and small boy to feed and very little money to do it on.

'Your Robert will come back one of these days,' Ceinwen said, 'and then he'll look after us all, such a capable man is Robert.'

Kristina felt a flash of fear. Why should Robert be spared when so many soldiers had died already?

Verdun, his meal finished looked longingly at his grandmother's knee warmed by the flames from the fire. 'Nana,' he said, holding out his arms, and Ceinwen, her face alight, took him into her embrace.

'There's a good boy then, have you eaten all your dinner?' She wiped his mouth with a tea towel, and watching them, Kristina felt warmed. Her child needed a family, needed people around him who loved him, for it seemed he was destined to live his life without the protection of a father. Kristina sighed. She could not get

Robert out of her mind. Her mother seemed to read her thoughts.

'Your husband will be all right, you'll see,' she said. 'If he's a prisoner somewhere in a foreign country he wouldn't be able to get word to us, would he?'

Kristina rose and began to clear the table. She was cold with fear. What if Robert *was* a prisoner of war? He might never return.

There was a knocking on the door and Ceinwen looked up at Kristina almost fearfully. 'I'll go,' she said at once, and Kristina bit her lip, fearing every knock at the door in case it was a dreaded telegram.

'Kristina, it's Mr Lamb,' Ceinwen said, stepping back and looking uncertainly at her daughter.

Eden entered the small kitchen. 'Kristina, it's so good to see you.' His face was drawn and pale but his smile conveyed real warmth and she felt so sorry for him in his grief. She watched as his eyes were drawn towards where Verdun stood near the fireside, and she knew that somehow Eden had learned the truth.

'I wanted to see my son.' He looked pleadingly towards Kristina. 'You should have told me about him long ago, Kristina, I could have done so much to help you and the boy.'

Suddenly Kristina felt panic rise within her. She drew Verdun closer to her as Eden came towards them.

'Look, Kristina,' Eden said reasonably, 'I mean no harm to you or to my son, but I'm so alone now. Don't begrudge me a little time spent trying to get to know my child.'

'How did you find out?' she asked and Eden smiled with a flash of his old charm. 'Old Nurse Freeman told me everything.' He smiled. 'In any case, anyone with half an eye could see the likeness.' He touched her shoulder. 'Think for a minute what I could do for the boy. He'd have money, position, everything he could want in life.'

'No!' Kristina found it difficult to breathe. 'He's *my* son, you can't take him away from me.'

Ceinwen spoke up quietly. 'Don't be hasty now, girl. You know we are finding it hard to manage, you with no money and all. Let Mr Lamb help you at least.' She moved nearer to Kristina. 'No one is going to let him take the boy anywhere, it's all right.'

Kristina looked up at Eden. 'I don't mean to be cruel, but Verdun is Robert's son, not yours. My husband was there at the birth, and ever since he has been a fine father to Verdun. Nothing can change that.'

'What have you to offer him?' Eden said. 'Look around you, Kristina, will you let my son grow up in poverty?'

'He's *not* your son, Eden,' she said hotly. 'Go away! Just leave us in peace.'

Eden turned away from her and opened the door allowing a blast of cold air to rush into the kitchen.

'I wish you hadn't come here, upsetting us like this,' Kristina said in a low voice. 'Now please go away and leave us alone. Please.'

Eden looked haunted as he stared at her and then at Verdun, and Kristina almost weakened, wanting to ask him to stay a while. Eden moved slowly to the door and closed it quietly behind him. But Kristina knew Eden well enough to understand that he would never give up. Now that he knew the truth, he would do everything he could to take Verdun from her, and suddenly she was afraid.

34

Nia was now a rich woman, her own modest wealth augmented by Colin's money, but she would have given away every penny if only she could have him back again. She missed his sensitivity, his calm common sense and most of all she missed the happiness and the feeling of security she knew when she was in his arms.

She sat up in bed, drained by her grief, not wanting to get up and face the day. As she lay against the pillows in the darkened room, she could not help but relive the feelings of despair of those first dark days when she had heard of Colin's death. She had been struck with a feeling of terror that was mingled with disbelief. She moved in a nightmare world from which there was no awakening, and the nightmare continued as she lost the child she'd been carrying. She was bitter and angry that her last link with Colin had been so cruelly taken from her.

Mrs Preece entered the room and stood uncertainly at the bedside. 'Are you feeling better, Mrs Singleton? Everyone's been asking after you.'

Nia nodded and turned her face away. She didn't want to talk or eat or even live.

'I've got to talk to you, Mrs Singleton.' Mrs Preece's tone had become brisk. 'I managed breakfast 'cos the hens been laying, see, but there's nothing in the cold pantry for dinner or supper. We got no meat or fish and I've been going without too, mind.'

Nia roused herself out of her apathy and pushed back her tangled hair. She must do something, see to the mundane tasks of running the house. In all conscience she could not expect Mrs Preece to stand in a queue a mile long and wait perhaps an hour in the cold for a scant piece of ham or some poor quality pig's trotters. It was time Nia used the influence she had over the traders of Swansea to the advantage of her household.

'I'll be getting up today, Mrs Preece,' she said wearily. 'If you can find me some warm clothes from the wardrobe, please.'

As she washed, she was aware that the water was cold. There was very little fuel available but she could always call in a favour. There was no need for the house to be uncomfortable. Nia felt a surge of energy. She had neglected her duties and most of all neglected herself. What would Colin have thought of her weakness? He would have been sadly disappointed in her lack of character.

Once dressed, Nia took stock of the kitchen. There was no butter or sugar, and though rationing restrictions were the law, Nia had never needed to adhere to them at all closely. How people managed on twelve ounces of sugar and four ounces of butter a week she failed to understand.

In the sitting room, there was only a small fire of sticks and paper, and Nia sighed. She had been remiss indulging in her grief at the expense of Mrs Preece who was old and unable to face the cold and the shortage of food.

Nia made a few telephone calls and then moved back into the kitchen. On the table stood a wooden box with pieces of straw jutting out through the slats. 'What on earth is this?' she asked, lifting the lid. The smell of chicken broth filled the kitchen even as Mrs Preece closed the lid quickly.

'It's my war effort.' She smiled, her rosy wrinkled cheeks reminiscent of a dry apple. 'I heard about it in the greengrocer's, see, and used the scraps from yesterday's dinner to make a soup.'

'But how does it work?' Nia asked suspiciously. 'Straw and newspaper can't generate heat, surely?'

'I don't know about that,' Mrs Preece said doubtfully, 'but if you bring the pan to the boil on the gas ring and then put it in the box, it finishes cooking on its own.'

Nia looked at the long coal cooker that dominated the kitchen, and moved to open the door. It was clear that the cooker had not been lit for some time.

'You've done very well, Mrs Preece,' Nia said, 'but there will be no need to use the box after today, for I'm having coal delivered.'

'Can I give it to my sister, then?' Mrs Preece asked, and Nia nodded rather guiltily. She had not known that there was a sister.

'You may take some eggs, too,' she said. 'And perhaps a little sugar. We'll see how much we've got in stock.'

She returned to the sitting room, and kicking off her shoes curled her legs under her for warmth. It was time she checked on her offices. If she failed to keep on top of her managers, she couldn't blame anyone but herself if standards were not maintained.

At the outset of war, when civilized life had seemed to come to a halt, when cinemas closed their doors and music halls remained empty, it seemed there would be little call for betting offices. But then, slowly, business resumed and there were always the small meetings and the dog racing on which punters wished to bet. She knew there was no need for her ever to work again, but poring over figures, working out odds, taking risks, were all part and parcel of her life. She had not been brought up a bookie's daughter without some of the excitement rubbing off on her.

But so much had been dead in her since the day Colin had walked out of her life never to return. It seemed like yesterday. The shock and grief were still as great, for she had not been given a chance even to say goodbye to him. Long weeks had passed since then, endless weeks when she had kept to her bed and wished only to die. But now, even though she still ached with the loss, she had come to realize that she must go on. She could not give up on life, however badly she felt. She had to make an effort to pick up the pieces.

It was late afternoon when Mrs Preece announced a visitor. At first, Nia was about to refuse to see anyone, then she realized that Eden Lamb was standing in the doorway. He was wearing the same sort of high-necked jersey that Colin used to wear, and he looked ruggedly handsome with white flecks in the darkness of his hair. Suddenly she realized that he too had suffered, for he had lost his wife Bella at the same moment she had lost Colin. The thought made her warm to him.

'Come in, Eden,' she said. 'Sit down. The fire is lovely because we've had some coal delivered today, you see. We'd run out of everything in the last weeks. Oh, why am I talking such rubbish?' She went to him and raised her lips to his cheek, and Eden held her for a moment in silence.

'I came to find out exactly what happened, if you can bear to talk about it,' he said at last. He moved away from her and settled himself easily in a chair. 'It's insane, I went away to sea a husband and came home a widower. I can't believe it.'

Nia sighed heavily. 'I'm sorry, Eden. In my own grief I didn't give you a thought. I'm very selfish, forgive me.'

'Tell me,' he said, and taking a deep breath, Nia forced herself to go over the events of the night of the air raid.

'Bella needed help,' she said raggedly. 'Her lights had all gone haywire and she telephoned Colin. She didn't know who else to contact.' It was difficult to go on. So many times she had tortured herself with 'if only'. If only Bella had not phoned Colin, if only he had been out at the time, if only, if only until she'd nearly gone mad.

'I know it's not easy for you,' Eden said softly, 'but please, I would like to know it all.'

'There was an air raid.' She swallowed hard. 'It left over fifty of the townsfolk dead, including Bella and Colin.' She looked up at him, and suddenly she felt so close to him, for he was here with her, sharing her loss.

'Eden, how can we live with it?' Tears so long held in check overflowed, and great gasping sobs racked her. She felt as though she were dissolving in her grief and she reached out to the only person on earth who must know exactly how she felt.

Eden held her close, murmuring soothing words, smoothing back the hair from her flushed face, drying her tears with his handkerchief.

'We will support each other,' he said firmly. 'We will be friends, more than friends because we are bound together now.' He tipped her face up to his. 'Promise me that when I'm at sea you will write to me, tell me things, anything, about you, about the town, about the bombing. You must be my link with all I've cared about.'

'I will, I promise.' She sank back into her chair. She felt exhausted and yet refreshed, and within her there was a warmth because she was no longer alone.

As Eden left Nia's house and strode purposefully down the hill towards the town, his thoughts were racing. He had meant to speak to Nia about her friendship with Kristina, to ask if Nia knew anything about the boy's birth. But as he'd held her and felt her grief, pity had stirred in him, along with a feeling of protectiveness. Now he was away from the house, his mind was working more clearly.

He frowned thoughtfully. It would take time for her to get over her grief, but when she did he would be able to talk to her about his son. His son. It was a wonderful feeling, and however much Kristina denied the truth, he had only to look at the boy to know he was born of the Lamb family.

He looked at the docklands spread out below him and the sprawl of the town with gaps in the houses like missing teeth. How he loved Swansea, with its haphazard architecture, its old buildings, its teeming dock life. Once the war was over, he would settle down, bring up his son, and if luck was on his side, find love again with a fine woman who would bear him more sons.

443

He still grieved for Bella – he had loved her for her common sense, her wit and her cleverness – but he had to think about the future, make plans that included his son.

He made for the Burrows near the entrance to the docks, and moved inside the smoky atmosphere, suddenly needing to be in the company of men, men who had clear minds and easy emotions. And yet as he leaned on the bar, drinking his beer, he felt again the trembling form of Nia in his arms. He'd seen her face, beautiful with tears, warm into a smile as she looked up at him, and the memory made him feel good.

'*Bore da*, Mr Lamb.' A man stood beside Eden looking up at him with an ingratiating smile on his face, and Eden's first instinct was to tell the man to go to hell. The last thing he wanted was to be caught up in a conversation about ships and the war. He wanted to forget all that, at least for a day or two.

'Minding the boy I am,' the man said slyly. 'Ceinwen Presdey is my sister-in-law, see.' He paused. 'Wanted a ride on my horse and cart, he did. Couldn't say no to him, my own kith and kin, could I? Waiting outside, the kid is right now. Would you like to talk to him?'

Eden felt a lift of excitement. 'Aye, all right.' He gulped the rest of his ale before moving after the bulky figure of Presdey into the street.

The child was standing miserably in the cold, next to a ragged looking horse and cart. He was shuffling his feet against the icy pavement, rubbing at his reddened cheeks with small hands. Anger ran though Eden as he saw the thin coat, inadequate protection against the February weather. He wondered if he should dip his hand in his pocket there and then, but instinct told him that Presdey would spend the money on ale and the boy would see none of it.

'I have a proposition to put to you,' he said quietly, and Presdey leaned forward expectantly, listening quietly, nodding his head several times as Eden spoke.

When he was satisfied that Presdey understood what

444

he had to say, Eden lifted the child in his arms. 'You go back in the bar, I'll take the child, and don't forget there's a few pounds in this for you.'

He carried the boy the short distance to Ty Coch, and the warmth of the house wrapped itself around him.

'That's better, isn't it?' he said softly. 'What's your name, son?' The word slid easily from his lips, and Eden felt pride that this handsome boy with the same eyes and the same lick of dark hair was his own flesh and blood. Old Nurse Freeman had been right; the boy was the image of him.

'Verdun Jenkins,' the boy said, lisping slightly, and Eden lifted him to his lap in one easy movement. The child was too thin, he needed building up. Eden meant to claim him whatever it took, but for now, he was content to get to know his son, the better to gain his confidence.

'Would you like something to eat?' he asked, not knowing what sort of food would appeal to a child.

'Butty and jam,' the boy said eagerly, and taking his hand, Eden led him towards the kitchen.

Kristina moved impatiently from one foot to the other. The queue didn't seem to be getting any shorter. The cold bit through her thin-soled shoes, and as she rubbed at her hands she wondered if she would ever be warm again.

'*Duw*,' Ceinwen Presdey standing at Kristina's side spoke angrily, 'by the time we get to the counter we'll be lucky if there's anything left.'

The smell of coffee beans was tantalizingly refreshing, and Kristina sighed, knowing that she could not afford such luxuries.

'I hope that boy of yours is behaving himself,' Ceinwen said. 'You know Bill Presdey's temper is as short as our Tom's used to be. Don't get any better as he gets older either.'

Kristina pushed away her sense of unease. Her choice had been limited; either take Verdun out into the cold of the winter streets, or leave him by the warmth of the fireside with Bill Presdey.

'Perhaps I'd better go back,' she said worriedly. 'I wouldn't like to think of Bill getting short-tempered with Verdun.'

'You can't lose your place in the queue after all this time, mind,' Ceinwen said anxiously. 'We need some sugar and butter badly. You'd better wait, Verdun will be all right.'

It seemed hours before Kristina reached the counter of Taylor's general supply store. She took her rations and placed the butter and tea and sugar carefully in her basket.

'I'd like some potatoes, please,' she said, smiling at the portly man behind the counter.

'Running out of spuds we are,' the man said, rubbing his hands against his striped apron, 'but for a pretty girl like you I can find a few, I suppose.'

At last, Ceinwen and Kristina were able to make their way back to Lambert's Cottages. '*Duw*, I don't think I'll ever feel my feet again,' Ceinwen said softly. 'It's all right for the men. They eat hearty and don't think of us having to find the food to put in their bellies.'

Kristina made no comment. Bill Presdey ate well. He'd taken to dropping in quite a bit lately and half the time he ate Ceinwen's share of the food as well.

When she entered the house, Kristina saw with dismay that Bill was snoring in the chair, his stockinged feet stretched before him, his cap awry on his head. The smell of beer filled the room and it was clear that the man had been to some public bar or other. The fire was burning low in the grate and there was no sign of Verdun.

'Bill Presdey!' Kristina shook his arm roughly, fear making her voice shrill. 'Where's my son, what have you done with Verdun?'

Bill snorted and opened bleary eyes. 'For God's sake stop your bellowing, woman, can't a man get a sleep then? Ceinwen, see to the fire, gel. It's blutty freezing in by here. Oh, and find a nice frock. I'm going to give my sister-in-law a treat. You and me is going out on the town tonight.'

Kristina longed to slap him. 'Where's Verdun?' She was icy cold now, her hands shaking so much that she clenched them together in an effort to calm herself.

'Don't worry,' Bill was deliberately taunting her, 'he's all right. With Eden Lamb he is, see. Now stop fussing. The man's his real father, isn't he?'

'Oh my God!' Kristina said in a low voice, and Bill rose from his chair, a defensive look on his face.

'You ungrateful girl,' he said. 'I look after your kid and this is the thanks I get.'

'Oh, Kris,' her mother said, 'now don't go taking it out on Bill. He's only trying to help, means well he does, mind.'

Kristina rushed into the street. He would be at Ty Coch, that's where Eden would take her son. She felt like screaming in her panic as she pounded on the door of the Red House.

'How dare you take my boy?' She looked up into Eden's face as he opened the door. In his arms was Verdun, his small face flushed.

'Mammy.' Her son reached out to her and she took him, holding him close, closing her eyes with relief.

'Come on in,' Eden said quickly. 'I don't think the boy is very well.'

Kristina followed him inside. 'What are you talking about? If you're still trying your tricks to take my son away from me, well it won't work.' It was warm in the big house, fires burned cheerfully in the grate. It seemed that Eden Lamb and his kind would never be short of food or fuel. It just wasn't fair.

'Let's be practical,' Eden said. 'The child should have warm clothes. And he's too thin, he needs feeding. I can give him these things. Just look at him now, the boy's clearly got a fever.'

Kristina sank down into a chair, holding Verdun close. 'He is my son,' she said. 'Are you trying to say I don't look after him properly?'

'Look,' Eden said softly, 'you can stay here, just until

447

the child is better. The house will be empty while I'm away. You and Verdun could be very comfortable. You can't deny him that.'

She opened her eyes and looked directly at him. 'And when your next leave is due, what then?'

'By then I might well be dead,' Eden said. 'And in that event, everything would go to the boy as my next of kin. Can you find it in you to deny Verdun his birthright? He would have the best of everything; good schooling, warm clothes to put on his back, proper food.'

'No, thank you,' Kristina said dully, knowing he could give her son more than she could ever offer him. 'We don't want your charity.'

'Just accept my hospitality for a few days. That's not too difficult, is it? Stay here at the house, and for God's sake buy the boy some adequate clothing. I go back to sea in a few days. Time is short, I could be killed on my next trip. I want to give my son everything I have, I've no one else to leave it to. Just tell me he's mine and I'll see my solicitor before I go away again.'

'Verdun *is* very hot,' Kristina said in agitation, her hand against her son's forehead, 'but he has these fevers often and soon gets over them.' She looked up doubtfully, thinking of the cold bedroom in her mother's house and of Bill Presdey lolling near the fire so that no one else could feel the benefit. 'I suppose we could stay here just until Verdun's cold is better, but I'm not admitting anything, mind.'

Eden rose to his feet. 'I shall cook us all a nice supper, and in the mean time, you sort out the sleeping arrangements for you and the boy.'

He disappeared from the room, and Kristina held Verdun close. He wound his small, warm arms around her neck and clung to her, and tears came to her eyes. Would it be so wrong to tell Eden the truth, put his mind at rest before he went to sea again? After all, Verdun was Robert's son by law. Eden could not take him away from her by force whatever he thought. Anyway, he had thought better of those threats. All he wanted to do now was take care of Verdun's future.

She took Verdun up the stairs and found that a fire was burning in several of the rooms. It was clear Eden had been expecting her. She chose the bedroom where she used to sleep when she worked at the house. It was familiar and warming and it held happy memories of when she was young.

After supper, Kristina washed Verdun and put him in the large bed in her room. He snuggled down under the clothes and closed his eyes immediately. Kristina felt a gentle hand on her shoulder and turned to look into Eden's face. In the flickering firelight, his eyes looked clear and honest, filled with happiness as they rested on Verdun.

'The boy was conceived in this very bed, has that thought occurred to you, Kris?' His voice was soft and gentle, and Kristina moved away from him quickly, not wanting to encourage any arousing of old memories. She was confused enough without Eden playing on her emotions.

And they were still there, the feelings of desire for him. He could move her physically, but she knew that there was no love in her heart for him, for Robert was the only man she could ever love now.

She hurried down the stairs and Eden was quickly behind her. He took her in his arms and bent his head towards her. She pushed him away quickly. 'No!' she said. 'If you touch me again, I'll go home straight away. I'll go and do the washing up,' she said shakily, and hurriedly she moved away from him and crossed the hallway into the kitchen.

She was drying the last dish when the now familiar wail of the air raid warning rose like the voice of a banshee over the town.

'I'll fetch the boy,' Eden said. 'You get some blankets and put on a warm coat.' She heard him pounding up the stairs and she hurried after him, dragging open the

449

drawers in the great chest on the landing and throwing out some of the heavier blankets.

Eden reappeared. 'We'll go to the shelters. Come on, hurry, Kristina, bring only what's necessary.'

The bombs were falling on Swansea to devastating effect. Shops and houses were blazing, the windows of the stricken buildings shattering, flying outward in the heat. Kristina tried to keep up with Eden, but she fell over the railway lines in the darkness and lay for a moment stunned. Suddenly she felt very frail and vulnerable, and in that moment she knew she could not protect her son unaided. Verdun must be given every chance in life.

In the shelter Kristina crouched beside Eden with Verdun still asleep in his father's arms. She felt her fear evaporate as she saw some people playing cards as though nothing was happening and others knitting or sewing. Children were quarrelling or calmly playing. It seemed that no amount of bombing could quell the spirit of the people of the docklands.

She slept fitfully, aware of the drone of voices around her. When she awoke, a flare of fire was visible through the narrow slit of the doorway and she moved stiffly, aware that she had been resting on Eden's shoulder.

'Take the boy,' he said softly. 'I must get out and see if there's anything I can do to help. The town has taken a pounding, if I'm not mistaken.' Eden was the first to leave, then one by one the few other men disappeared from the shelter. Kristina tried to sleep again to pass the hours, but she was restless, afraid for Eden. What if the bombers returned?

Morning came at last and soon the women began to pack up in preparation for returning to their homes. Many of them would have no homes, a fact of which all of them were stingingly aware. But there was no complaining as they took charge of their children and their pitifully few belongings and ventured out into the day.

Kristina saw with relief that Lambert's Cottages had not been hit. She made her way towards her mother's house, struggling over the uneven ground with Verdun clasped tightly in her arms. She must let Mam know she was safe, for her mother would be worried after the way Kristina had walked out last night.

The house was empty, the fire unlit in the grate, the remains of a meal still on the table. Probably Ceinwen and Bill Presdey had taken shelter in the town and would be home presently. In the mean time there was nothing for her to do but take Verdun back to Ty Coch.

It was much later in the day that Eden returned home, his face blackened by smoke, his coat torn and dusty.

'It isn't finished yet,' he said, slumping into a chair. 'The Germans are going to hammer away at the town until every building is demolished.' He rubbed at his forehead. 'I think it might be a good thing for you and the child to get out of Swansea, somewhere a few miles away where you won't be in danger.'

'I'm staying,' Kristina said decisively. 'Come on, get washed and changed and I'll cook us a meal.' She turned and smiled at him. 'And thanks, Eden, for looking after me and Verdun so well.'

The blitz on Swansea continued that night. Kristina again sat in the shelter with Verdun asleep in her arms. As the bombs crashed against buildings and started glaring fires, she prayed that she and her son would come through the night alive.

In the morning, Kristina went home to her mother's house. It was still empty. She took Verdun's hand. 'Come on, boy,' she said softly, 'let's look for Nana.'

The centre of the town was devastated. Rubble lay in smoking mounds and some of the buildings were still on fire. Ben Evans's store was no more than a burning skeleton. Kristina stopped at a mobile canteen that had been touring the stricken streets and looked up anxiously. 'Have you seen anything of Ceinwen Presdey?' she asked the elderly volunteer, and the woman shook her head. Groups of ragged people stood stunned amid the rubble, hollow-eyed and desperate, and Kristina was filled with a sense of foreboding.

Many people were injured and were being ferried to a makeshift hospital, and Kristina, asking an ARP warden where they were being taken, followed them. But there was no sign of Ceinwen or Bill Presdey.

The dead were laid out in a church hall, and Kristina joined the relatives searching the rows of fatalities. She found them, lying side by side, and in the dimness of the church buildings her mother might almost have been asleep.

'Oh, Mam!' Kristina said in a broken voice. 'All you wanted was a night out on the town and you gave your life for it.'

'Come on *merchi*.' A kindly warden took her arm, 'come outside and have a nice cup of tea with lots of sugar in it, good for shock it is, mind.'

She let herself be drawn away. There was no point in staying, there was nothing she could do.

Verdun pulled at her hand. 'What's the matter with Nana?' he asked in a loud voice, and Kristina swallowed hard before answering him.

'She's gone to be with the angels, son.' She could scarcely speak as she left the church buildings and tried to look to the future, hers and her son's.

35

The sun was hot, there was scarcely any breeze, and the ceiling fan did little to dispel the humidity in the air. Outside, the bougainvillaeas were bright splashes of colour against the drying grass. It was difficult to believe it would be winter back home.

Roggen pushed back her hair. It was growing thick and long and it was high time she had it cut to a shorter, more manageable length. It was so hot – how she longed for a cool spring day in Swansea, when the daffodils were in bloom and soft rain bathed the greenness of the grass with diamonds of light. Suddenly she was immensely homesick. She longed for the ghostly mists that fell over the hills of Wales and for the patchwork quilt of the fertile fields surrounding Swansea. Most of all she longed to be reunited with her brother. She missed him so much, and she grieved for him. The shock of losing both his wife and his partner in an air raid must have been devastating.

Up until the time the news came about the deaths of Bella and Colin, Roggen had been able to put thoughts about the war out of her mind, but now she had fallen into the habit of devouring every item of news about Swansea in the papers. The town had been pounded persistently by German bombs over the past months, houses had been destroyed and the beautiful shops in the centre of the town reduced to ashes. There would be no lights gleaming in windows, only black sheets to fool the enemy.

She was alone in the house. The servants were having a day off, sulking no doubt because Mark had refused to give them the huge pay rise they were demanding. It seemed that they were becoming more and more reluctant to do the work around the house, and their attitudes were sullen, almost rude. One of the servants had claimed that they needed extra money to give to the Kongsis, which were the trade unions, in order to fight the war in China. Mark had described the claim as rubbish and had been curt in his refusal even to consider such a rise.

Roggen glanced at the clock. Mark should be home soon. He had been out most of the day celebrating with some of his friends from Australia who had arrived in Singapore some time ago. The first influx of Australian troops had been received with mixed feelings. To some, their appearance meant added security for the island, but to others, the threat of invasion was hammered home. Mark had told Roggen that the extra men were necessary, though how the war could reach its tentacles as far as Singapore was a mystery to Roggen. The port at Seletar was impregnable, everyone was agreed on that, and as for any army coming at Singapore Island through Malaya, covering miles of swampland and jungle – well, that was unthinkable.

She brushed back her hair and picked up an English newspaper, poring over its contents. It seemed that Mr Churchill, with his fine sense of oratory, was doing a splendid job in leading the coalition Government, and although Roggen could not agree with his principles, at least the man seemed able to raise the spirits of the British people.

News was often several days late reaching Singapore, but Roggen enjoyed reading about home. The small matters such as rationing seemed so amazing, for in Singapore there were no shortages at all. She and Mark had read with horror of the latest bombing of London, and though awful, the events were so far removed from the sun and the heat and the colour of the life she was leading now as to be a world in an almost forgotten dream. But she wrote to Eden often and waited eagerly for letters from home.

Sometimes his letters, though infrequent, were filled with personal details; his blossoming friendship with Nia who had been widowed at the same moment he'd become a widower, and then the amazing revelation that he had a son. And yet even that sort of happening seemed distant and unreal.

Eden wrote sometimes of world affairs. He told her how in the past America had wisely opted to stay out of the war. Roosevelt had appealed to Japan's Emperor, personally urging Hirohito to avoid war with the United States. But all the good intentions had been washed away some time ago when Pearl Harbor had been bombed by the Japanese.

The outer door opened and Mark swung into the house in his usual eager way. He did everything quickly and with an energy that always had the effect of spurring Roggen into action with him. He had a sort of force about him, giving the impression that if he wished he could move mountains.

'Mark!' Roggen rose to welcome him and as she was held in a close embrace she closed her eyes, enjoying the scent of him, the animal attraction that he had for her. And yet there was more than that between them; Mark's sense of humour, his strength, and his tenderness towards her brought her the sort of happiness Roggen had never known before. And most of all, they could talk to each other.

'Get us a drink, love.' He released her and moved to the verandah, staring out into the shade of the papaya patch at the bottom of the garden. His voice held a note she could not quite interpret. She poured him a drink and handed it to him, resting her head against his shoulder.

'There's something wrong, Mark. What is it?' She hugged his arm to her side, fear trickling through her. He sighed.

'It looks as if the Japs are out to rule the whole world,

Ro. I don't believe we'll be able to stop them, not here in Singapore, anyway.'

'What will the Japanese do next?' Roggen asked, seeing in her mind's eye a Britain overrun and defeated. 'Will they attack Britain, do you think?'

Mark shrugged. 'As far as I can see they've been too busy invading Malaya and the Philippines to bother about England just yet.' He smiled teasingly.

'But you believe they'll come here soon, don't you?' Roggen asked fearfully. She had heard of the Japanese, how they believed in death before dishonour. They would have no mercy on anyone taken prisoner.

Mark put his arm around her waist. 'Enough of all this gloom. We're going on a picnic.' He laughed. 'Well, knowing the crowd, it'll be more of a boozing party. We're going to watch the parade of Australian troops in Raffles Square.'

Roggen had never felt less like being in the company of some of Mark's boisterous friends. Several of them had taken up with English girls from the military bases of Singapore, and the entire crowd seemed to be bent on having fun. Laughter and high spirits were all very fine but sometimes Roggen longed for a quiet time when she and Mark could be alone. Lately those times were getting few and far between. It seemed that the people of Singapore were having a last frenzied fling.

'I'll just change into a fresh skirt and blouse.' Roggen's smile hid her misgivings. 'I won't be long.'

Mark drove to the square with his usual haste, the vehicle bouncing over tracks and at times almost becoming airborne. Roggen clung on to her hat, smiling to herself. Mark could never be accused of being over-cautious.

His friends were already at the square. 'Look,' Mark said, 'there's Mac and Tricia. Trust them to get a good position near the front of the crowd.' He abandoned the jeep and, taking Roggen's arm, propelled her forward.

'Hello there,' Mark said quietly. 'What do you think of this parade, then?'

His friend pushed back his hat and wiped his brow. 'The poor sods must be worn out marching in this heat,' he said lugubriously.

Roggen was soon tired of the marching and counter-marching. The sound of boots against the road seemed to ring in her ears like a death knell and she shivered a little in spite of the heat.

'Well,' Mark thrust his hands into his pockets, 'the whole of Malaya must have been stripped bare of men to put on this little show. If the Nips want to attack they'll never have a better chance.'

Mac laughed out loud and slapped Mark heartily on the back. 'You're right there, mate!' He leaned forward and his glance included Roggen. 'About tonight, what about a little nightclubbing? We'll all meet back here in the square.'

'Aye,' Mark said at once, 'that's a fine idea, right Roggen?' As Mark looked down at her, Roggen decided that she might as well go along with the suggestion, though she could have done with a night in for a change.

She nodded. 'I'll look forward to that.' She edged one foot out of a high-heeled sandal and wriggled her cramped toes, wishing she'd forgotten vanity and had worn something more suitable for standing on a hot pavement watching a parade.

She was relieved when Mark took her arm and began to swathe a way through the crowd. 'I need a beer,' he said as he led her back to the jeep. He swung himself up into the driving seat and held out his hand to her. 'Let's have a cold drink and go to bed for an hour. How does that strike you?'

Roggen smiled. 'It sounds very tempting, but if I don't do some cooking there'll be nothing for dinner. The servants are having the day off, remember.'

'Aye,' Mark said, 'I remember. Pretty damn strange they're acting, if you ask me. I wonder what's going on.'

'Oh, I expect it's just Wee and Oey having the odd tantrum because we wouldn't give them the rise in wages they asked for,' Roggen said. 'Can't be anything else.'

Mark set the jeep into motion. 'How about us going home, getting changed and then grabbing a taxi into town to have a meal and then go on and meet Mac?'

Roggen brightened. 'That's the best suggestion yet. Anything to get out of cooking a meal in this heat.'

Mark reached out and touched her shoulder. 'Not at your best in the kitchen are you, love, but you make up for it in other ways, so don't you go worrying about it, now.'

Roggen smiled. 'I never promised you a cook when I came to live with you.' She rested her head against his shoulder. 'But I try my best to please.' She touched his cheek lightly, and in response he leaned over and kissed the top of her head.

'Any more of this mawkish sentiment and I'll be sick,' he said, but there was a smile in his eyes as they met hers. 'And don't look at me like that or we won't make it past the bedroom door.'

Later, when she had bathed and dressed in a flowing off-the-shoulder dress of blue silk, Roggen sat on the verandah sipping an iced drink and waiting for Mark. She thought again about home and how she wished she could be there in spite of the bombing. It had occurred to her to ask Mark to go home with her, if only for a visit, but the seas were dangerous these days, and in any case, how could she take him away from his business?

He came in from the bedroom looking more handsome than usual in his tuxedo, his hair smoothed into some semblance of neatness. He smiled and her stomach seemed to turn over with love for him. Wherever he was, then she wanted to be there too.

They dined on Cantonese food. Roggen chose her favourite dish of *Kon lo mee*, shredded pork and chilli noodles, while Mark decided to start with the *dim sum*, consisting of many small delicacies. He began with steamed dumplings stuffed with meat and vegetables, and moved on to fried cakes filled with sweets. Roggen ate very little. She felt unsettled, almost uneasy. She drank a little wine and told herself not to be foolish. She was imagining things, making up problems where there were none. And yet her sense of foreboding was increasing.

Later, the taxi dropped them at the square where Mac and Tricia were already waiting. It was a clear night with huge stars glittering in a velvet sky, and as Roggen breathed deeply, she thought how much she wanted to keep this moment for ever crystallized in her mind.

It was good dancing with Mark. He held her close as though he would never let her go, and even when Mac teased him in a good-natured way, Mark did not relax his hold on her.

'Tonight, I will show you how much I love you,' he whispered, and Roggen clung to him, wondering at his words, for he was not usually so communicative. His feelings he kept to himself, showing her more in deeds than in words how he felt about her. He must be very worried about the threat of impending trouble. But she would not think about it, not now. For the moment, she would enjoy Mark and the wonderful feeling of being in his arms.

That night, as she lay in the darkness unable to sleep, Roggen was very conscious of Mark's nearness. She reached out a hand and touched him, finding comfort in the warmth of his skin. He stirred and turned towards her, taking her in his arms.

'Can't you sleep?' he asked, and Roggen pressed herself close to him, liking the way he was immediately awake and alive to her mood. She was a slow awakener, she needed time to gather her thoughts, but Mark was startlingly aware from the moment he opened his eyes.

She felt his arm around her shoulders as he drew her closer. His other hand sought her breast and as he caressed her, her breathing quickened. He could always arouse an eager response in her, and with him, for the first time in her life, she had learned the joy of complete fulfilment.

She felt his mouth hard and hot against her own, and she wound her arms around him and traced the muscles of his back with her fingers. His body was hard against her softness and she felt as though she were merging with him in the heat of passion.

He came to her with vigour, possessing her so wholly that tears of gratitude and joy burned against her closed lids. She whispered his name as she felt tremors of pleasure shudder through her, every nerve ending tinglingly alive.

And then they rested. Close together, they talked in intimate whispers, although there was no one there to hear them. The servants had left and had not returned, the house was silent except for the rustle of the sheets and the sound of muted voices. At last, Roggen pushed aside the mosquito nets and stepped out of bed.

'Shall I make us a cold drink?' she asked, moving to the window and staring out into the night.

'If you like,' Mark said, and his voice told Roggen that his inclination was to sleep. She smiled to herself as she drew on her négligé, then stopped, frozen, as a sound like distant thunder filled the room.

'What was that?' she asked, her voice suddenly thick with fear. She lifted her head, straining to listen. The sound was louder, closer, and Roggen felt bile rise to her throat. 'Mark,' she said, her voice heavy in the sudden silence, 'I think we're being bombed.'

Instantly, he was sitting up, swinging his legs from the bed, drawing on his clothes. He joined her at the window and stared into the night.

A high-pitched whine rent the air, and as Roggen covered her ears the noise crescendoed, screaming like a beast in its death throes. Mark pushed her to the floor and flung himself on top of her as the explosion echoed around the house. Roggen closed her eyes tightly, praying that this was some sort of nightmare and that at any moment she would awake and be safely in her bed.

When the noise had died down, Mark moved away

from her and stood in the window staring out. 'Singapore is on fire.' His words were chilling and Roggen got to her feet, finding that her legs were trembling so much she could hardly stand. Mark moved through to the hallway and drew on his jacket, and Roggen hurried after him, begging him silently not to leave her.

'I've got to go and see what's happened love,' he said. 'If you hear anything suspicious, take cover and on no account show any lights. But don't worry, I don't think the bombs are intended for us. The Japs mean to hit the centre of Singapore and put everything out of action.'

Roggen watched him leave in the jeep, and when he was out of sight she put her hands over her eyes and tried to imagine him as he'd been not an hour ago, making love to her. Abruptly, she went inside and turned on the radio. Perhaps she would learn something if the station hadn't already been bombed. She glanced at the clock. It was quarter past four in the morning. She fiddled with the radio for a moment, and soft dance music filled the air. She sat for a time staring at the radio as though willing someone to speak, to offer an explanation of what was happening, but remorselessly, the dance music continued.

Above the sound of the music, Roggen heard the drone of aeroplanes. She moved to the window and saw the enemy aircraft lit up by search lights from the ground. Trails of smoke reached up like fingers towards the planes, and one of them was hit. It seemed to spin for a moment before plunging downwards, flames leaping from the tail.

Roggen went into the kitchen and made herself a cup of tea, smiling a little ruefully as she acknowledged that old habits died hard. The warmth of the tea comforted her and she sat for a long time staring around the kitchen as though she'd never seen it before. And if she was honest, she had in reality seen very little of it. Spoiled by native servants, she had become used to having her every wish fulfilled.

When the dawn began to spread fingers of light into the room, Roggen rose from the table and moved into the bathroom. She bathed swiftly and then dressed in what she thought were her most sensible clothes – a light skirt and a loose blouse. Her flat sandals were well worn but she would need them if she was to walk into the town. One thing was certain, she could not sit around any longer just waiting for Mark to return, not knowing what had happened.

She had just left the track from her house when a car stopped beside her. 'Morning. Like a lift?'

With relief, Roggen recognized Mac's cheerful face peering at her through the window. She stepped eagerly into the car and smiled up at him. 'There's glad I am to see you!' She had unconsciously fallen into her Welsh way of speaking, and Mac looked at her with raised eyebrows.

'Say, what's this you're talking then, Chinese?' he said with a grin. He swung the car on to the main road and set off at a good pace towards the town.

'Sorry,' Roggen said, 'I'm so worried and upset I don't know what I'm doing or saying.'

'That's all right, mate, it's a bit of a stunner all right being attacked like that, but it won't last, so don't go worrying your little head over it. Just the Japs trying it on. They won't get very far now that we know what they're up to.'

'I'm very lucky you were out this way,' Roggen said, deliberately changing the subject. She did not share Mac's optimism. The Japanese were notoriously tenacious; once they got their teeth into anything, they wouldn't let go easily.

'Sure are. I won't say exactly who I was with, but a certain lady asked me over for the night while her old man was on duty, and who could refuse a lady?' Mac smiled in what he hoped was a mysterious way, though everyone on the island knew that he and Tricia Noble had an affair going.

'Well, I'm glad to see you anyway,' Roggen said in

relief. 'It would have taken ages for me to have walked to the town.'

'Too right, mate,' Mac said. 'And the roads might not be too safe this morning, either. It looks as if the natives have turned against us, or at least are keeping their options open, waiting to see which side wins before they get their backsides off the fence.'

Roggen had not thought about the possibility of the Malays and the Chinese and Indians changing sides, but if the way her own servants had behaved was any indication, then Mac was very probably right.

The RAF hospital had been demolished in the bombing and Roggen could see the airmen as well as a few civilians working among the debris. She caught sight of Richard, his face dusty, his collar unbuttoned. He glanced at Roggen briefly and then turned back to his task of moving the rubble. It was almost impossible to believe that this man was still legally her husband.

To Roggen's relief she spotted Mark's broad-shouldered figure labouring to move the mass of stones from the site. She called to him, waving her hand frantically, and he looked up and saw her. He came over to her mopping his forehead with a dusty handkerchief. 'You shouldn't be here, Ro,' he said. 'I'd much rather you were safe back home. Why did you let her talk you into bringing her here, Mac?'

Mac grimaced. 'I had no choice. She was all set to walk in. I just had to pick her up.'

'What's the news?' Roggen asked, deflecting Mark's attention from herself.

He shrugged. 'There's been some sort of cockup. One of the Catalinas is long overdue. The crew set off last night and signalled a sighting of the enemy from the Gulf of Siam.' Mark brushed back his hair. 'No notice was taken of the report, nothing was done about it, with the result that the Japanese fleet have landed at Kelantan.'

He touched her shoulder. 'Don't look so worried. The enemy are four hundred miles north of Singapore on the east coast of Malaya. They won't get down here for some time yet. But just in case, you are getting out of here on the first boat home.'

Roggen had other ideas about that. She would not leave unless Mark came with her. 'What's going to happen now?' she asked in a small voice, and Mark smiled.

'At least we'll have advance warning of any attack. The town will be blacked out and there'll be a reception committee waiting for any more enemy planes that come this way.' He looked around. 'I think we've just about finished here. There are no casualties, thank God, so it's all a clearing up effort from here on in. Come on, I'll take you into the town and we'll have a look at what's been happening.'

Mac smiled at Roggen. 'I'll leave you in the capable hands of my mate, then. See you later.'

'I appreciate the lift, Mac.' Roggen's thanks were heartfelt. She had not relished the walk in the growing heat.

Mark led the way to where he had parked the jeep. In his hurry he had more or less abandoned it on the side of the roadway and a Malayan boy was searching it, ferreting around like a small animal.

'Get out of it!' Mark said, and with a quick look from large brown eyes the child disappeared.

The incident bothered Roggen as Mark drove the jeep home in his usual erratic fashion. She pondered on the thought that even now frightened, confused servants could be plundering their house.

The business centre of Singapore seemed to have been the worst hit area and natives were busy putting out fires and attending to the injured. There seemed little anyone without medical training could do to help.

'We might as well get back home,' Mark said at last, and Roggen nodded her agreement. The sun was getting hotter and she had forgotten to bring a hat, which seemed to be a trivial enough complaint with people lying dead and injured in the streets, but Roggen was beginning to feel ill with the stink and the smoke and the gripping fear that had been with her ever since she'd heard the first bombs that morning.

The house was empty and, in spite of her fears, untouched. Roggen sank into a chair and kicked off her dusty shoes. Mark went into the kitchen and reappeared a few minuts later with a glass of iced coffee. He sat beside her and put his arm around her shoulders.

'You'll really have to leave Singapore, you know, love,' he said softly. 'Go back home and I'll join you in England as soon as I can tie up my business here.'

'Let's talk about it tomorrow,' Roggen begged. 'We'll know more and then we can decide how serious this business is.'

'It's serious enough that the Japs are bombing us,' Mark said firmly. 'I won't be able to rest with you here. Every time I go out I'll be anxious about you.'

'But there's bombing back home,' Roggen protested. 'Swansea has been hit and hit badly, not once but many times.'

'Well then, you can go into the country somewhere,' Mark persisted. 'I want you out of here. The Japanese are getting too confident. They must have something up their sleeve.'

'Well, you said yourself that they are hundreds of miles away yet. They can't do much harm while the main force is still in Malaya, you know that, Mark.'

He smiled and then leaned over and kissed her. 'Shut up,' he said against her lips. 'You are going to do what I say, woman.' His kiss deepened, and as Roggen clung to him, she knew that whatever arguments he put up, she would never leave his side.

Sitting in the kitchen staring at the sun shining in from the garden, Roggen was grieved that her life in her Eastern paradise was over, and silently she began to weep.

36

Nia Singleton was never short of anything. She lived a privileged life, cushioned by the black market goods she was always able to command. But Nia was not happy. She still missed Colin badly, but the pain was easing as time passed. She would never forget him, not a day passed that she did not grieve for him, but she was learning to live her life without him.

In her ears Nia wore the perfectly matched sapphires given to her by Colin just before his death. She prized the gems not for the clear cornflower blue of the true Ceylon Sapphire or for the thick gold filigree surrounding the stones, but because they were a gift from the husband she loved.

There were lines of firmness around her mouth, now, that had deepened almost to a look of hardness, and these days, anyone who crossed Nia Singleton would have reason to fear the lash of her tongue. Within business circles Nia was respected, if not well liked. She was too arrogant for a woman, or so many of her male colleagues believed, and she ordered her own staff with an iron hand.

She had been wise enough to invest some of her not inconsiderable fortune abroad before the war had taken a firm grip, and much of her money had been put into the manufacture and supply of arms. She no longer bothered her head with the business of betting offices, although she retained some interests in the more affluent areas of the country, raking in a respectable profit from the gambling habits of the wealthy.

She now lived in a huge house on the outskirts of the town. By any standards it was a magnificent building, reminiscent of a stately home. It was perched on the cliffs overlooking the sea, and almost every room in the house afforded a view of the bay and the sweeping coastline of Devon beyond.

Nia had a reputation for toughness that bordered on the ruthless, and only in private did she allow her guard to drop and the tears of loneliness to fall. And she was alone now, sitting in the silence of her large house. But she did not need anyone; she was the self-sufficient businesswoman who walked alone.

The ringing of the doorbell irritated her. She did not want anyone intruding on her privacy. She rose to her feet reluctantly as she heard the slow footsteps of Mrs Preece crossing the hallway. She had kept her on out of loyalty to Colin's memory, but the woman was really too old to be in service.

'What is it?' Nia's tone was frosty and the old woman ducked her head apologetically.

'Mr Lamb is here to see you. Blowing a gale out by the door it is, mind, and me not knowing if I should bring him in or not.'

Nia's irritation vanished as Eden moved past the old woman and came towards her, hands outstretched. If there was any person on earth she wanted to be with at this time it was Eden, who had shared her terrible sense of loss and who had been a source of comfort to her in the letters they shared.

'My dear Eden.' She found herself engulfed in his arms and after a moment's hesitation responded to his embrace. She kissed his cheek and smelled the cold of the winter's air on his skin. She held him a moment longer and then moved away and poured them both a large brandy from the crystal decanter that gleamed ruby in the firelight.

'You are looking more beautiful than ever,' Eden said, and his admiration was genuine. Nia knew that growing older had improved rather than impaired her looks. The darkening of her hair gave it a polished chestnut look and good living had helped her retain her youthfully fresh bloom.

'Eden, there's no one I'd prefer a visit from than you,' Nia said warmly, handing him his drink and sitting in the easy chair near the fire, crossing one slim, silk-clad leg over the other.

'Does that mean I'm invited to stay for dinner?' he asked, pushing back the fall of rebellious hair that curled on his forehead.

'Spend your entire leave with me if you can,' Nia said warmly, and meant it. With Eden, she felt her hardness soften. He had no wish to manipulate or use her, he was simply a good friend.

'I've got only a short leave,' he said. 'I shall be going away again soon.' He took a sip of the brandy and looked at her over the glass. 'In these troubled times I don't know when or even if I'll return.' He stared down at the glass. 'So I'd like to take you into my confidence, if I may.'

Nia regarded him steadily. 'Anything I can do, just ask.' She knew he would not take advantage in any way. Eden Lamb was a rich man, a self-sufficient man, and she could scarcely believe she could be of any help at all to him. She leaned forward and rested her hand on his knee. It was a gesture quite out of character and she found the warmth of him through the thickness of his rough, sea-going trousers quite moving. His words came as a bombshell.

'It's about my son.' He paused, and Nia stared at him in surprise. This was news to her.

'You have a son?' she asked. 'I didn't realize, when did this happen?' She felt a sense of outrage as though somehow he had betrayed her, but then he was nothing more than a friend, she told herself.

'Nurse Freeman told me the truth about the child's birth.' He caught a glimpse of her face and rose to stand beside her at once, taking her hands in his. 'It all happened before I was married to Bella. The boy is illegitimate, but one day, when the war is over, I want to make friends with my son, I want to make sure we get to know each other. Is that unreasonable?'

'No, so long as no one gets hurt,' Nia replied guardedly. 'What does the child's mother think about it?'

'Don't look so disapproving.' Eden smiled. 'I don't mean any harm to Kristina, indeed, on the contrary, I want to help her.'

'Kristina?' Nia sighed. 'I suppose I might have guessed. She always did think herself a little in love with you. But she's a married woman now. Don't you think her husband would object to your interest?'

'I'll deal with that when the time comes,' Eden said. 'But I want to know the boy is looked after. Would you, could you keep an eye on him for me?'

'How can I help you?' she asked, her voice grown businesslike. Eden need not think he could involve her in anything underhand for there was no way on earth that she would allow it.

'I'm putting all this badly.' He smiled his charming smile and in spite of herself Nia found her guard dropping a little. 'What I wanted to say is that I need to see my son is provided for should anything happen to me.'

The pride in his voice warmed Nia's heart. She stared out at the sea washed ashore by the wind and suddenly saw the whole picture. She remembered the swift way Kristina had married the man Jenkins, the unseemly haste of the wedding, the 'premature' birth of a child.

'How could I have been so blind?' she asked. 'Now I come to think of it, Verdun looks just like you. It's very good of you, Eden,' she continued. 'I'm sure Kristina would appreciate what you're doing. Have you told her?'

He moved closer to her. 'I'm making no demands on her, or on you either, but I would be happy for us to get to know each other better.' He smiled down into her eyes and there was no mistaking what he meant.

*

469

Over the months, Eden was a constant visitor at Nia's house whenever he was on leave. They talked a great deal, sometimes about the past and sometimes about the future they would have to face after the war was ended. They seldom talked of the night when they had both lost their loved ones.

One day Eden came home to Swansea knowing that his next foray out to sea would be more dangerous than any of the others. The cargo he would be carrying was arms for the British troops at some secret destination abroad. It was the last night of leave before he returned to his ship and he was spending it with Nia. 'One day, when this is over, we'll be married,' he said.

She smiled at him and leaned towards him. 'We both need companionship and someone to care for, so why wait?' she asked.

They were married by special licence a few weeks later. There was nothing Nia could not arrange if she wanted it badly enough. There were no guests, just two witnesses taken from the staff of the registry office, and afterwards Nia drove Eden back to her home in the gleaming car she had bought just before the outbreak of war.

She had given Eden a large room in the west wing of the house, the huge windows hung with olive green velvet curtains, the colour reflected in the deep, lush carpet. There was the added luxury of a dressing room and bathroom *en suite* and Nia was confident that Eden would be impressed, for the surroundings were rich even by his standards.

She ate sparingly at dinner and drank a little wine to calm herself, for to her surprise she found she was nervous, unsure of what to expect of Eden. She had at first believed their marriage would be one of mutual comfort and companionship, but something in Eden's bearing disturbed her.

He looked into her eyes and she felt herself responding to him. She touched his hand and he took her fingers in his, kissing the tips lightly.

'I think I'm a very lucky man, Nia,' he said softly. 'You are just the sort of wife I could wish for, attractive, intelligent, self-sufficient.'

'Hey,' she said shakily, 'no more compliments. I don't think I could take it.' But even as she protested she felt more alive than she'd done in a long time. She would never forget Colin and the love they'd shared, but neither could she turn her back on the present. She had to make a new life and now at least there was a ray of hope for happiness with Eden.

He reached for her, drawing her close, and lightly he kissed her mouth. She moved away from him, not wishing to be rushed, and he let her go as though aware of her feelings. She looked up at him. He was a handsome man and perceptive, too.

She stretched her arms above her head, and then realizing that the act could be construed as one of provocation, put them quickly down to her sides, but not before Eden's glance had skimmed over her small firm breasts.

'I think I'll go to bed.' She spoke the words baldly, not wishing to appear coy, but the slight rising of Eden's eyebrows brought the colour to her cheeks.

'That eager?' he asked teasingly. She moved from the table, throwing down her napkin, unused to the uncertainty and confusion that was paralyzing her.

'I'll be up in a minute.' Eden drew a cigarette from his gold case and held it between his long brown fingers. The movements were somehow sensual and Nia turned away, wondering at the emotions his nearness was rousing within her.

As she hurried up the broad elegant stairway, she felt the pulse beating swiftly in her throat. She wanted Eden to make love to her, she wanted the comfort, and yes, the thrill of being made to feel a woman again. She waited impatiently, sitting on the side of the bed, her satin gown falling in shimmering folds over her still slim, taut body, and then, as she heard his footsteps on the stairs, she slipped beneath the covers.

He came into bed silently, his hand softly caressing her shoulder. Nia saw Eden was close to her, his eyes half closed, his mouth very near to her own. She must have moved, reached towards him, for then she was being held close in an embrace and his lips were warm upon her own. She sighed softly.

He made love with vigour tempered by expertise. Eden seemed to have just the right combination of Colin's finesse and Joe Barnes's energy. She felt her body quicken, sleep banished, as her hands traced the outline of his back, moving over the strong buttocks, pressing him to her.

It was an experience that raised her to dizzy heights and left her moaning with pleasure, low, involuntary animal moans that did not sound like her at all. It was so good to feel alive once more, and Nia revelled in the feeling, treasuring it, for she had thought it lost to her for ever.

Later, he turned on the light and lit a cigarette, and leaned on one elbow staring down at her. 'You are a very beautiful woman, Nia.' He sounded a little surprised and she smiled. Eden returned her smile. 'I never expected to find such fire beneath the icy exterior you present to the world,' he said softly. 'I think you will be a wonderful wife, as well as a good mother to any children we might have.'

He traced the outline of her lips with his finger, unaware that she had withdrawn from him into some secret despair that was always with her. How could she tell him that the only child she had conceived she had miscarried, and that it was doubtful if the miracle of conception would ever happen to her again.

'What is it?' he said quietly, and she realized he was more perceptive than she'd given him credit for.

'I doubt if we'll ever have children, Eden,' she said. 'I'm already in my mid-thirties, remember. Anyway, I never was a very fertile woman. I only conceived once, and then . . .' Her words trailed into silence as he put a finger against her lips.

472

'Don't worry about it,' he said. 'After all, I have my son, and if another one *should* come along, so much the better.'

Nia felt tears burn her eyes. She was touched by Eden's consideration for her. He had aroused in her this night more emotion than she had expected to feel in a lifetime.

'I think I could grow to love you very much, Eden Lamb,' she said softly, and turned to him willingly as he took her once more into his embrace.

In Lambert's Cottages Kristina lay with Verdun asleep beside her. She had returned home from Ty Coch when she had heard of Eden's marriage. She didn't care that the little house in Lambert's Cottages belonged to Eden Lamb. To Kristina it was home.

She was foolish to be disillusioned by Eden yet again, but she'd believed his promises to look after Verdun's future. As always, he had been full of empty promises. She looked round her, telling herself she should be grateful for what she had. Her neighbours in Lambert's Cottages had been kindness itself, giving her food they could scarcely afford. Verdun fared well with cut-down clothing and the kindness of the people around. Kristina had left behind all that Eden had given his son. She would take none of his charity, not now that he was married again and had so easily forgotten his promises.

Verdun was now of an age to take a lively intelligent interest in things, and he was big and strong, looking every day more like Eden Lamb. Kristina was surprised that no one else saw the likeness, but then the people of the docklands took it for granted that the child's dark good looks came from Robert Jenkins. Robert. Was he lost to her for ever? Kristina still wrote to him every day, even though there had never been a reply. She missed him badly and prayed that a miracle would happen and he would return to her one day.

She felt suddenly lonely. She wished a letter would come from Robert, some small sign that he was still alive.

But she must not give in to misery, she must keep believing that he was alive. And yet as the time passed, hope was dwindling.

She rose unrested as the soft dawn light crept into the room and lit the fire quickly, wanting the room to be warm before Verdun was awake. She made herself tea as the kettle sang cheerily on the gas ring, and sat down at the table, hands curled around the cup for warmth.

She tensed as she heard a soft tapping on the front door. It was very early for callers. She moved the curtain and peered through the window, then drew a sharp breath as she recognized the broad figure standing on the step.

'Eden!' She held the door open and stared out at him, hostility in every line of her body.

'May I come in?' he asked, walking past her. 'I don't like to talk on the doorstep.'

'What do you want?' she asked, her voice cold. 'I'm surprised you'll show your face here. Won't your new wife be jealous?'

'I've brought Verdun some presents,' Eden said, ignoring her outburst, as he placed a brown paper parcel on the table. He smiled his usual charming smile. 'I'm sorry you didn't feel you could remain at Ty Coch. I only wanted what was best for you and for my son.'

'I shouldn't have taken you up on your offer in the first place,' she said. 'I don't belong up at Ty Coch except as a domestic anyway.' She moved towards the fire. 'We're going to be all right,' she said defensively. 'I'll be getting a job and I've arranged for one of Libba's aunties to look after Verdun during the nights. Please just go away and leave us alone.'

'Kristina, Kristina, listen to me,' he said softly, his eyes staring into hers. 'I only want to help you, I want to take care of you. Surely that's not wrong, is it?'

She looked down at her hands, moved in spite of herself by his concern. 'You don't owe me anything.' She felt tears burn her eyes. It was so good to have someone,

474

anyone to worry about her. She'd been so alone, so desperately alone.

'Look, Kristina, let me give you some money so that Verdun will have a good start in life. You can't be expected to manage alone.'

'He'll be made a gentleman, that's what you mean, isn't it?' Kristina said. 'You don't want him growing up like me.'

'Don't be foolish,' Eden said gently. 'I didn't mean that at all. Give me some credit for feelings. But you are quite right in thinking I can give Verdun the education he deserves. Why not let him live with me, at least part of the time, then when this damn war is over, I can really look after him.'

'It wouldn't work,' Kristina said, shaking her head. 'You don't understand, a child needs his mother.'

'The boy would be well cared for, I promise you that,' Eden said. He stared at her for a long moment. 'Do you want him to know only this in his life?' His gesture took in the bare floor covered only with rag mats, the wooden table whitened by many scrubbings, the walls of brick and peeling paint. He sighed softly and touched her hand. 'Look, Kristina, I don't mean to take him away from you for ever. Surely we could share the care of our son together. Make the right choice, Kristina, the only choice for Verdun's future security.' He moved closer to her. 'I'd like to make sure you are not without anything you want. If you like, I'll set you up in a pleasant house somewhere away from the docks.'

'No!' Kristina looked at him with tears in her eyes. 'I appreciate your concern but there's no persuading me, Eden, I must work this out on my own.'

He held up his hand. 'All right, go work in your factory or whatever, but remember, if you get weary of it all, I'm always there.' He rose and made for the door. 'I'll be back before I go to sea again. Just think over what I've said, Kristina.'

She heard the sound of his footsteps as he strode away

from the house, strong, firm footsteps, the walk of a man secure in his own rightness, his own ability to wrest what he wanted from life. Shouldn't she just let him shoulder some of the responsibility for Verdun's future?

In the bedroom, she stood looking for a long time at her son as he lay asleep, a tiny figure in the large bed. Tears burned her eyes as she crept in beside Verdun and drew comfort from the warmth of him and the clean smell of Pears soap that enveloped him. 'I'll never let you go, my lovely,' she whispered, and she was answered only by the sound of the water lapping the edge of the docklands.

37

It seemed to Roggen that the bombing of Singapore by the Japanese had become an event of monotonous regularity. At first the aerodrome was the main target, bombarded with small, anti-personnel bombs, but after a few weeks the whole of Singapore town was under constant attack, with the residue of bombs being discharged over Seletar as the Japanese left the area. In a way that was frighteningly ominous to Roggen, the enemy proceeded with absolute regularity, raiding the island at set times during the morning and afternoon.

She sat near the window, an unopened book in her lap, waiting for Mark to come home from work. She glanced at the clock expectantly, and as always at this time of the afternoon, she heard the expected drone of the enemy planes.

Her pulse beat swiftly with fear that she could not entirely control, and she looked up at the skies to see the familiar pattern of twenty-seven bombers flying in perfect formation. They must be obsessed with tidiness, the Japanese, or perhaps they were superstitious, believing that if they deviated one iota from their usual pattern failure would follow.

As though to emphasize her thoughts, over the radio came the complacent voice of a Japanese announcer, informing the inhabitants of Singapore that the main body of troops was massing at prepared positions ready to strike. In her heart Roggen believed every word of it, even though most people, Mark included, asserted it would never happen.

His latest attempt to get her to leave had convinced her that in spite of everything she wanted to stay with him. When he left Singapore, she would leave, and not before.

The door opened and Mark entered the room, his hat set at a jaunty angle. He grinned at her and poured himself a long cold drink, the angle of his head showing to perfection the strong bronzed line of his throat and the strength of his face.

'There's a ship leaving tomorrow,' he said, putting down his glass. 'The *Wakefield*. I want you to be on it.'

'There's no need to go on about it,' Roggen said softly. 'You know I won't go without you.'

'Look, love,' Mark crouched beside her and took her hands in his, 'the Japs are at Endau, that's only a hundred miles north of the Johore causeway, and most of the British forces have been withdrawn. It's dangerous for you to stay here.'

'Come with me then.' Roggen leaned forward and wound her arms around his neck, hugging him to her. 'Forget your business interests. What will they be worth if the Japanese capture the island anyway?'

'I'm just waiting for some money to come through, then I'll leave.' Mark kissed her forehead and moved away from her. 'But I can't work if I have to worry about you. Go on the *Wakefield*, love.'

Roggen set her lips stubbornly, and after staring at her for a moment in silence, Mark shrugged. 'All right, you little witch, you win. I'll come with you. Let's pack up.'

That night, as they lay together in the big bed, hands entwined, Roggen felt at peace with herself and her world. Her eyes closed sleepily and her mind was beginning to drift to thoughts of home. Swansea, the cool breezes blowing over the docklands, the scents of spices from the ships in the harbour.

She thought with happiness of Eden, of his marriage to Nia which he felt would bring them both the comfort and companionship they needed. He and Mark would get along very well, for both were tough men, used to getting their own way in the world and yet with a core of softness when it came to the women they loved.

Roggen longed to re-establish old friendships. She would talk to Kristina about her son, for Verdun was Roggen's blood kin. Soon, hopefully, Kristina would be the mother of other children – those of her husband, Robert Jenkins. He was missing, it was true, but in the confusion of war there was always hope, and Roggen prayed that one day Kristina would find the happiness she deserved.

Roggen gradually became aware that the droning sound she could hear was not in her head. She sat up quickly, her hand on Mark's arm. 'The bombers,' she said softly, as though someone might hear her, 'they're back.'

A shrieking noise suddenly filled the house. Roggen clung to Mark as the earth outside the building shook with the impact of the bombs.

'Come on,' Mark said, 'get dressed, Ro. I'm getting you away from here right now. Take just what's essential. I'll come back later for my papers and such.'

She pushed aside the bedclothes and in the darkness felt around for some clothes. She drew open a drawer and her searching fingers encountered a cotton skirt and a loose blouse. She dressed quickly, her hands trembling as the sounds of the bombing continued. The Japanese were not content with a lightning raid. They seemed to want the area devastated before they would give in and go away.

Mark drew her silently towards the jeep. Around her, Roggen could see that some of the houses were on fire, the flames illuminating the ground so that the remaining buildings were clearly visible. Mark set the jeep in motion, and Roggen clung to her seat as he drove swiftly away from the house. She felt entirely exposed as the vehicle bumped along the roadway, sure that the pilots in the planes above would see their desperate effort to escape the bombardment. They would come at any moment, bullets strafing the ground, and she, along with Mark, would be found dead by unsympathetic Malays who would perhaps bury them where they fell.

A flurry of bombs dropped like dead birds from the sky, and as Roggen looked behind her, she could see the house she had shared with Mark explode into flames.

'Our house,' she said softly, 'it's been bombed.' She put her head on Mark's shoulder, aware that tears burned behind her lids. Wiped out in a moment, the home in which they had shared the happy days and the beautiful nights when they had reaffirmed their love for each other. God, was this the end of everything? But the sounds of the bombing were dying away, the darkness enclosed the jeep and its occupants in friendly arms, and Roggen sighed softly.

'Well, Ro, we'll be on the *Wakefield* tomorrow for certain, and then we'll be heading for freedom.' Mark's voice was cheerful. 'There's nothing to go back for now. I've got what's important right here next to me.'

So suddenly that Roggen didn't afterwards remember what had happened, the jeep spun out of control, the front wheels plummeting into a ditch, and she felt herself flying into darkness, with the sky and the earth dissolving into a crazy kaleidoscope of patterns around her.

It was daylight when Roggen opened her eyes. She looked up to see Mark bending over her, frowning. She struggled to sit up, aware that she was in a strangely familiar room, but Mark held her back against the pillows.

'What time is it?' she asked, and she became aware that the thumping sounds she could hear were in her own head.

'Don't worry yourself about that, love. You've had a nasty crack but nothing's broken.'

Over Mark's shoulder a face appeared, and for a moment Roggen thought she was hallucinating.

'Richard!' she said, her voice cracking with weakness. 'What are you doing here? I thought you'd have gone home by now.'

'I brought you to Richard's, love,' Mark said. 'We were near the house so it seemed to make sense.'

'Thank you for your help, Richard.' Roggen was aware that the words were stilted and inadequate, but she was having difficulty in coming to terms with the suddenly changing events in her life.

'The *Wakefield*?' she said, and Mark shook his head. 'We've missed it, have we?' She heard her voice shake.

'Aye, we've missed it,' Mark said, 'but don't worry, kiddo. Richard tells me that a few of the people from the peninsula are waiting for a steamer to take them back to England. We'll get on that, all right?'

'We're all right here.' Richard's voice drifted to where Roggen lay collapsed against the pillows, eyes closed. 'The Japs won't get to us. Singapore is impregnable and all we have to worry about is the raids, which is no more than the folks at home have to put up with.'

Was Richard trying to be reassuring, or was he just naturally stupid? Roggen couldn't decide, and in any case she was too tired to try to sort anything out. All she wanted to do now was to sleep.

When she awoke again it was dark and the sound of excited voices penetrated the room. She sat up and felt instinctively that Mark was not in the house. She slid shakily out of bed and holding on to the furniture made her way towards the passageway.

The voice of the Malay girl who was Richard's maid could be heard clearly, and Richard spoke once or twice trying to calm her. This was no time for tact. Roggen wished to know exactly what was happening so she moved into the dimly-lit room.

'Sit down, Roggen,' Richard said at once. 'You look ghastly.' He handed her a glass of iced coffee. 'I think you ought to listen to what she has to say.' His gesture encouraged the Malayan girl to continue, and with a quick look towards Roggen she obeyed.

'It is a great and frightening sight,' she said haltingly. 'Convoys of lorries with soldiers and gun carriers went northwards. We believed the English when they said that the Japanese were beaten.' She shrugged and held out her brown hands as though in supplication. 'But we see now on the streets of Singapore carloads of European women and children, the rich Chinese and Indians all going south. What are we to believe?'

'Don't panic.' Richard looked towards Roggen. 'I am now attached to a motor transport pool. My job is to help with the evacuation from the mainland, but I still maintain we shall be safe here.' He paused and his eyes met those of the Malayan girl.

'I want you to go back to your own people, for if the Japanese should come, they have their own way of dealing with anyone who associates with their enemies.'

'I want to stay with you.' Mary was wide eyed. 'I no want to go away from you. I been with you a long time now.'

'I don't want anything to happen to you because of your loyalty to me. Please, just go, now while it's dark. Tomorrow I have to cross the causeway again into Johore. It is possible I will not come back, do you understand?'

The maid slipped as silently as a shadow from the room, and for a moment Richard stood, shoulders drooping. Roggen felt suddenly sorry for him; he could not be as confident of the island's safety from attack as he pretended.

'It may all be over before we think,' she said softly. 'Perhaps all the Japanese can do is bomb us and issue threats.'

Silently, Richard handed her a sheet of paper. It was a written warning from the Nippon Army asserting that the white devils had perpetrated untold atrocities on civilian Japanese and promising that revenge would be great. Roggen shuddered.

'Where's Mark?' she asked anxiously, and Richard straightened. He brushed back his hair which was streaked with grey and appeared to pull himself together.

'He went back to your place,' he said, 'He wanted to see if he could salvage anything from the ruins.'

Roggen wrapped her arms around herself and tried to quell the rising tide of fear that swept through her. If anything should happen to Mark she would not want to live.

Richard sank down into a chair. 'Tomorrow I'll be out on the road again, bringing in refugees,' he said softly. 'In case I don't come back, Roggen, I want you to know that I'm sorry for everything and I hope you and Mark will get through this in one piece.'

'There were faults on both sides, Richard,' she said, wishing it were Mark sitting there smiling at her, giving her the feeling he could conquer mountains. Poor Richard, he would not give anyone confidence, not even the little Malay girl who was so devoted to him.

Mark returned a little while later, empty handed. 'It's all gone, Ro,' he said. 'My business papers, the lot, burned.' He sank down beside her and she could smell the aura of smoke on his clothing. She wanted to go into his arms, to hold him close. What did she care about some old papers? When they got to England, she would have more than enough money to take care of them both.

'I reckon we'd better take to the road, kiddo,' Mark said, looking at Roggen thoughtfully. 'More troops and civilian refugees are moving into the town. I think we should get there first and set ourselves up where there's plenty of food and water, and then sit tight until the British steamer arrives.'

It hadn't occurred to Roggen that essentials such as food and water would be in short supply, and apparently it had not occurred to Richard either.

'You should be all right here,' he said in surprise. 'There won't be any more bombing, I shouldn't think.'

Mark ignored him. 'Do you feel well enough to move, love?' He touched her hair briefly with his fingers and Roggen forced a smile.

'There's a question to ask a determined Welsh woman! Of course I'm all right to move.'

'Well,' Richard shrugged, 'if you mean it I'll be taking the lorry across the straits to fetch some more refugees. I can take you as far as the town.'

'Right, mate,' Mark said decisively. 'That's it, then, we'll get moving, shall we?'

'What, now?' Richard asked, his eyebrows raised. 'In the dark?' He looked at Mark as though he'd gone mad. 'The roads are crowded, the place is a mess, we'll never get through.'

'It'll be worse tomorrow if everybody thinks the same way as you, mate,' Mark said. He started to move through the house and Roggen concealed a smile as she heard him open and close cupboards, packing away anything he thought would be useful to them.

The night was silent and except for the distant glare of flames it would appear as though the war had not touched Singapore. Roggen stood for a moment staring up at the sky. Here she had found disillusionment with Richard and here she had found the only man she could ever care for. She was grateful to Singapore for giving her Mark.

In the cab of the lorry, the smell of fumes hung heavily in the air. It would not be a comfortable journey but hopefully at the end of it there would be a short wait in civilized surroundings and then a boat ride home to Britain.

'God only knows where the rest of my squadron is,' Richard said as he set the lorry into motion. 'I'll have to try and search them out once I've dropped you off in town.'

'If I were you, mate,' Mark said, 'I'd join up with any outfit you come across. You haven't yet realized the state of chaos that exists round here.'

'I realize more than you give me credit for – mate,' Richard said in irritation. 'At least I'm trying to do something to help matters.'

'What, by bringing into the island more and more people who will be facing sickness and food shortages as well as bombing from the ruddy Japs?' Mark stared out of the window, his face expressionless.

'It's a sight better than worrying about stupid business papers.' Richard's voice had become more aggressive.

'How would you know?' Mark said, and there was a hint of amusement in his voice.

The attack from the air was sudden, shattering the silence. Bombers swept in low over the island, loosing bombs indiscriminately and setting off a series of explosions that rocked the very earth. The vehicle lurched, falling drunkenly to one side. With a curse, Mark leaped down into the roadway and crouched forward, trying to see the damage in the darkness.

'Wheel's completely gone,' he said, rising to his feet. 'It looks like we've got a long walk ahead of us.'

Even as he spoke, the planes circled and returned and swooped low with the obvious intention of strafing any survivors with bullets. Mark pulled Roggen from the cab and thrust her to the ground beneath the tilting lorry. Roggen shivered, smelling the raw scent of her own fear mingled with the pungent smell of the earth beneath her knees.

'Keep still,' Mark said. 'It's unlikely they'll see us at night from the air, but keep under cover anyway.' He shielded Roggen's body with his own as the planes flew over once more, and then there was the sound of bullets rattling against the metal cab. Roggen closed her eyes, not believing all this was really happening.

'They nearly got us that time.' Richard was beside her in the darkness. He was sweating and she could feel his body trembling beside hers. Pity engulfed her and Roggen touched his shoulder.

'It's all right, I think they're going away,' she whispered. And they were. The sound of engines was dying into the distance and suddenly Roggen felt sick. Her head was aching, and for a moment her vision blurred. Mark lifted her to her feet.

'All right, Ro?' he said, his hand beneath her chin, gently lifting her face so that he could look into her eyes.

She clung to him, burying her head against his shoulder, drawing strength from him. She wanted to pour out her feelings, to tell him that while he was with her she could put up with anything, but she knew him too well to lavish sentiment on him. 'I'm all right, love,' she said simply, and drew herself out of his arms, tucking her shirt back into her skirt.

They began to walk along the pitted roadway. The skies overhead remained free of planes, which at least gave them some respite, but Roggen felt so utterly weary that she could not put one foot in front of the other. She staggered and fell against Mark and he steadied her, holding her upright.

'We'll kip down here for what's left of the night,' Mark said decisively. 'I'll take the first watch and you, James, can take the second.'

Richard did not argue and Roggen was grateful to fall to the ground beneath a rubber tree and curl up in the short grass, easing her aching body. Who would have thought that she would be forced into camping in the open with no blankets, not even the protection of a mosquito net, and yet as soon as she closed her eyes she was asleep.

The days passed, with the small party seemingly no nearer civilization. Eventually they met up with a mixed party of military and civilians who were building a roadblock of grey stones. The men were piling one boulder on top of another in the optimistic hope that the frail barrier would keep out an invasion from the Japanese.

Roggen sank to the ground, glad of any excuse to rest, and aware that her head was aching and that she still had a very noticeable black eye, though if she had come by the injury when Mark's jeep was wrecked or when the

Japanese bullets drove Richard's lorry off the road she could not be sure.

She could hear Mark talking in a low voice to one of the soldiers, and then she felt Richard sink down beside her.

'God, will we ever get out of this hell?' His face grey with fatigue, he was trembling with weariness, and Roggen put out a hand to comfort him.

'Of course we will,' Roggen said with more assurance than she felt. 'We're not alone now, we've got plenty of help.'

Mark returned and crouched beside Roggen. 'We'll sit tight for now,' he said. 'Wait to see what happens next. We can't go on because of the shelling of the Bukit Timor road. Too damn accurate, those Japs are.'

'We should go across the straits,' Mark continued. 'Once across, we could take to the jungle and then the Nips would have a devil of a job finding us.'

'If you try anything so daring,' Richard said heavily, 'you'll be caught. Don't you realize, man, that the enemy are coming over the straits in their thousands?'

'Yes, of course I realize that,' Mark said easily, 'but can you come up with something better?'

Richard fell into silence, staring wearily down at his dusty shoes. He appeared like a small child who had been given a good dressing down from his father. Roggen felt only pity for him. She found it difficult to realize now that she had once believed herself in love with Richard.

The daylight hours stretched ahead with the small, bedraggled party of soldiers and civilians keeping out of sight. Artillery fire from across the causeway was incessant, and Roggen, like Richard, began to doubt there would be any escape. By noon there was a ripple of interest among the now apathetic group sitting behind the pitifully frail barrier of the stone wall. Two men in army uniform scrambled towards them, slipping in the dust of the roadway, gasping. Roggen followed Mark as he moved towards them and held a water bottle towards the nearest man.

'They're everywhere!' the man wheezed, breathless from running, sweat dripping down his chest between the torn remnants of his shirt. 'The little bastards have taken over the Imperial Palace and set up headquarters there.'

Roggen could scarcely believe what she was hearing. The beautiful Imperial Palace on the heights on the north side of Johore Strait was an elegant building of red brick and green tiles standing in splendid lawns. It had been built by the Sultan of Johore and from its strategically placed grounds Seletar as well as the Tengah aerodrome could be clearly observed.

'They're not so stupid,' Mark said grimly. 'What better vantage point could the Japs have than the observation tower at the palace?'

Roggen found her last remnants of hope fading. 'What are we going to do?' she asked.

Mark stood facing the group, a mixture of soldiers and civilians, who were obviously waiting for some sort of decision from him. Roggen could not help but be proud of him. Mark, it seemed, was a natural leader, and he took control now with little hesitation.

'We will camp here for the time being,' he said, 'and see if there is any counterattack from the Allies. If not, we split up and try to make our way off the island by raft or boat, anything we can lay our hands on. Once over the other side, make for the jungle. It's our only chance.'

No one disagreed, no one had a better plan of action to put forward, and Roggen could see that Mark's words had inspired hope, at least the hope of doing something other than sitting behind a fragile wall of stones, waiting to be captured.

Over the next days, Roggen's admiration for Mark increased. He led forays for food and water and generally kept the spirits of the men high. But it was the calm before the storm, a situation that could not last. It was growing dark one night when a sudden silence fell on the camp. Mark, sitting beside Roggen, tensed and lifted his head.

The silence continued, with only the barking of a distant dog to break it.

'Something's happened,' Mark said. 'Either the Japs have gone away or Singapore has surrendered.'

Roggen crept closer to him, aware that people were talking in hushed whispers. It was an eerie sensation, sitting in the darkness, waiting for the unknown enemy to strike.

She did not sleep, but lay beside Mark, eyes staring intently into the darkness as though she could see the enemy coming and, with Mark, make her escape. She was uncomfortably aware of the bite of the mosquitoes on her unprotected flesh and she pulled her skirt over her knees, trying to cover her feet.

Mark was awakened instantly by her movement. He sat up and searched in the bag he'd brought from Richard's house. 'I've brought you some of the maid's clothing,' he whispered. 'Here, get into them and cover your head. It's a good thing you've got dark skin, you should pass for a Tamil woman.'

He smiled and rubbed a handful of earth into her face. 'You'll pass,' he said briefly and drew her against him. 'If the Japs come, pretend you're not with us. You'd be safer on your own. Try to rest now. First light, you and me, we'll be off, kiddo.'

Roggen must have dozed a little for she was aware that Mark was gently shaking her shoulder, pressing a cup of water to her lips, urging her to drink it quickly. He took her hand and led her over the wall into the shelter of the rubber trees. The leaves around them seemed to rustle with life and it was all Roggen could do not to keep looking over her shoulder.

'I only hope those poor buggers we've left behind will have the wit to do as I've said and split up. There's no chance of a crowd like that going unnoticed. I can only hope they've got the sense to realize that.'

Roggen thought they had walked several miles when she became aware that the rustling behind them was more than just the breeze in the leaves. Mark stopped walking and drew her behind the trunk of a tree, his hand on her shoulder.

He moved forward suddenly and silently and then he pounced, dragging a figure to the ground, rolling over and over in silent anger. He was lifting a knife, the blade gleaming in the early sunlight, when he recognized Richard.

'Strewth!' he said. 'You mad fool, you nearly got yourself killed then. What are you doing lurking behind me in the trees like that?'

He hauled Richard to his feet and stood shaking him like a terrier with a bone. Richard was gasping, his cheeks bore a hectic flush, and his eyes were glazed. It was clear that he was in the grip of a fever.

'Good God!' Mark said. 'The poor sod's sick.' He sat Richard down on the ground and held the water bottle to his lips. 'That's all right, friend, just rest a minute,' Mark said reassuringly. 'We'll move on when you're feeling better.'

They sat for what seemed an eternity and then Mark helped Richard to his feet, his arm supporting the sick man. Roggen fell into step behind them and looked down at her sandals covered in dust. How could Mark make it with a woman and a sick man on his hands? He would be better off alone.

The sun was rising higher as the hours passed. Soon they would have to stop and rest, and then Mark would measure out the water. She could not bear to think about water. Her throat was parched and her tongue felt as though it were twice its normal size. God, and she had only been on the road a few hours. What would she be like after a few days?

At last, Mark signalled for them to stop, and thankfully Roggen sank to the ground. She dug her fingers into the short grass beneath the trees and closed her eyes. Suddenly, she heard voices, Malay voices, and Mark was pulling her to her feet, hurrying her through the trees. Behind them lurched Richard, gasping harshly.

'What's happening!' he asked weakly when at last he caught up with them. Roggen leaned against a tree, her body aching with the effort of running.

'The Malays will have gone over to the Japs,' Mark said, breathing heavily. 'Wouldn't you do the same if the people you suddenly thought of as friends upped and left you to your fate?'

Richard seemed slightly better. 'Can I please have some water?' he asked piteously.

Roggen was glad when night came so that she could sleep. Her body ached and her feet were blistered and bleeding but she did not want to complain. Mark had enough on his plate without her moaning to him.

She savoured the little water Mark allowed her, rolling it around her tongue before swallowing it. Then she settled down to sleep, having no difficulty this time, for she had never been so tired in all her life.

She was awakened suddenly and looked around fearfully, wondering if she was alone. Then she saw Mark, sitting up against a tree, looking at a map he held in his hand.

'Can I have some water?' she asked, her voice cracking, and Mark looked at her, his eyes unreadable.

'Bad news, kiddo,' he said. 'Our invalid has skipped off, taking all our supplies with him.'

Roggen sat up straight and stared at Mark in disbelief. 'You can't mean it! Richard was so ill.'

'Perhaps not so ill as he seemed,' he said. 'But it's no good sitting here moaning about it. Let's get on and find our own supplies.' He put the map into his pocket and helped Roggen to her feet. She suppressed a sigh and tried not to show that she was limping on swollen feet.

Mark led the way through the trees, walking strongly, his muscles showing between the tears in his shirt. Roggen squared her shoulders and followed him. Another hot, dusty day had begun.

38

The soft silver material slipped between Kristina's fingers and she watched its shimmering folds with a sensation almost of awe. On this fragile silk held by a plethora of ropes and wires a man's life might depend.

Outside the stores hut where she worked, the rolling wilderness of Fairwood Common, laced with mist, stretched as far as the eye could see, a lonely barren land where the horizon met the grey of the darkening skies. And yet the aerodrome could come alive at any moment, the Beaufighters and the Defiants taking off in a neat, orderly sequence, the drone of engines shattering the silence of the countryside. It was a sight that never failed to bring a lump of pride to Kristina's throat.

It was strange to be working, and yet rewarding too, for now she could keep Verdun well fed and well clothed. She had been dubious at first when some of the mothers of the area around the docks had got together and suggested a childminding scheme. But then she could see it made perfect sense; the older mothers with large families were nominated to stay at home with the children, releasing the younger women for war work.

When Kristina had volunteered she had expected to be directed to the munitions factory at Bridgend, but instead, the official looking woman behind the desk had given her a searching glance and told her she was too intelligent for factory work.

The following weeks she had spent training, and now here she was working in the stores at the aerodrome, wearing a smart uniform, feeling for the first time as though she was doing something, however small, to help the war effort. And what's more she had a little independence, for she was receiving two shillings a day.

'Hey, Kris, wake up.' The voice startled her and Kristina looked up quickly, the silk of the parachute slipping from her grasp.

'Sheila, there's a fright you gave me, come like yourself!' She rose to her feet and stretched her arms above her head, aware that her shoulders were aching.

'It's time for us to go off shift.' Sheila patted her already sleek hair and adjusted her jacket. 'I'm for a nice cup of tea at the canteen, what about you?'

Sheila Williams was a young woman, perhaps barely past twenty years of age, and yet she had a confidence that surrounded her like an aura. She was kin to the Williams family who lived in Lambert's Cottages, and since gossip passed between families on the docks like bush telegraph, Kristina had no doubt that her own business had been discussed and laid open for all to see. But so what?

The wind on the common was keen and Kristina shivered as she set out towards the canteen, her long strides covering the damp tufted ground easily. As she walked, she was wondering at how much her fortunes had changed. Once she had been secure as Robert's wife, her future assured, and yet now here she was wearing ugly flat shoes, striding across a no man's land where she felt she belonged to no one.

'There's quiet you are, Kris,' Sheila said softly. 'Not feeling bad, are you?' She slipped her arm through Kristina's. 'Why don't you go out with one of the boys once in a while?' she asked artlessly. 'I know you're married, but things go on in a war that wouldn't happen in peacetime, and you can't go on living the life of a nun.'

Kristina didn't reply. She couldn't begin to explain that she would not wish to become involved with anyone. The only man she wanted to be with was Robert and he *would* come back to her one day, she was sure of it.

'Them Americans, they love us Welsh girls, mind,' Sheila said, warming to her subject. 'They are saying that lots more will be coming here, be all over the place they will, mind. Goodie, goodie, I say.'

'Why don't you go out with one of our own boys from the aerodrome?' Kristina asked curiously.

'Oh, no, the Americans are much more exciting,' Sheila said. 'I went out with an American the other night. Lovely, he was, a real gent, mind,' she giggled, 'until he got me on my own!'

With a feeling of relief Kristina saw the dark shape of the canteen loom up before her. She was fond of Sheila, but her conversation was always one-track, about her latest conquest.

'Funny how they put them black Americans up on the racecourse, isn't it, Kris? It's as if they want them out of the way, sort of. I can't understand it myself, nice boys they seem, very polite, and some of them are so handsome.'

'You stay away from Americans,' Kristina said, feeling a hundred years older than Sheila. 'They will go home to their girlfriends and wives after the war, remember.'

'Aye, I'll remember that,' Sheila said giggling, 'but while they're here I might as well enjoy the chocolate and stockings and ciggies they keep giving me.'

The sound of voices in the canteen and the spiralling of smoke from many cigarettes welcomed Kristina as she opened the door. She sank into one of the striped chairs and eased off her shoes.

'Get us a cuppa, Sheila,' she said coaxingly. 'I'm dog tired and all I want to do is sleep.'

'Getting old you are, mind,' Sheila said good-naturedly. 'All right then, but grab me an ashtray while there's one going.'

'Hi there, Kris.' One of the girls leaned over her chair, smiling. 'We need another girl to come to the Empire with us. Don't be an old meanie, say you'll come.'

Kristina sighed. She applauded the efforts of her friends

who bought tickets for a show and then took it upon themselves to treat a few of the American soldiers to a night at the theatre, but she didn't really want to be part of it.

'What about Sheila?' she asked hopefully. 'I'm sure she'd be much more fun to go out with than I would.'

'Oh, no,' The girl shook her head. 'We don't want a man-eater in our midst. This venture is a friendly one, not an exercise in how to get as many American scalps in a week as you can.'

'Dottie,' one of her friends said warningly, 'I'd shut my mouth if I were you. The one of whom you speak is coming in to land directly on your left.'

'You've got to say yes,' hissed the girl. 'I know you're off duty Saturday night 'cos I've checked. Seven o'clock outside the Empire, be there.'

'What did *she* want?' Sheila asked, putting the cup down so hard that tea spilled into the saucer.

'Oh, just asking if I'd like to go out with them,' Kristina said vaguely, not wishing to be involved in one of Sheila's vendettas.

'Oh, aye, a night with the Americans, is it?' Sheila's eyes gleamed with anger. 'Well, they never ask me, but then I don't see why I should *pay* to take some man out. If they want me, they can do the paying.'

'Ah well, it's only a gesture of friendship,' Kristina said placatingly. 'I expect they will all be old married men, or else kids not yet knowing one end of a shaving brush from the other.'

Sheila was not to be deflected. 'Hey, you, Dottie.' She twisted round in her seat. 'Why didn't you ask me to come along, put a bit of glamour into the night?'

'Didn't think of it, sweetie,' Dottie said graciously. 'You're always so busy with your own little adventures, I didn't want to muscle in and spoil your fun.'

Sheila made a face. 'I'll bet! You're a jealous cow. You'd love to be given pressies by the Americans but as they don't fancy you, you have to pay some man to go out with you.'

Voices were hushed, heads turned, a cup chinked into a saucer and Kristina held her breath. Dottie rose to her feet, her face red, her lips poised to utter some cutting reply when, as if on cue, the ominous wail of the air-raid warning shattered the silence.

'Thank God for air-raid warnings,' Sheila breathed as she buttoned her coat and fastened her belt. 'I think that just about then I was going to get a right pasting.'

Kristina sighed. All this excitement was for young women; with the exception of some of the officers, she must be one of the oldest on the base. She should not be running out into the night, preparing to take up yet another stint of duty on top of her normal shift. She should be at home caring for her child. She looked up at the sky crisscrossed with searchlights, and fear, as always, rose within her as the drone of the aeroplanes drew nearer to Swansea. Oh God, she prayed, keep Verdun safe.

Saturday was a cold wet night and, as she stood in Oxford Street, Kristina wished she was anywhere but outside the entrance to the theatre. She glanced at her watch. She would give Dottie and her friends another few minutes and if they didn't put in an appearance, she would be off back home. But there they were, Dottie, two friends and four Americans who loped along the street as though more used to big open spaces than cramped, built-up Oxford Street.

'Hi there,' Dottie said, smiling as she drew a tall American towards where Kristina was standing. 'This is Gene. You're to take good care of him, mind, he's a nice married man with a lovely family of four sons.'

Kristina could see at once why she had been inveigled into coming. Gene was an older man, probably nearing forty, while the others were young and fresh, with the look of boys just out of high school.

'Hello, Gene.' Kristina forced a smile. 'I hope you are going to like the show.'

'Hi, honey.' Gene had a deep attractive voice and Kristina told herself firmly he was not being forward. All Americans called women 'honey' all of the time. 'What's on tonight?'

'I think it's going to be a medley of favourite songs,' Kristina said doubtfully. 'There'll probably be some of Harry Roy's music and there'll be a bit of Hutch and some Richard Tauber. I think the show is designed to suit everyone's taste as far as possible.'

'Well, I'm easily pleased,' Gene said, and taking her arm, tucked it within his own in a gesture that was friendly but not threatening. Kristina relaxed. Gene was probably wishing himself at home with his wife and sons, not standing in a rainy Swansea street with a stranger.

The theatre was crowded and as the little group filed into their seats there were curious glances cast in their direction. Kristina sat down self-consciously, glad of the darkness. She felt somehow as though she was doing something wrong, and yet all she was doing was offering the hand of friendship to an American soldier.

The music was not to her taste. The beat of the Victor Sylvester dance music, performed adequately but without the smoothness of the genuine dance band, seemed to pound at her temples.

'Want a candy, hon?' the kindly voice whispered at her side, and she took a sweet, not really wanting it but not liking to refuse. She smiled at Gene. He believed he was giving her a great treat and she didn't want to disillusion him.

Kristina was glad when the performance was over. The theatre was stuffy with smoke and her eyes were smarting so that she could scarcely see. She felt her arm grasped and Gene cut a swathe through the crowds, taking her outside on to the pavement.

There was no sign of Dottie and her friends, and Kristina could not help harbouring a sneaking suspicion that she had been 'lost' on purpose. She looked at Gene, not knowing what was expected of her.

'A cup of something hot?' he suggested. 'No strings attached, honest indian.' He laughed at her dubious expression. 'I don't know what you've heard about us, hon, but we're not really lecherous fiends waiting to take advantage of you pretty English girls.'

'All right.' Kristina smiled. 'We'll go to the Kardomah, have a cup of coffee and then I really must get back to base.' How she was going to get there, she had no idea. The last bus would have gone by now and the walk to Fairwood Common would be a long one. She had heard some of the girls mentioning taxi rides, paid for by the Americans, but she had no wish to impose upon Gene's good nature.

The Kardomah was half empty. Probably most people preferred to drink in one of the public houses that were scattered in abundance around the area of Oxford Street. Kristina sat down and rested her elbows on the table. 'How old are your sons, Gene?' she asked conversationally, and he answered her politely enough.

He waited until the coffee he'd ordered was placed on the table before them and then he smiled at her. 'Tell me about yourself,' he urged. 'Why is a beautiful young woman giving up her time to be with a stranger? The men must be buzzing round you like a honey pot with those gorgeous looks.' He smiled admiringly. 'That lovely hair and those big beautiful eyes, honey you are lovely.'

Kristina moved back in her seat, wondering if this was the usual conversation of the American soldiers who must be lonely for their wives. Or was Gene trying to get her into bed? If so, she might as well say goodnight to him here and now.

'Don't look so frightened, honey,' Gene said. 'I'm sincere, believe me, I've got no ulterior motive. Talk to me, Kristina, please.'

'My husband is missing.' She blurted out the words in confusion. 'I don't know if he's alive or dead. I have a young son. That's all there is to tell, my life is not very complicated.'

'I'm sorry.' Gene reached out and covered her hand with his. 'I'm truly sorry. This damn war has got a lot to answer for.'

Kristina finished her coffee and rose to her feet. 'I'd better get back to the aerodrome,' she said. 'I'm on duty first thing in the morning.' She pulled on her greatcoat, doing up the buttons swiftly and then drawing on her gloves.

'How are you getting back there, hon?' Gene asked, and Kristina shook her head.

'I don't really know. I'll walk, I suppose.' She moved through the tables towards the door. 'I don't mind. It'll do me good.' She tried to smile but the thought of the trek through town and then up the winding hill towards the desolate common was not an attractive one.

'I won't hear of that,' Gene said firmly. 'I'll order us a car. Wait here.' He moved to the desk and leaned over, obviously asking if there was a telephone. He returned a few minutes later, smiling in satisfaction.

'I'll take you back to the camp and then get myself off home. Can't see a lovely girl like you wandering the streets alone. There could be an air raid, and then where would you be?'

It seemed easier to let him take charge, and so Kristina waited within the warmth of the Kardomah until Gene beckoned her forward. As he held the car door open for her, she because aware of a tall figure standing beside her. She looked up quickly into the dark eyes of Eden Lamb.

'Hello, Kris.' He was wearing a dark jersey and a heavy topcoat, and, as always, he looked angry.

She stared back at him defiantly. 'How are you, Eden?' Her tone was polite and she watched as he stared first at the car and then at Gene holding the door open for her.

'How is Verdun, is he well?' he said sharply, and she knew he was wondering who was caring for the boy. She looked up into Eden's face, her eyes challenging.

'He's very well. Good food and good mothering have seen to that,' she said deliberately.

He looked down at her, his face unreadable. 'May I ask who he's with at the moment?'

'It's none of your business, but rest assured he's in good hands. I wouldn't be here otherwise.' She thought of plump Mrs Thomas who was Verdun's proxy mother while Kristina was at work. 'Oh, yes, he's in good hands,' she repeated.

Eden smiled, though his eyes remained dark. He pushed back his lock of hair and looked into the distance like a man enduring a most boring but necessary encounter. 'Well please remember this,' he said. 'I don't want to find that the boy is being neglected.'

'Neglected?' Kristina said in a hard voice. 'I wouldn't neglect my own son.' The tears of anger were thick in her throat, how dare Eden threaten her? At her side, Gene touched her arm.

'Come on, honey,' he said reasonably, 'it's freezing out here!' He ushered her into the car and Kristina saw a look of anger cross Eden's face before he walked away.

'Who was that?' Gene asked as he settled into the seat beside her. 'Not that it's any of my business.'

She turned to him, wishing herself anywhere but here with this stranger. She wanted to be alone with the anger that was gripping her.

'He's the father of my child,' she said flatly, 'and you're right, it is none of your business.'

Eden strode away towards home, his hands thrust into his pockets. It was a cold night, a damn freezing night, and he'd had a row with Nia earlier that day. He had tried to persuade her to take a short holiday further down the coast at the lovely bay of Rhosilli, and he had suggested that she would be better off remaining out of town. Nia had flatly refused to consider it and Eden had left the house with a mixture of anger and frustration.

His mood had not been improved by seeing Kristina on the arm of some smart alec American serviceman. He knew he'd hurt her. Some devil within him had driven him to speak cruelly, to accuse her of neglecting their son. But he felt he was justified. The boy needed a stable, capable mother, one who could teach him how to behave and who would be constantly with him instead of gadding about town.

Nia was waiting up for him, her elfin face looking up at him as though trying to gauge his mood. He kissed her cheek and ruffled her hair and sank down into the seat on the opposite side of the fire.

'I'm sorry we quarrelled earlier,' Nia said softly, 'and I've come up with a compromise.' She smiled and Eden saw the loveliness she possessed when she was happy. She was not a beauty like Kristina, never would be, but in her own way Nia had a style all her own and an unmistakable air of breeding. He was proud of her.

'I'm listening,' he said softly, and waited as she rose and poured him a brandy from the crystal decanter on the sideboard.

'I'll go to my Aunt Sophie, my father's sister. She lives in a sweet little market village in Somerset.' She handed him the generously filled glass. 'I stayed in Bridgwater when I was a little girl and I'll never forget the scent of the roses, they were so beautiful.' Nia smiled reminiscently. 'I used to push the petals into a bottle of water and make scent out of them. I thought I was so sophisticated.'

Eden took a sip of his drink. 'That sounds like an excellent idea. I'd be able to go back to sea knowing you were away from the bombing. Perhaps you could come home when I'm on leave.' He paused and stared into the glass. 'When will you go?'

'As soon as you go back to sea,' she said softly. 'I'll have a car and driver take me to my aunt's house, it will be no problem.' She smiled at him. 'I don't know how long I'll stick it, though. I couldn't bear to live in the country for very long.' She crossed one slim leg over the other and Eden met her eyes, reading the desire there.

He moved to her side and deliberately put down his glass. 'Come along, Mrs Lamb,' he said. 'I think it's high time we went to bed.'

501

As he lay with his wife in the darkness, Eden could not help thinking about his son. It worried him that Kristina was leaving the boy with someone and going out with American servicemen. What sort of effect would that have on Verdun?

Eden had been very lucky so far. His trips to sea had all been short ones, but who knew what the future would hold? Before he went back to sea, he had the satisfaction of seeing Nia climb into a gleaming chauffeur-driven car to set off on the long drive to Somerset. He moved inside the house then, and closed the door against the sight of the huddle of ruined buildings that Swansea had become.

Kristina had exchanged her uniform for her ordinary wool coat and had tied a scarf over her short, brushed-back hair. 'I'm off home now, Sheila,' she said cheerfully. 'I'm going to be with my son. He can have my undivided attention at least for a few days.'

'Lucky you,' Sheila said. 'As for me, I've planned to get my own back on Dottie and the other girls. I've hit on the idea of taking our own boys from the 'drome to the Empire, so there. Charity begins at home, I say.'

Kristina was glad to leave the bickering behind her. It all seemed so trivial when there was a war going on. But then it was the little things that probably kept everyone sane.

It took her almost an hour to get to the docklands but once there she was glad to be breathing in the familiar scents of home. She took her ration book out of her bag and on an impulse called into Libba's shop. She would take something nice for Verdun, he deserved a little treat.

Mrs Thomas's front room appeared to be bursting at the seams with children. 'Hello there, Kristina,' she said affably. 'Time off again, is it? Don't you girls do any work?'

Verdun ran towards her and Kristina held him tightly. 'Have you been a good boy?' she asked, and he nodded vigorously. 'Come on then,' she said, 'let's go home.' She held out some money to Mrs Thomas, and the plump woman put it away carefully in a tin on the mantelpiece.

Kristina got Verdun up to bed at last. She had played with him and talked to him until his eyes were beginning to close. She felt as though she could not get enough of being with her son. She heard a knocking on the door, and when she opened it Eden shouldered his way into the room.

'I want to see Verdun,' he said, 'just once before I go away. Is that asking too much? Please, Kristina, be kind.'

Kristina stared at him in silence and he moved further into the kitchen. 'All right,' she said at last, 'but don't wake him.' It was a strange feeling standing with Eden staring down at their son.

'He's a fine boy, Kristina, a credit to you.' He moved closer, and in the dim light from the lamp he looked so handsome, so warm and caring. He reached out his hand, and on an impulse Kristina took it. As his fingers closed around hers, she felt tears burn her eyes.

Quickly, she led the way out of the room and on to the landing. There, she turned to look up at Eden and he was very close to her, so close that she could smell the familiar, clean soap scent of him. Suddenly, his mouth was upon hers and she was responding to him.

She clung to him, forgetting everything but the need for warmth and human contact. Eden had been part of her life for so long. She knew his touch, the feel of his lips, and so she did not resist when he drew her into the bedroom. She had been so alone and so lonely, and it had been so long since she had experienced close contact with anyone, so very long. 'Oh, Eden,' she whispered, and even as he came to her, the tears ran unchecked down her cheeks.

Six weeks later, Kristina was medically discharged from the service. She had been sick and ill for some time, but only when she was examined by the MO did she realize she was pregnant for the second time by Eden Lamb. She sat in the park not seeing the trees or the grass or the placid surface of the lilypond. All she could think of was how she had betrayed Robert in the worst way any woman could betray her husband. 'Robert,' she whispered, 'Robert, can you ever forgive me?'

Robert crouched closer to the ground, hearing the rattle of rifle fire and the random explosions of shells as though they were distant memories instead of here and now realities. Around him lay the bodies of his comrades, mutilated beyond recognition, and the smell of death was all around him.

And yet his thoughts were with Kristina. It was as though she was reaching out across the miles to touch him. Love flooded through him, love and the determination to survive.

He must get away from the bombardment. There was no officer left alive to give orders so it was up to him to save himself. He raised his head. The rifle fire had stopped, and now might be his only chance. He began to run, weaving across the uneven ground, tripping over dead men in his flight for the group of trees that offered some protection. His heart was pounding, his helmet bit into his forehead, and perspiration streamed down his face, running into his eyes.

The explosion took him by surprise. There was noise and smoke and pain, and then there was nothing but a silent blackness.

39

The heat was intolerable, the leaves of the trees providing scarcely any barrier from the merciless sun. The pathways were dusty where the stunted grass had withered and died. The scents and sounds of the roadway were a distant backdrop; the low rumble of heavy traffic, the occasional calling of a Malayan voice all took on a nightmare quality. Danger seemed to be hiding behind every rubber tree, and Roggen had never felt so frightened and weary in her life.

Mark, moving on before her, held up his hand and Roggen stopped walking and leaned thankfully against a tree. She watched as Mark inched forward, and as she brushed the sweat from her eyes, she saw with a sense of horror what he was looking at.

The grotesque figure on the ground was black and bloated, the feet were bare, the arms flung out as though the body had been crucified. A short distance away was a bag and Roggen recognized it as the one Richard had been carrying. It was empty. Shock waves washed over her. The grotesque body was that of Richard, her husband.

'Come on, love.' She was aware of Mark beside her urging her onward past the almost unrecognizable figure on the ground, and she covered her eyes, not wanting to look again at the terrible sight of her husband's body.

'Seems as though the Japs got Richard almost at once,' Mark said softly. 'Shot through the head, poor bugger, but at least it must have been quick. We'll have to go careful, kiddo.'

Roggen's flesh seemed to crawl with fresh waves of horror. Richard might be weak, might have many faults, but he didn't deserve to die on a dusty pathway in Singapore. She no longer felt hunger, only a raw, desperate thirst. She didn't know how far they had walked; maybe ten miles, maybe twenty. She had lost track of time, but the beating sun overhead told her it must be near noon.

During the night, she had been frightened of the dark, clinging to Mark, hating the stunted grass, the bite of the mosquito and the nighttime sounds in the trees. And yet now she longed for darkness for respite from the heat of the day. How long would she and Mark have to keep on walking?

Mark drew her into the shade of a tree and motioned for her to sit. 'There's a house over there. I'm going to take a chance on getting us some water,' he said softly. She held on to his arm, not wanting him to go, but reason told her that if they did not drink, they would die. She nodded despairingly, then knelt and watched him weave his way towards the clearing. Her pulse began to beat a rhythm of terror within her head. At any moment she expected a shot to ring out, to hear a cry of pain, and she sank down on to her heels, desperately fighting the weak tears that came to her eyes.

Mark was back within minutes. 'We're in luck, the place is deserted.' He helped her to her feet and cautiously led the way towards the large house that looked so inviting, gleaming in the sun, the windows shining like diamonds. The place was sanctuary.

Inside, the house was in a state of chaos, the furniture upturned, the drapes and hangings torn. It was clear there had been a struggle. Mark righted a chair and Roggen sat down, her head in her hands. He didn't have to say a word; it was clear that the family who had occupied the house had been taken prisoner.

Mark brought her water and warned her to drink just a little. 'We'll take what food we can carry,' he said, 'and head for the straits. If we can find a boat we'll make our way over to the mainland under the cover of darkness. From there it will be hard going all the way unless we can find sympathizers who will help us.'

Roggen did not want to think beyond this moment when she was safe, sheltered from the glare of the sun, and with a glass of precious water in her hand. 'Can I have a wash?' she asked softly, and Mark shook his head, a smile turning up the corners of his mouth.

'Jeez, you look like a grubby little Tamil girl, Ro, and believe me that's the safest way to stay.'

She moved to a long mirror over an elegant sideboard and smiled at the figure reflected back at her. Mark was right; not even her best friend would recognize her looking as she did. The long robes were torn and stained and her face was tanned to a deep brown. Covered as she was in dirt and dust she did not look at all like a white woman. She longed for a bath, for the feel of soft clothes next to her skin, but Mark felt it was safer for them both if she remained as she was, and she trusted his judgement.

Along with her sense of humour, her strength seemed to return, and she moved into the kitchen to see what she could find for them to eat. There was some cold rice and a bowl of fruit, but very little else. She ate sparingly; she was past feeling hungry, and yet the food seemed to renew her. Hope flooded through her. If anyone could get them out of this situation, Mark could. She watched as he filled a bottle with water and tied it around his waist. He saw her glance and smiled.

'Don't worry, kiddo, we'll wait until sundown and then we'll be on our way.' He leaned back against the torn cushions on the cane sofa and settled himself comfortably, and though he seemed quite relaxed, there was an air about him of a cat waiting with one eye open in case of danger.

Roggen sank down beside him, her head on his shoulder, and wished they could remain here for ever, cocooned in a safe and isolated world of their own. She must have slept because slowly, she became aware of voices, and she opened her eyes to see Mark at the window, a gun in his hand.

'What's happening?' She moved towards him and stared out to where two well-dressed Europeans were talking together on the verandah. They both wore soft panamas and lightweight suits, and it was obvious that they were civilians.

'Perhaps they can help us,' Roggen whispered, but Mark put his finger to his lips, signalling her to be quiet. One of the men gestured towards the house and spoke in a tone of authority to someone outside Roggen's line of vision. 'He's speaking in Malay,' she said softly. 'At least they are not Japanese.'

'I'll go out there and talk,' Mark decided. 'You stay here until we see which way the wind blows.' He moved quietly through the hallway, and Roggen heard him opening the latticed door. There was a sudden silence as he confronted the men on the verandah. They seemed startled to see a white man appearing apparently from nowhere.

A small noise behind her caused Roggen to turn sharply. She froze as she saw a Japanese soldier standing in the kitchen doorway, holding a fixed bayonet before him. He was quickly joined by four other soldiers armed with rifles, who stood covering her as though daring her to move. Instinctively, she raised her arms, and looking into the unfamiliar oval faces, devoid of any expression but with narrowed eyes watching her every move, she suddenly felt terror well up within her.

One of the men barked an order and gestured towards the verandah. She stumbled outside to find Mark covering the Europeans with his gun. He took one look at the soldiers with rifles trained on both him and Roggen, and with a gesture of anger flung the gun into the bushes.

'Is this woman your servant?' one of the Europeans asked harshly, and Mark without looking at her, shook his head.

'This isn't even my house. You're not very bright if you haven't deduced that I'm robbing the place.' He was rewarded by a kick in the back from one of the soldiers, and Roggen suppressed a scream, knowing that her only defence now was the fact that she looked like a Tamil servant.

She found herself beside Mark, being marched towards a pathway that flanked the rear of the big house. She glanced at Mark but he did not look at her and she read his silent signal that she was not to speak or to act in a way that would draw attention to herself.

The narrow pathway joined a wider road where the traffic of lorries and tanks rumbled past sending up sprays of dust. Beside the roadway were grouped a mixture of Malays and Tamils watching the spectacle with wide eyes as though unable to believe in the sudden capitulation of the island to the Japanese.

Roggen stumbled once and was prodded in the back by a rifle butt, and she felt Mark tense at her side, his knuckles gleaming white as he clenched his fists. She moved ahead more determinedly, a numbness overtaking her as she walked mile after mile of dusty, fume-filled road, determined for Mark's sake not to falter.

It became clear that the party was heading back in the direction of Singapore town and Roggen's spirits sank lower with every step she took. What would happen now? Would they be imprisoned somewhere or would they be allowed to leave the island? After all, Mark was a noncombatant, a businessman, not a soldier, and she would have little significance to the enemy as long as they continued to think she was a Tamil.

Much later, as the troop passed through the streets, Roggen saw that the Chinese and Indians were free to come and go as they pleased. Clearly it was only the British, the 'white devils', who were to bear the brunt of the anger of the Japanese army.

Raffles Place seemed untouched and the lovely proportions of the hotel reflected back the brightness of the sun, its whiteness marred only by an occasional drift of smoke from the docks. A large crowd of Europeans seemd to be gathered at the front of the building. A party of women and children were being herded across the Anderson Bridge while the men stood in listless obedience waiting for orders from their captors.

Roggen found herself being pushed in the direction of the Mercantile Bank. Beside her, Mark was glaring at the Indians who, it seemed, had gone over completely to the Japanese and were now helping to control the mixed crowd of Asians and British businessmen. The latter still had an air of authority about them, as if they were expecting even now to buy their way out of an almost impossible situation.

Roggen felt safer among a crowd but she stayed close to Mark who, under cover of the press of people, squeezed her arm reassuringly. She risked a glance at him, and he winked fleetingly.

Behind her there was a sudden cry of pain, and she turned to see one of the huge Indians, dressed in uniform, clubbing an unfortunate Chinese to the ground. No one moved to help and the Japanese soldiers simply ignored the incident.

An Asian woman with a group of children at her skirts began to sob uncontrollably, covering her face with her hands. She rocked to and fro, her voice rising higher and higher. One of the younger children began to cry too, as though frightened by the excess of emotion, and impatiently a soldier moved forward, pushing his way roughly through the crowd. The woman was silenced by a hard slap and as she fell to the ground she stared up at the unfamiliar face in disbelief. She scrambled quickly to her feet, and with a quick movement of her arm she hit out at the Japanese soldier with all her strength.

His reaction was swift. His rifle butt caught her squarely on the temple and she fell soundlessly to lie still on the dusty ground. Her children squatted beside her in the dust, wide eyed. Roggen would have moved but for Mark's iron grip on her arm.

After that the crowd fell silent and the Japanese began to jabber away to each other in excited tones, looking speculatively at the motley crowd of people assembled in the street as though wondering what to do with them. At last a command was given for them to sit, and Roggen found herself crouching down in the dust of the street. Those slow to understand were helped with the boot or the rifle butt and Roggen hunched her knees to her chin, hardly able to believe what was happening to her. It seemed that one minute she and Mark had been enjoying life, dancing the night away, and the next they had been on the run from the invading army of the Japanese.

Now they were captives, sitting in a Singapore street with the enemy standing over them with rifles as though at any moment they might open up and fire, doing away with the problem of what to do with civilian prisoners of war.

Dusk fell and Roggen crept closer to Mark, huddling against the warmth of his broad back. He did not dare turn and take her in his arms, but shivering, she drew strength from his nearness.

She fell asleep and saw in a nightmare the bloated body of her husband with his face half blown away. Richard seemed to be trying to move, he reached out a blackened hand towards her, and with a small cry, she awoke.

It was raining and Roggen licked the moisture from her lips, realizing how thirsty she was. She had neither eaten nor drunk anything since the previous day when she and Mark had found the deserted house. Beside her, Mark stirred and she saw that his hair was clinging wetly to his forehead. A pang of love darted through her and she raised her hand as though to push the hair from his eyes. Then, remembering, she turned the movement into a resettling of the shawl on her head.

She lay awake for the rest of the night and sat up swiftly as she saw one of the Sikh guards kick the prisoners into wakefulness. He scarcely glanced at her and Roggen hunched herself forward. Nothing untoward had happened to any of the women prisoners but she would take no chances.

Once awake, the prisoners were informed by one of the Japanese soldiers that a ceasefire had been ordered the previous night, but that some foreigners had chosen to ignore the command. Therefore, all prisoners would be punished by the withholding of food and water.

The sun rose higher and the roadway where the prisoners were kept became unbearably hot. Roggen was sickened by the fetid smell of unwashed bodies. She glanced at Mark and saw that the stubble had grown on his chin, and his hair, soaked by the rain of early morning, had now dried into a tangle of curls. He looked incredibly handsome, so rugged and strong, and Roggen knew that somehow he would ensure that when the time was right, they would escape. He was not a man to submit quietly to captivity and so she must be aware, ready for any move he might make.

At about two thirty, a Japanese soldier shouted orders at the small crowd squatting outside the bank. Other soldiers, acting like sheep dogs, herded the people into orderly ranks and indicated that they should begin marching. Roggen kept as close to Mark as she dared, grateful at least to be on the move and out of the direct glare of the sun. She glanced round at her fellow captives and saw her own weariness reflected in their haggard faces.

Roggen found herself marching out of Raffles Square and towards the docks. Abandoned cars cluttered the roadway and the pavements were littered with boxes and cast-aside clothes. Japanese with fixed bayonets were hurrying in and out of shops, searching for hidden enemy soldiers, jabbering in high-pitched voices that seemed to sing out, adding to the chaos. Tamil labourers, under guard, were sweating to clear up the streets where bodies lay like discarded rag dolls and blood had dried into hard brown stains.

Roggen averted her eyes by looking down at her feet,

and as she was marched past the railway station on the Kepal Harbour road she noticed a tin of food lying in the gutter. She bent swiftly and retrieved it, concealing it in the folds of her clothing, but a guard, gesticulating wildly, drew her out of the ranks shouting something she did not understand.

Roggen drew out the tin and handed it to him and he took it, pushing her roughly back into the crowd of people. A little further on she saw another tin and alongside it a service jack knife. This time she was quicker and sighed heavily in relief as her actions went unnoticed. The knife she slipped into the neck of her robes, and the tin she tied into a loop of cloth from her torn skirt.

At first, Roggen thought that she and Mark and the rest of the prisoners might be heading for a ship in the docks, but it soon became clear that the small party was moving west of the docks and heading inland.

Roggen felt sweat running down her face and between her breasts, and her legs ached from all the walking she had done over the last couple of days. She sensed Mark behind her and felt him touch her shoulder briefly.

'Keep going, kiddo,' he said in a whisper. She dared not look at him, though she longed to fling herself into his arms and bury her face against him to forget the nightmare world of heat and thirst and hunger and crushing weariness that she found herself enduring.

There was a cry, and one of the Asian women fell to her knees, hands held out in supplication. There was a discussion among some of the soldiers and Roggen watched, glad of the respite, to see what the enemy would decide to do. She wondered fearfully if they would split the group and take the women and the few children among the crowd away, perhaps even set them free, but the guards simply pushed the Asian woman to one side and prodded the rest of the prisoners into moving forward again.

Roggen kept herself hidden among the men, and to her relief no one seemed to take the least bit of notice of her.

She had no intention of separating from Mark; they would see this nightmare out together, and together, she was confident, they would escape.

The smaller party of men was ordered to move ahead and the pace was increased. Roggen struggled to lengthen her stride, determined not to be left behind.

Suddenly, a burst of rifle fire shattered the silence, and Roggen heard Mark's voice behind her. 'The bastards! They've shot the Asian woman and her kids.' His step faltered and Roggen cast an agonized glance over her shoulder, warning him silently to do nothing. He saw her look and his jaw set grimly, but he marched on.

Roggen lost all sense of time, but darkness began to fall and she guessed it must be about six o'clock when the party was called to a halt. Before them was a rough clearing that once must have been a rubber plantation, and by the scents and sounds, she came to the conclusion that the party had made a turn and was now once again near the sea.

Ahead was a group of half finished atap huts on rickety supports, surrounded by deep coils of wicked looking barbed wire. It was a small camp with a narrow entrance gate, and Roggen almost vomited as she saw the gruesome remains of a dead Chinese hanging from a tree, his tongue black and swollen, his body covered with flies.

The small group was pushed into the camp and Roggen could see that it was already occupied by a mixture of Tamil women and Asians. With a sense of relief, she crouched down on the ground.

She saw then that Mark and the other men were being pushed into another yard separated from her by a wire fence. Anxiously she watched as Mark sank on to his haunches as near the barbed wire as he could get. Roggen inched towards him, slowly drawing the tin from the folds of her skirt. It was a tin of milk. She showed it silently to Mark who gestured towards a Tamil woman and her child.

The baby was dressed in ragged clothes and was

sucking hungrily at his thumb. Roggen nodded and surreptitiously handed over the tin to the woman, who grabbed it eagerly.

Roggen looked around her. Everyone within the camp seemed apathetic, without hope. Tired, hopeless faces stared sightlessly into the distance, and her spirits sank.

There was a stirring outside the wire and a Japanese officer strutted forward into the centre of the clearing. Alongside him a soldier placed a box, upon which the officer stood to address the prisoners. He barked out orders in broken English, but Roggen could not understand a word he was saying. Neither, apparently, could anyone else, because no one took the slightest notice, and after a while the officer gave up any attempt to communicate with the prisoners and stalked away, followed by the soldier carrying the box.

'I wonder what all that was about, kiddo,' Mark said in a quiet voice. 'Whatever it was I suppose we'll find out sooner or later.' He smiled at her through the wire. 'I'm proud of you, Ro, you've got guts.'

Nighttime came and with it the mosquitoes. Highlighted in the arc lamps that shone down on the prisoners, the small vicious insects attacked without mercy. Roggen lay alongside Mark and did her best to forget the gnawing hunger pains that gripped her and the smell of filth and excrement that surrounded her. She was alive and Mark was beside her, and for the moment it was enough.

Roggen awoke to the feel of a light drizzle on her face. She got up and, half asleep, moved towards the barbed wire fence. A burst of machine-gun fire flared just above her head and as she became aware of her surroundings, quick hands pulled her to her knees and one of the Tamil women shook her head in warning.

'Keep your head down, for Chrissake!' Mark called hoarsely. She could hear a woman weeping softly, and as daylight spread through the camp a young corporal the other side of the wire stood up and began screaming. Mark reached the young man in one bound and landed a punch on the point of the corporal's jaw that felled him instantly. Gently Mark set him down on the ground and returned to the wire. 'Shell shock,' he said quietly. 'Had to shut the bugger up, otherwise they might have shot him.'

The rain began to fall more steadily and Roggen put out her tongue to catch the moisture. As if in response, the rain increased and Roggen sucked at her fingers and putting back her head opened her mouth for the coolness to run into her throat. Mark spread out a piece of tarpaulin and shaped it into a bowl, and the rain gathered there, a shimmering, life-saving pool.

It was two days since she had eaten anything of substance. The rice and fruit of the previous day had simply teased her appetite. She knew Mark must be feeling hunger too, but he sat impassive, eyes alert as though he was constantly on his guard, which he very probably was.

The crowd of people in the camp stirred one by one, haphazard movements signalling that the dawn light was awakening the prisoners. Some of the Tamils produced food, and the woman to whom Roggen had given the tinned milk passed her some stale dark bread and a handful of rice. Mark took but little of the food she offered him, gesturing to Roggen to eat. She nodded her thanks to the Tamil woman and felt tears of gratitude come into her eyes as the woman handed her some strange-looking leaves and a betel nut.

One of the Australian soldiers took out a packet of Double Ace and with a knife cut the cigarettes into small pieces, passing them round among the men. Mark gave one of his rare smiles and accepted a light, dragging on the cigarette with satisfaction.

The nut was bitter but Roggen chewed on it determinedly, and surprisingly, after a time, it tasted quite good. She became aware that Mark was scrutinizing the coiled wire. Beyond it was a mass of vegetation about twenty feet high. She knew what he was thinking; if they could get through the wire, they would have a good chance of escaping unseen.

'Don't try it.' An Australian voice spoke next to Mark's shoulder, and he glanced up into the face of a young soldier. 'Just hang about, mate, these Japs will be booted out in less than a week, you'll see.'

'Think so?' Mark replied, but Roggen could see he wasn't convinced. 'What do they call this place?'

The soldier crouched down and took the stub of a cigarette Mark offered him. 'Pasir Penjang,' he replied, 'but according to my reckoning we're nowhere near Pasir Penjang.' The remarks were not very helpful and Roggen knew that Mark was irritated by the young man's vagueness.

'Look out,' the soldier said, 'there's going to be a roll-call of some sort.'

Japanese soldiers scurried about pushing people into lines, separating the Asiatics from the Europeans. The soldiers handed out pencils and printed forms, and Roggen stared down at hers in dismay.

'Careful, scribble anything down,' Mark said in a whisper from behind her. 'Make out that you're stupid.' He didn't smile though there was a glimmer of humour in his eyes. 'That shouldn't be too difficult.'

Where the form said 'next of kin', Roggen scribbled Eden's name, and then looked uneasily at the form. Perhaps she should not have written anything in English, but she would want Eden to know if anything happened to her. In any case, she did not know any Tamil. The paper was suddenly snatched away from her. It seemed that the Japanese were giving only a passing interest to the information written on the forms; in all probability, none of them could read English.

The sun was rising higher in the sky when the soldiers rounded up the party. Orders were shouted, and groups of twenty were counted out, Mark included in one of them. Two Japanese soldiers hovered around the groups with tommy-guns at the ready, and Roggen could hear one of the British soldiers talking in a loud stage whisper.

'Perhaps they're taking us to Changi. I've heard that some of the troops are being sorted out there.' The man glanced at Mark. 'That lets you out, you civvie.' His words were spoken without malice but Roggen could see by the set of Mark's jaw that he didn't take kindly to the sarcasm.

'Shut your mouth, you ignorant pom,' he said easily, and his half smile put the Englishman off guard. He fell back, not knowing how to take Mark's remark, which made both men even, Roggen thought with a glimmer of amusement.

The men were pushed roughly forward towards the gate between the barbed-wire fences, and Roggen bit her lip in fear. Where were they going? As the group marched forward they seemed to be heading towards the coast road, and Roggen pressed herself against the wire, desperately watching as the men disappeared from sight.

Suddenly, overwhelmingly, Roggen recognized the truth of the situation she was in; she was alone in a foreign country, simply another casualty of the war.

40

The sea washed shoreward against the rocks of the island of Islay in the Inner Hebrides, sending up sprays of foam that rose like a bridal veil only to sink again into the greyness of the sea. The weather was bad, which was not surprising, for to the west of the island lay an uninterrupted two thousand miles of Atlantic Ocean.

Eden looked out over Loch Indaal, a deep bay-like fiord that almost cut the island in two, and realized that the place had been well chosen as a gathering point for the convoy. The loch had the advantage of providing shelter from the deeper ocean beyond, and here the sea was comparatively calm. Whitewashed cottages clung to the hillside over-looking the loch, windows staring like blank unseeing eyes at the movement in the calmer waters.

Once the entire convoy, along with its escort, was assembled, the trip to foreign shores would be under way.

By noon the weather had improved and it was almost a pleasant day. It was, after all, early May, and high seas and storms should be the exception rather than the rule. The convoy of merchant ships was riding light on the heavy waters, among them the tramp steamer *Chware Teg II*. She was not a ship of grace, lacking speed and manoeuvrability, but she was sturdily built with a bow as straight as a Welsh cliff face, and a tall 'Woodbine' funnel providing natural draught for her good solid boilers.

Eden pushed back his fall of hair and stared over the grey waters at the other ships in the convoy. They had been joined now by the escort of United States and

519

Canadian naval ships and were ready to sail. He felt a sense of anticipation, almost of excitement. Soon, the forty-one merchant ships would set out to cross the Atlantic.

Eden's thoughts drifted to home, and a warm sense of satisfaction swept over him. It was good to have Nia as his wife. She was so very suitable. She was also a beautiful woman and he missed her greatly. He thought with a sudden feeling of shame how he had lain in Kristina's arms, enjoying her warmth and beauty. There had been an unexpected closeness between them that night because of their son.

Verdun. At the thought of the boy his heart was full of thankfulness. His son was handsome and strong and had the dark eyes and hair of the Lamb family. He also had the grace of movement of his mother, and already Eden felt much love for the child. If only Kristina could be persuaded at least to let him see Verdun sometimes, to take him out, get to know him.

He wondered if Roggen knew about Verdun. His sister had never been particularly friendly with Kristina, but it was possible that she might have heard gossip. He had not had word from Roggen for some time, though he was not unduly worried about her. He was aware that Singapore had been raided by the Japanese but he knew that most of the British civilians had left the island in plenty of time to avoid capture. Doubtless, when he returned to Swansea, Roggen would be there to greet him.

Glancing round at the convoy, assessing the situation, Eden felt not a little uncomfortable. The *Chware Teg* occupied an exposed position in the middle of the outer port column of the convoy, and his ship would undoubtedly be one of the first to sail within the sights of any U-boat around. A little distance away he could see the reassuring shape of the Canadian escort ship *Candida*, and his spirits lightened. The merchant ships were well guarded.

The niggling worry was that the convoy could sail at only seven and a half knots. It was a speed that suited the *Chware Teg* admirably but would slow the rest of the convoy down, making the ships an easier target for the enemy.

There was a difficult and dangerous journey ahead of him, that was a fact, and yet he was looking forward to the Atlantic crossing in a strange sort of way, for at the end of the trip there would be a short respite before the convoy sailed for home waters. Once ashore and away from the battle, he would write to Nia and urge her to stay in the safety of the country. He smiled to himself. His life was not so bad, he had a great deal to be thankful for.

The convoy was on the move at last. Steam rose up above the forest of masts and funnels, and the shores of the Hebrides grew ever more distant. Eden stared down at the chart before him on the table, and thought of Swansea. Yet much as he loved his home – the sights and sounds of the docklands, the scent of tar on old ropes, the salt breezes that carried the aroma of spices from foreign ships – for too long he had sat in his offices and merely planned the business of shipping. It had taken the war to bring out the sailor who had always been within him.

Once out of the loch and on to the high seas, the *Chware Teg* dipped and bucked like a cork, sinking low in the troughs and riding high on the crests. Waters swept the decks as the wind freshened, and Eden no longer had time to think about those he loved or of his home town of Swansea.

On board the *Chware Teg II* the mood of the men was tense. All were poised for action, knowing the Germans were near and would strike at any moment. Eden pulled a heavy coat over his dark sweater, suddenly feeling cold. He quietly gave the order for all crew to put on their life-jackets. He checked that the few guns the ship sported were manned and the lookout was doubled. There was little more he could do but wait.

He moved on deck and looked up at the sky, praying for clouds. But it was a clear night, the stars beginning to hang bright over the sea. A perfect night for any U-boat to attack. Eden was aware of the particular vulnerability of his ship; the position the *Chware Teg* held was exposed, to say the least, and even the zigzag course the convoy adopted would do little enough to outwit the enemy.

But all seemed quiet. 'Why don't the bastards attack!' Eden heard his own voice loud in the darkness, and he leaned over the side, staring down at the dark deep waters as though his eyes could penetrate through the waves to the depths beneath. He held up his wrist to see the time. It was a little after eleven o'clock. 23.00 hours. Time for the convoy to discontinue its tactic of weaving a crooked path through the sea. Now, he felt, was the moment of most danger, the time when the enemy was most likely to strike.

He was right. Two rockets soared into the darkness, bursting into a flurry of brilliant white stars. One of the lead ships was signalling for help. The U-boats had at last taken action. Eden ordered that the alarm bells be sounded, but it was simply a gesture, for everyone on board had seen the burst of rockets and knew that the fight had begun.

Eden trained his binoculars on the lead ship, expecting the flare of coloured lights that would indicate an emergency turn, but there was nothing. Puzzled, Eden returned to the bridge.

A few minutes passed and Eden found he was alongside the *Eden Dell* which had been leading his column. It was clear she had been torpedoed. Eden deliberated for a moment, wondering if he should forge ahead or try to go to the rescue of the stricken ship. The lookout on the port wing shouted a warning and Eden turned sharply to see the phosphorescent track of a torpedo cutting the waters, heading straight for the *Chware Teg*.

It was too late for any evasive action. Even with the wheel hard over it would take several minutes before the ship would begin to cant. Eden felt a knot of fear within him and he held his breath, waiting for the world to explode around his ears.

The torpedo took the ship in her port quarter, squarely in the cargo hold. The force of the explosion ripped the ship apart, tearing at the steel plates of her side as though they were made of paper. And the sea poured into the hold.

The *Chware Teg* began to list at once, and the beat of the engine became a frantic tattoo in time to Eden's heartbeat. Then the engines died and the silence echoed through Eden's head like a death knell. His ship was going down in the darkness of the night. He must order his men to abandon the stricken *Chware Teg* and take to the lifeboats.

Eden shuddered, remembering the time before when he'd been adrift in a lifeboat, not knowing if he would live or die. He felt a surge of rebellious anger; this time things would be different. He intended to stay aboard his ship until the last of her funnels had sunk beneath the waves. If the *Chware Teg* was to go down, then he would go down with her.

There was a sudden, blinding light, a screech from the steam whistle which somehow must have become jammed. Eden tried to turn but something crashed down upon him, and the world was suddenly one of deep darkness.

The summer sun bathed the large gardens in a clear light, and the riot of roses around the numerous archways were full and blooming, with petals open wide, the rich scent permeating the summer air.

Nia had come home to Swansea and now she sat on a bench facing the sea, the sea that had carried Eden away from her so soon after she had found him. She held a letter in her hand and she re-read the typewritten words with a growing sense of disbelief. The document claimed that Eden was a prisoner of war in some Japanese camp.

It just could not be true, and yet the letter from the war office was clear enough. A list of people held in a Singapore prison camp had been collated, and Eden Lamb's name was there, plain enough for anyone to read.

She didn't understand. It was Roggen who was in Singapore, not Eden. She stared at the words as they danced and spun before her eyes. What had Eden been doing in Singapore? She knew the convoy had been heading for somewhere in the Atlantic Ocean; how then could his ship have ended up on the other side of the world?

Purposefully, Nia moved into the house and lifted the receiver of the telephone. She counted a Major-General among her customers. Perhaps he could find out for her if the letter was some kind of dreadful mistake.

She had to wait an hour for the Major's return call, and his voice was heavy with compassion as he told her that, unfortunately, there had been no mistake. Eden Lamb had apparently filled in the form with his own hand. 'At least, my dear,' the Major said briskly, 'you know your husband is alive and well.'

She thanked him and hung up, then sat staring at her hands, remembering her wedding day. She and Eden had planned to keep it a quiet affair but the news had spread around the town faster than Nia could put away her marriage certificate. But it hadn't mattered after all, because the townsfolk were so involved with their own lives that they had no time to spare for worrying about anyone else's.

Later, Nia went into town to do some shopping. It wasn't really that she needed anything – she could pick up a telephone and have what she wanted delivered – it was just that she felt she had to get out of the house, away from her worries about Eden.

It was in the coffee-scented atmosphere of Libba's shop that Nia saw Kristina and as she moved closer she realized her friend was pregnant. But surely Kristina's husband was missing? 'Kristina, how good to see you.'

Nia's voice was warm. 'Let's have a cup of tea together, my treat.'

Kristina stared at her for a moment, biting her lip. She seemed uneasy. 'I haven't really got time, I'm sorry,' she said, and Nia stared at her shrewdly.

'Something is very wrong, isn't it?' Nia said softly. 'Come on, I'll walk back to your house with you.'

A cheerful fire blazed in the grate and the small house glowed with warmth. 'Your little boy, is he all right?' Nia asked, puzzled at the way Kristina kept her face turned away. Had she had bad news about Robert? If so, they could worry together.

'Yes, Verdun's fine, thanks. With my neighbour, he is, she's very good. Sit down, Nia, I'll put the kettle on.'

Nia was suddenly uneasy. 'Kristina, what is it? You're keeping something from me. Tell me to mind my own business if you like, but I'm concerned.'

Kristina sank into a chair and put her hand over her eyes. 'There's no easy way to say this. I'm sorry, Nia, I'm having Eden's child.' The words fell like stones into the hot stillness of the room. The sun still slanted in through the windows though Nia was aware only of a cloud of darkness wrapping itself around her.

'It's not true,' Nia said, but she knew it was. 'When did this happen, Kristina, and how?'

'It was when you were away. He came to see Verdun. We didn't intend anything to happen, but it did and now, Nia, I'm once again carrying Eden's child.'

Nia rose to her feet, rubbing her hands together, conscious of her large diamond ring pressing into the softness of her palm. 'I don't believe you,' she said. 'You must have tempted him, you can't be telling the truth.'

'Look at me.' Kristina said softly. 'I haven't changed, not since we were young girls together. I never lied to you then, and I'm not lying to you now.'

'Oh, God! Of course you're telling the truth. There always was something between you and Eden.' Her shoulders drooped. 'How could he do this to me?'

Kristina stared at her in agitation. 'I don't know how it happened, and I'm sure Eden doesn't know either. I didn't dream of being unfaithful to Robert but it just happened. Two lonely people looking for comfort. I'm sure it didn't mean a thing to him.'

Nia began to weep. 'It doesn't really matter now. Eden has been taken prisoner. I may never see him again and yet I'm so hurt at his betrayal.'

'I'm sorry,' Kristina said. 'I don't know what else to say. It shouldn't have happened – I should have been strong – but it did, and now I'm paying for it.' She sighed. 'If Robert does come back from the front, I have to face him and tell him that yet again I'm carrying Eden's child. That's not something I relish doing, Nia.'

'How will you manage, financially, I mean?' Nia said, drying her eyes on a small scrap of lace. 'You can't work now, can you?'

Kristina straightened. 'I'm not asking for anything, Nia. I will work for as long as I can, and after that . . .' She shrugged. 'I'll manage.'

'No.' Nia said softly. 'Let me at least help you in some small way. I think Eden would want that.'

Kristina bit her lip. 'I couldn't take money from you, I just couldn't.' She was very pale and there were shadows beneath her eyes, and Nia found her anger draining away. She felt sorry, yes *sorry* for Kristina.

Nia rose to her feet with a new sense of determination. 'I won't hear another word. I'll make all the arrangements, you won't have to do a thing. The money will be there for you every week. Please, Kristina, it will make me feel better.'

But as she left the small house in Lambert's Cottages and made her way back home, Nia felt unhappiness settle upon her like a black cloud. She had given Kristina a lifeline, she was aware of that, and yet Kristina had so much more in life than just money. She had what Nia might never have – the joy of bearing Eden's children.

41

The August sun washed down on the golden crescent of Swansea Bay, turning the sea into an expanse of shimmering diamond lights. Kristina sank on to one of the dunes, tucking her skirt beneath her legs to protect them from the hot sand. Her spirits were so low that she wanted nothing more than to walk into the sea and let the cold waves close over her head.

She had been living for several weeks on the money Nia had placed at her disposal and she felt so ashamed and so humiliated. She could still see the pain on Nia's face when she learned the truth that Eden was the father of Kristina's child. And she felt sorry for Nia and for herself because now she was placed in an invidious position.

Kristina remembered how she had watched as Nia left the small house, feeling more ashamed about her lapse with Eden than ever for she had hurt one of her childhood friends. And Nia *was* hurt, that much was obvious. Kristina sighed. How could Eden take the lives of the people around him and wreak such havoc? And yet he was possessed of great charm of manner, he had an air of making the person he was with feel important which was so flattering and so transient. But that was unjust. She was as much to blame for her present worries as he was.

She had seen nothing of Nia since the meeting at her house. She heard rumours that Mrs Lamb might be moving away, going to the country, and she did not have the courage to find out if the rumours were true. If Nia wanted her privacy that was her affair and Kristina had no intention of upsetting her any more than she'd done already. She wondered if she should have kept the truth from Nia and lied about her pregnancy. But there had been too many lies, too many deceptions, and no good had come of them.

She lifted some of the hot, glistening sand and let it trickle between her fingers. Then determination rose up within her and her hand gripped the sand as though she could bind and hold it. She *would* work again, she would go back to the aerodrome. Once the baby was born, she would work to repay Nia's loan, then she would be beholden to no one. Mrs Thomas would take Verdun as she'd done before, and the new baby, too. She was wonderful with children and Verdun thought it a great treat to spend the night with her and the children of other women working on the night shift. He was with her now and Kristina was glad of the rest. She felt so tired these days.

As she stared out at the shimmering sea, she felt tears blur her vision. She felt without love, almost without hope. Robert might well be dead for all she knew, for though she still wrote to him each day, she had never received a reply. Perhaps he was buried beneath foreign soil somewhere and he would never come back to her. And if he did, would he want her now when she was once more carrying Eden's child. How could she even begin to explain to him the lapse that was to herself inexplicable?

She forced back the tears. What good would crying do? It would not change the situation one little bit. She rose wearily and turned towards the long arms of the twin piers reaching out into the sparkling sea. She would go home to Lambert's Cottages, hide herself away from the world and try to find some peace. Perhaps after a good night's sleep she would be able to think more positively about the future.

It was nighttime, the seagulls were silent, their mournful cries subdued by the darkness. All the world was asleep, but for Kristina sleep would not come. She turned over on her side, aware of a painful throbbing low in her stomach. She tried to ease the discomfort by the warmth of her hands but there was no relief. Indeed, the pain intensified as the night hours moved slowly forward.

She must have fallen into a half sleep for she opened her eyes to a sensation of pain and panic. She sat up, clasping her stomach even as the life blood flowed from her.

'God help me, I'm losing the baby,' she gasped. But the darkness closed round her silent and hostile. She moaned in pain and stretched her hand towards the water jug on the marble-topped table. She managed to reach a towel, quickly soaking it in cold water and pressing it against herself in an attempt to stem the flow of blood. She had never been so frightened in her life. Was she going to die here alone in the darkness?

Perhaps it was a punishment for not wanting the child. She felt guilt, hot and painful, rush through her, mingling with the physical pain. She rubbed at her head and felt the beads of perspiration run into her eyes. She stifled a cry as the contractions intensified and lay back wearily, knowing she could do nothing more to help herself. She drifted into a semi-conscious state where nothing was real.

She was being lifted then on waves where a golden light poured down upon her and where Robert was beside her, his strong hands helping her, washing away the blood, lying her down in soft, clean-smelling sheets. She was being urged to drink and she tried to lift her heavy lids, but the effort was too much for her. She sank back and with her hands held in a warm grip, she slept.

The refrains of a haunting melody woke her, and Kristina turned her head to the open window from where she could hear the sound of a concertina being played in the street. She raised herself and looked around. The sheets were clean and fresh. She allowed her hands to stray to her stomach. Had it all been a terrible nightmare?

But no, she was bandaged and bound, encased in swathes of linen, and Kristina knew that she had lost the baby. She felt a mixture of emotions run through her, relief mingled with guilt. She had not wished for the child to be born but she had not wanted it to die either.

Had she really seen Robert? Had he come back, apparently from the dead, or was he a figment of her fevered imaginings?

She tried to call out but her voice was too weak and her throat hurt. Yet she was filled with a feeling of euphoria and dimly she realized that she had been given some sort of medication.

The door opened then and Robert stood there, framed by the sunlight. His eyes were dark, unreadable, his lips set in a firm line. He looked thin and even more hawk-like as he stared across the room.

'Robert! Oh my lovely, thank God you're safe!' She lifted her hands but he did not move to take them and she closed her eyes against the rush of emotion. He was alive, he was really here in Lambert's Cottages. And from the look on his face, he hated her.

She looked at him once more in despair, knowing what he must be feeling. Here he was home from the war to find his wife miscarrying another man's child.

'The child was Eden Lamb's, I expect?' he said, and as Kristina nodded wordlessly, his shoulders seemed to droop.

'Well, one thing I'll say for you is that you're consistent.' His words fell sharply into the hot silence of the room. And yet he had been kind to her when she had needed him. He had always been there when she needed him, she thought in anguish.

'I've made provision for you,' he said, throwing a paper on to the marble-topped table. 'You'll be taken care of when I go.'

'Go?' Kristina struggled to sit up but she felt weak and ill. 'Robert!' she said, 'you are not going back to the front. You can't.'

He shook his head. 'No, there's no chance of me going back to the war. My leg was shattered by a German bullet when I escaped from the prison camp.' He looked at her without flinching. 'I'm lucky to be able to walk at all.'

For the first time she noticed the stick in his hand. He leaned upon it heavily and the new lines around his mouth told of the pain he had suffered.

'Where, then?' she asked, her voice shaking. 'Where will you go, Robert, who will look after you?'

'I'll be convalescing for a time,' he said harshly, 'but I told you all that in my letters. I don't suppose you even read them.'

'Letters, I didn't get any letters, and Robert, I wrote to you every single day of my life, I swear it.'

'Even while you were carrying on with your lover?' he said harshly.

She felt as though he had slapped her face. She pushed herself up against the pillows and stared at him pleadingly. 'Can't you let me explain, Robert?' she asked pitifully. 'I didn't have any letters from you.'

'There's nothing to explain, Kristina,' he said. 'And there's no point in lying. I sent you letters whenever I could.'

'Our house was bombed,' she said. 'You must have found that out for yourself or you wouldn't have come looking for me here.'

'Yes, and look what I found.' His tone was scathing and she lowered her eyes.

'I know how it must appear to you.' She faced him squarely then. 'But it's not what it seems, Robert. I didn't intend anything to happen . . .' His expression of disbelief stopped her mid-speech and after a moment she tried another approach.

'You saved my life, Robert. I'll always be grateful to you for that.'

'I cleared up the mess left by Eden Lamb. I seem to have made a habit of doing that throughout my life, but not any more, Kristina.' He sighed heavily. 'One thing to be said for war is that it makes the scales fall from your eyes right enough.'

She knew by his tone that the love Robert had once had

531

for her had dissolved into disillusionment, and she could not in all honesty blame him.

'I'm sorry, Robert, sorry for hurting you, and you such a good man.' She saw something like pain flicker in his eyes.

'No, not good, Kristina,' he said heavily. 'Just call me a fool for having loved and trusted you the way I did.' He stared at her for a moment longer. 'I suppose you are not entirely to blame. That bastard Eden Lamb will get what's coming to him one day, there's no doubting that.'

Kristina shivered, and Robert turned awkwardly and left the room abruptly, the door swinging open behind him. She heard the front door slam and then she was alone in the silence of the house. She put her head into her hands and wept.

Nia sat staring at the man who stood before her, his face drawn by pain, his eyes searching hers.

'Eden's not here, Mr Jenkins,' she said. 'I don't know where he is and if I did, I wouldn't tell you, not in the state of mind you're in.'

'I'd like to get hold of him and throttle the life out of him,' Robert said between his teeth. 'He's ruined Kristina's life and mine. Yours, too, if you only knew it.'

'Oh, I know full well what he's done.' Nia could not hide her bitterness. 'I know that Kristina's pregnant again with his child.' She lifted her chin. 'And yet I was the only one she could turn to for help.' She stared at him defiantly. 'I'll only help until the child is born. I think Eden owes her that much at least.'

'There will be no child,' Robert said, and she could see that the knuckles of the hand resting on his well-polished stick were white.

'What do you mean?' she asked doubtfully. 'I've seen Kristina for myself, I know she's pregnant.'

'Not any longer,' he said. 'Kristina has miscarried of the child, and I'd cheerfully kill the man who put her in such a position and then left her to fend for herself.'

Nia moved to the desk and took out a folded piece of paper. 'Read this,' she said heavily, 'and you'll see that whatever he's done Eden is paying for it.'

Robert read in silence. He glanced up at Nia and then re-read the words on the piece of paper. 'So he's a prisoner of war, is he? Then I'm sorry for him. The Japs are worse than the Germans. They believe in death before dishonour; any man who allows himself to be taken prisoner must be a coward, and as such is punished.'

Nia put her hands over her ears. 'Don't say any more, please,' she begged. 'It's hard enough for me to bear as it is. I thought by now I'd have heard from Eden, at least then I'd know he was alive.'

Robert went towards the door. 'I'm sorry for you, too.' He turned to look at her. 'You didn't ask to be treated so badly, and I'm sure you don't deserve it.' He paused. 'Let me know what Kristina owes you and I'll see that the bill is settled.'

Nia shook her head. 'It's nothing, it doesn't matter.' She sank into a chair, aware that she was trembling.

'It matters to me,' Robert said. 'Whatever she' done, Kristina is still my wife and I won't have her owing debts, not to anyone.'

'All right,' Nia said wearily, 'I'll send you a bill. Leave your address.' She didn't care much either way. What did a few pounds matter when her life was in tatters around her?

He scribbled on a piece of paper. 'I'll be at the hospital near Neath for a time,' Robert said heavily. 'After that, I don't know where I'll be.'

Nia took the paper without even glancing at it. 'Don't worry,' she said, 'I'll get it done as soon as possible if you're that worried about it.'

'I am.' Robert opened the door. 'I'm sorry.' He was at a loss for words. He had expected Nia to be hardbitten – he'd heard she was a businesswoman down to her fingernails – and yet here she was, hair hanging untidily over her face, her frock crumpled, her small feet encased in foolish bits of slippers, and her vulnerability touched him deeply. Eden Lamb had a great deal to answer for.

'Don't be sorry for me.' She glanced up at him and though her voice was harsh, there was the mistiness of tears in her eyes. 'I can take care of myself.'

He shook his head and moved out through the hallway into the sunlight without looking back. He did not need to take upon himself the worries of others for he had more than enough of his own.

When Robert had gone, Nia moved to look at herself in the mirror in the hallway. No wonder the man pitied her, she looked a wreck. Suddenly, she began to cry, great gulping sobs that shook her small frame. She cried until she could cry no more, and then she rose to her feet and moved to the bathroom with determination in her step. She might not be a successful wife, but at business matters she could excel if she put her mind to it. She lifted her head proudly. She had wallowed in self-pity for long enough. From now on she would forge ahead and be the best damn businesswoman Swansea had ever seen.

42

The sun was blazing overhead, shimmering, molten, torturing the prisoners behind the barbed-wire fence. Roggen edged stealthily towards where Mark lay exhausted on the ground. He had been away from the camp all day working on the docks, and his clothes were begrimed, his usually clean-shaven jaw covered in hard stubble. He looked awful and Roggen ached with love for him.

As if sensing her feelings, he opened his eyes and winked at her.

'Hello, kiddo, don't look so worried. It may never happen.' He sat up, flexing his cramped muscles. 'By the way, I've brought you a present.' He delved into his pocket and brought out some bananas and a rambutan, and handed them to her through the wire. 'Go on, enjoy them. I've had enough fruit today to last me a lifetime.' He leaned closer to her, shielding her from the watching eyes of the other prisoners as she ate.

'What did the Japs have you working on?' Roggen asked, watching the way Mark eased back his sleeves and rubbed at his arms as though in pain.

'There were some Tamils on the docks cleaning out the filth from the drains with shovels and long wooden poles.' He grimaced. 'The smell was God awful, believe me.'

'Oh Mark!' Roggen suddenly didn't feel hungry any more. 'They didn't make you work on the drains, did they?'

'Aye, that's exactly what they did do, and put the

Tamils on us to prod us into action if we so much as paused.' He smiled. 'The Japs are the most unpredictable lot. A Tamil took a swipe at me with his spade and I retaliated without thinking about it and knocked the man to the ground.'

Roggen watched him, breathless with fear at the risk he had taken. 'What happened?' she asked, and Mark sighed heavily.

'This Jap came up to me fingering his sword and I thought I was breathing my last, but the next thing I knew, he turned on the Tamil and gave the man a good kicking, then smiled at me and walked away.'

'Be careful, Mark, I don't want anything to happen to you.' Roggen shrank back as a guard came over to Mark and handed him a small piece of fish in a tin of rice, and half a cigarette.

'Thanks, mate,' Mark said, and once the guard had walked on, he passed Roggen the food. 'Go on, I couldn't face fish, not after all the fruit I've eaten today.'

'I'm not hungry, love,' Roggen said honestly. 'Shall I give the food to some of the women who've got children.'

'No!' Mark spoke sharply. 'Wrap it up and put it to one side. We may need it. There's no knowing how the Japs will treat us tomorrow.'

Roggen saw that some of the men were throwing the food aside, which was a bad mistake, for the Japanese guards seemed incensed by the waste and began to shout in loud voices, berating the prisoners. One man was severely beaten and left senseless on the ground.

'See how careful you have to be,' Mark said quietly. 'These men are like dogs, they can turn and savage at the slightest provocation.'

'You don't have to tell me that,' Roggen said quietly. 'I just hope and pray that you will remember it next time you have the urge to punch one of the Tamils.'

It was a relief when darkness fell and the fierce sun no longer bathed the camp in intense heat. At once, arc lights were switched on around the perimeter of the prison. The enemy took no chances. They made sure there would not be an escape attempt under cover of darkness.

Roggen moved into the hut nearest the fence, which she shared with the Tamil woman she'd befriended as well as a crowd of Asian women and children. She would far sooner be sleeping beside Mark, she thought worriedly, for it was in the dark hours of the night that she imagined all sorts of horrors, and fear was like a tangible taste in her mouth.

She lay for a long time staring at the chinks of light through the slatted sides of the hut, unable to sleep, thinking about Mark being forced to work like a slave every day. How long would he be able to endure the weariness and the blazing heat of the sun without his temper snapping?

She felt a movement at her side and tried to sit up, but strong hands were holding her. She was being pushed over towards the wall of the hut and she gasped as her head hit the ground. Probing fingers tore at her long clothing, pushing up her skirts.

The man silhouetted against the light was breathing heavily. He smelled of dirt and sweat, and his slanting eyes gave Roggen the icy feeling that one of the Japanese guards was attacking her. If so, she dared not call for help, for anyone interfering would be shot. But then she became aware that the man was raggedly dressed and was clearly one of the prisoners.

As he pulled at her clothing, Roggen hit out at him, her nails catching the side of his face. He said something she could not understand and she screamed out in terror.

For a few seconds, nothing happened, then the other women in the hut were awake and staring at the scene in confusion. Most of them turned their backs, obviously afraid to do anything to help, but some of them came forward and stood in silence as though wondering what to do. Roggen continued to scream until the man clamped his hand over her mouth.

The Tamil woman was the first to act. She hit out at the

man, who immediately struck her a forceful blow that sent her reeling to the ground. Roggen was conscious then of the other women beating at the man, tearing at his clothing, all of them talking unintelligibly.

There was the sound of high-pitched Japanese voices and the pounding of feet against the dry earth outside the hut. The Tamil woman acted quickly, pushing Roggen to one corner of the hut and then dropping to the ground and rumpling her clothing around her legs.

Roggen straightened her own skirts with shaking hands, and crouched among the shadows in the corner. She dimly realized that the Tamil woman was covering up for her. She must have seen through Roggen's attempt to pass herself off as a native and realized she was in danger of being discovered.

A group of Japanese soldiers entered the hut, bayonets at the ready. 'Tell what happen here? You.' One of the officers pointed to the woman as she quickly straightened her clothing. He had clearly taken in the situation at a glance, believing what the Tamil woman intended him to believe.

She spoke up as though in anger, pointing an accusing finger at the man who was still being gripped by the other women. The guard held up a light and Roggen felt almost sorry for her attacker. His face was grey with fear, his eyes bulging from his head.

The officer spoke in Japanese and the man was seized and dragged away. In the hut there was a sudden silence as the women melted into the shadowy darkness. Roggen spoke softly to the Tamil woman, trying to thank her, and the woman nodded briefly then turned away to lie down beside her child who was crying fretfully.

Roggen lay awake for a long time, wondering what had happened. Would the women be punished for taking matters into their own hands instead of calling the guards?

Eventually, she must have slept, because all too soon sunlight was streaming into the hut, and the men prisoners outside were roughly kicked awake to the accompaniment of loud Japanese voices. Roggen stretched her arms and then saw the Tamil woman glance warningly towards her. At once, she pulled down the loose sleeves of her dress and covered her head with the long scarf that had fallen to the ground during the night.

Outside, the sun blazed hotly, and Roggen, looking around for a glimpse of Mark before he left for the day's work, saw that the men were gathered at the edge of the camp in a silent, despondent-looking group. A Japanese guard spoke to them sharply and they dispersed. Carefully Roggen edged towards where Mark stood at the other side of the fence, glancing warily up at him, a questioning look in her eyes. She was afraid to speak in case one of the guards heard her.

'It's some poor sod,' Mark said quietly. 'He's staked out on the ground, his wrists and ankles lashed to bamboos. No one seems to know what he's done but we've guessed it's to do with the women, judging by the commotion last night.'

'He tried to attack one of them,' Roggen said quickly, 'but he didn't get very far.' Mark had enough to think about without knowing the truth. 'What will happen to him?' she asked, staring across to where the man lay spreadeagled.

'The idea is that the bamboo shoots will grow at the rate of a couple of inches a day, and they won't break, they are too strong.' He looked down at her. 'Don't think about it, love, it'll do no good.'

But Roggen had seen the implications at once. The man would be slowly impaled on the growing bamboos. She covered her mouth, feeling suddenly sick.

'The bloke brought it on himself,' Mark said reasonably, 'and the Japs are showing what happens to anyone who causes a disturbance in the camp. You can't really blame them, it's their idea of justice.'

One of the guards came over to Mark and carefully,

Roggen drew the scarf closer to cover her face. Out of the corner of the eye, she saw that the guard was holding out some cigarettes. Mark shook his head and spoke in Tamil, and after a moment or two of what appeared to be heated discussion, the Japanese soldier handed him a small bunch of bananas and a packet of Three Star cigarettes. Mark then delved beneath his shirt and brought out his watch.

Roggen's heart was hammering as she crouched on the ground. She was relieved when the guard walked away admiring the newly acquired watch.

Mark seemed ice cool. He carefully wrapped the fruit in his shirt and placed the cigarettes in his trouser pocket, well pleased with the deal he'd made. A packet of cigarettes gave him excellent bargaining power. He began to talk to an English RAF officer who was crouched beside him on the dusty ground.

'Do you reckon this place is just a transit camp?' Mark said quietly, and the officer nodded.

'I expect so, there's such a mixture here and the Japs are going to have to weed us all out.' He held out his hand. 'My name is William, by the way.' He glanced carefully at Mark. 'The rule here is don't volunteer too much info, not to anyone. The Japs have got a stool pigeon in the camp and God knows who it is.'

'Right,' Mark said. 'Want a fag?' He inched one of the cigarettes from his pocket and held it out invitingly.

'What do you want for it?' the man asked warily, and Mark smiled easily.

'Nothing at the moment, but you can owe me a favour, all right?'

The Japanese guards were ordering the men to assemble at the gates. 'Looks as though we aren't getting any breakfast this morning.' William rose to his feet with alacrity, prodded by the business end of the guard's bayonet.

Mark didn't look back as he was pushed into line near the gate. Roggen watched him, her heart in her mouth, praying that he would keep his thoughts to himself and be careful not to anger any of the Japanese guards.

As she watched the men leave the camp, she felt tears of hopelessness spring to her eyes. The sunlight blurred into thousands of particles of light and she bent her head quickly to hide her distress from the other women. A light touch on her arm startled her and she looked up quickly into the face of the Tamil woman who had befriended her. She was smiling, and the baby in her arms was asleep, the small dark face crumpled like a flower.

They both crouched on the ground, aware that the few Japanese guards left behind in the camp would relax now that the men had gone to work. The woman put the baby to her meagre breast, but there was scarcely any milk, and the child cried fretfully.

Roggen took out the hidden rice and fish and gave it to the woman who, after a moment, ate it hungrily. Roggen ignored the bite of her own hunger pains as she watched the woman enjoy the sparse meal. None of them knew when they would be fed again.

Mark stared at the sweating, labouring men around him. They all looked like bearded, ragged scarecrows, and he cursed the heat, the sun and most of all the Japanese guard who stood over him. 'You're a right dingo, aren't you, mate?' Mark insulted the guard with a smile on his face, and the man grunted and turned away, talking to his fellow guards, not understanding a word Mark was saying and indicating that he must be crazy in the head.

Mark returned to the unsavoury task of burying the corpses of the many Asians killed either by bombs or at the hands of the Japanese guards. He wrinkled his nose in disgust at the smell, and spoke to the guard in Tamil.

'How about letting us bathe in the sea after work?' he suggested. 'It wouldn't hurt to let us get a bit cleaned up, would it?'

The guard grunted but made no reply, and after a moment he jabbed Mark with his bayonet and ordered him to get back to work. Mark obeyed, knowing it was useless to rebel. He would only be rewarded with a beating or worse depending on the mood of the guards.

At last the order was given for the men to put down their shovels, and with a sigh of relief, Mark straightened his back to ease the ache. Wearily, the men fell into lines and began the walk back to camp. It didn't seem as though he was going to get his dip in the sea. He thrust his hands into his pockets; what if he offered the guard a trade, a fag for a bathe? He rejected the idea almost at once. A cigarette was no luxury to the Japanese. If he had another watch to trade, now, it might be different.

Suddenly, the bedraggled group was called to a halt and ordered to turn right so that they were facing an area of dusty scrubland. On the ground was the body of a Chinese woman naked from the waist down, lying in a pool of dried blood. She had been killed by a sharpened bamboo thrust through her abdomen.

'God only knows what they did to her before they killed her,' Mark said to William who stood, white faced, at his side. The men were kept there for over half an hour, and Mark muttered 'bastards!' and was slammed in the kidneys with the butt of a gun for his pains.

'This,' said the Japanese guard, 'is corrective training, teaching you to obey your masters without question. You may walk on.'

A few hundred yards further on, the company was again called to a halt and Mark glanced uneasily around him, wondering what other atrocities he would be forced to witness, but all he could see was three Australian officers under the armed guard of a group of NCOs. The Australian soldiers in the small working party were called to the front, and one of the officers held out a packet of Craven A cigarettes. Some instinct told Mark to hold fast, and he remained where he was, warily watching the proceedings.

The Japanese NCOs were not from the prison camp and had no idea what his nationality was. He half expected his own guards to give him away, but either they didn't know his nationality or they chose to remain silent.

The Australian officers began to smoke the cigarettes, all of them appearing uneasy and suspicious. Their fears were well founded, because with a suddenness that startled the watching men, the officers were suddenly kicked at the back of the legs, forcing them to kneel in the roadway.

Mark held his breath as a Japanese NCO stepped forward, swung his sword around his head three times and with a bloodcurdling cry decapitated the officer nearest to him. The other two tried to make a run for it but the rattle of rifle fire shattered the sudden quiet, and the men fell twitching to the ground. The guard cold-bloodedly walked up to the fallen men and shot them both in the head.

The Australians who had been in the working party were killed one by one and Mark felt anger clouding his vision as he stared at the remains of the cigarettes still burning in the roadway. He wanted to rush forward and land punch after punch on the sneering faces of the Japanese officers.

The man next to him passed out and Mark gripped his arm, gesturing for William, who was on the other side, to help. Together they held the man erect until he recovered consciousness.

'Now we go back to camp,' one of the guards said and headed the silent group of prisoners back along the road.

As though he were trying to comfort the men, one of the more humane guards called out in a loud voice, 'Tomorrow we go to docks to work and you will bathe in sea.'

As he walked dispiritedly back towards the camp, Mark knew that somehow he would have to escape before he went mad. The problem was Roggen. Could she survive a trek through the jungle even if they did manage to make it out of the camp?

As he neared the compound, Mark took stock of the

situation. The barbed-wire fence was fifteen, maybe twenty feet high. It would be impossible for him, let alone for Roggen, to cut through its thickness or try to scale the cruel wire barrier. The only way out was through the gate which was also made of barbed wire, though it was much thinner than that on the perimeter.

He was pushed through the gate by a guard irritated by his slowness, and as the prisoners began to disperse an order was barked out informing the weary men that they must stand to attention to meet with the new camp commandant.

'Surly looking runt, isn't he?' Mark said to William, and he smiled as a box was placed strategically for the small man to stand on.

'I am Colonel Nickar,' the Japanese said in stilted English, and William grinned.

'He's bloody well nothing more than a captain, the little pipsqueak. You can tell by his badges,' William whispered.

Colonel Nickar looked so much like a small, skinny bird of prey standing on his box, his head jerking forward, that one of the men in the group began to laugh. Soon they were all laughing.

'Have you ever seen anything so funny?' William said out of the corner of his mouth. 'It's just like something out of a comic opera.'

'Silence!' thundered Nickar, and turning, he issued an order to one of his men. Silence fell as the guards weeded out the tallest men from the bedraggled group. Mark quickly slipped off his shoes and bent his knees slightly. William was all right – he was a small man – and the guards passed both of them over.

'Yesterday,' shouted Nickar, 'some men escape, not good. We of the Imperial Japanese Army are good and kind, we are the liberators of all Asia, we must be obeyed.' He glanced around, aware that now he was holding everyone's attention. 'You will learn who is in charge, you must be taught a lesson.' He barked out a command and the taller men who were now standing to the side of him edged backwards as rifles were raised.

Mark knew at once what was going to happen. The guns spat forth death and in minutes the men lay dead in the dust of the compound. Some of the women screamed and Mark growled low in his throat, making an involuntary move forward. William's hand was strong on his arm.

'Keep cool, man, you can't help them now and you'll only draw attention to yourself.'

Mark realized he was right but the veins in his temple seemed to distend until he thought he would pass out. He didn't hear the order for them to be dismissed and it was William who led him back towards the shade of one of the ragged huts.

Later that night, the men were roused from sleep, pushed forward into the blinding glare of the arc lights and handed shovels. It seemed they were going to bury their dead.

In the days that followed the dreadful coldblooded killing of the innocent prisoners, Roggen found herself becoming steadily weaker. Her skin was peeling and sore and her lips were cracking from lack of moisture. The new commandant had restricted the water, taking away the barrel a day the old commandant had allowed and giving out one tin cupful instead.

The Tamil woman's baby cried most of the time and Roggen offered to take the child so that the mother could rest, but she shook her head, resisting all attempts to take the baby from her. One night, when the baby was crying more than usual, the guards came and took the woman and the child out into the night. Roggen watched in speechless fear, unable to do anything to help. Somehow, she was not surprised, only angered and pained, when they did not return.

The next morning, the prisoners were told to stand in the square and wait for their commandant. The sun blazed down fiercely and Roggen felt herself sway a little.

'Keep going, Roggen.' Mark was just a few yards away, looking at her through the wire.

'Bloody hell,' she heard him say, 'there's not many of us left, is there?' With a thrill of horror, Roggen realized that he was right. Many of the prisoners had died and many more had been killed by the Japanese.

At last, Nickar appeared and stood on his box so that he was elevated above the prisoners. His scrawny neck jerked forward as he spoke and Roggen felt her flesh creep as she watched him.

'Soon, we split you all up,' Nickar said. 'Native women go away to another place, they too much trouble here. Servicemen will be held but all civilians can go free.'

Roggen looked hopefully towards Mark but he shook his head. 'In a pig's ear!' he said hoarsely. 'What the bastard means is that the civilians are dispensable. We will all be shot, more likely.'

He motioned her to silence as Nickar continued to harangue the prisoners, urging them to be more diligent when working and to obey their superiors. Roggen stopped listening and wondered worriedly what would happen to them all.

When the crowd was dismissed, Mark beckoned her towards the wire. 'I've got an escape plan,' he whispered, 'and after that little speech, it's now or never time. We'll talk later.'

As Roggen watched the men being marched out of the camp, she felt fear gnaw at her and she realized that she was trembling in spite of the heat. She moved to the shade of the hut and sank down on to the dusty ground, and she was too frightened even for tears.

43

The water was cold and it lapped Eden's face, bringing him to slow consciousness. He gasped as the heavy swell caught him full in the face, and when he tried to move, he found that he was pinned by a weight across his chest. Remarkably, he was lying on a piece of timbering that was large enough to support him in spite of the twisted metal pressing cruelly into his flesh.

He fought the panic that swamped him as relentlessly as the waves, and tried to take stock of the situation. The seas around him were dark but he could just make out the looming shape of a ship to his port side. Beyond that, his own ship was slipping below the waves. The sea, edged with white foam, eddied around the sinking *Chware Teg*, and then she was gone for ever.

He wondered if he was destined to die here alone at sea. He thought of the women he'd left at home; Nia, whom he had betrayed, and Kristina, whom he had wronged. And Roggen, his sister. He would never know if she had survived the war or not. There was the sting of salt in his eyes, though whether brought there by the seas or his own tears he couldn't tell.

He attempted to drag himself into complete awareness as the darkness seemed to close in around him. He took a deep breath and after a moment forced his thoughts to return to the more immediate problem of his own survival.

Eden deduced that he could only have been unconscious for several minutes and so some of the ships from the convoy must still be within reach of him. He twisted his body as far as the piece of metal hull that pinned him to the timber would allow, and saw what must be the last of the convoy steaming towards him.

He wanted to call out but the sea filled his mouth, and gasping, he tried to raise himself higher. But it was useless. The weight upon him was too heavy. He rested a moment and then tried another tactic. He tore the shirt from his back, feeling the cloth rip where it was caught beneath the metal, and exhausted by the pain of his efforts he rested again until the ship was almost upon him. Then, frantically, he waved the torn piece of linen above his head, though with little hope that it would be seen in the darkness. The sound of the ship's engine was almost upon him and he wondered bleakly if he would be run down instead of rescued.

Miraculously, the ship began to slow, there was the scraping sound above him of a boat being lowered, and a cheerful voice called out to him.

'Hang on there, mate, we're coming to get you.' Eden felt humbled. These men, sailors like himself with families back home, were risking their lives by stopping to rescue him, knowing that their ship would provide a sitting target for the enemy subs.

'Hell's teeth, you've got yourself into a right pickle there, man, haven't you?' Eden could smell the man's good honest sweat as he tried to prise the metal away from Eden's body. 'Here,' the sailor gasped as he was joined by another man, 'Give us a hand, will you? This blasted piece of metal has got him stapled to the timber.'

The pain when the debris was lifted from him made Eden bite his lip in an effort not to cry out. He felt the blood begin to flow as he was being carried into the boat.

'You're lucky, mate,' the sailor said, 'we've got a doc here. He's going to take a look at you before we attempt to get you on board the ship.' He moved away, rocking the boat, and then someone was bending over Eden, fingers gently probing the wound in his chest.

'We'll be able to patch you up.' He deftly placed a pad

over Eden's wound and wrapped a bandage swiftly round his body. 'I'm Tom Grant, and – don't laugh – I was in obstetrics before the war, so babies are more my line than war wounds, but I reckon you'll live. Come on, let me just give you a jab and then we'll get you on board.'

Eden felt the needle sink into his arm, and almost at once his thoughts became blurred. He still felt the pain when he was being lifted from the rescue boat but somehow it didn't seem to matter any more. Dimly, he realized he was on the deck of the ship, then careful hands carried him into a cabin and put him gently on to a soft bed.

'Poor bastard.' It was the doctor's voice, 'he's seen the last of his war. The metal has punctured his lung and done heaven knows what else to his innards.'

Eden tried to lift his head but he was sinking into a soft, comfortable world where nothing could hurt him.

Nia was in the garden, cutting the last of the roses. The perfume from the flowers always reminded her of her childhood when she was friends with both Roggen and Kristina. But that was a long time ago. So much had happened since then, and yet somehow, through Eden Lamb, their lives had been inextricably joined.

Eden. It was so long since she'd heard from him. Was he still alive? She felt numb when she thought about him, for their marriage was over and done with, and she could not take him back, ever.

She placed a rose in her basket and drew a sharp breath as a thorn pierced her skin. She sucked at the small wound and there were foolish tears in her eyes. She *had* loved him and she could have forgiven him much, but not a betrayal committed in such a barbaric way on an innocent woman. And she was convinced that Kristina *was* innocent, the victim of a clever seducer.

She sensed, rather than heard, footsteps behind her, and casually she glanced over her shoulder. She dropped the basket of flowers as shock waves washed through her.

The rose petals lay scattered on the ground but she did not see them as she stared before her, wondering if she was seeing a ghost.

'Don't look so surprised. It really is me.' Eden looked sick and ill; his tall frame seemed to be wasted and his face was drawn with lines of pain, but his eyes were alive in the whiteness of his face and he was smiling down at her with more warmth than she'd ever seen in his eyes before.

She saw him tremble and knew it was from weakness and sickness, and very slowly she led him to a chair.

'What's happened? I was told you were in a Japanese prison camp in Singapore. Did you escape?' she said, trying not to let him see how shocked she was at his appearance.

'I was nowhere near Singapore,' he said in surprise. 'My ship was torpedoed in deep waters. Since I was picked up, I've been in a hospital up in Scotland with my arm strapped to my chest. Writing was rather difficult.' He smiled and leaned back thankfully, closing his eyes and lifting his face to the autumn sunshine.

'In any case, I didn't want to worry you. I imagined you'd think I was still at sea, and I wanted to be at least halfway fit before I came home. What made you think I was in Singapore, of all places?'

'Never mind that now, it was obviously a mistake. I'll get you a cup of tea.' Nia was concerned at his pallor, realizing that he was playing down the seriousness of his illness. And yet anger at his one act of unfaithfulness with Kristina warred with her pity.

He shook his head. 'No, I don't want tea. Stay and talk, please, tell me how you are.' He took her hand and she drew away. Eden looked disappointed at her reaction. He stared around the sunny lawns and his eyes held a faraway expression.

'And what's been happening in Swansea?' he asked. She knew that he was thinking of Kristina and his son, and the thought hurt. She could not help the sting of renewed anger as she wondered how much she should say. Her instinct was to accuse him, to shout out that he had pained her deeply by his betrayal, but how could she, with him looking so ill?

Eden sat up sharply, a frown creasing his forehead. 'I've just thought of something,' he said quietly. 'Roggen is in Singapore. Is it possible she's been taken prisoner and somehow our names were mixed up?'

'Oh, my God!' Nia said softly. Eden was very probably right. 'How can you find out?'

He shook his head. 'I don't know, but God, if she's held by the Japs then there's not much chance of her ever getting away alive.'

He put his head in his hands and Nia felt she should go to him and comfort him, but she couldn't, for it would be a gesture so foreign to what she was feeling.

She hurried to the kitchen and made the tea automatically, her hands trembling. She returned with the tray to where he was sitting, but far from being in control, she felt herself snapping.

'How could you, Eden?' The words burst from her lips and a rush of anger flooded through her as she imagined him with Kristina, speaking words of love, holding her close.

He looked at her blankly for a moment and then his thin face became even paler. 'I see Kristina has been talking to you, and I can't honestly blame her.'

Nia shook her head. 'Is that what you honestly think? Then you misjudge Kristina. She's no gossip.'

He sighed. 'Yes, you're right, but how did you know about us, then? And before you answer, I want you to know I went to see my son, not Kristina. Remember that.'

'He is *her* son, you remember that. And there's something else. You might as well know all the facts.' Nia looked down at her fingers. 'She became pregnant by you. The poor girl was living in poverty, she couldn't work, you see.' Nia couldn't keep the anger out of her voice. 'I found out because I pressed Kristina to give me an answer.' She sighed heavily. 'But she miscarried the child; her husband came home just in time to save her life, it seems.'

Eden pushed himself up from the garden chair, wincing with pain. 'I'm going to find out for myself what's happened,' he said, 'and after that perhaps we can talk about our marriage.'

Nia stared at him, her eyes hard. 'Do we have a marriage?' she asked quietly.

He moved out of the house with slow, breathless steps, and Nia felt pity, mixed with anger, as she watched him. But she was a determined woman and she had made up her mind; what she'd had with Eden Lamb was finished, over and done with. Wasn't it?

Kristina had recovered slowly from the miscarriage and somehow she seemed to have lost all her spirit. She sat alone in the house in Lambert's Cottages and stared at the wall, thinking of how her life had once been so tranquil when her son had been with her and she'd had Robert Jenkins as a good and true husband who really cared about her. What a sorry mess she'd made of her life. How she wished she could undo all the harm and all the suffering she had put Robert through. She loved him so much and now she had lost him.

The house was silent. Verdun was with Mrs Thomas who had been wonderful since Kristina's illness, asking no questions, though she must have been curious about the fact that Mr Jenkins had come home from the war and was not living with his wife.

There was a soft tapping on the door that brought her thoughts sharply back to the present. She got to her feet with a sudden flare of hope rising within her. Pausing to take a deep breath, she wondered if Robert had forgiven her and come back to her.

It was like a slap in the face seeing Eden standing there in the street, the light behind him. Even with the shadows in his face, she could see he looked ill. She instinctively stepped back from him and he followed her inside.

'It's all right, Kristina,' he said slowly, and even his voice was weaker, 'I just want to talk to you.'

'Sit down,' she said, putting the distance of the scrubbed wood table between them.

'I'm sorry, Kristina,' he said, 'you've had a rough time and it's all my fault.'

She sank into a chair, not wanting to remember the night she had lain in his arms, wanting him as he wanted her. 'Yes,' she said softly.

'You almost lost your life, is that right?' He leaned on the table and there were lines of pain around his mouth.

'Aye, but got over it, mind.' Kristina held her head high. She didn't want Eden's pity or his guilt, she wanted nothing to do with him at all.

'So I've broken up your marriage?' he persisted. 'Is it true that your husband has left you?'

Kristina sighed. 'Aye, Robert's gone and I can't say I blame him. What would you have done if you'd come home to find your wife pregnant by another man?'

'If I was in Robert Jenkins's shoes I'd feel like committing murder,' he admitted quietly.

Kristina rose from her chair and lit the gas ring beneath the kettle. 'We'll have some tea,' she said. 'You are not well, you shouldn't really be out and about.'

'I'll make it up to you, Kristina.' He ignored her remarks. 'I'll put this cottage in your name for a start, so that you and Verdun will always have a home.'

'Have your tea and go home,' Kristina said softly. 'You can't make it up. Don't you realize that I've lost the only man I ever really loved?' She heard the bitterness in her own voice and turned to him quickly. 'I'm sorry, that's not fair.' She handed him a cup of tea and sat down opposite him, making an effort to speak calmly. 'I don't want anything from you, Eden. Robert will take care of me, financially at least.'

He seemed a beaten man as he drank his tea and then

put down the empty cup. 'I can only repeat how sorry I am, Kristina,' he said softly. Slowly, he made his way to the door, and as she watched him leave it was as though a burden had been lifted from her shoulders. Eden had gone from her life for ever.

44

It was morning, and already the sun was burning down on the men standing in the yard waiting to be allocated work at Pasir Penjang prison camp. Mark stood next to William, who was looking at him apprehensively, both men wondering if they would escape the attention of the Japanese guard who was beating into line any prisoner who irritated him.

Mark felt as though his every bone ached, but compared to some of the prisoners who had been interrogated and even tortured, he was in good shape. He was worried about Roggen, though. She was looking so thin and drawn, and he didn't think she would last out if they stayed in the prison camp much longer. It was an added incentive to escape.

The guards had begun to move along the line, choosing the prisoners who were earmarked for 'special treatment' by the Japanese. One of the men, his face cut and swollen, fell whimpering to the ground as he was dragged yet again from the line for intensive and pointless interrogation. The man knew nothing, he was simply a private with the British army, but there was no accounting for the odd behaviour of the Japanese.

'Poor sod,' William said, and stiffened as one of the guards stopped before him. He looked speculatively at Mark before shaking his head, grinning and moving on.

'I think the Japs have got me tagged as a bit crazy,' Mark said in a whisper, 'and I don't care a damn so long as they leave me alone.'

They were marched out of the camp towards the

docks, and the guards amused themselves by forcing the weak or recalcitrant prisoners to move faster with the encouragement of a rifle butt.

'Why don't we get the entire working party to escape?' Mark said out of the blue, and William stared at him in amazement.

'Are you barmy? Twenty of us escape? Don't you think we'd be noticed?' He smiled without mirth, but Mark was deadly serious.

'Don't you see, it makes sense? The Japs won't expect us to do anything so daring, and in any case, you know very well what will happen to any of our party who are left behind. They'll be killed instantly.'

'Yes, you're right,' William said more thoughtfully.

Mark brushed back his hair. 'And with such a crowd of men making the escape attempt, it would be easier to get Roggen out.'

William nodded. He was aware that Roggen was a white woman and he sympathized with Mark's dilemma. 'Where would we make for?' William asked, warming to the idea. 'Perhaps across to Sumatra would be our best bet.'

'How about Australia?' Mark said, smiling. 'It's only about two thousand miles away, mate.'

'I doubt if we'd get that far,' William said softly, 'but it would certainly be great to try. I'll sound the other men out during the day.'

Mark tried not to show his elation as he worked at the unsavoury task of clearing out the drains near the docks. One of the guards came up to him and stood quite close.

'I promised you a swim today,' he said, and he stared at Mark quizzically. 'Don't smile or show you know me, but don't you remember I used to work for you?'

Mark glanced at him and then away again. A picture of the face and rather portly figure in civvies instead of the dour uniform of the Japanese army came to mind. 'Hell! You're Peachy. When did you join this lot?'

'Keep your voice down, please, Mister Mark.' He

allowed himself a smile. 'I've been here a few weeks now and I've given the Japanese the impression that you are a little mad. I hope you don't mind the liberty.'

'I don't care what you say, mate, so long as it keeps the monkeys off my back.' Mark looked cautiously at Peachy. He was of uncertain ancestry, probably Portuguese Eurasian, but he had lived in Singapore for most of his life. 'How did you get to join this lot?' Mark asked in a low voice, and Peachy, his back to the other guards, smiled.

'Simple. It was that or die.' He glanced cautiously over his shoulder. 'You must get out of the camp before the women are sent away,' he said quickly. 'After that, you will all be treated as dangerous prisoners and there will be no mercy for any of you. That's why, for old times' sake, I'm going to help you.'

Mark felt his spine tingle. He did not doubt for one moment that what the man said was true. 'Why should you care, what's your interest?' he asked warily.

'The Japs came and raped my eldest daughter,' Peachy said flatly. 'Now listen, I have a boat in which you can cross the straits. You can try to get to my brother in Sumatra. He's with the guerrillas there.' The man paused. 'But don't go in the daytime when I am on duty, otherwise my family will be killed for sure.'

Mark forced himself to speak calmly, though he wanted to shout out his elation. 'Where can I get this boat?'

'Wait a bit, it's getting to look suspicious.' The man turned away and shouted an order to some of the prisoners to work faster. He wandered away from Mark and for several minutes did not even look back at him. Mark began to wonder if it had been all talk on Peachy's part, and whether, when it came down to it, he had got cold feet.

But in a while, the guard came back. 'Come to my house in Paya Lebar, you know it?'

Mark nodded. It was a small group of houses, little

more than a village, a short distance from the Seletar airfield on the Serangoon road. About twelve miles from the prison camp, he guessed.

'Let me know what night you come so I will be ready for you.' Peachy walked away and Mark bent his back over his shovel, leaning towards William.

'You manage to hear any of that?' he asked, and William nodded.

'I got the gist,' he said softly. 'Do you think it's a trap and the Japs will be waiting to shoot us as escaped prisoners?'

'Possibly,' Mark said, 'but since when have the Japs needed an excuse to kill? No, I think the man's on the level. I was good to his family when he worked for me, gave him extra money for medicine when one of his kids was sick. He told me then he would always be grateful, but I never guessed how much that gratitude would mean to me.'

After work was finished, the men were marched to the sea front and with shouts of joy, the prisoners ran into the cool water. Mark felt the waves wash over his head and as he closed his eyes against the sparkle of the water, he realized this was the nearest thing to normality he'd experienced since being taken prisoner.

All the trappings of civilization had gone; the showers, the clean smell of soap, a good comb. Such trivial things, once taken for granted, all seemed so valuable now. And yet all he really needed was the primitive urge to survive, and Mark, surfacing from beneath the water, felt determination surge within him. He and Roggen *would* survive this war, come what may.

When he returned to the camp, he waited until the scant meal of rice and fish had been served and then he edged over to where Roggen was sitting alone. She looked so thin, there were dark shadows beneath her eyes, and the Tamil clothes hung on her so loosely that she looked as if a breath of wind would blow her away.

'Don't ask questions, but we'll be getting out of here

soon,' he said softly. 'We've got some help from an unexpected quarter.' He leaned closer to the fence. 'I don't want the guards getting suspicious.'

'Tell me more,' Roggen begged, but Mark shook his head.

'The less you know, the better.'

She leaned back against the wall of the hut and Mark pushed some fruit through the wires. Roggen shook her head, but he insisted.

'Come on, kiddo, keep your strength up. You're going to need it.' He felt anger burn within him that Roggen had come to this. She looked so weak and so ill, and yet a fire still burned in her dark eyes. She'd make it or none of them would, Mark swore to himself.

'I'm going to make some plans now, Ro,' he said softly. 'Try to rest. I'll come and tell you when everything's finalized. And don't worry, we'll beat the Japs yet.'

He moved to the perimeter of the camp and took stock of the situation. A plan so simple that he wondered why he had never thought of it before it began to take shape in his mind. Just through the first coil of barbed wire was a junction box with flex coiling almost towards where he was sitting. If he could reach the flex and cut it, disconnecting the circuit, ensuing darkness would enable the men of his work party to charge the gate, the weakest part of the fencing. In the confusion, he could take Roggen and make a run for it.

He edged up to William on the pretence of getting a light for his half cigarette. 'I think I've got it,' he said, hardly able to keep the excitement from his voice. He outlined the plan and William nodded thoughtfully.

'You have got bloody long arms, man,' he joked. 'A bit ape-like, in fact. But do you know, I think it's so simple a plan that it might just work.'

'I'd do it just before lights on,' Mark said thoughtfully, 'that way when the power is switched on the fuse boxes might all blow.'

'Good, when?' William's eyes were eager and Mark smiled, taking a slow drag of his cigarette before replying.

'What about tomorrow night?' He edged away from William and sat on his own, thinking the plan through. The success of it hinged on the possibility of him being able to reach the box which was quite a distance away. He could do it if William held the tough wire high enough for him to get his head through. He could just about reach then, he decided. He would also have to enlist William's help in lifting the thin wire around the women's compound, making sure Roggen was ready to run into the night. He would work on the wire in the darkness, weakening it so that when the time came, he and William could prise it apart just enough to let Roggen through.

William was passing the plan round the men one at a time and Mark, trying to read their expressions, saw hope light up the tired faces. He glowed with exultation. At least now there was a chance of getting out, and even if they risked a bullet in the back it was better than dying slowly of starvation or being tortured to death.

Mark decided he would tell Roggen at the last moment. No point in having her tense and apprehensive all through the night. Far better for her to get some rest. He lay down in the darkness with one worry nagging his mind; what if he or one of the crew was taken for interrogation? A man would not be fit to walk, let alone run, after an hour or two of 'special treatment'. He worked on the wire for a time until his arms ached, and at last he turned on his side. He must try to sleep. He needed to be as fresh as possible for the escape attempt, and worrying never got a man anywhere.

The next morning, Mark let out a sigh of relief as none of the men were held back for interrogation. He looked round him and smiled. 'Don't look so happy, blokes,' he whispered. 'They'll get suspicious.'

The day was steamily hot. Mark felt his muscles protest as he worked at clearing rubble from a bombed building. He was grateful when Peachy came up to him and offered him some fruit.

'It's on for tonight,' he said softly. 'We're going to be arriving at your house in pairs, hopefully.'

'Don't say more.' The man's voice shook with fear. 'What I don't know I can't tell, but I'll be waiting for you.'

William threw a piece of rubble to attract Mark's attention. 'Get some sort of weapon,' he mouthed, and Mark nodded his assent. He looked up at the sun beating mercilessly down on the sweating, labouring men, and he wondered if any of them would have the strength, when the time came, to make the escape attempt. But then desperation would lend the group vigour. They all knew the consequences if they should fail. Mark wiped the sweat from his eyes and bent over his work as though it were the most important job he'd ever done.

When Roggen heard the plan, she felt her head begin to pound. For a moment she felt paralyzed with fear, feeling she could not go through with it. But really there was no alternative. She would rather be dead than separated from Mark, not knowing what was happening to him.

Roggen was well aware of the rumours that swept the camp, and she knew that the men left behind would be less than dirt beneath the feet of the Japanese. Men were considered dangerous prisoners and would be treated accordingly.

'I'm ready when you are,' she said, forcing herself to be calm. But why was it Mark who would have to take the initial risk? Why couldn't some other man stretch through the barbed wire and pull out the cables from the junction box?

It was getting dark, and in a few minutes the guard would be leaving the guardhouse and making for the hut where the switchgear and generator were kept. The men were looking at each other expectantly, keeping a wary eye on the soldiers who were making their rounds.

Roggen felt herself tremble as William lifted the barbed wire to allow Mark to stretch his arm beneath it. A fierce barb bit into Mark's neck and drew blood but he didn't seem to notice. His fingers were still a few inches away from the electric cable. He inched further beneath the wire which was digging into his shoulder and his fingers were miraculously in contact with the cable. He gave a sudden sharp jerk and the wires were loose in his hands.

'For heaven's sake, get out of there,' William said. 'The guards are coming back.'

Mark moved swiftly, sitting on the ground, his face turned away from the guards who passed by seeming to notice nothing amiss.

Roggen sighed with relief. For the moment, Mark was safe. He whispered to her to move nearer the gate. 'Go on, and keep looking at me. I'll grab your arm and once the gate is down, run like hell!'

Roggen's heart was pounding with fear. She felt almost faint as she watched the thin Japanese soldier appear from the guardhouse and stand for a moment looking around him.

'Wait for it, kiddo,' Mark said, jovial as he always was in times of danger. He moved nearer to the gate where the rest of the men were seated, and Roggen followed him at a distance, praying that none of the guards would spot her and send her back to the hut. But it was dark and no one could see very clearly until the arc lights were switched on.

The Japanese soldier disappeared into the hut and Roggen, her mouth dry, waited for the light to fail. Would Mark's plan work as he'd anticipated? Or would the lights have a safety device that might make them work independently of each other?

The sudden explosion ripped apart the hut and lit up the night sky. Windows and doors were lifted into the air and fell back to earth in a blaze of flames. For a moment, the men stood in shocked disbelief, and then Mark shouted to them to move.

'Now, William!' The two men forced up the netting between the two camps and frantically Roggen squeezed through the gap. The men were rushing the gate. Some of them screamed as the barbed wire tore into their flesh, but they would not be stopped. One of the men took up a bamboo bar and with the help of some of the others pushed the gate up and over.

A handful of Japanese soldiers ran towards them. Roggen felt her arm grasped, and then she was being hustled through the heaving mass of bodies. She saw Mark strike a guard with a piece of wood and as the man struggled, he hit him again. He went down like a stone and Mark relieved him of his bayonet.

They were out of the camp then and running. Roggen's heart was beating so fast she thought she would die of fear. Behind her, she heard the spine-chilling sound of machine-gun fire, but Mark dragged her onwards through the tangled undergrowth, taking cover whenever possible behind the trees.

Then, suddenly, they were out on open land, running until Roggen felt she could not breathe. There was the stumbling of someone behind them and she saw Mark glance back uneasily.

'It's me!' William caught up with them in the darkness and the two men stood for a moment, staring at each other. 'Well done!' William said, his voice shaking with emotion.

Roggen felt Mark push her forwards. 'We must press on,' he said. 'We're at least a quarter of a mile from camp, but there's a long way to go yet.'

She followed Mark's lead as he zigzagged across the ground. After a while, he slowed his pace a little and Roggen struggled to get her breath. 'All right,' Mark said, 'we can afford to go a bit easier now we've reached the jungle.'

The grass was breast high to Roggen and she wondered what creatures might be lurking in its depths. Then she forced a laugh; she had just escaped from a Japanese prison camp and she was worried about spiders!

'We've been heading due north,' Mark said, taking a deep breath, 'but I reckon that to reach Peachy's house we should be heading between north and north east.' He looked down at Roggen. 'We'll hit the Bukit Timor road soon, but don't worry, we should be taken for Eurasians and if we see any Japs we'll hide in the long grass.'

Roggen nodded. She was too breathless to speak and when she grasped Mark's arm, he smiled down at her.

'You've lost your scarf, and your sleeves are torn ragged, but it's a good thing you're sunburnt or you'd stand out like a sore thumb. Lucky you're not a blonde.'

Suddenly Roggen thought of Kristina, tall and lovely with her golden hair, and for the first time, she did not envy her friend's fair beauty.

The Bukit Timor road was empty and dark and it was much easier going than the long grass had been. She didn't know how she managed to keep walking – the night was hot and she felt bone weary, unused to exercise – but she plodded on doggedly.

At last they came to a belt of rubber trees where it was cooler and very dark. Mark put his arm around her and held her for a moment. 'All right, Ro?' he asked, and hearing the concern in his voice, she made an effort to be cheerful.

'Of course I'm all right. I'm a strong Welsh girl, why shouldn't I be all right?'

She seemed to have been walking for hours and when she glanced back Roggen knew that they had skirted the town of Singapore. Low swathes of mist hung above swamp and jungle and Roggen wished herself out of all this and back in the safety of Swansea.

When the party neared Peachy's house, Roggen saw that some of the other men had made it to the meeting point. In all, there were about twelve prisoners crouched in the grass, eyes anxious as they stared around them.

Roggen caught her breath in fear as Mark began to ease himself forward. It seemed that he must take the initiative and approach the house. He disappeared inside and in the silence Roggen closed her eyes, wondering if the Japanese would be waiting to catch him in a trap.

After a few minutes he reappeared, and it took all her willpower not to run into his arms. He held out a wad of money but he was not smiling. He crouched down and spoke softly.

'Peachy is not prepared to go any further. The boats are miles away at Kranji Point and we'll have to get there under our own steam. But Peachy has given us some supplies and there will be cans of water on the boats.' He caught Roggen's arm and helped her to her feet. 'Can you make it, Ro?'

She nodded tiredly, knowing she had no option but to continue walking even though all she wanted to do was fall down on to the ground and sleep.

She didn't remember much about the journey to the Point. Her legs felt like rubber and a great thirst plagued her, but at last, through a daze, she could hear the lapping of water against the shore.

The mudflats were slippery but there, bobbing on the water, were two small boats. At least now she could rest.

Suddenly a shot rang out, shattering the silence. Mark lifted her quickly into one of the boats. 'Keep down,' he ordered.

She crouched trembling in the well of the boat, afraid to lift her head as the brief battle took place on the mudflats. 'Please keep Mark safe,' she whispered.

The silence was unnerving. Roggen waited in dread, each minute seeming like an hour, but then the men began to scramble into the boat, William first and then Mark, and Roggen felt sick with thankfulness. She held his hand in the darkness and there were tears running salt into her mouth. He leaned towards her.

'I think most of the others copped it,' he said in a heavy voice, 'but don't worry, kiddo. We're on our way home.' His words were optimistic, she knew that, but at least here they were together, tasting freedom.

565

It was perhaps two days later that the aircraft flew above them. Roggen felt half dead, the water supply put there by Peachy was long gone, and fevered by thirst, she had lost count of time.

'It's coming our way.' Mark's voice was hoarse. He sat up and shaded his eyes from the sun. 'It's not a Jap plane,' he said, but I think it's German. Just our luck.'

'Well,' William said in an effort to be reassuring, 'if it's a Jerry crew they might take us prisoner. Anything is better than sitting here dying of thirst.'

Roggen silently agreed with him. She didn't think she could last much longer. She watched the strange aircraft as it drew nearer and she saw as it came lower that it was some sort of seaplane.

'It's a Dornier,' Mark said as the plane landed in a shower of glistening spray.

Roggen watched apprehensively as the craft drew nearer and the door in the fuselage swung open. The man looking out at them was blond and fair-skinned, and Roggen felt faint with relief.

Mark spoke to him, then, turning to look down at Roggen, he smiled. 'It's all right, kiddo, he's Dutch.' He helped her to her feet and nodded to the man in the aircraft. 'Give us a hand.' He smiled ruefully. 'Don't worry, she's as light as a feather.'

Roggen felt her senses reel as she was lifted into the aircraft, and then lowered into a seat. Mark was beside her and, as she felt darkness sweep over her, all she knew was that she was in his arms and that they were on the first step of their journey home.

45

Kristina stood patiently in the queue at the grocer's, her shopping bag in one hand and Verdun clinging to the other. She was hungry but she was becoming used to not eating enough and she ignored the discomfort. Verdun was a growing boy and needed much more nourishment than the meagre rations allowed, and like most mothers, Kristina preferred her son to be well fed.

'Good morning, Kristina.' She looked up to see Eden staring down at her. 'Roggen is safe, she's on her way home. I thought you'd like to know.'

It was an excuse to stop and talk, Kristina knew that, and as Eden bent towards Verdun, she could not help noticing the unhealthy pallor that his still charming smile could not conceal.

'I'm glad,' she said.

Eden straightened. 'Nia finds it hard to forgive me,' he said, and she looked away. 'And I don't blame her,' he added with uncharacteristic humility. 'Are you still working up at the aerodrome?' he asked, changing tack, and she nodded.

'Yes,' she said guardedly. 'But Robert is very generous. We are well cared for, so there's no need to worry, mind.'

'I see.' Eden glanced at the other women in the queue, who were staring at him curiously. 'I'd like to talk, Kristina,' he said, 'just talk for a moment. Is that asking too much?'

'Not here,' she said quickly. 'Come to the house, I've got the rent ready.' She hoped her neighbours would think she was merely talking to Eden Lamb as her landlord. He lifted his hat and moved away, and Kristina sighed with relief. She was glad when it was her turn to be served and she could make her way back home.

Back at Lambert's Cottages, she set down her shopping bag and sighed. It would be potatoes and carrots for dinner again. There was a knock on the door and Kristina frowned. Eden hadn't wasted much time. But it was Robert who was standing on the cobbled roadway outside. He called on her from time to time, but he did so as a duty, nothing more. She knew that only too well.

'Come in,' she said and, as always, their eyes refused to meet. 'I've just got the shopping so I can make you a cup of tea with sugar in for a change.'

He put an envelope on the table. 'Here's some money, Kristina. I've got my job back on the docks and if you want to, you can give up work and stay at home with Verdun.'

She didn't know what to say so she busied herself making the tea while Robert talked to Verdun.

'I've had a letter from my Aunt Liv,' she said, making an effort at light conversation as she put the teapot on the table and covered it with the knitted cosy. 'The Norwegians think that the war will be over soon.'

'They may well be right,' Robert said slowly. 'It certainly is beginning to look that way.'

Kristina sat at the table. 'Verdun, go and wash your hands and come and have some bread and jam.' Kristina glanced quickly at Robert. 'Would you like some? I made it myself.' How foolish it seemed talking to her husband so politely as though he were a stranger. And yet how could she heal the breach between them? She could not bring herself to talk about the time, it seemed so long ago now, when he'd come home and found her sick and ill. He had been kind then, knowing how much pain she must have felt losing the baby, but once she was out of danger he had gone away from her unable to hide his hurt and anger. Should she try just once again to explain to him how lonely she'd been when she'd gone into Eden's arms?

'There seems to be plenty of work on the docks,' Robert said, and the moment was gone. 'Though there's not enough men to do it, which is why I was taken back there, I suppose.'

Robert still limped a little but he was no longer thin and ill-looking. He was a strong man, Kristina thought with a sense of pride. He would not give in to life easily.

He met her eyes and she looked quickly away, embarrassed at being caught staring at him. 'Robert,' she said hesitantly, 'I must talk to you, really talk, please.'

He rose to his feet in a swift movement. 'If it's about the past, there's nothing to say, is there?' He moved towards the door, his hunched shoulders putting an effective barrier between them. It was always the same, whenever she tried to explain. He just would not listen.

'Robert, it wasn't my fault,' she persisted. 'The baby, I didn't mean to . . .' Her words died away as he turned to look at her, and the anger she saw in his eyes silenced her.

'Oh, I believe you,' he said. 'I can quite see that neither you nor your lover wanted a child to complicate things.'

'He wasn't my lover!' The words burst from her lips. 'I didn't ask him to come here, nothing was planned.'

'Do you expect me to believe that you were forced?' he asked scornfully. 'You always wanted that man, you only came to me in the first place so that I could cover your shame and guilt by giving the boy my name.'

'Mammy,' Verdun came up to her and caught hold of her skirt, 'what's the matter? Why are you shouting?'

'It's nothing,' she said. 'Don't worry, Mammy's not angry.' Just hurt, she thought as she stared at Robert's retreating back, and yet could she blame him for his anger? She had betrayed his trust, there was no escaping the fact.

Kristina climbed from the bus and walked towards the aerodrome on Fairwood Common. She had not seen anything of Robert since their last argument and at night in her dreams she believed they were together again as they used to be, close and loving. She had not seen Eden Lamb either.

It was a lovely May day, and as Kristina went into the canteen, the whole place was alive with gossip.

'Sheila, what's going on?' Kristina said as she saw her friend coming towards her waving to her excitedly.

Sheila clasped Kristina in a warm embrace. 'Didn't you hear the news? The war is over, it's *over*!' she said excitedly. 'Hitler is dead, it's all finished!'

'Thank God for that,' Kristina said softly.

Sheila caught her arm and drew her into the canteen. 'Come on and listen to the wireless. Bugger the work, this is too good to miss.'

The girls were crowded round the set, listening with a feeling of relief to the well-modulated voice announcing that General Jodl had surrendered to General Eisenhower and that the next day, General von Keitel intended to surrender to Marshal Zhukov, the Soviet commander. It was Victory in Europe.

She didn't know afterwards how she got through the day. Hardly any work was done as the girls drank tea and talked about what they would do now that the war was over.

'Real thin stockings again instead of these thick things!' Sheila said excitedly. 'It'll be sheer bliss.' She hugged her knees. 'What's wrong with you, Dottie?' she called across the room. 'You look as if you've lost a shilling and found a sixpence.'

'Mind your own business, Sheila,' Dottie said waspishly, and Kristina intervened hastily.

'The first thing I'm going to buy is a new pair of shoes,' she said, 'something really fashionable.'

'Oh, yes, me too.' Sheila stared down at her sturdy flat-heeled service shoes. 'I'll be glad to be shot of these things.'

Dottie got up and left the canteen, and Kristina watched her with sympathy. Dottie had become involved, against her better judgement, with one of the

American servicemen, and it was obvious that he would soon return to his own country and to the wife he'd left behind there. If Kristina wasn't mistaken, Dottie was pregnant. She'd been pale and sickly for some days now.

'Hey, daydreamer, I'm talking to you,' Sheila chided, and Kristina smiled.

'When do you ever stop?' she said good-humouredly.

It seemed to Kristina that everyone in the town of Swansea wanted to celebrate. In Lambert's, street bonfires had been lit and excited children, including Verdun, were dancing around the flames.

Kristina had been given a few days' leave and now that the emergency was over she would leave her job and find something else she could do. She was determined that she must make something of her life, even if it was without Robert.

She was busy in the kitchen, scrubbing the table yet again, for Verdun always managed to spill something on the cloth that would seep through to the wood beneath. She sighed dispiritedly and put the kettle on the gas ring. She would make a cup of tea and not wallow in self-pity because she was alone. The war was over, she was alive and well, and so were her loved ones. She ought to be grateful.

A light tapping on the door startled her, and she paused for a moment, wondering if it was one of the neighbours inviting her to join in the celebrations. Mrs Thomas, perhaps. She moved across the room just as the door was pushed open.

'Roggen!' Kristina said in amazement. 'I heard you were home. Come and sit down, you look wonderful, so brown and healthy.'

Roggen laughed. 'You wouldn't have said that if you'd seen me when I got out of Singapore. I'll never grumble about putting on weight again.'

She drew a handsome stranger from the shadows of the doorway. 'This is my husband, Mark,' she said proudly, and the love and happiness that shone from her was touching to see.

571

'*Duw*, this is a surprise,' Kristina said. 'Sit down both of you, have a cup of tea. I was just making one.'

'We've been over to Ty Coch,' Roggen said, taking a seat. 'Mark and I are staying there for a while, just for a visit. I came over to see Eden. He's very sick, you know, Kristina, *very* sick.' She looked down at the cup Kristina handed her. 'Do you think you could let him have Verdun up at the house sometimes?'

Kristina nodded. 'I expect that would be all right.' She changed the subject abruptly. How could she explain that between them she and Eden had made a mess of both their lives? 'Was the sea crossing very hazardous?'

'It was a holiday compared to Singapore.' Roggen smiled. 'It was tough out there. I think you could say we had some hair-raising adventures before we finally got to Australia.' Her smile vanished. 'Richard died in Singapore, as did thousands of others.'

'It must have been awful,' Kristina said softly. 'I expect all you want to do now is to forget it.'

'We'll never forget,' Roggen said and then it was her turn to change the subject. 'Mark and I were married a few weeks ago, but we had to come home, we had to see Eden . . . perhaps for the last time.' She toyed with her glass. 'Eden is so dispirited, Kristina.' She glanced up. 'He and Nia have their difficulties but she is very concerned about him. She wrote and told me how ill he is. I don't think he has very long to live.'

Kristina felt shock waves wash over her. She had known that Eden was not his usual self, but she hadn't realized that he was so seriously ill.

Roggen frowned. 'God, coming home has brought back so many memories. An awful lot has happened to us since we were young. I can remember when I was so sure I could put the world to rights. What a naïve fool I was. I never saw the war coming and yet it has changed all our lives so drastically.' She smiled suddenly with a flash of the old fire. 'Though it does look as if the Labour Government will beat the Conservatives in the election in July.'

572

Before Kristina could answer, the door was pushed open, letting in a rush of sea air and the acrid smell of the bonfire. Kristina rose to her feet, her heart beating swiftly.

'Robert.' She tried to sound calm. 'There's nice to see you. Come in and sit down, have some tea with us.'

He entered the kitchen, his hat in his hand and frowned when he saw that Kristina had visitors, but Roggen adeptly broke the embarrassed silence.

'Well, it was lovely seeing you again, Kris, but we'd better be going. We have a lot of visits to make tonight.'

'Please,' Robert said politely, 'don't go on my account. I can always come back later.'

'No,' Kristina said at once. 'Please, Robert, stay for a while.'

Roggen stood up and Kristina attempted to keep the conversation light, though Roggen must have known at once that much was wrong with Kristina's marriage.

'We'll have to get together soon,' Kristina said brightly. 'We'll have a gossiping session, there's a lot to catch up on.'

Kristina moved to the door and suddenly her heart was beating faster as she saw a tall figure framed against the street lights. 'Eden!' she said in dismay.

'We're just leaving,' Roggen said swiftly. She picked up her gloves and hat. 'Eden, won't you come with us. I don't think this is a good time.'

Robert was on his feet at once, glaring at Eden. His hands clenched into fists as he squared his shoulders. 'What are you doing here?' he said angrily.

'You're right, Roggen,' Eden said, 'this is not a good time.' He moved away from the house, but Robert followed him.

'You've got a nerve,' Robert said in a low voice, 'coming here chasing my wife the way you do. And yet you allowed her to struggle alone with the mess you left her in. How she still gives you the time of day I don't know.' He caught Eden by the lapels of his coat and shook him as though he would empty the life out of him.

Eden tried to free himself but he had no strength. 'You are right,' he gasped. 'I've been all sorts of a bastard.'

'Don't, Robert!' Kristina said anxiously. 'There's no need for all this.'

Robert's eyes were hard as he looked at her. 'Still standing by him, I see. Well, you can have him. I wash my hands of him and you.'

'Wait,' Eden gasped, 'you have to hear the truth.' He took a deep breath. 'Kristina was having my child because I took her off guard when she was lonely and worried.' He paused to catch his breath. 'She didn't want *me*. It was you she wanted.' He fell back against the wall of the house, breathing heavily.

'Eden is sick, can't you see that?' Roggen had moved towards her brother, supporting him with her arm. 'Just look at him, really look. Don't you think that whatever he's done he's been punished enough?' Without another word, she led Eden towards his car, and Mark took the wheel. He slammed the car into gear and then they were away, sending up dust in clouds from the surface of the road.

'Mam, what's the matter, why was everybody shouting?' Verdun, his face blackened by the bonfire, a half-raw potato, hot from the fire, in his hand, stood looking up at her. Kristina drew him close and he put his arms around her waist, a worried frown appearing between his eyes.

Robert looked at Kristina and the silence between them was emphasized by the sound of cheery voices singing in the street. He took a deep breath. 'Well, it seems I've been too hard on you, Kristina,' he said, and it obviously cost him a great deal to make the gesture of reconciliation. When she didn't reply, he moved away and Kristina watched him for a moment in silence, a mixture of emotions racing through her; anger and pain and pride.

Robert was limping badly, his shoulders bowed, and suddenly she felt herself dissolve with love for him, her pride gone. 'Robert!' she said anxiously. 'Please don't leave me.'

He paused for a moment, his back towards her, and she waited in terror, believing he would walk away. But then he turned and looked at her, squaring his shoulders. Slowly, he began to limp towards her and she caught her breath, forcing back the tears.

He stood before her, staring at her for a long moment, his eyes, searching her face.

'I love you, Robert,' she said raggedly. 'Please, give me one more chance.'

He gave her one of his rare smiles. 'You think we can make this marriage work if we both try very hard?' he said softly. And then he took her in his arms, holding her close, his lips tender against her hair, and the tears were burning in her eyes.

The doors of Lambert's Cottages were closing for the night, the revellers going to their beds. The bonfire was burning low, the embers dulling like fallen stars. The sound of singing had ceased but as Kristina clung to her husband, it seemed that the air was suddenly filled with song. At last, the war was over, and for Kristina peace had come at last.